MORE BEAST THAN
PRINCE CHARMING...

BEAUTIFUL SINNER

VOL. 1

ELENA M. REYES

SUMMARY

These Men Are More Beasts Than Prince Charming...

Beautiful Sinner Volume 1 features three full-length novels packed with blood-pounding mafia romances where love is obsession and loyalty is laced with violence.

These men don't beg. They take.

And when their women are threatened...

They'll burn the world to the ground until they're back where they belong —pinned beneath them.

P.S. Read this if you love morally gray, unapologetic antiheroes who love hard and f*ck dirty.

Includes: SIN, COVET & MINE

DEDICATION

For the girlies who crave danger in a tailored suit and wicked lips that whisper… **"Mine."**

You know who you are. This one's for you.

CONTENTS

COVET

MINE

TRIGGER WARNINGS

This book contains dark elements that some readers may find triggering. These men are brutal and unapologetic; please read at your own discretion.

THIS IS A MAFIA ROMANCE SERIES AND YOU WILL FIND THE FOLLOWING:

EXPLICIT VIOLENCE
ON PAGE DEATH
EXPLICIT SEX (SPICY) SCENES
SEXUAL SPANKING
TORTURE/GORE
OBSESSED MEN
AGE GAP
FORCED PROXIMITY
SOME KIDNAPPING
MILD STALKING
VERBAL ABUSE BY ENEMY
MISOGYNY (NOT BY MMC)
TOXIC FAMILY

CRIMINAL ACTIVITY
VULGAR LANGUAGE

MALCOLM ASHER

I am both heaven and hell.
Sin and pleasure.
The Devil she never sees coming…

Everyone knows that Malcolm Asher owns Chicago. Nothing—not a single move is made in my city without my authorization. I'm ruthless. Conniving. Worshipped by those around me, and yet, it means nothing the moment my eyes meet hers…

Clear blue and innocent, the delicate doll on this stage holds me captive against my will. She's decadence personified—a corruptible angel I want to own.

I'm hard for her. Starving for a taste. Eager for her to feel me.

This little girl has no idea of the danger she's in within my presence. How I will make her crave the darkness I control.

How I will make her…*Mine*.

MALCOLM

"**M**OTHERFUCKING IDIOT," I hiss out, letting the steel door behind me slam shut. My head is throbbing—muscles coiling—as the urge to break the neck of the *piece of shit* errand boy my father asked me to hire runs deep. Ire flows like lava through my veins, and I need to get a hold of myself.

Rash emotions lead to stupid decisions. Errors.

Like the one I now need to eliminate. It was a mistake, and I know better than to ever mix familial ties with business decisions. Nevertheless, I gave in when asked, and here we fucking are.

Millions could have been lost. Charges would have been pressed.

Now, I'm left with no choice but to right a wrong that never should have been.

The feds are now looking into the Jameson family and its ties to the dealing of stolen weaponry and narcotics. Because of a simple fuckup— something someone heard come out of *Michael*, a person under my employ, I'm making every tidbit of information on the Jameson account disappear.

Nothing stays on that file. Not so much as a single cent.

My IT department is making it as if they never existed. Moreover, in this country, they don't.

A few steps inside, and the harsh scent of urine and perspiration invades my senses. My nose flares in disgust as I look toward the back—skipping over the three empty cells—and focus on the two near-naked men with their hands tied to a metal pipeline above their heads. Their feet are chained to the ground, limiting their movement.

They are the cause, and I am the effect.

Decisions have consequences. Repercussions. Rectifications that will appease the victims of their idiocy.

One spoke about things he doesn't understand, while the other tried to bribe the hand that feeds. Demanded that I kneel or else.

Because of that, tonight, I am their judge, jury, and executioner. The God each one will beg forgiveness to.

"Good evening." At the sound of my voice, one of the men looks up and his eyes widen. His bare chest is heaving with each rapid intake of air that does nothing to calm his nerves. Instead, his eyes lock with mine while a whimper leaves his split lip.

His fear is palpable, and it fails to move me. Motherfucking pathetic.

You knew better.

My eyes flicker to the other man and take account of the few bruises already forming on his face. He seems to be muttering a low prayer under his breath, tears running down his cheeks while his eyes look toward the wall past me. Avoiding his reality.

No begging. No pleading for leniency.

They're smarter than I expect. Know better.

Nothing pisses me off more than someone who can't accept their fate with dignity.

"Evening, boss," everyone answers, a low rumble that reverberates off the walls. Unlike other men in my position, I don't wait for my clean-up crew to arrive. Instead, they stand at the ready wearing protective gear and white masks. Their faces are bowed, arms behind their backs as I pass them on my way toward the two men who've caused me this unnecessary headache.

"Any problem getting them here?" I ask Javier, the head of my security and right-hand man.

"None." He's watching the two squirm, smirking as he hands me my favorite knife.

"Thank you." Taking it from his hand, I flick my wrist and admire the sleek blade. This small token came from my father the day I took over. A sharp blade with a solid gold handle—the exact replica of the one he kept inside his desk upstairs when he was the CEO of Asher Holdings. Back when the bank played a smaller part in the underground world of money laundering.

A phone rings, and Javier is quick to remove it from his pocket. I recognize it, and know it belongs to the gossiping fuck. Both men cease all movement, their eyes on me as I accept the phone from Javi's outstretched hand.

I know who it is. I know what he'll say.

Pressing the green button, I put the call on speakerphone and wait. Silence looms, and the harsh breathing on the other end comes from a man I still admire. Someone who should've taught his son a few lessons early on.

"What is your decision, Malcolm?" Straight to the point, his tone not showing his true emotions.

"What do you want it to be?" I toss back, walking slowly over to his son. A son that reeks of fear and his own piss. Who couldn't keep his mouth shut after I gave him the opportunity to work for me. Work his way up the ranks.

"Family is the most—"

At my godfather's lame attempt, I laugh. It's harsh and sardonic, causing another scared whimper to leave the men. "Save that sanctimonious drivel for someone who buys it, Henry. We both know it's bullshit."

"Agreed, but he is my only son." That I can understand. The need for a man to have a male heir, someone to take over. "Spare him and I'll pay for the damages myself. Buy the forgiveness of your client."

"What else?" I take the few remaining steps between myself and Michael, his son. His eyes are on mine, throat bobbing as words fail to escape. True fear has a way of paralyzing people, and their basic motor functions become nonexistent. "Because you'll be paying *me* every last cent either way."

"What do you want?"

"Blood." My reply is automatic, and so is my hand as I lash out, cutting a jagged line down Michael's forearm. His scream curls around the room—penetrates every square inch and then breaks his father's heart. At once, my lips stretch into a wide smile as a soothing calmness settles over my limbs.

Their pain brings peace.

Beside him, the wannabe blackmailer fights against his bindings. He winces but doesn't stop moving as the steel around his wrist cuts the skin there. "This is a mistake! Please, I'll never say another word about—"

Javier backhands him with the butt of his gun. "Silence."

"Malcolm, please. Don't do this to our family." Henry's voice rings through, cutting off the pathetic pleading of his son's friend. Same low-life punk that thought he could blackmail me. "Discipline them, but don't kill my son."

"I've learned my lesson," Michael adds, face tight with pain. "I'll do whatever you want...fix this...but *please*...no more."

"Interesting." Blood flows from the wound, dripping down and onto the concrete floor. It pools near the center—follows the small slope down and into the drain I had the foresight to add into the room's design when I remodeled the bank. This is the lowest floor, two below what the actual building plans show.

"Okay." Once more, I punish him, this time sinking the blade of my knife deep into his thigh. My fingers manipulate the steel tip, twisting it as I tear through muscle. Crimson splatters all over my white shirt, ruining another garment.

Michael's sobs turn into a loud scream as I pull the knife from his flesh. He writhes, bowing as he tries to move away from me.

In the background I hear his father's outrage, revel in his pleading, but it's still not enough. I want more.

More blood. More destruction. More compensation for my time.

Within my rage, there is also the compulsion to teach this boy a lesson he will never forget. Prevent him from ever doing this again—save his family both the embarrassment and grief.

"Untie him, Javier, and bring over a chair," I instruct, taking a few steps forward and over to the other man. A man who's currently giving in to his panic. That fight or flight response that is coded deep into our DNA. That helps people survive disastrous situations.

He won't be as lucky.

Javi unlocks Michael's handcuffs and lets him fall to the floor: a crumpled, bleeding mess. The sound of a chair scraping against the floor follows, and it's loud within this space. Heightens the anxiety.

"Get up and sit," Javier instructs, standing over Michael. "Show some appreciation for Mr. Asher's hospitality."

A few men in the room chuckle and I hold a hand up, effectively shutting them up. While Javier's words are funny, now is not the time to give in to amusement.

"My leg—"

"Isn't broken," I interrupt, not bothering to look back. "Shut the fuck up and move."

"Michael, I swear to Christ! Do as he says," his father pleads, choking on his own desperation. That parental urge to take care of his offspring. It's instinctual. A deep-seated need that I can understand—respect—even if it means shit at the end of the day.

It didn't change the disaster his son's stupidity caused.

Leaving Javier to accommodate our guest, I focus wholly on the other one. "Name?"

"Please, I…son of a bitch!" he howls, body cringing back as I slice through the back of his right ankle, then his left. It's a shallow cut. Just the first of many.

"Name?" I ask once more, the tip of my blade slowly sawing back and forth over the back of each calf—going lower with each cut until the sharp edge slices over the first. Just enough to hurt. For him to slowly begin to drip down all over my floor.

"I told you my name that day inside your office." Another lie.

"This is your second offense. You get one more."

"But it's the truth." No, it isn't. His eyes shift downward and a shiver runs through him, giving away his nervousness. Fear.

Moreover, he has every reason to be scared.

"Last chance," I grit out, stretching my neck from side to side while my hand clenches around the golden handle. Adrenaline pulses through my veins—licks at the tips of my fingers as I drive the knife forward and into his stomach. Deep enough that I feel as it tears through flesh. Blood seeps from the wound, but I want more.

Twisting the blade, I pull it halfway out and take a step back—leave it right where it is below his belly button. "Are you ready to be honest with me now?"

"I'm telling you…fuck!" he yells out as the heel of my shoe kicks the weapon in deeper. I bury it—lodge it within his stomach where only half the handle is left visible.

Michael shifts in his chair, trying to stand, pulling my attention back to him. "Please stop."

"Why should I?" Another strike; this time I land a punch to the right side of his friend's ribs. He cries out a curse, body trying to fold into itself. It's a mistake, one that causes him to freeze when the pain magnifies.

"Please stop. I'm not lying."

"Boss, we're so sorry. It was a huge—"

Michael's word die as Javier places a gun to his temple. "Placing a bullet in you will be a pleasure, one that my boss won't begrudge me for. Keep testing his patience."

"Michael, please, son, stay quiet!"

With a smirk, I nod at Javi and watch with pleasure as he pistol-whips the idiot across the face, breaking his nose in the process. "Listen to your father, Michael."

"No more," he says, his tone tinged with pain. Regret.

I can almost taste his acceptance. Can see the glimpse of resolve in his eyes.

"That's up to you. If you sit there silently, things will progress without further incident. Talk, and…" I trail off as Javier lands a second direct hit, and a gash opens over the bridge of his nose. Rivulets of red pour down his face and neck, staining his chest with his life's essence. "Understood?"

With his right eye beginning to swell, Michael nods and looks back at the piece of shit still strung up. At the man who befriended him with one goal in mind: getting to me.

He's finally understanding that someone needs to pay, and it's either him or…

Grabbing the end of the knife, I pull out the handle, leaving the blade inside. At once he screams, the anguished sound rending the air as I slide it up his flesh.

More blood seeps from the wound; my hands are soaked. "Lying to me was your biggest mistake." His pain is not enough. Another inch up, and I stop. "Your second was not being smart enough to hide your tracks."

At this his eyes widen, lips parting to deny what we both know to be the truth, but I shake my head. Moreover, the idiot listens for once and closes his pale lips.

"Your name is Phillip Mitchell…" the knife slices upward a bit more and he strains to move away from me "…and you take on certain jobs for the head of EMB Financial Group. The same man I turned down three weeks ago, when he asked that we merge a certain department—the one you demanded twenty million dollars for in exchange for your silence."

I pause and look down, admiring the clean line that starts below his belly button and stops at the center of his abdomen. It's deep, but not enough to kill him yet, although the internal damage is done.

His life's essence is slowly bathing my floor with each drop that splashes below.

"End me already," Phillip groans, head lolling forward from the loss of blood. He's dying.

"Not until you tell me why Jonathan sent you."

"He didn't."

"Then who?" Because we both know he isn't working for himself. Phillip is nothing more than a low-level soldier—a follower—and this entire bullshit scheme didn't come from his simpleton mind.

I've read his rap sheet. Know where he lives and whom he associates himself with, and none have a position of wealth or power in Chicago. They're nothing more than thugs and "wannabe" gangsters that admire TV crime lords and wish to live a life of infamy.

"No one—"

"Bridgeport. That is where your mother lives…is it not?"

Phillip nods, tears running down his cheeks. "She has nothing to do with this. Please, don't hurt her."

"Then tell me who the fuck sent you," I snarl, lip curling over my teeth as I fight the instinct to strike once more. "Tell me, and she'll be taken care of for the rest of her life. She will want for nothing. You have my word."

Resignation flashes in his eyes, and they close. Another choked sob leaves his throat as his life slowly fades, each breath harder than the last.

"Tell her that I love her."

"Done."

"His name is Alton Foster."

I nod but say nothing. I knew this also, just needed confirmation before I rain hell on a man that doesn't respect our rules. Being somewhat new to Chicago, he is stupid and arrogant. A dead man walking, he has no idea the kind of war he just unleashed.

Before Phillip could take his next breath, I pull a gun from my back and shoot him once between the eyes. A mercy kill as two voices shout out —the one on the phone full of despair while his son fights against the hold my men have him in.

I'm done with the theatrics and put the gun back in its place. Everyone watches me as, with absolute calm, I pull the knife from Phillip's dead body and walk back toward my godfather's only child. My hands and knife are a bloody mess as I grab a fistful of his hair. "Hold your tongue out."

"Malcolm—"

"Be grateful," is all I say, grip tightening until his eyes water and I can literally feel as the strands break between my fingertips. "Now open and do as you are told."

"Anything but this."

"Would you rather join your *friend* in the next life?"

"I didn't know. You have to believe me."

"The sad part is that I do," I say, letting go and grabbing the handkerchief Javier holds out for me. He takes my place and digs his fingers deep into Michael's jaw, holding so hard that the latter gives way and opens. Michael's tongue peeks out, and with no patience left, I grip it using the small fabric square between my fingers.

Tears run down his face as I give it a harsh yank and then slice it clean off.

He sobs while his father is silent. Accepting.

I don't kill the dumb fuck, and both know that can change in the blink of an eye.

"Now you can never speak of that which you do not know. You cannot put your life in danger or make friends with idiots that see you as easy pickings. Learn this lesson, own your mistake, and I will speak to you again in a month." Michael nods, whimpering in pain while my men help him up. Hold his weight. "Next time, I will not be so forgiving. Never betray me or this family again."

MALCOLM

I'M PREOCCUPIED.

My mind is replaying the last line inside the email my informant —the FBI agent—sent over mid-afternoon. It flashes on a loop:

Eagle. Claw. Fly.

Those three simple words cause my hands to clench and the leather beneath my hands to groan in protest. It's been a few hours now since Michael was taken from here and his friend disposed of, and yet, as I connect more dots, the ire within me grows. Each tick of the clock throbs in time with the raging inferno rushing through my veins, and all because someone thinks they can take from me.

Because greed overrode common sense, and they forgot their place.

Alton Foster made a move that will cost him. He ignores the rules.

In our business, discretion is law. You hear and see nothing.

I don't care who you are or how you came to have the capital you hold; my job is to move it around and turn the dirty money into clean. Untraceable.

Owning one of the largest banks in the world has advantages, and I use every fucking one in my favor. With facilities in almost every large city inside the United States, Europe, and Asia—the high volume of monetary transactions—we are untouchable. Not unless you want to disrupt the nation's economy.

Something no government can withstand, especially one that's one fuckup away from another recession.

Laundering is a skill set. A calling.

One that brings about danger—a danger that I welcome. It's a rush that satiates a need within. To these criminals, I'm their best friend until something goes wrong, and I've proven more than once just how dangerous I can be. How I am the one they should fear.

Taking a man's life doesn't keep me up at night. Instead, it feeds the darker part of my soul.

Swiveling around in my chair, I face the lit-up Chicago skyline from my office. The chair creaks, the leather protesting as I sit back and admire the city below through my floor-to-ceiling windows. This metropolis never sleeps. Never stops.

A never-ending chess game that I move at my discretion.

The phone atop my desk beeps, and I drum my fingers on the chair's armrest. Two hours until my appointment, and the darkness within me vibrates with need. With a depraved hunger—a different kind of yearning —that hasn't been fully satiated in a long time.

"Hey, Malcolm?" my cousin Mariah calls through the door, waiting to be acknowledged before entering. No one enters this room without permission. They know better.

Other than myself and our security, she's the only person left inside the building, my cleaning crew and other employees having left an hour ago.

For a few beats, I don't answer. Instead, I stare at the city below. It's ten p.m. and while the working class celebrates the end of another long week, I plot. Think. While the lights shine bright on this September night and bars fill up, I prepare.

Most people never realize that they walk past a killer several times in their life. That evil resides next door. No one cares. Most ignore the danger that lurks as long as the darkness never reaches their door. A common mistake.

Instead, the passersby below stop to admire the facade of my building. Of the details carved in stone. Of the gold name stamped onto its front.

The Asher building is synonymous with money and decadence. All they see is sixty floors of opulence, and their greed blinds them from reality. Not a single person below would ever suspect the city's most eligible bachelor of being anything but perfect. That good looks and charms mean shit when you sit beside the devil and play in his backyard.

Just how I like it. This concrete jungle is unlike any other, and I own it. Every fucking single square inch of Chicago is mine. Run by me.

Not the mafia. Nor those that come from money.

No. Every move in this motherfucking city is made with my approval.

Mariah knocks this time; three quick raps against the wooden door. "Are you in here?"

Once more, I don't answer. Instead, I rise from my seat and take off my suit jacket. I lay it over the back of my chair and then undo the cuff links, tossing them next to a Montblanc pen my mother gave me on my last birthday.

My eyes survey the room, and a smirk crosses my lips. This office is so unassuming. So normal, and what you come to expect from a financial institution's CEO. Lavish, sleek, and nothing compared to the rooms just a few floors down.

Rolling the sleeves up to my elbows, I grab my phone and keys. My steps are slow as I make my way around my desk and to the door, pulling it open before she can try once more. "How can I help you?"

She rolls her eyes at my gruff acknowledgement, sliding the strap of her purse up her shoulder. "I'm heading out, *boss*. Do you need anything before I go?"

"Has the package been delivered?" I ask instead, ignoring the childish gesture. It's been a long day for everyone, and she's been on the clock since eight this morning. We're all tired—wound tight—and snapping at my little cousin won't help us get out of here any quicker.

"Dropped off an hour ago and is being treated by his father's private physician as we speak."

"Good." Giving her a gentle shove, I close the door behind me. "Any issues?"

"Other than Henry calling nonstop?" Annoyance crosses her features. "No, but the old degenerate has been at it every ten minutes for the last hour."

"What the fuck does he want?" At once, my ire returns in full force. Today, they were blessed by me—should consider themselves beyond lucky that Michael is still breathing. Something that I could still reconsider. A quick drive and a bullet from my gun could remedy that.

"Easy, cousin." Mariah lets out a giggle, her top lip curving up at the end. "He's just trying to kiss your ass?"

At that, I bark out a harsh laugh. "More like afraid of how many zeroes that bottom dollar will include."

"Do you need me to come in tomorrow? I will if you do, Malcolm." She pulls her cell from a pocket in her skirt and types something before hitting send. I'm not surprised by her offer. Both Javier and Mariah are always willing to step up when I need something taken care of in a rush.

"You just want to see him cry," I say, patting my front pocket. *I'm missing my keycard.*

"Guilty." No denying. No shame. Her phone pings then and she looks down, smiling as she reads the text. "I'm not the only one, either."

I know. "Is Javier waiting for you?"

"Yes, but that's not a definite answer. We can come in and fine-comb the system for any trace that could have been missed?"

"No."

"No?"

Smiling, I guide her toward the elevator and call for it. Being so late, the door opens quickly and I guide her inside. "It's taken care of, and I'm not accepting a visit from Henry until late next week. Get out of here and go enjoy your weekend with your boyfriend."

"Pity. Aren't you coming?" she says, her expression showing confusion.

Pressing the *Door Close* button, I shake my head. "I will, but I need something from my office first."

"GOOD EVENING, MR. ASHER," the hostess greets as soon as I step through the club's door. It's a private estate on Lake Forest with over five acres of privacy surrounding the twenty-eight-bedroom home. It's the perfect retreat for the rich and deviant—convenient at only a forty-five-minute drive from my building at the heart of The Loop.

The clientele here is diverse. Those that like to succumb to their kinkier side without public knowledge. This mansion accepts everyone without judgment, and each floor handles a different kind of play.

I nod but don't say a word, my eyes giving her uniform a once-over. It's burlesque-inspired today and leaves very little to the imagination. However, she does nothing for me.

Too much makeup. Hair overly teased and sprayed. Too easy.

I'm picky about who I fuck. Whose pussy I let tighten around my cock.

Used and abused will never be for me, no matter how hard they chase. Offer what they consider a valuable trade—something I could easily have delivered to my home at any given moment.

A man like me is very desirable to a gold-digging trophy wife. At six foot four, I exude dominance and power, and yet, it's the light green eyes that draw them in like a moth to a flame. My looks open doors, but no one has been able to fully handle my insatiable thirst for sex. My demand to take charge and own.

Not that I have wanted to find a woman, either. *Not since my one mistake.*

I want soft and sweet. Dependent and innocent.

The perfect little cock slut I can bend to my will, someone that I won't find here.

The women that work in this club are okay with being nothing more than a sexual object. They enjoy the attention. Get off on being used by every member who chooses to have a taste of the forbidden.

This place isn't about having an intelligent conversation or finding a deep connection.

People come here to fuck:

Each other.

The staff.

Or watch.

I'm here for the latter. I will never touch a whore, but watching is part of my religion, and this club caters to me, my needs, very discreetly.

There hasn't been a woman in over eight months worthy of my cock. My come.

"Will you be needing an escort to your room?" This girl is new. The last one knew not to speak to me. "Or do you have any last-minute requests tonight, sir?"

"No. Nothing else will be needed." I hold out the special black keycard with my name embossed for her to see.

"Of course, sir. Enjoy your—"

I walk away before she finishes, striding inside and into the main reception area. The music is loud and vibrates through every cell in my body. Heightens my cravings. All around me people are dancing—grinding to this deep and hypnotic bass—while giving in to their baser desires.

The room is dark and open with a winding staircase off to the left. It's all wooden floors and paneling, floor-to-ceiling windows, and the deep red drapes they use to accent them. It's high, stoned arches and intricate carvings—gold antique fixtures and expensive furnishings.

Old Victorian meets debauchery.

A few dominants, a group of three, stand off to the left of the dance floor with leashes in their hands and a naked submissive at their feet. Across from them, a couple is fucking while those on two long couches watch.

There are moans and whimpers. Commands and guttural growls of pleasure.

However, nothing calls to me outside of my destination. My oasis. A quiet room where a reward awaits me.

People look at me—some try to pull me into their conversations as I make my way through the crowd, but I don't stop. My body is wound so fucking tight, the blood in my veins a volcanic rush of hunger that pulls me deeper into the mansion.

I've never felt this kind of rush before, at least, not at this level, and it's euphoric. Almost maddening as I give in to the pull, an almost palpable magnetic chord that's guiding me toward my sanctuary.

I don't stop until I'm outside the door three floors up. There, I pause and take in a deep breath while reaching down to palm my cock. Give it a hard squeeze that does very little to alleviate my almost violent yearning to come.

Sliding the key into the door, I crack my neck while waiting for it to unlock. This room is owned by me. Never to be used by anyone else.

A private gift given by the asshole that owns the club to pacify a personal debt.

"Fuck," I spit out, teeth clenching as my dick throbs against the zipper of my pants. Another stroke of my hand, and the green light blinks to signal it's open.

A rough exhale leaves me as I turn the knob and open the door to a room the size of a master bedroom. Two steps and I'm inside. The lights are dim, and the heavy riff of a guitar plays in the background on low.

The large room is empty except for my chair and a small stage with a metal pole that runs from floor to ceiling. There's nothing sexier to me than watching a woman dance—lose herself in her movements while the tension mounts. Watch her become needy with each inhale, the shakiness of her limbs as I command her to spread her thighs and slip a single finger inside.

How her thighs quake.

How her pussy clenches in need of more.

How she begs for me to fuck her.

Something that will never happen, and it's in my denial that I find a release.

I'm a voyeur. A killer.

A depraved son of a bitch that can take a life with no regret, and then come from pulling pleasure from a willing whore.

Striding across the room, I stop at my throne. An antique chair with its intricate wooden carvings and velvet upholstering—it holds this dark tone of both goth and sex that I love.

The hint of depravity hidden behind an expensive price tag.

The music within the room grows louder and I turn, humming the tune as the stage becomes illuminated. Adrenaline—the high that comes from killing that asshole—and the anticipation has me throbbing.

Desperate for a release.

Taking my seat, I sit back and press the small red button atop a table to my right. Not twenty seconds pass when the door at the other end of the room opens, and then closes with a muted thud.

Picking up the bottle of gin from the glass table beside me, I pour a few fingers into the tumbler while ignoring the performer. There's an electrical current flowing through the room, an energy that unsettles me as much as it excites.

"Come forward," I demand, yet don't look up. Instead, I take a sip from my glass and enjoy the spirit on my tongue. Close my eyes as the crispness, with just a subtle hint of citrus, pleases my palate.

"Where do you want me?" a delicate voice asks, and my heart thumps harshly inside my chest. Tries to claw its way out as my eyes snap open.

"Fuck." It leaves me on a pained groan as the music fades, and all I see is her.

She's not one of my regular girls.

She's young. No older than twenty.

She's breathtakingly beautiful and sweet.

My little doll.

MALCOLM

SHE'S DEFINITELY NEW and *innocent*.

I can almost fucking smell it on her. Can literally see the naivete inside those expressive eyes. Eyes that look away when mine bore into hers.

Something I find myself quite enjoying. That shyness. How lost she is.

It's there in the delicious touch of pink that sweeps across her cheeks and then down the soft curve of her neck. It exudes from her every pore as she nervously wrings her hands—the small hint of fear I took notice of before she began to avoid my gaze.

And fuck me if this doesn't both piss me off and turn me on.

While she takes in every detail of the room, I bask in the tension that's building between us; her uncertainty and my hunger.

Because there's no denying that I more than like what I see.

Unlike Michael's fear earlier tonight, hers makes me hard as fuck. Causes my entire being to pulse in time with each deep inhale she takes.

How the fuck did this delicate little thing end up working here?

She's not like the other women here. A blind man can see how out of place she is.

That she's more than likely inexperienced.

Not that it matters much. The journey is of no consequence to me when her destination is this room. With me.

I want her. Will have her. But more importantly, I won't share her with anyone in this place.

This little girl has no idea that I am the devil she never saw coming.

She will be for me alone. My personal tiny dancer.

That decision has me reaching down and undoing my belt. With a harsh yank, I toss it across the room. There's a clang—it's loud inside the quiet space—and she jumps. Finally fucking looks at me.

Bringing the glass to my lips, I take a sip and savor the herbal note of my gin, all the while my eyes roam her small frame. She has no idea what to do with herself, and for some reason, that pleases me.

I want to touch her.

Taste her.

Possess that genuine purity that causes an ache—an uncontrollable yearning to grow within me.

"Closer, sweetness." Neither of us miss the gruffness in my tone, how each syllable rumbles up my chest until it's a low and guttural growl.

"Yes, sir," she whispers low, taking her first step toward me. My eyes traverse her short frame, devour each piece of bare flesh I discover. Take in the rich, dark brown of her hair, and how each loose curl sweeps, then bounces around her bare shoulders.

This tiny morsel of sin is a natural beauty with wide, doe eyes in a rich cerulean tone. So expressive. Beautiful. She reminds me of a fairy tale princess. The kind that every dirty motherfucker covets and wishes to corrupt.

My gaze travels lower then, taking in her delicate upturned nose and the small smattering of freckles. Then to her bee-stung lips with the natural hue of a ripened berry that I want to see stretched around my girth.

Her skin is luminescent under the stage light. Soft, and with the barest hint of a tan. As if the sun kissed her skin. *My bite marks will look glorious on her.*

Next, I take in what she's wearing…

White and in soft lace. A short little dress that enhances her larger-than-a-handful-breasts—it's tight and revealing—displaying the sweet little tips that constrict under my perusal. She isn't wearing a bra, and my mouth waters while my cock gives a harsh jerk inside my pants.

Below her bust, the material flows out a tiny bit, but not enough to hide the flat of her stomach and wide hips. Her legs are long and toned, and her tiny feet bare.

This girl is petite, yet curvaceous. A tight little body meant to be fucked. Taken roughly.

Tilting my head, I watch her nervous habits take hold. How she leans most of her weight on her right foot. How she keeps biting that juicy bottom lip the closer to me she gets.

"Stop." At once she does as I ask a few feet away from me, eyes wide and staring into mine. Motherfuck, her shyness is delicious. Heady. "Twirl for me."

"As you wish, sir," she says, taking in a deep breath before letting it out slow. Her nipples are hard, pushing against the lace that leaves very little to the imagination. The sinuous curve of her body is tempting, so delicate, and I watch, enthralled, as she closes her eyes and performs a simple pirouette to please me.

"Again," I demand, voice rough and hands clenching. "Slower this time."

"Of course." Once more, she rises onto the balls of her feet and lifts one leg higher in what looks like a flamingo's stance. Her body holds this position for a few minutes, head held high to elongate her neck, before she slowly begins to spin. This turn is slow, a controlled move that shows off every inch of her flawless form.

The way she moves, every minute shift, shows me that this woman is a dancer. A trained one, at that.

What the fuck is she doing here?

Once more, that question floats through my mind and I know the answer will not please me. Something about her is throwing me off, and it's not my desire to own her soul. It's the sudden worry—that gut instinct that I follow blindly.

If anyone's hurting her, not even God himself will save them.

"I'm going to own you, beautiful. Destroy what you know and become your everything," I mutter low, rubbing a hand across my jaw. Watching as my little beauty turns three more times before I hold a hand up. "Stop." Again, she does, eyes shining bright and cheeks looking flush. "Come pour me a drink. Three fingers' worth will be enough for now."

A nod is all I get as she walks to me, hips swaying with each move. She tries to step around my parted thighs, but as soon as she's within my reach, I stop her. Fingers on her hips, I guide her closer—to take her rightful place between my legs—while reaching over for the bottle.

And fuck me if the feel of her pliant flesh beneath my fingertips doesn't cause me to shiver.

Limbs shaking, too, she follows my command. The bottle clanks against the glass table as it almost tumbles from her grasp while I lean forward. Pressing my nose against her midsection, I inhale deep, pulling her sweet floral scent into my lungs and groan.

Fuck, I throb. Both hate and love how I react to her mere presence.

Her quick intake of air lets me know she isn't unaffected by me. Not that it matters much. I'll train her—overthrow her senses—into craving me.

"You smell like sin," I grunt against the fabric of her dress, nose skimming a tiny bit lower as my hand holds her in place. "But do you taste as decadent?" She doesn't answer. Doesn't so much as breathe. "What's your name, little Twirl?"

"My name?" she croaks, and it's hard to keep in my amusement. I also don't miss how she doesn't question the nickname.

"Yes. Your name…" I nip the fabric but keep myself from marking her "…full name."

Slightly shaking, she pours my drink and then sets the bottle down. "It's London—"

"London what?"

"London Foster."

That last name isn't very popular around here, but I do know one family with it. One that has been living in my city for eight months. Same one whose head of the family is an egocentric asshole who's made some bad investments as of late. Stuck his nose where it doesn't belong, and that idiotic decision will ruin him.

All of them. Her.

However, she might be the one to pay the biggest price. She's just become even more precious to me. London is collateral, but I'll take care of her. This doesn't diminish my hunger; if anything, it multiplies tenfold.

But I don't say any of this as my mind runs through different scenarios. No, instead, I give her a smile and a tap to the back of her thigh. "Beautiful name for a beautiful girl."

"Thank you, sir."

"Call me Malcolm." Something I've never done before, but I need to hear her say it. Say my name. Not "sir" or "Mr. Asher." I find myself wanting this to be personal. Comfortable.

That, and lowering her walls makes it easier to take ownership of someone who has no idea that a predator is hunting. Calculating. Taking account of every minute detail in order to win this dangerous game.

"Malcolm," she whispers a moment later as if tasting my name on her tongue. It's a sinful delight to hear her pronounce each letter—to take in how a miniature smile forms on her lips after. "Anything else I can do for you, Malcolm?"

"Dance for me."

"W-what?" It's a shaky exhale as I kiss the area beneath her belly button.

"Dance for me, London." I gift her a few more soft kisses. "Get up on that stage, eyes closed, and dance for me. Let me enjoy you just a little."

My eyes stay on hers as I give the request and then sit back in my seat. I eat her alive as she nods and takes a few steps, all the while facing me. It's almost as if she can't find the will to pull her eyes away, and I mother-fucking enjoy watching her almost trip while making her way toward the stage backwards.

Once at the edge of the platform, she halts and gives me a soft smile. "Any particular request? Music you want me to—?"

"Slow." The word is out of my mouth before she finishes the question. "I want it slow, Twirl."

"Okay." She mouths the word *slow* and turns, giving me a small tease of the plump cheeks almost spilling from the dress's edge. It's ridden up, and with each move, I get a small taste of what will be mine.

"One more thing…" She pauses and tilts her head, listening to me. "Once the song finishes, you walk out without another word. Without looking at me." I'm hard. Throbbing. But instead of reacting like the animal she's making me feel like, I breathe in and take a sip of the drink she poured.

"Understood."

While London looks through the selection I have pre-approved, I undo the button of my pants and lower the zipper. While she nods to herself and hits play, I take my shirt off and toss it somewhere. While she shakes her head, tousling her hair, I pull my cock out and stroke myself once. While she gets up on the stage, back to me, and rolls her hips as the first strum of a guitar rents the air, I lick my lips.

I can't control my urges—this hunger that causes a hiss to escape through clenching teeth while she sways to the sensual beat. Can't stop myself as I swipe my thumb over the head, collecting the beads of pre-come there and spreading it.

This is foreplay. Makes my plans sweeter.

London dips low then, her knees spread wide apart while she arches her back. She bounces a few times, making the dress ride higher until the small string currently residing between two luscious cheeks becomes my focal point.

I fuck my hand with each gyration. With each arch of her back.

But nothing compares to the moment she stands, turns around, and with her eyes closed, skims a hand down the center of her chest. How she follows each beat—every single note in the song with absolute perfection.

She's glorious in her element. Dancing as if no one else is inside the room with her, she rises onto the very tip of her toes while those hips sway. London's moves are precise. Like a serpent enticing—hypnotizing while she prepares to strike.

And fuck, do I love it.

My fist pumps in time with her every move. My hips rise, giving into the lust burning through my veins.

With her foot on pointe, she lifts the other leg straight in the air into a vertical split and I growl, the sound loud within the room. She hears it. I know it. Moreover, that second—the minuscule moment in time when she falters causes my stomach to clench.

Move my wrist faster.

Following my instruction, she twirls for me in a slow circle.

My little Twirl. My little ballerina.

London holds her poise with grace. She doesn't realize as she turns that the white fabric between her thighs stretches tight, giving me a small glimpse of the sweet pink I want to devour.

Her labia is visible. So is a small patch of wetness.

My orgasm is almost violent as I focus on the proof of her arousal. *Even the innocent fall.*

"Motherfuck," I grunt, grinding my teeth as the first rope of come shoots from the tip and onto my stomach. Pulsing—I'm fucking throbbing as the second and third follow, coating my hand and then abdomen. Every single nerve ending in my body is a live wire and breathing comes second to watching her move, oblivious to my actions.

London doesn't stop, and I don't ask her to. Instead, I continue to stroke myself softly as the song comes to an end and she leaves.

She doesn't look back, but my eyes follow her out.

She doesn't speak, but I whisper an *I'll see you soon.*

Her life will never be the same after today.

MALCOLM

"SHE DANCES FOR NO one but me."

"Christ, Asher!" Liam yelps, jumping in his seat. He's been hiding inside this office all night, and as I walk in an hour later, I can see the why. He has a girl on his lap: late twenties, a redhead, and practically naked. The man is imbibing. Sampling what he perceives as his own merchandise. "You scared the hell out of me."

"Not my problem." Not waiting for an invitation, I take a seat across from them and lean back. Watch him squirm while the girl begins to play with a loose curl around her bare shoulders. "Now, about London."

"Figures." His companion mutters low, something he ignores. Knows better than to acknowledge, but I don't miss her grimace when he tightens his hold on her midsection. "But it's true."

"Shut it, Stacy."

"No, Liam. Let her talk…" I narrow my eyes at her "…finish. Say what you need to say."

"She's too innocent for a place like this. Too inexperienced, and I worry certain clients will eat her alive."

I almost smile at her perceptiveness. She's right on both accounts, and I won't be the only one to take notice of Twirl's naïveté. However, I'll do more than that. I'm going to consume her and make her dependent on me.

Show her brother and father before they take their last breath that I own them. Destroy without a single repercussion. Alton chose their lives' path, and I'm now fate here to collect.

At my silence, Liam becomes nervous. Curious, while his body language shows discomfort. "I apologize if London ruined your night. Did she upset you?" His worry is almost comical—full of apprehension that I will lash out. *Pussy.* "She'll get better. It was her first day and dance."

His words please me. I was her first.

It's an egotistical response. Feeds my need as an alpha to dominate and conquer.

To own. Be everything she will ever need.

"This man is just going to use her," Stacy mutters under her breath, but I hear and so does Liam. It's obvious she isn't quite sure who I am and that she worries about London, so I let it slide this once.

However, how loud she's now popping her gum in a show of annoyance is downright disrespectful. *Motherfucking nasty habit.*

"Don't concern yourself with London. Just make sure she doesn't dance..." my glare settles on the redhead and she dry-swallows the gum "...much less goes near any of your other clients."

"I'll see what I can do." Sweat beads at his brow while he frowns. Thinking. "I scheduled her for one more client tonight. A friend of a friend."

Sitting back, I take a second to rein in my rage. Breathe in deep while looking around the spacious room. It's opulent, heavily furnished, and predictable in its display of wealth. The paintings alone in this room would set him back millions—stolen originals come with a hefty price tag.

And then there is him.

Heavier set, hair dyed to hide his greys, and an expensive Cartier on his wrist. A wife and a few teenagers at home while he fucks anything that walks. He doesn't discriminate. He doesn't care as long as his dick gets wet.

Be a real pity if he loses it all.

"Find her."

"I can guarantee her starting tomorrow?"

"She's getting ready for her next client now." They speak in unison, but my attention stays on her. That's when I notice a few things aside from her trashy appearance.

This woman doesn't look like the rest. She's fidgety; lipstick smeared a bit and pupils dilated.

There isn't a single doubt that she is high.

Leaning forward, I wave a hand. "Explain."

"Ummm..." she looks at Liam and he nods, squeezing her once more "...London's in the dressing room now; her next private show is coming up. Saw her there right before I came to bring Mr. Kravitz his coffee."

"How long ago was this?" Coffee my ass. I see the small mirror and blade atop his ostentatious desk. The white residue left behind on it. The small open bag. *Idiot.* "How fucking long?" I spit out, hand slamming atop the desk when they both go mute. "Answer me."

"Thirty minutes ago," she stammers while the color drains from Liam's face. There's much he needs to account for, but not tonight. Tonight, he needs to stop London from getting up on another stage.

"If she makes it inside that room, I'll put a bullet in each of you." At my threat, she gasps while he nods. Knowing that I won't hesitate. Haven't in the past. "Find her. Pay her for the entire shift and then send her home with one of the many drivers here tonight."

"But, Malcolm—"

My glare cuts him off. "Let's hope for your sakes she hasn't stepped a foot inside."

IT TAKES another twenty minutes for them to find her, and it's pure luck that they do just in time. With her hand on the doorknob, and in another innocently indecent dress, Liam's plaything stops London.

Pulls her down the hall while I watch through a monitor in his office. Witness—hear as Liam greets her inside what looks like an employee lounge and asks her to sit. How he tells her that her second dance is cancelled, but that she'll still be paid in full. See him hand over the envelope I personally approved of, along with a tip.

A little something extra from me.

My little Twirl doesn't know how to react, her facial expression full of confusion, but she accepts with a nod. She doesn't argue. Instead, she heads inside the dressing room to change and grab her belongings. And in her normal clothes, London is exquisite.

Motherfucking...*cute.*

In a velour tracksuit with sneakers and her hair up high in a messy knot, she looks beautiful. Mouthwatering.

She has this girly innocence I crave to devour.

"Soon, Twirl," I say low, running a finger down the screen as she's being taken to the parking area set up for employees. "For the rest of our lives, I'm going to be all you know."

For as much as this girl brings out an animalistic desire in me, there's also an odd need to take care of her. It makes no sense. This sudden yearning to own her isn't solely brought on by her relationship to Alton, no.

I want her, and I'm not one to deny my instincts. My very nature demands that I make her mine, and I will.

And after I've satiated my lust and taken care of her family, I plan to explore these other *feelings*.

Later. Much later.

Now, my curiosity lies in a different area.

I make my move the moment the town car pulls up; my own vehicle awaits me at the mansion's doorstep. Grabbing the key, I enter and turn the fob just in time to see them drive down the driveway.

"Where are you heading, pretty girl?" I whisper, following behind them down a winding road. The highway is only a few miles away, and we merge left onto US-41 heading south.

For seven miles I follow close behind, only easing up a bit as traffic picks up while we get on the I-94. There're more cars than I expect for this time of night; a few semis and some drunken asshole yelling from the passenger side window about a basketball game we won.

And while the world around us zips by and the bustle surrounds me, I don't lose sight of her car.

They're heading straight for Chicago's downtown area, and it makes no sense. *Why are you here?*

The town car stops near my building, across the street and one over to be exact, at a garage meant for my employees. No one else is outside. No other car waiting for her.

"What the fuck is she doing?" Turning my headlights off, I pull over a little way down and watch her exit the vehicle. She says something to the driver and waves him off before turning around and walking up the small ramp where one of my security guards suddenly appears.

Someone who has been working for my family for over twenty years. Who I consider to be loyal, and trust.

Earl smiles and helps her with her bag, even says something that makes her throw her head back and laugh. A part of me wants to slam his head into the pavement for being so at ease with her, but I know him and his wife. A woman he adores.

From my position I can see that he's not looking at her with lust. No. There's something else there…

They disappear out of sight, and I'm tempted to follow.

Find out why Earl's letting her park here? Ask him how he knows—

Right then, a conversation we had three days back comes rushing to the forefront.

Sir, would you mind if a family friend parks here at night? She has a job that's far, and needs somewhere trustworthy to leave her own vehicle while she commutes…

Family friend. That's what sticks out the most since they haven't resided here long.

As more pieces come to light, something doesn't sit right with me. I don't know what Twirl's hiding, but I know Earl enough that he will never agree with what she's doing inside that club. He will borrow the money before letting her dance.

"Hurry the fuck up." The clock on my dash blinks with another minute passing, and I find myself growing anxious, my patience thinning.

A push of a button and my doors unlock. Hand on the handle, I'm pushing it open when headlights flicker near the building's exit. But then I am furious for a completely different reason.

"I'm going to burn that son of a bitch alive," I hiss, fingers clenching around the handle. A rusted piece of shit—what can barely be considered as a safe vehicle—passes in front of me, pausing at the corner to turn.

A thousand and one scenarios run through my head, and neither is better than the last. Why would a girl that comes from a somewhat affluential family sell herself for money?

Moreover, it's not for pleasure. Not because of a kink.

This is starting to smell like desperation, and I don't like it.

Within seconds, I am right behind her. Something she doesn't notice. Something I'll teach her to be aware of with time.

An old Toyota Corolla from the '80s with a muffler that's close to falling off and chipped paint isn't what she deserves. The more I see the car struggle to gain speed or change gears, the more my protective instincts grow.

Pressing the phone feature on my steering wheel, I hit number two and wait.

"Everything okay, Malcolm?" Javier asks after only two rings, sounding half asleep.

"Meet me outside of the Fosters' house."

"I'll be there in thirty." He doesn't question me. There's some rustling, and my cousin's voice in the background grumbling about the time. She'll get over it. "Are we going in together, or am I delivering a message?"

"*We're* delivering a personal invitation."

"A personal invitation?" he says slowly, sounding full of interest and confusion.

"That's it. Just a friendly visit."

"Something you aren't telling me here, Asher?" The man knows me, but now isn't the time to sit and discuss. We have tomorrow for that. Right now, all that matters is my little Twirl making it home safely.

That I assess her surroundings. Figure out her motives.

"I won't take *no* for an answer."

London

"WHAT DID I just do?" My legs are shaky, body trembling as I exit the private room. It's surreal. I feel lost, and yet, I won't deny that having his beautiful green eyes on mine made me experience the kind of excitement I've never been privy to.

Is that what having the attention of someone you find attractive feels like?

Even worse? I know what he did.

I could hear his grunts of pleasure while I danced for him. Know the exact moment he found his release, and I won't deny that my skin still tingles. That my panties are wet.

Does that make me sick? Weird?

With the cards I've been given, I should be running. And yet, here I am. Trying my hardest to calm down and move away from the corridor before he finds me a panting mess. A quivering ball of confusion that's using the wall for support.

Because he wasn't what I've been expecting. Not at all.

In my head, the men I've pictured since taking this job were bald, fat, and sexist.

Handsy. Disgusting.

However, what I got didn't fit the preconceived man in my mind.

Malcolm isn't any of that.

No. Not at all.

He's not the man the other girls told me is cold and distant. A dangerous animal that isn't to be trusted, but for some inexplicable reason, I do. Inside that room, I didn't experience fear or anxiety. Not once.

It's the opposite. With him, there's calm.

He didn't ask for extra privileges like the others. Like I know some of the other women here agree to. Enjoy.

Something that I might need to accept if the price is right. If my desperation sinks to a new low.

Malcolm's touch—I can still feel the possessiveness in his hold—was gentle yet firm. It didn't come with the repulsion I thought would accompany it. Not once did I feel like a whore.

Like the virginal idiot I am deep down.

The kind that in desperation ran to a total stranger's door asking for a chance.

The stereo clicks off then and I push myself off the wall, rushing down the hall before Malcolm opens the door. There's an empty room on this floor that Liam told me to use in case I want a breather, and right now, I'm needing more than that.

"Jesus, what is wrong with me?" I whisper, out of breath as I close the door and *his* opens a few doors down. My back to the wooden structure, I close my eyes and focus on his steps as he passes me and continues down the hall.

Heart pounding and hands clammy, I try and regain some semblance of composure, but it's hard. Too hard, when behind closed lids all I see is him.

That man is the textbook definition of tall, dark, and handsome. I'm petite against his harsher planes—soft curves to his muscular frame. The way he wore that suit, tailor-made to define every solid inch, is sinful, and yet the way he removed said jacket, rolled up his sleeves, and popped a button up top made my knees weak. Add to that the bold tattoo on his right arm, the skull with dark shadowing and bright blue eyes, and I'm left a literal mess.

And what's worse, *I* like it. Him. A lot.

His smile made me feel warm inside.

How his attention never left me still causes goose bumps to break out down my arms.

He's the kind of man no one survives from. A total destruction of one's senses; he's the hurricane I didn't see coming.

Jesus, London. Snap out of it.

Malcolm is a client. *A client.*

He's paying for a service, while I need men like him to reach my goal. He's nothing but a means to an end.

Shaking off thoughts of him, I wait another ten minutes before slipping out of the room and then taking the private stairway down to the employee area. It's a large space with three separate rooms attached; a locker area, changing room, and an employee lounge for a bit of relaxing.

Moreover, while Liam's a smooth talker with a penchant to come off as creepy, he's been very accommodating to my fears. To the years of distrust that have been scaring me.

My contract isn't like the others here:

No touching under my clothing.

No full nudity.

No sex unless I consent.

Liam knows who my family is. Why I'm here.

He's sticking his neck out by helping me, and that's something I appreciate. I know that having me dance for his clients will make him money, but he didn't have to hire me. Could just as easily told me to leave.

He doesn't have to offer me a way out. A possibility with hope.

This mansion whose walls hide secrets is exactly where my father and brother wouldn't be. I heard them one night saying as much, talking down the members and owner, making plans to out someone important.

They made the place out to be morbid and disgusting, while I find this a sanctuary.

Quick money. A way out from under my family's thumb.

My brother wants more than he should. Becomes braver with each night that passes, while my father sees me as a way out of his mounting debt.

They spend faster than either can produce and demand that I help maintain their lifestyle one way or another. I don't want to be a part of either of their schemes, much less what they are planning at the moment…

They want a war. Money. Power.

I need to be far away when that happens. They want to become what they will never be, and I refuse to become the casualty of their greed.

"So?" Stacy, Liam's assistant and a performer here, asks. She's by the small kitchenette preparing coffee, and she's not doing it right. There's splattering everywhere. "How did it go? Was he rude?"

"Not at all," I answer truthfully, walking toward her and shoving the cup deeper under the machine's percolator. No more splashing coffee.

"Thanks." Stacy gives me a sheepish grin. "I'm not exactly the Susie Homemaker type."

"Do you want to be?"

"That's weird, though." She waves a hand in the air, ignoring my question. But I see it in her eyes. Stacy wants to be, just in her own way. "All the girls complain he's a giant asshole. That he never let any of them physically near him. You dance, but don't touch."

That's the last thing I want to think about—someone else performing for him—but then the last part hits me. I did touch him. He initiated our contact.

Closing my eyes for a second, I relive the last hour and a half of my life. How reluctant he was to let me go.

Why am I different? Not that I say this aloud. Never. I'm new here and know how easily people can turn on each other. How someone can destroy who you are just because.

Instead, I find myself shrugging, opening the small fridge beside us to pull out a bottle of water. "Seriously, no complaints. He made me feel sexy, not stupid. I thought for sure I'd fall on my face and cry."

"Girl, that happened to me once. It's how I met Liam!" Her laughter makes me grin, the earlier tension dropping as we both fall into giggles. That fog he put me under starts receding and each breath I take is easier than the last. *I can still feel his touch. His warmth.*

"For real?" I ask, trying to act nonchalant, hoping she doesn't realize the sudden high pitch in my voice.

"Swear on my favorite pair of Manolos."

"That's one hell of a story to—"

"Take it from me, kid. Learn from my mistakes." Her mood change is instant. From happy to almost heartbroken. As if her uppers are making her crash. "Don't get attached. These men won't give you a fairy-tale ending."

Grabbing the now full cup, she places it on a tray with a sugar bowl and creamer. Not another word is said as Stacy walks out, leaving me in a state of confusion.

Why would she say that?

I'm not here looking for a man. I'm looking for an escape.

Besides, even if I did find him attractive, Malcolm has heartbreak written all over him.

"You're home early," I hear the moment I step in my father's house. Not that this surprises me, but it's wishful thinking that being early tonight would give me enough time to escape. To slip inside my room undetected.

It didn't.

Instead, I find my brother sitting inside the living room in his favorite leather chair with a glass of what looks to be cognac. His eyes are blue like mine, but a few shades darker. He's tall where I am short and muscular where I am slim. Our facial features differ, and personalities are like night and day.

Alton stares at me in a way that makes me feel uncomfortable. Makes my skin crawl.

"The diner closed early tonight," I say, letting the heavy wooden door close behind me. Even the low, muted thud it produces makes my body jump in place. "Bad batch of meat made a few people sick."

"Are you sure you weren't fired, Lola?" God, I hate that nickname now. Reminds me of Mom. She gave it to me, but now only he uses it, and each time it hurts. Cuts deep. Alton knows this, I've told him as much, yet the glint in his eyes tells me he doesn't care. He enjoys this sick game; there's a smirk on his face, a slow licking of his bottom lip before he takes another sip. "I'll be more than happy to hire you as my—"

"All is fine. I promise." The lie slips so easily past my lips as I walk deeper into the house. I have no choice. If they find out where I'll be spending my weekends and how much I'll be making, things will get worse. They'll take every dime, and Alton will demand that I serve him too. "I'm back on tomorrow for an overnight shift."

"Come here."

"Alton, I'm really tired. Can we talk tomorrow?" *Or never.* Slowly, I edge closer to the stairs that lead up to the bedrooms. My bedroom.

"I'm not fucking asking you. Come. Here." The bastard pats his lap, spreading his thighs apart, and I freeze. It's not the first time he's tried this, demanded that I get close, but dodging is my specialty and this time my saving grace comes from our father.

"Why the fuck are you home?" He stumbles in, almost falling over the entryway's carpet. Dad looks unkempt and reeks of alcohol. The cheap kind. His hand snaps out, grabbing onto my arm to stop his fall and bruising me in the process. Fingernails digging in, he rights himself. "If you got fired, then you know the alternative. Get me that money, London."

Before I can respond, a hand slips around my waist, pulling me back. "Enough, old man. Let's not upset my little *Lola.*"

"Of course, son. You're right..." he digs his fingers in deeper, making me whimper before he lets go "...marking her isn't going to help me."

A harsh shudder runs through me as I choke on a sob. Just feeling them close, much less touching me, makes me sick. They know this. Get off on my fear. "Can I please go upstairs now? I'm tired." Even I can hear the desperation in my tone.

Lips, Alton's lips, press against my temple as he squeezes me one last time. "Head on up to bed. We'll finish our—"

He's cut off by a sudden banging on our front door. Everyone stops, and I don't miss how fast Dad straightens himself. How he clenches a hand.

"Are we expecting anyone, Alton?"

"Not that I know of," he says, already pulling out his phone to check the front door camera.

There're cameras everywhere here. This isn't a home, more like a jail cell.

Whatever pissing game they are trying to play can end badly.

I'm not an idiot.

I know what they do and how much they owe a powerful family in Miami; a debt they are forcing me to pay while they live their lives in peace. That my brother's thirst for authority will end bad. His greed will be their downfall.

There's one lesson everyone, no matter what walk of life you come from, has to learn.

Don't bite the hand that feeds.

And for people like them, the mob is their God.

"Son of a bitch," Alton spits out, hands clenching around his phone a second before his eyes flick to mine. There's something in his stare. A subtle hint of fear. "Get upstairs and don't come down."

"Son, what's going on?"

"It's Asher's right hand."

"At this time?"

"Who?" Dad and I speak in unison, and immediately I wish I kept my mouth shut.

"None of your business. Get the fuck upstairs." Alton's pissed, his nostrils flaring while he grabs my arm and pulls me in the direction of the stairs. His hold hurts. He doesn't care that I trip or that I crash into the banister; he wants me out of sight.

"Jesus Christ!" I yelp, trying to pull out of his hold. "Let me right myself." And as the last word slips past my lips, a gunshot is heard and a bullet lodges itself in the wall nearest to my brother.

No one moves for a minute. No one breathes.

"Open the fucking door, Foster. Don't force my hand," a man calls out, his voice deep with a hint of a Spanish accent coming through. "You have three seconds."

"Don't say a word," Alton threatens, pulling me behind him while nodding at Dad. And like the blind man he is, our father listens, opening the door to a man dressed in a crisp suit holding a gun.

"Evening." His tone is friendly, yet it's his eyes that let on to just how dangerous he can be. What he will do if push came to shove. "Thank you for accepting this early morning visit."

"What can I do for you, Javier?" Alton asks, shifting his body to cover more of me. It has the opposite effect, because I see how this man's eyes slightly widen at the sight. There's curiosity there, and surprise, but no hostility toward my persona.

"I'm here to deliver a personal invitation."

"An invitation?" my dad asks, looking as confused as I am.

"Yes. An invitation." While this Javier talks, his eyes remain on mine, and yet I don't feel any distress. It's clear he is trying to make out my role here. Figure out who I am. Suddenly his phone chimes and he pulls it out, reading something and then answering. "You are aware of who Mr. Asher is, no?"

"Yes," Alton grits out, once more pushing me further behind him. "What does he want?"

"He requests your presence tomorrow for brunch at the Asher estate." There's a slick smile on his face. He's getting a kick out of how uncomfortable the men in my family are. "Eleven a.m. sharp—we don't take kindly to tardiness."

"My father and I will be there."

"All of you."

"She has nothing to do with—"

"Are you a Foster, sweetheart?" he asks, ignoring the men protesting.

I'm like a deer caught in the headlights.

If I lie, will it come back to bite me in the ass?

If I say the truth, will I get caught up in their mess?

"You don't need to answer—"

"The next time you try to intimidate her into not answering, Alton, we're going to have a very large problem on our hands. *She* can speak for herself."

Tensions rise. My brother's muscles coil tight and like an idiot, he reaches back and that's when I see a gun. More confirmation to set off my worries. Cements my rush to get the hell away.

The intent is there. Pure stupidity.

"I am," I say before things escalate further. "I'm the youngest child."

"Then I apologize ahead of time." Before anyone can blink, a second gun is in his other hand and he points them at my brother and father. My scream is loud. A natural reaction. "Hands off the weapon, Foster. Place them where I can see them."

He does along with my father. "Tell Asher we will be there. Tomorrow at eleven."

"All of you?"

"Yes." I'm the one who answers. Even if I catch hell after he leaves, I want this over with.

Whatever comes tomorrow, I'll get past it.

Working is all I have left, and it's my way out from underneath their thumb.

I just hope that this Mr. Asher understands that I'm innocent. That I'm not like them.

MALCOLM

"**W**ANT TO TELL ME why I left my bed to visit that asshole in the middle of the night?" Javier asks, slipping inside my car across the street from their house in Hinsdale. I'm all too familiar with this gated community, know people that live here, and as she showed her keycard and the gate unlocked to let her in, I followed.

He's waiting for an explanation, but at the moment, my attention is on their house. All the lights downstairs are on, and I can just make out the form of a man pacing in front of the living room windows.

He looks agitated, waving his hand angrily at something or someone.

"I don't like these fucks." Something isn't right with this family. Their arrival here a few months back made waves, but I let it slide as a favor to a friend. Same friend that he owes.

I've been patient while watching the recent boost in cocaine running through the southside, however, the Jameson situation is where I draw the line. Forcing me to make a phone call and change plans.

I'll pay Thiago the money in exchange for his life.

The oldest son of Marcus Foster is a fuckup. A pompous asshole who thinks he's invincible, and power should just be given to him.

A mid-level dealer with a death wish.

"Agreed."

"Was she in the room?" Stretching my neck, I lower the window and spark up another cigarette. The fourth of the night. I'm wound tight, muscles coiling, and nothing seems to calm me. Every cell in my body demands that I break down their door and take her.

Somewhere between the club and her house, my thoughts have become clear. The voice inside, that animal I keep under control in front of the world, demands that I save her. Her innocence is titillating, exciting, and also London's downfall.

Why are they hiding her? That thought is churning within me. Bringing out a side that only the few women in my family ever see: a protector.

Deciding to stay inside the car was a last-minute decision. A hard one.

Tomorrow. But it made the most sense.

I'll deal my cards then. Twirl will be inside my home, within my protection, and I can control how and when I approach.

Her brother and father are full of envious desires; they'll be too busy plotting to realize that she's already met me. That I've already taken ownership of the youngest in the family. That they are dead men walking.

Getting her alone won't be a problem.

"She was."

"And…" Taking a deep pull of smoke into my lungs, I hold it for a few seconds before exhaling through my nose.

"His demeanor as he stood over her was possessive." For some reason, I am not surprised by this. I've been expecting this confirmation. Fire flows like lava through my veins as more pieces of this puzzle fall into place, and I have no doubt that my London is looking for an escape. To get away from them.

Question is, though, what do they want her for? How does she play into any of this?

Maybe she knows who I am and is… I stop that thought in its tracks. My Twirl is innocent, of that I have no doubt. Reading people comes with this line of work, and that girl is afraid of the world, not looking to dominate it.

There are two reasons why anyone, of their own free will, sells their body for profit. Desperation, or because you like it. You need the money, or get off on the depravity.

May God have mercy on their souls, because I won't. I want their blood on my hands, and nothing cements that more than seeing London's tiny figure standing at a small bedroom window upstairs.

The dim lights surround her like a warm halo. She's so fucking beautiful, and in that moment, I vow to protect her. Kill every single member of her family if they are the cause of her pain.

"What am I missing here?"

"Not now."

"Are we leaving?"

"Not now," I grit out, teeth grinding as London wipes her cheeks. She looks sad—pensive, while looking up into the night sky.

"This is about the girl." Not a question, and I don't answer. "Something isn't quite right in that house, Malcolm. The way they tried to keep her hidden, the fear in her expression…"

"What did Alton say about my invitation?" Twirl moves away from the window, and after a few minutes, all goes dark. *Good night, baby.*

"They'll be there."

"Good." Nodding, I take the last pull on my cigarette and flick the butt toward the asphalt. "I want a file on London Foster on my desk by ten a.m. Everything on her."

"Just her?"

"She's the only one that matters."

"Sir, your guests just arrived," my security at the gate announces through the intercom, and my eyes flick to the center screen across from me. I see the car. A shiny and new Mercedes in white that looks nothing like the rusty scrap of metal Toyota my Twirl drives. *Mistake number one.* "Do I let them pass or…?"

"No search. Open." I'm not going to scare London.

"As you wish." The gate opens, and they drive up until they reach the roundabout, where another member of security waits for them. You can see the looks of envy on the two males, while London looks uncomfortable. The worry is plain to see as it flashes across her delicate features.

I can't have that. After today, I want this to be where she finds safety.

Closing her folder, I put the information in the top drawer to my left and lock it. I've read enough to understand the mystery behind their actions.

What her miserable family fails to realize is that in my world, people talk. They are always willing to sell you out for a profit, something two of Alton's street pushers were all too eager to do.

My sweet little Twirl is nothing more than a pawn to the two Foster men, and it all stems from a lie. Something her mother took to her grave when she suddenly died four years ago, leaving a sixteen-year-old girl to fend for herself after a robbery gone wrong.

Or so the police report says.

One, to get out of a growing debt, he's been shopping around her innocence. Tempting the sick fucks he surrounds himself with into desiring the cherry between her thighs for a hefty price.

The other, he wants to dominate—intimidate her into becoming his whore. Alton wants an heir, but not from his fiancée, the submissive idiot who dotes on him because of his make-believe status. That gold-digger isn't good enough. He wants London. Wants to fuck her while parading the other around town.

Alton believes that London is his. His way into a hefty sum of money that she'll receive on her twenty-first birthday. A child will bind them together and is leverage in case she rebels.

Neither of these plans will come to fruition. I will never allow it to happen.

Two certificates have been signed, and I am the executioner.

"Malcolm?" Mariah slips inside wearing a huge shit-eating grin. I'm sure Javier has something to do with it. That she knows. "Magda's attending to them in the parlor, and Javier is standing like a pit bull guarding your package."

"Don't be obnoxious."

"Don't ruin my fun."

"You're lucky that I love you, little cousin. So very lucky." Pushing my chair back, I make my way around the desk and reach her at the door. "Make friends." There's no need for me to elaborate. She understands.

"Got it." Mariah nods with a smirk. "By the way, she looks sweet."

"She's untouchable."

"Thought as much," she muses, eyeing my black jeans, plain T-shirt, and boots. "Why aren't you wearing your typical overpriced suit? I approve of this, by the way."

"I want her to feel comfortable here." It's the truth. The last thing I want is for her to feel intimidated by me.

"Who knew you could be so sweet?" Slipping her arm through mine, she tugs me down the hall and toward the voice of London's father, who is asking for a whiskey neat as I enter. No one notices me, but I see the dynamic. The men are in suits and sitting with a leg crossed at the knee, arms stretched over the back of the couch—a mimicking pose—while Twirl looks like she wants to disappear within the cushions of her chair.

She looks beautiful; there is no denying this as I stand and watch. However, the expression of distress and the way she tugs at the hem of her knee-length, bright pink bandage dress, tugs at my chest. You can see that she doesn't want to be here, and while it's my fault, I'll also be the one to right every wrong for her.

She's no longer alone.

My eyes skim down her sweet face and pouty lips to the decadence of her collarbones when I notice a discoloration mars her soft skin. Lower, I find a few more down her arms, and the growl that builds in my chest is unstoppable. It's loud and full of fury, shaking me where I stand as I catalogue every bruise.

"Don't scare her. She's good for you," Mariah whispers, passing me while making her way toward an equally-as-quiet Javi. His eyes meet mine and I nod, signaling the first move in this game.

"Hey, man. Good to see you again," Alton says, voice dripping in fake politeness. Hand outstretched for me to shake, he stands, completely ignorant to the nonexistent restraint I'm functioning under. "Thank you for the *sudden* invitation."

Taking his hand in mine, I squeeze hard enough to feel a knuckle buckle and dislocate. The pop is subtle, but no one misses his accompanying curse. "It's Mr. Asher to you, Foster. I won't correct you again."

"Understood," he grits out from between clenched teeth, rubbing his sore hand. "How can we help you, Mr. Asher?"

Fuck, I want to bash his skull in and watch the blood drip from every wall in this room. The carnal desire for retribution ignites within me, and I want to feed the monster within.

Because everyone has one. That wicked urge to take matters into your own hands and right the wrongs you've been dealt, and while most people ignore that voice, I revel in mine. Need it.

The fingers of my right hand twitch as it lowers to my side, and the cold steel behind my back beckons me to end this bullshit game that he will never win.

And I almost do, until I hear the soft gasp that escapes her, and our eyes meet for a brief second. Her distress is clear to see, and so is the subtle blush that sweeps across the apple of her cheek.

My little Twirl doesn't know how to react. What to expect.

While her brother and father are looking at the dipshit's hand, I send her a soft smile. She returns the small gesture and then quickly looks down before anyone sees her.

I remind myself that his moment will come when my Twirl isn't here to witness. Never in front of her. She's not ready for my darkness…*yet*.

"Mr. Foster…" her father begins, standing up beside his son but he doesn't offer me his hand "…is there a reason for this sudden request? Have we offended you somehow?"

"Marcus, have you ever heard the saying: *no bad deed goes unpunished*?"

"I-I have." Marcus swallows hard while his eyes shift toward his son. "But what does it have to do with our being here?"

"Everything." Looking at Mariah, I hold up a hand. "Please give Miss Foster a walk through the gardens while I have a word with her family."

"Of course." Her smile is huge as she gives Javier's arm a squeeze and then walks toward a still-as-a-statue Twirl. "Let's leave the boring men to their business while we go grab a treat from Magda's kitchen. She makes the best double fudge brownies ever."

I can see that she's not sure what to do, and I'll be fucked if she asks for permission from these assholes.

"Go on, London. Enjoy the treat."

"Lola's fine, Ash—"

My glare shuts him up, and I also don't miss her expression of disgust at the nickname. "Did I ask for your opinion on the matter?"

"No."

"Then I suggest you learn to speak when spoken to." With that, I look back at Twirl and Mariah. "Enjoy yourselves, girls. This will be a little while."

"Of course, dear cousin. Take your time."

And it's as they walk out of the room that I catch a glimpse of the naughtiness she keeps under lock and key. There's a small smirk on her lips, a brightness in her eyes as she mouths the words *thank you.*

I am the sole person in this world she should ever fear, and the only one that will never harm her.

MALCOLM

THE MOMENT THE LADIES leave, Alton shifts his angry glare my way. I know what he's going to say, but before the man further embarrasses himself, I walk over to my chair.

The same one that London was occupying a few minutes ago. I take in a deep breath, filling my lungs with her soft floral scent, and it takes everything in me to hold in the groan of pleasure.

There's a low chuckle that meets my ears a second before Javier takes a seat to my right, but I don't address his amusement. Instead, I arch a brow at my guest.

Two sit. Two stand.

"Are you waiting for an invitation?"

"How do you know my London?" Marcus asks, not moving to follow directions. He's fidgety, brow showing a hint of perspiration. Reeks of guilt.

"Sit down." I'm done with being pleasant. These two fucks need to understand just how vulnerable they are. "If I have to repeat myself, you'll each walk out with something broken. Understood?"

"Crystal." Marcus tugs on his son's uninjured hand to sit across from Javier on the opposite couch. For a few minutes we're quiet, my eyes on Alton while his grow uncomfortable with each second that passes. *Pussies.*

I have all the time in the world; my Twirl is safe.

A throat clears, and I shift my gaze to Marcus. "Speak."

"I'm sorry, but you must understand that as her father, I worry. How do you know London?"

Her father. Her father. Christ, this man is playing with the kind of fire that eviscerates, leaving no trace behind. It would be so easy. A flick of my wrist and two bullets is all it would take to eradicate the world of this filth.

"That's the wrong question, and we both know that." Leaning forward, I keep my eyes set on his. Let him see the fury burning behind this calm facade. "The correct one, is what *don't* I know?"

"Why are we here?" This time it's Alton who speaks up.

"Another stupid question." Standing up, I walk over to my bar and pour myself a few fingers' worth of gin. I can feel the stares on my back—the tension mounting—and I revel in it.

"Yet you give us no answer."

A chuckle escapes me, and I take a sip while walking back to my seat, savoring the crisp notes of citrus while the two asswipes squirm.

Another human trait that most cannot control: their nerves. Those ticks that are a part of our genetics—the makeup of our identities that controls reactions.

The shaking of limbs.

The twitch of a jaw.

The bouncing of a leg like the older man before me.

"Congratulations, Alton. You're as stupid as I thought you were."

"What the fuc—"

The click of Javier's gun stops him. "Try again, and be respectful. Do not mistake his generosity with patience."

"My apologies. No disrespect meant, I'm just..." He takes in a deep breath while shifting in his seat, using the same hand with the dislocated knuckle to push his weight toward me. He's in pain. Wishing he could retaliate against me—be me—but instead, is once again reminded to know his place.

I nod at Javi and he lowers his weapon. "Carry on."

"Please understand," Alton grits out, rubbing his hand, "I'm just concerned for my family. My sister isn't aware of our family's dealings, and yesterday's late-night visit has shaken her. I just want to make sure that everything between us is cool. That—"

"Save the bullshit spiel, Foster. We both know where your worries lie." I grab a small remote from atop a side table and point it toward the wall across from me. At once the whirling of a motor reverberates through the room as a faux wall moves up, exposing a hidden television screen above the fireplace.

Father and son look at the screen with trepidation that quickly turns to horror when a single image appears a second later. The color drains from their faces as reality smacks them.

It's his guy. The same piece of shit I personally killed less than forty-eight hours ago.

"Why are—"

"No more lies. No more playing dumb." The next photo is a close-up of his injuries. Each deep gash my knife made. Another shows his lifeless eyes and the gunshot wound that killed him. I leave the last one up. "Before you leave today, I want you to take a single lesson with you."

"Please let—"

"I know everything that happens in my city. Each move you make. Each breath you take."

"This is all a misunderstanding, Mr. Asher," Marcus begins once more while his son's eyes remain on the television. "Nothing that can't be talked over. We don't know why this young man involved us in anything."

Idiot gave himself away. *Fucking amateurs.*

"And who said that he involved you in anything?"

"But you said..."

"That I know it all. Take that as you wish." Standing up, I press a few buttons to hide everything again. Javier follows my lead, and we both walk to the room's entrance where I pause to address them again. "Today is nothing more than a friendly reminder. A warning, *dear friends*. Don't cross me, and mind yourselves—this isn't Miami. Thiago isn't who you should fear here."

It doesn't take long for me to find her.

She's alone and sitting on a small bench surrounded by roses. They're in full bloom, a small window of time here in Illinois that allows us to enjoy warm weather and the beauty of nature. It'll be gone soon enough; in a few weeks the temperatures will drop, and all this will die.

And yet, she stands out as the most exquisite flower of all.

Delicate and soft.

Decadent and sweet.

The innocence to my sins.

"I knew you would come," she says without looking up, in her hand a long-stemmed rose with a single petal still attached. The rest lay at her feet. "Mariah wasn't very secretive, nor was she a good actress."

"Is that so." I chuckle, coming closer. Just a few tiny steps separate us, and the fucking pull she holds over me is maddening. An invisible cord that controls me. "I'll be sure to tell her as much."

"Why did you demand that we visit today? Are you going to tell them about…" she trails off, embarrassment coloring her tone. "This is such a mess."

"I'll never say a word." Seeing her in distress makes my hands clench, but if I touch her, this conversation won't happen. My need is too strong, and I have very little control left when it comes to her. "Trust me."

"But I don't know you."

"My intentions will be very clear soon."

"That's very cryptic, Malcolm," she sighs, shoulders dropping low. "Is this some kind of game? Because if they find out I work at that club, I'm dead."

"That's something I will never allow. Never." Taking the remaining steps between us, I lift her chin with the tip of my finger. Force her bright blues on mine. "This isn't a game, Twirl. To me this—"

"Why do you call me Twirl?" she interrupts, and if she were anyone else, that would annoy me. However, even while being inquisitive, I find her utterly adorable in her purity.

London has the upper hand here and has no idea.

"It's simple, really." My finger skims down her warm cheek, following the soft trail of flesh until I reach the edge of her dress. A dress that I know she hates; I fist the material and in a single tug, pull her against me. The material stretches, showing me her strapless bra and a peak at her flat stomach, but I focus on her reaction instead.

"What the!" London yelps, stumbling into my chest at the sudden move. Her soft to my hard. Her delicate to my animalistic desires.

"Quiet, sweetheart. Let's not attract the attention of my guards." Wrapping my arms around her waist, I draw her in close, run the fingertips of my right hand up her spine until reaching her nape. My fingers wrap around the base, tilting her head back to face me. "I just want a little more time with you. Just us."

"You're so confusing," she mumbles, but I hear her. I also don't miss the small shivers rushing through her. The goose bumps on her skin. How she never pushes me away.

"No more than you are." I dip low and place my forehead against hers, lips hovering. "I'm still trying to understand what this undeniable pull is. Why I can't keep my hands to myself when you're near."

"You can't?" Fuck, how naïve she is rocks me. Sends a shock wave of pleasure through every limb, and I can't stop myself when I pull her even closer. Let her feel me. And she does. Those doe eyes widen and her lips part, her breath coming out in small pants against my mouth.

"I can't stay away. Not even if you asked me to." That realization should rock me, but it doesn't. Instead, it pulls everything into focus. I will bring the world down to its knees for her if she so much as asks. I will kill to own her. "My intentions aren't noble, Twirl. I want you. All of you."

"I don't know what to say," she whispers, cheeks flushing as her eyes wander to my mouth. "My family will never allow us to—"

"They are for me to worry about, baby…" I lick my lips, a move she follows "…leave everything to me."

"I don't know how. I depend on myself." The heaviness in her words breaks something inside of me. They'll pay for her sadness with their blood.

"Past tense. I'm here now." Moving my lips slightly to the right, I kiss her cheek with tiny little pecks, each one lingering longer than the last, driving her own need to surface. Her huff of frustration when I nip her chin tells me as much.

"Okay." It's an unsure whisper. London has no reason to believe me, but right now she's being led by the yearning for human contact. Her desire for my lips mirrors my own, and I groan loudly when she connects her mouth with mine.

"*Fuck*." My hands tighten their hold, cementing her body against me. Preventing her from pulling those plump lips from mine. She's soft and sweet; her taste sets off a chaotic explosion of hunger that shakes me, and I can't stop myself when I take a little more. My tongue parts her lips, sliding inside and entwining with hers.

Her touch is tentative, yet she doesn't back away. Instead, Twirl shows her own desire with little mewls of pleasure. How she fists her own hand in my hair to keep my mouth over hers.

London's acceptance of my dominance in this instance has me harder than steel. Almost demonic in my thirst to be buried deep inside her warmth.

"More," she moans low, a kittenish sound that shoots straight down to my cock, and I flex against her. Give a harsh jerk that brings me back down to reality.

I will have her, but not today. Not when we can be interrupted at any moment.

Slowing the kiss down, I embed my teeth into her bottom lip for a second and pull back. Her breathing and mine is labored, chest heaving as we slowly regain our composure.

"I'm going to need you to head back inside now, Twirl. Follow that path…" I point to the left of us "…and Mariah will be there. She'll take you back to where your family waits for brunch."

"What about you? Where will you be?"

"I'll be a few minutes behind, but I have eyes on you. Trust me."

She nods, gifting me a soft smile. "I'll try my best."

"Thank you, beautiful." Before she can take a single step, I press our mouths together once more and breathe her in. My nose skims the delicate skin from her lips to ear, where I pause. Kiss her pulse point. "I call you Twirl because you remind me of a ballerina. So pretty when you move, with the poise of an elegant swan. You're very distracting, London, and I'm enjoying each moment of madness."

London

"HOW WAS YOUR WALK?" Alton asks as soon as we enter the dining room, and I freeze up. His hand is wrapped in a dishtowel with what I can only assume is ice, and while his smile is friendly enough, I know better than to believe it. The truth is in the tightness around his eyes.

Did he notice my reaction to seeing Malcolm enter the room? Fear of his anger causes my hands to shake and for my body to want to withdraw into itself.

I couldn't stop myself then, no matter how hard I bit the inside of my cheek when Malcolm's eyes met my own. When his stare, so full of heat, ate me alive. Everything from last night came flooding back; his touch and the soft kisses he lay on my stomach while I poured his drink. How he took my scent into his lungs and groaned into my dress. All of it, every lustful moment hit me, while mixing with an uncontrollable horror that my family knew my secret.

But now, add to that my brother's calculating stare, and once more my panic ensues. I know him. Alton's thinking of ways to pin this disaster of a meeting on me.

Because with him, I am always to blame. Has been that way since Mom died a few years ago. If a glass so much as breaks in the house, even if I am not there it falls on my shoulders.

Their hate toward me makes no sense, but I no longer deny it. I've done nothing wrong except exist, and yet to them, it's reason enough.

Why weren't they like this when Mom was alive?

Why do I always feel like I'm missing a huge piece of a puzzle?

"It was a lot of fun," Mariah answers for me before I can come up with a lie, walking toward the side of the table where Javier is waiting. "Your sister has quite the keen eye for décor—colors, and I might need her help soon. Redecorating my loft will take some time, and another female point of view will come in handy. Don't you think, dear cousin?"

"I agree." Malcolm enters the room from the opposite entrance. Immediately the atmosphere changes once again. This time an electrical current of desire swirls all around me, and staying in place is difficult. My body throbs in his presence, while my levels of distress lower.

I feel weirdly…*safe*. Something that baffles me.

His presence dominates every square inch of this room while pushing my fear back. It loosens the tightening noose, letting me breathe.

Malcolm stops at the head of the table and looks at me, then at my father. The warmth from just a few minutes prior is completely gone. "Will that be a problem, Marcus?"

No one misses how he asks my father and not the head of our family. Something that infuriates my brother, and in a sick and perverse way, causes a smidgen of giddiness to flow through me. His lack of respect for the men in my family is clear to see, and I find myself delighting in the fact that the shoe is on the other foot for once.

That they'll experience inferiority like I do day in and day out.

"What do you think, Alton?"

"I didn't ask him for his opinion, Marcus, but yours. Now, answer the simple question."

My father nods his head, his lips thinning. "Yeah, that'll be fine. London could use new friend."

More like any friend. I'm a prisoner in my own home, the home my mother's father left her, and the only time I see the outside is when I work. No school. No fun. All I'm good for is to cook and clean—to bring home money so they can make payments to the Riveras.

Or spend it on some idiotic idea.

And let's not forget the poker tables my father frequents almost every other day.

We're lucky that Mom's family came from money and that our house is completely paid off. That when we came back from Miami after another failure from Alton, we had somewhere to live.

"Perfect." While Javier grabs Mariah's chair to pull it out, Malcolm does the same with mine, smiling at me, but then just as soon his eyes narrow. "Why are you full of bruises, Ms. Foster? Did you have an accident recently?"

Dad chokes on his drink while Alton looks at me, daring me to say anything. What's worse is that I know Malcolm saw these earlier, but why put me on the spot like this? Why mention it now in front of them?

"Just a minor slip last night," I lie, and he knows this. The way he glares toward the men in my family lets them know he isn't buying a single word coming out of my mouth. That he's doing this on purpose. That he's paying attention to even the most minute thing. "It's nothing, Mr. Asher. I'm clumsy."

I hate having to cover for them, but it'll be worse if I don't. Alton has never hit me, but I fear that day isn't too far into the future. The more I deny him, recoil from his advances, the angrier he gets.

Moreover, if he does, my father will never stop him. He'll never disagree or go against his prodigy.

Malcolm purses his lips, eyes hard. "No more clumsiness, London. No more bruises."

"Okay," I whisper, hating the way everyone stares at me. At the purplish marks left behind by the men who are supposed to protect me above all else. "I'll pay better attention to—"

Just then, a stomach grumbles loudly and Mariah laughs. "Sorry. I missed breakfast this morning due to work."

Thank God that works and the tension level drops as her boyfriend and mine—

No, not mine. I can't allow myself to get lost in him.

Malcolm asks me to trust him, and I'll try. However, my plans won't change.

He is a customer and a means to an end. My mind can't negate that. I'm so close to getting out of this clusterfuck, and it's the only thing that matters.

Their chuckles bring me back to the present and I know that I missed something, not that my brother or father notice the distress I am suddenly under. The confusion. Instead, they reach to serve themselves while Magda continues to bring in trays of food.

But *his* eyes aren't fooled. No, those deep seafoam eyes stare at me. See me.

Realize the danger I live under.

Moreover, it's in that dark stare that I get lost in once more. That I find myself wanting to lean toward. My skin tingles and heartbeats accelerate— my body is in tune with his every exhale, and for a second, I give in and hope. Make believe that he's here to rescue me from this hell of a life.

Trust me, he mouths again, and God, I want to.

I just don't know how.

MALCOLM

I ARRIVE AT THE office on Monday, the sun bouncing off the mirrored windows of the skyline while the streets begin to fill with morning commuters. It's early, but something doesn't belong in the picture before me, and I exit my car, making eye contact with a maintenance van across the street.

They aren't the best at hiding or looking for surveillance cameras—my guys had them on their radar within the first ten minutes.

Two of them.

The first is an older man, portly and with a mustache that hasn't changed since the seventies. He's someone I've dealt with before in the past and have a certain level of respect for. A man who still follows his moral compass.

A serious FBI agent. Has integrity.

Marcelles can't be bought and treats other with basic human decency. Even a motherfucker like me—a criminal—can appreciate that.

However, the other guy looks to be fresh off the Quantico farm. New in the field from the intel my own employees have given and the encrypted email my informant within the bureau sent a few hours ago.

No older than thirty, he's got sandy blond hair cut low and a medium build—average height and weight. Fidgety, he seems itching for action and can't stay still for long, which gives them away. You can't have a successful stakeout with someone leaving their post every thirty minutes on the dot to light up a smoke.

"I'm a bit insulted," Javier says, exiting the car behind me. He falls in step as we walk toward my building; neither the bank's lobby nor the offices above are open yet, but the financial district is full of nine-to-fivers arriving at work.

At that moment my all-black Navigator pulls away from the curb, merging into traffic and ignoring a horn. With the commute being horrendous Monday through Friday, a driver comes in handy.

"Agreed." I stop and turn, looking down at my watch. It's thirty to nine and I'm sure they'll be visiting before my ten a.m. coffee. I'm half tempted to wave just to move the process along; I have things to do and my girl to see. Being apart from her isn't sitting well with me.

I don't trust her brother or father to not do something stupid.

It's also why the man I have watching her has authorization to shoot first, no questions asked.

"Wonder why?"

I shrug. "To be honest, I expected more fanfare than this."

Not that they will find anything. The servers were wiped before the dawn of Saturday morning and the paper trails burned. Every trace of the Jameson name has been erased from our system in the aftermath of Michael's idiocy and Foster's greed, leaving nothing behind on our dealings or the physical money.

Money that I took ahold of and moved out of the States for security reasons.

No money. No evidence. No case.

"It's odd how very few have interest in that sale?" His phone pings then and he ignores it, which I raise a brow to. "It's an alarm your cousin set up on my phone. Woman is driving me insane with this multivitamin she wants me to take. Some crap she found in a TV informercial."

"And you aren't?"

"Nope. Just humoring her."

I shake my head at that with a chuckle. "Not surprised. You just can't say no to her."

"That word doesn't exist in her vocabulary, and I blame your parents and hers for that little gift."

The van's driver side window lowers a smidge then and the red tip of a cigarette becomes visible. We both look; I make it a point to let them know I'm aware they are there.

Marcelles has to be fuming inside that vehicle. Angry at the fact the moron he's working with doesn't understand the concept of being inconspicuous.

"Two, and one is green."

"Saw that." Javi brings his cup of coffee up to his mouth and takes a sip. For a man that holds no qualms in getting his hands *dirty*, he has an unhealthy love affair with whatever a caramel macchiato is. "For sale, though?"

Turning back to my building, I shrug once I reach the front doors of the Asher Building. "Possibly."

"Do we approach and make an offer on the land?"

"Not yet." They're listening. I know this. See the minute shift in a device they have hidden under a tarp and chain combination. What looks to be just sheet rock material being secured to the roof and side of the van. They went with blending in and not high tech, a mistake if you ask me. "Let them approach me first."

* * *

"Mr. Asher, you have some visitors," Mariah says through the intercom a few hours later, her tone saccharine sweet—her way of addressing me when someone doesn't know who she is. "Are you busy, or can they pass?"

"Let them in." I sit back in my chair and make it a point of not shutting down my laptop. Let them see what I am working on; there's an architect's 3D model of my new bank in Shanghai on the screen along with the paperwork that gives away the logistics, cost, and timeframe for it to be up and running. I hide nothing, because by the time they always come demanding entry, the evidence they hope to find is gone.

"Of course, sir." There's no click from her side, letting me know she didn't disconnect, and I pay closer attention. "Right this way, gentlemen."

"Do you like working for him?" It's the younger one. Marcelles knows who she is. Knows better. "Does he treat you right?"

"Jesus," I mutter under my breath, amused by this.

"I hate it." And you can hear the pout in her tone.

"Why? Has he ever done anything to—"

"My cousin is forcing me to order his lunch every day. To file stuff in those big metal boxes with drawers." There's a cough, not sure from who, but it holds a hint of a laugh. "My nails look like crap at the end of each shift and my curls lose their volume. This is hell on earth."

"I'm so sorry you—"

"Christ, Shawn," Marcelles snaps, silencing his partner. "Mariah is Malcolm Asher's cousin and secretary. Whatever angle you're trying to play...just stop. We're not here for anything other than a word with the owner."

"Always a pleasure, Paul." Mariah laughs, the clack of her heels following her to my door. She pauses just outside and gives a knock. "May I?"

Brat. "Yes." The door opens and she enters first, walking behind my desk and taking her position to my left. They follow her in, stopping behind the two chairs on the opposite side. One looks normal and the other overexcited. "How can I help you, agents?"

"How did you know?"

"How are you, Malcolm?" they reply in unison, but my attention is on the older man. He extends a hand out for me to shake and I reach across my desk to do so, ignoring the now visibly annoyed toddler beside him. "How's your father?"

"Battling boredom at the golf course."

"Since when does Anthony golf?"

"Since my mother decided that they needed to be handier around the house in their old age. Her *honey do* list is a mile long, hence the new appreciation for golf." I can see that this small talk is angering the other man. Shawn doesn't like that a criminal—although I've yet to be indicted or convicted of anything—is acting as if their visit is of no consequence.

He doesn't appreciate that his *partner* isn't rude or demanding shit. He has a lot to learn. About me. About the way the world works.

Unless you have solid proof and come with an arrest warrant, you can't touch me or my belongings. And even worse, the fact that I'll never see the inside of a cell or receive anything other than a slap on the wrist grates on some people's nerves.

If I go down, so does the precious economic standing—luxuries—some high-ranking members of government enjoy. More money runs through this bank than any other in the United States, Europe, and China. Hurting my empire will crumble theirs.

No more hush money.

No more lobbying.

No more power.

Even if it tastes rancid in their mouth, I'm to be treated with respect.

Moreover, Shawn hates it. I see it in his face.

His eyes narrow and nostrils flare. "We need access to every deposit made into the United States from clients outside the country. Everything from late July to now."

"Is that so?" I scratch my chin, flicking my eyes from him to Marcelles. "His first job?"

"Yes."

"So, he knows procedure?"

"Yes." Poor man looks embarrassed.

"I'm right here," Shawn sneers, and it's hard not to knock his teeth back into his skull. "We have reason to believe that your bank is aiding in the illegal move of drug money."

"You're accusing me of a federal crime. Be very careful with that, agent. Your career can go—"

"Are you threatening me?"

"I'm stating a fact." I narrow my eyes, leaning forward in my seat with both hands flat atop my desk so I'm not tempted to reach for the gun. My eyes remain on his, even after Marcelles tries to intervene. With a single hand up, I stop him and direct myself solely to a now visibly uncomfortable Shawn. "I'm going to let your disrespect and unprofessionalism pass this one time. Take it as a will of good faith because you are new and clearly don't do your homework before throwing that badge around. What you're doing is overstepping the boundaries, the same laws you are pretending to uphold, yet feel as though you can now trample because of what? What is the point of this visit other than to harass and throw out weightless allegations?"

"We were told by an informant that this bank has ties to the Jameson family," Marcelles says then, his tone calm and without accusation. "We're just trying to follow up on a lead, Malcolm. Before a warrant is brought forth, we were hoping for your cooperation with this matter."

"Our conversation would've stayed on a friendlier note…" I tilt my chin in Shawn's direction "…had he not opened his mouth."

"Can we have a look or not?" Shawn tries to reinsert himself into our conversation, but I don't acknowledge him.

"How do you want to do this, Marcelles? Should I call my lawyer?"

"He will leave, and I'll handle this myself."

"I'm not going anywhere."

"If he does, then we have a deal." I nod, and the old man's posture relaxes a bit. "He needs to get off my property and not come back until he learns respect and how to follow protocol."

"It's a deal. I'll speak with my supervisor now and be back within the hour."

"Director Monahan will never agree to this," Shawn hisses through clenching teeth. "He'll never make a deal with—"

"Luther Monahan is someone I've known since I was a child and would not put up with his agents being obtuse and arrogant. Watch your tone and the way you conduct yourself." At my words, the cockiness in his stance deflates and worry seeps in. "You don't seem to realize just who you're dealing with here. Who I am. Look me up—learn a thing or two, and then when you're ready to apologize for basing your judgement on idiocy, you may come back."

"I'll never apologize to—"

"It's time for you to leave, agents. Follow me." Mariah, who's been quiet, interrupts Shawn. Our eyes lock for a second and I nod, fighting the smirk that wants to curl on my lips. "Mr. Asher has a day full of meetings, but I'll be available to handle everything with you personally, Marcelles."

"Agreed, and thank you." While I know Marcelles doesn't buy that I'm one hundred percent innocent, he still sticks to the rules. Doesn't overstep or accuse, because thrown-around insinuations can become defamation lawsuits.

"This is not how this works. You can't just kick me out," Shawn tries once more, his tone with Mariah a lot less arrogant. I also don't miss the appreciative looks he's giving her, ones that Javier will kill him for.

"Not up for negotiations." She walks around my desk and doesn't stop until reaching the door. There, she waits for them with a not-so-patient look and it's funny to watch how quickly they follow instructions. "Now, let's get you out and let Mr. Asher get back to work. He's a busy man and can't entertain nonsense."

And as they walk out and head toward the elevators, I only have one thought:

I'm going to enjoy watching the life drain from his body at Javier's hands.

MALCOLM

I FIND MYSELF standing over her bed two days later watching her sleep, the same way I've been coming into her home since Sunday night, using a copy of her key made with an imprint in clay, to be with her.

That very day I set a few plans in motion to protect her, the first being my entry and exit out of her home without detection. It didn't take much work to trip Alton's cheap system. Thirty minutes and a few Red Bulls later, my best IT guy hacked the system, putting the recording of a quiet house on loop and disabling the alarm.

No alerts. No proof of my ever being here.

To protect her while she gets some rest. Make sure that no one disturbs her.

She makes me worry. I feel protective— need to feed this uncontrollable desire to be close.

I tell myself it's because I want to make sure she's okay, but it's a lie. A poor one at that.

Every minute she's in this house, I'm restless. Worry.

Her family isn't to be trusted; the assholes disappear at night as they plot my end. Try to find anyone willing to take me on as a job. Offering money they don't have.

Alton doesn't understand that I have eyes everywhere. That for the right price, people are always willing to talk and sell him out.

London turns onto her back then, the thick comforter covering her from view falling down and exposing her chest. I count each rise and fall while contemplating how much my life has changed. Just how far I'm willing to go to keep her.

It's been five days since she walked into my private room and danced for me.

Four days since I've had some peace where she isn't invading my every waking moment.

Since that first night, I've become her stalker. Always just a few steps behind her in some way or another, gifting her the invisible space she needs to get used to the idea of me. Giving her the illusion that I'm not around when in fact, it's the opposite.

I'll always be here.

"Malcolm," Twirl sighs in her sleep, completely unaware of my presence. "So confusing…"

Son of a bitch. Even her sleep talk is adorable. Makes me feel like a king when it's my name that passes through those plump lips.

Leaning over her, I skim a finger down her soft cheek. Enjoy the way she turns into my touch so innocently. Her response is automatic. "Salvation comes with sacrifices. Yours will be in his blood." I press the tip of my finger to her lips. Linger there for a moment as her warm breath caresses my skin. "Sleep, knowing that you are protected. I'll always take care of you."

My phone vibrates inside my pocket, alerting me to the time. Pulling back, I reach over and pick up her older-than-dirt flip phone to dial mine— the call goes through and after I hit the end button, I erase it from her directory.

Walking to the door without another backwards glance, I exit the house through the back door. It's almost five in the morning, and I need to catch a few hours of sleep before heading in to work. There's a new position I need to fill and soon; a personal bodyguard for her. A female.

My men are good, but any male in her presence rattles the cage of my demon's jealousy.

Pushes me past what I am comfortable with.

I'm going to be the only man in her life.

THERE'S a timid knock a few minutes after one in the afternoon. "You wanted to see me, sir?" Earl asks just outside my open office door. He's waiting for me to let him in, looking tired and full of worry—the deep wrinkles on his forehead crease and his brows furrow. "Is everything okay?"

I offer him a small smile to ease the tension and wave him in. "Come in and have a seat, please."

"Should I close the door?"

"Not necessary."

"Okay." There's a tray Mariah left before leaving for lunch with a few bottles of cold pop, water bottles, and a few pastries. He eyes them but makes no move to take one.

"You don't have to ask or be offered one. Take whatever you want, Earl." For this conversation I need him to feel at ease, to relax enough to be forthcoming with the information I'm after.

"Thank you." He gives me a sheepish grin. "I've been so nervous after Mary relayed your message that I missed breakfast and lunch today."

"There's no reason for you to be nervous. None at all." Standing from behind my desk, I grab a Sprite and walk over to the small seating area across the room, taking a seat in a leather chair. I point to the small sofa to my right and against the wall for him to follow; he does so with his snacks in hand and waits. Looks at me without making a single peep. "Please understand that what we discuss in here today is a private and delicate matter. That I'm looking to help someone I think is in danger."

"Of course, sir..." I raise a brow and he chuckles "...Malcolm. Sorry. I'm just not used to addressing my superiors by their first names. It feels disrespectful."

"It's not when I'm asking you to. You've more than earned mine." Uncapping my drink, I take a few sips and set it down on a small glass coffee table beside a plain manila folder. "And it's because of that trust that I come asking for help.

"Anything I can do, I will. You know that."

"I appreciate that." Sitting forward, I let my hands hang between my thighs. "I need you to tell me the truth—everything you know about someone we both know."

"Who?" he asks, nose scrunching up before taking a sip from his drink.

"Who is London Foster, Earl?"

The man splutters, choking on his drink while the pastry slips to the floor. Earl wipes his chin with a handkerchief he pulls from his front pocket, his eyes wide as saucers. "Whatever she did, I'll take responsibility for. It's on me. I'll pay for."

"That isn't necessary. I assure you—"

"Please, Malcolm. She's been through enough." I'm not one to be cut off, but in this instance it works. He cares for her, sees what I do, and I have no doubt that he'll help me. "Give her a break. I don't know what she did, but her home life is shit and Mary and I do what we can to help without her brother or father knowing. Those two pricks use her—the money her mother left her—"

"I know."

"What?"

"Earl, I'm not going to hurt her. I'm here to protect every single hair on that pretty little head."

"But why?" He looks at me as if I'm the devil playing God, causing me to laugh.

"Honest to God, I want to help her," I say simply after a few minutes, my amusement waning. *Own her,* but I don't voice that part aloud. Instead, I relax in my seat—controlling the part of me that demands answers. That wants to reach across and force the information out of him.

What stops me from doing so is his honest affection for her. The fact that I know London would be angry, and to me, that's unacceptable.

"How do you know her? What did she do?"

"It's her brother's head I'm after."

Earl runs a hand down his face, a deep sigh leaving him. "That asshole is not Amelia's son."

"Amelia is their mother, no?" I'm baiting. Already know this. What I want is the details that aren't on a piece of paper. Firsthand accounts of how Marcus weaseled his way in. How he and his son came to hold Twirl's future in their hands.

"She is *her* mother." He takes another deep breath and lets it out slow. He's trying to figure me out and what to say. If he can save her.

"Earl, I'm not going to hurt her…" there's a small folder on the table that I push his way "…quite the contrary, actually."

"What's this?"

"Open it." Shooting me another questioning gaze, he takes the folder in his hands and opens it. His eyes skim across each page, taking in every single bit of information inside. The who, how, and when of the Fosters' operations. But more importantly, how they are funding their schemes.

Because that is what they are. A low-level operation running on one grandeur fuckup after another.

"As you can see, I've already done my homework. I know their plans, old man, but I need you to fill in the blanks. Help me end this for her."

"Malcolm, why are you doing this? What did Marcus and his degenerate son do?

"Hurt her." At my words his eyes snap to mine, and in them I see the same hate that's been brewing within me. I'm not the nicest man—being seen as an asshole doesn't hurt my feelings—but the one thing I will never do is hurt an innocent. Someone who has nothing to do with this life I've chosen. "He put his hands on that which is pure."

"You care?"

"I do."

"And she will be okay? No harm will come to her?"

"London will never know fear again as long as I have breath left in my body."

"Okay. Okay." Earl pulls his wallet from his back pocket and produces an old, worn picture from inside. It's the picture of two women about the same age as Twirl is now. There's no doubt that the one on the left is a younger version of Mary, his wife, but the other is the spitting image of London.

Or in this case, my girl looks just like her mother. The resemblance is uncanny.

It also proves that there's a connection between the families.

"How did you all know each other?"

"Mary and Amelia were best friends. They grew up and went to school together...Catholic school at that." He chuckles as a small hint of pink touches his ears. "They were beautiful, but my eyes have always been for Mary, even though she was completely out of my league. They came from a somewhat upper-class upbringing while I was poor, not that it mattered to me. One look at Mary and I was a goner, something that amused Amelia. She didn't get it until she met Julian Conte her senior year of high school."

"Julian Conte? That names sounds very familiar."

"That's because he owned a chain of restaurants all over Illinois. Amore *was* theirs."

"Was?"

Earl nods. "He passed away when Amelia was still pregnant with London. Horrible car accident on his way home one night...he died on impact."

"Jesus." My poor Twirl's entire life has been filled with nothing but loss. Of her father. Of her mother. Her money and basic human rights.

"Yeah." Grabbing his drink, he takes a few sips while trying to gather his thoughts. "They fell in love. It was fast and hard and everything she ever wanted. Julian was good to her, there for her, and even in his death, took care of them. Everything he had was given to Amelia and at her death, it went to London."

Standing up, I walk over to the windows and look out at the Chicago sky. "However, it didn't go to her. Why?"

"When Marcus sunk his claws into Amelia, whose father left her some money as well, he adopted London and became the guardian of her inheritance until she turns twenty-one. He pushed and pushed and fought with her until Amelia took in his son and did the same. He manipulated her. Isolated her. Kept her from anyone and everyone that could see what was really going on."

"Where was her family? Why didn't anyone step in?" There're so many questions running through my mind. So many emotions.

I'm angry for her. For everything she was put through because of someone's greed.

Because that's what the fucked up situation my Twirl's in comes down to. Money.

"We tried," he suddenly snaps, but it's not at me and I don't interrupt him. You can tell he's angry at himself for not doing more, and I want that. Let him talk. Get it off his chest while I get the info I need. "Time and time again, we tried to reason with her. Prove to her that she was better off without his toxicity."

Turning to face him, I lean back against the glass. Expression neutral. "And what happened?"

"Mary had a really bad fight with her the year before she died." For a few minutes he's quiet, breathing choppy while he looks down at the last sheet of paper in the folder. The private investigation into Amelia's death. "She begged her to leave him after a particularly bad fight. He was cheating and when confronted, smacked her around a bit. I fought him for her, beat his ass, and then went over with a few guys to get her out of that house until she could evict him through the courts. Everything had been set and bags packed, when the asshole decided to take London out of school for a father/daughter day." Earl looks up at me then, his eyes holding so much sadness. "You know what's the best way to win any mother over?

"Love the child."

"Exactly. He knew that treating London like a princess would grant him forgiveness."

"I'm going to make this right for her. I'm going to take care of her."

"Amelia was a good mother that made mistakes, Malcolm, but I swear to you, all she wanted was for her little girl to have a family. The father that she lost." He stands and walks over to me, looks me in the eye. Pleading with me. "To the courts, he's in charge of her inheritance—the sale of the restaurant chain and her mother's money—and decides how her monthly stipend is spent until she turns twenty-one as per Amelia's will. All her life that little girl has been nothing more than a pawn in a game, and she needs someone to defend her. Care for her."

"I'm going to make him pay," I vow, extending a hand out, which he takes and tightens his grip. "Both of them will be avenged."

"Thank you."

"None needed." Just then my phone pings with a message from Javi.

> Breaking News on 32 ~Javier

Grabbing the remote from the coffee table, I turn on the large TV mounted on the wall. It's already on the channel when an image comes on, and I can't stop the smile that forms on my lips. There, in the middle of a quaint little shopping center's parking lot, is a white Mercedes Benz on fire.

Completely engulfed and unsalvageable. No victims or witnesses.

"Is that?"

"Yes. It's Alton's." The first of the many losses to come. This one is for the piece of shit '80s Corolla they have Twirl driving, while he leases a Mercedes on her dime. And if he gets another one, I'll burn that one and each that follows.

I'm going to take everything away from him. Slowly. Methodically.

"He's going to flip his shit," Earl snorts, smile as wide as mine. He's enjoying this as much as I am, but then turns serious. "Be good to her. Don't let them break her down like they did Amelia. Promise me you will save her."

"I'm going to do more than that." Taking my phone out of my pocket, I pull up her number and send off a quick text.

> Did you get my gift. ~Malcolm

It doesn't take but a few seconds for three tiny dots to appear letting me know she is responding.

> You are insane. ~Twirl

How did you know I needed one? ~Twirl

I don't know if I can accept this. ~Twirl

My reply is just as quick.

You can and will. You deserve the best, sweetheart. End of. ~Malcom

London

THE MUSIC IS LOUD as I enter the employees' lounge on Friday, walls vibrating with each pulsing note that comes through each speaker. There's a party tonight, a celebratory function with the CEO of a tech company—a bachelor's sendoff that includes a free-for-all with the staff.

A bride and groom will each own a floor tonight to have what they call a last hoorah.

I've been dreading this night; I know I'm on the schedule for a group dance, and I'm not looking forward to it.

It feels wrong. Like somehow I'm cheating, which is ridiculous.

That kiss is messing with me. His thoughtful gift throwing me for a loop.

He sent me a brand new iPhone when my old cell was about to crap out. But it was more than the thoughtful gesture—it's the text he sent after that gave my heart a jump start.

You deserve the best, sweetheart. End of.

The man is an enigma I want to solve, even though I should stay away.

It doesn't slip my mind that his package arrived fifteen minutes after my brother and father left for God knows where. That he somehow knew that I've been eyeing a rose gold one, setting a small chunk each week outside of my moving fund to do just that.

My father doesn't know just how much I make. They have no idea that the waitress salary they think I have doesn't even make up an eighth of what Liam pays me.

The phone in my hand beeps with an incoming text, which I ignore. I can't give in. Must fight it, whatever this is, even though I want nothing more than to get lost in him.

It's a week later and I can still feel the ghost of his lips on mine; I can't get him out of my head. He's there and refusing to give me a single moment of reprieve. Swear I can smell his woodsy cologne inside my room when I wake up each day.

Feel his lingering presence.

I'm going insane.

Every single day since then, all I do is think. I let him steal my first kiss, and it's creating ideas in my head—wants that before meeting him never came to mind. What I didn't think is possible for me until I'm far away from this place: hope.

For more. For peace. For everything.

Back at his house, the way he held my brother under his control, was sexy. Made me feel safe and untouchable—they couldn't treat me like dirt. As if I'm their property.

Malcolm is powerful and rich. He commands respect by merely entering a room, which is something I never thought to find attractive in a man.

He's not like Alton and the idiots he associates with.

My brother and father haven't spoken a single word to me since that awkward brunch. A few glares from Alton, yes, but no reprimand or recrimination. Instead, they spend their days in my brother's office trying to figure out who stole and set his car on fire. There's been yelling, cursing —glass smashed, but all behind a closed door, and that was more than okay with me.

Those few days of calm were a godsend. While they slept, I took care of the house and their mess, staying out of the way the moment they rose from sleep.

"Get it together, girl," I whisper under my breath, trying to shake off this feeling that sits heavy in the pit of my stomach.

I can see Stacy inside the employee dressing room with another girl from where I stand, one that I met just briefly the day I came asking for work. Neither notice me, and that's okay. The last thing I need is another person asking me how my night with Malcolm went.

Each girl is wearing tonight's uniform, which consists of a ruffled pair of booty shorts, tassels, and stilettos, all in white. While the men on staff usually wear a variation of boxers or briefs depending on the request, I'll take a wild guess that theirs tonight will be all-black and tight.

Everyone that works here is beautiful, and so much more comfortable in their near-naked state than I will ever be. More uneasiness settles deep into my bones. More doubt on how I will get through the night.

You need the money. You need it to get out. It's my mantra. On repeat as I square my shoulders and take another step toward the room.

My plan of going unseen doesn't last long when my foot catches on the threshold, and at once, their low whispers cease. Both girls look at me.

One with amusement, the other like she's trying hard to figure me out. It's almost comical, and had I not been freaking out about getting up on a stage, my giggles would've burst forth.

"Hi." I give a small wave, walking over to the wall where our performance schedules are. Skimming the name list, I find mine, and pause. What the…?

LONDON: ROOM 305
PRIVATE DANCE

My heart takes off at a galloping speed and my skin prickles with excitement. He's back.

"Someone did a good job," Stacy sidles up next to me, speaking low. "I'm happy for you, sweetie. You're not meant to be downstairs with the rest of us."

"Why do you say that?" I ask, looking over at her. The thin strap of my shirt falls, and it's hard for me not to fix it, but I don't move. Instead, I keep my eyes on hers, begging her to give me an answer that makes sense. "Please give me something."

Our last conversation became weird toward the end, and the way she left, odd.

Suddenly, my strap is fixed and another shoulder bumps into mine. "You are too innocent for this kind of a job, sweetie. We like what we do, love sex, while you look afraid of your own shadow."

Turning my face, I scrunch up my nose. "I do not...do I?"

She nods, a hint of warmth in her stare. "Sorry, kid."

"Yes, you do, London." Stacy interjects, pulling my attention toward her. "And don't take offense, but Sila is right. You're a virgin..." she arches an eyebrow for confirmation, which I give with a nod "...then take this as the best thing that can ever happen to you and keep him happy. Come in, dance, and feel at ease that he's the look-but-don't-touch type of client. That you can still walk out of here when you are ready with that V-card intact."

But he does touch me. He kissed me.

Why am I so different? "I'm in way over my head," I mutter low, but not low enough as they both hear and laugh. "Not funny, jerks."

"A little," they answer in unison, and this time I join them in giggles. The world I'm suddenly in the middle of is out of my depth, should send me screaming, but instead, I am full of butterflies in my stomach. A nervous excitement that I can barely hide from them.

And while they are right about everything they say; it doesn't quell my curiosity. The yo-yoing emotion dominating my body and mind.

I want. I don't.

Stay. Or run like hell.

Malcolm is like a roller-coaster ride. The kind that go up really high with a massive drop, and even though I'm scared of the unknown, getting on is all I find myself thinking about. Even when I know it's bad for me, that rush still flutters and tempts.

Confuses me.

"Your outfit for tonight is hanging next to your vanity, London," Sila says, bringing me back to the present. "It's per Mr. Asher's request." The look she's giving me—her grin—hints at something that I'm just not getting.

"Ummm, okay?" I shrug, not sure what this can mean.

"It's time to get ready."

"Still feel as if I am missing something."

"What Sila means to say…" Stacy rolls her eyes while also grinning "…is that you have a rack of clothing with dates for each beside your dressing area. All from him."

"All from him?" Are they messing with me?

Trust me.

Trust me.

Trust me.

"London, you only dance for him. Take a look at that schedule again."

My eyes shift to the wall and the piece of paper hanging on a corkboard. Finding my name doesn't take long, and neither does seeing what room I'll be in. Every night I'm scheduled says the same; he will own me every Friday through Sunday for the foreseeable future.

Throwing an arm over my shoulders, Stacy gives me a squeeze. "At least with him you'll be away from the craziness…no one will bother you."

Room 305: Private Dance

Why would he do that?

Or better yet, why do I like it so much?

MALCOLM

TWIRL ENTERS THE ROOM five minutes before our time is set to begin. It's Friday night, and I need her, my body's wound tight from denying myself the pleasure of her touch. From only watching her through a small screen or sitting beside her a few hours at night when she's sleeping inside that tiny bedroom.

For her, I've gone from voyeur to stalker, and I'm not the least bit ashamed.

And knowing what I do now, my killing of her family is a gift to humanity. They deserve the worst. Will receive a punishment befitting the crime.

"I can do this," she whispers then, pulling my attention back to her. For tonight, I vow to focus and make this solely about her. Give her something no one has ever before.

A choice.

London is stunningly beautiful; her steps slow while making her way toward the stereo and picking up the remote. That's when she notices the piece of paper there. A small note asking her to follow my instructions:

Hit play.

Face the wall.

Close your eyes.

Count to ten.

Fuck, I've missed her.

Miss her looking at me with sweet and curious eyes. Miss seeing the want reflecting back at me.

Her breathing escalates, and the remote in her hand slips to the floor as a shiver runs up her spine. This between us is palpable—an unstoppable force we can't control.

Can't deny no matter how much I know she's fighting it. Hearing her tonight while she spoke to the girls through a speaker inside Liam's office only confirmed what I already know…

Twirl is afraid.

Too pure for this son of a bitch that will break down every one of her walls. The more I see—learn about her—the stronger my urges become. The more the idea of us cements itself in my head.

"I'm going insane," she whispers to herself, oblivious to my presence within the room. Just how I want it. I'm hiding in the shadows. Nothing except her stage is lit up while I watch and sip from my drink. "Why am I letting him get to me?"

Because you want me. Because I'm as under your skin as you are under mine.

Twirl stretches her neck from side to side, shaking her limbs out to expel the tension. It's a waste of time; we're meant to explode. To burn hotter than the motherfucking sun each time we come together.

It takes her a few minutes, but London bends at the waist to pick up the small control. The little dress; a flirty light yellow number with a sweetheart neckline and short hem rides up, giving me a peak of the silk panties underneath. The ones that carry my initials at the upper right hand corner.

A guttural growl builds in my chest at the sight, but I fight it. Swallow my desire while palming my hard-as-steel cock, the thin dress pants doing little to contain the visible bulge—the throbbing against the metal zipper.

I want to fuck her. Own her.

Bury myself so deep within her pussy that she'll feel me for days after.

Ride her so hard that the imprint of my dick will forever be etched into her walls. Mine will be the only cock she'll ever know. Ever want.

Closing my eyes, I take in a deep inhale. Try to regain composure when the music begins. A slow and sensual beat meant to entice the senses. That blatantly expresses my desires.

The hunger to taste every single inch of her.

My eyes snap open as the first riffs rent the air. I wait for her next move.

Her acceptance.

London takes her time, and I am in no rush.

I count down the seconds until I see her turn and give me her back. Another harsh exhale leaves her, arms shaking, and I quietly stand.

Another minute and she tips her face down. I follow her move with one of my own. Then another, and it's when I'm halfway across the room that I hear her.

"One, two, three…four," she whispers to herself, and then pauses. London tilts her head as if listening for my entrance. *Tsk, tsk, baby. Come on. Finish for me.* Holding my position, I wait for her to begin again. Sixty seconds pass, the intro for another song begins, and she gives in. "Five, six, seven…"

Before Twirl can say eight, I'm right behind her, her back to my front, and my hands clench as she whimpers out a shaky *nine*.

We both need this. To be close. To touch, and before she utters the next number, my lips are at her ear. Kissing the shell, nuzzling her fragrant skin. "Ten."

"I knew you were here." London's skin breaks out in goose bumps, a tiny map of sensitive flesh that I nip as I follow the path down to her collarbones. Nipping her there, I soothe the sting with my tongue. "F-felt you."

"Is that so?" I ask, wrapping my arm around her midsection. The stomach muscles clench beneath my hold as she gasps at the sudden movement. "Why do you think that is, Twirl? Why can you feel my presence?"

"I don't know."

"Don't lie to yourself." At my words, London turns in my arms, eyes slightly narrowed. And fuck me if I don't like this glimpse of fire. "Something you want to say, Ms. Foster? Any questions?"

"There is."

Dipping down, I nip her bottom lip. "And?"

"Why am I different? Why are you doing all of this?" There it is. What's eating her.

Curiosity is a bitch and one people don't quite know how to tame. That inquisitiveness gets them into situations they have no business digging into. Or in this case, it will open a box she isn't quite ready to receive.

The attraction is mutual. Our desires match evenly. However, the life she's been given has created this defense mechanism she can't help but hide behind. It's easier for her.

"Are you sure you want the answer?"

"Yes." The pleading in her eyes—the desperation in her voice dictates my next move. Before she can protest, I grab a thigh in each hand and lift her up, wrapping them tight around my waist. A small squeak escapes, but there's no protest as I carry her back to my chair.

Instead, she wraps her arms around my neck and holds tight. Presses her cheek to mine while her lips whisper something that's too low to hear but end with *dangerous.*

Taking a seat on the wide chair, I tap the table and the bottom stand illuminates with a low light. There's just enough room for her to straddle me comfortably, and I push her back a bit so I can focus on her flushing face. On the brightness in her eyes.

On every fucking question and doubt that I'll erase—decimate in order to own this precious doll.

"This is better." Not a question, a statement. Being close is right. The only way this talk will work.

"Agreed." London moves her upper body back, but her hips stay just a few inches from my cock. So fucking close that I can feel her heat. Her thighs are exposed, the dress riding up just enough to give me a glimpse of her sweet, virginal pussy. "But my face is up here."

There's a hint of amusement in her tone, and I shrug. "Not going to apologize, Twirl. I find you utterly perfect."

"You're a smooth one, aren't you?"

"I don't lie." Bringing both hands to her hips, I bring us flush while spreading my fingers wide over her lower back. She's heat. Softness. Feels like the perfect sin, and I've yet to have a taste of her decadence. "With me, you will always know where we stand. What I am thinking. There will be no secrets between us."

"Why do you keep saying there's an 'us'? I don't know you." As she says this, there's a minute shift of her hips. It causes my cock to flex against her, to throb, while those cerulean eyes become heavy. "Tell me."

"Ask me the right question," I grit out, fighting my own desire to devour her.

London stares at me, swallowing hard as she finds the right words. And the moment she does, it's a glorious sight. Her back straightens, the subtle shift pressing her core harshly against my girth while she licks her lips. I groan at the natural sensuality she displays, not holding back—wanting her to see just how much I desire her.

"Tell me, Malcolm." Her hand, small and soft, cups my chin. "I need to know why I'm suddenly feeling as though my freedom is within reach." London's exhales are heavier, soft little pants over my lips. "Who are you? Why are you here for me?"

"You want to know why I always want you close?" My right hand leaves her hip, fingertips skimming up the center of her back until I reach her hair. Hair that I grab a fistful of so I can tilt her head back enough to lick a path from her neck to chin. "Why I can't stop reaching out for you?"

"Yes," she mewls out, hands moving down to my shoulders—grabbing onto *me*.

"Are you sure you're ready for that answer, sweetheart? Because there's no going back after I say the words."

"Please. I need to understand."

Nodding, I tighten my hold and appraise her. Rejoice in the mirrored hunger I see reflecting back at me. "What would you say, Ms. Foster, if I told you that I want to own your soul? That I want to make you mine. Tie you to me in every way a man can."

A whooshing breath leaves her. "I'd say you are crazy and that we don't know each other. My family isn't going to allow this."

"So, you have already said," I hiss out when I feel her thighs clench.

"Because it's the truth. My brother—"

"I'm more of a monster than prince charming," I interject, putting a stop to that idiotic thought he's put in her head, "but it doesn't change our reality."

"And what reality is that?" Another song begins, a heavier beat that pulses through the room. It sexy. Enticing. "You haven't even asked me what I want yet."

"Because I already know." With my other hand, I grab onto and stop the slow roll of her hips. The unconscious dancing she's been torturing me with. "You want out from beneath your family's thumb, London. To feel safe again and free-fall into this explosiveness between us."

Her entire body freezes. "How do you know?"

"You're running, and that stops here." With a soft touch, I run soothing circles over her skin with the pad of my thumb.

"Still doesn't explain how—"

"Sweetheart, there isn't a single move made in this city that I'm not aware of. That doesn't reach my ear."

A slight flash of fear passes through her eyes then. "Then you know that...?"

"That your father and brother are scum? About the money they owe the Riveras back in Miami and their plans here?" My fingers dig a bit into her hip, but I release her before their imprint appear on her skin. I'll never mark her out of anger, only pleasure. "Yes, I do. And mark my words, baby...they will pay." *For everything they've stolen from you.*

"But how?" With her hands on my chest, she tries to stand but I hold firm. "Why are you doing this? I have a plan. My mind was made up."

"*Was* being the operative word." Bringing her face down to mine, I kiss those bee-stung lips with a bit of the manic hunger I possess. My tongue seeks hers out the moment she groans against my mouth, prying her slightly parted lips apart and taking what belongs to me.

She's tentative in her own exploration, slowly running her hands up my chest and then neck, until she finds purchase at the nape. There, she embeds her slim fingers into my hair and tugs, creating a shooting rush of pleasurable pain that settles on the tip of my dick.

I flex against her, and she whimpers.

I press her down harder, and her thighs tremble.

I want to come all over her softness, but before that can happen, I'm going to gift her tonight.

Slowing the kiss down, I suck the bottom one between my teeth and bite down. "Tell me you want this? Admit it to yourself that you want me."

Heavy-lidded eyes stare at me, so open and honest. "I do."

"Thank you," I say, pressing my lips to hers once more. "Twirl, I need you to know that I'm not a good man. That I have and will do things that you won't agree with, but I promise you one thing…you will never fear me. The world might see my wrath, but you never will."

"I don't know why I believe you, Malcolm, but I do."

"Good." Grabbing her hips, I stand her up between my spread legs and sit back. Scratch the stubble on my chin as she squirms before me. "But enough with the heavy for now. We'll come back to this another day."

"Another day?"

"Yes, and we will finish this…" I give her a pointed look and she nods "…but right now I have a present for you."

"A present? More than the phone and all the clothes you had delivered to me?" She's baiting. Wanting me to admit my possessiveness.

"I'm not going to apologize for monopolizing your time here. You dance for me." It's not a request, and this girl just smiles. Not at all upset, which makes me happy. "But yes, I have a small token, just so you see how serious I am. That this is about more than getting between your thighs."

"Are you saying you don't want me?" The playful tinge to her tone makes me chuckle. London is more relaxed in this moment than I've seen her to date. Like a weight has been lifted from her shoulders.

"Baby girl, my biggest wish is to impale you on my cock. To watch you choke on a scream as I split you in two." Her mouth drops open and those soft cheeks flush. She's not put off by my words; the way she shivers and comes closer is evidence enough. My girl likes a dirty mouth. "But not tonight. Tonight, I want you to choose. We do what you want."

"What I want?"

"Anything and everything. Even if that means you walk out that door and go home to bed."

London

WHAT I WANT?

What do I want?

It's a question that no one ever asks me anymore. Well, not since Mom left this earth to find peace in heaven. I see now that she was the only one that cared for my well-being. The one that taught me to dream big and fight for my happiness.

It's why I am trying so hard now. Why I'm willing to sell my body if it comes to that.

Things weren't always the way they are now. I remember days of warmth and happiness. When money was the last thing on anyone's mind.

But then she died, and so did the peace I had. Working here to find my freedom is all I have left. It's my last promise to her memory.

However, looking into his green eyes, my metaphorical walls crumble. They don't stand a single chance against his devilish grin with just the right amount of sweet that causes my thighs to clench. A subtle movement he doesn't miss.

Fighting my desire for him isn't working; it's the true meaning of a losing battle. He makes me want more. Makes me want to let go and live.

"Tell me, Twirl." Malcolm sits up, running the tips of his fingers up each leg. "I'll give you anything you want." Slowly, he finds his way to my waist where his fingers almost encompass my abdomen—all the way around with little room left between his fingertips, showcasing how tiny I am.

Something else I like about him. Find attractive.

Malcolm Asher is the epitome of all things male. The literary equivalent of what I've read about in books when describing a true alpha.

He's dangerous, and from what I have seen, those around him show nothing but respect in his presence. And yet, with me he's shown another side; it's still rough, yet not intimidating. He's not trying to force himself on me, but instead, make me want him.

And I do. God, I do.

The man is handsome, dominant, and pushes every single one of my buttons. Gives me a boost in confidence—makes me feel comfortable in my own skin.

I'm beautiful to him, but will I survive if things blow up in my face?

"I don't know how to answer that, Malcolm. What I want isn't going to suddenly appear."

Those fingertips dig in—the small bite of pain feels good. "Don't fight it, baby. Just let go." He makes it all sound so simple. Like my wishes are his command, and that's very dangerous for me.

However, the more his stare penetrates mine, I find myself unconsciously moving. Straddling his thighs once more, my dress bunches up around my midsection as I press our bodies close. No room between us.

"I want my freedom, Malcolm." Laying my forehead against his, I give in. Saying aloud what I've kept hidden for years. "I want to feel alive."

"Then it's yours." He groans, flexing his hips against the shallow roll of mine. And *Christ,* I feel every solid inch. How thick he is. How much he wants me.

Wants this between us, and more so because I'm the one who's initiating this contact. Because I want him too.

Seeing his physical desire—the hunger in his eyes creates a heady reaction in me. It's freeing. No pressure whatsoever as I give in to my own wants.

Just let go.

He's in my head. Under my skin.

Prickling at my senses and chipping away years of repression.

"That's it, beautiful. Take what you want," he groans, tightening his grip, yet it's my hips that move above his. It's my control that keeps us at a torturous pace.

Everything in this room disappears. Consequences have no meaning; where we are or how we met. That no longer matters to me. I don't care that he's a client, is dangerous for me, and hates my family.

All I can concentrate on is what he makes me feel, and I let my instincts guide me.

"You make me want things, Malcolm. Things I shouldn't think about until—"

He crashes his mouth to mine before I can finish. It's urgent and rough, a raping of my senses that shreds the last bit of sanity I'm holding on to.

This time when my hips buck against him, its hard and fast, sending a lightning bolt of pleasure through every limb. A feeling I chase with another gyration, more closeness.

I want to feel his skin on mine. Every solid inch, so I settle for unbuttoning his shirt. "Get it off," I whimper into his mouth, trembling as the last button slips free and the shirt reveals a strong chest below.

That's when I see it. He has another tattoo.

On the right side of his chest is the large image of an owl in black and white with an all-seeing eye held tight in its claws. It's beautiful, with bold lines and its intricate shading. The entire thing stands out against his slightly tanned skin, and I'm not the least bit embarrassed by my reaction to this.

It's visual. It's automatic. It's instinctual.

I rub myself against his cock with hard little bucks of my hips while pushing the offending fabric back over his shoulders. My thighs clench with each roll, fingers tracing over his hard pecs and lower, over each solid indentation of his abdomen.

He's strong. Defined. All man.

"Fuck," he grunts out then, and it's the sexiest sound I've ever heard. His hands wander lower to my bare thighs and flex over my skin; he's fighting back his own need to take over. To touch me where no other man has. To claim what he believes is his. "Corrupting you, sweet girl, will be my greatest achievement. I'm going to enjoy watching you become my beautiful little slut. My every-fucking-thing."

Those words on anyone else's lips would incense me, but with him, I shiver with pleasure. Become wetter, the proof of my desire coating the front of his pants.

"I'm so close," I breathe out, choking at the end on another moan as one of his large hands pushes me back to sit up, changing the angle. Thick and throbbing, he takes over my movements, arms flexing as he guides my body over his.

"Come for me, Twirl. Let go."

"Please," I beg for more. My limbs are thrumming with pleasure and my heart is racing. A delicious orgasm licks at my senses, almost there, when he releases my hip and brings a hand to my throat. "What are—"

"I'm not going to ask you again." His fingertips trace my neck; his thumb, with the symbol of a cross tattooed on his skin, settles on my lower lip. Just sits there, while the rest of his hand spreads, caressing my neck. "Come for me."

"I-I... oh *fuck*," It leaves me on a cry that borders on painful. I'm gone. No longer in control over my body as pleasure zips through me. Burns me.

Nothing has ever felt this good. All the others given by my own hand now fall under the mediocre category.

"I can feel you clenching, baby. Seeking my cock," he grits out, stilling beneath me. "Son of a bitch, you're going to feel so good taking every inch of me as I claim you. When I finally steal that gift you've kept for me."

Even as he twitches, pulses, Malcolm's eyes stay on mine. And it's the animalistic hunger in them that takes the very breath from my lungs.

Another rush of pleasure takes over me and I fall forward. I can't breathe. Can't move.

Yet his hands are everywhere, slowly bringing me back down with every caress. It takes a while, but when I find my breath again, I look up and find him smiling down at me. It's a soft look, one that tugs at my heart.

That I'm not prepared for in the least.

"You okay, sweetheart?"

Blood rushes to my cheeks, and I bury my face in his neck. "I have no control with you."

"That's not a bad thing."

"It's a dangerous thing for me."

At that, he pulls me from my hiding spot to face him. "What are you afraid of? I'd never hurt you."

"My family—"

"Has no place in this conversation, London. It's about me and you." He leans in and presses a featherlight kiss to my right cheek and then left. To my forehead and then chin. "Don't fight me, baby. Don't fight us. Let me take care of you."

Christ, I don't know what to do.

I'm attracted to him. Feel safe.

"This is crazy. I don't know you, have no idea how any of this will work." Everything he says is exactly what I want to hear, but is it the truth? Or is it what he *thinks* I want? Because I feel a little caught in the middle of whatever is going on between him and Alton. "Give me a little bit of time. Give me a reason to stay."

"Okay."

"Okay?" I ask, a little confused at how easily he gives in. "Just like that?"

"Yes, just like that." Malcolm taps my thigh, signaling for me to get up. Immediately, I panic that he's leaving. It comes out of nowhere, over-whelming me as I stand with shaking knees. He sees this and follows me up, wrapping an arm around my waist to keep me steady. "I'll give you what you want, but I'm always going to be one step behind. Chasing you. I'm not giving up, just letting you catch up." His head dips down, lips brushing my own, once, twice, before he nips the sensitive skin. "Now get dressed. I'm taking you to pick up your car."

"How do you know my car isn't here?"

"Better question is whose building are you parking at?"

THERE'S noise coming from the kitchen area when I enter the house a few hours later. It's past my usual time of return—the sun is up and the streets full of people on their way to church for Sunday mass.

Blaming Malcolm for this would be easy. For taking me to breakfast and spending an hour and a half doing nothing more than sitting beside me at some small café inside his building, but I won't. Truthfully, I don't remember the last time someone made me feel this way.

At peace. Comfortable.

I ate while he watched, a sinful smirk playing on his lips each time I bit into the heavenly strawberry pancakes the cook made. The one instance he spoke outside of crooning about my beauty or to tell me he hasn't been with anyone in more than a year—his refusal to accept mediocrity—was to ask if my family said anything after we left.

Did they give you crap over me? Question you? He worries, and I find that sweet.

No one so much as looked at me when we got home. I was told to disappear.

That didn't relax him. Instead, he grew pensive. Picking up his phone a few minutes after, he sent out a text before returning his attention to me. And even as we said goodbye beside my car, because of his refusal to let me walk in alone, there was something in his eyes that made me shiver.

Not because I fear him. Not at all.

It's more of an *I see him*. Know that he's capable of anything to be the victor in the end.

My ears are on high alert as I close the door with a muted thud. So low, I doubt they know I'm home. No one's yelling, which is a good sign, but for some reason my defenses are on high alert.

I know them. Know how they function.

Last Saturday's brunch with the Asher family is still on their minds. How he made them look weak, churning within their gut as hatred flows through their veins.

Toeing off my shoes, I pick the sandals up and walk toward the staircase. I don't want them—Alton—to come and find me; avoiding him is for the best right now. What I did a few hours ago with Malcolm is dangerous for me—I'm playing with fire—and I don't know if I can hide it. The unadulterated happiness he brings.

Because he does. He's giving me a small semblance of hope.

Tells me that I am not alone anymore.

My bare foot hits the landing when a hand grabs my arm. "What the?"

"About time you showed up to make breakfast," a woman I've never seen before says, her acrylic fingernails digging into my skin right where my father's marks are fresh. "Hurry up. We've been waiting."

"Get the hell off me." Without care, I swing my arm out while trying to shake her off, and she teeters on what are ridiculously high heels.

"You bitch!" she shrieks, breaking skin as she holds on tighter.

I'm falling backwards and I grab onto the banister to keep myself up, smashing my elbow into the wood. "I'm not warning you again." I can feel a few drops of blood weep down my arm where she's tearing the dermis. "Let. Go."

"You need to learn some respect."

Cocking my other arm back, I move to strike when another arm appears, halting mine before it connects. "We don't hit our guests, Lola," Alton tsks, looking at me with disappointment. "Especially one that is family."

"Family?" I'm ignoring the other comment; it's hypocritical and a bait. He's looking for a fight. "Your conquests are nothing to me."

"Brittany is my fiancée, and you will respect her."

"Goes both ways."

"Don't push me, kid. Know your place and shut your mouth." Taking a step closer, he bends a bit at the waist, putting his face a hair's breadth from mine. "Better yet, I need you to talk. You need to answer a few questions for me."

"Tell that to your—" His hand wraps around my throat, silencing me. Alton's grip is tight, nothing like the pleasurable one of Malcolm's, and I'm panicking. My body thrashes against his, and I claw at his hand in desperation, something that amuses him by the grin on his face.

"Don't get brave, little girl. This is my house, and I own you," he spits out, pushing me backwards. There's a step behind me and I tumble, the edge of the second and third landing digging into my back while the room grows quiet.

This is a first, and it shocks more than it hurts. I'm angry, my body visibly shaking as he towers over me with the smug rat he calls a fiancée smirking.

"I won't tell you again." Alton spits out, his hand coming down to cup my cheek, but before he can, I pull back. Stand up before he tries to touch me again, ignoring the shooting pain traveling up my backside. "We need to talk, London. Now."

"Not interested. Good night." Turning, I give him my back and place my foot on the next step.

"We aren't done," he thunders, while his girl laughs as if this is the funniest things she's ever seen. Makes me wonder if she's high herself.

"I am." Another step. If I can take two more up without him following, it'll give me the space I need to sprint up. However, his next words stop me in my tracks and a whooshing breath leaves me.

"How the fuck does Malcolm Asher know who you are?"

"I—"

"Answer me, Lola. Are you fucking me over with him?"

"Please, as if a man like that would ever look at her," Brittany interjects, venom coating each word. There's a hint of jealousy there that I just don't understand.

For exactly thirty seconds I pray to come up with an answer that will save me. That he will believe.

It doesn't come, but the sound of a knock on the door makes everyone pause.

MALCOLM

Javier looks over at me, and I nod. He grabs his phone, sending a text to the car in front of us with three of my men awaiting orders.

I heard enough a few minutes ago to burn this entire house down with its occupants inside.

Fuck, do I want to end this shit. Kill every single one of them, but I need to handle things in a way that benefits Twirl. That takes back what has been stolen.

They are lucky that I now know what I do.

That my P.I. gave me new information corroborating what Earl said before I left for the club last night. Not fifteen minutes after reading, I found myself rushing to meet her while spitting out orders for my men to be here this morning. We were just a few minutes away, and two streets down waiting for Mariah, when things escalated.

Whoever put their hands on her will lose the use of said hand.

Even though the biggest infraction of all is mine by leaving her alone for the twenty minutes between her arrival and my cousin knocking on their door. Everyone was with me awaiting orders. No one watching her home.

Eyeing the folder on my dash, I take a deep breath and center myself while the girls leave the area.

What those papers prove is the only thing stopping me.

My wrath has no mercy when it comes to her, and those first few documents sent me into a blind rage. A fury I still feel pumping through me but had to rein in while with my girl.

Because she's just that. Mine.

The second I saw that innocent face and sinful body; I gave in to the desire she brought forth. This need to protect and devour. Break and hold together.

I will make her crave the darkness I control. Accept her own demons.

This house and the belongings inside, what's left of her mother and father's estate, belongs to London. Everything, and it's all she has left of them. She's the sole heir as per the will and testament, something that these two have lied about. Misused. Stolen.

And while memories carry people through grim times, the value of a physical reminder is priceless. I won't take that from my girl.

"Baby, who was that?" Alton's fiancée's voice carries through the small listening device Javier left behind on his visit. It's by the front door where this whore decided to stake her bullshit claim of hierarchy over my Twirl.

That's going to cost her. Them.

"What the fuck was his cousin doing here?" Marcus asks, a slight slur to his speech.

Without saying a word, I flick the headlights on and off. Within fifteen seconds five car doors open and each one disperses to a different area of the house.

One at the front.

One on each side.

And the one that walks with me as I enter the house through the unlocked back door. He'll wait for me there until I exit or give my second signal.

Their home is a nice two story with brickwork facia. It's over 3500 square-foot design has five bedrooms and three bathrooms with the smallest of all being London's. The back of the house is where the spacious kitchen resides, and it's filthy.

Empty beer cans litter every available countertop space and the overflowing garbage bin. The eat-in nook area has a few stacks of cash, an open bottle of prescription pills, and a blade beside it. There're plates in the sink, pots with something charred, and cigarette butts all over the floor.

It's disgusting, and if they expect for Twirl to clean this up, they have another thing coming.

Grabbing a barstool from behind the island, I place another listening bug underneath and then take a seat with my Glock on my lap. Right in the middle of the room, I wait while listening to them talk in the distance. Mumbling about her leaving and the state this house is in.

That they are hungry, and don't like my family close to her.

Marcus is the first one to enter and at the sight of me, he freezes. He doesn't fully step in, more like stops at the entrance and looks at me. Just stares.

Holding a finger up to my lips, I tell him to keep quiet.

The other two take their time to follow. They're kissing, stopping a few steps behind the father and their focus is on each other. On wandering hands and swapping spit.

They sicken me.

"What can I do to calm you down, baby?" Brittany croons, her hand moving down his chest. "Prove that this isn't a big deal. Malcolm Asher would never—"

"Can answer for himself," I interject, and their two heads snap my way. Marcus isn't moving, and his son and whore aren't very hospitable either. "Do come in."

"H-how did you get in?" Marcus asks, his eyes shifting around the room, looking for either an out or a way to defend himself.

"We've had this discussion before, Foster. Don't ask stupid questions."

"As you wish, Mr. Asher. Why are you here, then?" There's an expensive-looking knife set a few feet from him and he shifts, moves closer. I see the intent and on my next inhale, I raise my gun and release two bullets.

One blows away the knife set.

The other goes in and out through the old man's shoulder.

"Fuck," he yells out, staggering back while holding his arm. The sleeve of his light blue, unkempt dress shirt is quickly becoming saturated. Rivulets have become one large spot as blood runs down to his fingertips and pools on the floor below.

His wide eyes are on mine while I just raise a brow. "Be grateful this one missed my target."

"Oh my God!" the woman screeches, her tone grating on my eardrums and I am tempted to shoot her.

"Silence her." Alton doesn't move and I fire another shot, this one right by his head. This time they both flinch; an inch or two to the left and his earlobe would've been taken clean off. Or worse. Either would work for me. "That is my last warning."

"Brittany, go upstairs and lock—"

"Wrong. She doesn't leave." Bringing my other hand to my face, I scratch my jaw. I'm tired and in need of a shave, but that will all have to wait. There's a small field trip we will all be taking this morning before I can enjoy the rest of my day.

"I have nothing to do with this," she whimpers a second before Alton smacks his hand across her mouth, silencing her. He leaves it there for good measure while pulling her by the waist closer to his body. Tears run down her cheeks, leaving tracks of her mascara and liner in their wake, and I don't feel sorry for her. Not one bit.

Brittany looks pathetic and weak, just like Alton wants her to be. A whore for his pleasure, while London evades his every move. She's aware but doesn't have a lick of remorse. She's here for the money.

The lifestyle.

"Oh, but you do." With that, I stand and head to the door. Opening it, I stop at the threshold and look back over my shoulder at the three idiots. "You have thirty minutes to clean this shit up. All of it. If you are late a single minute, I will let one of my men collect a finger for each consecutive sixty-second period. Understood?"

"Malcolm, what—" At my glare, Alton swallows hard and nods, his eyes shifting between his injured father and me. "I apologize, Mr. Asher, but I have to ask…what's going on? Why are you here?"

"The clock is ticking. Hurry up, and you'll receive answers."

<hr />

Twenty-nine minutes later, we're on our way across town toward the Washington Park area. The guests inside my car are semi-silent as I drive with Javier as my passenger; the Fosters are looking out the window while the woman cries, muffling her low whimpers with a hand over her mouth.

Not a word since Carmelo, my guy watching the back door, gave me the all good. The room was clean, and they were ready to leave.

Now, though, as I take the scenic route toward the self-storage units they use for business purposes, I find myself tensing. Full of this adrenaline—a demand from my body for retribution. There's this thirst for blood that I can only fight for so long as my muscles strain against my rigid composure.

The more I think about everything they've done, the angrier I become. The more my pulse rises, I feel a red haze fall over my senses. Every cell in my body thrums, and I flex my hands on the steering wheel as I park in the empty lot.

No one's here except for the owner, a man who for a few bucks sold me the three units full of merchandise: coke and electronics.

"Get out," I say and step out myself. The early morning sun feels good on my face, but you can already feel a small chill in the air. Autumn is slowly creeping in, and with it, the change in seasons can be drastic. From one spectrum to the other.

Without looking back, I walk toward the unlocked front door and open it. There's no one inside as per my request, and the office door is wide open so I can shut down their security feed myself. Not that I completely trust them, but I accept the gesture with as much good faith as I can muster.

Javier walks in behind me and takes charge of their system, turning the power off and also using a signal scrambler for added protection. What happens here will stay between those in attendance.

Leaving him at the front, I make my way toward the storage units with my men and the Fosters in tow. Theirs are in the row second to the back and on the left; the sole occupants of that space. Secluded and with minimal foot traffic.

However, more importantly, what greets me makes me smile.

Each one is open, and the merchandise inside being accounted for by other members of my staff. The heads of my auditing department have things in crates with the quantity, product name, and the street value already on a neatly written note.

"You can't do this," Alton thunders, his hands clenching at his sides while his girl and father just look. Mouths open and eyes wide, they watch as their investment—the buy-in being part of my girl's monthly stipend—is being confiscated, and the three million they were counting on making disappears. Her brother's face turns red and his chest heaves with anger. "My business has nothing to do with yours, Asher. I don't owe you anything."

"That's where you're wrong."

"What the fuck—" Every man on my payroll pulls out a gun and points it at their heads, silencing his rant before it begins. He pales and shrinks bank, bumping into an annoyed Carmelo who shoves him off.

"Can I shoot him, boss?"

"Careful, Alton," I hiss, ignoring his request for now and take a step closer, and then another. I don't stop until I'm right in his face, hand snapping out to wrap around his neck. Similar to how he held London. "You're treading on thin ice as is."

"This is all a misunderstanding." His bullshit words fall on deaf ears. Alton thrashes and I tighten my hold, pressing on his trachea. Enjoy how with each breath his body fights to get free but can't.

"Be grateful that I'm starting off slow. That retribution will come in steps." The longer I hold him, the weaker he becomes, and when his knees buckle, I push him back toward Carmelo. "Help him find his footing."

"Please stop," Brittany whimpers, face splotchy and nose running. "Can we all just stop and talk about this. I'm sure that—"

"Why?" Marcus cuts her off then, finding his voice, his tone is low, but it carries a hint of rage. His eyes stray toward his son. You can see that he's full of worry, but the man is smart enough not to move. He doesn't even try to comfort the fiancée who looks close to passing out.

"*Why*, he asks?" Looking toward this hall's entrance, I nod at Javier and not ten seconds pass when the entire place goes pitch black. The woman screams, and a few muted thuds follow.

The sound of bodies hitting the floor.

In my head, I count to sixty and then clap once. The sound is loud, reverberates around the large space and bounces off the metal doors. A click is heard, the kind of noise that comes from the flipping of an electrical breaker, and then section by section comes back on.

A smile crosses my lips at the sight that greets me. Three people are on the floor, kneeling a few feet apart. Two males and one female; each one has a guard.

She's crying.

Alton is fighting to regain his composure.

Marcus is holding his arm tight to his chest as the wound once again seeps blood. My eyes shift to the guard standing behind him and zero in on the red-stained skin of his thumb. I don't say anything, but my smirk gives away to my pleasure.

From the corner of my eye, I see Javier hold out five fingers letting me know how much time I have left. Other guests are due to arrive soon, and there are a few things to discuss before then.

The Fosters' first locker has a chair inside, and I grab it. Place it in front of Alton. "Look at me," I say, and with the tip of my shoe push his face up. You can see the anger boiling within—feel his hatred of me. "Keep them here and pay very close attention. Do you understand?"

"I do."

"Good." With a swiftness he isn't expecting, I pull out my knife from a small holster on my ankle and slide the smooth steel across his cheek. Press just deep enough to leave a superficial wound from his cheekbone to the corner of his bottom lip. Blood seeps to the surface and a few drops glide down his face. "Don't ever fuck with what's mine again."

MALCOLM

"BUT I HAVEN'T DONE—"

My hand across his cheek, the same one I just cut, silences him. "Speak when spoken to, not before." Gathering some of the red on his cheek with the tip of the blade, I rub it into his skin, letting the sharp edge scratch at the cut. "We had this same discussion a week ago, and yet here we are. Going over the same bullshit. Wasting my time."

Javier comes over then to drop a folder with both information and a set of pictures in front of him. Every single one has a date and time stamp on them. They show a blatant disrespect for my personal belongings.

I sit back, crossing my arms over my chest. "Go on. Look at them."

Alton does as I tell him, picking up the paperwork first with shaky hands. He flips through each page, face pale and head shaking back and forth. "No. No!"

Those papers hold the transcript of a conversation he had three nights ago with a buddy of his and mine. Someone I use from time to time to deliver verbal messages to clients in the business of importing drugs into the US. To Alton's bad luck, this man owes me a favor after I took care of his mother's hospital bills, and he recorded their talk.

A call where London's *brother* asks him to help him both rob and kill me, the latter by cutting the brake line to one of my vehicles. More than likely, the SUV my driver uses.

"Yes. Now, pick up those pictures."

"Mr. Asher, you have to believe me. This is all a lie. I don't understand why I'm being framed or…" His father's scream of pain cuts him off, and he looks over to see my guy dig two fingers into the wound this time. Marcus is sweating, shaking as the shock of pain ripples through his body.

"Pick up the photos."

"Please, son," he begs right before another scream rips from his throat. More blood. More pain. His father's body trembles as the finger imbedded into his flesh is taken out, and staying on his knees is no longer an option. Marcus falls forward, the cold cement cushioning his fall as he lies in a fetal position.

"Please, Asher. No more."

"Listen to your father, Alton. Look. At. Them."

Trembling fingers drop the papers in hand and pick up the photographic proof of his idiocy.

There's ten of them in total, and each show different moments within the last few weeks where he stuck his nose where it didn't belong. Where he made a move to inconvenience me.

The first few are nothing special, except for the third, which shows him paying off Phillip. How they stupidly made this transaction while standing outside of my building in the middle of the financial district two weeks before his death. Three in the morning and within the shot of my security cameras when no one is around to question them.

Which also begs the question of where my men on the clock were?

A large metal door at the end of this hallway opens and closes with a loud bang. A group of people enter, two with hoods on their heads, but my eyes are on the man at the center.

"Good morning," I say, standing up to greet my guest with my hand out toward him. He's the main victim in the giant mess of a hindrance. "How are you, my friend?"

"Could be better, mate." Casper Jameson grips my hand tight before pulling me into a hug. "Bloody traffic here always gets me in a mood."

"You're a native, Casper. You should be used to it by now."

"Semi native, thank you very much." He's the only person I know whose accent is a crazy mix of British with hints of Chicagoan. His family and their operations are run out of the UK with connections all across Europe and the east coast of the United States. Guns, marijuana, and cocaine are his favorite poisons, and I am the magician that makes all profits look legal.

Strip clubs.

Laundromats.

Car washes.

All businesses that deposit quantities in cash day in and out.

This last run should've been simple. It wasn't, and I now need to make reparations.

"Four months a year is enough to qualify."

"Fuck you, and never." He laughs, slapping my back. Others around us chuckle, but just as soon it all dies down. "Now, how are we going to fix this, Malcolm? Cause we have a lot of money being held up by—"

"I have it all," I interrupt, and he raises a brow, his questioning gaze set on mine. "Before the feds got ahold of it or put a pause on the transaction, I froze everything. Moved the capital offshore, and my guys did what they needed to do to make everything disappear."

"So we're good, then?"

"No. Not in the least." Tilting my head toward Alton and his father, I sneer. "We won't be okay until I make an example out of this asshole and his family."

"Who are they?"

"The orchestrators." At once he pulls his gun out and points it at Alton, but before he shoots, I push his hand down. "They are mine, Casper. All three."

"Then why tell me, arsehole?" he hisses, nostrils flaring. "This delay is costing me a shipment coming in tomorrow night. With the heat on my operations, the weapons supplier isn't feeling comfortable."

"Because I want them to watch you leave this warehouse with every single *ounce* of their merch." That's when he sees the bricks wrapped in plastic; barrels upon barrels of Columbian pure snow. "The coke and electronics are yours to do with as you please. Dump them in the river for all I care, but they won't make a fucking cent in profit."

"Apology accepted, bloke." Walking over to one of the containers, he pulls out a small knife from his jeans and rips a brick open. With the tips of the blade he takes a small amount and tastes it. Nods to himself in approval. "I'll take it all."

"Done." Looking at a very quiet Alton, I smirk. "Load it up. Three trucks are outside waiting, and Casper's men will drive them away."

"Understood." Javier whistles and within minutes, everything is gone. As if it was never here.

"Thank you, Malcolm. I know my business is always safe with you…"

"But?"

Casper looks pensive as he walks back to me, his eyes shifting between the men with hoods and the three on the floor. "How will we make sure this never happens again?"

"Like this." Carmelo comes forward then, a box in his hands. "Go on. Open it."

"If it's a bloody snake, you arse, I'll shoot you."

"Open it." I laugh, knowing how much of a pussy he is when it comes to reptiles. Goes to show that no matter how dangerous or big you are, everyone has a weakness.

He does, and then looks at me. "What the pissing hell is this?"

"Two tongues. One for each man that played a part in this."

"Michael?"

"Knows to never betray his family again. Losing his was his penance."

"He's family…no?"

"Then he should know better. They all do now."

"And the other?"

"Belonged to Phillip Mitchell. A low-level criminal that he…" I point at Alton "…paid to try and extort me. His idiocy cost him his life."

"Thank you." He tosses the box toward a still-crying Brittany who scrambles back with a shriek when they land a few feet from her leg.

"When can we continue with the transaction? Will it be while I'm still here?"

"Give me three weeks to make some moves."

"Done." Casper extends a hand for me to shake. "I'll be heading out, mate…I'm hungry and need to make another pit stop before heading home."

"Of course, but before you go…" Javier lowers the hood from the two men and stands back while I pull out my gun and fire two shots. One in the neck and the other in the chest. The men fall to the ground and no one moves; all eyes are on me. "They weren't very vigilant during their shifts and let people make illegal deals on my property. For that they paid the ultimate price."

I still have one more rat to deal with…

"What's fair is fair." He turns to leave, but before he does, I speak again, halting him mid-step.

"There's a simple request that I want witnesses for."

"Of course, brother," Casper says with a nod, turning back to fully face me.

With my eyes set on Alton's, I walk over and pick up the last two photos in the bunch I gave him. It's of my Twirl. In the first, she's smiling wide while looking up at the sky with her eyes closed. However, the second is of her inside Mariah's car where she fell asleep. The one my cousin sent me seconds after I walked out of their home so they could clean.

Her neck is red, fingerprint marks visible across her sensitive skin.

Skin that should only bear my marks. Only my teeth and fingertips marring her flesh as I enjoy her body.

He looks down at them and then back up to me. He's catching on. My message is clear, but just in case, I crouch down to his level and meet his hard stare. "If you ever lay a finger on her again…" I grab his, the one with the dislocated knuckle, and hold it against the cold concrete. With the butt of my gun, I slam down on the bone. Four solid blows and there's a crack; I'll give him credit for holding his scream in. "Touch her— fuck with her —and I will dispose of you a small cut at a time. Filet your flesh and then feed it to your dear old father while you watch. It'll be a slow death. Agonizing. One that I will take immense joy in, Foster."

"I love my sister," he chokes out as I slam the gun down once more. I don't buy the concern.

He wants her under his thumb. To control. To use her as he pleases.

Over my dead body. "As of today, she's mine. I'll be taking her, moving her in with me as part of my payment."

"My daughter is innocent…please don't do this, Mr. Asher."

"Save the fake concern, Marcus. You're just upset I'm removing the cash cow from within your grasp." Standing up, I take a few steps back, ignoring his shocked gasp, and right my clothes—wipe my hands on the wet towel Javier hands over. "It's a done deal. Come near her…hurt her again…and what happened today will seem like a happy memory." Flicking my eyes to my men, I give them a nod. "Get them up and out of here. Clean it, and then close shop. For today we are done, and I have somewhere to be."

"Are you really letting us go?" Brittany asks, voice low.

"Because you're a woman, I've been extremely nice to you. Don't push it, Brittany…because a piece of shit like you doesn't deserve to breathe the same air as her." With that I walk out with Casper, and after agreeing to meet sometime during the week, I get into my car. They can handle everything from here; I need to get home. Need my own reward.

MALCOLM

"SHE'S UPSTAIRS SLEEPING," Mariah says from her seat at the breakfast nook inside my kitchen. She brought her here at my request. To my house outside of the city. To rest. To relax so I could attend to her. "Poor thing is exhausted. Her neck and arms, Malcolm…fuck…tell me you broke theirs?"

"One has a bullet hole in the shoulder, while the other has a mangled hand. Will be quite useless from now on." Walking over to the counter, I drop my keys and phone after shutting the latter off, something she notices and raises a brow. "No interruptions until Monday morning after eleven. The meeting with Jameson was held today, instead, and the one with Benjamin from accounting needs to be pushed back until one."

"Anything else, *sir*."

"Is Magda here?"

She snorts, the sound so unattractive. "I already gave her a paid weekend off. Give me some credit here."

"Then no. Not a damn thing other than you leaving." *Not until after I speak with London about moving in.*

"I love you too, grouchy. Consider it done." Picking up her coffee cup, she walks to the sink and leaves it inside. "I'm happy for you, cousin. Enjoy the time off and be good to her."

"I will be." Leaning back against the counter, I wipe a tired hand down my face. "We both can use some rest after I shower. Unfortunately, I'm wearing some of their sweat and blood. It was profuse."

"Better than Michael who peed himself inside of Carmelo's jeep. Idiot thought they were taking him out to kill him," she says with a laugh, walking past me while her hand shoots out and connects with my arm. "Is Javi outside? Because I don't feel like driving."

"Brat." It's my mature reply before I pick her up and carry her toward the front door. A quick press of two fingers on the push release, a kick with my foot, and the door opens.

"Put me down, jerk! I'll call aunt—"

"There you go." Literally deposit her outside. "And to answer your earlier question, when isn't Javier waiting for you?"

"Touché." Her smile is beaming.

"Goodbye."

"Be patient."

"You have ten seconds to leave my property before I—"

"I got her, man. Go get some rest…it's been a long morning." Javier takes over and throws his personal headache over his shoulder. He strides off my front porch with her cursing our names while wearing a smirk—the woman is certifiable and I love her, but right now, I want everyone gone.

Slamming the door shut, I toe off my shoes and then slip the shirt over my head. My pants drop next, and I pick everything up while making my way upstairs and toward a special laundry chute. One that leads to a small incinerator inside my basement which deals with these kinds of messes.

The moment I open the small door behind a painting, everything whirls to life and heat sweeps across my face a minute later. Ten minutes and all is gone. Mere ashes that no one can decipher.

I am left in nothing but a pair of grey boxer briefs in the middle of the hallway when I close the latch and the machine turns off. My sole focus now is finding Twirl and wrapping myself around her. Enjoy every single second of peace we have together before I flip her world once again.

But first, I need a shower.

SHE'S THE SWEETEST VISION. Perfection in its purest form.

Twirl's laying in the middle of my bed when I enter the room twenty minutes later fresh out of the shower. She's cuddling my pillow, hair fanning out like a halo around her while a few drops of water roll down my chest from my still somewhat wet hair.

The towel in my hand doesn't bother to stop a single one as I focus on her.

How soft she looks.

How warm she must be.

How perfect she's going to feel against my body when I finally take her.

It's been a long twenty-four hours, and while I'm bone-deep exhausted, my cock still throbs beneath my sweats at the sight of her. Find her utterly delicious while her plump lips part and she tightens her hold on the pillow, choking the fluffy material.

"Need Malcolm. Stay," she sighs in her sleep, shifting her arm.

I've never wanted to be the victim of a headlock more in my life.

"How can she be so sinfully sweet?" I ask myself, shaking my head as I drop the towel and fully enter the room. The door closes behind me and I press a button beside it that darkens my windows another few shades.

However, I can still make out the feminine curve of her hip as she shifts onto her side. London is sinuous. Decadent. And the closer to her I get, my body comes alive.

I feel her all around me. Her soft floral scent fills every single inch of this room, while the sight of her here, in my room, my house, fills me with warmth.

She brings out emotions in me that make no sense. That I've never thought to experience. Didn't care to because the women around me were all after two things: my cock and money.

The notoriety that came from having my name attached to theirs, something Twirl doesn't care about. I truly doubt she knows who I am or what I own.

She's refreshing. Sweet.

I always want her close.

My last relationship was a disaster waiting to happen.

A slap in the face. A lie.

And at the end, when I put an end to us, I didn't feel anything. I didn't love her. Never did.

Love: a word that didn't fit my life outside of family members. Those that hold blood ties to me, and yet, no one brings out in me what London does.

With her, I crave a bit of tenderness. To fuck her raw and then cuddle her close.

Somehow, she's broken down walls made out of reinforced steel, getting under my skin.

Placing a knee on the bed, I climb up, careful not to shift too much and wake her. The mattress distributes my weight as I lower myself beside her, slipping beneath the comforter to move closer.

Even the simple set of pajamas Mariah put her in feel sinful.

Her body heat sears me in the most delicious of ways. Slowly, and even though I should wake her—let her know she's with me, I wrap an arm around her midsection instead and pull her closer. The second her back meets my chest; I feel the tension drain from me. My entire being sags into the mattress while my lips press a soft kiss to the back of her neck.

This is enough for now. Just holding her and knowing she's safe is enough.

London startles at the move, shooting up from the bed while trying to remove my arm from around her. "Don't touch me, Alton," she whimpers, and my heart breaks. My entire being freezes as her fear rocks the both of us.

She needs me. Those words are the sole reason I stay in this bed instead of heading out once more to hunt her pig of a brother down. To dismember her father.

"Twirl, it's me," I croon low, flipping her onto her back so she can see my face. However, her eyes remain closed as a tear slips down her cheek.

Her bottom lip trembles. "Please, open those gorgeous blues and look at me."

"Malcolm?"

"I'm here."

Her small body stills and after a few deep breaths, she meets my stare. A heavy sigh—relief settles in as she realizes that she's not at home. That she's safe. "How?"

"You okay now, sweetheart?"

She nods, but then her brows furrow. "What are you doing here?"

"What's the last thing you remember?" Keeping my tone soft, I lay beside her but keep an arm around her midsection. Nothing inappropriate, just letting her feel me. Get used to my touch.

"Telling Alton I was heading to bed after he…" Trailing off, Twirl brings a hand up to touch her neck—grimacing at the tender flesh there. That's also when I see the angry lines down her arm, the hint of blood near the edge of broken skin.

My eyes move back to hers. If I see those marks again… "What did he do?"

"I don't want to talk about that." She shakes her head, eyes pleading me to drop it. London opens her mouth a few times and then closes it while her eyes survey the room. "How did you know where I…did Mariah call you? Because she appeared out of thin air, telling everyone we had an appointment with a designer that I never agreed to. She all but pushed me into the shower, gave me fifteen minutes to change, and I don't remember much after that."

Her rambling is adorable.

"That was all me." With my forefinger, I run soothing circles over her stomach. "I sent her."

"Why?"

"Because I don't trust those assholes, and I was right." I'm not telling her about the small listening device or the men that have been watching. Not yet. Because there is a small part of me that needs to deal with the guilt I feel for being late. "Wish she would've gotten there sooner. That I drove you home instead of letting you go alone after breakfast. I'm sorry."

"This isn't your fault." Turning to face me on her side, she cups my jaw while her thumb sweeps across my skin. "None of this falls on you. Please believe me."

"But it does." Nuzzling her palm, I turn my face and kiss the center. "You can't change my mind on that."

"Agree to disagree for now…" she shrugs "…I guess."

"You're cute."

"You're handsome," she counters, and a ghost of a smile curls up at the corner of her mouth. "Still doesn't explain why I have a half-naked man trying to seduce me? Or how you got into my room without me hearing you."

"Afraid I'm going to bite?"

"Not one bit, but that doesn't answer the question."

"Through the door for that last part." I let out a low chuckle at her glare. Can't help myself and I lean forward to nip her chin. "And for your information, this is my home. I told her to bring you here. To me."

"Why?" Her body stiffens for a second, head shaking. "I'm not ready to have sex," she blurts out, "It's too soon and contrary to what happened last night I'm—"

"We need sleep, London." Pressing my forehead to hers, I stare into her eyes. Let her see the truth in my words. "I brought you here so we can rest without anyone interrupting. Just rest."

"Really?"

"Yes. Just sleep." I lay back to prove my point.

"Thank you." Two simple words, but they hold so much weight behind them. So much gratitude as she settles once more, and of her own accord moves closer, settling next to me with her head on my chest. She melts into my gentle touch, each stroke of my fingers up and down her side, soothing figure eights that soon have her closing her eyes, a serene look on her face. "Can we talk some more later?"

"Anything you want."

"A girl can get used to this."

Kissing the crown of her head, I let my own eyes close. "Sleep now, Twirl. I've got you."

That's my last thought as sleep takes me under; *I've got you.*

I'm never letting her go.

London

FIVE YEARS AGO…

"YOU'VE GROWN UP so fast, Lola," Mom says out of nowhere, startling me.

"Quit sneaking up on me, old woman!" I shriek, a high-pitched sound that only teenage girls can reach, and it makes her laugh. Me, not so much as my heart tries to beat right out of my chest. "Or do I need to buy you one of those bracelets with the tinkling charms? Maybe a cowbell?"

"Brat." Still smiling, she shakes her head. Yet those blue eyes continue to appraise me.

"You suck." Moving away from the vanity, I grab my phone and close it before she sees the beauty website I'm looking at. Or worse, reads the article giving advice on something she has no business knowing.

"And you're spending far too many hours looking at yourself in the mirror, young lady. What gives?" Walking inside, she follows me until we reach my bed. Sits next to me when I refuse to answer. "Something you want to tell me?"

"Not really. Nope." That's my first mistake. You never answer too quickly. "Everything is fine, I swear. Was just looking at a new braiding technique I want to try out."

"Cool…" Mom sweeps her long brown curls over her right shoulder "…let me see. I'm always looking for ideas."

She's not buying it.

Crap.

Double crap.

"How about we do this later? I'm supposed to meet Kristine—"

"What's his name and age, London."

"What are you talking about?" Avoidance is key in this situation. Last thing I need is for her to tell Dad, who will tell Alton, and then I am left to deal with his wrath. He hates all of my friends—forbids me from ever dating anyone. "It's just a simple hairstyle."

Mom purses her lips. "And I was born yesterday."

"More like a hundred years, but…"

"Funny." Wrapping her arm around my shoulders, she pulls us back so we're lying down with our legs over the edge of the mattress. For a few minutes we stay silent, just looking up toward the ceiling, when she lets out a long and tired sigh. "I've let that crap with your brother go on for far too long. I've always chalked up your bickering to sibling antics and paid no mind because once he got older, his attention would shift. Marcus says it's nothing when I bring it up, that with age he'll stop picking on you, but you're hiding things from me because you're worried—"

"I'm not, Mom. I swear."

"Then tell me what's going on? Why the sudden swoony smiles when you get a text or—"

"His name is Santiago, and he moved here from Spain a month ago," I whisper while my face heats up, eyes refusing to meet hers. "He's cute and all the girls are crushing hard. We've never spoken until last week when he invited me to sit with him at lunch. That's it."

"And…"

Turning my head, I scrunch up my nose. "And what? Not following."

"Child, I swear to God." Mom mutters something under her breath that I don't hear before grabbing my hand and giving it a squeeze. "Did you have lunch with him or not?"

"Once. Yeah."

"Did you have fun?"

"He's pretty awesome."

"Then that's all that matters," she deadpans; the look she's giving me all knowing. Aware of my worry when it comes to Dad saying I'm too young to date and Alton being an even bigger jerk. "One day, baby, a man is going to come into your life and sweep you off your feet. He will become the center of your world, as you will be his. Don't hold back because of fear or what someone will say. When that moment comes, years from now, you promise me to hold onto it with both hands and never let go. Savor each moment you have together because tomorrow is never promised."

"Mom, I'm only fifteen and it was just lunch. Not that serious."

"I'm not talking about today, Lola. But one day it will happen... trust me."

PRESENT

"...HOLD onto it with both hands and never let go. Savor each moment you have together because tomorrow is never promised."

I awake with a start, but don't move. Her words come back, and I can't help but question if this is what she was talking about. Is Malcolm my person?

However, that question will have to wait since I notice something else...

There's a weight against my back, yet it's not crushing.

A warmth surrounding me, yet it's comforting.

I've never slept so at peace. Happily. Completely letting my guard down with not a single bit of fear over what could happen when my defenses are down. No one here is going to harm me.

I know this, Malcolm showing me as much with every single one of his actions.

His respect for me. For not taking advantage of me.

For once, that little voice deep inside that always warns and keeps me alert is silent. Resting. Free.

"Feel so good," his sleep-roughened voice murmurs, arm pulling me tighter to his chest. I don't know how long we've been like this, but the proof that we haven't moved much is in the position we still lie in—my back to his front with his arm beneath my head. "How are you feeling?"

"I'm good." More than, and I almost say this when a human need presents itself. My bladder is full and unwilling to wait, so I push his arm up and squirm to the edge of the bed, when he tugs me back.

"Where do you think you're going?"

"Bathroom," I say, turning to look at him from over my shoulder. "Point me in the direction, and I'll be back in three minutes."

"Can I count you down?" Another tug and I'm face to face, lips an inch apart at the most. "Do I win something if you take longer than that? I think I should."

"Aren't you playful in the…what time is it?" The way he stares at me causes my face to heat up.

"Who cares, and only with you." His lips ghost mine, soft little pecks that melt me in place. "The door right across from us and hurry up. I'll make us something to eat."

"You can cook?" This surprises me, and it also doesn't stop me from stealing one more kiss before I pull back and slide off the bed. I don't pause to look back at him until I am on my feet and a few inches away, out of reach. "Or are you going to ask Magda to whip something up while you take the credit."

"Being sassy looks good on you." Malcolm scratches his bare chest, a move I follow. "Eyes up here, sweetheart."

"That's my line." Where these bold replies are coming from, I have no clue, but I like how freeing it is to be around him. How I don't feel like I have to walk on eggshells around him.

Malcolm is powerful, and yet I am not intimidated. Never have been. With me he is different, and I like it.

"First of all, the bathroom is right behind you," he drawls, eyes roaming my body and pausing at the two hard tips I'm trying to ignore. The second I slid off his bed, I realized that my thin lace bra hid nothing. That the cool air over my skin while a hot guy—*he* looks at me—is a very bad combination for my modesty. "And second, Magda has the rest of the weekend off. It's just us here and I want to keep it that way."

"Just us?"

He sits up, abs tensing as he holds himself up with one hand. "Problem with that, Twirl?"

I swallow hard. "No. None at the moment."

"Good." Malcolm scratches his jaw. Same jaw that has the most mouthwatering five o'clock shadow I've ever seen on a man. It makes me want to lick him. "Now hurry up before I pick you up and steal a sample of the sweetness between your thighs."

Those words don't register at first, but when they do, I turn around and all but run into the bathroom. Lock the door as his laughter follows me inside and my cheeks heat up. It's not the first time he's implied this. Making me his.

Voicing what I know he wants, and I'll be the biggest hypocrite if I deny wanting it too.

Because I do. I want more. So much more.

However, at the moment it isn't right. There's something I want from him first.

He's earning my trust.

"Girl, get it together," I whisper, looking at my expression in the mirror of his vanity. What I see staring back at me in the mirror is surprising; I'm smiling, and my eyes are bright—cheeks flushing because of his words and the truth behind them. Because for the first time in a long time, someone cares.

I'm not one hundred percent ready, but the same want is there chipping away at my fear.

With him, I'm not afraid or focusing on the finger-size purplish marks my brothers left on my skin. I'm not obsessing over the way Alton let Brittany treat me—the broken skin she left behind when she dug her nails into my skin. Malcolm doesn't feel like the stranger he is for all intents and purposes, and while the man isn't shy about voicing his wants, his actions are showing me he also cares.

It's because of him that Alton wasn't able to do more damage.

He's making me want to stay.

Shaking the thought from my mind and the dangerous road it will travel down, I begin to disrobe, dropping the pajama set Mariah shoved into my hands as soon as I set foot inside this home. They were new, with a tag, and in my size. Made me suspicious, but exhaustion made me compliant and I changed out of my clothes.

The light blue romper set with flowers and my tan sandals are some-where in his room. At least, I hope, because his wall-to-wall shower looks so inviting and I plan to relax for a few minutes inside.

The bathroom is spacious and white. Every surface, even the décor is white—expensive, with subway tiles throughout and a very spacious custom claw-foot tub.

It's modern and clean. Beautiful.

Too much for a single man.

Its showerhead system reminds me of the one Alton has in his shower at home. Not as fancy, and I know which knobs to turn. Three separate heads come to life at once, and the bathroom fills with steam pretty quickly.

It's an open concept with just a half wall of glass at the end where the water pours from, and I step inside. The hot water feels amazing on my tired body. A moan passes my lips when I turn around, giving the jets on the wall beside the nozzle my back. Tension drains, and yet there's a new kind of energy buzzing around me.

More so when I grab his shampoo to wash my hair. His scent, so masculine and all him, surrounds me. Embeds itself into each one of my pores as I wash off. Massage the lather into my hair and then let it run down my body; a gentle caress that only heightens my need to have his hands on me once more.

I want him to win me over.

Grabbing a bottle of conditioner from the same brand, I pour some into my hair and let it sit while I lather the rest of me. Touching myself inside his shower creates images of us. Where it isn't my hands but his, where he's whispering filthy things in my ear as I shatter in his arms.

The first swipe of a finger over my clit sends a shock wave of pleasure through my body so strong that my knees shake. Every muscle contracts, and on the second, I rub harder, tiny little circles over my trembling bundle as my walls pulsate and throb.

I'm so close, and I've barely touched myself.

This is all over him. His face and voice.

An image of him pushing me up against this very wall with a leg over his hip.

My fingers travel lower and to my opening. I'm wet, and it has nothing to do with the water pouring down my sensitive skin. Circling my entrance, I slip a single digit inside to the second knuckle.

"*Fuck*," I whimper, body almost shaking from the need to find a release. Slowly, I push my finger in and out of my tight hole. Four pumps, and then I push a little more, adding a second. Walls locking down, I press the palm of my hand against my clit and shatter. Come apart with a silent scream and panting breaths.

It's the most I've ever done sexually.

At home, I've never felt comfortable enough to explore. Always afraid of Alton finding me.

Or worse, wanting to touch me.

But here, I let go and as I slide to the cool tile floors, I find myself smiling. Body limp and at ease.

What this man does to me. What I know I'll let him do in the future causes another rush of pleasure to zip through me and I close my eyes— focus on my breathing when I hear his voice coming closer. Calling something out to someone five seconds before his hand knocks on the door.

"Did you finish, Twirl?"

"Yes," I manage to squeak out, and the door handle jiggles.

"Babe, can I come in?" There's a hint of amusement in his tone.

"I'll be out in a minute." Scrambling to my knees, I rinse the evidence of my private desires and shut the water off. "Give me ten…just need to get dressed—"

"I'll gift you twenty. Your outfit is on my bed."

"Okay." Grabbing a fluffy white towel, I wrap it around myself and open the door. "Can you pass me my clothes?"

His throat bobs harshly as he swallows. "I am completely fucked when it comes to you, and I'll never complain over it." Malcolm turns then and walks back to the door, almost crosses it when he pauses at the threshold to look me up and down once more from over his shoulder. "You are simply mouthwatering, sweetheart. Makes me hate my parents for interrupting the quiet morning I had planned for us. I don't want to share you with anyone, not even them."

"Your what?" His words make my heart beat fast and palms sweat, but his parents being downstairs is going to cause me to pass out. "Repeat, please."

"My parents, Ms. Foster. Hurry up…" he licks his bottom lip, eyes on my bare legs "…I want them to meet you and then leave. In and out. I don't think I can handle more than a thirty-minute visit right now."

MALCOLM

WE'RE SITTING AT the breakfast nook area of my kitchen when she comes downstairs wearing her cute little outfit. It's short and flowy and she looks beautiful. My mouth waters as her hips shimmy with each tiny step closer.

Beside me, my parents are oblivious to her entry. They continue talking about a week-long trip to the Dominican Republic they've been wanting to make, that Mom almost has him ready to book. She wants my input—to agree with her—and I'm ready to offer them my jet if they leave now.

To get out so I can enjoy my time with London.

"Son, are you even…" Mom's words trail off, and I can only guess why. Twirl is standing beside me, her hand on my shoulder, squeezing, silently asking me to help her figure out what to do, but I won't. With me, she is fucking free to act as she wishes. To fit her own mold and not the preconceived bullshit someone else pushes on her.

Dad clears his throat then, a small smirk on his lips. "Want to introduce us, son? Cause if you don't, I can't be held responsible for your mother's next action."

That seems to snap my mother out of her gawking; she turns and smacks him in the arm. "Don't be an asshole, dear. First impressions matter."

"Yes, *sweets*." He winks at London, and it does the trick as a low giggle escapes her. "Much better. No need to be nervous around us."

"Sorry. I just wasn't—"

"We crashed your lazy afternoon. No apologies needed…" she waves her off, and then raises a sharp brow at me "…where are your manners? Name, Malcolm. Introduce us the correct way."

"This is London Foster." They know the name and what their greed almost cost the business. "This is new, and we're taking it slow."

"Is that so?" Dad's eyes meet mine, and the softness from a moment ago is now gone. There's only a reprimand and anger. At what? I have no clue, nor do I care.

"She has nothing to do with her asinine family's affairs," I hiss from between clenching teeth, hands in a fist. "Quite the opposite, really."

"Malcolm!" Mom yells out, eyes wide and bouncing between a now-stiff London and my father. "And really, Anthony? When have you known him to be anything but diligent."

"I'm sorry my family is an issue for you. They are for me too, and I'm working on moving away as we speak. Fearing for your life isn't fun, sir." My girl tries to take a few steps back, but I don't let her. If anyone leaves, it will be him. "Let go, Malcolm."

"No." This is her first lesson. An introduction into my world, and she will rise above it.

Fuck whoever points a finger. Even if it's someone in my family.

Since her mother died, all she's done is let others step on her. Manipulate and mistreat; it ends now.

My father has never been a saint and needs to remember that. Just because he's retired now, it doesn't mean that the sins of the past are now null and void. Much less would he be okay with anyone pinning those on my mother's head.

"I'm leaving, okay? This is just another reason why—"

"Stop. Breathe, sweetie." The words don't come from me, but my mother who is now standing beside London and giving her a hug. Her green eyes, a few shades lighter than mine, glare at my father until the man shrinks back in his seat. "He's an old grouch that seems to have forgotten to take his anti-asshole medication this morning. If my son says you're one of the good ones, then that's all I need."

"What did he do now?" Mariah calls out, entering the kitchen with an amused Javier in tow. In his arms are two pastry boxes from a Ukrainian bakery in town. "I swear, lately you've been on a roll, old man. First with Dad yesterday, and now London. *Tsk, tsk.*"

I'm not going to question why everyone's here, although I know it's my cousin's idea. She wants them all to meet. To see me falling for a slip of a girl with more honor and pride than anyone I've ever met before.

"Why am I being ganged up on?" Every eye in the room except London's turn to look at him. His indignation almost makes me laugh. Almost, because if she leaves, father or not, I'll kick his ass. "I did nothing wrong. Wanting an explanation isn't a federal crime; I'm on her side here. If I'm looking at anyone with questions, it's my son. Doesn't anyone else see the issue here? The bruising and deep scratches?"

"Watch it." Narrowing my eyes, I lean forward in my seat. "I've never hit a woman, much less hurt someone important to me. Don't criticize what you don't know when you have no right. You have no moral high ground to stand on."

"Why else would she be here?"

"What the hell is that supposed to mean?"

"Welcome to the family, London." Mariah pulls her from my mother's hold, shaking her head while navigating an in-shock Twirl out of the room. My mother, on the other hand, is glaring at my father and Javi remains quiet. He's used to our craziness. To the fights and loud voices.

They make it to the entrance before my girl stops abruptly. Watching her turn with fire in her eyes is thrilling. Makes my cock throb at the sight of her anger. "You know nothing about me, and yet you judge. You know your son, and yet don't trust his decision to have me here or his motives. Malcolm," she says, a dainty finger pointing straight at him, "has been nothing but kind to me when my own family hurts me. Respectful and even sweet within his own gruff personality. He's given me hope that I'll be more than okay."

"Anything else, *Dad*?" I sneer while my chest fills with pride at her words, her defensiveness making me feel like a motherfucking king. As much as I don't like seeing her uncomfortable, anything that awakens her passion—that tiny demon fighting to be set free—is a blessing.

No more hiding. No more fear.

"Yeah. Just one more thing." Anthony Asher stands from his seat and walks over to her, his gait slow and without aggression. When he reaches her, Mariah moves to step between them, but then moves to the side at the last second. Before London can flee, or I can lay his ass out, he's hugging her tight. Whispering something in her ear that only she can hear and then nods. When they pull back, she's smiling. "Hungry?"

"Kind of." She steps out of his embrace, kisses his cheek, and then walks back to me. No one speaks. No one even questions what he's doing. Instead, we watch as she takes her rightful place, standing beside me, and entwines our fingers together. Gives them a small squeeze that pulls the tension right from my body. "Can I help with anything?"

"No can do, Miss London. You're a guest." Javier smiles at her while placing the two boxes of pastries on the counter. "Sit and enjoy yourself."

"But, I can—"

"Hey." Turning her face to mine, I tip it up with my finger and lay my forehead on hers. Ignore everyone's looks while keeping my voice low so only she can hear. "Are you okay? If you want them gone, say the word and it's done."

Because even a murderer like me has family issues. Boring and mundane ones. Ones that make a member look like an asshole, but in the end it's swept under the rug because it comes from a good place. We'll never be angels, but we do care.

You fight and make up because you love them. Forgive and forget because those closest to you will do the same when you fuck up. Kill those that have done wrong toward them, and then come home to a mid-afternoon brunch or a late dinner with all the fixings.

This is my normal, the side of me I want her to see the most of.

Because money and blood take up a substantial portion, but they're not the entire pie. A life with me will be insane, dangerous, but will have moments like these to fill the void of normalcy even the most depraved need.

Even if Dad's behavior came at the worst time, I know it's not malicious. Not that I'm going to let this go. He has some explaining to do, but for now I'm shifting my focus back to her.

"It's fine. Promise."

"Swear it."

"Scout's honor." She holds a pinky up for me, those sweet lips curling up at the corner. Lips that I can't help but nip.

"Fine," I grunt against their plumpness, "but they get one hour before I kick them out regardless. Today is about me and you. You're not working this weekend…" *or ever again* "…Liam agrees that you need some time off and you will be paid by me."

"But," she splutters, not knowing how to answer.

"But nothing." Another bite. "Agree with me, Twirl. You know you want to."

"You're so stubborn."

"And?"

"Fine. One hour."

"One." Nodding, I pull back and direct her toward the seat next to mine. "Sit down, babe."

And just like that, it's back to normal. The late lunch my parents had catered is set on the table, chairs are brought close together, and everyone digs in. No one cares about the mini showdown or how much more comfortable we would be in the dining room.

We eat. Talk. And I enjoy the softness of her upper thigh underneath the table.

"YOUR FAMILY IS NOT what I expected, but I like it…them," she says later in the evening, head on my thigh while we watch some poorly made horror flick. The kind that goes straight to DVD and only a sub-culture of people like. Everything is bad, mind numbingly so, but she loves it. Finds some of the "morbid" scenes funny. "Especially Javier. He's hilarious."

"He's a trip when we're together like that. At work he's a different person, so please don't get offended if he's ever short or serious. It's not personal. He just has to be as the head of my security."

"Is that his official title on paper?"

"It is."

"Hmmm." Twirl nods, mulling things over. "And what is it that you do, Mr. Asher?" Those big doe eyes watch me, lip caught between her teeth. She's looking for a lie that isn't going to come.

"I am the owner and CEO of Asher Holdings Bank here in Chicago. We're the second largest bank worldwide, with the one at The Loop being our home base. We have financial centers all across the United States, Europe, and Asia who deal within four business groups: commercial, investment, wealth management, and private global banking."

"Wow."

I laugh. "It's boring, really."

"Sure, it is. Boring…" she rolls her eyes at me, reaching up to flick my lip "…my brother just loves to associate himself with the most monotonous people—those that have never so much as gotten a parking ticket are his peeps."

"You are something else, Twirl."

"And I need the truth. I'm not dumb."

"Then how about a tit for tat. I've shared something with you, and now it's your turn." Grabbing her finger, I bring it up to my lips and bite the tip, soothing the sting with my tongue. "Tell me something."

"Anything?" Her mock glare only makes my cock jerk.

"Anything."

"Okay. I'll play." She turns on her side to face me better, the low lighting in the room dancing across her soft features. It also accentuates the smattering of bruises on her neck, and it takes everything within me not to go after Alton again and break his. *Soon. Very soon.* "I've been a dancer for most of my life…" I open my mouth to say I know as much, but she makes a *zip it* motion "…talk and I stop."

"So bossy." Slowly, I stroke the marks on her neck with my thumb. Just gentle sweeps as to not distract her, but to soothe, and then lower to her arms where the deep scratches are red.

"Get used to it." *That mouth is going to earn her a few spankings in the future.* "As I was saying, Mom put me into ballet classes when I was around four, and I did well, stuck with it for a few years, but that kind of dancing wasn't my passion. I just went along with it until I stumbled, literally, into a lyrical class down the hall from mine. It changed everything for me. The way they moved, the graceful lines of their bodies as they told a story, was eye opening."

"How old were you then?"

"Almost twelve, and I nagged Mom to death until she gave in." Pain laces her every word.

"So, you are telling me ahead of time that you're a nagger?"

That did the trick; the sudden sadness in her eyes is gone as she smacks my chest. "Jerk."

"Never said I was a saint."

"I don't need this abuse. Maybe I should head…shit." London sits up suddenly, panicking, trying to right her clothes and smooth down her hair. "I need to go. Marcus and Alton are going to kill me."

"They can never touch a pretty little hair on your head again."

She pauses her frantic movements to look at me. "What does that mean?"

"You no longer live there, London," I say, pulling her back to sit beside me. "After what happened and the enemies they've gained, I can't let you live there any longer. Not when you're in danger and they will sell you to protect themselves."

"But where will I go? I have no one and—"

"You have me. My family." She lays her head on my shoulder, and I kiss the crown of it. "I'm here and not going anywhere. This is fast and sudden, but stay with me. You can have your own room if you want…just know that I expect nothing in return."

"That doesn't sound right at all. I know them, Malcom," she says instead. "Alton wouldn't allow it."

I shrug, and she looks up at me. "He gave in with no problem."

"You did something…didn't you?" Her tone isn't accusatory. If I'm reading her right, she just might be a tiny bit relieved to leave that hellhole. "Tell me."

"Broken hand and a gunshot wound."

"Funny, Malcolm. Real funny."

"More like well deserved, but okay."

"You're serious." Still no anger or worry; she just wants clarification.

"As a heart attack." I steal a quick kiss. "Another movie?"

"Why am I not bothered by this?" For some reason, *that* seems to bother her. The lack of emotion. Empathy when it comes to her abusers. "Does it make me a horrible person to be kind of happy about this?"

"Does it make me a monster for pulling the trigger or smashing the hand?"

"Not at all."

"Then fuck it." Grabbing the remote, I pass it to her. "How about that next movie…"

"In your bed? For some reason, I'm really tired." As if to prove her point, a deep and long yawn escapes her. Also don't miss how she chooses my bed over the others. "Whatcha say?"

I'm not the least bit surprised by her exhaustion. It's a lot to take in and she'll need time to process, which I'll give her. What I won't allow is for her to ever feel bad for them. Whatever lot they receive in life, it's well earned.

Instead of answering, I stand and sweep her off her feet. Pull her close to my chest while walking to the steps and up, and it's once I'm there that I remember something I wanted to ask earlier. "What did my father whisper in your ear in the kitchen? Did he apologize?"

Her head snaps up from its place at my neck, her smile cheeky. "Better than. He said, and I quote: *This one's going to keep you on your toes, kid…*" I almost laugh at how she deepens her voice to mimic his "…*I'll shoot him and anyone you ever need me to.*"

MALCOLM

"WHY ARE YOU up so early?" London asks shyly from the entrance to my office. Sleep rumpled and in just my T-shirt, she looks delicious. Warm and soft. It's why I left the bed shortly after she fell asleep. Each sigh from her lips made me throb.

The remnants of pre-come on my pajamas is the proof of my desire for her tight little body.

I want to fuck this little doll. Break her.

But I want her desperate and ready for it. Begging me to.

And she will. That's why I'm not rushing it.

Instead, I savor every single piece of concrete that deteriorates from around her mental walls. Last night is evidence of that. How she turned toward me, body molding to mine with a leg thrown over my hip. How she asked to wear a shirt of mine instead of the sleep set that Mariah gave her.

Every single move she's made since realizing that this is my home has been with me in mind. Touching me. Sitting beside me. Even the food she served me when everyone else made their own plate was without conscious thought.

It's a natural instinct. That desire to take care of me, just like I'll always do for her.

And even though she hasn't said anything about moving in, I know she's staying.

"I had an email that needed my immediate attention." Also not a lie. However, what's inside that correspondence will have to wait. I have more important plans. "And it's not early, Twirl. It's twenty to twelve."

"Everything okay? Do you need me to…wait, it's almost noon?"

"No and yes?" I push my chair back and pat my lap.

Rolling her eyes, she takes her time walking around my desk and coming to a stop between my legs. Twirl leans back against the desk, her expression showing amusement. "That made no sense, Malcolm. Give me full sentences, please."

"Brat," I playfully growl at her, taking ahold of her hips and pulling her closer. Close enough that I can sit up and press my nose against her stomach. That I can wrap my arms around her and nip the skin above her belly button. "Yes, it's almost noon. And no, you aren't going anywhere."

"Okay." She rakes her fingers through my hair, and my eyes close. "So, what are the plans for today?"

"First, I want you to never stop doing that." It feels so good, soothing, and when she gives the strands a not-so-gentle tug, I almost fucking attack. The little shock of pain settles on my already hard cock, and I pulse. My entire being tenses while the minx giggles above me. "I'm tallying every single infraction for a later payment. Keep testing me, sweetheart."

This time, her blunt nails scratch my scalp. "Pay attention, Mr. Asher, and answer the question. Plans?"

"We have a date."

At that, she pauses. "Do we, now?"

I nod, nuzzling her abdomen while one of my hands skims down her thigh and then calf, only to follow the same path up. Two times I do this, each one stopping at the hem of my shirt. "The entire day is planned and set to begin after you have breakfast. I'm going to spoil you a tiny bit today."

"Do I get a say?" She's trying hard to sound put off, but I can hear the smile in her voice.

"You get to say *yes* and *thank you*." Propping my chin on her skin, I look up and catch London fighting back a grin. "Want to start now or when we get there?"

"Instead of being a jerk, why don't you feed me or point me in the direction of the kitchen? I got lost three times trying to find this room, and it's on the first floor."

"As you wish," I say, standing to my full height and pressing every inch of my body against hers. My fingers at her hips dig in and hoist her up, causing her to wrap those perfect thighs around me, bringing her core to rub against my cock with each new step I take out of my office and to the other side of the house.

Bright blue eyes look at me with a spark of desire I want to feed. Nurture.

I don't pause or fuck her against my walls like I want to. Instead, I bring her inside, place her atop my granite countertop, and step back. "I made waffles earlier and left them warming, but if you want something else, just say the word." My voice is gruff, a literal expression of how wound tight I am.

Feet dangling over the edge, she looks at me with wide eyes. "Waffles sound good." London licks her bottom lip, and I follow the move with hunger. With a throbbing cock.

"How many do you want?"

"How many are left?"

Parting her thighs, I step between them and her heat sears me through layers of clothing. It's taking every last ounce of strength to not push her shirt up and exposed her panty-covered cunt. "As many as you desire."

"Two will do for now." Her tone is breathy, and I also don't miss the way her chest expands with each deep inhale.

"Okay." Leaning forward, I nip her chin. "Coffee or juice?"

"Orange juice now and Starbucks later?"

"Absolutely." Taking a step back, I run my fingers down her thigh and to her knees. "I'm going to get your plate and step back into my office for a few minutes. You have two hours to eat, shower, and do whatever it is women do to get ready."

"But I have no—"

I quiet her with a finger over her lips. "Already taken care of. Everything you need is in a bag on my dresser. Trust me."

"Is the blindfold really necessary?" she asks from beside me, mouth in a pout while I drive to our destination. It's been like this for the past twenty minutes, and I find myself enjoying her petulant act.

Because it is one. Showing just the barest hint of a smile when looking ahead.

Or when I answer with a playful grunt.

Something that a few weeks back would've annoyed me, I now find entertaining. The reactions she pulls from me are different, possessive, and full of contentment.

A balance I didn't have before.

"We have fifteen hours left in this trip," I say just to fuck with her and almost laugh when her head snaps in my direction. "Catch a nap, Twirl. It's going to be a while."

"You can't be serious?"

"And if I am?"

"The scary part is that I'd still want to go." There's so much heaviness in those words. Truth.

There's something between her and I that while I still don't understand completely, I can't deny, and neither can she. We fit. Work in a way that brings out the best in each other.

She brings equilibrium, while I give her confidence.

She calms me where I give her freedom.

I protect and offer a chance to reclaim her life.

She gives me her. A chance at an honest love.

"Why is it scary?" I ask, pulling into the parking space designated for special clientele. The place is somewhat empty now, only a few spots in use as people leave to beat traffic. Putting my Maserati in park, I take her small hand in mine and intertwine our fingers. "Do I scare you?"

At my words, the slight tightness around her mouth loosens. "Not at all. Why would you even think that?"

"Curiosity." Turning her face to mine, I slip the blindfold off and then wrap my hand at the nape of her neck. I bring her face closer to mine. "Because even at my worst, London, I will never hurt you. The world could burn to the ground and it wouldn't faze me, yet you—you I would kill for. Trust me."

She licks her lips, eyes on mine. "You say that a lot...*trust me*...and the thing is that a large part of me already does. More and more every day."

"Good." A rough exhale leaves me at her words, but there is one thing I need to make clear. "The only time I will ever break you is with my cock, and I'll make sure you love every single second. That you beg me for more."

"My being a virgin doesn't bother you?" she asks, stammering as her face turns pink with embarrassment, once again reminding me just how innocent she is.

"The opposite, really." Leaning over the center console, I kiss her. Part her soft lips with my tongue and steal the very breath from her lungs. "Knowing I will be your first and last is... *Jesus,* London, I feel like a conqueror acquiring the world's greatest treasure. You are my reward in this life, and I plan to keep you happy. You will never want another man, and it won't be based on threats or bullying, but because no one will ever treat you like I will."

The next kiss is more possessive than each before, giving her a glimpse of the animalistic hunger I'm keeping under a tight control for her.

Fingers flexing over the back of her neck, I tighten my hold and tilt her head. Angle her to my liking and kiss her like I haven't before. No control or slowing down, I want London to accept this part of me and yearn for it.

To know that while she is my equal in our day to day, in bed I will own her. Will possess her with each touch.

And then, when I feel her body tremble, I let her go.

Releasing my hold, I sit back and watch her squirm for me. Take in a few deep breaths while gathering her composure, but I see the effect.

The outfit I bought for her is simple and comfortable, but at the same time hides very little from me. A pair of black yoga pants that molds onto her every dip and curve, a white tank top with a matching lace bra that shows how hard her nipples are, and a pair of low UGG boots to keep her feet warm.

It's not cold outside, not the near freezing temps we're used to, but the evening air still has a small bite to it. Enough that I gave her an old hoodie of mine to use if she needs it.

One that has my name on the back. A gift from my mother I never put to use, but now I appreciate.

"Wow," she whispers low, almost to herself.

"You're perfect." My eyes flicker to those kiss-swollen lips and then to the time on my dashboard. "However, if we don't stop right now, I'm taking us back home and locking the door."

"What?"

"We're here." Turning the car off, I get out without replying, adjust my cock, and walk around to her side opening the door. "Come along, Miss London Foster. We have a date to begin."

Twirl puts her hand in mine, letting me pull her out. She stands a few inches from me. Looking at me. "It's getting harder and harder to pull back from you, Malcolm Asher. Very hard."

"I've never had a choice when it comes to you." A click of my fob and then I find myself walking with her hand in mine. We make it just outside the parking area when she stops, finally realizing just where we are. "You okay?"

Her mouth is gaping, and her eyes show excitement. "Oh my God! Which one are we doing?"

"Both."

"You brought me to the Planetarium and the Aquarium. Malcolm…" my name is a sigh on her lips "…you're killing me. I never stood a chance."

"Does this mean you approve?"

"This means… *I love it*." And this time, she controls me with her lips.

London

THERE ARE A FEW moments in your life that mold your future.

Losing someone you love.

Becoming an adult.

Then, there is that split-second where your heart and mind connect. Where it recognizes a significant shift and the happiness a new arrival brings. Where you feel the worry you carry slip through your fingers, and the world around you fills with brightness.

That perfect instant is where I am right now, watching as Malcolm slips his fingers below the surface of a shallow tropical pool. He's wiggling two digits as a stingray comes close enough to touch. His face is calm as the animal pauses just beneath his hand, letting him pet it with soft strokes. It's the most serene I've seen him, and I'm enjoying every single second.

From the different attractions—mammal or reptile exhibits—he's been attentive and informative. Sharing with me what he knows, how he's secretly an animal documentary lover, and how it's his go-to when he wants to decompress.

How much he admires snakes but hates them close unless it's behind a glass enclosure.

How Shark Week is something he never misses and wants to share the next one with me.

It's a normal conversation. Not what I've come to expect from a man like him.

From the men my brother associates with.

More so, after he confessed to hurting Dad and Alton. That my home now is with him.

What should've been shocking isn't, and I'm finding myself being swept away by a deep sense of relief. I'm not upset with him about either one. It's the opposite.

With my hand over my heart, I can say that I'm happy right where I am. With him.

I'll even confess to wishing I'd been a fly on that wall when it happened.

What does that say about me?

I can't think about that now because what comes to mind is worrisome. I've never been a vengeful person, but ever since meeting Malcolm, it's something that comes to mind from time to time. A churning thought that fills me with the need to see them pay.

If I go back home, how long would it be before Alton's abuse turns sexual?

Focusing on Malcolm again, I push the fear of that thought away and shake off the darkness it brings. Instead, I admire how casual my date's dressed. Not that I don't appreciate him in a suit, but there's something extra sexy about a man in joggers and a T-shirt combo. For some reason those grey sweatpants he's wearing have become a weakness.

It's sporty, yet accentuates his solid form. That, and each time his arms wrap around me from behind, I feel him. Every solid inch.

Thank God the area we're in is almost empty and he's staying close. Because for as much as the man is possessive of me, I find myself feeling the same.

"Aren't you going to try?" His voice is sexy. Smooth as whiskey.

"I like watching you instead."

His eyes meet mine, and there's a hint of something dangerously provocative flash in them. "You like to watch?"

"You?" I give him a coy look from under my lashes. "All the time."

"Dangerous creature," he mutters, but I hear. Also notice the flex of his cock when he turns to me, wet hand at his side while taking the remaining steps between us. Malcolm presses the entire front of his body to mine, and the room becomes hot. An inferno of desire only he can bring forth.

"I'm not the dangerous one here." It sounds needy even to my own ears.

"You know, one day I'll forget the definition of the word slow and just take you."

"I never said we had to go at a snail's pace, if you…Malcolm!" I find myself with my back to his chest and a secure arm around my hips where he lifts me with ease. My feet are a couple of inches off the ground and I can't help the giggles coming out of me.

We look ridiculous.

The few people mingling around just look at us while he not so casually walks me out of the aquarium without another word. He doesn't stop, not when someone recognizes him and asks to have a word, nor when the pathway from the aquarium to the planetarium fills with people.

He's like Moses and the sea of people make room for the rich lunatic holding his date like a toy down the pathway.

It's not until we come to the Adler entrance that I sober a bit. It's closed.

"Hey, you can put me down now. I can walk back to the car."

"Back to the car?" Instead of releasing, he just turns me around in his arms. Like a ragdoll, he manipulates my much-smaller frame to his liking, and I find myself enjoying it. Feeling delicate and at his mercy is sexy. "Are you ready to call this date over?"

His brow creases, and I reach up with my thumb to smooth it out. Don't like him upset. "Not at all, but we can go somewhere else too."

"I'm so lost, Twirl."

"The sign says closed for the general admission crowd."

"Oh, that. Fuck, you're adorable." A soft smile graces his mouth and I can't stop myself, pressing mine to his for a small kiss. "Can I get another?"

"After you explain why we aren't leaving."

His arms tighten their hold on my hip and lower back. "Because we aren't the general population, sweetheart. I bought out the After Dark show tonight so it's just you and me."

"Are you serious?" Tears spring to my eyes. The gesture is more than sweet and totally unnecessary. "You don't need to spend money to impress me, but the thought you put into this is appreciated. Thank you."

"None needed, sweetheart." He sets me down, sliding me over his rigid length and then offers me his hand. Ignores the small whimper I let out. "Ready to have your mind blown by my chivalry?"

I laugh at that, wiping the one tear that escapes. "You and chivalry don't belong in the same sentence."

"So little faith," he admonishes with a tsk from the back of his throat while placing my hand at the crook of his elbow. When I turn my attention to the entrance again, there's a man now around Malcolm's age waiting for us with a smile and tray with two champagne flutes.

"Welcome to the Adler After Dark experience, Mr. and Mrs. Asher." Extending the drinks toward us, he waits until we each take a glass before speaking again. "We're so thrilled to have you with us tonight."

"Thank you," is all Malcolm says. No correction on the names or the title, which isn't mine. Instead, the man looks a bit smug about it. While I, on the other hand, don't know what to say because the way his last name and my first sound together isn't unappealing. It's too soon to think about it, but not off-putting. "Everything set up…?"

"My name is Dean, sir, and yes. We are ready to proceed as you please."

"Perfect. I appreciate that."

"It's our pleasure." Once inside the Rainbow Lobby, he takes us toward the center and stops at the crossroads that lead to two separate exhibits. Dean turns to face us in front of two signs, each pointing in a separate direction. "Do you wish to dine with the moon first or peruse the stars?"

I'M NERVOUS.

Excited.

Out of my mind for what I'm going to do but can't stop myself. Control this need that's been burning—being fed by his attention all day. A never-ending game of foreplay.

It's been a constant bout of attention and lingering touches. Playful one moment and then sinful the next. Roguish smiles thrown my way, and then ice-cold glares toward anyone that tried to get close. If the guide at Adler's Planet Nine Show or the waiter's eyes strayed my way for too long, I was pulled closer.

He's possessive, and I like it. More than.

It's ludicrous that he gets jealous because I can't stay away. No one registers when we're together, and even when not, my mind is always on him.

Why does everything with him feel so right? Makes sense?

Even now, as he walks around the bed to turn down the sheets, I can't help but find the action sexy. Perfect. Full of those little gestures that people overlook but to me are everything.

"Are you going to stand there all day watching me? Or is this a new habit we are forming?" Malcolm asks suddenly, a hint of amusement in his tone. I notice how much he does that with me—laugh, he lets go of that rigidness that scares the hell out of people; with me, there's none of that. "Not that I mind."

The muscles in his bare back flex as he tosses aside another decorative pillow, while his low-slung basketball shorts give me a small peek at the deep V of his hips. I can also see how much he likes my attention. The outline of his cock is unmistakable, and my mouth waters just a tiny bit.

I wonder how he tastes. Will I be able to handle him?

And while the fear of pain is still there, that he won't fit, I want him.

"I'm just admiring the view." Malcolm Asher is built like a baseball player: tall, strong, with well-defined muscles. His tattoos stand proud against his fair skin with a hint of a tan, colorful details with dark edges that tell a story. Gives a warning.

Every single one I have seen has a matching theme that is quite clear; I see all. The eyes in their bright blue, an almost identical shade to mine, are a reminder that he has people everywhere, just watching. The owl on his chest stands for intelligence—Malcolm is wise and attentive to details; he doesn't make mistakes. Dangerous.

"Want to do so from a better vantage point? Or are you scared I'll bite?" Smug bastard.

"Please do." The words are out of my mouth before I can stop them, but it's the truth. If my reply surprises him, he doesn't say anything. Instead, he just looks back at me from over his shoulder with a smirk. It's almost as if he can read my thoughts.

All day—since I met him—I've been more vocal with my thoughts. What I like and don't want. There's a certain level of ease that's been missing since Mom died.

With him, I have no fear. No repulsion or wanting to get away.

It's the opposite. I want more.

Closeness.

Touches.

To fully live my life.

"I've told you that sassy mouth is going to get you into trouble."

"So you've said, but..." Trailing off, I push off the door frame and take two steps inside. I do test his control. Push him into taking things a little further than some cuddling or kissing.

To play a little. Touch a little and explore.

"Last chance to get in this bed, say sorry, and get some sleep." It's a barely controlled growl, and my thighs clench. His fists are at his sides when he turns to face me fully, matching my two steps. Closer. "I want you, London. Fucking hunger to taste that sweet little pussy between your thighs, thighs that tremble at the mere sound of my voice. Don't tempt me, sweetheart...I'm trying here for you."

I swallow hard, shivers running down my spine. "Maybe not all the way, but a sample...shit!" Before I realize what's happening, I'm airborne one second, and on my back the next. Pinned beneath him from head to toe, his larger frame hovers over mine while those piercing green eyes roam.

He doesn't speak. Just looks. Takes inventory of every single inch of flesh on display.

The shirt I'm wearing is his. My panties are another pair he bought for me. My breasts are free and nipples tightening under his hungry gaze.

"You need to be honest with me, London." Jesus, the roughness in his voice causes goose bumps to rise on my skin. I'm sensitive. Aching in a way I've never experienced before. "Tell me what you want from me. What do you need."

MALCOLM

"YOU." SHE DOESN'T hesitate. Not for a single second. "I want you to touch me."

It's her truth. She needs this. Me.

No matter how crazy—the fast pace of our relationship—we both want this. Accept the cards fate has dealt.

"*Fuck*." It's a groan of mercy from my lips. Embedding my right hand in her hair, I angle her head to my liking before slanting my mouth over hers. Savor the top before tracing the bottom with my tongue. "I'm going to enjoy you slowly. Taste every single inch of this beautiful body."

"Please," Twirl whimpers, spreading her thighs to cradle my hips. She's soft and warm. Her heat sears me through the thin layer of my shorts, caressing my cock. "More...I need more."

My kiss is possessive, yet worshipping.

My hold dominant, yet loving.

Her taste is decadent, an addiction-inducing pleasure that pulls a growl from deep within my chest. It's loud and almost feral, shaking me while her thighs tremble—tighten their hold to try and keep me from pulling away.

"So fucking sweet. Addictive." Nipping her bottom lip, I travel lower, licking a path down her throat and to the neck of my shirt.

A shirt that's ridden up, exposing her legs and panties.

A shirt that's doing very little to hide her lack of bra.

A shirt that I rip right down the center with one harsh tug.

"Oh my God," London moans as I pull the tatters of cotton away from her skin, tossing it somewhere behind me. Her back arches off the bed, offering what's already mine, while goose bumps dance across her skin.

"Not God, baby. Just this motherfucker who owns you." Sitting back, I take in her wanton form. The softness of her skin and the gentle slope of each breast. How mouthwatering her small nipples are; a light pink tip that tightens under my perusal. "So pretty."

"I need you to touch me." London sits up, grabbing my wrist and pulling. And I let her. Let her guide me to her right tit that fits perfectly in my hand; she's just a bit more than a handful and perky.

I take her hard little bud between two fingers and pull.

A pink flush sweeps down her face and neck. It covers her upper chest, and the color is beautiful. I want more of it. A deeper shade, and I slap the very top of her breast, catching the puckered flesh with the tip of my finger.

Three smacks and I attach my lips to her nipple, flicking the sensitive skin as a grunt rips from my throat. Her smell is intoxicating, her skin soft as a petal.

"Malcolm." It's a cry, a low, keening sound full of a need that fuels mine.

"What do you need?" Pulling her in deeper, I flick the tip before biting down, then lick a path across her chest to the other breast. Her hips buck beneath me as I suckle her, but she doesn't answer and that won't do. Pinching the nipple hard, I lift my head to stare down at her. "Answer me. What do you need?"

She's breathless and panting and lost in her arousal. "For you to own me."

Good girl. I hum against her skin and suck a path down her breast and ribs, leaving small reminders of my hunger. Tiny bruises that mark my conquering.

Her stomach clenches the lower I go, a sweet giggle escaping as I reach her midsection, and then a groan when my lips caress her hip.

Taking the waistband of her panties between my teeth, I pull the material. White satin and with my initials at the upper right hand corner, I revel in their stretching and the small peak of smooth skin beneath. In her wetness seeping through.

My mouth waters and I release the fabric, letting it snap back against her skin. Nuzzle her. "How do you want to come, London? My mouth..." I lick the satin over her clit, and she cries out "...or my fingers?"

"W-what?"

"Pick one." This time I tap her tender bundle of nerves with two fingers. "Mouth or fingers?"

"I can't pick. No one has ever touched me," she hisses out, sucking in a deep breath as I smack her pussy once more.

I know she's a virgin. Love the fucking fact that the tight little hole between her thighs will only know me.

"So innocent, and yet you're greedy." Lowering my body to the mattress, I place a leg over each of my shoulders and inhale her sinful scent. She's so fucking wet and I've yet to touch her, the crease of her thigh glistening. "Are you willing to let me do as I please? Give you what I know you need without a single complaint?"

"Yes...anything. Just help me find—"

"Move your panties to the side and show me your pussy." Wide blue eyes meet mine, but she follows my instruction. Slow, and with a hint of excitement, her hand comes down to the edge of her panties and fingers the fabric.

Watching her dip a single digit beneath the silk is downright sinful.

With the patience of the saint I am not, I wait for her to show me. To open herself to me.

To trust me.

Because intimacy is just that, trust between two people that care about each other. Anyone can fuck, but sharing private and personal moments carries weight.

However, nothing could've prepared me for the rush of animalistic greed that rushes through me at the sight of her. *She's mine. No letting go.*

London is pink and glistening with her arousal, clit throbbing beneath its hood. Her scent surrounds me, a heady and saccharine smell that is uniquely hers. She's perfect, and with my eyes on hers, I take a lick from her opening to clit, laying a tender kiss on her mound.

Christ, she tastes like heaven and hell. Like she will be the end of me and then the rebirth.

And if I wanted to hurt Alton before, now I want him to die a slow and agonizing death. To watch her flourish at my side as he loses it all. While I place the world at her feet and worship this altar every fucking night.

Because I am. Before I pull the trigger, he will know that I own her. *Love her.*

"Son of a bitch." I drag my teeth across her clit as the reality of that thought slams into my chest. It's fast. Sudden. But the truth is there and always has been. I just never put a label to the emotion.

This tiny beauty beneath me is my person.

"Fuck." At once, her body arches up, back bowing as a moan leaves her. She's writhing—hips lifting toward my hungry tongue.

With two fingers, I part her lips and pull back to watch how her hole clenches. How the wetness gathers at her entrance and then slips down to the crack of her ass. An ass I want to bite.

And I do just that, right at the tip. I embed my teeth and press down hard enough to leave a mark and then soothe the sting with my tongue, loving her flesh with slow licks as I follow the path back to her pussy.

She swollen for me. So wet. And seeing her lost in the pleasure I give makes me feel like a motherfucking Titan. All powerful and indestructible.

Sliding my tongue through her slit, I eat her like a man possessed. Sucking. Biting. Devouring every drop of wetness she gifts me.

London fights against my mouth, wanting to move her hips, but I hold her down with a forearm across her hips. "My pace. My rules."

"Need you, please!"

My reply is a smack to her inner thigh and a quick flick to her clit. Then another. Taking the throbbing bundle of nerves between my teeth, I slip a single finger inside to the second knuckle. She's so fucking tight, walls gripping as they pulse—try to pull me in deeper.

Her innocence is there against me, and I don't want to break it. Not with my hands.

That treasure belongs to my dick.

"I want to fuck you," I grunt against her clit, and she claws at the sheets. "My cock aches to be inside you. To claim you." At my words, London's hooded eyes meet mine, her panting breaths accentuating the heaviness in her breasts. Her hard nipples and the slight sheen of perspiration that covers her skin.

She's a goddess. *She'll be my queen.*

"So good, Malcolm. God, that feels so good," she cries out when I pump in and out at a faster pace. Five rapid little jabs, before I pull my finger out and circle her clit, rubbing her in tight little circles while my tongue laps at her juices.

Fucks her entrance.

Blue eyes roll back, and her mouth drops open. Chest heaves as breathing becomes difficult.

Her reaction feeds my need to see her come. To have her bathe my face.

"Come for me, Twirl. Give me what's mine." And then I pinch her clit.

"I'm almost...*fuck!*" London comes with a scream, muscles clenching as her wetness drips down my lips and chin. It pools on the sheet below as I continue to love her, slowly bringing her down after a minute.

She's limp in my bed, but her smile is wide. Tired but relaxed.

Leaving her in the morning is going to be hard.

WE'RE SITTING at the dining room table when London finds me the next morning. She's fresh out of the shower and wearing a ridiculous pair of wide-leg pants and crop top in a light grey cotton. They look cute, but on anyone else the bottoms would look funny.

Yet, on her thick hips, they work. Accentuate that perfect body.

Pausing at the entrance, she toes the floor, looking a bit unsure. "I'll be in the kitchen...” Twirl points in the general direction it’s in “...anyone need anything?”

Shaking my head, I crook a finger. “Come here.”

At my words, a tiny smile crosses her lips. “Yes, sir.” However, the mock salute I’m given before she comes causes my dick to harden. *Sassy little thing.*

There’s a natural sway to her hips that I can’t help but watch. It’s sensual. Coquettish. A cock-teasing quality that she can’t control and isn’t aware of.

London isn’t conscious of her own appeal. Of her control over me.

A throat clears to my left, but I ignore the assholes and continue my perusal.

We’ve been working for a few hours now, preparing for the next few days and what I expect to be done while I’m gone. How they will handle the FBI agent lingering around my building downtown.

Vital information—both customer and transaction details, along with a few photographs of Shawn at a strip club—sit in front of me, and yet, the only thing I can focus on is my hunger for her. The desire to sweep everything off this table, witnesses be damned, and spread her out for me to enjoy is almost maddening. I’m not leaving without eating her pretty little cunt once more.

Getting on the plane with her taste on my tongue and scent on my lips.

However, it will have to wait, and instead, I’ll settle for a kiss on the mouth. Once she’s close enough, I reach a hand out and grab hers, pulling her down to my level.

Those blue orbs hold a hint of mischief—relief and happiness—when I press my lips to hers. “Good morning, beautiful.”

“Hi.”

“You sleep okay?” I ask, nipping my way down to her jaw where I take the skin between my teeth. “Feel rested?”

“I did and do.” She brings a hand to my hair and scratches the scalp, tugging on the ends. London does this a few times, eliciting a hum of approval. “Very warm and comfortable.”

“Good.” With the bottom of my foot, I push out her chair to my right. It scrapes against the wooden floors as I release her tender flesh and sit back. "Please join us."

"Are you sure?"

"Absolutely," Mariah answers for me, a hint of amusement in her tone. "Besides, you need to know what's going to occur over the next few days."

A lot is going on, and unfortunately, my plane leaves in a few hours.

Magda walks in then, a platter of bacon and eggs in each hand. She looks over at Twirl, her eyes lighting up. "Lovely to see you, Miss Foster."

"You too." London sits, grabbing the carafe of coffee and pouring a cup. "Thank you for breakfast."

"My pleasure, sweet girl." She leaves and comes back a few minutes later with some waffles and cut strawberries, the syrup and butter already on the table. "I'll be in the kitchen. Let me know if you want or need anything."

By the time she leaves, London has my plate ready and almost over-flowing with food. She places it in front of me and then fills her own. "Eat."

"Yes, boss," I say with a chuckle, and Twirl rolls her eyes. The other two follow her lead, silently piling on food, and then digging in as we ignore the paperwork in front of me.

I can tell that she's curious, but I'll give her credit for waiting. She's giving me the chance to explain. Giving me a chance to prove that she can trust me.

Once my plate is pushed forward, Javi and Mariah do the same, waiting for my next move. My eyes remain on hers, though. There are so many questions in them, a small hint of doubt that I'll erase.

"Twirl, I'm going to be leaving the country for a few days."

"What? Why?" There's a hint of panic in her tone. Her eyes look sad, but she'll understand that it's a temporary thing. I'll always come back to her. For her.

"There's a business meeting in Costa Rica I must attend, but I'll be back in three days." Beside me, Mariah pushes a piece of paper toward her. My itinerary. "That's the information on my flight, where I'll be, and how to contact me. Don't hesitate to do so if something happens...I don't care how small or inane you think it is...call me."

Grabbing the paper, she looks over every single line on the sheet. It takes her a few minutes, but once she's satisfied, London places it to her right and looks at me. "What am I supposed to do while you're gone? Do I move back and wait—"

"The fuck you will," I interrupt, my discontent clear. Leaning toward her, I take her chin in my grasp and hold her stare. Make sure that her attention is on mine and she doesn't misinterpret my words. "Your place is with me. In my home. Never, not for a single second, think that being anywhere but beside me is acceptable."

"But—"

"No." I shake my head, caressing her cheek with my thumb. "And I want you moved in when I get back. Everything you own and want to bring needs to be incorporated with mine."

"Okay, but I'll need some help."

"That's where I come in, Miss London," Javier says before I can. Her eyes are on mine, though, never wavering. "Your bodyguard and I will be here to get you moved in. You'll meet her tomorrow. Gina has been assigned to you, and while Malcolm is gone, so am I."

"New bodyguard?" She's lost and doesn't know how to assimilate everything we're saying. The concept of someone taking care of her is foreign.

It's new and scary.

Especially after what we did yesterday. The new intimacy.

And while breaking the news gently would've been ideal, I don't have the luxury. Her neck and arms bear the evidence of their mistreatment. I know their plans. Know how much they want her back, and I wouldn't put it past them to try taking her by force and making a run for it.

"Yes, and don't argue with me on this. You won't win." Bringing her closer, I brush my lips against hers as I speak. "Your life is about to change drastically, sweet girl. This is for your safety and my peace of mind. *Trust me.*"

MALCOLM

"AFTERNOON, SON," MY father says taking a seat across from me. He's smiling, looking a little cocky, and I put my newspaper down, placing it beside my drink.

He's a last-minute addition to this trip, and by the look on his face, he knows why he's here.

Father or not, the shit he pulled with my girl a few days back needs an explanation.

I'm not London, and I don't have a heart of gold.

"Thank you for joining me last minute."

"I've been expecting your call." Dad takes his seat, and a second later the stewardess places a whiskey neat in front of him. "Thank you, Ellen."

"Let me know if you need anything else, sir." And then just like that, she disappears from sight. The in-flight crew knows to make themselves scarce unless we call upon them after the doors close and the engines turn on.

My men are a few rows back and watching a basketball game while

Carmelo studies the information Javier gave him before this flight. He knows the drill, what I expect, and takes it seriously, which I appreciate.

"Get it off your chest." Dad's voice pulls my eyes to his.

"I will in a minute. Go ahead and get your story together." Grabbing my phone from the table, I swipe my finger across the screen and send Twirl a quick message.

> Taking off. Behave while I am gone, and I'll have something sweet for you when I get back.
> ~Malcolm

Her reply is instant, and it's hard to keep myself from smiling.

> I've always been an angel. ~Twirl

> Promises. Promises ~Twirl

My mind immediately goes back to just before we left for the airfield and I had her bent over the bathroom sink, legs spread, with my face buried between her thighs. To the way she whimpers every time I rake my teeth over her clit. The way she trembles when I dig my fingers into her hips, holding her in place.

I can still taste her decadence on my tongue.

See the fire in her eyes when she begs for more.

An attachment comes through, and it's a picture with some sort of filter that adds wings and a halo to her. She's glowing in it. Beautiful. Wearing the sweetest grin, with a small hint of the blotchiness from the few tears that fell when I kissed her at the security gate.

It's perfect. She's perfect.

Another text comes in just as I'm going to respond.

> Is it weird that I miss you already? You just left and I feel off without you here. ~Twirl

> Not at all when I feel the same. Call you when I land. ~Malcolm

"Happiness looks good on you," Dad says, pulling my attention away from her messages. "And your mother adores her, by the way."

"Why?"

His smile drops, and he gives me a grimace. "Shit didn't look good, Malcolm. That's the God's honest truth." Dad rubs a tired hand down his face. "Look at it from my point of view; a pretty girl, her last name is Foster, and she's wearing bruises on her neck and deep scratches down her arm...wouldn't you be concerned?"

Nodding, I pick up my glass and drain the rest of its contents. "I agree that it looked bad, but you made her feel unwelcomed in *my* home, and that's unacceptable. Pull me aside. Question me where she can't hear, but never in her presence again. Understood?"

Ellen appears then with a new drink for me; a gin and tonic with a cucumber and lemon slice, setting it on the table beside a cheese plate.

"Thanks."

"You're welcome, sir." Once more she disappears inside a small area up front for the staff.

"You're right. How I handled it was wrong, and I apologize."

"Accepted."

"I know you'd never hurt someone who's an innocent, son. More so, someone we both know isn't involved in her family's schemes, but I couldn't in good conscience not ask—"

"Wait a minute." Holding a hand up, I stop him. *We both know...* "What do you mean by that? You know her?"

"No." Dad picks up his drink and takes a sip, then another before putting it down again. He's not looking at me; his stare is on the round ice cube inside the glass. "I don't know London, son, but your mother knew Amelia."

"Through Earl?" Because that's the first thing that comes to mind. A few muffled curses come from a few of my men. They're yelling at the TV, and when I hold a hand up, they quiet down at once. "Is that how you knew London's mom?"

"That, and Julian Conte, her spouse, did business with us." Dad reaches into the messenger bag he brought onboard and pulls out a picture. He places it face down and pushes it toward me. "We ran in the same circles and did a few social functions together. They were a very nice couple who had shit luck with the *company* they kept."

I don't miss his emphasis on the word "company." Picking up the photo, I bring it up to my face and study the people in it. Mom and Dad are to the left, with Amelia, and the man I know to be Julian, in the middle. They're laughing at something, having a wonderful time at what looks to be a Christmas function of some sort.

However, my eyes focus on the last person in the group. His face is familiar, just younger in appearance. An angry asshole putting up the front of a good friend and enjoying himself while his date looks to be bored.

Marcus Foster looks the same.

Same miserable expression.

The devil in me recognizes the malice in him. His thirst for money and power. His willingness to kill everyone in his way to obtain it.

He's pulled the tail of the wrong demon this time.

"He knew her father." It's a statement, not a question.

"Yes."

"There's more to this story, isn't there?"

"That's what Earl believes, and so do I."

Placing the photo down, I look at my old man. "He came to you for help?"

"About seven months ago. He's worried about London's safety."

"Is that why...?"

"I reacted?" Dad nods. "In part, yes."

"You knew who she was?"

"Your mother wasn't sure—a lot of time has passed since we saw Amelia—but I knew immediately. Aside from the pictures Earl has shown me, she's her mother's spitting image." Leaning forward in his seat, he lowers his voice. "Malcolm, you have to know that my surprise wasn't at her being there, or not approving, but the shape she was in. Those women have been through enough, and I wasn't about to stand back and let her pay for a crime that isn't hers."

"Why didn't you come to me the moment Earl spoke to you?" I can't disguise the bite in my tone. The anger at knowing I could've saved her sooner.

"Because you made a deal with the Riveras."

Understanding dawns on me. "And they should've been dead by now."

"Exactly," he says with a heavy sigh, shoulders drooping a bit. "The last thing we wanted was for them to run, or worse. They'll kill her out of desperation, and then Marcus will gain total access to her inheritance. We couldn't run the risk of word getting back—"

"There's a rat," I deadpan low enough so only he can hear.

"You know?"

"I have my suspicions, and I'm letting the scum trap himself."

He rubs his jaw, eyes shifting to my men behind us. "You've always been ten steps ahead of everyone."

"Paying attention to details is my job."

"And yet something is bothering you."

"I failed her."

"No, you—"

"I did." Sitting back, I close my eyes and picture her face. That sweet smile and the soft expression she gets when I call her Twirl. "I should've never accepted the deal with Thiago and shut them down the moment they stepped foot in my city. I should've just paid the debt they owe and put them down like the vermin they are. There's a lot of *I should haves,* but I didn't, and now that's a wrong I'm going to rectify. London will never know pain again. Never feel fear. They will die so my girl can reclaim her peace."

"What are you going to do?"

"I'm going to paint a beautiful picture with their blood."

"WELCOME BACK, MR. ASHER," Maria and Juan greet me in the driveway of my vacation home in Costa Rica, their accents heavy. They've been with me for a few years now; a trustworthy, older couple that lives here and takes care of the property year round while I'm away.

They're here to cater to my guests and never ask questions.

They've never been reluctant to clean up a mess if things turn south.

But more importantly, they've never said a word about the business that's transpired.

"Happy to be back," I say, extending a hand out to Juan and then Maria. They each shake it, and then get right back to work on unloading the back of the rental. The men traveling with me are already taking their luggage down and heading toward a separate home, a smaller structure to the right of the main house, where they'll stay while we're here.

Except for Carmelo and my father. They will be with me.

"Has anyone else arrived?" Dad asks, exiting the SUV with his phone in hand. He's reading something on it, chuckling to himself, before typing a reply. "Or do we have time to relax for a bit?"

Maria pauses on the second step and looks back. "You're the first to arrive, señor."

"Perfect." Dad follows her up to the house while I survey the area. I'm sure he wants to call Mom and then rest for a bit, while I'm feeling restless. A bit edgy.

You miss her.

I do. Not going to deny it.

Being with her these last few days—having her close and drowning myself in her scent—was heaven, but I couldn't bring her with me this time. Not when she isn't ready to deal with assholes that walk around thinking women are here to only serve one purpose.

To be on their knees.

In time, she won't cower from those men. She won't so much as blink when they make a comment. London will know how to protect herself. She'll shoot first and let me worry about the consequences for her later.

That the only man she will ever kneel for is me, and that's because she wants to. Craves it.

Carmelo's voice meets my ears then and I tilt my head, catching the end of his instructions. He's walking my way with four others; two of them will man the security kiosk and the others will handle perimeter checks around the clock during our stay.

No one gets on this estate without my knowing. No one leaves without my permission.

This property is nestled on a private stretch of land between a waterfall and the dense Costa Rican jungle. Its lush vegetation surrounds the back, while the ocean is visible from the front because of the high vantage point of this cliff. The warm waters below and white sandy beach, with miles upon miles of solitary beauty, is only accessible by foot or short motorbike ride down a hidden trail that a select few know about.

It's beautiful, peaceful, and I have no neighbors for a few miles. The perfect place to host a man with just as much blood on his hands as I do.

He's one of the world's richest; a modern-day narco. A man that resides at the very top of every most wanted list in the world. Someone who values his privacy and ability to fly under the radar above all else.

Roberto Castillo is rich, smart, and someone who moves a lot of money through my bank. A loyal customer from a secluded mountaintop in South America who owes me a favor.

One I plan to cash today.

MALCOLM

"SO, YOU FORESEE NO future delays after the Jameson issue?" Roberto asks, sitting back in his seat out on my lanai, an ice-cold beer in his hand. His right-hand man nods beside him, yet the move is a bit sloppy. A bit drunk. He's sipping on his fourth serving of rum while Carmelo and my father don't move an inch.

Don't show any emotion.

Blank faces greet Roberto's question, and I bring my own drink to my lips, savoring the orangey hop flavor. "This business has no guarantees, yet I've never failed you. My record speaks for itself."

The smell of an open flame and meat permeates the air. Juan is at the grill while Maria prepares a few typical dishes for our guest; a few salads, rice and beans, fried green plantains and empanadas. It's been hours since my last meal and I'm starving, feeling a bit agitated by his lack of faith.

"It's not you I'm worried about per se…" he trails off and I tilt my head to the side, raising a brow. "There's been a few rumors. You know people talk—"

"About what?" No one misses the bite in my tone and his men tense, two reaching back to grab the guns tucked at their waistbands. *Idiots.* What they fail to realize in their cockiness, the bravado that anyone with power suffocates in, is that no one is invincible.

It's the most obvious that gets you killed.

Danger is always in front of your face, not hidden.

Like now, I scratch my chin and two of my men get into position, the scopes at the end of their semi-automatics barely visible from the roof's edge. A dangerous scenario for anyone that pisses me off.

Those snipers are on my payroll. Are loyal to me.

Roberto shifts his eyes to Carlos, who's busy laughing, not a single care in the world while I break down their actions. Mannerisms.

"Who's talking?" my father asks, his own hand clenching once before he grabs his own beer. "Please share."

"They're saying you're distracted by a woman."

"Is that all?" I laugh, a harsh, sardonic sound that fills the now-quiet space. And just as soon as it starts, it stops when I turn my hard eyes on a still-chuckling Carlos. The man is oblivious to my mounting ire.

"No disrespect meant, my friend." Roberto is a smart man. It's why he's still alive when so many have fallen before him. He thinks. Plots. Makes the right investments.

I recognize in him what he sees in me: no remorse.

In this business he needs someone to trust with his assets, and I make a fortune from each transaction. It works, until it doesn't.

At this moment, it's becoming a failure.

"I fail to see how my private life holds weight over my business."

"This came from someone close to you. A Jimmy Cross?"

His noose just grew tighter. "I know the name, yet it still doesn't answer why it should matter to anyone."

"To me, it doesn't. I just wanted to address—"

"See, boss." Carlos slaps a hand down on the table. The impact causes his drink to spill, and the asshole has the audacity to snap a finger at Maria to clean it. She makes a move to do so, but the shake of my head stops her in her tracks. Something he doesn't notice. Nor does he realize that three hands on this table have moved beneath the wood. "I told you Malcolm doesn't let a meaningless fuck control him."

"Enough, Carlos," Roberto hisses from between clenching teeth, a hand up but no call to action. To remove the asshole.

Shaking his head, Carlos grabs Roberto's bottle and drains what's left in two deep pulls. Once it's empty, he slams it down with a sneer on his face. "Pussy is a dime a dozen and most come attached to a whore—"

His head flies back from the impact of my bullet, blood splattering his boss and Carmelo. Neither so much as flinch. No other guns go off.

Instead, we watch as Carlos's body slumps with his head hanging at an awkward angle, red dripping from the exit point at the back of his head. It pools on the floor below and then spreads along the grout lines of my terracotta tiles.

There are small bits of flesh and bone fragmented by the force, sticking to the pillars and walls near his body. The scene is gory and a bit gruesome, and yet, I feel a sense of relief settle deep into my bones.

My agitation is somewhat sated. At once, I'm a little calmer.

"Thank you for that." That comes from Roberto; he's wearing a tiny grin on his face. "Motherfucker was driving me insane."

"Why didn't you just put him down?" I place my gun atop the table, and then pick up my drink to take a hearty sip. "The man was obnoxious."

"Idiot was my wife's cousin." Roberto shrugs, pulling a handkerchief from his pocket to wipe the few splatters on his face. "You know…" he waves a hand in the air "…family and all that shit."

"And this won't cause an issue?" Snapping my fingers gets everyone moving. Roberto's men take the body into a large storage I have in the woods, while mine will assist in preparing the corpse for transportation back to whatever family he has. Maria's already cleaning, abandoning her cooking for the moment, while her husband goes around the table refilling drinks and then replacing the ruined chair.

"Not at all, since he died at some bar with his hand between the legs of another man's wife."

"Poor guy." Carmelo lifts his bottle in the man's memory.

"He was a nuisance who took liberties which weren't his to take. I put up with him for my wife who took pity because he has no wife or kids. No one who really cared." Roberto sits back, nodding to himself. Thinking. You can tell the exact moment his attention shifts back to what's important; business. Why he needs me. "However, I have more important things to worry about than what story to tell my lady. We need to move the equivalent of half a billion dollars in six months, Malcolm, all in Mexican pesos this time. Five transactions coming from different states within Mexico starting in two weeks. It's going to an offshore account in Barbados, and then from there to Switzerland."

"Consider it done, but..." I pull out my phone and cross-check his last choice with an email from my informant. "Not to Switzerland. We're going to split the final destination between Uruguay and somewhere East."

"Uruguay works, but where east?"

"China. Shanghai, to be exact."

<hr>

I'M on my plane back to the US the next day around midday. Roberto left early this morning after a late dinner and then a few friendly games of pool, needing to reach the Panama Canal and ensure that a shipment of drugs passes through without incident.

He has men in that port, but one can never be too careful when money is involved.

Money moves the world, and it's the reason why so many illegal businesses exists. One hand washes the other, especially when a few bills are thrown at any complication that can arise, but people get greedy. Want more.

And the problems lie with that *more*. With the opportunity, those idiots make mistakes, and in his business, that's more common than one thinks. Even those at the top have to watch their backs of thieves.

Because everyone has a price. That golden number which makes them willing to take a life.

"We'll be landing shortly, Mr. Asher," my pilot announces, and I buckle myself in. This is a short pit stop that's unavoidable before I head home. To be honest, I should've made the trip the moment I found out he was released.

My eyes stray away from the TV in front of me and over to the window. The sun is high, and the waters off the Florida coast glisten in its light. The city of Miami is beautiful, loud, but hides a danger beneath its golden surface that many fail to see.

I see it, though. The allure. The mist of sin and carnal desires that turns people into criminals.

The wheels touch down on the tarmac, and I turn my phone on. Immediately it pings with three text messages; two from Twirl and one from Gina.

The woman has been with me for a little over six months, working as a daytime guard inside the Asher building. She's diligent, an ex-military medic who came home to nothing. Her family died, and the law failed to find their killer.

Javier knows her from when they were kids, vouches for her, and I've promised my help.

That alone has made her loyal to Twirl.

> They're both here just as you predicted.
> Cemetery entrance and waiting to approach.
> ~Gina

My fingers fly over the keys of my phone as the unbuckle seatbelt sign flips on and the pilot maneuvers the plane to the disembarkment point.

> Call Javier and have him meet you there.
> ~Malcolm

Three little dots appear on the screen before her reply comes through.

> Already done. I'm at one end of the road and
> he's at the other watching. ~Gina

> Approach made. Looks tense but the older
> Foster spotted Javier. ~Gina

With her response comes a photo of the three of them standing at a gravesite. They're too close, and my girl looks uncomfortable. She's wearing all black, a shirt and pants, and her face is half hidden beneath a large pair of sunglasses. The other two are of no importance, but I do smile a little when I see the bandage on Alton's hand and the sling on Marcus's shoulder.

> Good. They don't go anywhere with her. Keep close and alert at all times. ~Malcolm.

> Understood, sir. ~Gina

> Keep me updated. ~Malcolm

Giving her one last look over, I put my phone away and stand. My guards have already gotten off and are waiting for me just inside the private gate area. The plane will refuel here, and the crew will take a break while I meet up with an old friend.

The terminal is full of travelers as I make my way through the vast number of gates and restaurants. All overflowing, but even through this maze of faces, I spot Thiago Rivera easily.

He's alone, sitting at a table in one of the more upscale bars inside this concourse and nursing a drink.

The man looks different. He's bulked up and his features have hardened while in jail paying for a crime he didn't commit.

"I'm not surprised by your call," is his greeting, a small smirk on his face.

"Good. Then you know why I'm here." I extend a hand out for him to shake, and when he does, I pull him up into a man hug. "Happy to see you out, Rivera. That was a shit case and setup."

"I know." He nods, squeezing tight and then letting go to take a seat. "It's cost me something far more valuable than time."

"Then I won't take any more of it." Carmelo hands me a folder then and walks away. He'll wait outside along with the other two that stayed with me. Dad left for Chicago straight from Costa Rica via first class with a few bodyguards. "I want to liquidate their debt. The Fosters will owe me."

"Why?"

I slide the folder to him. "Open it."

Thiago flips it open and his eyes harden. Fingers twitching. "That poor girl is innocent. She's nothing like them."

"She's mine." At my words, he looks up and realization hits. Understanding, because he would kill anyone that touches his Luna. "Their lives will end by my hands. Agree or don't, Thiago, it makes no difference. This is a courtesy visit because of our friendship, but my compliance with our agreement died the very minute they touched her."

"Fuck the money." His large frame sits back, jaw ticking. "Keep it, burn it...donate it for all I care."

"Then what do you want in exchange?" I ask, mimicking his actions. My eyes are on his. Unwavering. "If not money...?"

"I'll be there to witness."

I nod. "Done."

"Good." He stands and I follow, walking out after tossing a few bills to cover his drink and tip. "Are you heading back home or staying in Miami for a few days?"

"My flight leaves in half an hour."

"Mom will be sad she missed you." He chuckles, and a bit of the man I knew before he took the fall for his brother seeps through. "She's been cooking all day for the party tonight."

"Wish I could, but London needs me."

"Say no more. Next time." He gives me one last slap on the back before pulling me into a hug. "Be good to her, Asher."

I pull back and match his shitty grin. "Are you going after Luna?"

"I am." His phone beeps then, and he pulls it out to read the message. At once his features darken, and the plastic in his grasp groans under the pressure of his hold. "Call me when you're ready to proceed."

"You okay?"

"Just have a girl to reclaim and a motherfucker to kill." Thiago turns around and leaves then, merging into the crowd while I make my way back to my gate. The plane is ready for take-off when I arrive, and I approve the change.

I'll be home in a few hours.

Hold her sooner.

Kiss those lips.

Pulling out my phone, I send her a short message.

I miss you, Twirl. ~Malcolm

London

IT'S BEEN SIX HOURS since he left, and I miss him like crazy. In a way that makes no sense. As if a piece of me is gone, and to be whole I need him back.

It's his cocky grin and smoldering green eyes. His filthy words and possessive touch. The way he commands respect by simply entering a room or how he treats me like I'm a precious doll.

Like he needs me just as much as I do him.

This is crazy—we're insane—but it works. We click. Connect on a level that I've never experienced before.

Mom's words come to mind then:

Hold onto it with both hands and never let go. Savor each moment you have together because tomorrow is never promised.

The two sides of him draw me in, pull, until my will becomes his. Because I find myself *wanting* to please him. Make him happy.

"Where do you want us to put these boxes?" Javier asks, pointing at the man named Jimmy that works for Malcolm. He's serious and a little weird, looking at everything and keeping tabs of the expensive items inside the living room.

He makes me feel uneasy—looks at me as if he knows me, or something that I don't. But instead of saying something, I don't.

For now, I'll pay attention to my surroundings and count down the minutes until he leaves. Until I can speak to Javier or Malcolm about the emotions he evokes.

My gut doesn't trust him, and Gina doesn't seem to either. I've caught her looking at him a few times, eyes narrowed and body tense.

Always standing closer to me when he's in the room. Like now, she moves to stand in front of me while speaking with Javi, blocking me a bit from view.

She did this at my father's house.

Never leaving me alone. Always near and alert, even though no one was home. No signs of Dad and Alton as I took my belongings and we drove away without a backwards glance.

I force a smile and point at the corner near the back. "It'll be fine over there. Actually, put them all there."

Not that there's many. Six boxes and once suitcase is all I packed, grabbing what's important and irreplaceable.

The money I've been saving that I hid beneath an old floorboard under my bed. A few photo albums, Mom's old jewelry box with what's left inside—what Dad hasn't been able to sell and gamble away. My clothes aren't much and take no space, while my books fill two boxes.

Everything else are things that Mom left behind for me.

Mementos, a box that's taped up, and in her handwriting, with knick-knack she saved from each one of my birthdays. Almost a lifetime worth of memories. It's been in my closet for years, from the day I found it in our attic underneath a blanket and beside the chest with my old baby items.

"That's all for tonight," Javier says then, bringing my attention to the three of them. "Jimmy, take the night off. I'm going to need you tomorrow morning."

"I don't mind staying. Help Gina with—"

"I'm not repeating myself." Javier's tone doesn't leave room for argument. It's final, and I watch how Jimmy forces a neutral expression on his face. "Report downtown at nine. I'll be there to grab you. We have an order pickup for the boss."

"Understood. Have a good night." With a final glance my way, he walks out with Javi following behind him. We don't say anything as we wait for Javier to come back; the feeling is mutual.

Something is off with him.

Instead, I busy myself by opening the first box, which has books. I pull them out one by one, stacking them atop a table until I can figure out where to put them.

Hopefully Magda can give me an idea in the morning.

"Want some help with that?" Gina asks after a while, coming to stand beside me. "I'm an amazing unpacker."

I smile at her. "How about organizing by color? I've always wanted to put them on a shelf in a gradient style; lightest to darkest."

"Sounds good to me." Gina starts with the ones on the table while I inspect a small book of poems that Mom always kept on her nightstand. There are scribbles in her penmanship, little notes on how a specific line made her feel. How beautiful they were.

"And that one?" Javier's voice cuts through my memories, bringing my focus to him. He's pointing at the small book in my hand. "Is that one going to the library like the rest? Or will they go in the office?"

"I was thinking about getting them sorted while he gets back. I'm not sure where to——"

"Sweetheart, he wants you to mix your things with his. Put them in the middle of the staircase and that man wouldn't care," he says, tone gentle. Javier walks casually to my stack and picks up an old copy of *Emma* that's been in my mom's family for years. "Or better yet, why don't I show you."

"What're you talking about?" My interest is piqued.

"Ten bucks says I can find the most out of place for it, and he'll love it."

"I want in on this." Gina wipes her hands on the black slacks she's wearing. "However, this needs to be ridiculous. Somewhere that'll leave him scratching his head."

"You're both crazy." I'm shaking my head, a giggle bursting through. "I'm in. Double or nothing."

"Done. Now..." Javi scratches his jaw "...where to put this?"

"I'm leaving that up to you. Just make it good."

"Or, you can both be neutral and let me?" Gina interjects, a wicked glint in her eyes. "Whatcha say?"

"Go for it." Taking the book from him, I hand it over. She walks away and toward his office, leaving me with the perfect opening to address my concern. "Javi?

"I know."

"Something isn't right."

"You have a good eye." He bumps his shoulder with mine. "Don't doubt yourself. If someone gives you the creeps, nine times out of ten, they are one. An off chance isn't worth the risk of your safety."

"Does Malcolm know?" Because I don't see him letting someone untrustworthy work for him.

"He does. Trust us."

SINCE LAST NIGHT I've been feeling off. As if I'm missing something—forgetting something important—and this morning at eight a.m. it finally hit me.

Mom died five years ago today. Taken from me by some asshole that only cared about the money she had inside her wallet that night, his next high, or God knows what, because to this day, he still hasn't been found.

Not a single trace. No one cares to look.

One minute she's here, and the next gone.

Moreover, that night I lost my entire family.

Dad hates me, and Alton no longer pretends to see me as a little sister.

At sixteen, I became an orphan. I was lost and desperate until just recently when Malcolm came into my life. And while a part of me mourns Mom all over again today, the larger part of me just misses *him*. Today, I just need *him*.

He's been in my life for such a short period of time, and maybe the rest of the world will think I'm insane for moving in with him, but deep down it feels right. Like I belong here.

"Are we stopping for flowers," Gina asks the closer to the cemetery we get. I've been quiet. Lost in my head as I try to fight the guilt for being more torn up by his absence than this anniversary.

Maybe it's because of how many years have passed.

Maybe it's because I don't want to spend the day alone like all the years prior.

Looking out the window, I shake my head. "I always pay for year-round service. The cemetery puts fresh flowers in my name, because I never knew when they'd allow me to come and do so."

For a second, I feel her eyes on me. Hear the sadness in her tone. "Is there anything you need from me? For me to do?"

Not unless you can magically make him appear.

"Just drive down to the end of this road and turn left. The second row after is where the family's mausoleum is." The cemetery is almost empty when we arrive around mid-morning on Tuesday, most people coming to see their loved ones over the weekend. It's an old and very large park, accommodating the affluential and rich. Those that can afford large buildings to house the final destination of the entire family.

Funny, it also serves to show me a cold, hard truth I've been neglecting up until this very moment. The women of my family are the providers. First Mom, and then I took up the slack when they didn't lift a finger to cook a single meal, and then there's the odd jobs to help pay bills.

"This one?" Gina points to a large structure, the only one near the end of this road.

"That's the one," I hear myself say, but I'm on autopilot now, literally asking one foot permission to move the other. "Right here is fine." My body feels heavy as she parks and I exit, and yet, I manage to hold a hand up when her car door opens. "I'm going to need some privacy, please."

"Completely understandable, London. I'm just going to stand beside the car and get some air."

"Thank you." I don't turn back to look at her, though. My eyes are set on the entrance to her resting place. One foot in front of the other, I walk closer with tears brimming. My chest feels tight and breathing becomes a bit choppy.

Being here. Entering this space and finding that it looks the same hurts for some reason.

Maybe it's because I'm the only one that cares.

Maybe it's because I feel like a failure for not standing up for myself.

Maybe it's because a part of my soul wants to unleash years of anger on the world for the unfairness of it all. And while I know it's not her fault, the pain still lingers.

I feel abandoned.

"Why?" I'm choking, emotions bubbling to the surface that for so long I kept hidden from everyone. From myself. "Why, Mom?"

"It was just her time, Lola," Alton answers out of nowhere, and I freeze. Where did he come from? How didn't I hear him enter?

"What are you doing here?" There's an edge of panic to my voice, my fight-or-flight instincts kicking in. *Calm down. Gina is close and nothing will happen.* "Did you know I would be here?"

London

"**S**HE WAS MY MOTHER, too." His tone is softer than I ever remember him using, and I'm taken aback by it. It throws me off. Turns my sudden fear into annoyance.

Since when? That retort sits on the tip of my tongue, but instead I step around him. He's misconstruing my question earlier. I'm not asking why she died; it's clear to me that life has a beginning and end that no one can predict. No matter how unfair it is, how much I miss her, it is what it is.

What I want is answers.

Why do they treat me like crap?

Why is Alton fascinated with me?

Why does Dad threaten me every time he can?

Just fucking *why*?

"I'll leave you to your visit, then," I grit out, waving a hand in the air before turning to leave.

"Wait." His hand shoots out to stop me—it connects with my arm and he winces, bringing my attention to the bandages around his hand. To the purple and swelling around his wrists. Alton notices where my eyes are and pulls it away. "That's a gift from Mr. Asher himself."

"Kind of like the ones you and Dad left on my arm and neck? Or how about the scratches your fiancée took immense joy in making down my arm." With the tip of my finger I point to each one, waiting for some bull-shit excuse or one of his threats. It doesn't come this time, and I'm not ready for the regret in his eyes as I look at him once more.

"I'm sorry," he says, his voice hoarse and low. "There's no excuse for my behavior, London, and I'm truly sorry."

"I don't know what to say." It's the truth, and I also don't feel comfort-able inside this enclosed space alone with him. "Maybe I should come back later. Go ahead and have your visit—"

"No. Take your time...you were here first." Alton gives me a sad smile, and it throws me off. This entire change of behavior isn't like him at all. *Did Malcolm hit his head?* He only mentioned a broken hand and bullet to a shoulder; did I miss him giving this man a personality transplant? "...Dad and I will wait outside. Please, just give us a few minutes of your time before you go."

"Again, why are you doing this?" I say, exasperation coloring my tone. "You don't care. Never have."

"That's where you're wrong, sis. You're everything to us." With that he walks out, leaving me alone inside the mausoleum, feeling lost and unsure. The sole thing giving me comfort is that Gina is nearby, keeping an eye, and she won't let anything happen to me. *None of them will.*

"This is such a mess, Mom." Taking the steps to where her plaque is on the wall, I lower myself to the floor right in front of it. I sit crossed-legged and look at her name, trace each letter with the tip of my fingers and then check the water level inside the metal vase. "What are they playing at? They've never come here. Not once since you died."

Silence. Not that I expect anything different, but outside the wind picks up and the stained-glass window above the entryway rattles a bit.

At this, a small snort escapes me. "Is that your way of saying run? That you're not buying it either?"

A memory hits me then, something she said to me on my fifteenth birthday. Dad fought with her that night. He was so mad over my gift; a girls-only weekend trip to California we never took because he forbade us from going alone.

"Apologies are empty when the actions prior hold malice. One thing is making a mistake, Lola, but when a person hurts you because they can—to make you feel small—that's not love. Never give someone the power over you to do so, baby." Mom cups my face, her smile sad. *"Don't make my mistakes."*

"I promise I won't." Leaning forward, I place my forehead against the cool marble. Lower my voice so Alton can't hear me outside. "Besides, Malcolm won't allow it. You'd love him, Mom. How he is with me. How he defends me."

The heaviness I've felt since last night lightens with each word I share. With how I gush like any woman my age would with her mom when she falls...

Christ. That train of thought stops me.

I can't lie to myself. Can't deny that I feel something special for him.

"I think he's my one. The guy you told me would come into my life and change it all." A shadow appears at the doorway but doesn't enter. Just stands there. "There's so much I want to share with you, and I will...soon. For now, please know that I'm happy—that I've found peace away from Dad and Alton. I love you so much, Mom. Always."

A few stray tears fall from my eyes, and I wipe them away. It's always hard to leave here, but today there's also hope blooming in my heart because for the first time in a long time, I'm not alone.

Standing from the floor and with one last touch to her grave, I walk out to face Alton and Dad. The two are standing close, whispering and looking like utter crap. *How did I miss this when Alton apologized?*

Their clothes are wrinkled. Unkempt.

Their hair is greasy and skin a bit pale.

Once I'm near, they stop talking while my brother gives me that pathetic look once more. "Can we go home and talk? I'm late for my next dosage of pain medication."

"No." Lowering my sunglasses over my face, I shrug. "If you need to go, then go. We can have this chat another day."

"Don't be difficult, London. We just—"

"Dad, stop. Not this time." My eyes shift toward Gina and notice her hand at her side, how her eyes are on the men of my family. Alton notices her, while Dad looks toward the other end of the street and I'm not the least bit surprised when I spot Javier there. He's casually leaning against the side door of his car, a grin on his face. It also explains why they didn't barge inside and forcefully remove Alton. "I'm not interested in going to the house, but I'll give you the chance to speak with me if you want, and I'll give you plenty of time to go and get your meds. Meet me at Rojo's today around five. Google it if you don't know where it is."

"Why can't—"

"That's perfect. See you there." Alton gives Dad a hard look and reluctantly, he nods. They walk away after a few minutes of my silence. I'm sure my attitude is throwing them off, and it surprises me too, but feeling safe does that to a person.

If only this didn't feel like a mistake.

Or worse, how do I get Gina and Javi to agree?

THEY'RE ALREADY HERE when I enter the Mexican restaurant at 4:45 p.m. on the dot. Sitting at a table near the back, they spot me, and the company I keep, the moment we enter.

It's the compromise Javier gave me.

They'll sit away from us, but within visibility. I have to be easily reachable.

That, or it's a no-go, and I agree with him. Alton's apology isn't making much sense—it goes against everything he stands for. In his egotistical mind, he's never wrong, so saying the words *I'm sorry* causes a danger sign to flare across my processors.

It's fake, no doubt about that, but why?

I slip into a chair across from Alton and Dad, giving them a tight smile. "Have you been waiting for long?"

"Just a few minutes," Dad answers, picking up his drink of what looks to be pop, and taking a sip. "We got drinks but were waiting on you to order."

"Have you eaten here before?" Alton opens his menu, flipping through the few pages in the binder. "Anything you recommend?"

"No, but I've driven by it a few times and it caught my eye."

The waiter appears then, in his hand a tray with fresh chips and a couple small dishes with salsas. He places them in the middle of the table. "Hi, I'm Miguel and I'll be your server today. What can I get you to drink, Miss?"

"An horchata is fine." He nods, and before he can ask me what I want to eat, I hold a hand up. "I'm not going to eat here; I'll be placing my order to-go a few minutes before I leave. Thanks."

"Of course, you just let me know when you're ready." Turning his attention from me, he looks at them. "And for you two?"

"Why aren't you eating with us? You chose this place." Alton ignores the waiter, directing his attention to me. A flash of annoyance crosses his features, but he hides it quickly.

"Please choose something, London." Dad isn't happy either, he's looking down at the menu, lips in a thin line as he makes his plea. A plea with a hidden edge of *do as you're told*.

"No, thank you." They hate my talking back. They hate anyone that challenges them.

Like Malcolm, who doesn't take shit and won't hesitate to let you know how beneath him you are.

"We don't want to argue. That's fine," Alton says then, his expression back to that sad look he gave me at Mom's grave. "I'll have the chef's taco tray; the six count is fine. Bring extra lime and another Modelo with them."

"Of course, and for you, sir?" he asks, not looking at my father, busy jotting it all down.

"I'll have a large chicken tortilla soup. That's it."

"Perfect. I'll put this in now and be back with your drink, Miss."

Once more the table goes quiet after the waiter leaves. It makes me wonder what's the point to this. Why ask to talk and say nothing?

I take in a deep breath and let it out slow. "Why am I here?"

"We wanted to talk with you away from *his* influence. Try to make you see reason, Lola." Dad shifts in his seat, grimacing when his arm hits the table's edge. He pulls it toward his body, the sling digging into his shoulder

—a shoulder where a small piece of bandage peeks out from the collar of his pullover. "He's using you to get to us. It's not love or whatever bullshit Asher said to turn you against us. Your family."

"Really?" His words sting, but I keep my expression neutral. With them, I expect the attack. They want me to doubt myself. "Is that the best you can come up with?"

"London, he told us as much." Alton grabs my hand atop the table, giving it a squeeze, and my body wants to recoil at his touch. I try to remove my hand from his grip, but he holds tight. "You have to believe us. You are nothing but a pawn in a sick game."

"Let go of my hand." I keep my voice strong. I'm a bit louder than usual so Javier and Gina can hear me. And they do. A chair scrapes against the flooring with the sound of footsteps following, getting closer to our table.

"London, a word please." Gina leaves no room for argument as she reaches for my hand in Alton's, and with a flick of the wrist, releases his hold.

I'm quick to stand, taking a few steps back while avoiding their gaze. "I need to visit the restroom anyway. Let's go." The bathrooms are across the restaurant, and we bypass an angry-looking Javier as we do. His phone is in his hand. Once inside, I turn to face her and let out the breath I've been holding since Alton touched me. "Thank you."

"None needed." Gina wets a wad of paper towels in her hand and places them on my forehead. "Next time your brother so much as breathes wrong, I'm shooting him. Anyone with a working neuron can see how uncomfortable you are with them."

"I'm more upset by the crap they are trying to pull. The things they are saying about Malcolm."

"Please tell me you don't believe—"

"No, I don't." Giving her a soft smile, I turn around and open the faucet to splash some water on my face. The coolness feels amazing against my flesh and it calms me. Helps re-center me. After a few more minutes of quiet, I dry my face and neck. "Come on. Let's get this over with."

"You don't have to. We can leave...just say the word."

"I know."

The restaurant is a bit fuller when we step out, with a large group blocking my way as I go back toward Alton and Dad. It forces me to walk around the group and staff helping them sit, putting me right behind their table where the two are oblivious to my presence.

"Fucking asshole has sunk his claws deep into her," Alton spits out before taking a deep pull from the beer he was nursing. "She's going to make this hard, and I'm taking it out on her ass the moment I get my hands on her. No more waiting."

"Calm down, son." Dad scratches his jaw, tilting his head toward an angry Javier watching them. "We can't act now...they have her under tight surveillance."

"Then when, old man? Because the longer we wait, the harder it will be."

"Eyes on the prize. Remember that." Marcus reaches over and grabs my drink, taking a few sips without shame. When the contents are halfway gone, he places the cup down, and turns to look over at the family with two screaming kids. "With the older cunt gone, the younger one won't be a problem. Stick to the plan, Alton. We sell her virgin holes, take her inheritance, and keep the pathetic bitch as a personal slave to bring in money."

"She's mine." Alton nods while it feels as though the floor beneath my feet has been taken from me. How can they be so cruel? How could I be so stupid to come here?

"Word." It slips past my lips in a low whisper, almost drowned by the busy restaurant, but Gina hears. Without asking any questions, she walks with me to the table and helps me grab my purse from its place on the chair beside mine. She guides me out of the place, ignoring their protests and the call of my name.

Nothing registers as we make it outside and continue toward parking.

Not when we pass our car. Not when another door nearby opens.

Nothing, until a pair of arms I know pull me inside the backseat of a large SUV and settles me on his lap. His touch awakens me then. Breaks down every fucking wall that once stood around my heart, protecting me.

The moment he whispers in my ear *I've got you*, I break down.

MALCOLM

SHE'S SHAKING. SOBBING.

Pouring out years of pain and anger caused by two assholes I'm going to kill. A slow death. Agonizing as I repay them with the same kindness they've given her.

The anger flowing through my veins is blinding. Consuming me while my limbs feel tight. Muscles tense—clenching as my desire for violence grows. It's been building since I landed, and Javier told me where they were. Why they were here.

I tried being civil for her sake. They should be thankful to still be alive.

Yet, the moment I step out of town, the lowlifes came out to play. Whatever they said, hurt her. Broke down that final reinforced-steel wall she hid behind to escape this pain.

And on the anniversary of her mother's death.

"I'm sorry, Twirl. So sorry I didn't make it back to you earlier," I whisper into the crown of her head while wrapping my arms tight around her small frame. She's against my chest, burrowing her face into my neck as the tears soak my collar. Her small, nimble fingers cling—hold on to the fabric of my shirt in a death grip as more teardrops flow. "Please don't cry. Seeing you this upset is killing me."

"No one dies from tears," she mutters low, then hiccups. The sound is cute. "And I can't stop them. Just so much—"

"I know." The car slips into traffic easily, taking the route toward my home. There's a minute nod against my skin and then a long, shuddering sigh. We don't speak as my driver maneuvers around cars or when the occasional horn is honked.

We just stay as we are while I run my fingers up and down her spine in a gentle motion. It takes a while for her sobs to calm and for her breathing to even out, letting me know she fell asleep.

London is clinging to me while I offer her support. I inhale her soft scent, pulling the floral smell deep into my being as I try and keep my composure. The more she relaxes, the more my ire burns bright.

Knowing she's resting gives me a chance to speak with Javier. He's sitting in the front passenger seat and fuming. He cracks his neck then knuckles, body shaking a bit.

"What the fuck happened?" I hiss out from between clenching teeth, my jaw ticking as I fight to keep my voice low. The last thing I want is to wake her up.

"Alton grabbed her hand and wouldn't let go..." he pauses, looking back at her with regret when she whimpers "...when we saw that, I got up and Gina took her to the bathroom. My eyes stayed on them the entire time after I sent the message, but they wouldn't look at me. By the time they came back, London heard something, and Gina took her out. When the Fosters stood to follow, I threatened to shoot, and they sat back down. My focus was on removing her at all cost."

"Okay." Shifting her a bit so she's more comfortable, I lay a kiss on her forehead. Then add another to her cheek that's still wet with tears. "In forty-eight hours, I want everything back in her name. Enough with the childish games."

"Consider it done."

I give him a nod and then look back down at the gorgeous girl in my arms. Skin blotchy and a slight mess, she still takes my breath away. Stirs in me a protective side no one, not even my mother, has ever seen.

"I'm going to make this right," I whisper against her temple. *They're going to pay for this in blood, and it's time I start collecting.*

"WELCOME back to the land of the living, sleepyhead," I say, startling her just inside the kitchen entrance, causing her to squeak. It's a high-pitched sound that I find...*cute*. Makes me want to bite her just a little bit. "Are you hungry?"

I've been awake for hours thinking now, weighing my options. However, after speaking with Gina and knowing what she heard, it's time we talk. No more waiting.

London needs to make a few tough decisions today. The first comes in signing her name on the dotted line of a few sheets of paperwork to regain the power over her future. I'll always support her, but as my equal and not someone who lets fear dictate her life.

However, I know that will come with time. With my patience and helping her see that what they did—how they treated her—isn't normal.

London narrows her eyes at me and huffs with a hand on her chest. "What are you doing hiding in corners?"

"It's hardly hiding when I'm sitting here finishing my breakfast out in the open." Pushing out a chair with my foot, I point to it with my fork. "Join me."

Her fake annoyance melts and the pain resurfaces. "I'm just not hungry."

Dropping my fork, I push my chair back and open my arms. "Come here." Her bottom lip trembles, and she comes to me with no other prompting. With her in my lap, I take her chin with two fingers and turn her to look at me. Let her see the honesty in my words. "Please, let me take care of everything. Let me help you fix the mess they've made for you."

"You spoke to Gina?" I nod, and she wipes away the two tears that have fallen. "How much worse is it than what I heard? How much do I need to prepare myself to hear?"

"I'm sorry, Twirl. I really wish it wasn't this way."

"Not your fault." London leans into me, forehead on mine. Her exhale is sweet and minty on my lips. "To be honest, Malcolm, you've done more for me than I can ever repay and—"

"I take care of what's mine. End of." Taking her bottom lip between my own, I suck on the tender flesh before releasing. "Your happiness is what I'm after. It's what gains me entry into my heaven...it gives me *you*."

"I've been so lost...scared." My girl takes a deep breath then and lets it out slow. The heavy sigh makes my own chest ache for her. For the weight those two assfucks are placing on her head. "Deep down I've always known something was off. With the way Marcus treated Mom. With Alton's sick fascination with me. That's not love. That's a mixture of hate and gaslighting—machismo at its finest. They just wanted us to be subservient and docile so they could do as they pleased."

"You're brilliant, sweetheart. I have no doubt that you'd be long gone by now."

Her small fingers play with the bottom of my shirt, absentmindedly swiping her pinky across my lower abdomen. My reaction is automatic, muscles clenching beneath her touch. "Do you think we would've met otherwise?"

"Of that I have no doubt."

"Yeah?" Her watery eyes lighten a bit, and a small grin curls at her lips.

"Yeah." Lowering my hand to her ass, I pat the luscious flesh so she stands. "Now, let's get you fed and caffeinated before we continue with this talk. And before you say you're not hungry...humor me."

"Do I have a choice?" I'm happy to see that even with the world she knew crumbling around her, my Twirl still has her sass. That she's not pushing me away.

She's hurting, and before the day is over, it'll only get worse. Today I'm staying home to show her what they've done—stolen from her. She'll learn that her father isn't Marcus and that Alton is a depraved son of a bitch.

They both are.

To free her, I have no choice but to break her heart.

I don't answer her. Instead, I pick her up by the waist and I stand us up, only to place her in my seat. There's a small huff, maybe even a slap to my shoulder, but she doesn't fight me when I prepare her coffee or when I place a plate of cheesy eggs and toast in front of her.

"Eat, and come to my office when you're done. I got a few emails to look at."

"Eye, captain." Twirl even gives me a mock salute.

"So bratty."

"You like it."

"I love it." The words slip, but I don't take them back. I do love her mouthiness and playful nature. Her positive outlook and hunger to experience everything life has to offer. "Now, eat up. You have thirty minutes before I come looking for you."

"How can they live with themselves?" London asks me thirty minutes later; the evidence I've given her so far lies on the floor where the folder landed after slipping through her fingers. She's shaking, begging me to make it go away, but I can't. I'm going to do what no one else had the decency to do, and tell her the truth. "My life has been nothing but a lie. One on top of another while the castle they built is now drowning me."

"It was never your mother's intention to hurt you, sweetheart, but she made bad decisions." I bend down to gather the folder and its fallen contents before taking her hand and walking us to a small seating area inside my office. Waiting for her signal to continue isn't easy when all I want to do is break those chains holding her down.

After a little while, London holds out her hand for the information again. "They're not my family."

Not a question. It's a statement, and I nod beside her. "No. They aren't."

"Okay…" she swallows hard, lip trembling "…how do I find out who my biological—"

"Already done." Pulling out the second sheet inside the file, I hand it to her. Just stay quiet as she reads every line with precision. I've seen the photos of her mother, and while they hold a resemblance, there's also a deep connection to her father's Italian roots. Her complexion, hair color, and even the slightly fuller lips come from his side of the family. His mother and sister were the same.

"Julian Conte," Twirl says the name slowly, tilting her head to the side. Thinking, the deep furrow of her brows and the faraway look in her eyes tell me as much. "I've heard that name in passing all my life. *Julian Conte*." Closing her eyes, she sits back against the cushions. Two tears fall, and she doesn't wipe them away. "You know, most fights between them ended with his name being shouted out by Marcus, and all this time, I just thought it was some model or actor from their youth that Mom had the hots for and he was jealous of."

London's sad eyes open and land on mine. "How did you find all of this? Why?"

"Beside my own concern for you?"

"Yes."

"Earl and Mary are terrified you'll end up like your mom. A shadow of herself."

"They know?" she gasps, sitting forward while I nod in confirmation. "Why the hell didn't they tell me anything? Why stay quiet all this time?"

"Because Marcus threatened to move you far away and cut all contact. With hurting you physically, and neither was willing to take that chance. They had no help, London, and did the best they could to be there for you."

"Jesus, this is…" she trails off, and I wrap her tightly in my arms as the first sob breaks free from her chest. Just hold her to me while the reality of what could've been seeps through, and we're not even at the worst. Where my suspicions lie.

Seeing her tears feels like a dagger to my chest. It hurts.

Caring for someone does that to you. Their pain is yours, and you will tear the world apart to take it away. Nothing has proven this fact to me more than seeing her this distraught.

The way London clings to me so desperately further ignites my need for their blood. I want her gripping me from pleasure, never pain.

Kissing her forehead, I breathe in her sweet scent. It helps calm me. Keeps my focus on her and not ending them. I made a promise that their end will be slow, and it will be. Each strike from me will leave them reeling—crying for a mercy I will never grant.

"They both love you but couldn't take on either of them. Not without help, because sadly, they know someone in the Chicago PD that covers for them."

Her head shoots up at that, blue orbs wide with fear. "Lieutenant Bristol. That's who they know…he and Alton went to high school together."

"Thank you, sweetheart." Slowly, I wipe the dampness from her cheeks. "I knew the whom, just needed confirmation on the connection."

"He's a cocky jerk. The guy has always given me the creeps."

"Did he ever touch you?" There's an unmistakable bite to my tone. If he has, the Lieutenant will be dead by the end of the night.

"Was he creepy? Yes, but never moved past a leer or comments on my looks. I swear."

"Okay." I'll leave it at that for now, but something still doesn't sit right with me about this man. Especially if he's covering for the Fosters because no one does anything without some sort of personal gain. His job is on the line and so is possible jail time if found out.

What did they offer him?

London grabs the file then and continues to look over each document, pausing on a particular one detailing the Conte family. The one she will never get to meet. "They're all dead?"

"All except for your cousin Aurora who lives in the Lincoln Park area. She's the daughter of your father's sister who passed away a few years ago due to complications from a kidney transplant."

"I have a cousin," she breathes out, and for the first time since we started this talk, Twirl smiles. It's a curious one with just a hint of excitement. "Mom was an only child and my grandparents died when I was small…I've never had anyone outside of the Fosters."

"Well, now you have my family, and we're crazy enough to keep you entertained for years to come."

"You'll probably give me greys early." And it's that comment that lets me know she'll be more than okay. The sadness lingers, but it won't be permanent. This opens the doors for her to another world, and I think that gives her hope.

"That mouth of yours." I give her a playful growl before leaning over to nip her shoulder. "But there's more to discuss, and I need your attention for a minute."

"What else?" There's trepidation in her tone.

"You're the sole beneficiary in your mothers will, London. Just you."

"That can't be right...they...Marcus told me...*fuck*!" She rubs a hand down her face. "It's mine?"

I get up and kneel in front of her, bring our faces level, and I'm proud to see some anger in those expressive blue orbs. "Say the word, and I'll proceed with getting everything handed back to you. The house is yours and so is the monthly stipend you get—and they've been misspending—until you turn twenty-one and receive your inheritance from Amelia and Julian."

"And the Fosters?"

"Karma."

"In that case...*word*."

London

FOR THE LAST THREE days I've been under a fog.

Just going through the motions as I make peace with what I now know to be the truth. Everything I knew is a lie. A tiny fib that at first seems innocent—a man finding love with a widow, wanting to take care of her and her small child as they navigate through their new normal. It has all the makings of the perfect daytime movie on one of the popular channels women fawn over.

But it's not like that in reality. This story is a nightmare that I have not fully awoken from.

How can I? For years, I was nothing more than a servant to those two men—the same two that were supposed to be family. My protectors.

I did everything they told me to. Have been working to help pay bills and fund their vices so I could escape their threats for another day.

I'm a joke to them. Nothing but a pawn.

Truth is that the more I read, the more it stings. The angrier I am.

"Sick assholes," I hiss out, putting my hair up in a loose bun before grabbing the next paper in the file Malcolm gave me. This one has Julian's information, and I read through it for the thousandth time. Seeing in bold black ink where he's from and the dynamic of his family makes me both happy and melancholic.

Happy because I can see they were good people. Sad because I will never have that with them.

You have Malcolm now.

And I do. God knows he's been a saint as I sort my head.

I'm safe because of him. Because he cares.

I want to stay for him. Make him happy.

However, right now my focus is on my father's life story on these next few pages:

How his parents were from Rome and came here when Dad was three.

What schools he went to, where they lived here in Chicago, and the pictures of my parents on their wedding day. The smiles on their faces brings one to my own, and how he looks at her reminds me of the way Malcolm gazes at me. It's that same sweet and unguarded expression that makes my skin flush and heart beat fast.

Then there's the knowledge that my father's buried in the same mausoleum as my mother. That they're resting together, and that every time I visit, he's there listening too. Dad's ashes lie in the space beside my mother's. Something she did without anyone's knowledge—without Marcus finding out—so she could be with him again someday.

The last few pages in this file explain the financial situation I'm in. What has been taken; the sale of Dad's restaurant chain, and how at his death, everything he owned went to Mom and then me. The details of two hefty life insurance policies are here too, and while the amounts surprise me, learning that Marcus knew my father before his death doesn't sit well with me.

A horrible feeling I can't shake churns within my gut the more I think about it. The more I stare at the few pictures that Malcolm put inside the folder.

Why would my father associate with a man like him?

My guess is that it all comes down to money.

Back then it was his or hers, and now it's mine. The Fosters want and have plans for it.

Knowing all these minute details helps me put together the pieces of a puzzle that were missing. Things that now make sense the more I think about it.

All my life I've thought that Alton and I are nothing alike. We differ in both personalities and looks. No resemblance whatsoever outside of our blue eyes, and his are a darker shade than mine. For years, I just thought that each kid took after one parent, but it's so obvious to me now how wrong I was.

Mom wouldn't hurt a fly, while Marcus doesn't care about anyone other than himself. She was selfless to his selfish.

"I've been so blind," I mutter to myself and rub my left eye. I'm tired. Just plain ol' exhausted but can't stop re-reading what these papers say. "How could Mom let him—"

"Breaking News," comes from the TV then, stopping my train of thought. The local anchor is on the screen and tilting her iPad toward her. Her face shows no emotions while her eyes are wide, looking at someone beside her and then at the monitor. **"An explosion occurred a few minutes ago at a warehouse near the South Side now known to be the headquarters of a local prostitution ring. Luckily, no one was on the premises when the blast occurred, and the authorities are searching for the identity of the owner."** She pauses and looks toward another camera. **"We'll have more for you soon as our team arrives on the scene. If you or someone you know has any information that can help arrest those responsible, please call the number on your screen."**

Doesn't Alton rent a building in the South Side? I know I've seen the rental agreement for it.

I HAVEN'T HEARD a peep from the Fosters in five days now.

Not from them. Not from my Malcolm about them.

Nothing. Not even confirmation of my suspicions about the explosions that took out a large building on the South Side.

It's almost as if they don't exist, and I like it. Love the peace and normalcy I'm experiencing.

Things that to other people are boring, I'm enjoying—from doing laundry to watching a cooking show during the middle of the day—there's no rush in my schedule or fear of someone's wrath. I'm just being me. Thinking. Figuring at my pace what I want to do with the rest of my life.

For the first time, nothing's off the table and everything has possibilities.

My life at the moment is domesticated bliss, while tomorrow I could go back to school and he'd be just as happy for me. He enjoys my cooking, more than Magda's, but will adjust if that's what I need. I am falling for this man more and more every day.

His generosity. How sweet he is with me.

How safe I am because everyone around us respects him.

The small things he does to let me know he cares.

Like now, I'm at the stove finishing our dinner as he walks through the door that connects the garage to the house. He's smiling at me with a long-stemmed rose in his hand. It's a light blush and in full bloom. "Honey, I'm home," he croons with this handsome-ish, cocky grin on his face that only he can pull off. His strides are long as he walks over, the dark pinstripe three-piece suit he's wearing looks delicious on his body. This man is perfection. "Miss me?"

"Someone's in a good mood." Taking the flower from him, I crook a finger, so he crouches a bit to my level. Without any kind of heels, it's hard to reach him even if I stand on the tip of my toes. When he does, I don't hesitate to kiss his smiling mouth. Just a quick peck, then nibble. "And thank you."

"I'm in a great mood." Malcolm wraps his arms around my body, pulling me closer. Chest to chest. "You're here, and the food smells delicious. What're you making?"

"Enchiladas two ways." My own hands explore. Caressing his arms and then shoulders, I dig my fingers in a bit on my way to the nape of his neck where I embed my fingers in his hair. "Then for dessert, I made my very first flan."

Making our dinner has become my thing. Gives me a chance to spoil him a bit.

Magda gave me complete use of her kitchen, and I gave her the afternoon off. She's been here for years and I didn't want to step on her toes, but when I mentioned wanting to do this, Magda just gave me a huge hug and told me to go nuts and have fun. That this is my house too.

"Fuck, I'm a lucky son of a bitch," he groans and then slants his mouth over mine. This kiss is hungry, a full possession of my senses as his tongue meets mine—caressing and tasting me. His body is wound tight against mine. Muscles clenching, Malcolm picks me up and places me on the countertop beside the stove, stepping between my parted thighs and pressing his throbbing length against my cotton-covered core.

The thin material of my shorts lets me feel him. All of him.

His slacks do little to hide his desire for me, and I want more.

To explore, and I almost say this when the timer goes off.

"Don't stop," I beg, but he pulls back. Just a few steps, but it does nothing to cool the need burning through my veins. "Ignore the food. Come back."

Malcolm shakes his head, that same shitty grin is back. "No."

"Why?" I pout, eyes wandering down his body and settling on the thick outline of his length. "I'll leave it in the warmer and—"

"I'm going to run upstairs and take a shower…" my mouth opens to protest, but the predatory gleam in his eyes shuts me up "…behave, and I'll eat you for dessert later, instead."

"Have I thanked you for dinner yet?" His lips skim my ear, causing goose bumps to break out across my skin. His breath fans across my neck and then lower when he nibbles on my shoulder. "Told you how fantastic it was?"

"Only about a hundred times." I'm sitting between his spread thighs on the living room couch with my back to his chest. His bare chest. There's some thriller movie playing in the background, based on a book he seems to love, but for the life of me I can't concentrate. I'm tense. Aware of every solid inch of him and this overwhelming need to please him.

Maybe it's because of how gentle he's been with me or the way he helps me sort through my thoughts. How he never fails to ask me what I want or what plans I have for us in the future.

How proud of me he was when I told him my desire to open a foundation that helps women escape violent situations. Victims—women and children—who have no way out of the nightmare they live in. People like myself; who escaped because someone cared enough to save them.

Malcolm inserts himself so flawlessly into my tomorrows, and I don't find myself minding his company one bit. I value his opinions. His intelligence.

Everything about him drives me crazy in the best of ways. I want more.

More time. More of his touch. More of these drugging little flicks of his tongue over the area right beneath my earlobe.

However, every time I try…he puts a stop to my advances.

He's waiting on me to heal from the lies that broke my heart, but what he fails to realize is that he put me back together again that same night.

"Well, it was amazing, and I appreciate the effort." His fingertips skim the edge of my loose tank top, dipping beneath the hem to caress my stomach.

"You're welcome, and none needed." It's a low keening sound that escapes without my permission. Slowly, those same hands wander high, over my torso and stop around my neck. One alone takes up the entire expanse, and I'm distracted by how unafraid I am of him.

His masculinity calls to the inner slut in me. How much bigger he is— his hardness to my petite form is a turn-on. It makes me think of more intimate moments where he could easily dominate me. Take me.

I want him to claim me.

"I'm going to enjoy spoiling you, Twirl," he whispers, tightening his hand so I can feel the thin metal chain he's holding against my throat. Where he's hid it all this time, I have no clue, but then again being distracted does that to a person. The charm digs into the skin a bit. It's cold, small and round, a delicate piece that he brings up to my face after letting go. "My tiny dancer. So beautiful and devilishly sweet."

"Malcolm," it's a breathless sigh. My eyes are on the thin, gold chain with a vintage locket hanging from it. The intricate design on it is beautiful, but what stands out is the delicate ballerina in an en pointe pose. "It's so pretty and too much. You've already—"

"Arguing with me will get you nowhere, London." Large fingers open the clasp and show me an old photo inside. "Do you like it?"

"How did you…?" My eyes water, and I turn to look back at him with a huge smile on my face. So thankful for this man. "Where did you get this picture?"

"I have my ways." His smirk is so sinful, his body mouthwatering.

"Put it on me." He does as I ask when I turn back around to face the TV. The fact that he went looking for a picture of my mother and me as a baby leaves me without words. And while there are three that I want to say, they evade me at the moment.

I might not have any experience when it comes to sex, but I know what I want. And I want him.

Not because I need to repay this kind gift, but because nothing will please me more than loving him. Showing him with my actions what I can't verbalize just yet.

Before he can protest, I stand and turn to face him. On my knees and between his, I place my hands on his thighs and squeeze the now tense muscles. Massage him slowly, all the while my eyes are on his.

His wander, though. From my baby blues, to my lips, and then to the now beautiful gift he's given me. Malcolm looks me up and down in this position; I can see the want in his eyes. Almost touch the fire that burns between us.

Our need is palpable.

Combustible.

And I'm tired of the words *no* and *slow*.

"London, you don't have to do this." He swallows hard when I bite my bottom lip. "My gifts don't come with any expectations."

"All the more reason to act on my own wants. This isn't for you…" walking my fingertips up his gym shorts, I pause at the waistband and pull the fabric back, exposing him "…this is for me."

London

MALCOLM DOESN'T MAKE A single move to stop me. Doesn't so much as breathe when I wrap my hand around his girth, fingers not fully touching as I pull him out. He's thick and long, absolutely perfect with velvet-smooth skin and a drop of pearl-like fluid at the tip.

There's a part of me that's scared. It's my first time touching a man like this, and yet excitement wins out. I'm curious.

I want to explore him. I want to taste him.

Enjoy the more intimate part of a relationship between a man and his woman.

Because that's what this is. It's clear to me that he is mine and I am his.

My mouth waters at the sight, and I lick my lips. "Show me, Malcolm. Teach me how to please you."

At my words, his entire body shakes. A deep rumbling sound forms in his chest, and I pull my eyes away from the perfection throbbing in my hand to meet his eyes. They're hooded, and the hunger in them causes my core to clench.

"That's a dangerous offer, Twirl." His hand comes over mine and strokes twice, the grip tight. "The way I want you is dangerous. Perverse. If you're not ready for all of me…want this, back off and head upstairs. This is your one out."

Mimicking his fluid motion, I pump him once on my own, causing him to groan. "Please."

"Are you sure?" It's a hiss, his hands clenching at his sides. He's holding back for my sake, and I don't want that. "I'll never hurt you, but I won't be gentle. Can you handle all of me?"

Instead of answering him, I do something that seals my fate. Ties me to him.

I lean forward and kiss the very tip of his swollen head, rubbing my lips back and forth once and then lick his essence from them. Then, just to push him further, I place him back inside his shorts and sit back on my calves, meeting his stare. Let him see in mine how serious I am.

How ready I am for every single part of him.

Malcolm gives me a nod and then that sexy grin I like. "Lose the top, Twirl. Show me those pretty tits." Without a second thought, I lose the simple cotton shirt and toss it somewhere behind me, followed by my bra. He sucks in a breath but doesn't say anything, his eyes roaming, caressing the curves of my breasts. "Come closer and arch your back. Tell me to touch you."

That gravelly voice is a weakness of mine. Something so natural and raw, the tone of his voice—the hunger in it—send a shiver down my spine.

"Please," I whimper as my nipples tighten to almost the point of pain. Pain at being denied what I need.

Him. From that very first time inside the room at Liam's club, my world has been revolving around his. I belong to him. He's my happy place.

"*Fuck*, the neediness in your tone is delicious." Malcolm brings a hand up to my chest and cups my right breast, weighing it in his hands before pinching the tight little bud. He gives it a harsh tug, but instead of cringing away, I welcome the new sensation. The sting of pleasurable pain causes my core to clench and clit to throb. "You want this," he croons before giving the same treatment to the left. "Want me."

"Yes." I arch further, inviting him to take more. "It's you. All of you."

"Good girl." With the hand on my chest, he pushes me back a bit, and I scoot two steps back. He stands then, over six feet of solid muscle hovering over me, the outline of his thickness at my eye level. "Undress me."

My hands tremble. The thrill of the moment travels through my body, goose bumps rising as I use his thighs as leverage to stand to full height. My face to his chest, I step into his space and lay a tiny kiss over the place where his heart is, then across his other pec as I work my way up.

I nip his collarbone, standing on the tip of my toes to reach his chin where my teeth dig in just a tiny bit. "I trust you, Malcolm."

"Say it again." His hands take hold of my hips and lift me off the floor so I can look at him in the eye. "Tell me."

"I trust you," I whisper before kissing him. Hungrily. Needing him to accept that for as much as he wants me, I can't be without him anymore.

His tongue in my mouth is demanding and I gladly submit to him, soaking up his every grunt for more. How his hold on me tightens when I swipe my tongue across his bottom lip. "Addictive little thing. So fucking perfect."

"We are. Perfect for each other." Slowing us down to a few soft pecks, I wiggle in his hold. Malcolm pulls back to look at me, but I arch a brow. "You might want to put me down."

"Do I?"

"You will if you want me to use my mouth in a more productive way." I make a show of licking my bottom lip in a slow swipe he follows. That causes his dick to flex against my hip.

Malcolm leans forward and takes the still wet lip and bites down hard enough for it to sting. "As you wish, sweet Twirl." He lets go after a quick kiss and lowers me, my body sliding against his until my feet meet the floor.

Once I have my balance, he steps away and sits down, the expression on his face similar to the very first time we met inside the club.

It's a bit of an angry hunger mixing with his natural edge that makes him dangerous for me.

And I'm wet for him. Soaking my panties and the thin boxers I stole from him.

Knowing that I want to feel all of him, I take in a deep breath and shimmy out of the shorts. My panties too.

Humming his approval, he makes a turning motion with his hand and I give him what he wants. Taking my position with one foot slightly back, I gift him three slow twirls and then on the last, drop back to my knees.

I crawl the few steps between us, coming to a stop between his parted thighs. "Lift," is all I say as I give his bottoms a tug. On the next pull, he does as I ask and rises just enough so I can take both items covering him off.

Our eyes stay connected as I toss his boxer briefs and shorts somewhere behind me. What sounds like glass crashes on the floor, but neither of us stops to look.

Instead, I lower my lips to his skin, trailing open-mouthed kisses up his right thigh. Let my instincts guide me. "I've never done this before, Malcolm. Never thought much about dating or sex. With you, though…" I nuzzle the soft hairs on his leg "…with you I want it all. Want to give you all my firsts."

"I'm going to cherish you, London. Give you the motherfucking world on a silver platter if that's what you wish for." His fingers thread through my hair, pushing the long strands back off my face before wrapping it around his fist. A tug has me hovering over his cock. "Now kiss it. Show your appreciation."

My tongue darts out, swiping over the slit before I lay tiny kisses from tip to base. "Show me how to please you."

"Open your mouth, baby." It's a hiss, his fingers tightening their hold as I follow the instructions, sliding his length through my parted lips. "*Damn*, you look beautiful like this. Worshipping my cock with those plump lips like the good little slut I knew you could be."

His words should offend me, but they don't. I enjoy them. Let them travel across my senses as this part of me I didn't know comes alive. Thrives beneath his touch.

"More," I say around his shaft, pressing my tongue against him before taking the tip between my lips and sucking. His hips buck before he pulls all the way out. He holds me above him, hard eyes on mine as a whine leaves the back of my throat. "Don't stop."

"Beg me," he growls, fingers tightening, and the stinging bite settles on my clit. "Beg me to suck my cock."

"Please let me suck your cock, Mr. Asher."

"Motherfuck." Slowly, he lowers my mouth down his shaft, rubbing the underside on my tongue as I hollow my cheeks. It throbs, his pre-come coating my lips when he pulls me up and off, rubbing himself over my lips with each pump of his hips.

I lick them. His taste off them. "More."

"My naughty little girl," he grits out, pushing in deeper, and my first instinct is to pull back. I gag as he touches the back of my throat, but his hold keeps me in place. "Relax, sweetheart, and breathe through your nose. Yeah…just like that…*fuck*."

He thrusts his hips a few times and stops, pulling me off so I can catch my breath. "Ready?" he asks.

I nod, not entirely sure what he means, before he guides me down again and I take him between my lips. The thickness of his cock makes me ache with the desire—with the need to feel him filling me, and my thighs rub together in search of the friction I crave.

"Let's see how much you can take." I barely get in a deep breath before his hips flex up and both hands push on the back of my head. The moment I begin to gag again, he holds me still, instead, giving short little thrusts into my mouth. "Swallow." It's a difficult task, one that earns me a deep groan before he begins pushing again. "I'll get this mouth trained. One day you'll take it all."

I gag again and attempt to breathe through my nose, and he pulls me off, leaving a string of spit connecting my lips to his cock. Once I get control of my breathing, he repeats, sliding to the back of my throat and holding me there as I acclimate to the sensation.

This time, when he thrusts up, I don't gag. Knowing what to expect calms me, and I look at him from beneath my lashes. Four quick pumps and I'm moaning around him, sliding my teeth over his skin on each exit.

"Fuck, Twirl," he groans before letting go of my hair, arms stretching out. "So wet and hot. That mouth is the definition of sin."

I pull back and take in a deep breath. "Did I pass, Mr. Asher?"

"You did, and you've earned a reward. One that you will swallow all of."

"Yes, sir." It's a whimper. A plea. I ache for him.

"How wet are you?"

I bite down on my bottom lip as I nod, my hand slipping between my thighs. I let out a shaky moan as my fingers swipe across my swollen clit. "Soaking and needy."

"Show me." Gathering up some of the wetness, I pull my fingers up to show them glistening. He grabs my wrist and pulls my fingers to his lips, his tongue lapping up the juice before sucking them into his mouth. "So juicy."

"Please."

"Rub that pretty little kitty while sucking my cock, London. Make me come." I love the commanding tone, crave it, and obey, because it's something I want just as much as he needs.

I wrap my hand around the base and take him into my mouth again. This time there's no instruction, no guidance. He wants to see how badly I want it, and I'm about to show him. Instinct and desire mingle and intensify, and I find myself moving up and down his length, sucking and lavishing the hard flesh with my tongue. "That's it, beautiful. Take me deeper, Twirl…let me fuck that mouth."

In that moment I realize another truth. There is nothing sexier than a man's moan. His pleading for your touch.

Taking him all the way back, I fight the urge to pull off and breathe through my nose. "Mmm," I hum and then rake my teeth down his length. The muscles of his abs contract and he throws his head back, closing his eyes and biting his bottom lip.

It's that sight right there that brings my hand back between my thighs, and I rub myself while working my mouth up and down his length at a rapid pace. I'm so close, thighs trembling. All I need is a little more to find my own release when he breaks me.

"Don't fucking move, and swallow every drop," Malcolm all but snarls, lip curling just a bit, and I pause. Follow his instruction and suck, hollowing my cheeks as the first stream of come coats my tongue. As the second follows, my own orgasm tears through me and I tremble, riding my fingers as he gives me every last drop.

When he's done, I lick him clean and lay my head on his thigh. My jaw hurts a bit and my body still tingles, but that is an experience I want to do again. And again.

Before I can fully catch my breath, Malcolm lifts me up and into his arms. Cradles me against his chest while tipping my face up to meet his. "Hi."

The softness in those gorgeous green eyes and the sexy grin cause me to giggle. "Someone's happy."

"Someone isn't ever letting his precious gift go."

"Is that so?" I nuzzle his cheek. "Because no one asked me if I agree to this."

"Babe, the moment you walked into my room that night, you lost all rights." Then, he surprises me with a quick and passionate kiss. Tasting himself on my lips, he groans and pulls back so I can see just how serious he is. "You're mine."

London

I'M IN BLISS. A wonderful period of my life where everything feels right, and I have no worries. It's like being a kid all over with the added bonus of having adult privileges.

In the last two weeks I've come to terms with the lies and betrayal. I've forgiven my mother because when all is said and done, she did the best she could. She stayed with a monster to give me the best life possible with the cards she was dealt. Out of her love for me, she endured so much pain with the Fosters.

I remember the shouts. Her cries. Her wanting to leave but staying because we were a family.

Losing my father must've been hard. I can only imagine the emptiness she felt, because I now understand what love does to a person. What you will do for them.

I'd kill to save him if it ever came to that.

Being with Malcolm, seeing his own feelings for me come to light with each action he takes, is humbling. Fills my once-beaten heart with joy. I'm in a better place because of him.

I love him.

His easy smiles. His charming disposition.

Even the darkness he tries to hide from me.

Every single facet of his personality calls to mine, and I accept him as he comes.

Dangerous and sweet. The perfect deadly concoction.

"We're here, London," Gina says, bringing me back to the present as we park in front of a Starbucks. "Are you coming, or do I get you the usual?"

"Nah. Give me a moment and I'll come in." Pulling my cell from my small purse, I send him a text.

> Getting coffee, and then heading home after a stop at the paint supply store. What do you want for dinner? ~Twirl

Putting it away for now, I exit the car and walk toward the entrance. Gina is just past the threshold when someone pulls on my arm.

"What the...?" My eyes shift toward the person; the curse on the tip of my tongue dies at the sight of Brittany. She looks just like the last time I saw her. Angry and overdone in the makeup department. Desperation swirls all around her.

"Aren't you going to say hello to your brother's fiancée, Lola?" Another tug, her hold painful, and I yelp. "Come give me a hug."

My head shakes, and before I can call Gina, the click of a gun is heard. She's right beside me, her Glock pointing at Brittany's chest. "Remove your hand. You have three seconds before I shoot."

She lets go and holds both hands up. "I'm just saying hello. No need for the hostility."

"Bullshit, and you know it." Gina steps between us further, pushing me back, creating distance between us. "Leave."

"This is a public—"

"Mr. Asher will be in touch," she spits out, interrupting Brittany who looks toward a store across the street. My eyes follow and meet the ones of a man I hate. Alton stares at me, then looks to Gina, and you can visibly see his disdain for her.

He mouths the word *I miss you* slowly then gives me a wave, and I shudder. I'm so caught up in my disgust that I miss the rest of their conversation. All I manage to catch is the sight of Brittany walking past us.

She's at the curb's edge when she turns to look back at me from over her shoulder. "I'll be seeing you soon, dear little Lola. Oh, and tell Asher he's welcome."

MY ARM IS a little sore after we get home. Her hold had been painful and my old fading bruises become a little red.

"Fucking great," I say, rubbing the area of my forearm when my phone beeps from somewhere in the foyer.

Forgetting the coffee, we came straight back. I tossed my bag on a table while Gina left to find Magda and some ice for my arm. After, she left to go and pick up the painting supplies which were my last stop for the day. I want to change the color of our bedroom walls from white to a grey-ish mauve color that caught my eyes on a design show.

That was an hour ago, and I'm still in a daze.

My vacation from them has come to an abrupt end.

Another beep and I follow the sound, finding the small device on the floor of all places. Picking it up, I swipe a finger over the screen and find ten texts and four missed calls. All from Malcolm.

> Something simple is fine ~Malcolm

> Or how about I bring dinner, and you wait for me naked on our bed ~Malcolm

> I want you to sit on my face tonight and ride my tongue ~Malcolm

A few others go on like that until the last one a few minutes ago.

> I'm coming home. ~Malcolm

Touching the small picture of him I have at the top of our message thread; I press the call button and wait. It barely rings once when he answers, the harsh rustle of wind on his end lets me know he's outside—more than likely heading my way.

"Are you okay?" There's some bite to his tone, but I know it's not with me. A car honks near him and then another. "Tell me you are okay?"

"I'm fine, babe. A little shook up, but fine...I promise." Opening the front door, I walk down the steps and down his driveway. My mind is racing, trying to fight off the fear seeing *him* brought on, and I need to keep moving. Put one foot in front of the other as I fight to find my calm.

"They should have never approached you. I'm sorry—"

"Not your fault." And it isn't. However, it does make me think. Makes me wonder what it'll take to rid myself of the men I thought were family. "Actually, I'm safe because of you. Because you care."

"I more than care. Never doubt that."

His words bring a smile to my face and I close my eyes, soaking in the meaning behind them. "I more than care too."

"I know." Cocky man. "Maybe we can call it a Netflix and Chill day?"

"Get back to work, Mr. Asher."

"London—"

"Chop *chop*, mister." The leaves to my left rustle, but I pay them no mind. This property is safe. "Go wrap up whatever you need to and then come home. We'll order a pizza and eat it in bed while watching that boring movie you had on last time."

"So bratty."

"You bring it out of me."

"Are you sure? I can come back with no problem."

"Positive. See you soon, babe." Disconnecting the call, I open my eyes and realize that I'm at the end of his long driveway. At the entrance and staring into the eyes of a man I've never seen before. "Who are you?"

"Are you a Miss London Gabriela Foster?" The way he says my name, as if he knows me, isn't sitting well with me. That, and how does he know my middle name? I never use it. "Please don't be alarmed, ma'am. I just want to talk to you."

I take a step back from the closed gate. "How do you know my name?"

"Can I come in and speak to you? I'm with the FBI and have some questions."

"Show me your I.D." *Where the hell is security?* I know someone is always guarding the entrance and back of the property. "If I do, can I come in?"

"You need to regardless." His eyes tighten at my answer, lips thinning, but he schools the expression quick enough. Back is the smile he gave me when I first noticed him standing here. It creeps me out. He creeps me out. "Never mind. Whatever it is, I'm not interested."

"Did you know that the man you're sleeping with is a killer?"

That makes me pause and step back, my anger rising. "Why would you say something like that? Show me your badge, or my next move is to call security and the cops."

"As you wish." He pulls out a small manila packet from inside his suit jacket along with a bifold wallet. Flipping it open, he holds it to the bars so I can read his name. The first thing I notice is he's part of the Federal Bureau of Investigations and his name is Shawn Hayes. "Satisfied?"

"Not really." Some would think this should put me at ease. It's the opposite. Makes it worse.

Why would a member of a government agency be here?

Why would he avoid showing me his credentials until I mention calling the police? If he's here under direct orders, he wouldn't care. He also wouldn't be fidgeting and looking back every few minutes.

A true professional wouldn't be skulking in a corner or giving me leering looks.

"Look, I'm not here to make you uncomfortable, Miss Foster." Agent Hayes comes closer to the gate, shifting his eyes to the area behind me. "I'm here to help you. Get you out of a situation that could end with your body in a morgue."

"What the hell is—"

"Malcolm Asher is a killer."

"Leave. Go before I scream."

"He killed his last girlfriend, London." Shawn opens the manila envelope and pulls out what looks to be pictures. His jaw ticks as he looks at the first, his expression full of ire as he tosses them at my feet. I don't look down. I don't move. Whatever is in those photos I have no doubt will haunt me. "Go on. Look down."

"Leave."

"Fucking look before I jump this fence and make you." The warning in his tone, the way his hand goes to his side makes me bend slowly, following orders. There's a glint that comes from his weapon as he pulls it out. "Look at what he did to her. Karina Hughes is dead because of him."

A loud gasp leaves me and my stomach heaves; what's in the pictures below is haunting. Will forever be etched into my mind. "No. No." I'm shaking my head, hands trembling as I flip to the next.

A beautiful girl.

Vacant eyes.

A bullet hole right between the eyes.

Her body with a bluish tint in a morgue, bruises littering her body.

Blood. So much freaking blood.

It's everywhere. Splatters. The floor and the wall behind her.

"He killed her. Took her from those who love her. Still mourn her."

"Leave," I say, my voice shaking, but get no response. When I look up, he's gone and I'm alone.

My body begins to shake, and breathing gets hard. Those empty, blank eyes are all I see.

Every image rushes across my mind in a fucked-up reel, a tiny horror movie that holds my life hostage. Fight or flight kicks in, and all I want to do is bolt. Run away from it all and never look back, however, I can't.

Maybe I'm crazy, but accepting this at face value feels wrong. Off.

Malcolm would never hurt someone he cares about. You know this.

"What're you doing, London?" a voice calls from the other side of the gate, the engine of a car running. "You okay? You're shaking."

My eyes leave the pictures and lock with Mariah's. "Help me."

Make sense. Tell me it's wrong.

Whatever she sees in my expression puts her in panic mode, and she runs back toward the gate's access panel. Her fingers work fast to push in the code, but to me everything seems to be happening in slow motion. Each breath is harder than the last.

This has to be an error. Please, God. Let it be wrong.

"What's got you so scared, sweetie. What're you looking…" Mariah trails off now, seeing what I am. She takes the pictures from my hand and pulls me with her toward the still running car, placing me in the passenger seat and even buckling me in.

I'm on autopilot, and it isn't until we pull into traffic down the street that I react. "Where are you taking me? What the hell is all this?"

"Who gave you those pictures?" she asks instead of answering me, making a right turn toward the expressway. "Please, London. It's important that I know where these came from."

"An FBI agent—"

She cuts her eyes to me. "A Shawn Hayes?"

"Yes, but why?" We're on an expressway with the signs indicating that The Loop is our destination. "What's going on? Why are you even here?"

"My cousin gave me the afternoon off and I decided to spend it with you. Was hoping we could get some lunch or watch a movie, but now that won't do." Cutting off an older man in a large SUV, she presses down on the gas of her BMW coupe. "You doubt him."

"My rational side is telling me to run, but my heart doubts what that agent said. The man I know, and the one Hayes painted, are not the same. Can't be."

"And what if he is?"

"Then there has to be a very good reason behind his actions." That's the God's honest truth. Deep down I know Malcolm is dangerous, my fam— the Fosters wouldn't fear him if he wasn't, but I still need an explanation. *I need him to make this right. Give me back the feeling of safety taken from me today.* "All I know is that right now, I'm scared."

"Of him?"

"Of everything." *Of knowing that either way, my feelings for him won't change.*

"All the more reason to go see him." With a high arch in her brow, she looks at me for confirmation.

"Would you take me back to the house or elsewhere if I say no?"

"Would I agree with it? No, but yes, I would."

"Thank you." I believe her. Just like I know that rash decisions can lead to catastrophes. That he's never been anything but good to me, and I have to believe in that if nothing else. "Now, take me to the Asher building. He needs to see these photos."

A small smile crosses her lips and she takes my hand in hers, squeezing. "Don't lose your trust in him, London. Not everything is as it seems."

MALCOLM

"YOUR UNEXPECTED IS HERE," Mariah announces around ten thirty through the intercom. I've been expecting this visit.

Have seen him skulking around; at the airport and outside my building. He's following a dead-end trail that will lead to nowhere.

"Let him in." I grab my cup of coffee and sit back in my chair. Waiting. There's a ping on my computer, an incoming email that I've been waiting on all morning from the developer in Shanghai, but it'll have to wait. The construction of my building is ahead of schedule and will be completed within the next eight months versus a year.

I'm happy with that. Opens the door for more business.

"Good morning, Mr. Asher." Shawn enters my office sans Marcelles. His cocky gait and grin—that *I know something you don't* attitude doesn't intimidate me in the least. However, I'll give it to him for having enough balls to continue his pursuit.

"Drop the polite act and get to the point."

"Is that how you want to play?" Shawn eyes the documents on my desk, trying to read something he'll never understand. It's in Mandarin and from the office of a powerful organization requesting my services.

To this agent's detriment, I've read his file. Know his strengths and weaknesses. While the man prides himself on his brute attributes, the skill of speaking several languages evades him. He understands some Spanish and Italian, but that's it. There's no fluency.

"Curiosity is killing you, isn't it." Not a question. And while he will like nothing more than to take a picture or the paperwork itself, that would be breaking the law. No warrant, and it's an invasion of privacy.

Inadmissible in court with the right amount of money thrown at it.

"One day you will fall, and I'll be there to expose you. Walk you out of this building in handcuffs."

"Is that right? Keep talking…please." With my cup, I point to both a camera and the intercom system that's still on. "Threatening a highly respected man, harassing him, won't look good for the agency."

"People like you make me sick. You have no right to record me—"

"This is not a public domain, Agent Hayes." Standing from my chair, I walk around it and lean back on my desk. Wave a hand around. "It's my building. My property, and I can surveil anywhere I wish to."

"Why were you in Miami recently?"

"Are you following me, Agent? Have I become an obsession?" I counter. If he thinks that knowing my travel itinerary will scare me, once again he put the eggs in the wrong basket. Had he been paying closer attention, my meeting in Costa Rica should've been the priority. "And to answer your question; we needed to refuel. I never left the airport."

"Where were you prior?" He's getting agitated, face red. "What are you hiding?"

"Am I under arrest? Do you have a court-issued warrant?"

"No, but—"

I silence him with a hand held up. "Get out, and quit wasting my time."

Hayes puts his hands inside his pockets and rocks back. "It's in your best interest to cooperate with me."

"Is that right? And why is that?" Javier and Carmelo appear at the doorway to escort him out, but I give a minute shake of my head that stops them. "Please tell me why that is."

"Think of those you love."

"I'd take that same advice, Agent Hayes. Be very careful who you threaten." Looking back at Javi, I signal him to come in closer. "Get him off my premises, and tell Mariah to get me in contact with Director Monahan. I'm done playing games."

"Consider it done, boss." Carmelo places a hand on Shawn's shoulder. "You can leave two ways…escorted, or on your own. Choose wisely."

Hayes shrugs his arm off, all the while his glare is set on me. "You'll be very sorry soon enough." With that he leaves, and both men follow. One to make sure he leaves, and the other to tell his girl to contact the FBI director.

This man is going to be a problem.

I can already see it.

Another loose end that needs to be cut off from this thread.

———

PRESENT…

AFTER MY TALK WITH LONDON, I'm calm enough to head back upstairs and get a few last-minute items done. With everything happening, I'm going to take a few days off and surprise her with a small vacation.

She needs this, and so do I.

I also need to feel those juicy lips wrapped around me. On a tropical island where it's only us and naked, the sun bathing her skin while I fuck her mouth. Take her innocence and claim it.

My mind revisits how well she took me down her throat a few days ago —how easily she gave in to her needs and handed the control over. Since then, I've eaten her out a few times and then came in her mouth as I stood above her, jacking off to the sight of her satiated face. It's done the job of calming me down, gave her the chance to embrace who she really is, but the wait is over.

"What do you think, Mr. Asher?" Li Qiang, my oversight director, asks. He's been working with the developer and a P.R. agency—transferring over to this location from North Korea to keep us on this new schedule. If we lose the momentum, have to change things again to accommodate a new completion date, it'll cost me more than the money I'm spending.

Customers, my clientele, don't trust those that are late. Constantly change times and dates.

"Contact Mariah tomorrow, Li. She's handling the final decisions regarding the grand opening and its guest list. What she says goes." There's a knock on the door, and I hold up a hand for them to give me a moment. "That's right. Okay, I'll let her know." Another knock, a bit more persistent, and I look up to find my girl and Mariah, both wearing matching expressions. He says something else, but my focus is on an upset Twirl. On the hold she has on an envelope in her hands. "I got to go. Call her at some point tomorrow and figure it out."

"O—"

I hang up before he finishes, already making my way to her. When I reach her, I take London's hand in mine and ignore the slight flinch. Whatever happened between our phone call and now has her scared.

It's like seeing that lost little lamb all over again from the first night at the club.

Shifting my eyes to Mariah, I level her with a hard stare. "What happened?"

"She had a visit to the house."

The moment those words seep through, my vision gets hazy and red. Anger rushes through every limb, and I have to take a few steps back. I don't want to make things worse, but the way I feel right now is nothing less than murderous.

"Shawn Hayes was at the house?" It's a barely contained snarl, and Mariah is smart enough to close the door to my office. She nods in confirmation. "What did he do?"

My eyes are on my cousin, but it's London that answers, pulling my attention toward her. She takes a few steps my way with a look on her face that I can't quite decipher. "He gave me these at the gate, and before you ask, when we were on the phone, I took a walk down the driveway, not really paying attention since I feel safe there. When I hung up with you, there he was. Looking at me and quite honestly, giving me the creeps."

"Show me." Yet I make no move to touch her. I'm shaking. Hands clenching.

"I'm not looking at those again." When I make no move to take the envelope, a flash of hurt crosses her soft features. She hides it under a mask of indifference, but I see it. All of her, while with trembling hands, she places them atop my desk. "Please look and explain, Malcolm. All I want is an explanation of why that man did this."

Nodding, I walk to my desk and open the now-worn manila packet. The second the first photo falls into my hand, I have to take a moment to breathe. That son of a bitch has no idea what he's just done.

"Empty this floor and the three beneath, Mariah. No calls or interruptions for the rest of the day," I say with my back to them, leaning with my palms flat on my desk. The pictures scatter in front of me, yet it's the one with her face, bullet wound on display, that I focus on. There's an eerie calmness taking over my body. Scenarios playing out and plans forming.

Shawn Hayes just signed over his life to me.

"Of course. I'll be with Javier downstairs if you need us." The door opening and closing follows, leaving just the two of us inside my quiet office. Her breathing and mine are the only sounds within.

On my next inhale, she's behind me. Close, her hand presses against the center in a supportive gesture. "Talk to me. Don't shut me out."

Not moving. Just touching. Her warm touch begins to thaw the ice flowing through my veins, but it's not enough. I'm going to kill this motherfucker myself. *My face will be the last he sees.*

"Before I explain, I need to know—"

"For a few minutes, yes, I did." Her tiny fingers move up my back, digging a bit into the tense muscles. "But I'm here, Malcolm. I'm here, so you can explain to me why this man sought me out. Why no one at the house...why security never came to remove him."

At her words, I turn around and lock eyes. Green on blue. "You're not upset about the dead woman?"

"Oh, I am." Her eyes flicker to the photos and then back at me. There's fear in them, but for some insane reason, it's not with me. "Something happened with her and you were involved, there's no denying that. Your reactions confirm it, but my question is *why*? Why did he personally deliver these? Why did he say that you took her from those that love her? Not past tense, but present."

Holding a hand out, I give her the option to take it and follow me. When she does without a second of hesitation, I feel some of the tension leave my body. With her hand in mine, I walk us to the seating area and sit with her beside me.

London makes a noise of disapproval at the back of her throat and lifts my arms so she can crawl into my lap. "Much better. Now talk."

Chuckling, I shake my head. "You're one of a kind."

She shrugs. "I am."

"Okay, before I explain, I need to know a few things."

"Shoot."

"What were his exact words, Twirl? When he showed you those pictures, what did he say word for word."

She takes ahold of my hand and begins to play with my fingers. "He said you killed your last girlfriend. That you, and I'm quoting him here…"

"Go on."

"Look at what he did to her. Karina Hughes is dead because of him," Twirl whispers, pleading with me to set things right. "Now, my question is quite simple. Did you—"

"I did." I'll give her credit for not getting up and running for the door. Instead, my girl gave a nod and kept her eyes on mine. Waiting for the rest of this story. "The girl in those photos is someone I dated for a while. It wasn't love or anything special, just a companionship based on our mutual needs. Hers for money and mine for appearance sake."

"So, you didn't love her?" Her question is so low I almost miss it.

"Not at all." I push back a stray piece of hair behind her ear, giving her a soft smile. "Karina was superficial and made a mess of everything she touched. While I did give it an honest try with her, nothing was there. No love. When I ended the relationship because quite honestly, I was tired of the bullshit and fake tears she used to manipulate those around her, it never crossed my mind that things would go so far."

London turns in my arms and straddles my thighs. Leaning forward, she presses her forehead to mine. "What happened to her. What happened to you?"

"I wouldn't take her back, and she got desperate. Angry with me and my family." I close my eyes, seeing that moment all over again. Reliving Karina's last moment alive. "Somehow she convinced my mother to have lunch with her at their home. The staff there found it odd, and Magda, who was filling in for the cook on vacation, called me to let me know. You can imagine I rushed over, London, and what I found put me in a blind rage."

"Tell me." Her lips ghost mine, just a soft caress. "I'm not going to judge you."

"Karina held my mother at gunpoint, making demands about money owed and wanting to be paid. She threatened her life. Held the gun, dug it deep into her temple while my mother sobbed. To this day, I hold no remorse. None. I didn't think twice about shooting her then, and I would all over again to save someone I love."

Wetness coats my cheek before I hear a sniffle. When I open my eyes, what greets my line of sight is comprehension and respect. Not a single ounce of judgement.

"You did the right thing, Malcolm. Had it been my mom, I would've done the same without a doubt." My girl swallows hard, lip trembling as her emotions pour out. It's been a crazy day for her. "I'm so sorry I ever, even for a second, doubted you."

"Thank you." I kiss her soft lips then, tasting her tears. It's slow and gentle as I wind my arms around her back and pull her in close. This kiss isn't like the others that overpowers and destroys our senses, where time seems to stop, and nothing but the other person remains. No. This kiss feels like coming home. Like acceptance and understanding. "And I'm sorry that he sought you out. That you felt alone in that moment."

"Something isn't right with that man or his visit," she says then, sitting back as a heavy sigh leaves her. "What a coincidence that I see Alton, Brittany, and this man all on the same day?"

Indeed.

Picking up the locket on her chain, I finger the ballerina. "This chain can never come off you, Twirl. It has a small tracking device inside, and until I put an end to the Foster men, I can't take the chance of something happening and not being able to find you."

"Say what?" Then, for some reason, she starts to giggle, her body shaking in amusement. That is, until she notices I'm not joining her. "You can't be serious...are you?"

"I'm not joking, London. Promise me you won't take it off."

"Do you think it's necessary?"

"Yes."

"Okay."

"Okay?" Hands on her thighs, I caress the soft skin in gentle strokes with my thumbs. "That easy?"

"Pretty much." She shrugs then, shifting a bit in my lap to get more comfortable. Her heat sears me through my pants, but for the moment, I have to ignore my desire for her. Have to pretend that I don't see how hard those little nipples are or how my mouth waters at the sight. "You've done nothing but take care of me without crowding, and I appreciate that, Malcolm. The things with my father...finding the truth for me...I can't thank you enough for that. I trust you, and if you say it's needed, then I'm following your lead."

"All I want is for you to be safe and happy." *And you will have that soon enough.* Taking a pause, I choose my next words carefully. Since we met, I've done my best to not push too hard and let her make up her own mind, but what's coming next isn't a request. She needs this. "That's why you and I have a date tomorrow at a shooting range and then some time at the gym after for sparring lessons. It's going to be our thing at least three times a week for the time being."

"We are?" Twirl can't hide her excitement at the idea, and that pleases me.

"Yes." With two fingers I grab her chin and bring her lips to mine. Peck them once, twice, and then stare deep into those beautiful blue eyes, wanting her to see the truth in my words. "I never want you to feel fear again."

MALCOLM

"**I** WANT HIM IN a cell within the hour. Presidential treatment," I hiss out, eyes on the screen in front of me, watching as the dumb fuck walks away from his post. The door to my office closes just as Jimmy looks past the camera and toward the gate, while on another screen, London opens the front door with her phone in hand.

She's not paying attention to her surroundings. It's something we'll address soon in training.

I'm happy she feels safe at our home, but in this world, you can never truly let your guard down. Being able to protect yourself and knowing what to do are things that'll come natural to her once I'm through. I've seen the gleam in her eyes—the hint of her own darkness below—and I'm going to nurture that tiny demon. Sharpen her claws.

On the monitor, she's just talking. Her lips curling a bit when she pauses near the end of the driveway, closing her eyes with a small smile on her face as the last bit of sun caresses her skin.

Beautiful, and you can see the appreciation for her looks on the leering look Shawn gives her. *He's a dead son of a bitch.*

My phone pings then and I pause the feed, flicking my eyes to the device. Twirl's name flashes with a message attached.

> We're home. Please don't be too late. ~Twirl

My girl left about thirty minutes ago after Gina came for her. While I love and trust Mariah, right now she needs protection. More than one available gun.

I'm past being civil or being rational. They've been poking the wrong beast, and I'll show my next hand soon enough. My ducks are in a row, and the last piece is about to make an appearance.

> Promise to be home before your show starts. Wouldn't dream of missing an episode of the cheesy goodness you love so much. ~Malcolm

Three small dots appear on the screen. Then they disappear. Then start again.

This goes on for a few minutes. However, once her reply comes through, I can't stop the laughter from bubbling out. That, or the way my cock twitches at her words.

> Was that sarcasm I detect in your letters? ~Twirl

> Are you being bratty, Mr. Asher? Do you need a spanking? ~Twirl

The thought of *my hands* reddening those luscious cheeks is very appealing. A cock-throbbing little fantasy I'll make a reality soon enough. I'll push her boundaries a bit. Make her crave more.

After the way she perfectly worshipped my cock, I know her desires match mine. That she's the one the Lord above used my rib to mold. For me.

London's been saving herself for me without knowing.

But more importantly, there's another truth I uncover with each passing day. My own confession.

This cheeky little thing means everything to me. I love her.

Careful, little girl. This man does bite. Spanks too
if you want. ~Malcolm

Her reply is instant. And so is the shiver than rushes down my spine and then settles on the tip of my dick.

Promises. Promises. ~Twirl

AT SIX ON THE DOT, I find myself walking down the stairway toward the holding cells a few floors below the bank. The lighting is low, and it takes me a moment to adjust as I cross the threshold and into a very interesting show.

They don't notice me, and that's okay. I prefer to watch for a few minutes.

Undoing my jacket, I lay it on a chair near the entrance as a laceration appears on Jimmy's brow. Next, my fingers undo the buttons of my shirt, one by one, and then leave it atop the jacket as Javier delivers another bare-knuckle blow to Jimmy's midsection.

Closely followed by two more, and the prisoner's screams mute the sound of the large door closing.

The air meets my chest while the energy within the room flows around me, taunting, igniting my need for blood.

For a few weeks now, I've been playing nice. I've been understanding.

That ends here.

Today, I begin my reign of justice.

Carmelo steps back from Jimmy, letting the man go so he can swing on the chain. He's bloody and crying, begging them to stop. Each of my men shake their heads, knowing that what comes next is the kind of mindfuck most can't handle.

"Shut the fuck up," Javier growls, fist connecting with Jimmy's jaw. The man's head snaps back as blood splatters the ground below and Javi. "Why did you vacate the security kiosk without letting anyone know? Why did you let Agent Hayes come and go as he pleased?"

"I was calling my pregnant wife back. She's been feeling off?" A lie. *Stupid, stupid man.* "Swear it, Javier. You can call and ask her."

"Bullshit." Carmelo walks toward a small table nearby and picks up a gun—he cocks it back and points it straight at his chest. "I'm going to give you one more chance to—"

"Enough." Everyone stops and looks at me. Two with a bit of mirth, and the last, Jimmy, with fear. A fear that manifests itself in perspiration and tears. To a rapid growing wet stain that appears at the front of his pants the closer to them I get. "He's telling the truth."

Relief, pure unadulterated relief pours out of him in tears. Pathetic.

"Oh, thank God," he whimpers, falling to the ground as Javier releases the locking mechanism on the pulley system for chains. "Mr. Asher, I don't know what's going on here. I've never done anything to jeopardize the business or those you associate with. I'm a worker. Just a foot soldier."

Another lie. Besides, no one ever mentioned him hurting my business. He gave that up himself with that comment. Not that I didn't already know this, but like every other fool, you give them leeway and eventually they'll hang themselves.

Jimmy Cross has been selling me out to the Fosters for a while now. He met with Alton just before they made the move to extort, and again just recently, running his mouth about London. He's one of the reasons why Roberto's wife is grieving the death of her cousin.

I nod, hand coming up to scratch my bare chest right over the all-seeing owl. "It's been a huge misunderstanding, Jimmy, and I apologize. Please let me compensate you for this unfortunate event."

"Only if that pleases you, boss." He looks up at me from the floor, the right side of his face swelling. "I'll be okay with a few days off just to rest."

"Consider it done." Turning to Javier, I give him a hard look. "Help him to a seat. I want him to witness how I deal with traitors. How I skin a rat and the man responsible for his beating."

"That's okay, boss. I just want to clean up and go home."

"Take a seat, Cross. Sit and enjoy the show." There's no room for argument, and he nods, letting Javier help him. Once he's comfortable to the right of the room, I walk to the door and open it, revealing a man on the floor with a guard holding a gun to his head.

The cleanup crew is silently awaiting orders too.

There's a gasp, but I ignore it. Instead, I raise a hand and snap my fingers once. The boys know what to do, and without a word they carry the asshole inside while Javier keeps Jimmy in his seat. His hold is firm, and while the fight or flight kicks in, my now-freaking-out employee can do nothing about it.

He knows the man as the owner of a bar he frequents. Someone he places bets with here and there over the season of our Chicago Bulls. To whom he lost a lot of money not long ago on a rigged poker night.

Jimmy doesn't consider him an enemy, but I do.

What they didn't consider into their equation is my finding out. People talking.

Frank Lewis is a personal friend of Marcus, one Lieutenant Bristol's uncle from his mother's side, and the man responsible for the meeting between the Fosters and Jimmy. For luring my employee away with the temptation of a paid debt and enough money to walk away from every-thing, including his wife. For planting ideas in his head that were never set to become a reality.

Marcus and Frank would kill him if their plan came to fruition.

Unfortunately for Frank, I need Jimmy alive for just a little bit longer. He's the head of the snake I must cut to terminate easy communication, to scramble their piece-of-shit wannabe network, and send them into hiding.

I want them desperate.

Afraid.

Crazy enough to make a few stupid moves.

My men drop his near-naked form between me and the ash-white secu-rity guard before taking their places once again. Frank's body hits the cold concrete hard and he groans, head bouncing off the ground as he tries to get into a fetal position but can't. It's slow. His limbs aren't cooperating.

Consciousness seems to be slipping, eyes rolling back, and I bring him back with a kick to his midsection. He cries out, shifting onto his back, choking on air while his body stiffens—trying to breathe through the pain.

Still, I land another. And another.

Each hit is direct and now aimed at his ribs. An area that is quickly turning an angry red while a welt appears from the tip of my shoe, the hard leather marking his skin as blood begins to pool at the surface. Bruising.

"Please stop," he begs, coughing. Frank moves a hand to block my next direct kick, but I move last minute, landing the blow to the side of his leg. "Let's work this out. I'll tell you anything you want."

"Anything I want? Is that right?" Kneeling, I grab his face, forcing his focus on mine. "What could you possibly say that will change the outcome here?"

His eyes flicker to Jimmy. "I know a few things."

"Humor me." I stand up and as I do, Carmelo and the other guard do the same with him, holding him up a few steps from me. "Tell me a story."

"Marcus Foster isn't your girlfriend's father. It was all a lie."

"Tell me a better story. Be original." Shaking my limbs out, I stretch my neck.

He eyes me with distrust, fear radiating off his shaking form. "Alton wants her for his own—" I cut him off with a right hook to his jaw. At once he goes stiff and begins to fall back. The sole reason he doesn't hit the ground again is my men.

"String him up." Jimmy's stench hits my nostrils, more potent now, and I turn to look at him. "Want to get cleaned up?"

"Yes, please." His voice is low. Meek.

"I'll take care of it." Javier moves to the wall behind him where there's a knob and he turns on the overhead irrigation system for this section. This one works with stinging pressure, pelting the walls and ground for cleaning purposes, while the dirty water flows toward the center of the room where a large drain sits.

When the four of us step back, Jimmy gives us a perplexed look. It doesn't last long when that first jet of cold water hits his beat-up face—the pressure stings—reopening the cut above his eyebrow—causing blood to flow down his face in rivulets. His companion in idiocy screams, now awake and freaking out when he realizes that he's strung up and without an escape.

We let them cry it out until all that's left are shaking bodies and weak pleas.

Carmelo looks at me then, and I give a minute nod. He leaves the room to retrieve something for me.

"Please make it stop."

"This is a mistake." They speak in unison, tones hoarse.

I step beneath the water and head straight toward Frank's body. Look him in the eye. "You want it to stop?"

"Yes."

"Then tell me a story."

"What kind?" You can see it on his face. The resignation. He's realizing that this is his end.

That his only choices are brutally or quick.

"The kind that'll make your last minutes on this earth bearable." If it weren't for how angry I am, I'd find this somewhat amusing. Walking over to the switch, I shut the water off and then level Jimmy with a glare that dares him to move. "Can you do that, Frank? Can you surprise me?"

"Yes."

"Good answer. Now, once upon a time…" I trail off so he can continue.

Fat tears run down his cheeks, his lip trembling. "Can I please have a mercy kill?"

"That's up to you."

Frank takes in a deep breath and lets it out slowly. "Once upon a time there was a young innocent girl who was hurt by the men in her life. Those men wanted the riches that belonged to her by birthright." His eyes remain on mine as I circle his body, listening to the bullshit I already know. What I want is confirmation to my investigator's findings. To get the answer to the last piece of this puzzle. "Her evil stepfather and brother were planning to…what's that?"

"What's what?" I say taking a syringe from Carmelo and removing the cap. Since he's taking his time, I'll force his hand and speed this up. "It's a special cocktail I have just for you. You see…" I sink the needle into his thigh and press down so every last drop enters his body "…when I met up with an old friend in Miami not long ago, he gave this to me when he hugged me goodbye. A token, if you will."

"What is it? Why does it burn?"

"It's rattlesnake venom. Raw and pure from a milking farm in Florida." At my words the panic begins. The more agitated he becomes, the faster the toxins travel through his bloodstream. Soon, he'll begin to feel some numbness in his limbs and begin to sweat. There might be some nausea or loss of sight…maybe even some bleeding as his organs begin to shut down. An unattended rattler bite is deadly. "Now, what were you saying about her twenty-first birthday? What are they planning to do?"

"Kill me," Frank slurs a bit, some spit escaping from the right side of his mouth. "Please. Just end this."

"Tell me what I want to know, and I'll gift you some mercy."

"What about my wife—"

"She'll keep the bar and be taken care of. Not that you ever gave a shit about her to begin with."

His head lolls back. "Tell her I am sorry."

"Done. Now say it."

More tears fall, and he has a tough time swallowing, so I offer him water from a bottle Carmelo thought to bring with him. The hemotoxin is working faster than I anticipated. That, or he's having an allergic response to it. Either way, I'm getting what I need from him.

"Thank you."

"None needed. Carry on."

With difficulty, he brings his head up and focuses his stare on me. "They're going to sell London's virginity to the highest bidder on the night of her twenty-first birthday. They want to break—pass her around to anyone willing to pay the fee—until nothing is left but a shell of a woman. Then, when his control is obsolete, Marcus wants to kill her after she signs everything over to him and Alton."

There it is. The ultimate goal.

His next intake of air is difficult, and I notice his face swelling.

Pulling my favorite knife from my back pocket, I flip it open and let the steel blade reflect a bit of the light in the room. "Anything else I should know?"

"You have a—" He doesn't get to finish as I bury my knife up his skull via his chin. The long blade lodges itself, and I twist the handle to make sure he's dead.

Frank's body sags against the chains and his breathing is no more.

"Clean this up, and take Jimmy home," I say while removing my knife. "He can thank me another day for killing the scum responsible for his pain."

MALCOLM

WHEN I WALK IN the door a few hours later, I find London asleep on the couch. There's a repeat of her favorite show playing, the women fighting about something that no one cares about, yet my girl finds amusing. The trashier the show, the more she loves it.

Taking the control from her hand, I turn the TV off and set it aside. My eyes stay on her beautiful face and pouty lips. On how she's smiling a tiny bit.

That innocence in her kills me. Makes me throb.

It reminds me of her inexperience, yet how eager to learn she is to please me.

"Sorry for missing it, pretty girl," I whisper, leaning down to nuzzle her soft cheek. "I'll make it up to you. Promise."

Being late tonight was inevitable. After disposing of Frank and having Jimmy taken home to his not-pregnant wife, I sat down to have a conversation with Javier and my lawyer.

Amelia's home is back in the legal possession of her daughter. A judge sided with London over the contest of the will, seeing that several changes were made the day of her death and the filing signature was wrong. As of today, at four thirty in the afternoon, she no longer has a guardian. The accounts are hers and the stipend will be deposited into an account I made for her in my bank.

No one has the right to touch a single cent of hers.

The Fosters will be served with an eviction notice tomorrow, and she won't be in Chicago when it happens. I'm taking her away. Giving us a break.

Javier has his instruction, and Mariah will hold the fort down, emailing me only when it's an emergency they can't handle.

"How do you plan to do that?" One eye is open, and she looks adorable in her fake annoyance. "Cause the episode you missed was epic."

"Is that so? Who fought with whom this week?" Slipping my arms beneath her body, I pick up her grumpy form off the couch and carry her into our room. Not once since moving in has she slept anywhere but beside me. "Or did the dude go to the strip club? Was he caught getting friendly with a dancer?"

"Neither." There's a pout in her tone, and I kiss her. Nip the plump bottom lip while she rolls her eyes. "The mother was tripping on his girl and they fought over dinner. Food and cheap wine went everywhere."

I lower her down to the mattress, laying her back so I can crawl over her body. "How can you watch those shows?"

Boggles the mind how much she enjoys these things.

"Cheesy goodness, boo. It's all in the cheesy goodness."

"Do you think you can give those up for a few days starting tomorrow?" I kiss her chin, then neck, licking a path down London's throat toward her chest.

"Why?" She arches to give me better access. "What's going on?"

"Nothing." I leave open-mouthed kisses across each breast, dipping my tongue between the two to tease the skin. "Just you and me…"

"You and me what?" she hisses when I drag my tongue beneath the edge of her tank and find a nipple.

I take the tight tip between my teeth and pull, sliding my teeth over the sensitive skin as I release her. "We're just going on a little vacation to a secluded island…a few days of fun in the sun and some training. Nothing special."

Twirl pushes me back to look at my face with a perfect brow raised. "You said what now?"

"Vacation starting—"

"When do we leave?"

"Six hours."

"Are you serious?" She's wiggling beneath me to slip away, but I lower my body fully atop hers. Lips to lips and chest to chest, I'm pinning her to the mattress. "Can you move?"

"No." My hands grab her legs and wrap them around my waist. "Not going anywhere."

"But we need to pack." Twirl tries to sound stern but fails miserably when it comes out a low moan.

"No, we don't." Flexing my hips, I let her feel me. How hard I always am for her. "I have everything you'll need already packed, sweetheart. My personal shopper took care of everything with Mariah's help. No need to rush. Just let me feel you a little."

THIS PLACE IS AMAZING," Twirl squeals, rushing up the coral-carved stairway that leads to the main house of this tropical oasis. She walks from the entrance to the living room with one goal in mind; she stands at the veranda with both hands holding onto the wood and takes in a deep, cleansing breath.

The warm sun, tropical trees, and the salt air will soothe even the most savage beast.

The place is huge and very private. Open space, the main house is made to blend the inside with nature—no windows or doors—just the cooling breeze and the sounds of waves crashing below surround you.

This luxury retreat is ours for the next five days. Just the two of us.

No outside distractions or problems.

No worries outside of how to entertain ourselves.

The staff here signs an NDA with each new renter that books, and they're to be off the island by sundown unless otherwise told to. They cook, clean, take care of setting up activities and disappear to a smaller island a short boat ride away that houses their accommodations.

It's the perfect vacation.

The de-stressor we need.

Where I plan to make her mine.

"I'm glad you approve." Walking up behind her, I wrap my arm around her waist. It's still early, and the warm waters of the Atlantic look inviting. "Care to take a swim with me?"

"Don't we need to unpack first?" There's a hint of a pout in her tone and I almost laugh. Almost.

"You're right. We should." My other hand travels lower, down to the edge of her short khakis with a side-tie that make me want to bite her. Kneel before her and undo the small knot holding the almost-indecent piece of clothing in place with my teeth. "It's the responsible thing to do."

"You're right, Malcolm. Adult first and play later?" Twirl pushes her ass against my front, grinding just a tiny bit. She's tempting me. I know she's craving—almost desperate for my touch—but I have other plans for us.

So, I grit my teeth and let her. Let her feel me. How I throb for her and her alone.

And when her arm reaches back to embed her fingers in my hair, I pull back. Release my hold a few seconds before the woman that cleans wheels our luggage toward the master suite. She doesn't look at us, just takes the pathway below us down toward a private bungalow.

"That was mean."

Ignoring her question, I reach back and pull my T-shirt off. Lay it on the back of a chair near us. "Did you bring a swimsuit in your backpack like I told you to?"

Blue eyes narrow. "Yes."

"Then hurry up and change in that bathroom beyond the wall. You have twenty minutes, or I come to take you with me as is."

"And if I say no?"

"Try me."

"I'm going to get you back for this," she huffs and walks past me, shaking those luscious hips while leaving the room. Walking over to the intercom by the wall, I press the number two for the kitchen and wait for someone to pick up.

"How can I be of service?" the voice of an older woman says as the clanging of metal on metal comes through the speaker. "Would you like something prepared for lunch? A snack, maybe?"

"Something light will do. We're going to take a swim and just need something to hold us over until dinner."

"Understood, sir. I'll work on that now and it'll be ready shortly." She pauses for a moment, and the sound of a door closing follows. "Any requests?"

"Surprise me." I remove my belt next and empty my pockets, putting the items on a coffee table. The shorts I have on will have to do. Looking for my trunks at the moment is a waste of time. Time I could be kissing her instead. Feeling her pliant flesh beneath my fingertips. "However, dinner needs to be followed to my every last detail. Do you have the menu?"

"Yes, sir." London walks out then wearing a tiny, itty-bitty little scrap of fabric that doesn't cover much and I find decadent. My eyes eat her up, cock hardening as she struts past me and down the stairway that leads down toward the beach and the rest of the island. Those hips tell me to follow. Her small giggle tells me she knows exactly what she's doing to me. "We have our instructions. Preparations are set to begin early this evening while you and your spouse ready yourselves for dinner. Once you are served and dessert finished, we'll vacate and be a call away if we are needed for any reason."

"Perfect. Thank you." I press the end button and before my slip-on Adidas are off, I'm rushing after her. When I make it down to the long stretch of beach on this side, she's facing the water with her soft skin glistening under the high midday sun. There's a hint of sweat on her with the scent of coconuts from the lotion she's applying on her arms.

Fuck, she bends down to get her legs, and that's the last straw for me. Before Twirl can make a run for it or evade me, I grab her by the hips and toss that tight, curvy body over my shoulder. She screams. Wiggles in my hold.

It's not a deterrent.

On her next shriek of laughter, I toss her in the water and then follow. I swim up to her when she rights herself, pushing her wet hair back and away from her face. Her eyes narrow while my smile grows.

"That wasn't very nice, Mr. Asher."

"Neither is your teasing." She goes to open her mouth, but I pull her in close and steal a quick kiss. "Besides, you looked in need of a cool off. What kind of a man would I be if I didn't take care of your every need?"

"CHRIST, THAT WAS AMAZING." London sits back, patting her nonexistent stomach. For the past ten minutes I've been watching her, ignoring my slice of the key lime pie so I can focus on how sinfully she ate hers. Those sweet, low moans. How she drags the spoon past her berry-colored lips after swallowing.

The way that tiny pink tongue peeks out to swipe the excess sweetness she missed.

It's been torture while I nurse my fifth of gin.

"I'm glad you enjoyed dinner, sweetheart."

Twirl smiles at me, pushing a wayward curl out of her face. "It's not just dinner, Malcolm. The entire day has been incredible…you're almost too good to be true."

"But I am, London." Bringing the glass to my lips, I drain the rest before placing it down. "I'm right here, and there's nowhere I want to be but with you."

"You're nothing like I thought you would be." Azure eyes twinkle in the candlelight as she leans forward a bit, showing me more of the cleavage that's teased me all evening. The flowing white maxi dress with a halter-style neckline is both sexy and innocent.

It fits her perfectly with just a high enough slit over her right leg to keep me hard all night.

She's the entire package. My version of perfection.

My little love.

"That's because you're the only person in this world that will ever see this side of me. Just you."

A touch of pink grazes her cheek as a smirk curls up at her lips. "Is that so? Why am I so special?"

"Because you are mine." Pushing my chair back, I hold out a hand for her to take. "Now, take a walk with me."

MALCOLM

MALCOLM," SHE SIGHS, LEANING her head back against my chest while taking in the scene in front of her: The lone bed sitting in the middle of the white sandy beach with gauzy drapery flowing in the breeze. The lit candles on a small table holds a bottle of chilled wine and chocolate-dipped strawberries. How the waves crash upon the shore a few feet from where we stand and the million and one stars that cast a soft light on us. "How? When?"

"I want you, London. Every piece of you for as long as I have breath in my body," I croon, lips skimming the fragrant skin of her neck. My hands explore lower, down her stomach to her hips where I grip her. Pull her to me. "You've changed my life. You're my everything."

"I feel the same way. You own me."

"Do I have your heart? Your trust?" I pause and wait. Needing to hear her say the words we've been holding in. Because I know she does.

It's in her eyes. The smile she gifts me. How she constantly finds a way to tell me what she hasn't with her actions.

Cooking a meal. Making my coffee and bringing it to me while I shave.

Accepting my family without preconceived notions or judgments.

By choosing me. Choosing to let me in.

"I do," she says, a low whisper in the wind, but I hear them. Loud and clear. They also make me think of a future where I tie her to me in all the ways a man can. "It's fast and our lives are crazy, but Malcolm, I…" Twirl takes in a deep breath and then lets it out slow "…I love you."

At that moment, my life began.

Everything prior was a warm-up. A build up to what—the man I could be.

Because her love is what makes me a man. I'm worthy of her.

Her love. Devotion. Trust.

Everything else could go fuck itself; she's what matters. Her opinions of me are what matter.

"I love you, too. So fucking much, London." Turning her around, I wrap my arms around her and lift her off the ground so we're chest to chest. My lips hovering over hers. "You're the only thing in my life that matters, and I'll spend the rest of my life showing you this. No matter what the future brings, what obstacles life may throw our way, my love for you will never be in question."

Watery eyes meet mine with so much emotion that my heart clenches. "Thank you."

"Never thank me for what I was born to do. Loving you is a gift."

"I love you," she says against my lips and on her next pass, I take possession of her mouth. Kiss her with every bit of my love—with the uncontrollable fire that burns within for the beauty writhing in my arms. She's hungry for me, fighting for control of this kiss as our teeth clash and tongues taste.

Her hands are in my hair as I undo the knot at her nape holding the dress up. It falls to the ground and I reach for her thighs once more to hoist her up. Fingertips roam her skin, down her back, and over her ass, where I find nothing.

I take a step back, much to her protest, but I want to see her like this. Naked and in the moonlight with the ocean behind her. *Fuck*, my Twirl is flawless. Beautiful.

"Like what you see?" she says while looking at me from beneath her long lashes. A coy look that's sexy, but it's the sassy bite behind the questions that makes her dangerous. At this moment, this singular second, I'm her prey as I take in her silhouette.

Those luscious curves and the dip between her thighs. The perkiness of her round breasts and the tightness of her nipples.

How there's a slight sheen on her upper thigh letting me know she's turned on. Needs to be fucked.

That I will be the only man to ever take her. Bring her pleasure.

"I love what I see. What I own." My voice is rough—deeper—and doing a horrible job at masking the mounting desperation. Hands clenching and unclenching, I take a moment to breathe and calm myself down enough to be rational. This is her first time, and I need to prepare her for my size. The pain is inevitable, but I'll do what I can to minimize it.

"You're wearing entirely too many clothes, Mr. Asher."

A chuckle slips at her words. "Am I, now?"

"Yes. Lose it all."

"Impatient little thing." Not caring for the shirt one bit, I tear it open and pull it off, sending the buttons across the sand. It's unimportant and in my way. My shoes and belt meet the same fate as they land somewhere, but my pants stay on for the time being with the button undone. She devours me with hooded eyes where she stands, a slight tremble in her body. "Now, can you do something for me, sweetheart? A little favor, if you will."

"Anything." It's a plea. A whimper.

"Good girl." On her next breath, I'm on my knees in the sand and holding a thigh up. "Take your leg and hold it high. Show me my pretty little pussy."

She does as I ask and pulls the leg I'm holding up to her head. The perfect vertical split.

It takes her a few shifts to steady her equilibrium, but when she does, this dancer is beyond graceful. London is perfection. A temptation I plan to bring to heel.

Bringing my face against her core, I take in a deep inhale and groan. My first lick is slow, a gentle flick over her slit, but that changes quickly when her taste invades my senses. I'm gone. Hungry. A beast giving in to his nature as I bury my face between her thighs.

My cock is hard and throbbing—rubbing against the fabric of my pants as I devour her pussy. I'm like a man possessed. Starving. Lost to his baser instincts as I lose myself in her taste.

It's uniquely hers and with a hint of honey. This come-inducing flavor that I can't get enough of.

Need more. All of it.

Swiping the flat of my tongue through her labia, I groan against her core as another rush of wetness coats my tongue. Each drop is sweeter than the last. She's my nectar of the gods.

Sucking those tender lips into my mouth, I take every last drop and pull back. Take in the rapture on her face above me. The light sheen of sweat and the perfect O of her mouth.

London's eyes are closed but snap open after I stop. "Don't. I'm so close."

"Close to what, Twirl? Tell me." It's a growl. An angry hiss as I slip a finger to the first knuckle inside, and her opening clenches. Her thigh in this position trembles. "Fucking tell me what you need, and I'll give it to you."

"Please!"

"Please what?" I pull it out, only to push in a little deeper. Slowly, I work her opening in short strokes until her hips begin to move of their own accord. She's using me, and I let her for a few more pumps—stopping when she doesn't answer. "Say the words."

"Make me..." the leg that's by her head drops a bit, and I use my free hand to smack her clit with two fingers "...shit!"

"Keep it up there or I stop." Another direct tap, harder, and her juices splash my face. Just a little. She hasn't come but is soaking wet. All soft and swollen.

"Please let me come. I can't...it's...oh God," she cries out as I add a second finger. I'm building her up. Want her tears and screams of frustration. Want her crazy. As lost to this powerful need as I am.

"Give it to me. That's it." Another rush of wetness escapes, and I am quick to lap her, finger-fucking her to an almost orgasm. Her body seizes, leg slipping just as her knees begin to give out.

I stop. Pull back as she's on the brink, and stand.

"No!" There are tears in her eyes, anger in her expression at my denial. However, I don't pay attention to either and swoop her up in my arms, carrying her to the bed as she whimpers.

Without a word, I place her in the middle and part her legs—silently dare her to move as I remove her wedged shoes and then my pants. Our eyes remain locked as I crawl between her thighs, stroking my cock a few times over her sex.

With the blunt head I rub her clit, mixing my pre-come with her wetness. She's slick and needy, arching herself toward me in invitation.

"Whose hungry little cunt is this?" I tap her trembling bundle of nerves with the head twice, and she throws her head back. That won't do. Two more slaps, and she screams. "Answer me."

"Do it, Malcolm. I'm yours...*fuck*!" Her orgasm comes fast and hard, stealing the breath from her lungs. Twirl shakes beneath me, head thrown back as the cries get caught in her throat.

"That's it, baby." I position myself at her entrance, sliding across her slit a few times to wring out every ounce of pleasure from her sensitive pussy. "Let me feel you."

"Malcolm...what...oh my God," she screams as another tremor rocks her. That's what I've been waiting for. This lost feeling. Her innocence coming to the forefront as she loses herself to the pleasure I gift her.

And on her next helpless whimper, I slam in, taking her cherry. "Son of a bitch," I grunt, grinding my teeth while trying not to move. To fuck her like my body demands I do. "So tight. Motherfucking wet heat."

Her walls pulse—hold me tight, yet I don't move. Now my focus is on her. Soothing her from what I know has to be painful. My hands stroke her sides and down to her thighs, helping to loosen the tightness in her muscles.

My lips are kissing any part of her I can reach. Saying *I love you* over and over again as she adjusts to my length.

After a few minutes, she cups my chin to look at her. "Malcolm, this...it hurts, but feels so right. You're right for me." A few tears roll down her cheeks, and I'm quick to wipe them away. Twirl turns her face into my palm and presses her lips to the center. "It's as if all this time I've been waiting for you."

"We were destined to meet. To love each other." Bringing my hand to her nape, I bring us closer and slant my mouth over hers. Just kiss her. No rush. This time I take my time and savor every sigh. How she hums in the back of her throat when I massage my tongue with hers.

The longer I kiss her, the more she relaxes. Melts under me.

London gives a minute shift of her hips, testing the feel of my cock inside her cunt with a few clenches. There's a hiss from her into my mouth, but it's not full of pain.

Tenderness? Yes, but a little pleasure too.

It's the same sound she made when I added a second finger earlier. Adjusting, but not averse to it.

"Move."

I press my forehead to hers. "Are you sure?"

"Yes." She arches against me, sliding a bit off before taking me back to the hilt. "I need this just as much as you do."

"You're my heart, Twirl." With her eyes on mine, I pull out and hold just the tip inside. Her opening squeezes around the head, clenching— trying to pull me back in as I grab her legs and wrap them around me. "Last chance. Are you sure?"

"I want the real you. Don't hold back," she says, voice steady. Her thighs tighten around my hips, fighting my hold. "Fuck me and cuddle with me after."

"I'll make this up to you." I slam back inside causing her to choke on her reply. My hips ride her hard, pounding into her without mercy.

The sounds of the waves crashing upon the shore and her moans create the perfect soundtrack. Nature and beast; I've given in to my carnal desires. Accept that this beautiful woman with her head thrown back and drowning in pleasure was made for me.

From my rib.

Her heat envelops me each time I thrust inside. My cock glistens with her juices; I can feel the sweet little drips rolling down between us and soaking the sheets. I'm hypersensitive—a thousand minuscule electric shocks dance across my skin at the sight below me.

The obscenity. She's so tiny compared to me.

Finding purchase on those thick hips, I raise her off the bed and gift her five punishing strokes in rapid succession.

"So good. Please don't stop," London cries out, fingernails raking down my chest. She breaks the skin, and I revel in the sting. Love how far gone she is to the pleasure I give her.

"Say my name," I grit out, snapping my hips and burying myself to the hilt as a harsh shiver rushes through her. "Motherfuck, baby. You are my heaven...my nirvana. Squeeze me again."

"Malcolm, I'm—"

"I know. Give it to me," I demand through clenching teeth, holding my own release back as her body lets go. Her orgasm borders on painful as the need to fuck her raw becomes unbearable, and yet, as her warm juices drip between us, I let her ride it out.

She's out of breath and beautiful, face flush and chest rising hard with every breath she tries to take in.

Once she's coming down, when the last of the aftershocks subside, I pull out and flip her onto her stomach. She yelps, but it soon turns into a wanton moan when I grip her hair in my fist, spread her thighs just a bit, and mount her from behind.

With her body flat to the bed, I fuck her. Pounding into her tight little body as my body covers hers from head to toe.

Fingers tightening in her hair, I tilt her head toward me. My lips leave open-mouthed kisses on her jaw before I lick her from cheek to neck. "You feel like perfection. Like *my* perfect little cock slut."

Son of a bitch, she's clenching around my dick in the most delicious way. Tighter like this, and in my next thrust, I force my way back inside.

"What's happening to me? Am I...*fuck*!" London arches, pushing against me as another orgasm rocks her, and I follow. With one more punishing thrust, I bury myself deep and let go.

"Fuck, yes, Twirl. Milk my cock," I grunt out, balls drawn up tight as I release the first stream of come deep inside her cunt. Three more leave me and mix with her own, creating a sticky, beautiful mess.

The sheets below are soaked.

She's panting with her eyes closed while I watch her.

Enjoying this moment of calm as my body settles beside her on the bed,

I tuck her beneath my chin with the blanket half over us. London is pliant in my arms, all soft and sweet with her head on my chest and a leg thrown over my hip.

There are no words said, but I feel them. Those three simple ones that, put together, are worth more than all the money in the world: I love you.

With her, I'm happy.

At peace.

She's my queen.

MALCOLM

"**A**GAIN, LONDON. THIS TIME, close your fist like I taught you yesterday. Keep your thumb on the outside and over your pointer and middle finger. Never under." I'm holding a trainer's punching pad up toward her, expecting the next hit to be full of frustration. She's tired, sweaty, and looks hot as fuck out in the middle of this beach wearing a pair of yoga pants and a sports bra. "You'll break it if you don't position it right."

"I should kick your ass for this," she grunts, landing a mid-kick into the pad instead. It has some power behind it, and I let out a grunt when she lands five more in rapid succession. "This is supposed to be a vacation, Malcolm. Fun in the sun and naked times...sex on the beach and all that jazz."

I heard this yesterday too, but with only another two days left on the island, this is not up for negotiation.

I'll cuddle the fuck out of her afterward. Spend the rest of the day with my tongue in her pussy while feeding her my cock. Making her choke on my girth as I bring her to orgasm multiple times like I did last night.

"Good. Harder." As I say this, I follow the path of a few stray beads of sweat as they gather at the edge of her bra. My mouth waters, and I swallow hard as the fight to lick her becomes almost unbearable. Her nipples are hard. Pressing hard against the thin fabric. "Higher."

"If I knock you down, can we stop for the day?"

"You can try." At that, London throws a jab that misses when I step aside. "Missed."

"Why are we doing this? What aren't you telling me?" Another combination: jab, jab, cross.

"The house is yours, and they've been evicted."

"W-what?" She falters mid throw, and both hands fall to her sides. "Say that again, and slowly. I feel like I heard you wrong."

"You won, sweetheart. Everything they took is either in a new bank account or portfolio. The house, bonds and stocks...your mother's wedding ring that I found in a pawn shop on the South—" I'm cut off by her body hitting mine as she jumps into my arms. The pad falls from my hands and I catch her mid-air, falling back into the sand and taking the brunt of the impact.

Then she's straddling me, and it doesn't matter. Her supple body covers mine, pussy to cock, and she gyrates. Strokes me through the thin fabric of my board shorts. I'm hard for her, throbbing against her core, but it's the smile on her face that holds my attention.

It's the look of a woman in love. Happy. Carefree.

"Thank you," she breathes out, her sweet breath on my lips. Her mouth hovers over mine and her hair falls around us like a curtain. *Fuck, she's beautiful.* "I just don't know how I'll ever repay everything you've done for me. For my mother's memory."

"You never need to thank me, Twirl."

"But I do, Malcolm." She kisses me then, a slow and sweet gesture that I feel down to my bones. I can taste her devotion. Feel her love. London pulls back after taking my bottom lip between her teeth, and she bites down hard before letting go. Blue eyes stay on green. "It's because of you that I'm alive and in love. You're my person, something I never thought I'd find. Love wasn't on my radar until you came along, refusing to let me go, and I'll forever be in your debt for doing so."

Tangling my hand in her hair, I hold her in place and return the kiss with a fervent one of my own. Its quick but full of passion and want. Of my adoration for her. After a minute, I slow us down to a few soft pecks. She whines at the back of her throat and undulates her hips, however, with it being so early and with the staff on the grounds, I stop us.

It hurts to do so, but I do. Stop her before she teases and gets fucked with a possible audience watching.

That would ruin this short vacation.

A dead body wouldn't be fun.

"Kiss me," she demands, fighting my hold.

"No."

London sits up then and narrows her eyes on me. "No? Explain that one."

"One; we aren't alone, and no one sees your pussy milking my cock but me." Immediately a light blush sweeps across her cheeks, and she gives me a sheepish look. "And second; you need to finish the last three sets. Faster you do, faster we get to play with some of my favorite toys."

"Sex toys?"

I can't stop the laugh that escapes me. It's loud and she moves to get off, but I just wrap her in my arms to keep her above me. Not being able to slip inside her tight, wet heat at the moment is one thing, but I love having her like this.

Close. In my arms. Feeling her warmth over my cock through the two thin layers of clothing separating us.

"No," I chuckle, laying a tiny kiss to her chin and then the tip of her nose. "Those we'll go shopping for once we get back. You want it, and I'll buy it. Nothing is off the table."

"Okay, then what?"

"Guns, London. I have a couple of my favorites here to play with."

"Seriously?" Excitement rushes through her, and she wiggles in my lap. At my groan, she rolls her eyes and pushes against my chest to be let go. "Come on, lazy. You're slowing me down."

"What happened to this being boring and hard and not vacation-like for you?"

"That's before you mentioned guns. I've always wanted to play with one."

"You shoot, not play."

"It qualifies if it's role-play. I plan on you bending me over before the day is through."

London

THE FEEL OF A gun in my hand is comforting.

Its weight is an extension of my hand, and the power I feel as the bullet discharges from its chamber cannot be put into words. It's freeing. I feel powerful.

Another shot, and I hit the target in the chest—the vibrations move through me, and I won't deny to feeling a thrill, arousal from his appreciative looks as I fire again and again.

The empty shells fall all around me as I empty this clip and then restock, all the while holding in the needy sound building within my chest.

Ever since Malcolm put that first Glock in my hand back on the beach, things have changed within me. That fear I've hidden behind disappears with each praise. My confidence grows—my hunger for him has become my life force.

The reason why I am living life my way for the first time.

As I raise my arms up, locking my elbows, he comes up behind me—presses the length of his thick cock against my ass. "How many times can you…" his breath skims my ear as those strong arms encircle my waist "…hit the bull's-eye on its head. Give me a number, Twirl."

"I-I can't—"

"Concentrate. Never let anyone or anything pull you from what matters. The possible threat." This time he leaves a kiss on my neck, then a quick nip. "Clear your mind and focus. I know you can…you're a natural with my gun. Just need a bit more practice."

"You're not being fair." It leaves me on a low moan as I lower my arms, leaning my head back to give him better access. "I can't resist you, Mr. Asher."

"Is that right? Are you wet for me?" His right hand skims down until reaching my core, slipping beneath the thin fabric of my tights to cup me. "Fuck, London. What made you soak your panties, sweetheart—the gun, or the idea of my cock slipping inside from behind as you pull the trigger."

"Do it," I whimper, bringing a hand up to wrap around his neck. "Take me."

The luxury of being with a man like Malcolm Asher is that this gun range is on his property. At the very back and near a secluded path, there's a small structure holding one room, a divider with a small counter for the occupant to place its weapon, and a pulley system that goes back enough to challenge the shooter. That's it. At the most three people fit inside comfortably, and the cameras inside go to his computer, not to the staff. No one but those he trusts the most practice here, and only with permission.

"You want my cock, little Twirl? Want me to fuck you?"

"Please." My back arches, rubbing my ass against his length.

"Please what?" His fingers part my folds, rubbing against my entrance before moving to tap my clit. "Fuck you or let you shoot this gun? Make you come if you can hit the target between the eyes?"

"Both?" There's no hesitation. Every time I think about him inside me, my heart speeds up and my pussy aches, but add a gun to that equation and it's downright perverse. "Should we put it to the test?"

"Is that a challenge, love? You think you can handle both?" I don't even have a second to sass him when his other hand loops the waistband of my pants and pushes them down over the swell of my ass. "Tell me."

"I can."

"Such a naughty little slut." His hands press on the small of my back, leaning me over the railing. "Grab the gun and fire the first shot."

"What do I get if I hit?" My hips gyrate once against him and I grab the Glock, cocking it. "Challenge me." There's something so dirty about this, and I want to push him. I want to be taken rough and quick.

The next thing I register is the sting of his palm on my right ass cheek and the heat that follows. "Concentrate, Twirl. Shoot." My body reacts before my mind catches up and my finger pulls the trigger. I miss the target completely. "Again."

The sounds of his belt coming undone fill my ears as I line the sights of the gun up. I try to push out the feel of his hand spreading me, of the hot head of his cock rubbing against my slick slit, but it's futile when his low groan—that almost feral sound rumbles through him.

"Oh God…please!"

"Come on. Shoot." I blow out a breath and fire just as Malcolm slams into me. I choke on my own breath at the overwhelming feeling of him. So good. So perfect. "Motherfucking perfect," he says, echoing my thoughts. "Just think of it as an exercise of shooting from a moving car."

"What?" I ask before he pulls out and slams back in, setting up a quick pace that jostles me. My arms go lax, head falling down as I get caught up in the pleasure. A hiss leaves me when his hand tangles into my hair and he pulls.

"You're not concentrating." I try to line the gun up again as his hips rotate, hitting an explosive part of me. "Hit the target and I'll give you the release you need."

"Fuck!" I fire, missing again, hitting the rotator chain. It ricochets, bouncing somewhere, but I'm not aware of my surroundings anymore. All I know and feel is him, his cock and his hold on me, his heavy breathing and the moans he utters in my ear.

"Again, baby. Focus or I'll finish over your ass." The next flex of his hips is fast and deep, stealing the very air from my lungs. "It'll be a win for me. I love to see you wearing my seed."

"Don't you dare," I grit out, focusing just long enough to empty the chamber. Every shot fires off in rapid succession, and I toss the gun away.

Adrenaline pumps through me, my skin tingles with excitement—I'm trembling beneath him.

I'm so close. So close.

And it's his next words that throw me over the edge.

"Good girl."

That's it. Two words and I clench around him while closing my eyes. I'm lost to him, to the feel of his every ridge rubbing my walls as he slams in a final time and comes deep within me. Spurt after spurt coats me— mixing with my own release as I slump forward.

Breathing is hard. Moving impossible, and yet, I still look at him from over my shoulder with a cheesy grin that matches his. "Best shooting lesson ever."

Leaning forward, he catches my lips in a quick and harsh kiss. "You hit the target twice. Congrats, baby."

***

"You're going to get us into trouble, kid," Gina says from beside me as we head toward the mansion where I met Malcolm. She's driving the large cargo van I convinced Carmelo to lend me with the promise that it's all to surprise his boss.

And technically, I'm not lying. This is all for him. Us.

To play a little. To pay him back for everything he's done for me.

My Malcolm is a voyeur, and as such, gets off on watching. So tonight, after he gets home, I want those gorgeous green eyes on me while I touch myself. Make myself come with nothing but the sound of his voice and my fingers.

Something I never thought I would do or want to try with anyone else, but with him I want to experience it all. The sexy. The perverse. The dirty and even illegal.

Jesus, a lot has changed since that first dance. Since his fingertips dug themselves into my hips and he told me to twirl for him.

The setup at the club—the small stage and his throne—isn't going to be hard to move. And I'm hoping that once I tell Liam what it's for, he'll be very receptive to letting me take it home with us. I'm sure someone there can load it up and one of the guards at the house can get it down.

"How much trouble?" I ask, taking a sip from my latte.

"Depends on how good of a mood he's in later. They've been too quiet since being evicted, and that worries everyone."

I've thought about this too. Why haven't they tried to reach me? Show up and demand I give back the house and everything they had power over.

While on the private island, I learned the final judgement from the judge dealing with my case. I won. Everything is mine again, and they had to vacate before we returned to Chicago.

Since then they've gone underground. Hiding from everyone.

Yet I have a feeling that my man knows more than he lets on. That he's biding his time before he strikes.

"We'll make it quick. In and out mission here." That appeases her as we pull up to the back of the house where the employee parking lot is. There's usually one guy watching the lot at all times, but this one I've never seen before. He waves us in without asking to see our IDs.

"I take it you don't know him?"

"No." My eyes stay on his as we pass, trying to decipher my gut reaction of distrust. "Let's just get this over with."

"Works for me." Gina parks near the back entrance and waits for me to get out. Together we walk inside and head straight for Liam's office. A few of the girls I met while here wave and I do the same, trying to ignore the naked state of their bodies. The tiny red welts one of them has down her arms and legs came from what I assume was a demonstration.

They're heading back into the main lounge area, leaving just us alone back here. The door is slightly ajar when I reach it, and Stacy's giggle meets my ear.

"You stop that," she says, and all that follows is his grunt. It doesn't sound like they're having sex, but I look at Gina and tilt my head so she enters first. "Oh my God, Liam!" More laughter. "Keep those hands to yourself."

"Knock, knock," Gina calls out while tapping her knuckles on the door. "Can we come in, and are you decent?"

"Baby, go see who that is." Liam's voice is rougher than usual.

"Coming!" It's hard to hold in my snort, but I do while Gina rolls her eyes. It doesn't take more than a minute for Stacy to peek her head out, but when she spots me her polite smile turns into cheesiness. "Get your butt over here and give me a hug, stranger."

"Hi to you too!" I laugh, walking in for the tight squeeze. "How have you been?"

"We're good except for Liam. He's a bit cranky after getting a root canal earlier today."

"Am not!"

"Yeah, he is." Stacy takes my hand and pulls me in behind her, leaving Gina to close the door. My eyes take her in then and notice this is the most clothing I've ever seen her wear: slacks, a cardigan, and a thin scarf around her neck. Like this, she looks like the average girl next door. When I look at her face again, she's smirking. "Shut it. I had to drive him to and from his appointment. Tassels and a thong would be frowned upon by the uptight trolls out there."

"Who are you…hello, Miss London." Liam smiles at me and stands, coming around his desk to shake my hand. "How have you been, sweetheart? That Malcolm being good to you?"

"He's perfect."

He eyes me for any deceit and when he finds none, he gives me a nod to sit down. "Good. That makes me very happy, kid."

I take the seat directly in front of his desk. His eyes are on mine as I take in a deep breath and let it out slowly. "First, I want to thank you for hiring me. For helping me the only way you knew how, Liam. My contract wasn't like the rest of the employees here, and I appreciate that."

"None needed." He waves me off. "You're one of the good ones, and while I knew the men here would salivate and it'd bring me money, I made sure it was at your pace. Your call to—"

"You didn't have to," I interrupt, because while he isn't one hundred percent noble, his chance saved my life. Gave me an out. A path to leave or, how fate played it out, toward Malcolm. "I know money was involved, but knowing who my brother and father are, you stuck your neck out for me, and nothing in this world could repay that. Thank you."

"Forget it." He levels me with a look that says I won't win. "Now, what can I do for you?"

"How hard would it be for you to gift me the items in Mr. Asher's private room? For me to pick up my costumes?" I ask, sitting forward toward him. "I'm trying to surprise the man—"

"Done."

"Thank you…oh my God!"

There's blood everywhere. On me. On the walls. Oozing from the bullet hole in Liam's head. Another three shots ring out and I throw myself to the ground. The person on the other side is hell-bent on emptying their clip before coming inside.

Screams come from what sounds like every direction. Stomping—it sounds like a scared herd of wildebeest racing through the mansion. Everyone here is running for their lives while this person continues to give us everything his weapon has.

My eyes find Gina's and she's reaching for her gun. "When I say the word, you duck behind his desk and don't come out. Got it? No matter what, stay hidden."

"What about you?"

"Don't come out." The fact she ignores my question fills me with dread —more so than the bullets flying throughout the room.

A shriek rents the air, and Stacy's body hits the ground. She's been hit in the shoulder and bleeding profusely. I crawl to her, ignoring Gina's curse or the way she tries to block me with her body as best she can.

"Look at me," I whisper to her, taking the loose scarf around her neck and using it to put pressure on the wound. "We need to get you with me behind his desk. Help me get us back there."

"It hurts to breathe. I can't."

"You have no choice, or we all die." My fingers are bathed in her blood. It's dripping down my wrist as I hold the fabric in place. "We don't have time to lose. Crawl and I'll follow."

Stacy takes ahold of the scarf and turns to crawl when the door is kicked open. Wood splinters and flies around the room. More shots are fired as Gina takes the first man down with a bullet to his neck. The one that follows manages to respond, but his shot barely misses her, and the flesh wound on her arm pisses her off.

The sound of empty shells falling fills the room and when all is said and done, the man is dead and so is the attendant from the employee parking area. He didn't have the chance to shoot.

"London, we need to go now."

"I can't leave her here by herself!"

"I'll be okay. Promise." My eyes snap back to Stacy who's already in motion; she's unsteady but moving aside a discrete area of wall behind Liam's dead body. It opens to a small cupboard-like notch in the wall where a human can hide inside. A tight fit, but she's small enough to be comfortable. "Get out, sweetie. Listen to her and go."

"Are you sure?" Adrenaline is pumping through my system. I'm jittery yet hyper alert.

"Go," she urges, already slipping inside. "Save yourself."

Those are Stacy's last words; they slip past her lips mere seconds before another round of bullets comes from the direction of the other room.

I'm scared, shaking as I look over at Gina, but as soon as she mouths *run*…I do so.

London

T HE WORLD AROUND ME dissolves into chaos.

Noise and destruction as I run out of the house with the unadulterated sense of fear lodging itself in my throat. Feet follow me—run behind me—but I can't tell who it is.

It might be Gina.

Might be worse.

All I know is that I don't look back. I run.

Run until the door opens with force, slamming against the outside concrete wall as I pass the threshold, and still I don't stop.

All I know is that it's not safe. That I must continue moving.

"Head to the car, London. Don't look back and get inside." Her words are comforting, give me hope as I hear the lock click on the van up ahead. The lights flash, and I extend a hand out to open the door.

I'm so close.

Just a little bit more…

The sound of screeching tires meets my ears, and the loud sound of a crash follows. From my periphery something—a large mass moves and falls to the ground, and it takes everything in me not to confirm my fears. In my heart I know it's Gina.

"Don't stop. Just don't stop," I mutter to myself, but the reaction is automatic, and I do so. She's there. Just there. Lying a few feet from me and to the right, unconscious and unmoving. A sob catches in my throat and I turn toward her, wanting to help or make sure she's breathing, when I am taken from behind.

Whoever bumps into me tackles me to the ground, and the hard pavement digs into my flesh. Breaks the skin.

A hiss escapes as pain shoots through my body and I buck my hips, try to wiggle out from beneath him. Because of that, there is no doubt.

It's a man. A large man at that, and his scent is familiar.

Oh God. Please help me.

Panic churns within, and I scream.

"No one left to hear you, little sis. Yell all you want…it only excites me." That's the last thing I hear as he covers my mouth with a dirty rag, and all goes black.

HUSHED WHISPERS and the feel of the car I'm in meeting a large pothole awaken me. I have no idea how long I've been out or where we are at this point, and I pray that we're still in Chicago. Darkness surrounds me, my body lying awkwardly on a bench seat inside of what I think is a van or truck, as I try to open my eyes.

I can't. There's something covering them, and my hands are tied behind my back.

Whatever road we're on is in bad shape. In need of repairs, and with the areas that Alton likes to frequent, that could be anywhere.

He likes the dirty and dangerous. Where no one will bat an eye and calling the police is forbidden.

Criminals don't snitch. They don't involve themselves with what doesn't concern them.

I'm a dead duck unless…

I wiggle a bit, just a discreet shift as to not draw attention to myself, and the low clink of my chain follows. It's small, but I feel the locket move across the thin chain, letting me know it's there.

That Malcolm has a way to find me.

I have to believe that.

That Stacy is alive and calling everyone she can. She knows Malcolm. The office must have his number somewhere. The fact that we won't be home soon is also a reason to come looking.

He will find me. Everything will be okay.

It becomes my mantra as I'm driven God knows where and with whom. Because I know Alton's not alone. The voices are a bit muffled, but I can pick apart his and Brittany's. Not that it surprises me; she's a piece of work and his follower. A sick individual.

But then again, sick fucks attract compatible individuals.

The car comes to a sudden stop then, and two doors open. A cool breeze fills the inside of the car's cab and with it, I get a hint of water. That specific scent that comes from a large body of water. Fresh and clean with just a subtle hint of fish.

"Lake? But which one?" I mutter under my breath, but then go slack again when another door opens. This one is near my feet, and I'm taken out like a sack of potatoes. Swallowing my yelp takes heroic effort, but more so my grunt when I'm thrown over a shoulder that digs into my abdomen.

"Take her inside," Alton says, and the man holding me tenses, his hand on the back of my ankle, clenching. "Go on. Wake my darling little sister up and secure her to the pole near the back."

"I'm not your puppet or employee. Watch it, or I pull the plug on everything." *Agent Hayes? What the hell?*

"My apologies, Agent. No reason to be so sensitive."

Another car pulls up, tires screeching, and this time I'm not able to hide my automatic response. If Hayes notices my body tensing, he doesn't say anything, but his tap to my leg is enough to make me still.

There's no yelling. No demands to let me go. No shot being fired.

Instead, I hear a voice that sounds familiar, but I just can't pinpoint. The person has heavy footsteps, clomping on the pavement until coming to a stop near where we stand. "As you predicted, the authorities are all over that place and no one has reported the girl missing. I've gone around the perimeter twice now, and it's empty. No sign of Mr. Asher yet."

"Good. Very good," Alton says, and then Brittany giggles at something. "Let me know when he gets within the property line. I want her to watch me kill him."

And then we're moving.

The bones of his shoulder hurt, pressing into me as we cross a threshold. We go from dark and fresh air to dank and cold. The place is freezing.

"Be quiet and behave, London. I don't want you to get hurt in this." Hayes walks deeper into the room and stops to lower me, his hands gripping my arms to steady me. "It'll be over soon."

"Why are you doing this? Do you have any idea how crazy Alton is? What he's going to do to me?" My breathing gets choppier as my chest gets tight. I have no weapon and my hands are tied. How the hell can I defend myself? "Please, I'm begging you…let me go."

"Now why would he do that?" An arm wraps around my midsection as the blindfold is taken off. Alton is behind me and Hayes in front. "His eggs are in this basket, Lola. The love of his life was killed by the asshole you've given yourself to, and he wants revenge. A man in love without his woman will go insane." His lips kiss my temple before he licks a path from cheek to chin, nipping my jaw hard before pushing me toward the agent. "Tie her up and gag her."

I stumble into Hayes but turn my head to glare at the man who was never really my brother. My enemy.

He looks like shit. Dirty. Still wearing a cast, but like the rest of him, it's filthy.

Nothing like the vain man I knew.

"You're not getting away with this, Alton."

"Want to make a wager on that, dearest?" His slimy grin causes my stomach to churn. The disgust must be visible on my face because his eyes narrow. "Something you want to say?"

"I hope he kills you—"

His hand meets my cheek, knocking me over, and I'm caught by his accomplice. Hayes pushes me behind him. "Keep your hands off her. Hurt her, and we're done."

"Fine. Just shut her up." Alton walks away, leaving me with another man that I see as a monster.

I don't say a word as I'm taken to the very back and my hands are secured to a metal post. Agent Hayes doesn't use handcuffs and I'm thankful for that, but the thin zip tie in his hand isn't going to be easy to escape either.

"Stay." His voice is gruff, and the look he gives warns me not to defy him. He doesn't go far and grabs a small metal chair by the only doorway in this place. It's a large room. Empty, and with a few dozen boxes stacked against the opposite wall of where I am. There's a second floor, but it's all dark and the windows are too high for me to reach except for one right across from the metal stairs. They look unstable but will have to do.

"Count of three," I mumble and take a step forward, ready to make a run when Hayes grabs my arm. "Let go."

"I wouldn't do that if I were you."

"Do you really expect me to sit here and wait for him to kill me?"

"He won't hurt you, London. I won't allow it."

At that I laugh, the sound rough and sardonic. "Really? You're going to stop him?"

"You have my—"

"Your word means jack after helping a criminal kidnap me to use as a pawn. The fact that you're willing to go this far for what? Revenge for a woman that didn't love you?"

"Shut the fuck up," he spits out, grabbing my wrist in a hold sure to leave a bruise. Hayes pulls me toward the pole, a hand on either side, and wraps the tie around them. It's tight, hurts a bit, but plastic isn't metal. "If you want to get out of here unscathed, I suggest not pissing off the only person here that cares if you live or die. To them, you're just the dessert after a gory main attraction. Remember that next time you open that slick mouth of yours, kid."

He walks away, kicking the chair toward me on his way out of the room. The heavy door clanks against the metal frame as it closes, leaving me alone.

With the toe of my shoes, I kick it closer and take a seat. Think.

The glass above me shows some light, so it can't be that late. Maybe four or five.

"How do I get out of this mess?" Leaning my head against the metal pole, I close my eyes for a minute or two, trying to remember this video on Facebook I once saw about self-defense and what to do if you're tied with zip ties.

You have to tighten them, leaving no space between the hands.

Extend your hands out with the palms facing each other.

Then you pull back as hard as you can.

Easy peasy.

"You seem lost in thought, Lola. Want to share with the class?" My eyes open and snap toward the sound of Alton's voice. When did he come in? Why didn't I hear him?

He's standing a few feet away and watching me with that same creep-tastic look in his eyes. The same one that's always made me wary of him. That he's not right in the head.

"Why can't you just let me be?" I ask, trying to buy myself a bit of time. He's a talker. Get him going, and he might not notice my actions.

"Because you're mine." He says it so calmly, so emotionless. Alton takes another step toward me, his hand reaching out, but instead, he drops it and turns around, giving me his back at the last second. His good hand is at his hair and pulling. His breathing is becoming agitated. "You just had to fuck him, didn't you? Had to give away the one thing that was going to make me enough money to disappear. He took your cherry and everything else that mattered in my life."

While he talks, I take the end of the zip and pull, tightening the cord. But as his words sink in, I pause and sit straight. "What do you mean, disappear?"

"Dad wanted to sell you to an overseas trafficker. That, or whore you out, while I want to keep you."

"You two are sick," I whisper, but it's not low enough and before I can turn my face, his fist connects, sending me back. The force is enough to break the hold of the plastic, my body landing hard on the cold concrete.

Blood drips from the cut at the corner of my bottom lip, and my head feels woozy. It takes a moment for me to regain complete visual of him, and even then, there's a ringing in my ear that's distracting.

He's angry. Visibly shaking as he lowers himself over me.

Trapping me against the floor so I can't escape. My legs kick out, but it does nothing to dislodge him. Instead, it makes him laugh, a hot, panting chuckle against my neck. He's hard, and I'm disgusted. Acid-like-bile rises up my throat as panic sets in.

No one is here. No one to stop him.

I want to yell. Scream, but the words won't come out.

"Even if you did, no one will hear you. This building is completely soundproof." His good hand wanders over my rib and higher, skimming over my breast before wrapping around my neck. Squeezing hard. Painfully so as to block my airways. "I'm going to fuck you as Malcolm Asher bleeds out in front of you, London. I'm going to break you, pass you around to anyone willing to pay for your used cunt, and then have you train my next whore while I spend every last dime your mother left you. You'll pay for your betrayal."

"You'll never get away with this," I manage to wheeze out, clawing at his hands to let go.

Alton laughs, the sound psychotic. "Did you know that Dad killed your father years ago by cutting his break line? That he planned—used your mother to gain access to Julian's wealth?" Another laugh, his face hovers over mine. Pure evil reflects in his stare. "However, I did something so much worse. I'm the one that killed Amelia, Lola…I pulled the trigger and now I'll own their little girl."

"You—" I don't get to finish as the door is kicked in and multiple guns are cocked.

MALCOLM

THE DOOR TO MY office is thrown open, and as I reach for my gun, Javier comes into view. He's angry. Full of agitation as he clenches and unclenches his hand, one that has blood dripping from the center knuckle.

"What's going on?" I'm already standing and making my way toward him. The man never reacts—he's calm and collected at all times—knows better than to barge in here like this unless it's an emergency. His expression makes me pause as I reach him, my stomach churning as the worst-case scenario plays out. "Where's London?"

"She's been taken. They're holding her at a warehouse attached to a power plant on Lake Michigan just outside of Milwaukee," Javier answers, and I nod. Take a moment to breathe as a rage the likes of which I have never experienced surges through my veins. It's sudden. Maddening as I grit my teeth and fight to not give in to the emotion.

Emotional reactions lead to mistakes. Bad calls of judgement.

She can get hurt in this process if I don't play my cards right. They don't want to hurt her, not when she comes with a price tag, but will to save themselves. Especially Marcus. He's been shopping her innocence— the one she gave me so sweetly—to the first son of a bitch with the right amount of zeroes at the end.

They know I'm coming but will never guess which route I'll take. How far I'll go to save her.

"Alton, Marcus, and Jimmy." It's not a question, but a statement.

"No Marcus, but we do have one Shawn Hayes assisting." This one surprises me, but then again, after what he said to London about Karina, I've been waiting for him to strike. Finding out she was his ex was the easy part. A few clicks and the world's your oyster; the internet has its pros and cons, and this is the perfect example.

A man in love with an old social media account from his days in college that he hasn't closed. That he hides from his job along with a creepy fascination for women who look like Karina. Photos of the couple. Declarations. The last post on his wall is of the day she left him.

It's a personal purging. Dark and full of bitter rage.

Yet it's the last line that stood out for me.

I'LL KILL HIM FOR US.
TAKE HIS EVERYTHING AND PLACE IT AT YOUR FEET.

"Where were they, and why the blood?"

"At Lake Forest, and I punched a wall."

My brows furrow as I focus on the first part of his answer. "Why the ·fuck would she—"

"London wanted to surprise you and they went to pick something up." *What could she possibly want from…that dirty girl. I'll turn her ass a nice shade of red for this after I kiss her stupid.* "They were in his office when shots rang out, killing Liam, injuring a girl named Stacy, among other patrons."

"And Gina?"

"Run over trying to get London out and into their car. She has a flesh wound and a broken leg but is otherwise fine. I have someone with her and Stacy at the E.R. for precautions."

"Who?"

"Carmelo."

Nodding, I scratch my jaw. "Where's Marcus Foster? One doesn't go far without the other."

"We have a tail on him. He's out by the pier and seems to be waiting on someone."

"He's not to leave." Not a request and at once, Javi pulls out his phone and sends out a few messages. Pings follow as I walk back around my desk and remove a black and white drawing of The Asher building given to me as a gift by a customer. It's large and heavy in its expensive casing, and the perfect size to hide the access panel behind my desk.

Placing my entire palm over the screen, I wait for the scanner to skim my hand and the section of wall to unlock. It does with a loud click, and I pull it open, entering my private collection of weapons here.

Javier follows me inside and grabs two assault rifles with silencers while I remove my suit jacket and hang it from a hook on the wall. I'm a man that appreciates the nicer things in life, and my holster is leather-made and one of a kind. Tailor made by an old Italian man in a shop where a billfold will run you a few grand easily.

Taking the upper-body holster, I slip it on and secure the strap across my midsection before taking my Desert Eagles from their place inside a drawer. There are a few magazines beside them, six to be exact, with nine bullets each, and I take those too.

I want them to hear each shot.

To see the gleam of polished silver as I empty a round into each body.

Once we're outside the weaponry room, I close the door and when the click signals it shut, I turn and open my top desk drawer. Atop a stack of papers is my favorite knife and I grab it, too, before walking out.

Mariah is at her desk when we do, and she's just as angry. Her eyes are cold, and no words are said as I walk up, kiss her forehead, and continue straight back and toward a door that no one uses here.

The private elevator will take me straight to my garage, opening the door mere steps from the car I keep on site. I open the door and enter, turning to look at my cousin who's already on her way to make my office appear as if nothing has happened.

Our eyes meet and she gives me a nod which I return, then looks at her boyfriend for the same.

Today, their blood will cleanse the streets of Chicago.

"I DIDN'T KNOW." Marcelles greets me near the pier's entrance with a serious look on his face. He's holding his hands up, taking a step back as I tower over him. Friend or enemy, everyone around me runs the risk of my wrath at the moment.

Blackness—that dark manifestation of my soul is clawing its way out and wanting to play. For every second they have London, I'll repay the world with my maelstrom of vengeance.

"Where is he?" My voice is cold, hand on the handle of the knife inside my pocket.

"Down below and not alone." Beads of sweat form at his brow, and he wipes them away. "He's with that officer you told me to look out for—"

"Bristol?"

"Yes." His phone rings, but he doesn't answer. Instead, he keeps his gaze on mine. "Marcus seems desperate, Malcolm, while the Lieutenant kept assuring him about some buyer. Those two are deep into some fucked-up shit, and I'll take them out if you need me to. Just say the word, and it's done."

"These two are mine. They all are." Agent or not, Shawn Hayes ran his luck and lost. There is no coming back from this.

"Understood. My loyalty has always been with you and our family, my career be damned."

"I know." And I do. Marcelles has been with us for years and has never betrayed that trust. He's an honest man, a hard-working agent, but loyal to only those in his family. He's my mother's cousin and went to school with my father and Director Monahan.

All sides interconnect and watch out for the other.

He's not a traitor. Neither is Monahan.

However, Shawn Hayes has proven to be more than a nuisance. He's a danger to society."

A rogue.

"The press release will go out to all major networks in three hours. There will be a manhunt."

"I'll make every second count." I turn and walk around toward the pathway below, when I pause and look at Javier. "Who's watching them now if Marcelles is up here?"

"Michael. The kid wants to prove himself and atone for his sins."

———

THREE MEN now stand right where Marcelles said they would be, talking in hush tones and with hands thrown up in the air as they argue over something. They don't see me or the others with me, and I use it to my advantage.

A moment to test one of my own.

Grabbing Michael by the collar of his shirt, I pull him beside me and hand over my gun. "How good of an aim do you have?"

He gives me a thumbs-up, mouthing *good* while taking my Eagle.

"Three men, and one is young," I say while waving a hand in front of us. "Shoot the one to the left in the chest, and I'll forgive you. Get a bullet in his head, and I'll welcome you back with a forgiven debt. You have one bullet…make it count."

We step back slowly, and he takes his stance. Michael raises his hands and aims with elbows in a locked position. His hand trembles a bit and he shakes his head to rid himself of the mounting nerves. The finger on the trigger twitches, but on his next breath he pulls, and Bristol falls to the ground.

The men turn our way, and Marcus pales but is smart enough to stay quiet as I walk over to inspect the shot. I'm impressed with Michael's accuracy and balls to take this risk when he still looks in pain himself. I can respect that. Forgive but never forget.

"Center of forehead and clean exit by the puddle beneath his head. Welcome back, kid."

Michael makes a humming sound, and I look back to see him place a hand over his heart. He's a good person that made a mistake. He paid for those crimes with blood and the removal of his tongue, took it like a champ, and I'll repay him for proving his loyalty when all is said and done.

"Who the fuck are you, and what do you want?" the older man beside a quiet Marcus asks. "This is a private sale. I've already paid for that cunt to suck—" He doesn't get to finish as I pull my knife out, flip it open, and slide it across his throat. The cut is deep enough to kill, and it splatters across myself and Marcus, ruining my white dress shirt.

I'll never know his name. If he has a family.

None of that matters when his intentions were to hurt the one I love the most in this world.

Blood flows from the open wound and he weakens, dropping to his knees in front of me. Fisting his hair, I yank his head back, stretching the torn skin, prompting more of his life's force to drip onto the wet ground below.

"Please," he cries, a gurgling sound as he begins to choke. "Please get me help."

"She's mine." His eyes widen at my words before I slide the blade once more, cutting his aorta. I drop him and let him bleed out while I turn to face Marcus fucking Foster. "Anything you want to say? Explain?"

"You can have her," he says, holding a hand out as if to keep me from advancing. It didn't. "All I need is five million dollars and two tickets to Mexico. Give me that, and you'll never see Alton and me again."

"Really. Just five?" Wiping the dirty blade on my pants, I bring the gleaming steel between us. "Why not ten? Fifty, even?"

"That would be very generous of you. I'd be forever—" The back of my hand cuts him off, the force of the blow causing him to stagger back and fall.

"I'm going to enjoy every single second of your death, Marcus." Standing over him, I place the sole of my shoe on his chest. "However, before that can happen, I have a promise to fulfill. I told you you'd have a front seat to Alton's end, and I'm a man who keeps his words."

MALCOLM

FUCKING IDIOTS.

We're about two hours from The Loop and on Lake Michigan, standing a little way down from a power plant outside of Milwaukee. London is here. Being held here. Her locket is pinging with a signal and coming from a run-down warehouse toward the east side of this property.

It could be storage.

Could be a structure that they've been meaning to tear down and haven't.

Could be that after the workday is done and employees go home to their families, someone has been letting criminal activity take place on the premises. Someone, like the balding fuck currently slumped over his desk chair inside the central office.

However, I will thank the man for having the CCTV live system off and the recorder looping through footage from last week. Saves me time.

Ready and in position. ~Javi

Hold ~Malcolm

My eyes scan the surrounding buildings and the lone structure where they hold London. No one seems to be on high alert. Monitoring the entrances. They're doing a shit job at surveillance.

Overconfidence is a disease many people suffer from. Too cocky. Too stuck within the *it'll never happen* mind frame, and this reeks of it.

Of narcissism on a level that is dangerous.

They're lazily watching the front and back, and yet, the few assholes Alton put together as guards are laughable. Incompetent. Five in total and spread out, the men all imbibing. High. Too busy snorting coke and playing with the cheap guns given to notice they're surrounded on all sides.

"Boss," Carmelo speaks low beside me, looking through a pair of binoculars toward the entrance. He left the hospital to join me after I sent Michael to take his place. "We have movement. Hayes and Jimmy are outside talking, and Alton has gone inside."

"And the whore?"

"Getting high as a kite inside of Alton's car." The car in question, a blue Mustang, begins to inch forward and then stop. It does this three times until Brittany lowers the window and sticks her head out, yelling out something to Hayes.

The man ignores her.

Jimmy ignores her.

She doesn't like it and pulls away from them to do a reckless donut between the building and a few old trees. The rubber burns on the asphalt, blowing smoke around the car as it spins. Any other time, I'd watch the idiot kill herself all day, but right now, I'll need her to stay alive long enough to become a scapegoat.

"How much did her supplier gift her?" Looking at my phone, I send a message to Javier.

Now ~Malcolm

Carmelo chuckles. "Enough to kill a bull."

"Good. Make sure she doesn't leave the property." Adrenaline pumps through my veins and I take my gun out, checking the magazine and cocking it. My body is vibrating with excitement. With anger.

The demon I keep hidden within wants blood and vengeance. To kill. To make them pay for every single minute of fear my Twirl has lived through.

I count to ten and crack my neck, watching as the guard walking close to where I stand hits the floor with two bullet wounds to the chest. My eyes close, and I wait for Javier's signal. For confirmation that everyone but the three main culprits are dead.

Two minutes pass and my phone vibrates. My eyes snap open to read his one-word reply.

Done. ~Javi

Good. Have them clean up and set the stage.
~Malcolm

Already on it. Meet you in ten. ~Javi

I pocket my phone and walk through the lot toward the entrance casually. Carmelo is already with Brittany, turning off the vehicle and pulling her out. She's screaming and throwing punches while Hayes and Jimmy scramble to grab their guns.

My steps don't falter as I raise my gun and fire three shots at Jimmy. The first misses by a hair, but the second and third lodge themselves deep into his chest. He staggers and I fire another two, this time hitting his stomach.

Blood drenches his shirt as his body falls. It pools all around him, staining the ground as he takes his last few breaths.

From the corner of my eye, I see Javier making his way to me with another two men.

"You're a dead son of a bitch," Shawn yells out as a bullet flies by my head. He fires another and again misses. I return the favor and don't, hitting his hand with the Glock. "Fuck!"

It falls to the ground and I put my own away, preferring to use my knife on him. "You want me? Come get me."

"Karina was too good for you, asshole." He charges toward me as I flip the blade out, his body colliding with mine as we hit the ground. Hayes is quick to mount me, throwing a punch that lands on my jaw. It cuts my lip, and I return the favor by embedding the blade of my knife deep into his thigh and twisting it.

His screams are loud. Like the bitch he is.

I'm quick to buck him off and stand up, leaving the blade in his possession. "Did that hurt, Agent? Need help?"

"You ruined everything." He follows me up to his feet, putting the bulk of his weight on the opposite leg. "We were going to be happy together. Had plans to elope."

"Quit lying to yourself. You never had the means to keep her happy."

"Shut the fuck up," he growls out, his hand on the handle of my knife. With a quick yank, he pulls it out, gritting his teeth as the shock of pain travels through his body.

But I don't. I taunt. Push every single button he has.

I begin to circle him, walking just close enough for him to reach if he dares. I'm counting on his rage. "She was a selfish and greedy whore that deserved all ten bullets I put into her body."

I'm ready for him when he lunges, and with a quick turn of my arm flip him over my shoulder. Shawn lands hard on his back but has enough mind to lash out when I turn, cutting my arm. It's not deep, but burns, and I punch him twice in retaliation.

His nose cracks, a sickening sound as blood gushes from the nostrils. "I'm going to kill you." Again, he makes a slicing motion, and I grab his wrist easily, bringing the knife toward his throat. He fights it, tries to push me off, but I use the momentum of my body weight to move the point of the blade to right below his Adam's Apple.

"Accept your fate with dignity," I grunt, adding pressure as the end pricks his skin. His mouth opens to reply, but before he can spew some other bullshit, I shove the blade straight through his neck.

Shawn's body goes limp after a minute and I stand, leaving the knife where it is for now.

"We have an hour between a tip being sent to the police and their arrival. Marcelles and Monahan will be shortly behind since this involves one of their own." Carmelo catches up with me as I pull out my gun with the full magazine and walk toward the door. "She's almost comatose and not going anywhere. Weapons are ready and with her fingerprints. Clean-up crew is staging the rest…let's get them out, and fast."

"Agreed." I don't waste another minute and kick the door in when I reach the entrance. Every gun beside me cocks, but it's my bullet that dislodges when I find him over her body on the floor. It hits his side, causing him to scramble off and land on his back.

London's eyes are wide and full of panic, yet behind that choking fear I see her relief when she spots me by the door. Without another conscious thought, she pushes herself off the floor and runs to me, jumping into my arms and holding tight. Every part of her wraps itself around me.

Tight, not a single inch of space is left between her body and mine.

Her entire form is shaking. Mumbling something that I can't quite make out, but when I try to pull her back a bit, she refuses to move with a shake of her head.

"I'm here, sweetheart. It's going to be okay."

"Not until he's dead." Twirl's voice comes through then, monotone and ice cold. "They have to die."

"Alton Foster was never going to make it past the end of this week—"

"Now." She shudders, a sob catching in her throat as she pulls back to look me in the eye. Those sweet lips I love tremble, tears rushing down her cheeks as I take in the bruise forming on her skin. How pale she is from the shock and trauma.

A million deaths wouldn't be enough for this fucker.

"Tell me how I can make this right for you. Whatever it is, it's done." My men move around us, Carmelo and Javier sending London sad looks. Alton is picked up from the floor and forced to sit in a chair near a pole. My guess is that's where he kept her—tied her to—by the broken skin of her wrist. "Seeing you like this is killing me, love."

"He killed her, Malcolm. They fucking killed my parents."

Motherfuck, he told her. "I know."

"You did? When…why didn't—"

"My investigator looked into their deaths, and the results of his findings were inside my email this morning. I'll show you the time and date if you need me to, London."

"I'm s-sorry, I—"

"Shhh, none of that. I'm not looking for an apology, and you've done nothing wrong." Lowering her to the ground, I wait until she's on steady feet and pull back. Force her eyes on mine with the tip of my finger. "Just tell me how I can make this right."

She nods and squares her shoulders, coming to terms with whatever decision she's made. "No one can, but you could lend me your gun."

"My gun?"

"Yes." Her eyes flick toward a groaning Alton, and that darkness I've seen glimpses of comes to the forefront. The tears stop for the moment, and her lip curls over her teeth in a snarl. The pain is there, but that need for retribution is growing by the second, and I understand it. Her. "Give it to me, Malcolm. No more questions."

"As you wish." I hand over my Eagle and watch as she gauges the weight. Admires its power.

Twirl looks at me then from under her long lashes, those beautiful blue orbs full of love and appreciation. "I love you." That's all she says, making her way toward her step sibling with slow and sure steps. She doesn't pause or so much as blink. Her arm doesn't shake when she raises it, nor does her finger twitch.

One pull. One bullet.

The kickback is stronger on this gun, but she manages to keep it steady somehow. Then again, the human body is capable of miracles when a person is determined.

At close range, she blows his skull in with no remorse. No tears. No screams.

Instead, she watches as his head flies back and the wall behind him is a work of art—eccentric splatters of blood and other matter.

He's dead, and she's safe.

One more to go after I adjust the crime scene. I'll take what I need and leave a high—overdosing Brittany behind to take the fall for both murders.

"Are you ready, love?" I ask, coming to a stop behind London. She's in our bathroom putting on a pair of diamond earrings I gave her for this occasion. The dinner downstairs is in her honor and with a very special guest.

She's a vision in her white dress. A Grecian inspired.

An elegant yet sinfully sexy white lace dress with a deep V at the front and a long skirt. It's tight. Perfectly molds against every dip and curve with a side split that I plan to rip later and fuck her while she wears the tatters.

"Pervert." Her eyes meet mine in the mirror. Those ruby red lips and soft brown curls accentuate the cerulean of her eyes. How bright they are. How devilish she is.

Because while this little girl will always hold a certain air of innocence about her, she's no longer pure. London's taste are ever changing. Morphing. As the week since her kidnapping passed, she has come into her own.

She wants this life. With me.

Craves the darkness I control.

There isn't a single ounce of remorse for what she did, and I'm proud of her. Have let her lead when it comes to how the Foster story ends.

"For you? Always." My hands skim down her spine, and she shivers. Over her ass, and she lets out the sexiest kittenish sound. "Ready to play?"

"With you? Forever." She turns around, and in her heels almost reaches my chin, which she bites. "Now, let's go celebrate."

As we descend the stairs, the noise of conversations infiltrates and her smile grows. My family is here, and she loves them as much as they do her.

The formal dining room is full when we enter. My mother and father, Javier and Mariah, and lastly Marcus, sit around our table. All dressed to the nines, while the last, like he's been inside of a padded cell and is seeing the light for the first time in years. He's skittish. Afraid. *Pussy.*

"Evening." All voices cease as we enter, walking to the front where I pull out London's chair and she waves to the room. A whimper comes from the opposite end, but we ignore him as we take our place at the head.

"You two look rested," Mariah comments, bringing her glass of wine to her lips and taking a sip. "Playing hooky looks good on you."

"Best nap of my life," I reply, winking at my cousin while the others chuckle. Magda comes in then; her dress is all black and for mourning. She walks around the room in silence and places a plate in front of everyone with a domed lid. Every plate is empty except one.

His.

A starving Marcus that hasn't eaten in over three days.

"May I?" comes from where he sits, a low and meek voice that resembles nothing of the man he once was.

"You may, but first I have an important question for you, *sir*." I stand and walk across the room to where he sits and pull a chair out beside him. Sit and wait for him to have the decency to address me. "Aren't you curious?"

The position I have him in is the perfect vantage point for the cameras recording this, a live feed that Thiago is watching from his home in Miami. Because while he understands the cause and effect—the rapid pace in which Alton was killed or how it came to be—for this one he wants front row seats to the show. Something London agreed with wholeheartedly when I explained.

Was actually her idea that we find an encrypted server through the dark web. Something that with money isn't hard to do.

"Where's Alton," he asks, instead, hands clenching atop the table. "Where is my son?"

"You'll see him soon enough." A giggle escapes London, and Marcus looks at her. His eyes turn hard, cold—the hate toward her is palpable.

"Sorry." I know her, and she's anything but. "Just remembered something I heard a few days back."

"Behave, love," I chuckle and look back at an angry shell of a man. A man that can never hurt her again. Whose last minutes on this earth will be spent in total misery. Because for as much of a piece of shit as Marcus is, the asshole did love his son. Is going to die because of his innate ability to see no wrong in him. "Marcus, the reason I brought you here today is because I'd like to ask you for London's hand in marriage. I promise to always take care of her. Spoil her. Place the world at her feet because she deserves that and so much more. I love her."

He doesn't say a word. He's fuming in his silence.

"Oh, honey!" my mother exclaims from across the table, clapping her hands together in excitement. "I'm so happy for you both. She's perfect for you and this family."

"Welcome to the family, London." This time it's my father who talks, and he raises his glass in a toast they all follow. And still, no response from the man who raised her.

"See how happy she is? How fucking beautiful?"

"Bring me to Alton. I need to see my son."

"Of course. But first…" I lift the lid of his dome where a decent-size portion of a filet sits in a reduction sauce. Specially prepared for him. "Bon appetite."

"I'll wait until after—"

I slam a hand atop the table, tipping his goblet of water over. "Pick up that knife and fork before I shove the entire plate down your throat."

All eyes are on his as he does what I ask, picking up the utensils and cutting into the medium-rare piece of meat. His hand trembles as he brings the small bite to his mouth and chews. There is no savoring. No appreciative noises.

Almost as if he knows…

"Can I see him now?"

"Another bite."

"Please, I just—"

"Two more."

Marcus nods, picking up the next piece and practically swallowing. A dry swallow at that. Then another, larger this time. When he finishes, he pushes his plate away and looks at me with hopeful eyes.

"What?" I ask, not understanding the perplexity of his expression.

"Can I see him? No more games, Malcolm." He's near tears. Beyond desperate. "Just let me see my son."

"You already have. He's been here the entire time." I've never seen the world come down on a person's head before, and the interpretation in front of me is amusing. The look in his eye—the retching that follows as the tears pour from him—it's nothing compared to what they were willing to do to an innocent woman for monetary gain. Leaning forward, I meet his stare with a devilish grin. Neither conforming nor denying his worst night-mare. "Make of that what you will."

"No. NO!" He shoots up from his seat, his blazing eyes set on London. "This is all your fault. I'll kill you, bitch!"

"I pulled the trigger, too." Twirl taunts, her grin matching mine. "My face was the last one that sick bastard saw."

"After everything we did for you? How we took you and that cunt—" He doesn't get to finish his sentence as London shoots him square in the chest, creating a domino effect. My gun follows, as does every person inside this room. A bullet for each member, and then two more for her parents.

Marcus Foster bleeds out in my dining room, a mass of failure. A product of greed.

"Thank you," my girl says then, pulling my attention to her gorgeous eyes. They are happy. Full of relief. "And the answer is yes. A thousand times yes."

"It wasn't a question, sweetheart." Taking her hand in mine, I slip the large princess-cut diamond ring I've carried with me all day onto her ring finger. Where it will stay until we leave this earth. "You're mine, and I am yours. Fated."

"Still saying yes." She's admiring it. How perfectly it fits.

"Never though you wouldn't." I pull her out of her chair, leaving the others to receive my cleaning crew. While we celebrate out tonight with family and friends, they'll take care of the man that'll soon become a distant memory. Leave nothing behind like his son.

"So cocky, Mr. Asher."

"Look at me…" she does, and whatever she sees in my expression melts her against me "…I love you." It's my vow. A promise. My truth. There will never be anyone else for me. No one would ever compare to the perfection in my arms.

"I love you, too."

My lips come down on hers then, and the world fades away. Her taste overtakes my senses, and I let her. She's the only person in this world with the power to destroy me, and yet, I know that my home will always be at her temple.

My tiny dancer.

EPILOGUE 1
London

"YOU LOOK BEAUTIFUL, cousin. The bracelet from Grandma Isadora looks perfect," Aurora says from behind me as I stand in front of the mirror adjusting the Swarovski tiara Malcolm insists I wear. He didn't want a veil or anything to cover my face because his queen never hides. Even this dress; with the sweetheart neckline and mermaid-style bodice in lace—how the bottom curves over my behind, accentuating one of his favorite places to grab—was bought with him in mind.

To please him. See his eyes shine with hunger as he takes me in.

That man. *Christ*.

He's changed my life in the best of ways. Completely.

I'm no longer afraid. I'm no longer running.

Because of him I have a family, love, and a chance to be anything and everything I want to be. No rush. No expiration dates. He supports me.

Like my wanting to find Aurora and tell her immediately who I am. To build a relationship when she could've easily told me to disappear. It's because of him that I didn't chicken out. That I have someone from my side of the family to walk with us down the aisle of this beautiful cathedral.

Just like Earl and Mary give us their blessing on my mother's behalf.

"Thank you so much for coming, and for this." I lift my wrist and inspect the delicate tennis bracelet with diamonds and sapphires through-out. It's my something borrowed and blue. "Having a piece of the family to wear today means more than you'll ever know." Turning to face her, I take in her appearance in the elegant little black dress I chose for her and Mariah. Take in our similarities. Like our high cheekbones and skin tone. The plumpness of my lips that seems to come from my dad's side. "It means a lot that *you* could make it. That *you* wanted to do this."

"I'm going to flick you if you thank me again, chica. Stop it."

"Ass," I mutter, but she hears and smacks my arm.

"Dork."

"You bruise me, and you'll deal with Malcolm." In the last few months since we connected, if I say something like that she laughs and hits me again. Our relationship feels like what a sibling one should be—what I've missed out on. However, this time she gets a pensive look instead. "What gives? What's with the look?"

"How well do you know his groomsmen?"

"Which one?"

"British and a complete lying asshole."

"Casper?" I ask, thrown off by the change in her demeanor. "Did he do something to you?"

"Other than exist?" At my nod, she lets out a huff that's full of annoy-ance. "We don't click."

"Why?" Because I get the feeling there's something she isn't saying. "Do I need to involve—"

"No. It's me." Now she's petulant, almost looks close to stomping her feet, and I've never seen her so out of sorts. Like she…

"Do you like—"

"I'm coming in," Malcolm calls out through the door a second before barging in. His eyes fall on me immediately, hungry and calculating.

"Aurora, we need a moment before the ceremony. Please find Casper and let him know I'll be down soon."

For a second, I shift my stare toward her and see that she's fluffing her hair a bit. "Of course. Just behave, kiddos. Leave the fun stuff for the after…"

The second the door clicks behind her, he's on me. Turning me around to face the vanity, he lowers my zipper carefully and then pulls the dress down. Lets the expensive gown pool at my feet as he takes in my nakedness.

"No panties, Twirl. Such a beautiful little slut." His filthy words cause a moan to slip from my lips, for my thighs to rub together. The way he's looking at me. How hungry he is…

"Your slut. All yours."

He hums in the back of his throat as two fingers slide over my slit, rubbing my clit in firm strokes. "He likes her, you know. Acting a bit like me when I met you."

"*Fuck*, I know. She's interested." It's a whimper. A plea for more. "I'll hook them up later."

"Much later," Malcolm growls out, burying two fingers deep as my body bows into the pleasure. They move in and out of me at a face past, bringing me close to the edge so fast my knees almost give out. "Hold onto the edge, sweetheart. This is going to be rough and fast."

My knuckles dig into the edge of the counter, trembling as he lowers his zipper. The bulbous tip skims my opening and I clench, needing him inside. "Please, Mr. Asher. Take care of the ache you…fuck!"

He slams in, grabbing my hips to hold me up as I begin to fall forward. His hips are punishing, taking me with fast strokes. "Quiet, London. You don't want the priest to hear your moans. How much of a dirty little girl you are."

I nod, hearing the threat in his voice.

My Malcolm is possessive of me.

Will kill anyone who so much as looks and lingers, something I secretly love.

How protective he is of the women he loves. How he treats me like his most prized treasure.

He shifts my loose curls over my shoulder and kisses the base of my neck where his tattoo is. A tiny owl that mimics his, just cuter. Bold and wise; a symbol of how I see him.

"I need you, baby. All of you."

"Always." He knows my body. What makes me clench, tremble with pleasure, and on his next stroke angles his hips to hit that spot inside me. Each of his thrusts is precise, hard with an edge of pleasurable pain that I crave.

Those fingers on my hips dig in, bruising me, and I welcome the marks. Live for them. They're a reminder of our passion. This nearly psychotic need we can't control.

Malcolm brings a hand to my neck and squeezes. The hold is tight— another way to show his dominance over my female form. I love it. Him. How those fingers wrap around my throat and pull me back to his chest, deepening each thrust.

"Oh, God," I whimper, my mouth going slack as his breath comes to my ear, a harsh, panting groan against my skin before licking the shell.

"Come on me, Twirl. Mark me."

"Malcolm," I yell out, standing on the tip of my toes as a rush of warmth flows through my limbs. Building in its intensity. Pulsing until breathing is obsolete and I come with a brutality that brings forth his own release.

"Son of a bitch," he hisses, burying himself to the hilt as his cock pulses within my core. Rope after rope filling me—running down my thighs as I try to regulate my breathing. And yet, as I find the will to move, my eyes remain watching him through the mirror.

How he tucks himself back in and then fixes his shirt.

How he runs a hand through his perfect mess of hair.

He acts like nothing just happened, while I'm out of breath and with blushing cheeks.

My simple makeup isn't ruined. My hair just needs to be fluffed a bit.

However, one look at my bright eyes and smile, and you'll know.

"You did that on purpose." It's the first thing that comes out after a few minutes. Malcolm is kneeling at my feet now, pulling my dress up and zipping the back. He stands to fix my breasts next, lifting each one into the built-in cup with no shame on his handsome face.

Like he didn't just set me up to walk down the aisle with his come drying on my thighs.

"You look beautiful, by the way," he says, stepping into my space once more after deeming me ready. His smile is boyish. Happier than I've ever seen him. "Breathtaking."

"You clean up well yourself." I fix his lapel, straightening the slightly crooked rose inside his breast pocket. "My Prince Charming."

"More like a beast, but I'll take it." He dips his face to kiss my lips. Just a soft peck. "Cold feet, or burning on a hot sandy beach?"

"I'm toasty warm and ready to become Mrs. Asher."

"Well then..." he steps back to offer me his arm "...let me walk you down the aisle toward your forever."

I giggle at that. Crazy man. "Is that even allowed?"

"My wedding. My woman. My rules."

EPILOGUE 2
MALCOLM

LONDON STANDS WITH our little prince in her arms as our family surrounds them. My parents, Aurora, Mariah, and Javier are all here with their little one, Charlotte—a baby girl born almost nine months to the date after their wedding, and who owns Javi wholly.

Beside them is Stacy, who now runs the club for me as the majority shareholder as per Liam's will. Even being the bastard that he was, he made sure to take care of her the only way he knew how. He left everything to me that had to do with the club, making sure she wouldn't be out of employment.

She's a good employee who's proven herself loyal, has become a good friend to London, and who Carmelo adores.

A group of adults varying in age, and they're standing there watching the kids in action. One sleeping and being an angel, while mine is the center of attention.

But he was like that during the pregnancy, too. Kicking and shifting—keeping her up at night—but London always had a smile. So happy and grateful that we were starting a family after months of negative test results.

I knew it was the stress. That once her body began to relax and accept that her nightmare was over, it would happen.

And it did with the biggest blessing.

Maximus is awake now and clapping in that adorable way only toddlers can, with a cheesy grin, a head full of dark brown curls, and an enthusiastic disposition that has everyone in attendance eating out of the palm of his tiny hand.

Future dictator that he is.

Kids are brutal. Demanding. Lovable in that you-do-what-I-say-or-there'll-be-mutiny until I get my way. Like father. Like son.

And I want another one.

He reminds me of myself. Even at two years old, he's observant. Likes order and for his rules to be followed without complaint.

Makes me motherfucking proud while his mother just rolls her eyes. Tells us to chill or the one who runs the house will let us starve. My staff fears her more than me.

It's a beautiful thing.

London is kind and generous, but that kitten has very deep claws when it comes to how our home is run. She likes to be hands-on. Cooks and cleans, only asking for help if it's too high or her attention is needed elsewhere.

Over the years, I have learned to not fight this. A happy wife means a happy life, and I like getting my dick wet every night.

"Congratulations, bloke," Casper says, walking up to me from the crowd and giving me a hug. He's smirking at me, while his eyes stray every few minutes toward a giggling Aurora. She's ignoring him while making faces at my son, and you can see how frustrated he is by her refusal. Something happened between them while we were on our honeymoon, yet neither wants to explain. "Not many have the guts that you do, Asher. Out in the open like this..."

"Interpol can look but can't touch. Not in this country, at least." With the success of my Shanghai location, I've built two more in major Asian cities. The ribbon-cutting ceremony today for the Hong Kong building in the middle of their financial district is my largest. My customers here include a few syndicates, but the main source of transactions come from the counterfeit market: the purses, shoes, and clothing that are sold in the States and in a massive quantity.

Those items are produced all over Asia, but they come to this location to secretly deliver deposits. China would be too obvious for those following the paper trail, and it doesn't hurt that the government here loves me.

Love my business motto and the money I bring to the country's economy.

If they thrive, no one asks stupid questions. Cheeks turn while they shake your hand.

"You have my respect."

"And money. Don't forget that." My eyes scan the large crowd, and I spot a few of my other clients milling about, each with their families and happily celebrating out in the open with no fear of repercussion. My success is to their benefit.

As my empire grows, so do the risks. However, the rewards outweigh them.

Money rules the world, and I dominate the market.

That's what sets me apart. The fact that I have no fear.

"Very true, and I also think it's time our families grow. Unite."

"What do you have in mind?"

"Is London still looking to sell her childhood home?" Once more his eyes flick toward my wife's cousin.

I raise a brow and nod. "Yeah, why?"

"Is Aurora still working at the foundation with her?"

"Yes."

"Then Chicago is about to become my permanent home base."

Two warm hands wrap around my midsection then, interrupting, and a head sneaks under my arm. "Hello, gentlemen."

"Hello, Mrs. Asher." Her smile is wide, so fucking sweet each time I call her that. "Ready to go?"

"Just about. I'm waiting for Aurora to leave with Sam—"

"Who the fuc...fudgesicle is Sam?" Casper corrects himself quickly, shooting us an apologetic look. "Where is she going?"

"Aurora?" She's playing coy, and I narrow my eyes.

"Yes," Casper grits out, his eyes on the woman standing a few feet from us and talking to a couple from the new office here.

"She said something about a prior engagement with Sam. Not sure if it's the guy, or..." And just like that, Casper stalks off in her direction. We hear the gasp that follows, a curse or two, and then the crowd laughs as he throws her over his shoulder and leaves. Not that Aurora put up much of a fight. Even from her upside down position, I can see the sly grin she's fighting back.

The same one her cousin isn't.

"Who was the mastermind?"

"I have no idea what you're talking about, husband. I'm an angel."

Wrapping my arm around her waist, I pull her in close and lean down just enough to nuzzle the soft skin of her neck. "I'm going to punish you for that lie. Make you choke on my cock as you beg for forgiveness."

"Promise," she mewls low, smiling out into the crowd. "Are you going to make it hurt?"

"Where's Maximus?" My lips kiss the shell of her ear.

"Your parents are taking him. Giving us the night off to explore the city."

"Is that so?" Her nod is my reply. "Then head upstairs to my office and strip down, Twirl. You're going to dance for me like that first night before I split you in two. I want us to explore the option of baby number two and make it a reality."

"I don't think that's necessary." The tone she uses makes me pause and pull back enough to look into her eyes. The radiant blue is glistening with unshed tears while her bottom lip trembles. In that moment as reality hits me, I fall in love with her all over again and thank God for putting her in my path. For gifting me the privilege of loving her. "I found out a few days ago, Mr. Daddy. Asher baby number two is already on its way and growing strong."

"I love you so much, London. So fucking much." Without giving a single fuck about the people around us, I lift her into my arms and leave the stage toward my building. I don't stop until we're alone and locked away at the very top overlooking the city.

Not until her clothes and mine lay in tatters somewhere by my desk.

Not until I feel her bare skin against mine and I'm buried deep inside her against the floor-to-ceiling windows. Her back to my chest.

Because this is where I find my heaven. The temple I repent to.

I love her slowly. Tenderly.

Thanking her with every kiss for giving me my babies. For trusting me with her heart.

I pour my heart out to her with every thrust. With every moan I draw from her shaking body, and when she reaches her peak and turns to look at me from over her shoulder, I whisper, "I love you," into her mouth as we break apart and come together again.

My life is crazy. Thrives on danger and moments of chaos.

Yet with her I find my balance.

The reason to be a better man.

And I'll spend the rest of my life ruling this world so I can gift it to her every single night.

She will always be my Twirl. My best friend. My queen.

CASPER JAMESON

I'm a sinner. A criminal.
The beast that will never let her go...

Everyone in England knows the name Casper Jameson. They know that I'm a cruel bastard with no regrets when it comes to dealing with those that cross me. They fear me; a man with no morals. Someone cold—without a weakness.
Until I see her...

She's beautiful; a delicious temptation standing across the room from me without a care. Unaware of the danger that lurks—that this man wants to consume her.

I'm going to own her every sigh.

Taste her every moan.

Drown in her pleasure.

Let the bloody chase begin.

CASPER

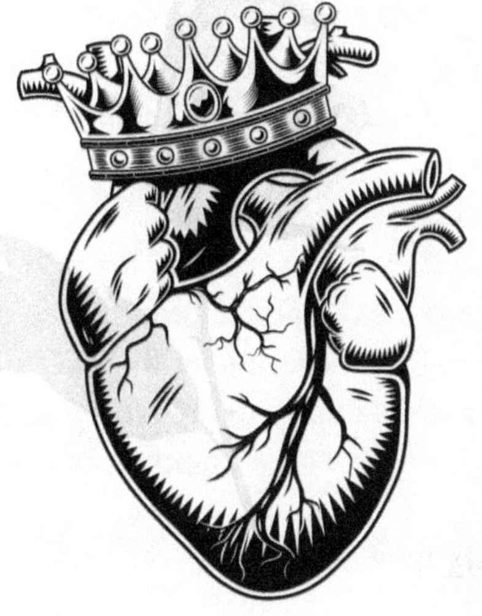

"**S**CREAM FOR ME," I whisper against her soft skin, licking the few beads of sweat that roll down the back of her neck. Tasting. Savoring this decadent little body that caught my bloody attention just a mere three hours ago. "Say my name, love."

My demand is met with more wetness. She's swollen; ready to be fucked like the horny little beauty she is. Like my perfect dirty fantasy.

This woman is a temptation I shouldn't imbibe tonight, but I ignore rationality and indulge. Take without concern for the state of my business or my family. With her skin against mine, I don't give a fuck about the gun shipment we lost forty-eight hours ago because of some bloke's incompetency. Because of his greed.

A reality that is dangerous. For myself. For her.

I should be ending that man as we speak, but I'm not. I should be spilling his blood as payment, but I'm here, and God himself couldn't pull me away from *Aurora*.

"Please," the beauty against me mewls, and I throb against her core. I focus on her wetness as it rolls down my girth, caressing every solid inch as I slide between soft, bare lips. Thrusting twice, I spread her slickness while my pierced head rubs against her clit from behind.

Her back is to my chest. Her body against the solid wood of my door.

She's made me break my rules.

I brought her home. For her, I've behaved like the good little boy I'm not, until the moment we stepped foot inside my manor. Now, all bets are off. Moreover, waiting to reach my bed when my hunger's near demonic is impossible.

My need is almost debilitating. It controls me.

And I'm going to make sure she feels me for days after.

This little one-off has me throbbing, beads of pre-come mixing with her slick cunt as I pull back from between her thighs. Thighs that still hold her silk panties midway down, limiting her movements. Her little black dress, the kind that doesn't allow for a bra, is thrown somewhere behind me along with my clothes.

In our haste, everything was ripped off almost savagely and left in tatters.

"Oh God." Another whine comes from the back of her throat, a needy little sound that travels straight down the center of my spine and settles on the tip of my length. Her hips undulate, trying to rub faster—to create the friction that I'm denying her. "Don't toy with me. I need you to...*fuck!*"

"Louder," I say with a groan, slamming inside in one fluid thrust and then pulling back slowly, just far enough so the head touches her entrance —caressing the tiny hole that clenches in search of more. "I want everyone on this street to hear whose cock you want." Pressing my lips against the back of her neck, I inhale deeply, pulling the soft scent of cherry blossoms with a hint of vanilla deep into my lungs. "Say it, sweetheart. Tell them who you're crying out for."

And I'll gift her my cock, as much as she wants it tonight, but first I want to breathe in her need for me. I'll feed off that desperation that show-cases our humanity, giving in to its animalistic nature.

"If you don't move, I have a hand—" She doesn't finish, choking instead on her cry of pleasurable pain as I snap my hips forward. My strokes are relentless, almost punishing, but my sweet victim takes it with her head thrown back, meeting me thrust for thrust.

Grabbing a fistful of dark hair, I turn her head toward me and take her lips in a heated kiss. It's sloppy and hard for her to concentrate, but I don't slow down. Instead, I enjoy how lost she is to the pleasure.

It's intoxicating. Delicious.

I revel in her cries. How her fingernails dig into the wooden door. How she rises onto the tips of her toes as I hit a particular spot deep inside when I change the angle of my thrusts.

"What were you saying?" I taunt, mimicking her American accent. There's a Chicagoan lilt to her tone that I find sexy and ironic; she's from the same city I spend a couple of months in each year. *Dangerous indeed.* "You were threatening me?"

"Who the hell...*oh God*!" she cries out, a sweet sound I revel in as I hold her in place, fingers digging in to the point where I know she'll walk away with my mark. And I like the thought. More than I should.

It's frustration and want and everything we shouldn't crave, but motherfuck, it feels good. Too bloody good. Being buried balls deep as her body trembles in my hold, fighting to move and reach the orgasm she so desperately yearns for, is nothing short of nirvana.

Releasing her hair, I bring my hand down between us and smack her clit with two fingers.

Her reaction is automatic; pussy clenching and body arching against me. A harsh shiver runs down her body and into my own, causing my eyes to close.

The feel of her walls choking my cock is heaven.

The screams of pleasure are my brand of heroin.

"You are going to be nothing but trouble," I hiss from between clenched teeth, my eyes on the way her arse bounces against my thighs. It's obscene, the sight of her tight body taking everything I give her. Skin slapping against skin, I fuck her with no remorse. Without reprieve. "Such a beautiful chaos."

"Please, Casper." A gorgeous surrender. Her eyes meet mine from over her shoulder, heavy-lidded and hazy with lust. "*Fuck*, I'm so close."

She's a vocal one, and I love it. Love each sound that slips past that pouty mouth, a delicious shade of red that I've kissed off and spread down her cheek.

Aurora looks like the sweetest mess for me. Like a bad decision under the design of a priceless jewel.

Like a gem. The kind I'll covet.

"You want to come?"

"I need—"

"Me." It's a growl. An angry sound that erupts from deep within my chest and I pause my movements, keeping myself deep within her walls. "Say it. You need me to make you come."

"I do." It's low and breathy, and my balls grow heavy with those two words.

However, I need more. It's a nagging little voice in the back of my head that demands I make this right.

I need to see her.

Watch her face as she comes.

A hiss escapes me as I pull out, my hardness immediately missing her warmth, but I grit my teeth and before Aurora can protest, I flip her position. On her next breath, I have what's left of her panties in my fist and I slam her back against the door with those perfect thighs around my waist.

Her sweet pussy sits just above my cock. Her juices coat the head in a soft caress.

"What are—"

"Hold on to me." That's the only warning I give her, letting go of the ruined fabric as I drop her weight, sliding back inside in one forceful thrust. One hand cradles the back of her neck, keeping our lips pressed as I maneuver her hips with the other. I'm not gentle. There's nothing soft about the way I guide her over my length.

Fast and hard. Near painful.

The only part of her touching the door is her upper back, and even then, it's almost hovering. Aurora arches, body bowing in my hold as pleasure rocks her small frame. And yet, as my assault rises into a nearly manic state, her pussy grips me tighter—almost holding me hostage.

If that's what she wants...

"Motherfuck," I grit out, slamming inside once more and then holding still. Her pussy massages my length, walls pulsing. "Shit, Gem...you're going to pull the come from me just like this." Slipping a hand between us,

I ignore the use of the nickname and place my thumb over her clit, adding pressure. Just hold it there as her hips do all the work. She's wild against me, body moving, hips gyrating as she rides me in small little strokes. "That's it, love. You feel so good."

It's the most exquisite pain.

"It's never been like this," she moans out, fingernails digging into my shoulders as she uses them for leverage. Taking her pleasure from me, and while I'm a man that dominates in every facet of his life, I find this incredibly sexy. Watching her has my abs contracting—muscles coiling—as I fight the urge to take the control back. "Why?"

A question I don't have the answer to. It's never been like this for me either.

Never have I yearned to watch a woman fall apart in my arms. To drown in her pleasure.

Moreover, I'm not ready to analyze it. Not yet.

"Come for me." I massage her trembling bundle of nerves, hard little circles that cause her eyes to roll back. That won't do. Not at all. I need her pretty hazel eyes on mine. "Look at me."

At once, they do as I say. Her stare locks on mine.

I inhale her exhale, lips sweeping against hers.

"I'm so close, Casper."

"Then fall." I tap her clit with two fingers. "Give me what I want." Bringing both hands to her hips, I hold her tight and then raise her above the head. Just high enough that the swollen tip can slip inside without guidance. "Come for me."

"Need more." A tear. A plea.

"You only need what I give you." Then, because I'm an arsehole, I drop her once more. Without an ounce of care, I impale her—gift her that last push over the proverbial edge she needs. It's pleasure and pain, and the feel of her release is my sweetest torture.

"*Fuck.*" One word sums up our need perfectly. My hips piston in and out of her warmth as she comes with a scream, and a light sheen of sweat shines across her flesh. My mouth waters at the sight of her wild abandonment and I lick her chin, biting down on the soft skin as I follow her into bliss.

Her orgasm slams into me, milking my cock with each pulse of her walls. It's tight and hot. Messy. *Perfect.*

"Christ." I'm panting against her lips, kissing her slowly as spurt after spurt leaves me, mixing with her juices as I keep a slow and steady pace. My strokes keep her on the edge, riding her release until she becomes sensitive and clingy—holding onto me with her arms and legs, pulling me closer.

I almost hate how perfect she feels. Almost.

After a few minutes of trying to calm her breathing, Aurora pulls her face from mine, a now shy smile on her lips. "Wow."

I chuckle at that, pushing her matted hair back from her face. "Agreed, love. Agreed."

We don't move. Both just watch the other.

Neither give a fuck that our mess is running down my cock and probably splattering the marble floors beneath us. At this moment, nothing else matters. Not even the ringing of my mobile somewhere in the background can pull me away from her.

Those warm and sated eyes.

Those kiss-swollen lips.

That rich, dark hair that curls down the middle of her back.

And it's that kind of power that pulls the next few words from my lips.

It's without conscious thought. Without giving a shit about the consequences.

I'll deal with whatever comes...*later.*

"Spend the weekend with me?"

CASPER

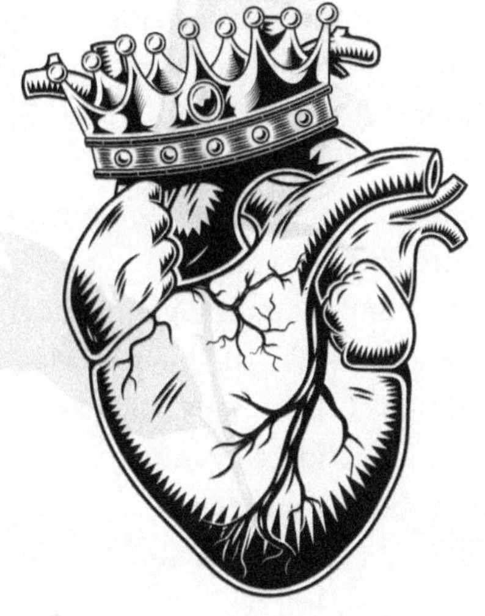

I NOTICE HER the bloody second she comes into the room. There's a shift in the air, a different kind of energy that sweeps over my over six-foot-two frame as I take in every delicate detail of her body. How she walks. How the little black dress she wears clings to each sinuous curve.

This girl commands the attention of every drunk arsehole without an ounce of effort.

From my seat, I have a view of every inch of this pub; from its entrance to the bar, to the small dance floor off to my left where bodies grind to the beat of some chart-topping artist. The place is full to the brim, and yet, she's all I see. All I can seem to focus on, taking into account every minute detail while all around me people continue to slam back pint after pint.

Each swing of her hips is a call to the animal within. A taunt.

The woman she's with stops a few tables from the one I'm occupying near the back with my men: a setup of high-top seating, and along the wall, two private booths. They greet another couple already sitting there with a small handshake, though hers is more on the distant side, the kind you give a stranger. A bit timid.

She shifts a bit—head bobbing to the music—and I follow the move, lowering my eyes to roam her small frame and liking the way her hip juts a bit to the side. Naturally coquettish, she's small but thick where it counts. Young, but legal. A beautiful little thing with the face of an angel and a body made to worship. At no more than five foot three and no older than twenty-two, she's all hips and thighs and has a gorgeous face with hazel eyes and plump, berry-colored lips.

Moreover, it's that mouth that first caught my attention.

How she throws her head back, laughing at what someone at the table says. How carefree she looks. How those lips stretch wide and her eyes close for a brief moment before meeting mine.

We hold each other's stare. Not moving.

And then that mouth parts in slow motion, her tiny pink tongue peeking out to sweep across her bottom lip, sealing her fate. At that moment, every single thought of retribution leaves my mind. My hunger morphs into something wickedly delicious.

I need that tight body on her knees.

I want her breasts encasing my thick cock as I slide between them.

I want her wetness running down my length, bathing me as those hazel orbs stay on mine.

"Sir, are you all right?" someone says from beside me, but I pay them no mind. Not when my prey turns as some bloke taps her bare shoulder. I'm out of my seat and across the room before I can register the action, but there's no ignoring the red-hot ire that burns through my veins at the sight of the pompous wanker.

I want to punch the idiot. Break the hand he touched her with, but before that can happen, he catches my eyes and pales, stumbling in his haste to get away.

Then, I'm five steps from her and pause as my rage turns into an inferno of lust. My hunger renews as the soft scent of cherry blossoms infiltrates my senses, and I bite back a groan. It's all her. The temptation and want and this lust that has me throbbing—beads of pre-come already rolling down the tip and shaft.

It's also why I take the remaining steps and bend to place my lips next to her ear. Why I revel in the way she shivers for me. "What's your name, love?"

THE NEXT MORNING I awake to her weight on my chest. To the same hunger that propelled me to take her—to manipulate this doll to my liking for hours on end—until she finally cried out in defeat.

Spent and exhausted, Aurora fell on top of me and didn't move. Not even when I placed her beside me so I could clean up, and then came back with a washcloth to wipe the evidence of my hunger from her inner thighs. Thighs that now bear perfect little marks in the shape of my fingertips, light purple and spread about—from her upper legs to those supple hips— that stand out against her lightly tanned skin.

They are the perfect reminder of the pleasure I gave her. Of what she willingly gave to me.

I also recognize that there's no sense of panic in me.

We didn't use a condom. There hadn't been anything to dispose of, and yet, I don't have a single worry about *what could be* or the *what ifs*. My mind is at ease for once. Calm.

A foreign feeling, but I'm not questioning it either as her words from last night come back to the forefront; a mumbled confession as I pushed her against the door after slamming it closed and taking possession of her sweet mouth in a kiss. It was a promise. A plea for me not to stop.

I'm clean and on the pill. Christ...you're so...I-I haven't been with anyone in over a year since my last breakup.

And I gave in after my own reassurance of being clean. Over and over.

"Why my pub, Gem?" At my question, she lets out a cute sigh and snuggles closer, burrowing her nose into the crook of my neck. The sensation tickles, but I don't want to move her. Take away the sweet warmth of her pussy so close to my cock.

If anything, I want to bury myself deep within those walls once more. Hear her screams.

"Casper," she whimpers low in her slumber, lips skimming across my skin in an unconscious taunt. I'm hard—throbbing—as I press my length against her bare leg over my hip. It's a dangerous position for her. Too easy for me.

All I need to do is move a little lower and...

I'm interrupted by the obnoxious ringing of my mobile atop my night-stand; it's loud within the silence of the room and I worry it'll wake her up, however, she doesn't so much as stir.

Gem is definitely a heavy sleeper, I muse; a low chuckle vibrates through my chest as the device rings three times and then goes to voice-mail. There's a beep that follows, a few seconds of silence, and then the blasted tone blares again, causing my amusement to cease.

The person on the other end is a persistent arsehole.

I also know why he's calling. What he's waiting on.

Life or death; it's a delicate balance that I control with a flick of a finger. With the sharp edge of my blade.

It's mine to decide—to take their last breath—and I close my eyes for just a second. Just a little longer, and those two deep breaths give me a moment to take in her softness and how at ease I feel with her near.

And with that ease comes another dose of reality:

The thought of getting rid of her hasn't crossed my mind once.

It's the opposite. Something I don't quite understand yet, but I want her here.

She's a reprieve. She's not just a fuck that I can ignore after.

Aurora is someone I want to see again. *Have again.*

My phone beeps then with an incoming text and I carefully move Gem, settling her against the space I vacate. It's selfish of me to want her here with the kind of business I run, but I'm greedy if nothing else. Hold no remorse over it. Something about this woman has caught my attention, holding it captive while making me crave more.

Of her. Of us.

Of the explosion I barely got a taste of last night. Those hours weren't enough.

Leaning over her slumbering form, I press my lips to hers while inhaling the scent of sex and cherry blossoms that still lingers on her skin. It soothes me. A seduction, and I'm more than tempted to crawl back onto the bed and part those legs so I can explore her heat once more, but I don't.

Instead, I whisper *soon* against the pillowy flesh of her mouth, nipping her bottom lip a final time before backing away. *We're not done.* And it's the bloody truth.

Naked and rock hard, I grab my phone and send off a quick text to the cock-blocker without reading his message. He will know what it means. What I expect.

Twenty. ~Jameson

Just as soon as he received it, three dots appear on my screen. However, I don't wait to read his confirmation. I'm already walking across the room and into my closet to pick out something to wear. And it takes less than three minutes to do so, grabbing a pair of denim trousers and a simple black vest without underwear.

I don't like them.

The guest bath I'll use is downstairs and as I exit the room, I pause to look over at a slumbering Gem one last time. To take in how tiny and decadent she looks. To acknowledge how her allure, the pull, is just as strong as it was last night.

Complications can be fun.

And a complication she is.

The second the door closes, there's a shift in me. Raw and ireful energy. With each step I take down the stairs—away from her temptation— I welcome the change that courses through my body.

The space between us brings back the cruel animal in me. The devil beneath the facade of a saint.

The real me.

Entering the bathroom, my eyes shift toward the large mirror and I take in my expression for a second. Gone is the smile I had for her. Gone is my relaxed state. What looks back at me is a killer.

I'm a handsome face with a cruel smile.

Green eyes that seem to glow in the lighting of this room.

Muscles that coil as I remember the two hours before noticing her:

The final report from the dock where the theft took place.

The surveillance photos of that night.

The proof of who sold the merchandise. Who bought it.

My men had forty-eight hours to gather every last bit of evidence on the betrayer and buyer. Whose name is attached. Every bloody fucking detail sits atop my desk inside the pub where I met Aurora.

"Blessed be the wicked," I tell my reflection and then walk toward the shower, turning the setting to my liking. Steam builds rather quickly within the grey and white bathroom, the water coming down from four shower-heads with various pressure settings as I step inside. It cascades down my back, but I feel no relief, nothing but a craving for retribution that grows with each tick of the clock.

I don't linger as I'd like to. I don't jerk off to take the edge off my hunger for her, like I need to.

Instead, my neck stiffens further as the weight of this family finds its rightful place: back on my shoulders. I stretch it from side to side, causing a loud pop to ring throughout the shower, and yet, the tension doesn't lessen. If anything, it becomes more pronounced. Aggravated by the blatant disrespect to those I care about.

Nothing happens in London without my knowledge. Without my approval.

And yet, someone decided to play God for the day and stole from me.

It's an insult. A slap to the face. *They put an innocent in danger.*

I'm also calculating. Taking into consideration her sleeping form upstairs.

Because she will know the truth. She will run. Something inevitable, and it fucks with my already vexed mood.

"Why are you really in London, Gem?" I mutter low, making my way out of the bathroom once dressed. My manor in the Kensington area is sacred and always protected. And while it's Sunday and my staff has the day off, I have three guards and my two male boxers—outside these walls —to keep those who are curiously stupid, out.

These men will lay down their lives for me. Are loyal. Hold no qualms about shooting first.

They also know to never enter without permission, so when a knock comes as I head toward my office on the opposite end of the house, I make them wait. Family or not—my men or not—it doesn't matter.

It's a rule taken straight from my own version of the ten commandments:

In this world, I am their King.

The one responsible for their fate.

A male shadow looms through the frosted glass of the front door. "Oi, you in there, bro?" Another knock sounds, a bit harder this time, and I walk over, pulling the front door open so my guest can come inside.

"Don't make another sound," I spit out, eyes narrowing at the man who looks a lot like me, just six years younger than my thirty-two. "My office, and no deviations."

"Rough night, mate?" my cousin, Callum, jokes while raising a brow. His lips are quirked up at the corner, a shitty smirk that all the men in my family seem to have. "That pretty little thing not—"

"Don't." That's all I say, and the amusement drops from his face. In this moment I'm not family, I'm his boss. He eyes me for a second but doesn't comment. Instead, he nods and walks off in the direction of my home office, entering, while my eyes shift briefly toward another room at the top of the stairs.

Last night I gave in to her temptation and let the game of Russian Roulette take its natural course, however, today is different. I don't regret Gem, my time with her, but that must all take a back seat for now as I walk in a minute after Callum.

Even if I have to chase, she'll be my reward after.

The space is large and holds an air of old luxury that intimidates most that enter. The interior furniture is a mixture of dark and natural tones, wall-to-wall built-in bookcases to the left, and a large desk in an imported teak wood that sits center stage. The walls are painted in a deep royal blue with one white stripe at the center of each.

Rare Gothic paintings litter my walls—expensive and found throughout the black market—that depict the depraved curiosity people have with death. Demons, blood, and sexual deviancy stare back at you no matter where you sit, and it makes even the most decorated killers uncomfortable.

Then, there is a collection of weapons on display. Old and new. My favorites, and a few cruel contraptions from the medieval ages with purposes that reek of horror.

Some are loaded. Some no longer work. Some still hold a few dried drops of blood from their last kill.

And right there in the middle of it all sits someone I trust with my life. Waiting. Callum has questions, but he won't ask. Instead, he cracks his somewhat bruised knuckles.

"Did he give you that much of a fight?" I ask, tilting my head in the direction of his hands as I pause beside the chair next to his.

"Nah. That's just the consequence of fighting a spider," he says, holding two fingers together to show me its size. "Bloody thing kept running."

"What kind?" The phone in my pocket buzzes with an alert and I pull it out, swiping my finger across the screen. It's the motion-detection camera near the stairs and it shows Aurora stumbling down still half asleep, wearing my vest. Looking for me.

From the screen, I watch Gem continue down and catch glimpses of her from different angles. There are so many directions she could head, but as if pulled by an invisible string, her steps come closer across the foyer, and it's that camera with her face in my line of sight that I focus on.

"Daddy long-legs."

"Are you fucking kidding me?" I bark out a laugh to help guide Gem. Walking around the desk to take a seat, I place the phone against my computer monitor so only I can see. *That's it, sweetheart. A little bit more.* "Let me guess…you gave the wall a bunch of fives to kill it?"

"It was an instinctual reaction." No shame for his stupidity. Instead, he shrugs while stretching his hand out. "Caught the bloke on the third punch. Not that bad."

"And Otto?" Because while his story is entertaining, it's unimportant. That, and this will kill two birds with one stone. "Where's the cunt now?"

"Taking a nap near the Eye. I transferred him before coming here."

"Good." Most people don't pay attention to their surroundings, especially those that are vacationing. A tourist destination is the perfect way to mask the danger that lurks. You blend in. No one looks at you twice. No one asks questions as they imbibe the spirits you serve.

This business is overlooked on the daily as just another pub. A large two-story building with a roof-top establishment, a kitchen down below, and a hidden floor beneath where no one is allowed without my presence. And I like it that way. To hide in plain sight.

Every single one of my endeavors is the same way.

"Have you decided yet?" he asks then, pushing his hair back from his face. While mine is the same dirty blond color, his is long enough to keep in a bun. "Because what that son of a bitch did doesn't deserve your mercy."

"Is that your suggestion?" From my periphery I see a shadow loom near the still open door. There's no going back. "That he die?"

"Yes, but you know I'll follow your lead, cousin."

"I know." Reaching over, I open the top drawer to my right while looking at him to avoid the temptation of seeking her out. My favorite toys in the world lay there; two steel karambits with silver handles given to me on my sixteenth birthday by my grandfather. They're both engraved with my name on the curved, four-inch blade; a sleek and deadly design that lets me get close enough to feel the flesh give way beneath my assault.

Taking one out, I slip one finger through the circular end and the rest around the handle tightly. The weight feels good in my hold. Like an extension of me.

"Are we—"

"He pays in blood." There's a low gasp from just outside the door, so low that Callum misses it but I don't. I also don't miss how she rushes away and up my stairs to probably get dressed and then flee. That's okay, though...

I won't allow her to get far.

Not after how good she felt beneath my fingertips. How *right* we were.

She was tantalizing. Delicious. A cock-hardening manifestation of femininity that will try and slip through my fingers but won't get far.

I will chase.

We're not over.

Aurora

"**W**HAT THE HELL is wrong with me?" I ask myself for the hundredth time, rushing up a stranger's staircase with my torn dress in hand—stumbling in my haste to find anything to wear and leave. To get the hell away from someone I have no business being near, much less sleeping with.

I let his smile last night lower my inhibitions. Let the feel of his fingertips skimming my arm guide me closer.

A mistake. Monumental.

Christ, I'm an idiot.

Fear and lust and desire still linger over my skin. I feel him. His touch.

And I hate how I love it. How I crave him again. How even after I heard him sentence someone to death, I want more.

Of his danger. Of how he made me come alive last night.

Of the pleasure...

But I can't. Casper Jameson is something that can never be. He's the physical embodiment of what I'll always run from.

"Get it together and focus, Aurora." His room is in my line of sight and

I enter, running inside while I avoid looking at his bed, a large, king-sized monstrosity with an almost black wooden frame and headboard. It's regal. The lines are sexy, and it sits in the center of the room with soft white sheets strewn about.

It's the mess we made. Where he took me over and over again for hours on end.

Where I let him.

My thighs clench, the slight sting of pain making me look down and lift the seam of his shirt that smells just like him—woodsy with a hint of whiskey—that I found lying over a large chair in the corner of the room. It's a white Oxford that fits me like a dress, and it also made me blind to the marks he's left behind.

His fingertips. His touch.

It's more proof of my idiocy. A map of his desire.

"It's a one-night stand and nothing more." I repeat these words three times, taking in deep breaths as my heart accelerates. As my hands begin to shake. "Get in and get out."

My head whips from side to side, searching for anything else I can wear because his shirt, without panties, won't do. He tore them from me last night, leaving them unwearable. That, and I don't have the time to search them out.

I need to get far enough to call a cab before he comes up. Finds out where the hell I am.

That's when I take in an armoire on the left wall. It's large, a piece from the same line as his bed frame, and should have what I need. At least, I hope.

Walking over the sheet I let fall off my body when I went looking for him, I reach the large piece in a few steps. I'm on autopilot as I open the first two drawers and find plain undershirts. The one below has some gym clothes, and so on. Each one is full to the brim with things that don't fit my much smaller frame, and I toss everything onto the floor before noticing a pair of basketball shorts that I think will be a bit tight on him.

"These will have to do." Slipping them up my hips, I realize immediately just how wrong I am and almost laugh. Almost. They're huge, and

I'm running out of time. He could come up at any minute and see the mess I'm making.

Tying the strings of the shorts as tightly as I can, I roll the waist twice and then test them by shaking my hips from side to side a few times. They fall a bit, but not enough that I will become bottomless as I walk. *Good enough.*

Next, I begin the search for my shoes. The problem with that is the heels won't work.

They'll be a hindrance. Slow me down.

"Bingo," I mutter low, opening a drawer to find socks. Lots of them. In all styles. Which makes it perfect since the kind I'll need sits atop the bunch and to the right, an old-school pair of over-the-calf socks with two black bands across the top. I put them on; they're large but perfect, warming my legs while covering me to the knees.

Sure, I look like a clown, but I'm covered and comfy. Now all I need is my...

"Crap, my purse." Last night in our rush, I tossed it somewhere behind him, not caring about the contents inside. My phone and wallet are inside, and so is the hotel's keycard and a card with the address. "I'm such an idiot."

It's also the reason why I've never had a one-night stand before. The uncertainty. The danger of an unknown person and their true intentions.

And yet you let him have you so easily. Can't deny that. The intensity as our eyes met across the room, charming green on my hazel, and then the heat that scorched my veins. The harsh lick of desire rolled down my spine as he sipped his drink, never taking his gaze from mine.

It made me weak. It made me want to take a chance.

And now here I am. Paying the price.

My breathing picks up a bit at the thought of seeing him again. Of being close to a man that is wrong for me.

The kind my mother warned me about.

Of not having an out.

"Just go downstairs and explain my family is waiting on me." It's not a lie per se. Just that our meeting was yesterday, not today, but he doesn't need to know that. It'd give me just enough time to—

A door opens and closes loudly downstairs, then nothing. No noise. No footsteps coming up the stairs.

Unconsciously, I move toward this room's entrance, turning the knob and then pulling it open just a smidge. Just enough that I see no one in the corridor or near the top of the stairs. Moreover, at that very moment, I release the breath I didn't realize I was holding in.

He's nowhere in sight and that works for me, gives me the opening I need. That maybe, just maybe, I won't see him again.

As soon as the thought crosses my mind, I feel a pang in my chest—a tiny and annoying thump that I ignore for the time being. If not forever. Deciphering what it means could be disastrous for me.

A repeating of the cycle.

Opening the door further, I tiptoe out and toward the stairs, making as little noise as possible. My heart rate accelerates, beating faster with each step closer to the top landing. Even more so when I notice a figure, tall and intimidating, near the door and to the right. Fear and excitement course through my veins, but I don't stop.

I'm on autopilot. Moving without conscious thought until I meet the eyes of the person there.

It's not him. Not even close.

This man is dressed in a black suit, his features hard and that of an older man, maybe in his late forties. His appearance is serious, and yet there's a hint of a smile that comes through as he reads the disappointed expression on my face. It's unavoidable. Can't hide it.

Confusion with a hint of regret simmers, and my heart does that stupid thump once more. I should be happy, but I'm not. I should be relieved, but instead, all I feel is used. Unimportant and stupid for making a big deal of what obviously isn't.

There stands this stranger with my purse in hand, waiting for me, while I was just another notch on his bedpost. An easy lay.

"I'm an idiot." All that worry for nothing when he wants me gone; a realization that stings and confuses me further. This is exactly what I should want. What I need.

"What was that, Miss?" he asks, voice rough as if he's a heavy smoker, while he moves closer to the bottom step. "Everything okay? Do I need to call Mr. Jameson—"

"No."

At my quick denial, he nods and holds out his hand with my belongings. "In that case, the car is ready when you are."

"The car?"

"I've been instructed to deliver you back to your hotel."

"Lead the way, then." What else can I say? I feel dismissed. Like a fool.

Luckily, the man does as I ask without further prompting, turning on his heel to open the front door where I see a sleek black sedan waiting for me. Its ignition is already on, and before I can reach for the door's handle, he's rushing to open it, letting the muted thud of the front door closing follow close behind.

A sound that reeks of finality. Of a goodbye I should want but bothers me when just a few minutes prior, I wanted to leave.

Doesn't matter anymore. It's for the best.

And it is. Casper Jameson isn't someone I need to further mix myself with.

Silence fills the inside of the car, a looming quiet that makes the voice in my head loud. Wondering. Questioning the last twelve hours and my actions.

Why did I sleep with him?

Why do I feel so restless?

My mind is a constant loop, an uncensored movie reel of our night together and then what I heard from outside his office. Moreover, there's a miniscule part of me that knew to not go home with him, and I still did.

"What's your name, love?" a deep, husky voice whispers in an English accent, lips lightly brushing the shell of my ear from behind. He's close. Close enough that the scent of whiskey with a touch of wood and spice infiltrates my senses, and I bite back my hum of approval.

It's sexy. Alluring. I also know who it is before turning around.

His heavy-lidded eyes have been following me throughout the roof-top pub for the last thirty minutes, almost since the very moment I walked in. Tempting me. Causing my nipples to tighten in anticipation.

And I've been waiting for him to make a move. To approach.

Since that first glance, I've been watching too—catching his stare every few minutes while we play a game of cat and mouse—getting lost within those hypnotic green eyes. While I appreciate just how handsome he is.

How his top lip curls to the right, a cocky little smirk that makes butterflies erupt within. How his defined and lickable jaw ticks after each sip from the glass in his hand. How his dirty blond hair flops a little over his forehead, a chaotic mess that my hands itch to pull on.

Even from where I stand, a couple of feet from him and at another small high-top table with a girl I met at the hotel today, I can tell he's tall. Muscular. A sinful surprise I wasn't expecting but want.

This man is the perfect British specimen, and I want a taste. A little of the dominating persona that stands out amongst the sea of drunk bodies all around me. There's just something about him. Something delicious. Something that calls to me.

Turning around, I look up at him from beneath long lashes. "I'm Aurora...and you?"

"Casper." He winks, picking up my hand and bringing it to his lips. Soft lips that skim across my knuckles. "And I'm your date for the evening."

At his response, I giggle. "Is that so?"

"It is."

"Miss, we're here," the driver says, snapping me back to the present. I've been so lost and inside my head that I never gave him my hotel's name or the address.

"How did you—?"

"Mr. Jameson." That's all he says before exiting the car and coming to my door behind him, an action that tells me the subject is closed. He's not divulging the how or why.

"Thanks..." I trail off, hoping he'll at the very least give me his name. He doesn't. Instead, Casper's employee gives me a nod and walks back around to his door as I watch. No more eye contact or smile, he leaves me there as he enters and then slowly pulls off the curb to merge into very busy traffic.

For a few minutes, I just stand there, still lost inside my head, when a body sidles up next to me. It's a familiar presence. Someone I know will reproach my actions even though they don't have a leg to stand on.

"You're late and you look horrible," he says after a minute, tone calm. Too calm.

Without looking over, I let out a heavy sigh. Just not in the mood. "Why are you here?"

"Because daughters shouldn't stand up their fathers."

CASPER

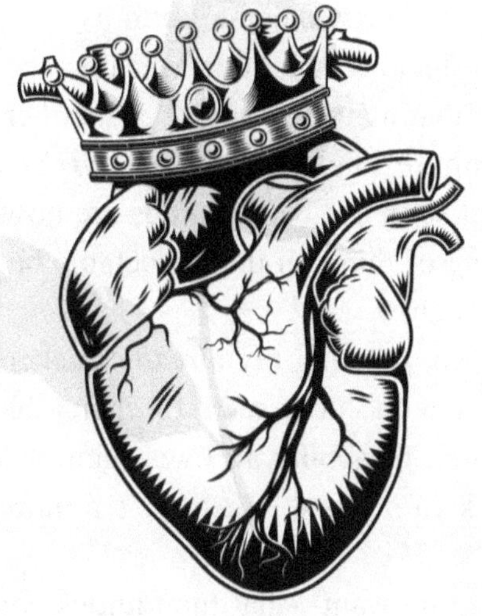

I DON'T FOLLOW HER. It's not necessary.

Not when I send a quick text to one of my men outside the minute she rushes upstairs to get dressed. He's under strict instructions to make sure she gets to her hotel safely and then stay close by. To give me an update on her location every thirty minutes on the dot, no exceptions.

I want to know everything. The what, where, and how.

To know if she so much as coughs until I come for her once more.

Because we aren't done. Not at all.

But first, I have somewhere to be, where good little girls should never step a single foot inside.

The moment my front door closes and I see her enter the awaiting car from my security feed, I push my chair back, pocketing my phone and the two custom karambits. I walk out without another word to my cousin, knowing he has more questions, but I couldn't give a bloody fuck about them. Now isn't the time for bollocks or even a little ribbing, something that as my right hand he understands.

His footsteps follow mine out of the room, but we part ways as I head upstairs to collect something I'll need. Taking the stairs two at a time, I reach my room and find it in complete disarray with clothes—my clothing —strewn about. She's emptied every drawer of the armoire in her haste to leave. Plain vests, gym shorts, pajama bottoms, and even a few pairs of joggers are atop my bed and on the floor beneath.

However, none of that matters when I see that her little black dress lies in tatters near the furniture's bottom drawer. *Must've brought it upstairs in her rush.* The scrap of satin she calls panties are nowhere to be found, but she left with something of mine on that delectable body, a reminder of me, and for now that's enough.

"Good girl," I groan, palming my already thickening cock through the outside of my trousers as the faint scent of cherry blossoms infiltrates my senses. I'm hard for her, throbbing all over again, and want nothing more than to bring her back to my bed, but there's a more pressing matter that needs my attention.

And it's the anger, the want—that tumultuous combination that causes me to grit my teeth and walk over to a small compartment hidden behind a painting of the London skyline at night. There's a small safe there. One of the many throughout my two-story home that provides easy access to an arsenal of weapons.

This one, though, doesn't hold much outside of my favorite chrome Colt 1911 and the custom holster for my knives. Punching in a four-digit code, I grab each, and then the extra magazines ready and loaded beside them.

I'm not changing, but I do choose a pair of old combat boots for this particular meeting with Otto. He's the kind of man that will appreciate my way of handling this type of situation, the less-than-formal setting, and after lacing them tight, I walk out.

Each step toward my private parking structure next door is loud against the floors. It echoes, follows me as do the two men awaiting my orders outside. No one speaks, they just follow.

When I purchased this property, I bought the one on either side as well because I like my privacy. Because money talks, and a few extra zeros on any check will buy you anything you desire.

Once inside my garage, I point toward the two black Range Rovers while walking toward another small panel near the entrance. It's a small box with a fingerprint reader, and I place my thumb at the center. Then there's a click, and the sliding of a panel which reveals ten sets of keys.

I grab the ones to the left on the top row and press the unlock button on the fob. At once, doors open and then close.

Turning around, I notice Callum still outside while holding a hand out. "I'm guessing you're driving alone." My response is to toss him the set that belongs to the Rover where two of my men sit inside. "We'll follow, and security will be here within five minutes to replace the men coming with us."

I nod and get inside my own car, taking off toward the Eye. It's a thirty-minute drive that I cut down to fifteen, weaving in and out of traffic as drivers around me press down on their horns—glaring at me in annoyance while my car cuts them off at close range.

There's a rush of excitement that comes with the art of scaring the piss out of them, and even more so when they don't know it's me. That moment at red lights as they send curses my way—waving a fist or flicking me off—and I lower my tinted window to show my face, is priceless.

The closer we get to the touristy area, the thicker the congestion on the roads becomes. There are buses and people walking, all looking up toward the landmarks we're known for and snapping selfies.

They aren't self-aware. Ignore danger.

These wankers don't care—they ignore the fact that a man like me will run them over without an ounce of remorse for being arseholes. And what's worse, no one will lift a finger against me. To turn me in.

Pulling into my private parking spot behind my building, I turn the ignition off and let out a perverse chuckle. I'm so close to parliament; to where all the lords of this great country hide away for hours fighting the good fight while men like me break their laws. I defy them, metaphorically flip them off, and not one will rise against me.

Callum follows, parking in the spot next to mine, and gets out a minute after, rushing to fall into step with me as I enter the kitchen's back door. Eyes lift as I make my way through, but quickly shift away when they take in my facial expression. Faces are lowered and all movement ceases;

nothing can be heard outside of the sizzle of a deep fryer and the two or three pans on the burners.

I look at the manager on shift and give him a nod. No words.

His reaction is automatic, almost running to hold a finger on a nondescript button near the large walk-in coolers. It blends in with the other two there that manage the lighting and a backup fan for emergencies. Eyes on mine, he waits for me to enter my office before the fake wall begins to lower, sealing us inside.

No exit.

No entry.

It's out of sight and with soundproofing thick enough that I could blow the blasted building from below and no one would realize until it's too late.

Inside the room and behind my desk, there's a large bookcase the size of a door—a mobile bookcase that opens with the slight pulling of an old copy of Romeo and Juliet that Mum thought was funny to place there and use. Moreover, unless you know it's there, the entrance is undetectable. Clever in that hiding-in-plain-sight kind of way, and I can appreciate the subtlety.

Callum gives the book a small tug and the lock disengages, moving the wooden structure an inch or two forward, giving us a peak at the darkness behind it. A void that for most who enter is the entrance to hell, while I find the dark and morbid relaxing. A release.

My men enter first, walking down the stairs that lead to a large and open space, then they wait for me; three men with heads looking straight ahead while a low whimper meets my ears. It's a fascinating sound: fear. The way someone crumbles as reality sets in when I walk inside the room.

However, I make Otto wait. Fuck with his fragile mind the way he screwed my business.

My family's money. Took food right from their mouths.

His disloyalty, the way he took it upon himself to sell and profit from what isn't his, doesn't warrant any leniency from me. Especially after I gave him a job when his family—wife and two kids—were on the streets without a pound to their names. After I got him cleaned up. After I put them in a home that same night and made sure his family was taken care of while his training down at the pier began.

He earned more than most because of the women in his life.

None of that seems to matter, though, when greed becomes a prominent driver in a person's life. They don't think. Don't process that shit could go wrong and you will find yourself staring at the end of a murderer's knife.

Once again, I crack my neck, shaking my head from side to side as another pulsing energy begins to flow through my system. It's a heady concoction. Almost as delicious as Aurora's pussy.

Placing my holster, knives, phone, and gun down atop my desk, I shake my arms out, loosening my limbs. The room is cool, and yet I'm a raging inferno as the moment begins to settle. As I let my need for blood to spill take over.

Rationality and compassion have no place inside this meeting.

I pull my vest over my head and then fold the cotton fabric, leaving it beside my gun. A gun I won't be taking with me. This sentencing will be more of an intimate affair. Hands on.

To the victor goes the spoils.

"Please." It comes from the floor below, a yell of desperation that pulls a smile to my face. "Mr. Jameson, I'll work the debt off...do anything you need me to. Just don't..." a broken sob follows and I've yet to make an entrance "...my daughters and wife need me."

I don't answer.

I don't utter a single word as I put my holster on, securing the leather strap down each side of my chest, and then pick up each karambit. In the low lighting, the steel gleams, a sharp contrast to every single item within the space. It's weight feels good in my hand, like an extension of me, but I don't plan to use them yet.

No. I'm nothing if not fair.

Placing one in each holster, I turn and walk toward the stairs, taking them down to the all-dark room. My men await orders. Await my decision with their heads straight ahead while the traitor squirms under the scrutiny.

The man in question, *Otto*, is kneeling on the cold concrete floor. His shadow shakes and a chain rattles with each move. But louder than anything else is his breathing—harsh intakes of air that seem to choke him as his lungs close up and panic sets in.

"Lights," I say, and someone flips the switch a second later. Everyone in this room knows the rules except my guest, and they quietly take position, blocking the stairs behind me. Only one way in and one way out. "Look at me, Otto."

His eyes, which have remained on the floor, meet mine and they are a horrified blue on my light green ones. They're terrified—almost accepting of his fate—but a small speckle of hope still peeks through. One which I hold no qualms about stomping out.

He thinks I have a soft side when it comes to his daughters because of their young ages.

It's almost sad. Almost.

Otto doesn't say anything as I tower above him, bare chested—the black ink on my skin bold against my flesh—and with a smirk on my lips. Not as I take in his near naked and bruised form. Not even as I wrinkle my nose in disgust at his stench; a combination of sweat and piss hits my nostrils.

My eyes leave him, and I take in the small tray beside his body with an empty plate and cup. There's a tiny piece of tomato and lettuce on the all-white dish and a crumb here or there. It's evidence to just how far my mercy goes; he's been fed, the room is at a cool temperature, and the leash around his neck has enough leeway that he can move about a bit.

I've become the bloody saint of all demons.

"You've disappointed me."

CASPER

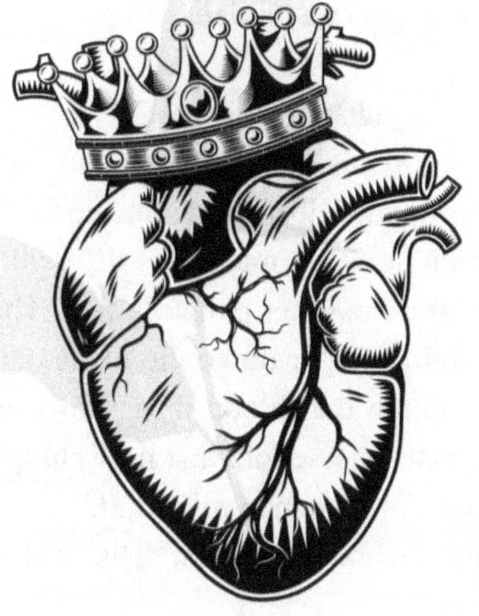

"M R. JAMESON, I—"

"Silence." Taking a step back, I look over my shoulder toward Callum, who comes forward. He takes my place as I walk over to the wall on the left, stretching out my limbs with my back to Otto. The sound of his restraints meeting the hard concrete floor come a second later followed by the grunts of pain as he tries to stand.

"Am I being forgiven?" the wanker asks, a slight tremble in his tone.

"Mr. Jameson has granted you the privilege of fighting for your life. You'll have—"

"I said I was sorry. That I swear to pay off every single quid...*fuck*!" I turn my head slightly at his yell, barely catching the movement of Callum's strike and then him resuming his stance.

"Interrupt me again and the boss won't begrudge me a few minutes of fun. Understood?" There's a moment of silence, then an almost too-low-to-hear whimper that my cousin lets slide. "Good. Now, as I was saying..." footsteps move about, almost pacing "...you will have ten minutes to either knock out or subdue Mr. Jameson and then walk out a free man. No repercussions or debts. A clean slate."

"May I ask—"

"You will have your choice of weapon from those we provide. Choose wisely, Otto, because you get one choice."

"Guns?"

Callum chuckles. "No guns are allowed."

"Unless he manages to make it upstairs and takes my Colt from the desk." Turning to face them, I lean back on the brick wall with my knee slightly bent. Both men look at me with different expressions on their faces: one amusement and the other palpable fear. They also watch me as I pull out a knife and run my finger down the blade, slicing my thumb. It's a nice little cut—deep enough that blood drips down my hand and onto my wrist, showing the ungrateful arsehole just how sharp this blade is. "It's the only way to make sure I don't change my mind."

Otto looks at Callum, who just shrugs. "His rules, mate."

"Is there any other—"

"No." As I say this, Jeffrey, a guard, walks toward a small area behind the stairs and pulls out a cart. He brings it toward us, stopping before Otto, and lifts the sheet covering the few items it holds: an assortment of knives, a pair of brass knuckles, a baseball bat, and crowbar. "Pick."

"I…please…can't we—"

"Choose, or I'll do so for you. You have ten seconds." I snarl, lip curling over my teeth while my hand clenches around the silver handle as I slip my thumb within the circular hole at the end. For now, I'll only use one. That's all I'll need.

His hand trembles as he reaches out toward the assortment I've provided. They hover over the crowbar for a second, fingers almost skimming the iron, but then changes his mind at the last moment. For some reason, Otto picks up the aluminum bat, weighing it in his hands, and then takes a step back.

"Is that your choice?" At my question, Otto nods and my men retake their place by the stairs. The cart goes with them, and a harsh pounding begins to fill the room. It's an abrasive beat. An angry guitar riff that clears my head—flows through me as I give him my back. "The first strike is yours—make it count—there won't be another chance out of here."

I take three steps forward and close my eyes. In that moment the room stills, and I focus on the movement inside the room. How Otto lets out a long shuddering breath and then lets out a heavy grunt while rising the bat above his head, holding it there as his fear wages against the need to survive.

It's a natural reaction. We all have the need to protect ourselves at all cost. To kill if it means we get to head home and be the same useless bastard we were the day prior.

Because this isn't about his family. His wife and kids.

Not in the least.

His gambling addiction is his downfall. The reason he's in this room and minutes from death. He's lost money—owes someone that wanted my shipment as repayment—and he agreed with a little compensation on top. Stupidity overruled common sense.

Like now; if he were smarter, he'd keep his noises down to a minimum. He wouldn't shift his weight from foot to foot, dragging his feet on the cold concrete and kicking the chain that was his leash.

He also wouldn't take so long to make a decision. To strike.

But then again, I expect this. It's why I'm good at what I do.

Over the years, since I was a young bloke, my father taught me to rely on more than just what's in front of me. To pay attention. To focus.

It doesn't matter if you're inside a packed stadium, the mind has a way to block out distractions. To pick apart movement and keep track of a threat. Use that. Hone it.

Kill without mercy, kid.

That's why when his arm lowers, bringing the aluminum bat with it, I duck out of the way, letting it barely graze my shoulder as I shift. I follow his action with a counter of my own, turning with my karambit's blade open and in his direction while lowering toward my target. The cut is across the back of his knee—I feel every second in slow motion as the knife slices through flesh and ligaments—leaving an almost surgically precise line while his upper body follows the movement of a missed swing. It's a bloody thing of beauty how he falls.

How the blood rushes out through the open wound.

How he cries out in pain, unable to stand.

How his eyes snap to mine, full of horror.

I'm behind him with my hand in his hair and yanking his head back before the scum can even think to try and crawl away. His life's essence seeps from the deep wound, pooling around him and staining my boots—boots that I use to stomp down on his left ankle. Once. Twice. I don't stop.

Not until I hear the bone crack. Not until it's broken and at an awkward angle.

"Please!"

"Please what, arsehole?" I sneer, ready to end the dumb fuck. He owes me for much more than a missing shipment. For stealing from me. "Tell me why I should let you go?"

His eyes, wide and full of panic, settle on mine. "It was a mistake…it'll never happen again, Mr. Jameson. Just please. My kids."

His kids. His kids.

Bending at the waist, I place my lips near his ear and bring my blade to his left nipple, digging the tip in. "Did you stop when you smacked Melinda around? When you beat her in front of the girls?"

"I've never—"

"What about when you walked out on them two weeks ago to fuck a whore?"

"That's not—"

"Liar." In one swift move, I slice down, leaving a deep wound in the exact same place he kicked her a few weeks ago. It's not lost on him either as he chokes on his mistake. It's another rule of mine he broke: we take care of our family. "What was the first thing I told you after taking you in? After giving you the help you asked for?"

"To never…fuck!" My blade slips lower, opening the area over his ribs. I can feel each one. It's almost like playing a xylophone. "No more. I can't take any more."

"You'll take what I give you." To punctuate my point, I turn the curved tip of my karambit and follow the path to his belly button. With a slow cut, I take my time parting his flesh and then embedding the four-inch blade within.

I let him bleed while his body fights to coil into itself—to move away from my hold.

And because I'm a generous bloke, I release his head after a few minutes and remove my blade. "Don't move." His reply comes in the form of a whimper and then a nod; his body's sweating profusely. "Callum?"

"Yes, Boss?"

"Bring our guest a glass of water."

"Of course." Behind me there's movement, the footsteps of more than one man as things are put into place. Jeffrey brings a file with him as Callum offers my guest a drink. Both are put in his line of sight—given to him—yet he doesn't move.

"It's rude to not take what's being offered," I say, taking the file from Jeffrey while giving him a nod. Silently, he moves away and retakes his place while my cousin and I watch the crying cunt. "Take it."

"Casper, I—"

Callum strikes him, a closed-fist punch to the face that snaps Otto's head to the side. "He's Mr. Jameson to you."

"Relax," I say, tossing the file on the floor in front of him. Its contents spill out: photos, a bank statement, and the deed to a new home. They show a life he will never live with those he claims to love. Their future. Their security. Their peace. "Hurts, doesn't it?"

"What's this?" Otto eyes the picture of his wife and kids, his loss of blood making it hard to move. To raise his hand. "Where's my wife?"

"Safe." In the first picture his wife and girls are smiling, sitting out on the back porch while eating ice cream. In the next, she's taking them to a new school. A private and very expensive one. "Building a better life."

"They need me." It comes out low as his body sways a bit.

Walking behind him, I yank his head back once more and force his eyes to mine. I want to be the last thing he sees. I am his end. "No. They don't." With that I bring my karambit to his neck and slice his throat clean from one side to the other. Blood splutters and stains my skin, while Otto chokes on his last breath. Releasing my hold, I let his lifeless form buckle and hit the ground while I take the glass of water from Callum. I pour a bit onto my hand over his body to wash the blood off. "Did he show up?"

"Yes." He chuckles and passes me a small towel. "We have eyes on them as they talk near the hotel's elevator bank. I'll forward you the pictures now."

"Good." Taking the cotton, I clean off as much as I can. "I expected as much."

"Is that why you didn't ask him about Boston? About the sale?"

"It's not necessary when I already have what I need." Stepping over the dead, I walk to the stairs as my men move to the side. "Clean it up and burn the body."

"Yes, sir," they say in unison as I take the stairs up with Callum following close behind. I know he has questions. "Spit it out."

"Did you know about—?"

"Doesn't matter to me."

"It's a problem, cousin."

I nod, a cocky smirk on my lips. "This problem is mine."

Aurora

"THAT'S FUNNY COMING from an absent father."

"You know it wasn't like that. I had no choice—"

"There's always a choice. We just weren't yours," I spit out, clenching my hands into tight fists as I turn, leaving him alone in front of the hotel's entrance.

"For the love of God, Aurora." It's a hiss, low and heavy with a warning I ignore from behind me. His footsteps match mine, entering the almost-empty lobby a second or two after, and following close as I make a beeline for the elevator bank. "We need to talk. Where were you last night? Who dropped you off?"

What he fails to understand—accept—is that I'm not in the mood for this. That I'm not a little girl he can control. That I just don't have it in me to explain *why* his predicament means nothing to me.

Especially while I'm riding a rollercoaster of emotions that I've yet to understand.

My mind is still on him.

His scent surrounds me.

How it bothers me that he just sent me away without another word. *Casper Jameson.*

"None of your concern. And no, we don't need to talk," I throw over my shoulder. Besides, these conversations always lead back down the same hurtful path: he abandoned us. We meant nothing to him when push came to shove. "You made your decision a long time ago, Matteo. Leave me out of your future endeavors."

"Don't call me that. I'm your father and—"

"You didn't raise me. Don't give yourself a title you haven't earned." I'm but a step or two from the *up* button, and just as I lift a hand to press it, I'm whirled around to face him. The eyes that bore into me are the same shade as mine. My father's hold isn't threatening or hard, but his expression is full of anger mixed with regret, a sadness that makes my brows furrow and chest clench.

It also causes me to look away, surveying the room to make sure we aren't attracting attention. That, and to compose myself. To not show him that I care.

Because I've never seen this man be anything but the hardcore criminal he is: the head of the biggest mob in Boston with connections all across the US and South America, Brazil being his biggest suppliers.

That, or the cocky and shrewd real estate mogul.

But with him, there's never an in-between. Criminal or unscrupulous businessman.

Matteo Cancio is known for being a cruel and egotistical man with no patience, and yet, right now, he looks almost defeated. Almost hurt by my rejection.

"Will you ever forgive me? Your mother did before she—"

"How's Samantha, by the way?" I cut him off, eyes snapping to his and narrowing at a man I barely know. My heart hardens all over again at his almost statement. At his reminder of what I lost. "Does she know you're here and visiting your bastard child? That you're offering me something that belongs to her son?"

He flinches at my words but regains his composure quickly. "You know we're divorced, Roe. And more importantly, it belongs to my firstborn...you."

"How quickly I've come to matter in the last few months. How easily you find me now that you want something from me."

"Why are we fighting?" he says, his fingers flexing on my arm as if he's afraid the moment he lets go, I'll bolt. "Aurora, I flew all the way out here because you promised to hear me out. You skipped dinner yesterday, and I sent you a message saying I'd be here at one."

"When did I confirm this?" I raise a brow.

At least he has the decency to look away. "I waited in the lobby hoping to catch you."

"So, you're stalking me?"

"It's not stalking when you agreed to hear me out," he counters, nose flaring a bit in his annoyance. I also know he hates this, that he finds the begging beneath him and believes I should just fall into line, but it's not happening. I'm not afraid of him. "And I've never done that to you. It's the one promise I made to your mother and kept."

"Again, no." I snort, the sound not attractive in the least as I ignore his last statement. His words hold no value to me. Not after years of being let down. This man is an unbelievable manipulator and nothing else. The poster child for *give an inch and they'll take a mile* kind of personality. "That's not how our conversation went at all, *Father*. I mentioned a vacation in Europe, and you decided to crash and make this about my duties as your child."

"I love you, Aurora. Please believe that if nothing else."

"Liar." As soon as I turned twenty-one, his call came. He thinks now is the perfect time to create some kind of bull-crap bond after years of missing visits, important dates, and remembering that I existed all around. Our time together over the years has always been few and far between, his attention always on my mother's life and never on me. I'm the forgotten one he now needs. "And quit avoiding my question. Samantha?"

Releasing his hold, he takes a step back and runs an agitated hand through his hair. "You know we're divorced."

"Because she cheated."

"Because we both made mistakes. Horrible ones." His cell phone rings somewhere on him, but he chooses to ignore it. A first for him. "With her, it was never about love."

"And yet you married her anyways," I sneer, my disdain for him and his actions clear to see. "This is your bed, and you will lie in it."

"Roe, I—"

"Don't. No excuses." An older couple comes near us then, and I move to the side with a smile on my face. "Good morning."

"Morning," they say in unison, looking between my father and me, noticing the tension—but choosing smartly not to comment. They mind their business while waiting for the elevator and then they enter, letting the doors close while avoiding our stares.

"As you can see, this isn't the best place for this type of conversation…" he tilts his head now in the direction of a crowd of what looks to be tourists that are gathering nearby "…why don't we go to lunch after you clean up, instead? I'll wait for you here and—"

"No." I take in a deep breath and let it out slowly, giving myself an extra minute to gather my thoughts. To come up with a better way to tell him to leave and never come back that doesn't use my favorite four-letter word. "Listen, Dad…I'm trying here. Really trying to keep my composure, but your insistence is making this very difficult. I already told you, I'm not interested. My answer hasn't changed. It's the same as when we spoke in Chicago and Boston. You chose a marriage of convenience over my mother's love. Over being my father. I owe you nothing."

As the last word slips past my lips, a man I've seen once, when I agreed to visit my father's Boston office three months ago, reaches us while holding a phone out. He's tall and handsome, but in that generic sort of way with dark hair and brown eyes in a black suit and shiny shoes. Too put together. Nothing about him is as effortless as the man I spent last night with.

The man I vow to forget. To leave behind as a memory of my night in London.

My father takes the cell phone, covering the receiver. "Who is it, Dominic? I asked not to be interrupted."

"It's Lucas, sir." For a brief second the man's eyes shift toward me, and I don't like it. His stare. I don't know why he rubs me wrong and I shift from foot to foot, something my father doesn't take notice of.

Instead, at the mention of his ten-year-old son's name, Matteo Cancio smiles. It's the kind a loving father makes. The kind I've never seen directed at me. "Thank you." Then, like I've watched him do all my life, he holds a finger up and walks away without another word.

Because he just expects me to wait. To be here while he leaves me with someone I don't know—who makes me uncomfortable—while he attends to his real life.

The one I'm not privy to. The one I want no part in.

If I wasn't good enough as a child, then as an adult, I just don't care. *I'm done with him.*

Giving him my back, I take the few steps between myself and the elevator button, pressing the small circle. It lights up and a whirling sound follows as the elevator comes down. "Tell him I said no."

"Mr. Cancio didn't say you could leave." Dominic is much closer than I anticipate, and as I turn around to tell him exactly what his boss can go do, I bump into his much taller frame. I stumble, almost tripping on his foot, but his tight hold on my arm keeps me upright. "You'll wait here until he returns."

"Let go."

"Learn your place," he spits out, eyeing my clothes with disdain and a hint of something else that I can't quite identify. His proximity makes me uncomfortable. "You also look like trash. A man in his position can't be seen with a—"

"A what?" I snap, trying to yank my arm out of his grip. Thank God the group from before has left and the couple near the sitting area is oblivious to us. "Leave a mark, and it's your head."

"I'm his second-in-command. Well above a whore."

"So, you think his daughter is a whore?" How the hell does his right hand not know who I am? How much of a secret have I been kept from everyone?

"His daughter? Cancio has a daughter?" The shock is evident and all the answer I need. I've been kept a dirty secret, a thought that hurts, but I can't focus on that now. Not when his reaction causes his grip to loosen just as a ding rings clear from behind me.

"Yes. He does." Eyes on him, I step back, one foot after the other until I'm inside the car and pressing my floor's number. And it's as the doors begin to close that he realizes his mistake, stretching a hand out to keep them open. However, before he can come inside, I'm holding the taser my mother gave me years ago. It's small—almost untraceable—and does the job, forcing him away from the doors he stops from closing.

"Motherfuck," he hisses, shaking his left hand.

"Touch me again, and I'll show you just how much his daughter I am."

<hr>

THE SECOND I'm back inside my room, the walls cave in. My emotions overflow in rivulets of hurt down my cheek, and no matter how much I wipe them away, another tear follows its path.

I'm angry and overwhelmed—choking on confusion and physical exhaustion. On my regret and need. On a push and pull that makes no sense, and no matter how badly I want to let go—fall apart at yet another reminder of how little I mean to Matteo—there's another, more prominent desire: to flee. To get far away from this city and the last twenty-four hours.

Away from the memory of someone who's just like my father. A criminal.

With that thought in mind, I stumble toward the hotel's closet and pull out my luggage; a midsize piece that I'll gladly tote through any train station or airport in order to escape and forget. To not seek him out— demand an apology—by going back to the pub where I met him.

Rushing into the bathroom, I stop at the vanity to collect my things when my eyes glance up. "*Christ*, I'm a mess." My dark waves are a tangled disaster from Casper's fingers, from the way he wrapped the long strands around his fist and tugged. A memory that causes my nipples to harden and rub against the soft fabric of his shirt. The sensation pulls a low moan from me as yet another tear falls, its track creating a charcoal-colored line down my cheek and toward my kiss-swollen lips. Lips that tingle as if he were kissing me. "Out of everyone I could've slept with, why him?"

Casper represents everything I loathe, and yet a sick part of me wants another night. To feel as alive as I did under his fingertips. *How can I want his touch after hearing him sentence a man to death?*

After what happened downstairs? Seeing my father should deter me. I shouldn't be flip-flopping from one extreme to the next within the same breath.

One second I want to punch a wall and then cry. Then, the very next, I want to find Casper and smack him for making me feel this unstable.

"Get in the shower," I tell myself, forcing my fingers to come up and undo each button of his dress shirt. It's torturous and slow, but I manage to peel it off while watching through the mirror and cataloguing each small bite he left behind.

On my breast. On my collarbones.

Then, when I lower his shorts, the purplish fingerprints stand out on my hips. Yet another reminder of my stupidity.

Closing my eyes, I count to ten and reopen them. Then I do it again. And again.

Each time I look at my reflection, I let go of a little guilt and forgive myself for being human.

"I won't see him again. I won't repeat my mother's mistake." Pulling his socks off, I step into the shower and turn the faucet to as hot as I can stand it. I'm in a rush to put this all behind me, to wash him from my skin. Lather, rinse, and repeat; I let what's left of his touch flow down the drain in a rain of vanilla suds before stepping out and drying off.

And it's after brushing my teeth and collecting his clothes from the floor that my phone begins to ring. It's a ringtone I know. A ringtone I have no plans to answer.

Instead, I bring everything in my hands to the bed and dump it beside my open luggage. I never really unpacked, and it's a blessing as I pull out a pair of yoga pants and tank top from the very top, then my underwear from a separate small pocket attached to the lid.

I'm dressed before the ping of a text comes three minutes later.

I have my toiletries in hand as the next message comes in.

Five in total, and I don't reply to any.

My focus is on packing up, closing the luggage, and slipping my feet into a pair of trainers for the long trip ahead. This change in plans will put me in Ibiza a few days early, but the extra cost will be worth it. Money isn't an issue thanks to my inheritance, and this is an expense I can justify without thinking twice.

My mother would approve of this change in plans and so would my best friend, Aliana. She's holding down the fort back home, and I'd like to think she'd slap me for letting a man get to me this way. For not using my better judgement. *Or she'll cheer me on for getting some.*

That last thought isn't helping, and I block out everything around me, tunneling my focus on getting the hell out of this place.

I can't run the risk of seeing Casper again.

I don't want to be anywhere near my father.

CASPER

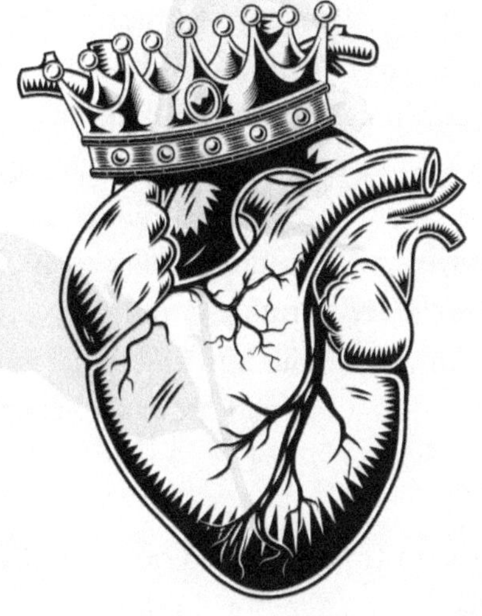

I'VE BEEN WATCHING her since my arrival in Ibiza two days ago.

Just watching. Cataloguing her mannerisms. Taking in every bloody detail without the outside world interrupting the voyeur-like tendencies that have risen since my meeting Gem.

She's become my own personal show. This sad little doll who hides her pain from the world and I want to make smile again.

Because I see her. What she hides.

Aurora knows what I am because I'll never hide that, but I'm also not the one she's truly running from. Her past is dictating her future, and that won't bloody work with me.

After she left London, I took forty-eight hours to do my homework while one of my men tailed her. While he made sure she was safe and not being followed, I confirmed my suspicions on her ties with Matteo Cancio; a father/daughter relationship with no real bond.

The video feed I procured through the manager was enlightening to say the least. As they spoke in the hotel's lobby near the elevator bank, there was a coldness—clear unfamiliarity between the two. Her body language showed discomfort and distrust, while his was nothing but frustration. No warmth. No clear connection.

Then, there's the lack of his involvement in her life.

She's his firstborn. His heir. And yet, Aurora Conte doesn't carry his last name. She doesn't so much as have a security detail.

Her father has the same resources I have—knows where she is—but chooses to leave her unprotected. Not so much as a location tracker was found on her phone by my hacker, Ezra, after breaking into the device.

Why?

It's an arsehole move, but useful as I took over the position and put a man on her I trust. Alexander is ruthless and very much committed to his husband. He has eyes for no one but him and understands what I'm capable of. Knows that I won't hesitate to end him and his spouse if so much as a hair on her head is touched.

I'm protective of her.

The second my private flight touched down on Spanish soil, I sent my man back home with a message for Callum. We still have visitors in London, and I want him to follow their every move—to make sure Matteo doesn't change his mind and comes after Aurora.

That, and to pinpoint the location of my guns.

Because they're still inside the country. No container has left the port or has been transferred since the theft. No manifesto for export has been reported by my employee at the docks, either.

They've gone ghost, and I want them found.

My phone buzzes atop the small beachside table then and I look down, reading the quick message from Callum.

> Flight booked for tomorrow back to the States.
> Ten in the morn. ~Callum

I pick up the phone to reply but stop when movement from the pool catches my attention.

"Christ," I groan low, taking in her delicious curves as she exits the pool, and then as she walks toward the lounger she's occupying. Aurora is a vision; drops of water skimming down her body as the sun kisses her skin —the light-golden tone making her look like a goddess. She's temptation and heat and the definition of femininity while crawling onto the beach chair and then lying face down.

Her arse—the bottom curve with just the hint of my bruise—is on display as those tiny black bottoms ride up a tiny bit, molding onto those plump cheeks that make my mouth water.

She's a pleasurable puzzle I crave. A drug I will indulge in soon.

My mobile buzzes again in my hand and I look down.

B.O.L. for a container to Massachusetts just went through. Code? ~Callum

Registered Name? ~Casper

Three tiny dots appear on my screen while he types.

It's to Cancio. ~Callum

Code to proceed? ~Callum

Bringing the two fingers' worth of whiskey to my lips, I take a sip while considering my options. It'd be so easy to take back what's mine with quick retribution, but something doesn't quite add up in this equation. It reeks of a bloody rat.

His actions back at the hotel don't add up with just how alone she is. How unprotected.

This bothers me. Nags at me.

She needs me. A truth I'm coming to accept with each tick of the clock. With the way my eyes always stray to hers.

I don't hesitate on my reply, fingers flying over the screen.

Green. ~Casper

His reply is immediate.

Are you sure? ~Callum

I smell something foul. ~Casper

Then I'll find the source. ~Callum

With that, I pocket the small device and stand, throwing a heated glare at the arsehole serving drinks behind the hotel's bar. The bandage over his nose should've been enough of a deterrent—my visit and then the broken bone—to keep his bodged-up mug from looking in her direction, however, he seems to need a reminder.

The bloke doesn't see me approach and neither do the people milling about. They're all too busy watching a group of women letting loose and dancing, stumbling as their inebriated state becomes evident.

The moment the blonde trips into the pool, most rush to the edge in order to help or get a closer view of the hot mess, and I move closer. As her mates yell and the lifeguard dives in, I stop right in front of him.

His eyes widen. He pales. "Sir, I—"

"Not a sound," I warn, and before the crowd dissipates, I grab him by the hair and slam his face down against the stone edge of his bar top. At once, a gash appears on his forehead and blood spills from the cut, while his scream is muffled by the cries of panicking women. He's pathetic, afraid, and I laugh—a sinister little chuckle that makes him tremble. "Don't so much as breathe in her direction, lad. I'm watching."

With those parting words, I pat his cheek and walk away. I have plans. A surprise.

Before the end of the night, Gem will know the lengths I'll always go to find her.

To have her.

How I want more of us.

For her, I've become a stalker. The lion in our private game of chase.

UP UNTIL A FEW DAYS AGO, I had not slept with a woman in months, and she'd been a true one-off catered by the private club in Chicago's Lake Forest. They know of my appetite. Of my rules. Of what I demand.

Anonymity.

No names. No conversation. And my cock wrapped tight above all else.

Those encounters were few and far between; once or twice during my four-month stay in Illinois each year because I don't do relationships. I don't trust easily. I don't want a woman who hangs off my arm or spreads her thighs at night so she can spend millions on some bullshit that only impresses the snobby arseholes that frequent elite establishments.

The easy type that see a man in my position as nothing more than a bank account.

Moreover, with my job—lifestyle—I couldn't afford that kind of a distraction.

However, the day I met this woman, something within my rationality changed. Made me want more.

A thought cemented by the hardening of my cock as I watch her in that tiny towel fresh out of the shower. Walking toward me. Toward the darkened corner of the room I sit in, unbeknownst to her.

Aurora pushes her hair over her left shoulder with a delicate hand, stretching her neck as drops of water disappear beneath the fabric of her towel. Tantalizing. Mouthwatering.

I want to follow the path of those rivulets with my tongue.

"Fuck, Gem." It's a low groan. A hungry warning.

"Casper," she says, and it's a bit breathy. No screaming or even a hint of shock in her expression. Instead, those beautiful eyes meet mine and they're full of curiosity and want. With the same cheeky fire of that night a few days back.

"I'm here, love."

At the term of endearment, she swallows hard while goose bumps rise across her flushing skin. "I knew I wasn't going crazy. There's this insane pull and I...*Christ*...by the pool...I kept looking, trying to find you but couldn't. Yet I knew. I knew you were here."

"Good." I push the small button on the lamp atop a table beside me. It illuminates the room, a soft glow that makes her look almost ethereal.

Like my perfect wet dream.

"It's insane and makes absolutely no sense." Aurora shakes her head then, those wet tendrils moving across her collarbone. "Why did I sense you near? How is that even possible?"

Standing, I take the few steps between us slowly, almost predatory, stopping when there's only an inch of space between her almost naked body and mine. "I'll never be too far." Slowly, I bring a hand up and cup her face, reveling in how she nuzzles my palm without conscious thought. How she rubs her thighs together, a slow movement I don't call attention to. "But you know that already. Don't you, Gem?"

"Do I?" She pulls back a bit but lets the tip of my thumb rest against her bottom lip. An action that is followed by the quick swipe of her pink, soft tongue across my skin—by the warmth of her breath as a pant escapes.

"Careful." My voice is rough, exposing my undeniable yearning. How close I am to taking those lips and then her body.

"Sorry?" The way she phrases it like a question shows she's anything but.

"Not your fault I find you dangerous."

Her eyes widen and a rosy tint dances across her cheeks. "Me? Dangerous?"

"Completely." With that, I let my hand drop and take a few steps back. I have plans and won't ruin them by giving in to the temptation so soon. "Now, how about you get dressed and join me for dinner. We have reservations for eight."

"We do? When did that happen?" Gem is trying hard to fight back a smile, but I notice the twitch in her upper lip immediately. This girl is crazy, beautiful, and not denying my request.

"While you were having lunch."

"And if I say no?"

"You won't."

"How do you know that?"

"Because, Gem—"

"Why do you keep calling me that?" Fuck, that mouth. That sass. How she questions everything makes me hard. Has me throbbing. More so when she arches her defined brow and places a hand on her hip, waiting, demanding an answer.

Reminds me of an angry kitten. Cute and with claws.

Three steps forward and I have her heat caressing my skin, her scent—soft and feminine—infiltrating my senses. She consumes me, and yet, I'm also aware of every little thing. Notice how the flush on her cheeks travels down her neck and over the top of her breasts. How her lips part, a sweet little pant escaping her mouth as I bring my face closer.

I want to kiss those lips. To taste her again, but not yet.

"What are you doing?" It leaves her on a shaky whisper.

"Nothing at all." Turning my face, I trail my lips up from her cheek to her ear, releasing a rough exhale there that makes my Gem shake. To make this little noise from the back of her throat that causes my cock to jerk hard within the confines of my trousers, beads of pre-come rolling down the sensitive skin. I can feel each one. How they coat my piercing and then the fabric of my trousers. "Be ready by eight and I'll tell you."

"Tell me what?" Aurora arches her neck to give me better access.

"Why you're my Gem." Then, because I can't help myself, I nip the skin she's offering. A bite just shy of pain and that will leave my small mark. "Eight on the dot."

"Eight." It's a moan. A plea for another.

"Yes," I hum and stand up to my full height, towering over her small frame with a smirk. Loving the dazed look in her eyes, the quick rise and fall of her chest. How I affect her. "See you in an hour, love."

"Okay."

Leaving is hard, but I do so without another word.

I'll give her the next sixty minutes to prepare for me. To get her thoughts in order, but that's it.

I'm ready for her to meet me as I am.

The devil behind the eyes of a saint.

Aurora

THE SECOND HE walks out, I let out the breath I'd been holding. I'm shivering and my legs feel weak. I'm confused and angry and feel elated all at once.

I've been expecting him. It's why I didn't scream. Why I let him get close and then convince me to attend this dinner.

This effect he has on me isn't fair, and he uses it to his advantage. He gets under my skin, and I forget the reasons why *we—I—*shouldn't.

Like his similarities to my father. What I heard inside his office. How he had his employee see me out.

That last one stings the most, which is hypocritical since I was already looking for a way out. I know this. Admit it. However, the mind is a torturous bitch, and mine seems to hate me since I woke up in his bed. It won't let me rest, agree with the rational side of me.

He's nothing but bad news wrapped up in a handsome package. A beautiful disaster.

This man has heartbreak written all over him, and I'm going to be damaged goods after he leaves. Because all men do that in the end. They come and conquer and then disappear into the night with nothing but the occasional smoke signal left in their wake if you're lucky.

I don't want that life. His kind of life. The kind my father gave my mother and me.

And what's worse, I have a feeling he knows more than he lets on. That he sees more than I want him to.

"Why didn't I just tell him to go?" I ask myself aloud, but the answer is pretty obvious. Even with all those strikes against him, I want Casper. Want him near. Desire his lustful wrath.

There's something about him that pulls me in; I wasn't lying when I told him this. Just like I'm aware of his presence, that dominating force that takes over any room and makes you take notice:

Of him.

Of just how dangerous he is.

That night at the club, I felt it. Let it consume me.

Let him take over my senses—rationality—and I followed his lead. With him, I lowered my inhibitions and let the almost painful need that bloomed at his touch dictate my actions.

I slept with him without a condom.

I begged for more.

I became a needy whore without an ounce of shame.

My thighs clench at the memory of his rough hands, and I place my palm on the door to hold myself up, leaning my forehead against the cool metal for a second. "Why is he here?"

Another question with a simple answer: me.

For two days now I've felt him near, could smell that lingering scent of wood and spice in the air around me. Haunting me. Making me doubt my sanity as I looked around but couldn't find his handsome face.

And even as he evaded my eyes, I knew.

In a sick way, I felt nothing but relief when he spoke from the darkened corner of my room. I like that he came for me. More than I should, and it brings forth a tumultuous mixture of emotions that I'm not ready to decipher.

"Maybe I am going insane?" Damn him, I'm yo-yoing again. Going from one emotional extreme to the next as I did back at his home. It's making me unstable. Agreeable. Too curious for my own damn good. "Or maybe I'm just an idiot when it comes to him."

Not a question. My actions prove as much.

My curiosity will be my downfall, and I'm walking straight toward it.

Turning, I head toward the closet in the room and grab a little taupe-colored faux wrap dress that I bought in London during my afternoon outing. It's sexy, comfortable, and fits me like a glove. Then, I peruse my shoes and grab a pair of nude, embellished-buckle heels and the pearl drop earrings inside of a small case with my jewelry.

Normally, I don't wear anything outside of a bracelet with a large charm my mom gave me when I turned sixteen, but today calls for some-thing extra. At the very least, I want the man to suffer. To want what I'm not going to give him.

I've become certifiable. Playing with the devil.

It thrills and scares me all in the same breath. Makes me feel guilty but alive.

This combustible attraction pushes me to seek out answers to questions I shouldn't have but can't deny.

Once I have everything in my hand, I walk back out and cast a glance at the hotel alarm clock, realizing I only have forty minutes left to get ready. "I need something with lace," I mumble under my breath, mentally checking through what I have with me. I never took my lingerie out of my luggage, choosing instead to leave the suitcase inside the small sitting area and above the coffee table there. The lid is closed but not zipped, and I flip it open to the small compartment. I know what I'm looking for: a black and lace pair of boy shorts and a bralette in the same material.

The bra doesn't do much in the lifting department, but mine are perky and this just gives my nipples an extra barrier of protection against his charm.

With everything laid out atop the bed, I drop the towel and get dressed. Everything fits me just right, and as I walk to the bathroom to do my makeup and hair, I decide to go the natural route. Just a bit of mascara, my winged liner, and a hint of gloss on my full lips.

Then, I leave my hair to air dry. Grabbing the mousse atop the counter, I dispense a healthy amount and work it through my hair, scrunching the raw waves and giving them an extra bit of bounce. It's the perfect complement to the atmosphere; the sea salt in the air and the waves crashing upon on the shore.

Besides, if he pisses me off, I can go from date night to a club like this. *Keep telling yourself that.*

Ignoring my inner thoughts, I open the faucet to wash my hands, when there's a knock. Three simple raps against the metal door and my thighs clench—heart trying to beat out of my chest as my panties dampen.

I know it's him. Casper.

It's that same crazy electricity that flows through my system when he's near.

Another knock follows a few seconds after, and I give myself one last look in the mirror. "Just dinner, Roe. Behave and don't lose yourself."

Easier said than done, because the moment I open that door a few seconds later, I know it's a lost cause. Every single cell in my body comes alive, and I thrum with excitement. With that dangerous edge of fire I'm currently playing with.

I'm going to burn for this.

He's going to ruin me.

"You look motherfucking delicious, Gem."

"So, tell me a bit about yourself?" he asks from beside me just as I lift my forkful of saffron rice to my lips. "Where are you from? Tell me about your family."

Putting the utensil back on my plate, I take a moment to sip from my wine glass instead—trying to find the right way to phrase my answer without explaining just who my father is. How similar they are.

Because my mother wouldn't be a hard or long topic; I don't speak of her in detail. It's not necessary, more so after saying a certain four-letter word that makes others uncomfortable.

However, Matteo Cancio is another beast. One he will grill me on. Ask me questions I don't have answers to.

These men don't have a reason to know about each other. They should never meet; Casper's in the UK and my father in Boston.

There should be no business ties. These two worlds should never collide.

Besides, it's not like I'll be seeing Casper after this. *You hate liars.*

"You're saying my accent doesn't give me away?" I say instead, changing the subject while waving my right hand in the air. My eyes are on his, watching, and I catch the moment a hint of amusement flashes through his eyes. As if he's privy to what I'm doing. "What?"

You're hiding something yourself, hypocrite.

"What's *what*?" he counters, taking a sip from his own glass, savoring the full-bodied red he chose to accompany his steak. Watching him swallow is a sinful experience—the way his throat bobs is sexy, and he knows this. The curl at the corner of his top lip tells me just how aware he is of his appeal. "Be more specific, Gem."

"Fine," I huff, finding my opening. The perfect way to avoid. "How about you tell me about the nickname? What does it mean?"

"So tit for tat."

"More like I want answers, and you owe me." I lift a bitch brow, while on the inside I'm relieved he's following. That I won't have to lie.

"How'd you figure that, love?" There's something in his tone that I can't quite decipher. His posture is completely at ease while a boyish grin spreads across full lips. Lips that I want to taste. Remember how good they felt against my own.

Focus, Roe. Don't let him jumble our conviction.

Taking in a deep breath, I let it out slowly while squaring my shoulders. I won't be dissuaded. "Because you sent me away the morning after via your employee without a goodbye. Because you followed me here—imposed yourself on my vacation—without me ever sharing my location. Because you were inside of my hotel room, waiting, as I took a shower without my giving you a key." I tick each point off with my fingers, mimicking his posture, my voice at an even decibel. "What are you looking for?"

"You." A simple answer that causes goose bumps to rise on my skin. "I'm here because of you."

I let out a small huff. "Explain, Casper. I deserve more than that."

The waiter comes around then, pulling my attention away. "How's the food? Is there anything else I can get you?"

"No," we reply in unison, remaining quiet until the man is out of earshot. A minute or two passes and I'm beginning to get frustrated, the silence more than awkward.

"Ask me." Casper's low words pull my eyes back to his warm green ones. My breath catches inside my throat; the softness in them isn't something I'm expecting, and my traitorous heart thumps harshly within my chest. "Ask me again why I am here."

"Tell me." My own response is a whisper. Almost afraid to hear his response.

To face what his words could mean.

Sitting forward, he extends his left hand toward me, palm facing upwards. Long fingers wiggle while the handsome devil raises a brow; it's an invitation. A welcoming gesture that I can't turn down.

I place mine atop his and a current—this inexplicable feeling begins to flow through my limbs. It's heady. Pulling me in closer by this inexplicable and invisible force.

"That's why. Right there." His thumb runs across my wrist, over my pulse point that thumps wildly beneath his fingertip. "There's something about you, Aurora Conte, that pulls me in. That I can't get out of my head." His hand grips my wrist then and tugs me over, enough so that I'm but a few inches from his face. Tasting his every exhale. "That same desire is what put me on a plane to Ibiza so I could steal another kiss."

"I don't—"

Casper shakes his head, telling me he isn't finished, and I close my lips. "Want to know why I call you Gem." It's not a question and yet, I still nod. Waiting with bated breath for another confession. "You're my Gem because you're trouble under the disguise of a priceless jewel. Rare and hidden, but once found, they come attached to a heavy price tag. A life of servitude."

"What are you trying to say?" Because I need more clarification. To understand.

His fingers intertwine with mine and tug, causing our lips to meet. At once, that spark of desire and life and warmth reignites, seeping into every single cell in my body. Making me move closer. Moan as he sweeps his mouth over mine, once, twice, and then parts his lips, letting me taste him as he releases a rough exhale.

"What I'm saying, love, is that we'll be fucked in this together."

CASPER

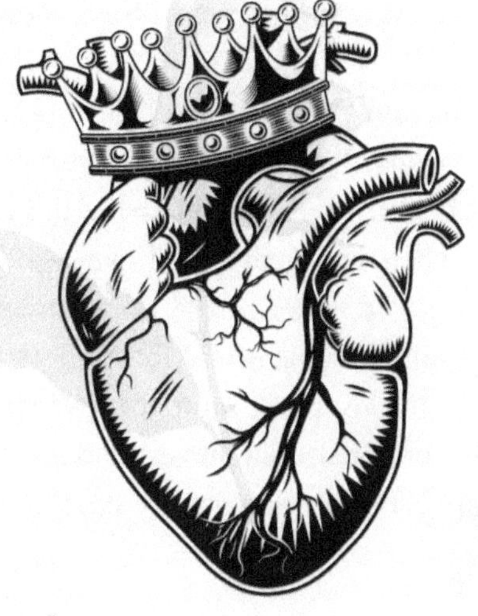

"SO, THIS IS ME," Aurora says as we stop in front of her room door an hour later. She's a tiny bit tipsy, smiling and fucking adorable while looking up at me.

We've done nothing but talk, eat, and drink—laugh—all night. Just being. Something I don't have the luxury to do, but with her seem to effortlessly fall into.

I've also held back from kissing those sweet lips again for the sake of showing I *can* be a gentleman if I so choose. To show her that I'm not just after what's between her thighs, that torturous heat that I can feel through the fabric of my trousers. That I want to drown in.

I'm here for more than that.

I'm here to get to know all of her. Figure out why I can't stay away.

Just a taste. Just one and I'll leave.

"Are you sure, love?" I close the gap between us, pushing her against the solid metal, one hand on her hip while the other is flat on the door beside her head. "What if it's mine?"

"You're not staying here." It's a matter-of-fact response that pulls a small chuckle from me. "I would know."

"If you say so."

"I do." Then, her brows furrow while nimble fingers dig into her small clutch, bringing the keycard up to her face. "Says room 916...that's mine?"

"Then I guess it is."

"Told you." The look she gives me is full of sass and fire—of a playfulness that makes my length twitch against her lower abdomen.

Motherfuck, she's beautiful. Adorably erotic in these tiny bouts of softness that come forth when her guard is down. And I like her like this, relaxed and without the purse in her lips or the stiffness in her posture.

Right now, she's languid against me. Melting into me.

Without realizing, her body seeks mine. My warmth. My touch.

While her shoulders are pressed against the door, those hips are slightly pushing forward. Small gyrations against my cock that cause me to grit my teeth.

"Behave."

"Why?"

Instead of answering, I bring the hand at her hip up, skimming up the center of her chest and pause at her throat. Aurora swallows hard and my fingers stretch out over the expanse, tightening just a bit to see her reaction.

It's automatic. Sensual.

Those hazel eyes close and lips part, my name slipping past those lips on a sacred moan. "Casper."

That sound breaks me, and before she can take her next inhale, I slam my lips to hers. I pin her body against that door, tilting her head back as I devour her natural sweetness. It shakes me and pulls an almost animalistic growl from deep within my chest as I part her lips, caressing my tongue with hers as I take more.

As she lets me. As I dominate the kiss.

And fuck me if she isn't a responsive little thing.

Her clutch meets the floor and those small fingers embed themselves in my hair, tugging at the ends to pull me closer. "I shouldn't want this, but I do," she mewls, a low kittenish sound that settles on the swollen head of my cock and I thrust against her. It's pleasurable pain. It's a guttural need.

It brings rationality back and I slow down our kiss to a few soft pecks. Because while I want her—fucking crave her—I want her to trust me. To beg me. To call on me.

Stepping back, I bend down and pick up her small purse and the phone that slipped out. I don't look at her as I do this, nor do I ask her for permission while entering my phone number into the device.

"What are...why?" Aurora huffs, frustration and want ringing clear through her words.

"I'll see you in the morning."

Gem snatches her belongings from my hand, eyes narrowed. "I'm not a toy."

"And I'm just a man," I counter, loving how her eyes immediately shift to the bulge in my trousers. "A hard-as-fuck man."

"Then why—"

Placing a finger over her lips, I shake my head. "Because I'm trying to be more than the arsehole you think I am."

At once, whatever rebuttal she had evaporates and the soft girl from a bit ago returns. "Okay." There's a hint of a blush on her cheeks that makes my mouth water, even more so when she turns, fumbling with the card and its slot. Her hands are shaking, breathing a bit labored.

On the third try, the light turns green and her hand turns the handle, pushing the door wide open. Her right foot moves, entering the threshold, and I press myself one last time against her back, pushing her soft tresses over one shoulder so I can lay a tiny kiss below her ear.

"If you need me, I'm right next door. Sweet dreams, Gem."

HER BODY CALLS to mine like a siren's song.

An unrelenting tune set out to destroy the last of my mental stability. Not that there's ever been much there; I'm a proud arsehole without an ounce of shame. Without remorse.

Being a criminal is second nature.

Taking a life is as easy as breathing.

And yet, with her, I'm different. Hard as fuck but relaxed. Enjoying myself without the itch—the need to get my hands dirty.

Like now.

I should be in London and putting a bullet between her old man's eyes. Killing the three men he brought with him, especially the one with a wandering eye. Eyes that continuously strayed toward my Gem.

I saw it in the video and pictures while she argued with her father. His interest was plain to see. The dumb cunt wanted a taste of her forbidden fruits.

I'll be taking care of him myself when the time comes.

Pacing the length of the room, I stretch my neck, trying to control the insatiable hunger Aurora creates. My need is growing. Each time the clocks ticks signaling the passing of another minute, I'm wound tighter, hands clenching as I try to behave. To not seek her out.

So, I pace again. Then once more.

There's nothing but a wall separating me from her temptation. Nothing but a door with a lock that I have the key for.

It would be so easy...

"Fuck," I grit through my teeth, palming my thick cock through the thin cotton of my lounge pants. The material is soft, sliding down my length with each jerk of my hands and leaving behind a wet spot right below the waistband.

Another firm stroke and the bulbous tip slips out, meeting the cold air and pulling a hiss from me. Hot and cold, it feels good—bobbing on its own accord—and I lower the bottoms over my hips.

It slaps against my lower abdomen and I take hold, wrapping my fingers tight around the smooth shaft. Pumping my wrist one, twice, I swipe my thumb over the head and piercing, flicking the metal.

A shock of pleasure runs down my spine and it's mediocre at best. Moreover, I'm afraid everything after Aurora will fit that profile.

That nothing but her pussy will ever be enough.

Tightening my fist, I close my eyes and focus on the scent of cherry blossoms that still lingers from when she clung to me. How good that tight little body felt against mine. The warmth between her thighs as she gyrated—

My mobile pings with an incoming text and my muscles clench. Needing. Wanting.

Another text.

"Lord, please give me strength." Opening my eyes, I walk over to the nightstand and grab my phone with my unoccupied hand. My thumb swipes across the screen and what meets my eyes is the devil's temptation.

It's my redemption and cross.

Gem is lying down with a sweet little smirk on her lips while wearing my white Oxford, the same one the little thief took when running from my home. The first three buttons are undone, giving me a small peak of her breasts, while those hazel eyes dare me to come. To take.

And I will.

Fuck it.

She wants to play with fire. So be it, but on my terms.

I told her all she had to do was ask. To tell me what she wanted, and I'd be there.

But this picture was a dare, not a plea.

Giving my dick three harsh strokes, I remove my hold and pull the lounge pants up. There's a decent-sized sitting area in this room and I walk toward it, taking a bloody seat at the center of the couch. I'm throbbing, needing to come, but I ignore the pain and set an alarm instead.

Her punishment will be the desperation that builds as I make her wait.

My reward will be her screams of pleasure as I mark her soft skin with my come.

***

Two hours later I'm pushing the hotel's keycard into the scanner and slipping inside her room, keeping my movements as quiet as possible while Gem sleeps. She's unaware and at my mercy.

The room is dark except for a small sliver of moonlight coming in from the large window to the left of the bed; it takes me a minute or two, but my eyes adjust, and I take in her curves. Aurora is face down and semi-covered with a half thrown blanket over her hips and my long sleeves to keep her warm.

Her lower body, though, from that bottom curve where arse meets thigh, is bare. Looks soft. Ready for me.

And I'm hard for her—throbbing as I leak pre-come down my shaft; the drops roll over my piercing before marking my pajama bottoms. It's proof of my desire. My weakness for her.

For her, I've become a gluttonous bastard willing to live in hell in order to enjoy this slice of heaven.

Poor girl has no idea of the devil's trap she's fallen into.

My feet carry me closer and I stop at the edge of the bed, lowering my pajama bottoms before placing a knee on the mattress. It dips beneath the weight, but she doesn't wake up. Instead, a light sigh escapes her pouty lips and she lifts a leg higher.

Unconsciously opening herself to me. An invitation I accept by climbing up and kneeling just over her dainty feet while fisting my length, stroking twice. Harsh strokes that cause another pearl-like bead to pool at the tip and then fall, this time right over the arch of her foot.

Motherfuck, the sight is sinful, the heat coming from her skin maddening.

I can almost taste her sweetness in the air all around me.

"Fucking perfection." And she is. Those words hit me in the gut the second they pass through my lips, and I accept their weight.

From the moment I laid my eyes on her face, I've become an addict. Wanting more. Needing her closer. It's something that makes absolutely no sense, but I'm not fighting either.

It just is. We just are.

Moreover, it's this pull that has me crawling over her sensuous body with a throbbing cock and pressing my mouth to the corner of those pouty lips. The act startles her awake, but I just peck them again. "It's me," I whisper, nuzzling her cheek before giving her chin a small nip.

At the sound of my voice, her body loses its rigidness. "Casper, what...*oh!*"

My body covers hers, thick cock pressing against her arse. "You pulled the wrong lion's tail, Gem."

"You left me hanging." Subconsciously, she pushes back. Back arching as she gyrates beneath me. No fear. No pushing me away. "I waited for you."

"I know." Placing an elbow beside her head, I put most of my weight on it while using the other hand to trail down her body. Softly. Slowly. Barely there caresses as I make my way toward the bottom edge of my shirt that has ridden up. The end sits halfway over her arse, but it's not enough. I want her bare from head to toe. Pinned beneath me. Writhing for me.

Fisting the material, I lower my lips to her ear and groan. Release a harsh exhale over the fragrant flesh of her neck as I push it up higher, not stopping until the expanse of her back is against my front. "Little girls that taunt deserve to be left wanting."

The simple contact burns me. Sears me from the outside in as she moans low from the back of her throat. "No games. I *need—*"

"Tell me." It's a rough grunt, my hips thrusting against her bare cheeks.

Aurora turns her head then, hazel eyes locking on mine from over her shoulder. "I want you."

Three words that promise nirvana. Gift me her submission.

"Lift up a bit." She does as I ask without another prompt, giving me just enough space to slip a hand between her and the mattress. There are two buttons which hold the top in place, and I undo those quickly, parting the material before pulling it off and tossing it aside. She's not wearing panties and I don't hesitate to cup her pussy, spreading her wetness with the tips of two fingers.

I follow the length of her slit, just slightly adding pressure on each pass and on her next whimper, I bury them deep.

"Oh God," Gem releases a tiny moan then, walls clenching as she tries to pull me in deeper. Her hips undulate against my hand and I pump them in and out a few times, slowly dragging my fingers against her walls before pulling out and replacing them with my dick.

The bulbous tip runs from her folds to clit, and then back again. Once. Twice. And on the third slide, I slam in to the hilt, causing her to choke on a scream.

"There's my girl." A warm rush of wetness coats me on the second stroke and I groan, holding still for a second to enjoy the tight squeeze. How her walls flutter around me. "This beautiful little pussy missed me."

Not a question. I know she missed my touch; her photo proved as much. Aurora wanted to test me—push me to act without her admitting our truth.

Together we're an exquisite explosion. An unavoidable catastrophe we will morph into a beautiful beginning.

"That feels...so...*more*," she whimpers, bucking back against me as she rises up on all fours. That sinful body never stops moving, though.

Working herself on and off my length, Gem motherfucking rides my cock, hard. Her arse bounces. Her wetness coats my inner thighs and balls.

Balls that grow heavier each time she clenches.

Pleasure rips through my limbs as the perverse sound of her wetness becomes the soundtrack of this moment.

My eyes roll back and my hands grab her hips, fingers digging in as I retake control. Pulling out, I don't allow her to move. I don't allow her take what she needs.

"Don't move," I hiss out, gritting my teeth when my piercing grazes her entrance. A harsh shiver rushes down my spine and my muscles lock down.

I'm close. So close.

But not without her. She'll always come first.

With my knee, I spread her legs further apart, forcing her body low to the mattress with mine following. From head to toe, we were one.

And through it all she never stops looking back at me. Those hypnotic eyes on mine. Those parted lips moaning my name.

But that's not what breaks me. What annihilates the last shred of my control is the slow glide of her tongue across her bottom lip before she closes her eyes and mouths the word *fuck me*.

That's it. I'm done.

I'm not letting her go.

A truth that has me slamming back in to the hilt on my next breath. It clouds my senses and I lose myself in her. In her touch. In her scent.

In the way she arches against my hold to match my strokes, pushing that round arse back. No matter how hard I take her—fuck the imprint of my cock into her walls—Aurora stays with me. Matches my every thrust with a gyration of her own.

"Casper, please...I need you—"

"You have me." Fisting her hair, I force her head back and eyes toward the headboard. The deep arch changes the angle—it's deeper—and I bring my lips to the area just below her ear. Kissing. Nipping. Licking a path down to her neck where I nuzzle the lightly sweaty skin. "*Motherfuck*, you have me."

And it's as the last word passes through my lips that she clamps down, body seizing as her orgasm hits. I don't stop. Instead, my strokes become almost punishing with how out of control she has me. Seeing her come undone is my ultimate high, and my own release follows hers two strokes later.

"Christ, you're tight. So fucking good." It's messy; I spill every last drop inside and don't pull out—rope after hot rope mixing with her juices and dripping onto the sheets below. The entire room smells of us, and it's a heady scent that I've come to crave. Need.

As we lay there trying to regain our breathing, silence fills the room. Her slick body writhes as the aftershocks of her orgasm begin to subside.

Neither of us say a word, and the more she relaxes, I do too. We can talk tomorrow. For now, I let the slow rise and fall of her chest lull me into a semi-conscious state.

She feels too good. Like *home*.

CASPER

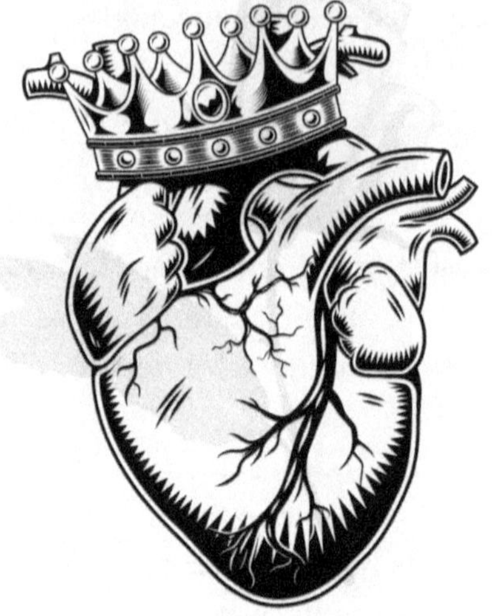

"WHY IS SAYING NO to him so hard?" Aurora whispers from her position on my chest with a leg thrown over my waist, breath skimming across my skin for the fourth time. It's been like this for the last thirty minutes or so while I pretend to sleep. While I lie completely still with my arm thrown over my face, covering my expression while ignoring the twitch of my cock. How much I want her again. How we're both naked. "Handsome asshole." Christ, it's hard to hold in my smile at that, but I do. More so when a huff follows a few seconds later. "Why me?"

Her questions don't upset me; I expect them. If anything, I'm amused by her reactions.

Find her cute.

I'm becoming a total wanker for this woman.

A realization that doesn't bother me. Not one bit.

I'll always be the same depraved arsehole, but with an exception now. Gem *is* the exception.

My wrath will never reach her. She'll never be buried beneath the weight of my darkness.

She shifts her position again, hand sweeping across my left pec where a large tattoo of a Cerberus sits in all black with eyes in white, giving it a sharp contrast. It's bold and depicts who I am deep down; a man not afraid to shed blood for the well-being of my family. Her tiny fingers caress the skin over the head at the center, softly, an action I doubt she's even aware of making while watching me. Waiting. Looking for some sort of magical bloody answer to her dilemma.

Why she can't resist me. Why she gave in again.

Like now, another annoyed grumble escapes her while she tilts her pelvis against my hip. Tempting me with her bare sex on my skin. Making my mouth water as her wetness seeps into my skin.

Tight, wet heat.

"Need help with that, love?" I say, my tone husky as my hands skim down to grab her thigh before she can pull away.

Something she tries a second later as she jumps in place. "Shit!"

"Easy, tiger." Green eyes meet shocked hazel ones as I tighten my hold, placing her thigh right over my hard length. Throbbing against her.

"What is wrong with you?" Her stare hardens and the arm that a second ago was flailing comes down over my abdomen where the Jameson name is in Old English across my flesh. The slap had some strength to it and I grunt, loving the sting of pain as her leg rubs my cock. Then, her eyes turn to slits, lips pursing. "How long have you been awake and listening?"

"Not long," I lie, keeping my face neutral. "How long have you been awake?"

Her expression morphs, mimicking mine. "Not long."

"Is that so?"

"It is."

"Little girls shouldn't lie."

"This girl learned a long time ago that wolves are never truthful." Those words stop my reply. The teasing joke sitting on the tip of my tongue disintegrates as I take in the flash of sadness that crosses her eyes—*I see her*:

How her brows furrow for a brief second.

How her lips purse.

How those hazel eyes lose their brightness and she looks past me to avoid any questions.

And while this all unfolds, I digest what those words could possibly mean with a father like Matteo Cancio in her life. What she would have witnessed growing up. Been a part of.

"What the fuck did that arsehole do?" Those words are out of my mouth before I can stop them, dripping with venom. Because I'll kill him without a second thought if Matteo is the cause of her pain. I'd kill anyone for her.

A truth I accept with honor.

The more I'm with her, feeling those soft curves melt against my flesh, I accept it. This.

She's precious, like a jewel. Moreover, I protect what's mine. And she is just that, even if she fails to recognize it.

"Who?" Gem tenses in my arms, her voice low but steady. Those eyes won't look at me, though, not even when she places her hand atop of mine on her thigh and taps it twice. "And loosen the grip a bit, buddy."

"Sorry." A word I've never said to anyone but my mum.

"It's okay."

I relax my fingers but don't let go. Instead, I massage her leg in slow, comforting circles, up and down, until she loses the hard posture. Once she relaxes, I bring my lips to the back of her head and kiss the crown. "What did he do to you?"

"Who…" she stops, swallowing hard when my hand trails a little higher on her thigh "…who are you—"

"Whoever the wolf was that broke your trust."

Hazel orbs snap to mine, head shaking. "It's not what you think."

"Then tell me." Simple as. I know most of their story, but some things can only be shared by those involved.

"Why don't we get up and—"

"I'm not letting you hide from me." Slipping out from beneath her, I sit up against the headboard and then pull her with me. Closer. Skin to skin. She doesn't complain as I situate us, her back to my chest while her arse sits between my parted legs. Nor when my hand traverses slowly up to her hip, giving the flesh there a soft squeeze. "Talk to me. Let me in."

"Why should I?" Gem says this so low I almost don't hear her.

"Because I'm not him."

"But that's where you're wrong. You couldn't be more like my father if you tried." Aurora mutters a very low *fuck* after her confession. Her confirmation.

"Explain." Pressing my lips against her temple, I lay a tiny kiss there while taking her scent into my lungs, soothing us both. Her anxiousness and my need for her. Now isn't the time to do anything but this; I need her walls down. I'll confirm her suspicions, but I'm not him and won't pay for those broken plates. "What does your father have to do with me?"

"Everything." Aurora takes in a deep breath and then lets it out at a very slow pace. Almost as if she's extending the silent moment after admitting such a heavy truth. And I let her. Let her gather her thoughts and say the words we both know are coming. "All the men in your industry are the same."

"Industry?"

"Participants in illegal activities."

"I don't agree with your earlier statement."

"Of course you wouldn't. Men in your—"

"You mean criminals."

"Just like that…what the hell!"

I lift her like a rag-doll and position her to straddle my thighs, her sweet pussy but a few inches from my cock. "Better?"

"I'm not a toy."

"You're adorable, love."

"And you're unbelievable," Aurora says incredulously, ignoring the compliment while crossing her arms over her chest. Her well-defined brow is arched and lips thinned, trying to look mad when we both know she isn't. If anything, she hates how easily I've gotten under her skin. "You aren't even going to try to deny it?"

"Should I?"

"How high in the ranks?"

"I'm the head of the Jameson Syndicate."

"Christ." She closes her eyes and throws her head back, muttering something unintelligible to herself.

"Share with the class, Gem."

"Why me?" That question isn't directed at me, and I don't reply. Instead, I just wait. Leave her to reconcile the truth with what she already knows. "But then again, I knew it. I heard you sentence that man to death while your men listened. You sent me home with an employee that looked more like a hired hit man than a driver."

And yet, she remains with her perky arse perched on my thighs. Straddling the devil reborn.

While talking to herself, Aurora turned her face from mine, but I rectify this with the tips of two fingers. "Eyes on me always. I don't like it when you look away."

"Why are you doing this?"

"Why are you fighting this?" Now, our mouths hover and her lips slacken, that tiny pink tongue coming out to wet the bottom one as I come a little closer.

She looks down at my lip and then up again. "We shouldn't."

Not that we won't. No real conviction behind the words.

For a minute or two I hold her stare, and then when a small whimper slips past her lips, I slant my mouth over hers, kissing her deeply while the arguing girl in my lap succumbs to my touch. Moving closer. Matching my hunger.

Tiny fingers embed themselves in my hair and pull, eliciting a deep grunt from me as she presses her core against my cock, wetness coating my taut skin. It's a move I welcome and reciprocate with a hard bite to her lower lip that I soothe with my tongue.

I swallow her moans.

I can feel each drop of her juices as it rolls down my shaft and onto my balls.

Moreover, she's proving my point. She might hate what I do, but wants this. Me.

Slowing the kiss, I peck her lips twice more and pull back. "Are you going to run again?"

"Yes, run." The lost look on her face is comical and I chuckle, loving how easily she gets lost in us. It's natural. Alluring. "If you do, Gem, I'll follow. Remember that. I'll always be but a few steps behind."

Something about those words resonates with her, but they also cause her to frown, an action that causes my heart to clench. I can literally feel her sadness, and it's the most intoxicating yet confusing thing.

Why do I feel so connected to her?

"Please don't make promises you won't keep."

"I'm a man of my word." Bringing a hand up, I cup her face and rub my thumb across her cheek. "Can you try and believe that?"

She shrugs. "Promises are broken every day."

"Who let you down?"

"I've seen this story in the past, you know." Aurora closes her eyes then, a sad and wistful smile on her lips. It's the most unguarded expression I've seen on her. "My mother met my father when she was eighteen and fell head over heels in love with his bigger-than-life persona. A few years older than her and charming, the man was in Chicago for college— her freshman year to his third—and they became inseparable. It was a whirlwind romance, the kind where she claimed to have been swept off her feet and made to feel like a princess. Almost two years later, that same love resulted in me." My sweet girl pauses to reach for the sheet bunched up by my hip, pulling it over her shoulders.

"Are you cold?" I ask, rubbing her hip beneath the fabric with my free hand. "Need me to turn up the temperature?"

"No, and a little." Gem nods. She leans forward, pressing her forehead against mine. The move covers us both and causes my hand on her face to fall. I want to protest, love the feel of her skin beneath my fingertips in any capacity, but the private cocoon brings a level of comfort in her body, so I choose to remain quiet. "Now, back to my story on why we are completely wrong. Why this will end in disaster."

"That's bullshit and you know it, love. You can feel it."

"As I was saying." My mouth opens, the rebuttal sitting on the tip of my tongue, but she shakes her head. "You asked me to let you in, and now I'm saying to just listen."

"Okay."

"Thank you." Her wild brown tresses move across her skin as she situates herself a little down my lap and away from my cock. For this conversation it's better this way, even if I miss her soft warmth immediately. So, I focus on the long strands as they sweep over her shoulder and the top of her perky right breast, on how they move with her every inhale.

After a minute, I push them back, letting my hand linger on the back of her neck. Massaging the tense muscles there until she releases a sigh. "Go on, Gem."

"Sadly for her, his love came with an expiration date," Gem whispers and I stop all movement, keeping my hand where it is as I take in the painful lilt to her tone. The small shake in her limbs. "His engagement to another woman three years after I was born broke my mother. Annihilated her trust in men while he just moved back to Boston and assumed his role. She had no notice. No knowledge of the plans my grandfather had for his prodigal son—the same man that didn't even know I existed until I was five and a knock came to our door."

"Your father is a cunt, Aurora," I say, keeping my voice soft. "End of. No real man does that."

My girl sits back then, taking my face between her hands, while the expression in her eyes begs me to understand. "He walked away because *the family* came first. Not us. Not his child. The business demanded, and he gave in always." Two fat tears roll down her cheeks and I quickly wipe them away with my free hand, watching as her bottom lip trembles. "So, you see, I know all about what's expected from a man like you."

"The blood on my hands, or the type of man you think I am?"

"I'm the daughter of a mob boss, Casper, and I'd be a hypocrite to judge you for what I'll never crucify my father for. However, I do hate that he left us. That he chose the business above us, when we would've proudly stood at his side."

I nod in understanding. "Did he provide for you at all?"

"My mother came from a pretty well-off family, and whatever money he gave her each month, she put away in a savings account for me." Even her shrug is listless. The hurt and exhaustion this topic brings is palpable. "But when it mattered, when I needed him the most, he was never there. I know the disappointment and heartache that follows, Casper—I saw it every day—and I refuse to follow down that same rabbit hole. It's why we can't be anything more than these last few days. I won't repeat their history."

"I'm not him."

"You have the potential to be worse." That's the rubbish she's fighting to believe, but I won't allow it. This woman, beautiful and a bit heartbroken, has a hold on me that refuses to budge no matter how hard she pushes. Fight this. Us. "Until the very end, she waited for him."

Past tense. And while I know there's more to it—her mother's story—I'll wait for her to come share on her own, confirming what I already know. I also don't need to ask for clarification on something that if you read between the lines is clear to see.

"I'm not walking away, Aurora. Can't." Needing her closer, I grip the back of her neck and guide her lips to mine until they're almost touching. "All I want is the chance to show you. Let me in, gorgeous. Get to know me before placing me in a category I don't belong in."

"We don't even live in the same country, for God's sake." It's a weak rebuttal at best, and we both know it. One that I don't answer to, and her sigh of defeat a few minutes later is an admission of that same truth if nothing else. "Just don't hurt me. I don't think I can handle any more disappointment, Casper."

"I don't think I ever could." At my words, her body falls against mine and I wrap my arms around her much smaller frame. This is her giving an inch, and it's enough for now.

Even if she doesn't realize it yet, Aurora has already let me in.

Slowly. Effortlessly.

I'll show her who I am, too.

I might be a bastard. An unapologetic arsehole.

But I'm not a liar.

Aurora

T HE NEXT TIME I awake, I'm alone in bed.

There's a cover thrown over my body and the scent of fresh coffee lingering in the air—that, and the low hum of his voice coming from the room's balcony. There's a gravely timbre to it. A low and dangerous thrum that's both hypnotizing and scary.

He's not yelling. However, the angry cadence makes me sit up, throw my legs over the edge of the mattress, and stand up. The need to be closer becomes overwhelming the more alert I become.

"Why can't I fight this pull," I whisper under my breath, reaching over to grab the same bedsheet to cover up my nakedness. Before it's secure around my torso, I'm walking closer to where he is. Each step makes my body ache for his touch. Each inhale bonds my DNA with his scent.

I've lost my ever-loving mind.

Coming to a stop just before the partially-open sliding glass door, I admire his form. This view gives me the perfect view of his other persona. Casper's but a few feet from me and facing the Mediterranean Sea, wearing a pair of pajama bottoms and nothing else, hair disheveled, but the danger radiating off his skin sears me.

I can feel it.

This almost choking presence that makes goose bumps appear on my skin.

The corded muscles in his back are tense and the hand not holding onto his cell phone is gripping the veranda tight, almost choking the metal frame.

This is not the man I fell asleep against just a few hours ago.

This is not the charismatic devil who made me question my logic.

No, this man is ire personified. Angry and every bit the reason I ran.

And yet you still want him.

"How the hell did this happen?" he snarls, stretching his neck from side to side. "Where was she?" *She? There's a she?* "I don't give a bloody fuck that it was mid-morning and on West End near Burberry, Callum." There's another pause as the other person speaks, but Casper only seems to become more agitated. His chest expands with each breath, a rapid succession that worries me. "Why was she alone? Where were her bodyguards?"

"Who is she?" I mumble under my breath, too low for him to hear as my mind goes straight for the worst-case explanation. There's a woman in his life that means a lot. That's important enough for his reaction to be so severe.

It stings. Literally takes the breath from my lungs, and tears spring to my eyes.

This is why we—

"Dad, where's—" The sudden crack in Casper's voice stops me from completing that thought. I'm frozen in my spot, watching as his mood flips once more. How his head drops a bit while listening to his father's account of whatever happened. "And where's Mum now? Who's attending her?" Moreover, I feel like an asshole. Like utter crap for thinking the worst when something is wrong with his mother. "Is she...don't lie to me." There's another pause. "Okay."

His posture is different, the shift exposing his concern and fear. Seeing him like this hurts me. Reminds me of days when I was in his same position.

And it's that concern that brings me outside, stopping just behind him. His head tilts to the side, letting me know he heard me, but he doesn't look back.

However, the moment I wrap my arms around his midsection, he exhales. It's rough. "Tell Callum to...yeah...thanks. See you soon." The second he hangs up, Casper's turning around and pulling us chest to chest. His lips are on my temple, breathing me in while I hug him tight. "I have to—"

"I know."

"This isn't what I had in mind for today." He pulls back a bit after a few minutes, causing me to look up. "There's been an accident with my mum and—"

I silence him by placing a finger over his lips. "No need for an explanation, and more so when it comes to your mom. I understand and don't hold it against you...I was the same with my own."

"You keep speaking in past tense."

I give him a sad smile. "That's because she died a little over two years ago." *And still hurts just the same.*

"I'm so sorry, love."

"Thank you."

His phone pings three times in his right hand, one after the other, and he nods. "That should be my flight info."

"Then don't let me keep you." I take a step back, but his own hold doesn't let me get far. "Go on. It's okay."

Bringing his hand to my face, he sweeps his fingers across my cheek in a soft caress before cupping it. "This isn't the end of our time together, Gem."

"Focus on your mother, Casper." I'm shaking my head, trying to keep my own emotions in check. To not let him see that this sudden goodbye hurts. Because it does. To me, this is it. "I'll be fine."

"Look at me."

"You're going to be late."

"I own the fucking plane and they can very well wait. Look at me, Gem." Reluctantly, I let him tip my face up. Our eyes meet, and I can't hold back the small gasp that escapes. Nor can I stop myself from moving closer, pressing my chest once again to his.

"Please don't make this any harder."

"I'll come for you, sweet girl. Expect my call." Then his lips are on mine, kissing me with so much passion I can't think straight. Can't understand anything past the feel of his mouth against mine and the taste of him on my tongue. It's quick and fast and desperate. Sexy. It also breaks me into a million and one pieces.

Pieces that I doubt will ever be put back together correctly because as Casper walks toward the door and exits, two truths smack me in the face.

I'll never be the same.

There's no place like home.

Without a second thought, I rush back into the room and make a dash for my phone on the nightstand. There's a lump in my throat that shouldn't be there; I shouldn't be emotional when it's for the best that he left.

And yet, my eyes prick with tears as I dial my best friend's number—hands shaking so much that I almost drop the device while waiting for her to pick up. There's this sudden need in me to run and hide and lick my wounds, which is absurd, but I can't stop the loneliness from creeping in.

"Come on," I grit out with the phone cradled between my neck and ear. The closet is but a few feet away and I walk inside with purpose, pulling things down from the hangers without a care if they rip; it's all inconsequential at this point.

There's a click from the other end after the fourth ring, and Aliana sounds out of breath. "Yolo! How's the vacation going?"

I swallow hard, pushing my emotions back so she doesn't ask too many questions. "It's going."

"What's wrong?" she asks, her tone holding alarm. "Because that doesn't sound like you're having fun on this European escape. Are you hurt?"

If only she knew the truth.

Physically? No. But emotionally I am a mess for reasons that don't compute.

To be honest, nothing does at the moment.

Even after telling Casper all the reasons we shouldn't.

After he assured me we should.

I'm lost. Inexplicably and without a doubt confused about what is wrong and right. My path in life has been set for years, but his arrival has shaken that. Made me want something I've never craved before. Not like this.

He's wrong for me, but I forget all of that when I'm in his arms. And it's that belonging that I chase.

It's idiotic, I know, but I can't control it either.

"I'm sick with the plague," I lie, sniffling at the end from fighting back tears. From choking back my truth. "For days I've been feeling off and today it hit me full force. I'm miserable."

"Did you see a doctor? Did you eat something bad?" Her concern guts me. I hate liars and now because of *him*, I am one.

"No, but I am going to be booking my flight back home. This vacation has been the worst."

"Are you sure? Maybe you'll feel better tomorrow and can enjoy the view?"

"Between this and my father's visit in London, I'm done. I want to go home."

"He showed up? Seriously?"

"As a heart attack."

"Fucker," she hisses, and I can see her in my head rolling her eyes. "He won't give up."

"No, he won't." Grabbing a pair of cotton hipsters and a sports bra, I drop the blanket and put her on speakerphone while putting them on. The more we talk, the more I begin to relax—shows me how much I needed my friend these last few days. *Christ, it's only been a few days.* "But that's not as much of a surprise to me as my stubbornness is to him. I won't budge, and he hates it."

"Like mother, like daughter." She laughs, and I can't help but smile.

"Proud of it too." Then, there's an old pair of jeans I brought with me in case I'd do a walking tour of some sort and wanted the comfort. Those I shimmy into and pair them with a vintage concert tee from my New Kids On The Block obsession phase. "Besides, why should I play nice? I owe him no loyalty and have no desire to play the puppet."

"You're okay with the family entrepreneurship?"

"Are you with yours?" I counter, because she's the only person who can understand where I stand—on a slightly smaller scale but still gets the shift. Shady politicians run in her family, while mine is the crime boss funding campaigns to push certain agendas.

"Touché." There's the sound of a doorbell from her end. "About time."

"Food?"

"You know it."

After a few seconds of silence, I let out a long and tired sigh. "I'm coming home, Ali. I need to be home."

"Are you sure there's nothing else bothering you?"

"No." *Yes.*

"Then just come home." No judgment or further inquiry, even though the small huff on her end tells me she isn't buying my excuse entirely. "Send me your flight info and I'll pick you up."

"Thank you."

"I got you, boo."

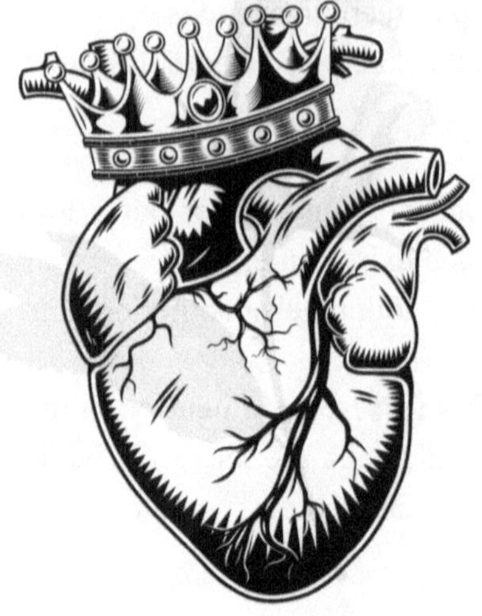

"I'M SO SORRY, BROTHER."

I hear the words, but I'm not quite understanding them. There's a haze that creates fogginess, then the rapid beating of my heart—a thundering war drum inside my chest—that makes it near impossible for me to digest Callum's words.

What he's saying to me can't be right.

There's no fucking way that...

"Son, can you hear me?" Dad's face comes into focus then. He's leaning down to get a good look into my eyes, and it's his red-rimmed ones that slam me back to reality within the hospital's waiting room. In that instant, sounds and light rush back to the forefront as I watch his own emotions burst forth. A man that for most of his life has been stoic is breaking apart at the seams. "I know this is hard, Casper. Fuck, this is hard, but I need you here with me. "

He. Needs. Me.

He. Needs. Me.

"Who?" That's all I say as I look away from a man I admire but would love nothing more than to give a bunch of fives to in that moment. One or two solid punches to the mouth would help this growing need for violence that's slowly consuming me. This pain is eating away at my rationality like a disease.

Had he been with her instead of staying back to talk shit with my uncle.

Had he insisted she take more than one guard.

Had he, my mum...

Motherfuck.

I can't say it. Can't think it.

"Casper, we have someone in custody. The sack of shit claimed to have information on her—"

I'm out of my chair and in his face before Callum can blink. "Don't finish that sentence."

"Cousin, I know this is painful."

"You know fuck all at the moment," I seethe, chest heaving as my vision becomes hazy. The anger and hurt and pure venom flowing through my veins makes it hard to understand anything, and yet the words he said to me upon arriving continue to play on a constant loop.

"Aunt Penelope died on the operating table."

Those seven words broke something inside of me that will never be repaired. No one ever wants to think of a parent dying. Of the pain it will bring.

Then, with that sadness comes a regret that I'm not ready to deal with; she will never meet my Gem. A beautiful girl that I walked out on without looking back because the sadness in her eyes made it difficult to do so. She herself has been in my position. Dealt with this all on her own because her bloody cunt of a father forgot how to be a real man.

Because real men don't abandon their families.

Because real men don't skive on their responsibilities.

Because a real man takes care of those he considers his.

I stretch my neck from side to side. "Where is he?"

"Beneath the pub."

"Good." Turning my head slightly, I look at my father. "I'll have everything taken care—"

"We planned for this, son. Your mum..." He pauses to clear his throat as a single tear rolls down his cheek. I know this is hard for him. She was his everything for over forty years and I'm fighting to remember that. "Y-your mum and I planned for this when you two were boys. Granted, I thought I'd always go first, so I took care of everything to make it easy for her. She picked the flowers and location while I put together the rest."

"That's not what I'm talking about." My voice is terse, and Callum gives me a look that screams *not now*, but I can't control it, nor do I want to. My emotions are high, a battle between ire and sorrow that's suffocating me.

There's nothing I can do to fix this, but at the least, I'll avenge her. My beautiful mum didn't deserve her lot. Didn't deserve to have a bunch of delinquent arseholes as family.

I'll gut the son of a bitch that did this. He and anyone else involved are dead men walking.

"Let's take a walk, mate." Callum puts himself between us, and I didn't realize I'd moved. "We don't need to be fighting. Family first."

"I left for less than four motherfucking days," I yell out, fist pounding my chest hard enough that the sound in the room makes a passing nurse jump. "Four days, and my mum, bro. My mum…" I trail off, unable to finish.

"Casper," Dad says then, the tone in his voice one I haven't heard in a while. Not since he was *boss,* and I look back at him through narrowed eyes.

"Yes."

"Find him and bring him to me."

"You can have the scraps when I'm done." With that I walk out, pausing just long enough to squeeze his shoulder on the way out. I'm angry. Fucking furious, but I love him, and past the tumultuous emotions swirling within, this isn't his fault.

He won't feel my fury, but the rest of the world won't be so lucky.

———

THE PUB IS empty when Callum and I arrive.

It's quiet, the streets almost empty, and the night holds an edge of eeriness that mimics my mood at the moment. Even the few people walking to their cars or entering another eatery are quiet and with their heads down.

No one makes eye contact. No one so much as breathes in my direction.

Closing my eyes, I take a moment to help my mind settle. To focus on what's important: the death of an enemy.

"Jeffrey is the only person inside," my right-hand says, and I open one eye to meet Callum's. "How do you want to handle this? We can wait outside if you like?"

"Just you and me." I shift my Glock to behind my waistband so the arse doesn't see it upon my entering. Not yet. They can become intimate after a friendly chat.

"Send him home?"

"No. He can clean up afterward." The back door is just a few feet from me, and with each step I take closer, my muscles tighten and hands begin to clench and unclench. Death is close.

I can feel it all around me; a heady sensation overtakes my senses whenever I take a life.

Because while the man below didn't plan or pull the trigger, he helped by not coming to me.

The door is unlocked when I turn the handle, and my foot has not fully crossed the threshold when a scream rents the air. It's masculine and reeks of fear, making goose bumps appear on my skin.

All doors and the divider are open inside the dark kitchen. Moreover, I follow the sound without pausing. Don't need to.

Step after step, I make my way through my office and then down the staircase that leads to my playground. The lighting is soft and music even plays in the background, a song all football fans know by memory as a war cry for their team.

And there in the center of it all is a man around my age that I've never seen before mouthing what I think is a prayer. It's the same lip movement over and over, and it causes my glare to deepen while I take in the rest of him.

His hands are bound above him to a small metal pipe and his chest is bare, bruises and a few deep cuts littering his upper torso. Lower, I take in the streaks of blood that meet at the center of his chest and then flow as one down to his lower abdomen, staining his beige trousers.

The red liquid is dry, and his skin looks pallid. A bit sickly.

"My condolences, boss," Jeffrey say lowly from the prisoner's left, and the man's eyes snap to mine. It's obvious he knows who I am. They widen at the sight of me, his fear growing the closer to him I get.

I give my man a nod in appreciation for his words. "Wait outside and close the door behind you."

"Of course. I'll await orders." His footsteps are loud inside the room as he exits, but more deafening is the harsh breathing of the arsehole tied up in my prison. He's fighting against his restraints, pulling hard enough that blood appears at his wrist as he breaks the skin there.

Bloody idiot.

Callum takes his place behind him while I stop a few inches from his face. Eyes on his. "Name?"

"This is a mistake, sir. I don't—" He doesn't finish as my hand across his face silences him, snapping his head back and jostling his entire body as it sways.

"Answer the question and nothing else," I say, my tone even. I'm watching him, cataloging his reactions to make sure the idiot doesn't pass out from fear before I get what I need. Because fight or flight is quite an interesting thing. Causes reactions in people that they simply can't control, and escaping into your own mind is one of them. "Name, mate. If I have to ask you again, it will hurt."

"Andre Gellar."

"And where are you from, Andre Gellar?" Because his accent is American. Callum meets my eye from behind him and I nod for him to proceed, beginning to push the buttons of my long-sleeved vest through their respective holes. One by one they become undone and Andre watches, sometimes flinching if I make a certain rapid movement with my hand. He does so again when I take it off and toss it somewhere behind me. Still no answer. "Last warning. Where the fuck are you from?"

"New Jersey."

"Where in Jersey?"

"Patterson."

I crack my knuckles. "And what exactly is a man from New Jersey doing in London?"

"Just on vacation. I swear to you that...*please!*" he cries out through a split lip, blood rushing to the new cut after my strike. "This is a mistake."

"The mistake was running your mouth and claiming you set up the hit on my mum." His mouth opens to deny this, but before he gets a single word out, I bring my closed fist forward and clock him in the nose. The sound of it breaking, bone crushing behind the hit, only ignites the fury I have within.

I don't stop after one punch. I land one after another as a red haze overtakes my senses, using his face as a punching bag without feeling the stress on my knuckles. If anything, I want to feel that kind of pain—to forget for just a few minutes that because of this cunt and whoever is working with him, I lost the most important woman in my life.

Another bare-knuckle strike lands across the bridge of his nose and the skin gives way, opening to form a gash that bleeds profusely, splattering across my hands and bare chest.

"No more." It leaves him on a nasal whimper, and I stop for half a second to admire the damage. "I'll tell you anything you want to know."

"All right." I stretch my hand out, head tilting to the side as I appraise that sack of shit. "Talk."

"Mr. Jameson, I'm just an errand boy."

"Gathered as much. Talk." Turning away from him, I walk toward the back and grab a folding chair, bringing it with me to sit in front of his bloodied form. My eyes connect with Callum as I do, and he moves into position with a large plastic bag in his hand behind him. "Amuse me."

"My job was simply to deliver payment to the man hired to make the hit." Andre swallows hard, trying to see what Callum has in his hand from the corner of his eye. "He was supposed to kill a male member of your family, not your mother. It was a mistake."

"I want names," I grit out. Now isn't the time to fully lose control, at least until I get the information I need to proceed—to unleash my wrath on those who crossed me and mine.

"I've never met the man hired by my boss—" His airflow is cut off by the plastic bag closed over his head. At once, his body thrashes as breathing becomes difficult with the lack of oxygen. The expression on Andre's face is of pure terror a second before the material becomes foggy.

Callum removes the bag. "Tell us the truth."

Andre is gasping, face red and eyes a bit bloodshot. "I swear on my—"

I pull my gun from the waistband of my trousers and cock it, holding it up in his line of sight. "Let's try this again, Mr. Gellar. Who pulled the trigger?"

"Before making the delivery, I'd never seen the man before."

"I'm beginning to lose my bloody patience here, mate. You have three minutes to give me the name of your boss and the hired help." Still no answer; the arsehole is too busy watching the Glock in my hand. To help him along, I fire a warning shot to his kneecap. "Clock is ticking."

"Motherfuck!" he yells out, body trying to fold into itself as the rush of pain hits his nervous system.

"Names." This man has got to be the most incompetent man I've ever encountered. Bullet hole in his leg, battered face, and my cousin behind him ready to suffocate his arse, and still he doesn't speak up. Instead, he whimpers, a pathetic little sound that grates my nerves on a level that leaves me with little choice. "Again, Callum."

"Of course, boss." Callum places the bag once more, this time tightening the plastic so it molds to his facial features as he sucks in a desperate breath. "I loathe liars," my cousin seethes next to Andre's head, finally letting his own emotions out as he pulls the bag off a minute later. My mum was like his own. Probably more so since Aunt Miriam lives to travel and pretend that what funds her expensive lifestyle isn't drug and gun money. "Give up those names or it's your life."

"All I know..." he coughs, bloodied spit dribbling down his chin "...is that the guy lives on and off on a Caribbean island and takes on jobs like these as a hobby." Andre takes another pause, and I raise a brow. There isn't much time left in my countdown.

"Carry on, bloke. Today is not the day to test me."

"Please. I have a wife and kid on the way."

"No, you don't," Callum interjects, yanking his head back, exposing his neck. "When Jeffrey picked you up and offered you cheap pussy to strike a conversation, you told him you were newly divorced and desperate for an easy fuck.”

Andre flinches when I use the barrel of the gun to scratch my chin. “His name is Mauricio Hernandez and he was paid $500,000 in cash to do it.”

“And who the fuck do you work for?”

“He lives in New Jersey but is looking to take over the state of Massachu—” Andre doesn’t get to finish as I put a single bullet between his eyes. That’s all I needed to know.

CASPER

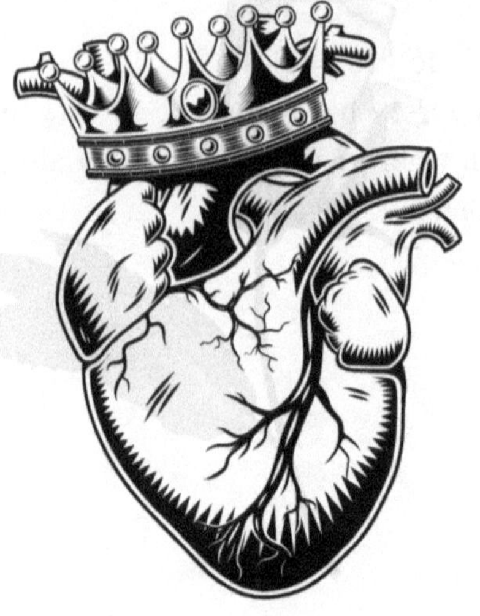

THERE ARE SIX OF us carrying my mum's casket down the row of the cemetery where she's being laid to rest. We own the entire area where the family's mausoleum is—toward the back end, away from others—and the surrounding graves; about thirty of them outside of ours.

My grandfather bought them just in case someone who works for the family needed one, an example we continue to follow:

A Jameson always takes care of their own.

And we will. My mum's guard who died protecting her, who took six bullets while trying to save her, will also be buried here in a private ceremony for his family. He will receive full honors, and they will be under our care for the rest of their lives. My care.

It's also that sense of loyalty that brought so many here today to pay their last respects. It's why everyone, including a few of the wives, are carrying and not concealing it. With our family being well known in the UK, many are out to see for themselves—to catch a glimpse of us in our private moment of grief. Magazines, international newspapers, and even social media bloggers turned conspiracy theorists are out to feature this story.

They have no respect.

Especially this one son of a bitch I'm seconds away from putting a bullet in the body of: a particular reporter for the largest network news station. He's cocky and pushing the boundaries; he's continuously getting closer with his phone out and recording our walk.

My father is at the front with mum's brother and I'm at the back, eyes on the man who just took another step.

"Leave it, brother. I have it," Malcolm Asher, a business associate and long-time friend, says from beside me. His voice is low so only I hear, and I flick my eyes toward him for a second, giving him a small nod that he understands. We're cut from the same cloth. Trust each other. "Ignore him until later. Javier will keep the man entertained for a few hours."

At the mention of Javier, his right-hand, I notice the reporter's gone. Not a single trace of him left behind, nor is there any commotion from the bystanders dissecting our every move.

Either way, I don't question it.

Know better than most that people have one-track minds and easily miss the obvious. A person could get stabbed in the middle of a concert surrounded by large bodies of strangers and not a single person will remember seeing the attack. It's why corrupt governments get away with so much.

Distract the mind and kill without repercussions.

We walk a few steps further and reach the open mausoleum, a tall Victorian building that houses our grandparents and now will have my mum. Everyone halts their steps and the employees help us put her down gently into a lift of some sort that will help them place her safely within.

And the moment we do, the skies open and a light sprinkling of rain begins to feed the earth. Her favorite flower, large pink peonies, are in full bloom, and I walk over to the nearest growth and pluck a single one as the priest begins to talk. I tune him out. I tune everyone out; my focus is on her.

My memory of her baking cookies after my football games.

The look on her face when I graduated from secondary school and then got my acceptance to Oxford.

The first time I killed a man, an arsehole that tried to rob me, and she helped me wash his blood from my favorite coat.

Mum was always there. Always.

My throat bobs harshly as I swallow back my emotions. This hurts. My anger and guilt are a heady combination, but showing any weakness is forbidden.

Not in public. Not until I avenge her death.

"Your mum would've loved these," my father says, coming to a stop beside me a few seconds later. He's been a pillar of calm these last few days, but the tremble in his hand as he reaches for a flower speaks volumes. "Thank you."

"Thank me when I bring you the head of her killer."

He gives me a barely perceptible nod. "Are you heading back to the US?"

"Soon."

"We need to talk."

"We will, but not for a few days." At my response his mouth opens, but when I look over at him, the rebuttal dies. I don't know what he sees in my eyes—grief or regret—but his backing down helps.

Right now I'm not okay.

I'm a ticking time bomb.

"...*let us pray.*" The priest's words meet my ears and I turn around, taking in how every head bows. How they all begin to recite their own plea to God above for her soul and our solace.

I don't join them.

Instead, I walk over to her casket and place the peony atop, hand lingering. My eyes close and my chest feels tight. My entire body shakes with the painful rage I have to swallow.

This is goodbye for now.

"I love you, Mum," I whisper, lightly tapping the coffin. "And I promise this will not go without punishment. I'll bathe the street with their blood in your name."

I'VE BEEN BIDING my time. Waiting.

Settling my affairs for when the time comes, and I decide on a change of scenery.

I'm also letting those playing this game move the chess pieces into the position I want.

They think I'm clueless. That I've given up as not a single attempt to find the hitman has been made.

That is, until now.

Something, the piece of shit inside of an abandoned warehouse in West Hendon Broadway, once used by union workers as their headquarters, doesn't know. The lights are on and I can hear the heavy thrum of a guitar throughout, but no security outside.

My eyes shift once more to my informant. "Are you sure?"

"Yeah." He's tweaking a bit; jerky little movements show how badly he's feigning for a hit, and yet his only request is that I pay his mum's hospital bills. "Bert was given the guns three days ago as payment for getting Mauricio out of the country. They led him out through the Chunnel to Paris where he later took a flight back to Guatemala."

"Guatemala?" I say, looking over at Callum who's raising a brow. That's Central America, not the Caribbean, but close. Close enough that he could jump back and forth with ease while withholding just where he lives.

Smart little cunt.

He's also a dead arsehole.

"That's what Bert told someone on the phone a few days ago." Tilting his head to the side, he nods to himself. All the while, his fingernails are tearing into his forearms and leaving deep welts in their wake. "I was emptying the trash in Bert's office when it happened, and no one looks at the tweaker as a threat, so he carried on as if I wasn't there. The plan was to take out your father or uncle, an older male, but they were just as happy with it being your mum. They wanted to hurt you, hurt your business, while a larger play is being made. You're a pawn in a bigger game, Mr. Jameson, and it all leads back to Boston."

"Why are you putting yourself in harm's way?" Callum asks, but I know the answer. I know because this man could've asked me for money and drugs and a plethora of shit, but he didn't. He wants his mum taken care of.

He loves his mum.

He understands they are not to be touched, and doing so is crossing a line there's no coming back from.

"Because I may be an arsehole, but what they did was wrong. Mums are sacred."

"Thank you," I say and reach out to stop him from tearing off more skin. "Now go back to the car and wait there. I'll take care of the rest."

He nods and walks off back in the direction he led us without another word, and I turn around. Look back at the building. Watching for movement.

"You trust him?" Callum steps up beside me, checking the magazine in his Glock.

"I do." *His loyalty just bought him a second chance at life. One, I'll make sure he succeeds at.*

"Then so do I."

Pulling out my own weapon, I raise a hand and then point in two separate directions. My men, six in total, know what to do and disburse without a verbal command. Two of them will take their position at the back of this building, and the other four will guard the sides. Two men at each possible exit while Callum and I walk in.

Literally step right inside the building while the wankers inside are too high to notice.

There are tables littered with old needles and cheap liquor. Bodies; a group of five men and two women are naked—taking turns fucking in each available hole—while flying high as a kite. Moreover, in the middle of that group of grunting animals is the man I came to pay a visit to.

Bert Holmes is a nobody trying to play the role of a top dog. A petty dealer at best.

I've let his business slide with the agreement that I take fifteen percent clean off the top and he stays in his lane. This deviation—betrayal—will cost him his life.

"Everyone with a pussy between their legs has one minute to get the fuck out." At the sound of my voice all within freeze, shocked expressions traversing their features before the scrambling begins.

One man to his left reaches for his trouser pocket, but before he can pull anything out, I shoot him in the head. A clean entry and exit wound near the center of his skull leaves blood and fragments of what looks to be his brain on the woman closest to his dead body. Her screams follow; she's struck with fear and doesn't move while the other woman runs out naked without looking back.

"Miss, you have thirty seconds before I do the same to you." I smile down at her, pointing my gun at the man behind her when he makes a sudden move. My finger on the trigger twitches, his fingers skim over the butt of his gun on the floor, and I shoot. Once. Twice. Three bullets into his chest and he bleeds out at her feet. "Ten seconds."

"Please, I'm just here to entertain—"

"Get the fuck out," I snarl, walking forward, taking her by the arm and then pulling her to her feet in one swift move. That's when rationality hits and fight becomes the predominant behavior. She's thrashing in my hold as I all but drag her toward the door. Yelling at me. Begging. I ignore it all.

"Make a single move, arsehole, and I'll shoot," Callum hisses, stepping forward only to plant his foot on another guard's head. From the corner of my eye, I see his head snap back but don't pause my steps.

"I won't tell anyone." The woman is in tears and still not recognizing my chivalry. Not realizing she's a few feet outside the door. "Don't kill me."

Looking down at her tear-stained face, I lower my voice so only she hears. "Leave and don't look back. Don't so much as think of this night again. Agreed?"

"Yes."

"Good." Taking off my button-down, I give it to her and stay in an undervest. "Now, go."

"Thank you." When she takes off a second later, I head back inside and lock the door behind me, taking in the sudden change in the large and dirty room's dynamic.

My men are now inside and standing around the still-alive men on their knees with Bert at the end. All heads are bowed, and some are shaking.

Their fear is palpable. The bloodied bodies of their friends with vacant eyes lay before them as a reminder of what is to come.

"Good evening, gentlemen," I say, coming to a stop before the first one, another nobody that falls to the ground as I empty the rest of my magazine into his body. "Let's try this again...shall we?" Coming to a stop beside the next man, I pull out a second magazine from my back pocket, I change it out and then cock it, all the while pointing the barrel at his head. As I do this, the putrid scent of urine hits my nostrils and I tsk in disgust. "*Good evening, gentlemen.*"

"Evening," the three of them mumble, voices shaking.

"Good job." It's patronizing, more so when I pat the pissing lad's head. "You can follow orders."

"Casper, what is—"

Callum backhands Bert with the handle of his gun, shutting him up and breaking his large nose and two front teeth in the process. "Speak when spoken to."

"Today is not the day to test me, Holmes." My eyes shift to Jeffrey for a split second. "Find them and bring them here."

"Right away, sir." He takes three of my men with him and they walk toward the back, directly toward the unlit section where I know his office is. Their footsteps are loud, more so as they move items out of their way— boxes, a few tarps, and then there's the subtle sound of a click.

One by one, lights come on. Each dingy fixture illuminates my belongings.

My guns. My property.

Jeffrey removes another tarp and finds a rolling container with wrapped bricks inside. He picks one up, weighing the contents in his hand, and then walks back over, leaving the other three to catalog what is there.

I've brought a large semi with me and they already have instructions to load and leave, which they do silently as one of my employees exits the building. The sound of a large engine follows, the headlights shining our way as he parks it and then they begin the retrieval process.

"Watch them," I command, and those three fuckwits do at once, shaking from their kneeling positions. For almost half an hour all that is heard is the sound of items being moved—wooden crates scraping against the floor and out the back loading area. One by one they disappear while Jeffrey stands beside me with a gift for my troubles. "Rubbish or worth it?"

He tears a corner of the wrapping off and tastes it. "It's very cheap quality."

I nod. Expecting as much. "Callum, please help Mr. Holmes to a chair."

"Oi, you heard him." Callum presses the trigger, shooting the pompous arse in the thigh. "Get up."

"This is all a misunderstanding. We can come to—" Bert shuts the fuck up, gritting his teeth after I shoot his other leg. He forces himself to a standing position, wincing as pain radiates throughout his body and blood runs down both limbs. Taking a step forward and then another, he doesn't stop until he's standing right in front of the chair my cousin pulled out for him.

"Do you need an invitation?" Callum waves a hand in the air, the same one with the loaded gun and finger on the trigger.

"I'm sorry." No, he's not. He's just fucked and knows it.

"Silence." The two still on the floor whimper at my barely contained snarl and I shift my attention toward the employee standing behind them. "They so much as move a muscle or cough, shoot them. A bullet for each minute twitch and sound."

"Yes, boss."

"Now, let's have a little chat, old friend." Jeffrey and Callum have moved a table in front of Bert and have added a chair for me, which I take, turning it around and straddling it backward. "How have you been?"

"Casper...this can be fixed." He's sweating profusely, body trembling from either the blood loss or nakedness, as I stare him down. His hands are up in a gesture of surrender, not that it means shit to me, but the longer I glare, the more nervous he becomes. "I didn't have anything to do with your mum...I swear."

"You swear?" Placing the gun down on the table, I pull one of my karambits out from my right pocket and flip open the blade. Its blade glimmers in the low lighting. "Is that right?"

"Yes, I—"

"I want your hands flat on the table."

"Okay." Bert does as I ask, palms face down, but he eyes the knife with distrust. And he should. "Casper, I can help you find the man responsible. I-I didn't...*fuck*!" His scream rings loud inside the warehouse, the echo bouncing off the walls as I embed the blade straight through the center of his hand and down between his middle finger and pointer, tearing the flesh in two.

"Your words mean fuck all to me." Bringing the bloody knife up, I wipe it on my vest before tearing the cocaine brick right down the center. A little bit of the white powder falls to the table and some on my trousers as I push it across to him. "However, you will be helping me. Talk."

"Are you going to kill me?"

"Are you going to talk?"

"Casper, I've been loyal to you and the Jameson family." Before I can reach across and snap his fat neck, Callum slams his face down into the powder. He holds him there, forcing Bert to pull the substance deep into his lungs as he fights to catch his breath. "Please!" He coughs, hands pushing against the cheap wooden table, the mangled fingers failing to grasp the edge.

After a minute, Callum pulls him back. "Ready to talk?"

"All I know is what I was paid for." He coughs, gagging while his pupils dilate. His speech is also becoming fast, chest heaving rapidly as the high begins to ascend. "Mauricio lives in Guatemala, but that information stayed between Nico Savino and me, as a precaution."

"Who's Nico Savino?"

"He wants Boston and now the daughter." Bert wipes his brow, only managing to smear blood across his face. "You're just the catalyst for that to happen."

"How am I involved in this?"

"You rejected his sister a year ago in Chicago during a visit. Does the name Antonella ring a bell?"

"No. It doesn't."

"She bloody remembers you, mate, and so does he. They wanted an in here—an alliance—to destroy Cancio." Bert suddenly shoots up from his chair, the pain from his wounds now nonexistent. "Is it hot in here? I'm sweating bullets."

"Why didn't you come to me when they approached you?"

"They offered me your position; I'd be an idiot not to accept."

"So you let an innocent woman die…my mother…and all because of your greed." Not a question, and he knows this. Sees the murderous rage that I am fighting to keep under control until I get what I need. He's a nobody in a long chain of bodies that will bleed for her death.

"I'm truly sorry for that." Bloodshot eyes meet mine, and in them, I see euphoria mixed with a hint of death lingering in the background. "Your mum wasn't something I was made aware of until after, Casper. She wasn't supposed to die."

"You're just as guilty."

He ignores the last part, fanning his face suddenly. "Christ, my heart feels like it's going to beat right out of my fucking chest. Can you turn on the fan?" Then, like the piece-of-shit lowlife he is, he walks over and does another small line and then smiles at me as if we're best mates.

Stupid bastard.

With him so close, I can't stop myself. Don't want to. Without blinking, I stand and reach out quickly with my blade open, slicing across his face. From orb to chin, I open a deep gash.

However, he doesn't so much as notice the deep cut or the profuse amount of blood falling now down his face. It's a testament to what a person can do or withstand while under the influence of a narcotic.

"Sit," I grit out, waving at Jeffrey to help the idiot. Which he does, pushing him down hard enough that one of the chair's legs break from under his weight, and it's a domino effect if I ever saw one.

His body falls forward, tipping the table as they both crash to the floor; the blow hits the dirty concrete below a second before his face follows. His inhale is deep and so is his groan. They both pull more into his system and he begins to seize, body shaking as breathing begins to get difficult.

I don't help him. Instead, I kneel beside him to pick up my fallen gun— a barrel that I use to place at the back of his head while placing my lips near his ear. "Never betray your master."

There are choking sounds coming from him, thrashing and jerky movements. Using the back of his head, I push the tip of my Glock deep into his skull as I stand.

Then, after a few minutes, all movements stop. His breathing is slow, almost nonexistent, and we all stand there watching as he gets closer and closer to an overdose with each deep inhale.

There's no regret in me when it comes, either.

Fuck him. Fuck them all.

I have the information I need and a girl to look out for. That I need to get in contact with.

And while I haven't been in Chicago in the physical sense, I still have eyes on her. Eyes that give me a report of her day every single bloody night that I'm away. She's protected. Will always be as long as I have breath in my body, and if this Nico wants her, he'll have to kill me himself.

Gem is mine.

"**M**OMMY, WHAT'S WRONG?" I ask, pausing at her doorway on my way to my own room. She's sitting in her little nook, what looks to be a letter in hand, and crying. It's not the kind of sobbing that attracts attention. No. This is silent and choking; her eyes are closed while tears fall, ruining her always-impeccable makeup.

I've seen her upset before, but never like this. This feels different.

Like whatever is in her hands will cut deep. Has cut deep.

"Baby girl, I need you to give me a few minutes," she manages between uneven breaths, not looking at me. But I don't listen. Instead, I drop my book-bag on the ground and enter, not stopping until I'm right in front of her. She's shaking, and my ten-year-old heart hurts, a feeling coming over me that I've never experienced before.

It's worry and fear and I know it has to do with Dad. He's the only one that makes her cry. "Is Dad okay?" I ask first, needing to know more than anything because while he's not the best father, I do love him. Wish he was here and not in Boston. "Just tell me. I'm a big girl and c-can handle it."

Whatever she hears in my voice makes her tearful eyes snap to mine, *her expression morphing into one of tenderness. "He's alive and without a single scratch." There's a hint of bitterness in her tone, but I don't say anything and nod. "But we do need to talk, Roe. How about you go and change and meet me downstairs in twenty or—"*

"Now, please."

"Aurora, I said—"

"Mom, you're starting to freak me out. Please."

"Okay. Okay." Standing from her seat, she gives me a sad smile, wiping under eyes with the pads of her fingers. "Give me two minutes. Drop off your book-bag and come back."

I nod, turning to walk out of the room, but before taking a single step, I turn around and hug her. Wrap my arms tightly around her midsection. "I love you, Mom. You know that, right?"

"Of course, baby. And I love you."

"Always and forever?"

"To the moon and back." Mom kisses my forehead then and pulls my arms from around her, squeezing my hands before letting them go. That haunting expression on her face is almost gone, but not quite. It's like a Band-Aid on a wound; covers the cut but doesn't make it go away. It's there hurting beneath the surface. "Now, go. I'll be here waiting."

"Be right back." I leave her there and almost make it to the door when she speaks again, making me pause.

"When you grow up, Aurora, I need you to find a man that will love you completely. Solely." It's a whisper full of so much emotion that I'm hit with another wave of hurt. I don't know if she wants a reply, but I still nod my head so she knows I'm listening. That I understand her. "Your happiness to him must come first, and you'll live to do the same for him. Never settle, baby girl. Never. No man that causes you a moment of pain due to selfishness is worth the heartache. You deserve the world. Never to be an afterthought."

I awake with a start, my body breaking out in a cold sweat as it's done every single time this memory re-emerges in the shape of a dream for the last few weeks. Ever since coming back home to Chicago a month ago—since my time with *him*—I've been off-kilter and can't shake these mental pictures.

I'm unfocused and questioning things.

My beliefs and life choices.

What led me to where I am now.

Because I remember that day to the very last second when I finally fell asleep:

The news that broke my heart. The tears that followed from both of us. The acceptance that I would never have a family—a real one—where my father lived with us and we were happy together.

Because just a few weeks after my eleventh birthday, Matteo Cancio and his wife announced the birth of their first child, a son, through a magazine article. The Bostonian businessman, as they were more than likely paid to portray him, was ecstatic about the arrival and looked so in love while holding the days-old infant.

It was an exclusive he gave this publication in exchange for good press. To help sway the way people saw him before his insider trading case of all things.

He's an asshole, but smart. He has never been caught or convicted of a single crime.

That day as I read the article, I lost a bit of my innocence, too. Every single word was a stab to the heart, and more so because he didn't tell me himself. No. I had to find out as a stranger would.

All of my hopes for a better relationship died, and so did the way I viewed my father.

Grabbing my cell from the nightstand, I look at the time while ignoring the four missed calls and sigh. "Great, it's almost six," I grumble, knowing that it'll be nearly impossible for me to fall back to sleep and with my alarm set for seven, I push the covers off. I'm tired and don't want to but throw my legs over the edge anyways. Grudgingly, I stumble a bit and manage to keep myself upright, walking into the en suite bath while hissing as the bright lights come on when the sensor picks up my movement.

My reflection in the mirror shows my displeasure. The bags under my eyes from lack of sleep show how unhealthy this all is.

And even though that dream makes me relive a hard memory, I know that its resurfacing has everything to do with a certain British man whose presence I can't evade while awake or asleep.

This same man has yet to contact me.

To so much as send a text message to assuage my thoughts.

Because I still hear his promises when I close my eyes. I remember how those hypnotic green eyes watched me from between my thighs while bringing me to orgasm.

I want him but despise the very thought on the same breath, more so as each day passes without a single call.

"What the hell is wrong with me?" I ask my reflection while taking my tank top off and then panties, hating how my eyes lower to the places on my torso where his marks are fading. The imprint of his fingertips on my skin is almost nonexistent and I miss them. I miss how alive he made me feel. "I can't be with someone like my father. A liar."

And it's with that thought that I walk over to the shower and turn the faucet, letting the water heat up before stepping in. It feels good on my body and for a second or ten, I just stand there while the warm water soothes my tired limbs before lathering. Something that I quickly realize is a mistake.

Not now. This needs to be an in-and-out situation.

My hands over my body, slippery from the suds—a woodsy scent that reminds me of him—makes my nipples harden into stiff, throbbing peaks. It's been a month since I felt the delicious ache Casper leaves behind and I'm needy. Aching as the image of his handsome face haunts me.

I hate how much I want him again. How easily I would give myself to him.

How if I slip a hand between the juncture of my thighs, I'll find my pussy slick and not from the water.

"*Christ*, I need help." And I'm also now in a rush because the temptation to touch myself—to come—is near maddening. Each inhale dares me to do it. To let my mind wander back to those hours where he took me over and over again, exhausting my body while leaving me afloat on a blissful cloud. "Wash, rinse, and out," I chant while doing so, fighting with myself when all I want is to give in—and I almost do, but the phone pinging on my countertop stops me.

Turning the handle, I shut the water off and step out, grabbing my towel off the rack before walking over. My hand touches the screen without picking it up, a quick swipe that nearly sends me stumbling back.

> I miss the sweetness of your pussy on my tongue. ~Casper

> How your walls choke my cock when you come. ~Casper

> I'll be seeing you soon, Gem. ~Casper

Three quick texts that scare and excite me more than they should. They have me on edge and breathing hard. Thinking. Craving. Swallowing hard.

No. No. No, damnit. I need to get my mind off him and forget. I need to move on and thank my lucky stars that I didn't get in any deeper. I return the favor, ignore him like he has me for these last thirty days.

If only my heart would listen to my head.

"So you've been a bit distant lately?" Aliana asks as we walk out of the women's shelter I inherited and run. It's late, easily almost eight at night, and I'm dead on my feet. "What gives?"

I can't help but be irritated by her question each time she asks, even though it's not her fault. To be honest, it's no one's, but I just haven't been myself since coming home.

Between the dreams, my father's insistence, and thoughts of Casper, I'm fried. Beyond exhausted, and she sees this. My best friend since middle school knows me, is worried, and I just don't have a way to explain the craziness my life has become since my trip to London.

So, like the hot mess I've become, I evade. Take a moment of silence to just look around the front grounds of the Conte House while ignoring the *tap tap tapping* of her foot.

This place was my mother's. Her dream that I continue to carry on and make thrive while doing so.

Sure, I could've gone to school to become a doctor or lawyer, but that was never my passion. This is. And after graduating high school at seventeen, I immersed myself—worked with her every single day until she couldn't—in order to take over.

Hell, this has been my second home since the age of fourteen when it opened; I've worked in every department. From helping in the kitchens to CEO and everything in between, I've done them all and with pride. It's my way of honoring her memory.

To keep her dream of helping women get out of toxic environments—to leave the men that broke them down—alive.

This place keeps me close to her memory. Every successful case helps to fill the void that her death left behind.

Aliana clears her throat. "Quit Ignoring me."

I let out a tired sigh. "I'm fine. Just really tired—"

"Finish that sentence and I'll kick you," she deadpans, pulling on my arm so we stop at the end of the sidewalk that leads to the parking lot. "Look at me."

"What?" Turing my head, I find her brown eyes narrowed, searching my face for the answer as to why I'm so distracted. A little lost. Although I'm sure it's pretty clear to see that I have a problem named Casper Jameson that follows me around. Like a ghost. Like a life-altering realization, nagging at me from the back of my mind.

"Talk to me."

Out of all the words she could say, why those? The same ones he used back in Ibiza between rounds of mind-blowing sex. When he caught me with my walls down and I was most vulnerable. Open to him.

"Maybe I'm just hungry and in need of a strong margarita?"

Releasing my arm, she pulls out her phone. "Uber? I'll treat while you spill?"

"There's nothing to..." I trail off as my own phone goes off, and it's a text from him. His special ringtone. Then, because I have no control when it comes to this man, there's an automatic pull at my lips. They curl at the right, a cheesy grin, while her eyes get an evil glint to them. "Don't."

"Aren't you going to look?"

"Nope."

"Why?" She reaches for the device in my hand, but I pull back before she can snatch it. "I knew it!"

"Stop. It's nothing." My attempt at nonchalance is met with a laugh. "I'm serious. It was a one-time thing that—"

"You had a one-night stand?"

"It was more than one night."

"You hoochie!" *Christ, the decibel of her voice is loud.* "Who and where? Are you dating him? Do I know the dude?" My eyes shift around us, hoping no one heard, but I'm not so lucky when two volunteers a row down in the parking lot look our way. They wave, but the one to the left adds his version of a flirty grin to it. "Poor guy. He's going to be so sad when he realizes you're taken."

I shrug with a grimace. "Lawrence just isn't my type."

"No one has been since that douche bag, who shall not be named, that you dumped months ago." Ali raises both hands in a "praise the lord" gesture and I laugh.

"You're so extra, babes."

"And you're so not getting out of this." My shoulders drop, causing her to giggle and clap. She won and she knows this.

"Fine. Just hurry up and call for a car." *I'm going to need alcohol courage for this. A lot of it.*

"Yay! I can't wait to..." I don't hear the rest of her excited speech as my eyes stray toward the cell I'm unconsciously holding up. My right index finger swipes across the screen without my permission and I read his words. A gasp gets caught in my throat and my skin prickles with excitement.

With a need so palpable, a harsh shiver runs down my spine.

> I need you. ~Casper

Aurora

"OH MY GOD," Ali says for the sixth time since I began my story, vibrating in her seat inside our favorite Mexican restaurant. Just those three words. Nothing else. It's almost like she's a scratched CD, which would be funny if it wasn't due to my stupidity. "I'm shook."

Yup, she is definitely cheering me on. Why did I hope for anything different?

"Can we drop it?"

"We most certainly will not," she counters while wagging her brows. "Now, tell me..."

"For the love of all things holy, Aliana. What now?"

"Was he huge? Cause I'm living vicariously through you at the moment." Her lips purse in an exaggerated pout as I choke on the remaining drink in my glass. "I haven't had a single date in months."

"I'm not discussing that," I hissed through clenched teeth before faking a smile for the older couple a few tables away. "And can you tone it down a bit, chick? You're drawing attention."

"Why are you being so overprotective if it meant nothing?" Aliana grabs our shared pitcher of margarita and pours us another drink before bringing the glass to her lips and taking a healthy sip. "This is some pure hot epicness and I'm happy for you."

"And you're a dork."

"We came to that conclusion back in junior high, babes. Remember when I did the Macarena—danced my heart out for the talent show and won the creative award?" She waves me off, but her eyes are analyzing my expression. The woman is like a dog sniffing out a juicy piece of meat. "Now, tell me the truth. How did he make you feel?"

I laugh, remembering her trying to guilt-trip me into performing with her. "Still not answering—"

"Is this seat taken?" a voice says from behind me and I stiffen, my entire body tensing. The anger I experience is instant and so are my biting words. "What are you doing here?"

"You and I both know the answer to that, Aurora." He pulls the chair out from beside me and sits, waving over some random waiter to take his drink order. The server doesn't hesitate, most in the country knowing who he is, and making him wait like a normal person is a no go. "Scotch on the rocks," he says before the man can ask.

"Right away, sir." Then he hurries off to do his bidding while I sit in my chair quietly seething.

"Leave."

"You left me no choice." His eyes shift to my companion and smiles. "Hello, Ali. How are you, sweetheart?"

"I'm good, Mr. Cancio." She looks at me with a *what do we do* expression. "Working hard and taking some business classes at night."

"That's wonderful to hear." My father nods to himself as the waiter drops off his drink. "And you, dear? Still running the women's shelter?"

"You know the answer to that."

"I do," he muses and brings the glass to his lips, taking a slow sip and then savoring the amber liquid. "Which is why I am here with an offer."

"Maybe I should go?" Aliana says, shifting uncomfortably in her seat. "Or do you need—"

"There's a car waiting to take you home, Miss Rubens. I appreciate your understanding."

Her eyes meet mine and I nod. "Yeah. I'll see you tomorrow."

"Okay. Goodnight, sir." Her smile is a bit forced, but he doesn't seem to notice. That, or he doesn't care.

"Goodnight."

Pushing her chair back, she stands and grabs her purse. "Want me to pick up breakfast tomorrow on my way in?" In other words, our conversation isn't over.

"At nine in my office."

"Love you, boo."

"Love you, too," I say and then she's gone, leaving me alone with *him*. A him I turn to stare at with impassiveness. "Talk."

"Why are you avoiding me, Roe?" The tinge of annoyance makes me bristle, but before I can respond, Matteo holds a hand up. "And don't give me the crap about my absence or the business; you've never ignored my calls before. We've never gone so long without so much as a hello."

"May I speak?" At his nod, I snort. "That was rhetorical."

"Can we please cut the attitude?"

"Can you stop stalking me?"

"I'm not stalking you. Not in the way you think."

"Then how?" I demand, pushing my mostly empty chimichanga plate forward. "Because popping up at random places I'm visiting constitutes as that. You *are* having me followed."

"I'm not."

"Lie to me again and I'll—"

"You might not believe this, but I do know you." Sitting forward, he places both elbows on the table. While his stance is relaxed, I know he's uncomfortable. That talking about his feelings isn't something he enjoys. "I know the kind of books you like to read, that you hate to exercise but love to swim and that Mexican food is a weakness of yours. Just like your mother, Roe...this place was a favorite of hers."

Those words pierce me. They soften the stiffness in my posture, and I slump in my seat. "So you randomly picked this place because we like tacos?"

"No." The smile he gives me is sad. As if he's remembering something. "I chose this place because every Wednesday you two would have dinner here without fail."

"How would you even know that?" Because Christ, since when does he care?

"Believe it or not, Bianca and I spoke every Friday night to share our week. This meal was always the highlight of it...you were always at the top of her priorities."

"She was an amazing mother and I never doubted her love for me."

He nods, a sad smile on his face. "I'm sorry for making you believe that I didn't care, Roe. I also know that the failure of our relationship does fall at my feet, kid, but I'm trying. At least give me that. Trust that I do care."

"So you keep saying, but actions...or better yet, years of your inaction have proven the *opposite*." Matteo opens his mouth to argue, but I hold a hand up. "Which begs the question: why are you here now? You're not retiring at the moment, and by the time you do, you'll have Lucas to take over. If he's your pride and joy, why not mold him for the position?"

"You're right, I'm not retiring just yet, but...and here's the *but* you're missing; I'd like to within a year. I want you in my life, Roe. Want to give you the place I should've years ago as my firstborn and heir." He reaches across the table and takes my hand in his, giving it a squeeze. "And while the rejection hurts, I know it's my fault. I did this to our relationship."

Those words bring tears to my eyes that I refuse to let fall, and I choke them back. "I don't know what you want me to say or do, Dad."

"I know." Releasing my hand, he sits back and picks up his drink, taking a hearty sip. "Which is why I have a proposition for you."

Mimicking his pose, I take a sip of my margarita. "A proposition?"

"Yes."

"Go on." I'm curious if nothing else.

"How would you feel about coming to Boston for a few days next month." The word *no* is on the tip of my tongue and he notices this, shaking his head. "Before you shoot me down, hear me out."

"Okay."

"I'd like for you to come down and meet some people...see the business, and not just go by what you have in your head. There's more to our name than the illicit side of things, Roe. Just give me a chance to show you that."

"It's a complete package. One doesn't go without the other."

"It does, but all I'm asking for is a few days of your time."

"And if I say no?" I raise a brow in challenge.

He gives me a grimace. "I'm really hoping you don't."

"Why that face?"

"I have one more proposition if all else fails, and I know you won't like it."

"Then don't ask me."

"Just come to Boston with an open mind."

"Give me a few weeks and I will." This has the word mistake written all over it, and yet I don't turn him down like I should. "However, I need you to keep one thing in mind…"

"What's that?"

"I make no promises."

<hr>

THE NIGHT AIR is a bit chilly as I exit the restaurant, leaving my father inside to settle the tab since he insisted on paying. I've already ordered an Uber to come and pick me up, much to his annoyance, but tonight isn't the night to push. I've acquiesced, made a promise to come and see him— spend time with a man that I still really don't know.

Checking the app, I realize that the driver is still a good eight minutes away and sigh. "Hurry up, dude. All I want is my bed and—"

"How are you, Miss Cancio?"

I know who it is before I turn my face, not at all shocked to find him lurking. He looks the type. The kind that is always waiting and biding his time to strike.

Dominic reminds me of a snake in the grass, and I hate how immediately uneasy I feel with him.

"It's Conte."

"Excuse me?" His expression shows a perplexing look that I'm not buying.

"I'm sure you've done your homework by now." Looking back at the restaurant's entrance, I'm hoping for my father's appearance. "Right-hand men are usually more on their game than what you showed in London. The same mistake wouldn't be made twice."

Dominic pushes off the wall, gait slow as he comes closer. "You're right. I'll give you that."

"Then why pretend?" I ask, raising a brow, holding my position because I'll never show just how uncomfortable he makes me feel.

"I'm just trying to make conversation, Aurora." Dominic raises both hands in a showing of peace, stopping a few feet from me. Close enough that the harsh scent of his aftershave tickles my nose. "Our last encounter was unpleasant and that's my fault—something I owe you an apology for, if you give me the chance to."

"Go on."

"Okay." At my quick response, he smiles, and it does nothing to soften his features. "I'm very sorry about what happened back in London between us a month ago and would like to make amends. That's not me, and my shitty day shouldn't have been taken out on you."

"Thank you." He seems sincere, and I'll take it with a grain of salt. Still don't trust him, but I'll play nice for now. At the very least, make it less unpleasant when I eventually see him in Boston. "I appreciate that."

"I'd also like to invite you out for a few drinks tomorrow. To get to know each other a little better."

"That sounds a lot like a date."

He shrugs, that grin turning into a smirk. "I would like it to be."

Not happening, buddy. "I'm sorry, but I'm seeing someone."

"Who?" he says, an accusatory tinge to his tone that has no place being there. That, and I don't miss the flash of anger on his face.

It's quick, but I saw it. Don't like it either; he has no place to feel any kind of way when it comes to my persona.

"That's none of your—" I'm interrupted by the ringing of my cell and I look down, noticing right away that the area code is foreign and at once, a smile tugs at my lips. Excitement fills my belly because it has to be him. No one but him has my number that doesn't live here. "I need to take this."

"I see."

"Have a good night."

"You too, Miss Conte." The emphasis on my last name makes me look up, but I still swipe a finger across the screen, accepting the call. "We should be seeing each other again, and very soon."

I don't answer. Don't have time to, either.

My Uber pulls up then and just as I reach for the car door, Dominic opens it for me in a show of chivalry that doesn't come off as genuine. It's the one thing I've been blessed to inherit from my father; I can spot bullshit a mile away.

And he reeks of it.

Before stepping into the car, I give my father's employee a nod while bringing the phone to my ear. "Hey," I say, and then close the car door without acknowledging him again. There's something not right there and the next time I see Matteo, we will be discussing it. *I just hope he listens and doesn't brush me off.* "It's been a while, Mr. Jameson."

"Too fucking long, Gem."

CASPER

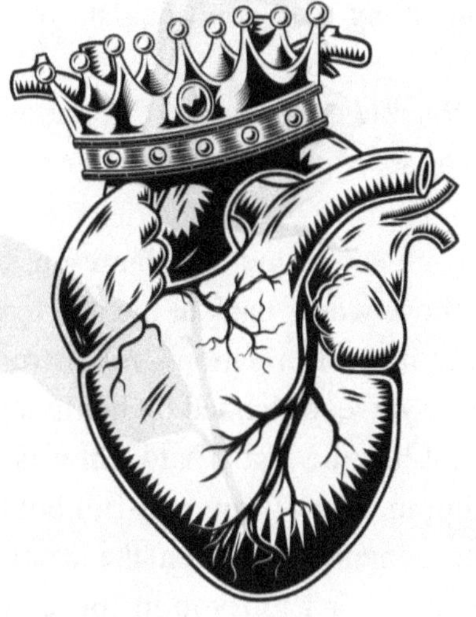

"*TOO FUCKING LONG, Gem.*" And it's the truth. The moment those words leave my lips, their weight settles on my chest and I realize my mistakes...

The first being leaving her without me. Open to some wannabe cunt sniffing around what doesn't belong to him. Her bodyguard, Alexander, lets me know about my little friend Dominic. Of him asking her out on a date, and even though I'm not physically there to break his face, I interrupt. Made sure to call where he could see her expression at my call. The smile on her face, which her bodyguard sent me a picture of.

Then, there's another area I bodged up; I didn't call. Didn't communicate like I should've after leaving her so abruptly, and if anyone would have understood, it's her. My Gem would've been there for me.

I'm an arse.

A car horn sounds in the distance before she releases a sigh, yet I feel no animosity. "Where have you been? It's been weeks, and I was worried about you."

"I'm sorry, love, but—"

"But what? Talk to me...wait...give me two secs." She pulls the mobile from her ear to answer someone, telling them to turn left at the end of the road. *Where is she?* Then it hits me. It's Wednesday, and that's Mexican night with Aliana. Something they don't deviate from. "Sorry, Uber driver took a wrong turn."

"It's all right." A chuckle escapes me at her adorableness, the first in a while. This shyness that seeps through when her guard is down. "Are you heading home?"

"Don't change the subject on me, Mr. Jameson, but yes I am. Now, let me in." Her throwing those words back at me, the teasing tinge in her tone, and the fact there's been no recrimination—no distrust—cements what I've known since the moment my eyes landed on her in my pub.

She's special and not like the rest. That Gem was meant for me.

So, I give in. Taking the top off my half-full bottle of whiskey, I take a sip before placing the container back on the center console. "My mum passed away a few hours after I left you in Ibiza, Aurora." From her end there's a soft gasp and then heavy breathing, the kind one makes when emotions choke you—when tears form at the corner of your eyes. Listening to her, I let out a heavy breath of my own, sitting back while staring at my childhood home. Taking in the guards on duty as they make their rounds while pretending to ignore me. "A hired assassin took her from us, and...and it's why I left straight for the hospital after my cousin delivered the news. It's why I've been gone and uncommunicative."

"*Christ*, Casper. I'm so—"

"I know, sweet girl." The tears in her voice gut me and I rub a hand over my chest. This weird connection we have, even thousands of miles away, is palpable. It lets me sense her emotions as if they're mine. Clearing my throat, I grab my drink and take another sip, focusing on the slight burn it leaves behind instead. "You're too perfect to be anything but, and while I appreciate it, right now I just need you. For a few minutes, I need nothing but you."

"You have me." It's low and soft and soothes a part of me that's both in pain and restless. That wants to bring back the bloody bastard I killed earlier tonight just to watch the life drain from his body again, a drop of blood or inhale of coke at a time. "Can you stay on the phone for a few minutes?"

"I can."

"Can we FaceTime where you are?"

"We can."

"Good, now hush. Just don't hang up." Then, there's some rustling and the jingling of keys. A car door opens then closes, there's a muffled good-bye, and she's back. Her breathing is a soothing balm as I roll down my windows and light up a cigarette, pulling the earthy smoke deep into my lungs and then release it slowly. We do this for a few minutes, just being, and I enjoy the silence by taking a few deep drags and then toss it out the window, ignoring the man that picks it up and then returns to his post. And I'm still looking his way when she lets out a snort. A cute one. "I don't know why I'm nervous all of a sudden. You've seen me naked."

I know this is hard for her. It's easy to see the pain Aurora tries to hide whenever her mother is mentioned—when she revisits the memories, and yet, the small joke is made for my benefit. To ease my tension.

I'm falling helplessly for her. Without an ounce of struggle or restraint.

"And I think about it—you—constantly."

"Accept, perv," she says, and I close my eyes to picture that decadent blush of hers. "I'm waiting."

"So impatient, little girl," I chastise and then do. Pulling the device from my ear, I press the FaceTime button on the mobile. A click. A few seconds. A beautiful face staring back at me. Her expression is soft, and those expressive hazel eyes are full of unshed tears she's refusing to let drop. She looks exhausted but happy. Unguarded and peaceful. "Hi."

"Hello, love." Her smile is blinding at the term of endearment, a sweet little curl of her lips, and I can't stop myself from swiping a finger across the screen. From wishing she was here so I could taste that berry-colored mouth. "Let me see you."

"Naked?" At her words my cock twitches, an automatic response.

"No, but if you're offering..." I trail off, raising a brow suggestively. And while I'd love nothing more, now isn't the time. It'd be a cruel punishment for the two of us. "But seriously, Gem. Just pull the phone back and let me see my girl."

"Your girl?" she questions but is already placing the device somewhere that holds it up and allows her to stand back, giving me a full view of her beautiful body in a pair of painted-on denim trousers and a sky-blue vest with her company logo on it. The top is tight and has a few splatters of paint—accentuating her larger-than-a-handful breasts—while the denim trousers have a few bleach stains on them, the kind strategically placed by the designer with rips at the knees.

Comfortable yet sexy. But then again, the woman could wear an old potato sack and I'd still find her attractive. A cock-throbbing fantasy.

"Yes. Mine." Bringing my hand to my chin, I rub my thumb across my bottom lip a few times. "Rough day at the women's home, love?"

"Why do you say...wait. How do you know where I work?"

"Own, Gem," I correct. "You own the place."

"Fine. Own it." She huffs, pulling her long hair down from the high ponytail she had it in. It tumbles down her shoulders, the waves with curls at the ends framing her face. "I never told you anything about where I work, Casper. Did you pull a file on me?"

"Had it waiting for me at my desk the second I left you at the hotel."

"No shame, huh?"

"None when it comes to you." I'm not going to deny or lie to her.

Tilting her head to the side, she purses her lips. "That should really piss me off."

"And yet it doesn't." Not a question, but a statement. "A part of you likes the fact I'm obsessed with every minute detail. Infatuated with you."

"I will neither confirm nor deny that." Aurora shimmies out of her trousers, letting them drop to the ground while giving me a peak of a light purple pair of cotton panties. They're molded like a second skin, outlining the perfect little pussy my mouth waters for.

At the sight, my cock gives a harsh jerk within the confines of my trousers, beads of pre-come rolling down the tip. "You don't need to."

"What else do you have in that magical file on me?" A yawn escapes her then, and I shift my eyes to the clock on my dash. It's late, and I feel a little guilty for keeping her. I'm used to being awake at this time—it's well past three in the morning here and I'm six hours ahead. "Is the math test I failed my senior year in there, too? Or what about the time I got suspended for punching a kid in the year below mine for trying to touch my ass?"

"Give me his name."

"My father threatened him personally when he found out." Gem rolls her eyes, but you can tell she finds it amusing. "He made him pee his pants while his father watched, and then apologized for him being a creeper."

"So he kissed arse, then?"

"Absolutely. Now, about that file..."

"That's a topic to be discussed later. When you're more awake." She pouts, looking at me with this sassy little expression that I want to kiss off her face. "How about I put you to bed instead?"

"How?"

"Take me to your room and lay me on the bed beside you." My father is standing at the door looking toward my car, probably wondering why I haven't come inside, but I ignore him. He's been having trouble sleeping since mum passed, and I find myself stopping by every other night to make sure he's okay. Tonight, though, he called me later than normal and can wait a little while longer. "I'll keep you company until you fall asleep."

"You'd do that?"

"Pretty girl, I'm starting to realize that there isn't much I wouldn't do for you."

"Something you want to tell me, son?" my father asks the very second I take a seat across from him in the living room. His features are hard and lips thinned; the sign of an impending reproach. Not that I've gotten many over the years, but the few I did were memorable.

"Spit it out." Because quite frankly I don't have time for whatever stupidity he wants to impart. How he wants to act like he has an active role —his old one—in our organization. "I'm tired and have no interest in playing a game or going around in circles. You have something to say, just say it. What did you ask me to come over for?"

He sits back and regards me, something that in my early teens intimidated me. "You know I still have some pull of my own, Casper. That I know about—"

"I'd be very careful in choosing your next words, Dad. Don't start something with me you won't win."

"I'm not the enemy here."

"And she is?" I hiss out, gritting my teeth in order to not say something that will cut deep. My anger toward him hasn't waned completely. It's there, festering, and made worse by his audacity to look into Aurora. And while I understand the circumstances, I still hold him partially responsible too.

"Her arsehole father—"

"Did not kill Mum." At the finality in my tone, his mouth snaps shut. "There's a family trying to overthrow Matteo Cancio and keep her as a prize. Something that I'll never allow to happen."

"How are we involved, then?" There's less hostility to his tone, but the stone-cold expression is still very present. His narrowed eyes are pleading with me to make him understand. To make it easier. "Why did I just bury my w-wife?"

And it's at that very moment, as his voice cracks, that my anger toward him evaporates. It's just gone. Seeing him break, the tears that spill forth and then the tremble of his hand as he rushes to wipe them away, are proof that he's living with a pang of guilt that's crippling him. Choking him.

"I'm going to need you to listen very carefully. Can you do that?"

"I think it's best if I head to bed. I'll see you in the morning."

"No. You need to stop and listen." Sitting forward, I let my hands hang between my parted thighs, eyes on his. "It's not your fault."

"I should've been there."

"It's not your fault."

"I see it in your eyes, son. I let you both down and—"

"It's not your bloody fault," I all but snarl, slamming a hand atop the vintage coffee table my mum spent hours restoring during one of her phases. "There are two fucking cunts responsible and I have their names. *I* will go to the ends of the earth if I have to in order to bring you their heads. They did this and will pay with blood. You have my word."

He nods but holds a hand up. "I want to be there."

"Done."

"Thank you." His head tilts a bit then, and this time the way he's watching me is different. "Is she worth going to war for? Because we both know it will head that way if you step in to protect."

She's more than that. "Aurora is mine."

CASPER

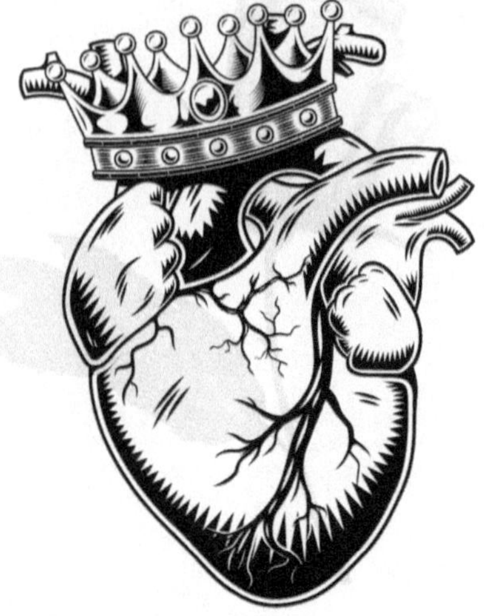

IT'S BEEN WEEKS, and nothing on the whereabouts of Mauricio. Not a fucking sign of the son of a bitch has been found. He's gone deep into hiding, and now I have another matter to take care of at the moment. Aside from not seeing my Gem since Ibiza, I now have a monetary transaction being investigated by the United States government.

They made a move to seize the wire, to tack it onto Asher Holdings as a launder attempt—to expose him for what we all know he is. The man is an arsehole with brass balls unafraid to do what he does best: move money for criminal organizations, without fear.

I make it, and he *cleans* it.

However, what was supposed to be a simple transaction has been compromised by two very stupid individuals. One by greed, and the other by trying to impress a useless cunt below him.

He let his ego talk for him, and that's a big *no no* in this business.

You see, hear, and know of nothing. You don't talk. You don't try to make moves outside of your lane or it will cost you.

Pulling out my mobile, I send a quick text to Gem.

> Morning, beautiful. Any plans today? ~Casper

My plan is to surprise her later. To fuck my beautiful Gem like the perfect obsession she's become.

> Hey! How's it going? ~Gem

> And my plans are the following today: nothing, couch, junk food, and Netflix. ~Gem

> Sounds amazing, love. Rest as much as you can today…Skype later? ~Casper

She's typing just as I hear a man scream from the inside and I chuckle. *Bastard is having fun.*

> We can most definitely sexy Skype later today.
> 😌 Around 8 p.m. my time? ~Gem

Fuck, she's perfect. My perfect.

> It's a date. ~Casper

I reply back to keep up the charade. Let her think I'm far away…it'll be much sweeter that way.

Pocketing the device, I refocus on the issue that brought me back to Chicago without my letting Aurora know. It's why on a late Sunday morning I find myself opening a large metal door with enough force that it bounces off the wall, and the resounding bang that follows causes a woman to cry out.

Jeffrey and Callum are with me—leaving the three other men outside— walking just a few paces behind and with the hoods of their black sweat- shirts over their heads. The hallway is long, but there at the end is my friend kneeling in front of a man—while a few close by are on their knees.

The concrete is already stained with someone's blood.

"Good morning," Malcolm says, standing up to greet me, extending his hand out while the woman whimpers again. Something that isn't the norm;

we don't harm women this way. We have more civilized ways to make them cooperate. *What did you do to find yourself in this mess?* "How are you, my friend?"

"Could be better, mate." I grip his hand in mine and then pull him into a hug. "Thank you for the *help* at the funeral with the reporter. My father and I are very appreciative." My whisper is met with a barely perceptible nod. Just enough of a movement to let me know he heard. We don't know what happened to the man, nor do we care, but he was never seen again. Pulling back, I pat his shoulder twice. "Bloody traffic here always gets me in a mood."

"You're a native, Casper. You should be used to it by now."

"Semi native, thank you very much." The motherfucker just laughs, rolling his eyes as someone groans from behind us. Malcolm Asher's crazy matches mine, and it's one of the reasons we work so well together. With global operations, he provides certain money management services that a family like mine requires.

He sets them up. He watches over them.

Strip clubs.

Launderettes.

Car washes.

All businesses that deposit large quantities of cash day in and out. It's almost like recycling in a sense; the dirty and unusable goes in and the clean and untraceable comes out.

"Four months a year is enough to qualify."

"Fuck you, and never." At my reply he laughs, slapping my back. The men around us chuckle, but just as soon it all dies down, the seriousness resettling in. "Now, how are we going to fix this, Malcolm? Cause we have a lot of money being held up by—"

"I have it all," he interrupts while I raise a brow in question, not understanding what's going on, especially after our last phone conversation where he asked me to be here today. "Before the feds got ahold of it or put a pause on the transaction, I froze everything. Moved the capital offshore, and my guys did what they needed to do to make everything disappear."

"So we're good, then?" *Why am I here?*

"No. Not in the least." Malcolm tilts his head toward two men I've never seen before. I take in both his hostility and how they cower under his glower. "We won't be okay until I make an example out of this asshole and his family."

"Who are they?"

"The orchestrators." At once, I pull my Colt out and point it at the younger of the two males as my ire resurfaces to the forefront. This cunt set my operations back and that's un unforgivable offense, but before I can shoot, Malcolm pushes my hand down. "They are mine, Casper. All three."

"Then why tell me, arsehole?" I hiss, shrugging his hand off. "This delay is costing me a shipment coming in tomorrow night. With the heat on my operations, the weapons supplier isn't feeling comfortable."

"Because I want them to watch you leave this warehouse with every single *ounce* of their merch." As the last word leaves him, I notice the few men attending to barrels upon barrels of bricks wrapped in plastic. "The coke and electronics are yours to do with as you please. Dump them in the river for all I care, but they won't make a fucking cent in profit."

"Apology accepted, bloke." Walking over to one of the containers, I pull out one of my karambits, a smaller version of my two back home, and rip open one of the packages. With the blade's tip, I take a small amount and taste it. Nod to myself as I realize the quality at once: Columbian pure white. "I'll take it all."

"Done." Malcolm looks down at the younger male with a smirk. "Load it up. Three trucks are outside waiting, and Casper's men will drive them away."

"Understood." Javier whistles and within minutes, everything is gone. As if it was never here.

"Thank you, Malcolm. I know my business is always safe with you…"

"But?"

Walking back over to my friend, my eyes shift between the men with covered faces and the three on the floor in front of them. How pallid the older man looks. The blood he's lost on the floor. "How will we make sure this never happens again?"

"Like this," Malcolm says, and Carmelo comes forward then, a box in his hands. "Go on. Open it."

"If it's a bloody snake, you arse, I'll shoot you."

"Open it." He laughs and so does Callum behind me. They know how much I despise reptiles. I'm an equal opportunity hater when it comes to them—a weakness those closest to me find hilarious. Me, not so much.

Opening the box, I look back him. "What the pissing hell is this?"

"Two tongues. One for each man that played a part in this."

"Michael?"

"Knows to never betray his family again. Losing *his* was his penance."

"He's family…no?"

"Then he should know better. They all do now."

"And the other?"

"Belonged to Phillip Mitchell. A low-level criminal that he…" Malcolm points toward the younger male "…paid to try and extort me. His idiocy cost him his life."

"Thank you." Because I do appreciate the gesture. Tossing the box containing the two appendages toward the crying woman, I hold in a laugh when she scrambles back with a shriek when it lands near her leg. "When can we continue with the transaction? Will it be while I'm still here?"

"Give me three weeks to make some moves."

"Done." I extend a hand for him to shake. "I'll be heading out, mate… I'm hungry and need to make another pit stop before heading home." *Is that what she is? My home?*

"Of course, but before you go…" Javier lowers the hood from the two men and stands back while Malcolm pulls out his gun, firing two shots. One in the neck and the other in the chest. The men fall to the ground and no one moves; all eyes are on him. "They weren't very vigilant during their shifts and let people make illegal deals on my property. For that they paid the ultimate price."

"What's fair is fair." I'm not going to argue that point when I'd do the same. Turing to leave, I take two steps when he speaks again.

"There's a simple request that I want witnesses for."

"Of course, brother." I turn back to fully face him and watch as he sets his eyes on the younger man, walks over, and the picks up two photos from the ground. His eyes roam the picture and soften for a split second before hardening all over again. They're cold and threatening as he crouches down to meet the other man's stare. "If you ever lay a finger on her again…" He grabs his hand, the one with what looks to be a dislocated knuckle, and holds it against the cold concrete. Then, without an ounce of care, he slams the butt of the gun down on the bone. Four solid blows and there's a crack; the man doesn't so much as whimper, but the tears in his eyes give away to his pain. "Touch her— fuck with her—and I will dispose of you a small cut at a time. Filet your flesh and then feed it to your dear old father while you watch. It'll be a slow death. Agonizing. One that I will take immense joy in, Foster."

"I love my sister," he chokes out as Malcolm slams the gun down once more.

"As of today, she's mine. I'll be taking her, moving her in with me as part of my payment." I'm surprised by his reaction, but at the same time can't judge. *Seems the arse has met his match, too.*

After a few quick orders to his men and a final warning, we leave, both heading out while cries and whimpers follow in the distance. We don't talk, but I can't help but fuck with him before getting into my car. "You been holding out on me, mate?"

"No more than you have."

"What's that supposed to mean?"

"Means I'll share when you do."

HALF AN HOUR later I'm at her door after dismissing her guard for the night. I want him gone—to go help the others store the cocaine at a warehouse I own here, while the electronics need to be shipped to a seller in South America. They have just a few hours to get it done because everyone except for Jeffrey and Alexander are heading back to England at first light while I enjoy my Gem for a few days.

While I gorge myself on her decadence. While I remind her of just how good we are together.

My breathing is heavy and cock hard as I knock. Almost pounding my fist as the desperation to see her becomes near maddening. It's been too long.

This tiny woman has me going insane, feigning for a taste.

"Christ, woman, open the bloody door," I hiss under my breath, listening for any sign of life from the other side of the door. No more than thirty seconds later I sense her near, that inviting pull ever-present and throbbing the closer to me she gets.

I hear the padding of her feet.

I can just make out the low gasp that escapes her, an almost undetectable little sound that makes my cock throb as she sees my hungry expression through her peephole.

I see the exact moment she begins to turn the doorknob and then yanks it open in her haste to reach me.

Then, we are face to face.

Breathing the same air.

Mirroring the same need.

I have no idea who attacked first or how we ended up an upright mass of tangled limbs, but all is right in my world the second those sweet lips meet my own.

Aurora

"How?" is all I manage to get out between kisses, the slanting of his mouth over mine as he robs me of coherency and the front door slams shut. I'm surrounded by him and yet it's not enough. I don't think anything ever will be.

"Later. Talk later," he hisses as my nails rake down his chest, leaving deep welts behind while I follow the trail down to the waistband of his jeans. His abs clench the lower I go, muscles contracting as I pop open the button and begin to lower the zipper. My fingers push it down slowly, taunting him, and a rumble builds inside his chest—the vibration running through me a second before I'm turned around by a hand on my hip. The other fists my hair and tugs it back. "Room."

"I want you." I'm breathless and giggling and enjoying the tight hold he has me in. I want to stay as I am, in his arms and being manipulated.

There's something so sexy about it, the way he can pick me up with ease or bend me to his liking. How palpable his hunger is.

It's physical and literal. Can't be denied.

"Room, Gem." His lips trail down my temple and cheek, not pausing until reaching my neck where he embeds his teeth. It stings but feels like heaven. The pleasurable pain flows through my skin and brings every nerve ending to life.

I'm hypersensitive. Throbbing with need.

I shouldn't want him as I do.

I shouldn't give in as easily as I do.

My problem is that every question that starts and ends with him has one answer: I do.

I'm screwed. Utterly screwed.

"Down the hall, first door on the left," I manage to say on a whimper, pointing in the general direction as I throw my head back and close my eyes. Loving the feel of his teeth raking down my skin, how his fingers dig into my hips and hold my ass tightly against his hard length.

Casper nods, the movement subtle as he kisses the spot he's abused. "I've missed you, love. So fucking much and it makes no sense. It's driving me insane."

I'm not sure if those words are meant for me, they are spoken so low, but they warm me from the inside out. Causes my heart's cadence to speed up, a rapid *thump thump thump* that seems to pump only for him.

I've never experienced this type of connection before. This kind of yearning.

I'm afraid and excited and probably stupid for allowing it to continue, but it can't be stopped. This combustion is meant to happen for better or worse.

"I've missed you too." No sooner have the words passed my lips that I find his hold on my hair tightening, forcing my back to arch in a manner that puts his mouth over mine. Devouring. Showing me with his dominion how much of me he already owns.

"Say it again. Tell me." It leaves him on a growl a second before one of his hands leaves my hips and travels to the barely there tank top I'm wearing. Casper fists the material between his fingers and tugs once, forcing the cotton to dig into my skin as the sound of it protesting seems loud within the room. Another pull and it stretches, a tear forming at the thin strap, ripping the elastic material from the seam and exposing half my right breast. "Say it, baby girl. Tell me what you need. What you missed."

"You." And it's the most honest answer I can give him. All these weeks I've been going through the motions, trying to fight my attraction to him or the rabbit hole it could possibly lead to. Deny how much his morning texts mean to me, though sometimes far between, they make me smile. "I just needed you."

"Fuck, I can't go so long without seeing you. Feeling you against me." Another sharp pull and the other shoulder strap breaks, leaving me exposed to the cool air and him. My nipples tighten into stiff peaks and my thighs clench as I wait. Anticipate his next touch. He doesn't make me wait long, though, cupping a breast in each hand as he forces me to take two steps forward. And then another, all the while his lips are at my ear. "Lead me to your room, Gem."

"Please," I whimper, arching my chest into his hands. "Can't wait that long to feel you." Then, to further prove my point, I do what I've been fantasizing about in the darkness of my room late at night.

I walk away from him and step fully into my living room, not stopping until I'm beside the loveseat. His footsteps follow mine; their heaviness causes goose bumps to break out all over my skin. For my thighs to dampen as the soft lace panties I'm wearing become soaked.

There's no need for words. This is a moment to just feel.

To take. To satiate this building fire we have burning within.

Bending over the couch's armrest, I expose my desire to him. "This is what I need."

"Could you be any more bloody perfect." It's a statement that he follows up by dropping to his knees behind me. By pressing his lips to the curve of my ass, the area where cheek and thigh meet, and then skimming across to the other. Casper does this a few times before nipping the skin below the lace as he pulls the material aside with his teeth.

The cool air meets my labia and I shiver. The wetness coating my lips is visible to his hungry eyes.

"Casper, I...*oh God*!" His mouth is against my clit and a harsh shiver rocks through my body. Just the mere act brings me to the precipice of an orgasm. I'm shaking for him, panting for more, but all I get is a low *shhhh* to behave. "Please. *Please.*"

He doesn't hurry, though. Instead, he explores me. Tastes me.

Those lips part and then his tongue flicks at my engorged bundle of nerves. Each swipe, the hungry way he moans into my tender flesh, causes my knees to shake. For my hips to undulate against his perfect mouth as his tongue slips lower until he reaches my entrance.

My entire body clenches as he dips the tip inside and holds still. "More."

I don't receive a verbal response. Instead, there's the sound of his belt coming undone and then the lowering of a zipper. Goose bumps arise on my flesh and I try to push back, to take more, but he pulls back with a tsking sound.

It's a reprimand I meet with defiance as I slip a hand between myself and the armrest, but that doesn't work out; if anything it ignites a ferocious anger in him. His hand meets my cheek, three times in quick succession that steals the air from my lungs.

It stings, but immediately spreads warmth through the area as I choke on a moan.

He spanks me again. Then again. Alternating between the right and left, different areas before giving one last swipe with the flat of his tongue from my clit to rosebud and then he stands.

His pants lower to the ground behind me, trapped by his shoes. His shirt is tossed somewhere, and a second later something made of glass crashes to the ground.

And I don't care. Don't lift my head to look, because nothing matters more to me than the bulbous tip of his cock running through my wetness, coating his flesh before stopping at my entrance.

"Say it again."

"I need you."

One of his hands gathers my hair at the back, fisting the tresses as he turns my head, putting his lips right at the corner of my mouth. "I need you too." Then he slams in, one swift move that causes my toes to curl and eyes to close.

This feeling is what I've been missing. Needing desperately.

Pulling out slowly, he lets me enjoy every solid inch of his cock before sliding to another entrance, one I've never given to anyone. At first, my puckered hole clenches as the fat head and metal slide over, but soon I find myself pushing back beneath his hold. Find myself finishing what I tried to do earlier, and I slip my hand between the couch and my pussy, shaking in his hold as my fingers make contact with my swollen and sensitive flesh.

"Bad girl." It's a growl, a menacing declaration a second before he places his other hand on my hip and pins me against my fingers. Pressing. Giving me just enough friction to keep me on edge. His hips jut forward a little then, the head of his cock pushing against the tight hole, when he pulls back. "That's mine and I'll be coming back for that soon, but for now…"

"Oh, God!" I'm a whimpering, sensitive mess when he enters my core again, and I clench my walls to keep him right where he is. Not that he pauses or lets me. Now he's relentless. Fucking me like I've needed to be all these weeks.

Fast and hard. Almost punishing.

Only he can invoke this painful pleasure; I choke on a scream as I tremble and my wetness wets us both. It's quick and nothing I was prepared for.

"That's it, love," he grunts above me, lips at the back of my neck. They part and his breath is a caress on my skin a second or two before his teeth lock down. The bite hurts in the most blissful way, taking me higher as he pistons in and out. "You feel…*motherfuck*, you're my ambrosia. My heaven and hell."

But it's those words that put me over the edge. That destroy me.

Between his cock, my fingers against my clit, and how honest he is in his need for me…I'm done.

I'm his. Completely his.

My wetness coats us both, soaking the fabric of my loveseat, but nothing registers more than the pure groan of pleasure from his lips after another pump of his hips. I'm limp beneath him, taking everything he gives, but as I feel that first rope of his come release inside of me, I come alive. My back arches and walls hold him tight as another orgasm rocks me from head to toe.

It's explosive and I'm gasping for breath.

I can't register anything around me but the blissful wake of this release.

"Casper." It leaves me on a reverent moan so low I doubt he even hears me. My eyes are drooping, and sounds are becoming muffled. I'm weightless and falling.

And yet I still hear his whispered words a second before all goes black.

"I'll never let her go."

Aurora

"Y OU LOOK MIGHTY at home in my kitchen, Mr. Jameson."

"I look mighty everywhere, love," he replies, not missing a beat or turning around; instead, he continues to put food on a plate. My eyes shift to the counter beside him and they widen, taking in the crazy number of Chinese cartons on my counter. It smells amazing and my stomach growls. "Grab something for us to drink, and back to the living room you go."

"Aren't you bossy, too."

That earns me a wink from over his shoulder. "Always, so behave."

My thighs clench. "And if I don't?"

The items in his hands are put on the counter and he turns, leaning back against the granite. "Would you like another time-out, Gem? Want me to put you to bed?"

"Please."

"Tease."

"You're the one looking delicious in my home."

"You're the one looking at me with hungry eyes, sweetheart. That's an unfair tactic."

"All's fair."

"Dangerous," he mutters under his breath, but I hear and giggle. "That's it. You brought this upon yourself." I blink twice and he's striding my way, reaching me before I can run, and picks me up. Automatically my legs wrap around his waist, exposing my naked core. The shirt I found of his on my side table—where the picture frame now lying in pieces on the floor once was—is doing a horrible job of covering my body. "Just a bad little girl."

"Is that a deal breaker for you?"

"More like seals the deal." Then his lips are on mine and a hand is exploring lower, over my ass cheek and between my thighs where he encounters my desire for him. Two fingers slide between my slickness, spreading it around before slipping them inside. "But you already know I'm wrapped around your tiny little finger."

"Are you?" I moan as he pumps those digits in and out slowly.

"Irrevocably." But instead of making me come, he pulls those fingers out, dragging them against my walls before circling my entrance twice with the very tips. "And it's because of that pull on me that I'm going to lower you to the ground, pat your arse, and send you to the living room. It's late, and you didn't eat after I attacked you. Let me rectify that."

"Okay." Because what else can I say when he's looking at me with warmth in his eyes? "What would you like to drink? Beer or a Coke?"

"Lager would be lovely."

Nodding, I walk over to my fridge. "I got you."

"Yes, you do."

<hr>

"How do you spend four months out of the year in Chicago and have never done the Gangsters and Ghosts tour? This is a staple, dude!" I ask him a few days later after being wrapped up in each other for the last forty-eight hours. The people around us continue to walk diligently behind our tour's host, but we pause with two very different expressions on our faces.

I'm almost appalled by this and it shows. "Seriously, I just can't with you right now."

"Gem, think about it." He's chuckling, shoulders shaking as the guide stops at another location on his map of The Loop, this ones near the Asher Building. From where we stand, I can hear him talking about a specific incident that made the headlines in the late 1920s. "Why would I need information like this? I was born into this life. It's who I am."

"Oh, come on! Everyone needs this in their life." At my exasperation, he puts his arm around my shoulders and pulls me in close, pausing while the others doing this tour gasp at the information being given. They're listening intently to the history of this city's most notorious gangster and how prohibition laws brought forth the reign of these men as the need for certain illicit activities grew to high demand.

It's like any business.

If you tell a consumer no, they want it all the more. Good or bad for you; people want what the government says you can't have.

"Sweetheart, look at me."

"Say please."

He turns to fully face me, the hand on my shoulder dropping to my waist, fingers grabbing onto a belt loop. "I'm going to enjoy putting you over my knee."

"Is that so."

"Yes, you lovely little thing." One tug and I stumble forward, chest to chest, leaving no room between us. His heat sears my skin and my nipples tighten, stiff little peaks that poke through the thin material of my bralette and vintage band T-shirt. "But you'd like that, wouldn't you?"

"Maybe."

"Bad girl." His lips meet mine for a quick, passionate kiss before, in a move I'm not expecting, he turns me around and guides me forward. Our group has continued to walk down the street and is currently in front of what used to be a speakeasy owned by the biggest mobster of that era.

"Oh, this is an interesting story from that time." Grabbing his hand, I yank him with me toward the tour guide, forcing myself to ignore the lust he awakens in me with each simple touch. Ignore how right his hand on my lower back feels. "This one is all about alcohol, prostitution, and guns."

"Aren't they all?"

"Just pay attention, Jameson. He's getting to the good part." My voice is louder than I intend, and an older lady with a fanny pack looks back at me with a stink eye. "Sorry." She nods with pursed lips, wrinkles on point and full of displeasure, while I try to fight back my own amusement. "And you…" I shift my eyes to my date and elbow him in the ribs "…don't provoke me."

"What's the fun in that?"

"Learn now and I'll give you a special kiss later."

"That's all you had to say."

"Thank you."

"Can I get a preview of that kiss now?"

"Listen to the middle-aged guy retelling our past."

"And I'm the bossy one, love?" Casper says, then tilts his head to the side, those green eyes still showing mirth. "By the way, how many times have you done this tour?"

I shrug. "A few."

"Dozen?"

"More like five or eight."

"Five or eight?" he whispers, raising a brow.

"We liked the ghost part a little bit more, and it became a tradition to do it every year around Halloween after I turned sixteen. It was our thing, you know?" I look away from him and focus on the building in front of us. There's so much history in this city that people tend to ignore—forget the ways in which it molded who we are today. It's one of the reasons Mom and I did these crazy tours. In a sick way, it keeps us connected to who we are and where we come from. Especially with who my father is and what he represents. "We did corn mazes, old jails, or an asylum or two if the time permitted, and then at the end of the month, this tour. We knew all the monologues by memory, but it's still fun in a morbid sort of way."

"We?"

"Mom and me."

"Sounds like your mum was a lot of fun." The small chuckle that escapes him is a bit wistful, and I can understand it. Mine's been gone a few years, while his has only been a month; thirty days is nothing in the grand scheme of things. "Mine was a chicken when it came to anything like this. Dad, though, he's got issues."

"A fan?"

"A wee too much. Even my curiosity has limits."

"Folks, I'll give you a few minutes to take pictures and wander the area. Our next stop is in fifteen," the guide says, and the murmurs around us grow. People take off in different directions, yet stay close enough to hear further instructions. Us, though…

We stay right where we are. For the third time today, Casper has wrapped an arm around my shoulders and pulled me in to his side, nestling me against his much taller frame. While cameras go off and questions are asked, we breathe in and out while just being.

It's our second official date and while not the norm and probably silly for him, I love that he let me pick our activity. That he's letting me indulge in something I haven't done since my mother passed away, and while it's not October, it's close enough that I feel festive.

Fall is just around the corner, and this year doesn't seem as heavy as the ones in the past. Or maybe it's because I don't feel alone.

I have him here at the moment and that's all that matters. All I will allow myself to focus on.

"How do you feel about blues music?" I ask after a minute or two, trying to hide my smile when his stomach rumbles.

"It's very relaxing when I'm cleaning my guns. Why?"

"And Creole cuisine?"

"Never had it but I'm liking where this is going."

"Good." Turning to face him, I rise to the tips of my toes and nip his chin. "Let's skip the rest of this and get a late dinner. There's an amazing Blues Club not that far from here that serves the best gumbo I've ever had outside of Louisiana."

"You sure? Cause I'll wait until—"

"Come on. Let's get you fed, big boy." At my words, his eyes darken and that cocky smirk spreads across his lips.

"Can I eat you instead?"

"I'm definitely on the dessert menu."

"I REALLY HATE GOODBYES." I also hate the gut feeling that this separation will be a long one.

"Then don't say it." Casper wraps his arms around me tightly, pulling me against his chest as I wipe away a few stray tears that have escaped. "Because I won't. This is more of an *I'll see you later* kind of thing. Besides, we have a date coming up soon and I'm very much looking forward to this Skype sex you mentioned."

At that I look up and find that cocky little smirk on his face. "You're a pervert."

"When it comes to you..." he shrugs "...no doubt. But you already know this, Gem. I don't hide my hunger from you."

No, he doesn't. If anything, the man is the opposite of what I expected in that department. His need to touch—to feel me close at all times—is adorable in the sexiest way possible.

It matches his ruthlessness. The darker edges of his persona that always loom within my fingertips, but I'm yet to fully grasp. But I've heard it, seen the change in his expression when he speaks to those who work for him. Especially Callum, his cousin, who I've yet to meet but have heard them talk on speakerphone when he thought I was still showering the day of the mobster tour.

"What are your plans, Casper?" I ask instead of pulling him into the bathrooms here and bending over a final time before he leaves. We're at the airport now, waiting on word from his employee that the private jet is ready, and holding on for just a little bit longer after five days of normalcy.

Of bliss. Of minimal outside interference.

I took the time off while he delegated. Being the boss has perks, and Ali was nothing short of ecstatic to help me. More so when she heard his voice in the background the morning, I called in. Then there's Casper, and while I know men like him never travel alone, his guard was always out of sight. He kept his distance and I appreciate it—enjoyed every last second because I don't know when I'll see him again.

Something that just last week I thought to be for the best, but today makes me sad. A bit bitter because I wish things—our lives—were different.

In another place and time we would've met, made eye contact while exchanging numbers and then made plans. Then, that one date would've turned into two and then three—months and years with a proposal thrown in the middle—that leads to the elusive happily ever after that all women dream of since childhood.

He would be my prince and I his princess.

However, reality isn't that easy. Nothing in life really is.

I live here, and he's in England.

I want nothing to do with my familial ties, while he's the head of a British mob family.

I promised to never make my mother's mistake, while he is the physical embodiment of a catastrophe waiting to happen.

Would I ever be able to accept him like this? So much like my father?

"Quit overthinking, love. It'll be hard, but we'll make it work." I look up and he's smiling, looking calm and without a care. Nothing like the killer I know he can be.

"Why are you always so sure?" I ask and inhale deeply, pulling that rich scent of woodsy man in that I'll miss like crazy when he's gone. "This is a disaster—"

He cuts me off with a bone-melting kiss.

Casper fists my hair and pulls my head back, slanting his perfect mouth over mine and parting my lips. His tongue caresses mine and I shiver, greedily slipping my fingers through his hair to pull him closer. To express my urgency.

Something he reciprocates.

An animalistic growl builds in his chest and I tug on the longer strands at the back again, nipping his top lip. "Why do I need you so much?" I ask him, but his answer comes in the form of his hold tightening, keeping me in place.

Its sexy and dominating and I whimper for him like the desperate girl I am.

It's the kind of kiss that robs you of all your senses and stops time. The kind where everyone else in the world disappears and it's just you and him.

No one else. All alone and savoring—drowning in each other's taste.

Casper nibbles on my bottom lip, teasing little nips that bring goose bumps to my skin before he trails across my cheek and lower. There's a low whine that comes from me, my need to have his mouth back on mine, but that's silenced quickly as he sucks on my pulse point.

It stings, but I enjoy his marking. Can't find it in me to deny him this.

"You know why I'm calm?" he asks against my neck, tone gravelly. "Know why I can get on that plane without a single shred of doubt?"

"Please." It leaves me on a whimper as he nuzzles my sensitive skin. I *need* his confirmation. *His* word that we won't be another repeated story.

"I can do this because I trust us." He nips my earlobe, and the quick sting travels straight to my clit. My thighs clench. "I can do this..." Casper swallows hard "...because for the first time in my life, I want a relationship. Look forward to this journey and coming back to you, Gem. And lastly, I can do this because in a not-so-distant future, we will always be together."

At his words I freeze and then pull back. Heart racing. "What does that mean?"

"It means that I need you to trust me. That you'll have faith in me."

"How long will you be gone this time?"

"I'll be back the moment I put a bullet between the eyes of those responsible."

"And I'll wait." His conviction—trust in us—helps me make the decision without a single second of hesitation. If he believes, then I will try my best to push all doubts back. I'll give this an honest try.

"And I will come back. Always." Leaning forward, he presses his lips to my forehead and breathes me in, lingering for a minute before walking away. He only looks back once before going through the small tunnel to the plane, and that one look made my heart thump with excitement.

It says he'll be back.

For me. For us.

Aurora

THERE'S NOTHING WORSE than being roused from a deep sleep by the blaring of your phone in the middle of the night. Your restful dream is interrupted, and the world comes crashing back in full force, startling you. Your heart races, palms begin to sweat, and you immediately begin to think the worse—fear that someone you love is hurt or…

In my haste to grab the small device, I reach over and knock my lamp over where it crashes to the ground and the glass part breaks. *I need to invest in plastic home furnishings. Since meeting Casper, things break all the time.*

"Shit," I mutter under my breath, fingers tapping all around the night-stand until they skim over the screen, and just as I fully grasp it, it stops ringing. I don't move and wait to see if a voicemail or another call comes through…

Nothing. I'm surrounded by absolute silence once more that brings no comfort.

Sitting up with my cell in hand, I bring it toward my face and unlock the screen, directly searching the incoming call log. The last call came from an unknown number; a 609 area code that I've never heard of before.

Seeing that it's not someone I know gives me immediate peace and I calm down. My breathing begins to normalize, and I relax.

They don't call again, and I put the cell back in its place atop my nightstand without giving it a second thought. It's early and I have to be at the home by eight for an early meeting. That, and I'm due for a Skype date tonight after having to cancel last week.

It's the only way to stay sane while Casper and I are apart. In the three weeks since he left, we've made plans and made the effort to keep them. Kept our promises of always talking and no shut-outs.

For this to work, communication is key.

But how long can this long-distance relationship work? Will he ask me to move or will he come here?

Ignoring those plaguing questions, I settle once more and close my eyes. Go back to that last kiss at the airport and remember how at home I felt with him. How right I know we can be for each other if I just trust him not to hurt me.

It's what helps me drift off and forget about the rude wake-up call.

MY ALARM WAKES me up at exactly 7:05 and I glare at the thing while fighting the urge to fling it across the room. I'm tired, hangry, and not in the mood to so much as move a muscle.

I'm sore, and with that soreness comes a kind of cramping I'm all too familiar with.

Aunt Flo is here, and that hateful bitch just loves to annoy me. She appeared somewhere between the wrong number calling, the sweeping of the broken lamp, and then my need for water about an hour later. I hate her, and she made her presence known with a series of vengeful, ovary-crushing cramps that had me near crawling, but like the righteous woman I am, I kept it in check and threw back some ibuprofen with water.

It's what we are taught to do from the moment this *time of the month* arrives.

Throwing my legs over the edge of the mattress, I stand up and stretch my back. It feels tight but eases with every contortion until something pops and I feel the relief. "Much better."

Today is a very important day and I have to be on my A-game; a back spasm is the last thing I need.

After a few more bends and twists, I grab my phone and make my way into the bathroom. There's a certain playlist that I like to use for days like this, and I open the Spotify app on my phone. Before I do that, though, something else catches my eye.

There are a few text messages from an unknown number. Ten to be exact, and I click on the first.

6:00 a.m.

> You will learn your place, little girl. ~Unknown

What the hell?
6:03 a.m.

> I don't tolerate that kind of behavior. ~Unknown

6:07 a.m.

> You touched what isn't yours. ~Unknown

6:10 a.m.

> His blood will be on your hands. ~Unknown

They go on, each one showing mounting frustration at being ignored. They also bring a feeling of dread to the pit of my stomach. These messages aren't a mistake.

They are clearly for me. Evidence that I'm being watched.

An observation turned reality when I read the very last message sent.
6:15 a.m.

> A whore just like her mother for a man that's a
> known killer. ~Unknown

The phone slips through my fingers and crashes to the ground, a large crack forming at the upper right-hand corner. This scares me. Brings a series of complications into my life that I don't know how to handle.

It's clear to me that this message came from someone who knew both my mother and father. Of their relationship and my place in that story. I've always been kept on the sidelines, but people talk. They know who I am, and all my life I've been looked at differently because of who Matteo Cancio is.

Something that up until today I've brushed off and kept going. Not letting him define who I am, but this, *this* is very different. There's an underlying threat here. Moreover, they also know of my relationship with Casper—an association that's in its infant stage.

The question now, though, is who? Who would have the guts to send this?

I need to tell Casper.

My first thought is to call him and ask for help. I'm not naïve, nor will I ignore this.

I know better. I have seen things, even as my mother tried to protect me, that other kids haven't. My father never hid who he is, and on the rare occasions where he picked me up for a visit or a weekend stay, he never stopped being boss.

Business is business and to the Cancios, it comes above everything. If it meant making a decision while at the dining room table while his wife glared at me, so be it. If it meant leaving the room and having the cook keep me occupied in the kitchen while profanities were being hurled, so be it. If a sentence had to be carried out somewhere in the backyard of his private estate—deep into the forest behind the property, then so be it.

I know what being in this life entails and as much as I hate what it represents, the family it took from me, it's part of me. A part of me I try to ignore, but it's still there and has come to the forefront now that I've been seeing where this connection with Casper goes.

My second alarm goes off then and I'm pulled from the racing thoughts going through my head. "Shit!" I yell, realizing that in all this craziness I've forgotten to get dressed. "Christ, I'm going to be late today of all days."

This meeting is too important, has the possibility of a large donation that will help us expand the operation to a possible second state.

I'll tell him tonight. Everything will be fine.

Taking a few deep breaths, I calm myself and then send Aliana a quick text.

> Running late. Explain later. Hold the fort until I arrive. ~Roe

At once, three dots appear on the screen.

> And the meeting? Are you okay? ~Ali

> Not really, but I'll explain after. Just keep him there until I arrive. ~Roe

> I got you. ~Ali

Knowing that's taken care of, I walk straight into the bathroom and toward the shower. The motion sensor has already picked up my movement, so I quickly strip and turn on the faucet, letting the water run almost scalding before getting in.

This is a mission-impossible-like situation and I lather, rinse, and repeat faster than I ever thought humanly possible. Once out, I check my phone on the counter for the time and blow out a big breath of air. I have thirty minutes to get dressed and then drive twenty minutes to the home.

"Clothes. I need clothes." Running out, I make a beeline for my closet and pull out a retro three-quarter-sleeve pencil dress with a belt in charcoal that I match with a pair of black leather strappy botties with a platform heel. It's comfortable and cute and after adding a winged liner, leaving my curls down, and adding a nude lip stain, I take a selfie.

This one is for Casper and goes with a caption: *BIG MEETING. WISH ME LUCK!*

I know he's busy and probably won't see it right away, but I send it anyway. Hoping he responds in the off chance. At least that's what I thought because just as I grab my purse, keys, and a bottle of water, my phone rings with his special tone.

And I'm smiling. A real one.

"Hello."

"Morning." He sips something, I can make out the sound of ice inside of a cup, and then there's a groan. It's low and throaty and will be the death of me. "You look beautiful. Absolutely stunning."

My nerves calm at once, and the earlier scare is pushed to the back of my mind until later tonight. "Thank you." It comes out shy and I feel my face heat up. "It's a huge meeting, and I'm kind of nervous. It's the first step into looking for donations to help with our expansion."

"I'll match whatever they give you today."

"You sound so sure."

"How could anyone say no to you. I know I can't." Someone says his name and I know our time is about to end, but it means everything to me that he stopped his day to call. "Sorry about that. My cousin tends to be on the loud side."

"It's okay. I know you're busy."

"I miss you," Casper says then, taking me by surprise. My lips part, and just as I'm going to tell him that I do too, he continues. "And knock them dead, beautiful. Shine like the precious Gem you are. I'll call you later tonight."

Then he's gone and I'm still smiling like a loon. He has no idea how much those words mean to me. How much more at ease I feel now.

They also serve as a reminder that I need to grab my gun from the safe.

It's always better to be safe than sorry and he'd want me to carry.

———

"GOOD MORNING," I say, walking into my office and placing my purse atop a small table against the wall before turning to face the occupants. Ali is looking at me with nothing but relief on her face while my could-be donor gives me a smile. "I apologize for being so late, Mr. Asher. Something came up that I was not prepared for and—"

"No worries, Miss Conte. Things happen." Grabbing his cup of coffee, he takes a sip and then places it back. "And it's Malcolm. Please call me Malcolm."

Behind him Aliana fans herself and it's hard, but I do manage to keep my eye roll in. Yes, the man is handsome and exudes a powerful aura that can't be denied, but I only have eyes for a certain Brit. He haunts me day in and day out without mercy, and I want to keep it that way.

I extend a hand, which he takes and then shakes it. "Then please call me Aurora."

"Deal." He sits back and regards me quietly, and I take that as my cue to move this meeting along. A man like Malcolm Asher doesn't like to waste time.

"Speaking of...?" I trail off as I take a seat behind my desk, matching his cool demeanor.

"Right to the point, Aurora. I appreciate that." Malcolm nods and pulls out a folded piece of paper that resembles a check from the inside of his suit jacket. He places it atop my desk and then pushes it forward in my direction. "If you need more, please don't hesitate to call me. No questions asked."

"I don't understand." For a split second I look over to where Aliana was a minute ago and find her gone and my office door closed.

"Go on. Open it and ask your questions."

Picking up the paper, I unfold and read. "Why?" It's all I can think to ask as I take in the half a million-dollar check in my hand. "Why are you doing this?"

"Look at me, Aurora." And I do, completely flabbergasted and unsettled; I know my expression mirrors this. "There's a reason I am doing this, and her name is London Foster, although, her rightful last name is Conte."

"Wait, what? Who is London Fos—"

"She's your cousin, Aurora," he says softly, but to me it's as if he's shouting the words right into my ear. "Your uncle Julian had a daughter with his wife, Amelia."

"He had...has a daughter?" And I believe him. I grew up hearing that name from time to time—from my mother and grandmother while alive— and how sad they were because of a choice she made. Christ, my head is spinning, and nothing makes sense, but I also can't deny that hearing this makes me smile. A smile that falls just as quickly and I voice my next thought. "But why would my mother hide this from me?"

"Amelia was in a very abusive relationship, Aurora, and out of concern for her daughter, she made your mother promise to stay away. To not get involved, although she did communicate with her every chance she got. It was your mother who helped her change her will and accounts over to London before she died."

I nod, understanding more than he can ever imagine; I see the damage abuse leaves behind every single day. "Is London safe now?"

"She's with me."

"With you?" *Is he saying that...*

"London is my life." And now it all makes sense. She's his girlfriend, because had he married anyone, the entire state of Chicago would know. This most eligible bachelor has a following.

"Does she know about me? About her family?" I can't stop the tears that spring to my eyes, not when the only family I have left on my mother's side was being abused and I couldn't help. Didn't know she needed me. "When can I meet her?"

"Not yet, but I'm sure she will be in contact soon." Malcolm scratches his jaw and then looks down at the watch on his wrist. "I'm not hiding this from her."

"Thank you." It's the least I can say, but those words carry all of my gratitude.

"All I ask is that you're there for her, Aurora. She's going to need you." His eyes are on mine as he says this and, in that moment, I see the other side of him people whisper about. He loves her and is protective. Won't tolerate bullshit when it comes to her.

And that just earned him my respect.

CASPER

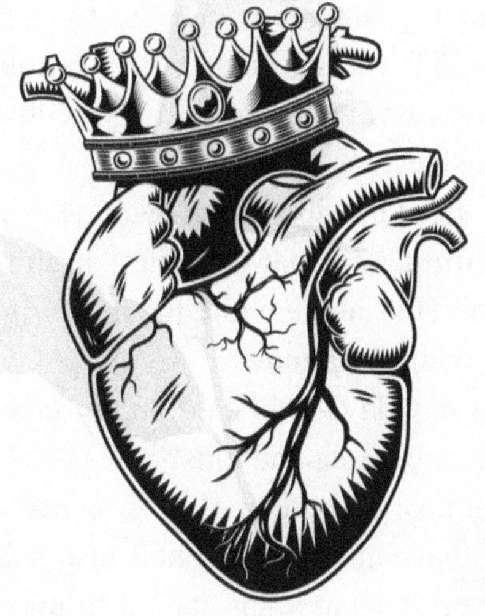

I STARE AT the picture she sent me an hour ago one last time, ignoring Malcolm's confirmation that my wire has been completed before pocketing my mobile and exiting the car. I know he's going to see her today; her guard was able to slip inside her office undetected while she went to the on-site kitchen for lunch and saw his name in her planner. It's how I learned of a few interesting facts after having Ezra look into this for me.

Learned just how tiny this world is.

My girl has a cousin, and my friend is completely taken by her. And it's that small fact that kept me from forgetting our friendship and making a pit stop in Chicago to put a bullet in his brain. He's like a brother to me, but when it comes to Gem, I'd burn the world to the ground for her.

Two car doors close a few seconds after mine, and my men fall in line on this sunny East Coast day as I walk up a pathway that leads to an Ocean City property. We're in New Jersey, and the owner doesn't know I'm here.

Not one person can pinpoint my location, and it will stay that way as I hunt down Mum's killers.

Not even a friend I have in town who's providing me with the facility I'll be using for today's meeting. He knew I'd need it, but not when, and said it was mine for whenever I decide.

Well, today is that day.

"Sir," Archie, a new guard recommended by Jeffrey, calls my name. He's his childhood best friend and an ex-British soldier in need of work with connections that are valuable, especially with the changes that are coming soon to our business.

I pause, tilting my head but don't look back. "Speak."

"Sir, we have confirmation that our guest hasn't left the house since yesterday around eight. He's alone while the new wife is in the Dominican Republic vacationing with girlfriends."

"I see." There is a few-days-old beard on my face at the moment and I rub my chin. "Is there an ex-wife and kids?"

"They live in an apartment complex in Patterson where her older brother and mum also have apartments. She's also had to take a minimum-wage job, working overnights at a gas station to make ends meet since he barely passes her a hundred fifty a week."

"What's his net worth?" Because with its size and location two blocks from the beach, this home is easily worth more than seven hundred and fifty thousand.

"Bank statement shows a balance of three hundred thousand, but if we add cars and homes, probably a low million."

I turn my head to look back at Archie. "Transfer every last bloody cent to the children's mother."

"It shall be done," he vows and pulls out his mobile, shooting a quick message to Jeffrey, who is awaiting orders with my hacker in London. It pings a few seconds later and he shows me the screen, confirming my thoughts.

> Ezra is already on it. We were awaiting
> confirmation to proceed. ~Jeffrey

Pocketing the device, he takes his place slightly behind Callum who's been silent. There's something bugging him—he's been off since the last time we were in Chicago—and we haven't had time to talk.

But I see it in the deep pull of his eyebrows and tense posture.

Meeting his eyes, I raise a brow, silently asking if he's good. If he's focused.

His reply comes in the form of a nod and tap to his chest with a closed fist.

Nothing else is said as I turn my head and continue up the path with my gun in hand. It's a sweltering day and I'm glad I dressed down for this occasion. No suit or tie or cuff links—instead, I brought with me a pair of denim trousers and a pullover, both in black. Easier to hide any stains that might come about before we leave.

There are two steps onto a small porch that lead to his door and I don't pause to knock. Raising my foot, I land a solid kick to the wooden structure and send it flying backwards and into the home. It rings loud throughout the silent room, and then we have a commotion upstairs.

Two screams. Two male voices call out to each other at the same time from opposite ends of the second floor and then rush toward the center stairway with weapons drawn.

Two bullets from my gun and the one I'm not here for falls to the ground with a neck and chest wound. He'll bleed out while I deal with this arsehole.

"Who the fuck!" the other yells, switching between panic and worry for the man slowly dying beside his feet. "Luis, get up. I need you to get up, pana."

The man coughs, the spittle red and running down the side of his cheek and onto the floor. This action repeats itself as breathing becomes difficult and his throat cannot perform the simple function of swallowing.

He's choking. Gagging on his life's essence.

And then he stops and the man I came here looking for screams, an agonized sound that brings a smile to my face. It gets the blood pumping harshly through my system. Excites me.

If there are two things in this life that can get me hard, it's the thought of my Gem's pussy and the blood that drips from an enemy's veins.

Seeing their life slip away.

"You have two minutes to come down those stairs." At the sound of my voice, his head snaps up and so does the shit-for-an-excuse gun in his hand. "I'd be very careful with that, mate."

"Hijo de puta, I'm going to...*fuck*!" The gun is no longer in his hand but on the floor, courtesy of Callum who lets out a low chuckle.

"Oi, my apologies, bro. My finger slipped."

My eyes shift to his amused face. "I'm going to start calling you butterfingers."

"I'm not that bad." Callum shrugs and I roll my eyes, looking back at the man bleeding from a hole in his hand.

"You only have a few seconds left, Felix."

"Who are you?" he screams, but I see his intent, taking a few steps back. The cunt wants to run. "What do you want?"

"Your head on my mantle." And just as I predicted, he takes off toward the rooms upstairs, slamming a door closed behind him as the three of us shoot out in different directions.

Archie goes toward the back and out the door.

Callum to the front with his weapon drawn.

And I take my time walking up the stairs. Slowly. Without a single ounce of haste.

At the top of the landing, I turn to the left and turn the handle. It's not locked, and I don't waste my time. The next room is the same, but the third one is the key to finding the slimy fuck.

One kick and it flies open, the cheap wood splintering and flying throughout the room as my eyes land on his huddled form in a corner. He has another gun in his shaky and uninjured hand, pointing at me with the fear of God in his eyes.

"I'll shoot."

"Go ahead," I say and take another few steps in his direction. "It's you or me at this point."

"What do you want?"

"And there's the billion-pound question: *what do I want?*" Scratching my jaw with the barrel of my gun, I continue my walk. Coming closer. Cornering him. "Money, I have. Power is mine. However, there is one thing..."

"I don't know you...you...you break into my home and shoot my brother-in-law. Threaten me." That trembling hand brings the gun up a little higher and he aims it at my head. "Do you have any idea who I am? What I can do to you?"

There's a small wooden chair in the corner of the room and I grabbed it without fear, flipping it around to straddle the seat. Then, I eye him. Just stare from my place near the end of the bed, and as the seconds tick by, his nervousness becomes more pronounced.

"Ask me who I am." Not a question. I'm challenging his bullshit notion of being an alpha in a game where he barely knows how to wipe his arse. "Ask me my *fucking* name, Felix De La Vega."

"Who are—" He's cut off by my bullet to his kneecap. "Motherfuck!"

"Does the name Casper Jameson ring any bells, Felix?"

Felix's face is ashen and his eyes are wide; the anger from before is still there, but now the predominant emotion is fear. "No. No. No."

"Si. Si. Si, motherfucker," I mimic his pathetic tone. "And would you like to tell me why or how you remember my name?"

"I-I took on a—"

"A job that is going to cost you your life, Vega." Standing from my seat, I kick it out of my way as I make my way over and crouch down in front of him. His finger twitches as I do, and his gun goes off, shooting me in the arm. It's a clean entry and exit; I don't flinch. Instead, I bring my face closer to his with my shitty grin firmly in place. "You're the man Nico Savino came to when looking for a trusted contract killer. True or false."

"True," he whimpers out as I dig the barrel of my gun into the wound on his leg.

"And you gave him Mauricio's information?"

"Yes."

"And you know both men well?"

"I do...*please* stop."

"Okay." I pull back and he lets out a breath of relief. "For now."

"For now? What are you—"

"We're going on a little trip, you and I."

Aurora

"**I**'M GLAD YOU came, Roe," my father says as I step into the all-black Denali SUV outside of the Boston airport. He's sitting in the back as always while two of his men are up front, and I breathe a sigh of relief to see Dominic isn't one of them. "It's good to see you."

"Good to see you too." Pulling my phone out of my small purse, I check once more to see if I have any missed calls or messages. There isn't, and it makes me sad that I've come to expect it. It's been two months since our last call; a Skype date where he was distracted and after five minutes of stilted conversation, was called back to work. Then, there's the last few messages; sporadic at best. They've been short and basic.

I couldn't even come to him with my concern over the anonymous text I received. You can't talk to someone who just isn't there, and I'm thanking my lucky stars that nothing came of it because there's no one to turn to. All I have is my gun and an accurate aim to depend on.

Heck, I don't even trust the man sitting beside me all that much—if anything, his visit is a test to see if we can ever have a normal relationship of any sort.

But Casper and I; we're missing the element of heat that makes me feel alive.

His mind just isn't with me. He's obsessed with vengeance.

Doing something that even though I hate the separation it's created; I understand. Truly do.

Losing his mother the way he did, violently and cruelly, would do that to a person. Casper is out to find those responsible, and all I can do is be supportive and wait. Understand. Because if the shoe was on the other foot, I would expect the same as I hunt down the animal responsible.

I am my father's daughter, and forgiveness is a concept I struggle with. More so if you hurt someone I love.

The traffic at this early hour is heavy and the drivers in a hurry, cutting each other off while others curse and make hand gestures in a lewd fashion. Goes to show you that no matter where you are in the world, rush-hour traffic sucks and brings the worst out in people. "Where are we off to first?"

"You just got here, kid. No rush."

"Really?" Because this man is not known for being laid back.

"Yeah." He chuckles, making a show of silencing his cell phone. "How about we get some breakfast and then go to Salem. You haven't been in ages and the weather's nice out."

"Only if we can go to The Friendly Toast for breakfast."

"Done."

"Thank you." I smile at him, really excited about going to the place Ali talked about after her visit last Halloween. "It comes highly recommended and it's waffles. What's not to love?"

Dad looks at me then, his expression softer than I ever remember seeing. "Believe it or not, your happiness means everything to me, Aurora. And while I've been shit at showing you this in the past, I plan to remedy that."

I don't reply to his statement and he sits back, following my lead. Maybe we can talk more another day, but for now I just want to relax a bit, eat, and spend some time with him where I'm not hurtling reproaches and he's not demanding that I do as he pleases.

For once, I just want to be his daughter and he my father with no anger on either side.

———

Where are you? ~Casper

It's the message I found once dressed this morning after going to bed with a throbbing headache. A headache that's ever-present and won't be getting any better until I put an end to the hot mess I currently find myself in. Because this is exactly what I thought it to be.

True to his word, Matteo kept all talk of business nonexistent for the first forty-eight hours. It was nice. Felt almost normal as we hung out and did things that I never thought we'd do together. Even his security detail made sure to keep a distance—to not disturb—as we reconnected, and I grew at ease with the idea of spending time here. With staying at his home instead of the hotel I'd booked prior to my arrival.

Also, doing something as simple as visiting the Salem Witch Museum and then walking the downtown area afterwards made me realize that a part of me wants him in my life. I'm not fully sure to what capacity and if I can ever depend on him, but I want him there.

The third day was completely different, though. The man I've been expecting made a very memorable appearance…

"You want me to what?" I seethe, gripping onto the chair's armrest and digging my fingernails into the leather. It's the only thing keeping me in place. It's preventing me from hurtling things across the conference room and at his salt-peppered head. *"No."*

"Just calm down, Roe. It's not that big of a deal and –"

"Christ, something is very wrong with you. How could you even begin to think I'd consider this idiocy? That I want any part in your scheme!"

"You have more of a choice than I ever did, Aurora. More than my father did…please…just consider what I am putting on the table."

"So, let me get this right…" A sardonic laugh escapes as I begin to tap my fingernails on the large wooden table, a long one where he's smart enough to sit on the opposite end with his PowerPoint presentation that

must've taken him all night to prepare. "Either I step up and take over as boss, or find a husband who will? Did I sum that up correctly?"

"You make it sound—"

"Archaic?" I finish for him, eyes narrowed. "Because what you're proposing is the same bull crap that took you from us. A marriage of convenience to some random man I've never so much as met before."

"Dominic isn't a stranger. You've met him in London and he's a great man. A dependable asset who knows the ins and outs of my company and day-to-day activities. He'd be a great husband if you choose to go this route, and who knows, maybe someday you might even fall in love. All is possible if you give it a chance." Matteo's sales pitch is completely in the tank after this.

Had he not said that name. Offered him to me like some prized stallion.

I'm done.

"No," I say and stand up, gathering my purse from beside me. "The answer will always be a no. I'm not you, and I'll never play this game."

"Do you have a problem with him? Is there something I'm not aware of?"

"How well do you know him?" I counter, raising my brow.

"He's been with me for years. Came highly recommended by a family friend of Samantha's."

"I don't like him." Plain and simple.

"What did he do?" Matteo asks, his tone now serious. Worried.

"He's pushy and rude and quite honestly, I have no interest in the man. That, and there's something about him that doesn't quite sit well with me. Like his anger when I—"

"Okay. I get it," he interrupts, rubbing a hand down his face in frustration without letting me finish. "We can shelve the Dominic subject for the moment, but don't ignore the other half of my proposition, Roe. I also said you could take over on your own and find a husband to stand beside you within the time frame of a year. Find him on your own while I expand the Conte House to an international level."

"Your help isn't needed."

"It was your mother's dream to do so."

A low blow and I bristle, gripping onto the wooden edge so hard my

knuckles turn white. "Her dream was to love and grow old with you, Dad."
My barb is just as sharp and it cuts him deep, the immediate flinch as if
I've slapped him the perfect tell. "Something of which you will never
know…to be with someone who holds your heart, and I will not follow in
your footsteps. I've met someone—"

"Who?"

"That's none of your concern."

"You're my daughter and I have the right to ask. To make sure he's
good enough."

"For me or your precious family affairs?"

"You always come first," he hisses, slamming a hand down on the
folder in front of him. "You've always come first."

"Bullshit." I don't believe that. He's never proven so.

"Just answer me this much?" His tone softer now, but I can still detect
his own anger beneath the surface. "Are you happy with him? Does he
treat you right?"

"My world is bright when I'm with him." And that's all I will give him.
Because the king of give and inch and he'll take a mile *would make things*
difficult if he knew who I'm seeing. To be honest, I'm surprised Casper
hasn't brought it up after pulling the file on me. Maybe he just doesn't care.
But my father is different in that sense and will think it somehow leads back
to him. That he'll use me to get to him. "This is also where I'm warning
you not to interfere if you want me in your life. This is where I draw the
line."

Instead of the reaction I'm expecting, of demands, Dad just smiles and
nods. "Okay."

"Okay?" I raise a brow, not buying it.

"I'll drop it for now. Maybe we both need to rethink our approach."

"The answer will still be no tomorrow." Declaring that my third option,
I walk over to him and kiss his cheek in a show of mild affection and then
walk out without looking back. Knowing that it's best if I book my ticket
back home for the following night.

The phone in my hand goes off, and it's my second alarm. It's fifteen
minutes past eleven and I need to get a move on. I promised to meet him at

his central office in the heart of downtown Boston, a large building near the center that is recognizable by all that see it.

Because not all Cancio businesses are illicit.

Because his money is not all dirty.

My father has two great passions in his life: power and real estate. He dominates both.

The man is also known for being a real estate mogul with properties, high-rise towers all across the US and a few abroad. It's one of the reasons why nothing has ever really been pinned on him. He's too good. Too smart. He knows too many people in high places who are always willing to help him.

"Just message him back," I mutter under my breath as I pull Casper's text back to the screen, reading it for the tenth time since finding it. It came in sometime during the early morning hours and along with it, there was one missed call a few minutes prior. Nothing else. No voicemail to let me know if something is wrong. If he is okay. *Where are you?* "He would know if he called."

But that's what we've come down to since the last time we were together; a here and there that I hate. I feel disconnected from him, and enough is enough. Considering the time difference between London and Boston, my fingers fly across the screen to reply, but I'm stopped from hitting send by a knock on the door of my room.

Thinking it's the estate manager with some sort of message from my father— a cancellation—I rush to open the door and it's a mistake. The kind that makes your skin crawl and breathing speed up slightly. "How can I help you, Dominic?"

"May I come in?" he asks instead of answering, trying to step around me, but I block his path and keep him on the other side of the threshold. I don't want him inside my room. I don't want him near me.

"No." There's something about this man that rubs me wrong. A gut feeling that makes me cautious. "Whatever you need to discuss can be said downstairs, and I'll meet you in the living room in ten minutes."

A flash of annoyance crosses his face, but it disappears just as quickly and is replaced by a slick smile. "Do I make you uncomfortable, Aurora?"

"Not at all."

"I think I do."

"Good for you." If he thinks I'll back down, he's got another thing coming. "Now, wait for me downstairs and we'll speak then."

"Maybe I don't want to leave. Maybe I want to be closer." Dominic takes a step forward and I do the same, not giving him the opportunity he seeks. At once, the harsh scent of his cologne infiltrates my nostrils, making me want to sneeze. He smells nothing like Casper. Nothing like the woodsy scent mixed with his natural essence that makes my knees weak. "Maybe I'd like to take you to dinner tonight and get to know you better."

Even upset with him, I miss the jerk. Can't deny it.

"I've already explained that I'm seeing—"

"Casper Jameson isn't good enough for you, Aurora."

Everything within me freezes, and my hands ball into tight fists beside me. I'm angry and uncomfortable and worried. It reminds me of those messages I received. Of their emphasis on my relationship with Casper.

Messages I've pushed to the far back of my mind as the sender hasn't made another move. Messages I'm yet to tell the man I'm supposed to be with about since he's never around. Not here for me like I knew deep down would happen.

"How the..." I'm seething, almost shaking in my indignation "...why the hell are you concerning yourself with my personal business? Who asked you to?"

"It's a personal choice."

"Is it, now? Or are you doing my father's bidding like a good little boy?" I challenge, arching a brow while crossing my arms over my chest. A move he follows with his eyes, licking his bottom lip, and I clear my throat. "Eyes up here, jerk, and answer my question. Did my father put you up to this?"

"No, but I doubt he'd approve of that asshole fucking his little girl."

"Leave."

"There's no need for this hostility, Aurora." Dominic's eyes are still on my chest, and when I clear my throat in annoyance, he just shrugs as if to explain that he can't help himself. "We got off on the wrong foot, but I want to change that. Just give me a chance to—"

"No." I have no interest in him. Not going to beat around the bush.

"And I suggest you back off. That man who you claim isn't good enough is a jealous bastard and doesn't take kindly to others sniffing where they don't belong."

"Really?" He laughs, and the sound sends a shiver down my spine. "Is this the same man who's been ignoring you? Who's left you all alone and defenseless?"

"Get out or—"

"I will if you agree to one date."

"You will because just like my father..." I lean in close and make a show of batting my lashes in a dramatic fashion, grabbing the door handle while his attention is on my face "...I have an amazing shot and I carry. Don't test my patience, Dominic."

With that, I slam it in his face and engage the lock.

From this side, I can just make out his low curses and then the sound of him walking away. And it's when I'm sure that he's gone that I breathe out a sigh of relief. For a second my shoulders drop and tension evaporates, but then on my next inhale it all comes rushing back in a chaotic tsunami of emotions. My mind swirls with questions. My body shakes as the hidden fear of the last few minutes makes its appearance.

However, one thing stands out above the rest:

Why does Dominic know about Casper and his absence?

Then, there's a scarier thought: *Why does he care?*

Aurora

"**H**OW WONDERFUL IT IS that you're still here, Aurora." The last person I thought I'd see says as my foot hits the bottom step. Our eyes meet and at once I'm taken back to all those years of attitude—mistreatments and not-so-subtle jabs at my mother and me. Matteo's ex-wife stands at the entrance to a smaller sitting area to the right of the door, waiting, her look calculating in that fake fondness she's forcing as an expression. "It's been too long since you've come to visit us."

I don't miss her emphasis on the word *us*.

"My apologies, Samantha…I've just been so busy with work." Matching her bullshit act of decorum, I walk up and give her a kiss on the cheek and pull back. "How have you been? Are you here looking for Dad?"

"No. I came to see you."

"Me? Why?"

"Can't a stepmother—"

"How about we get a little more comfortable?" Walking past her, I step into the small living space and take a seat on one of the oversized chairs, motioning for her to sit across from me. She follows a few seconds later, taking a pretentiously demure seat with a smile on her face. "Would you like something to drink?"

"No. I'm good."

"Okay then." Crossing my legs, I let my true emotions come through my expression. No more sugar coating or playing pretend. "What do you want, Samantha? You never cared then, and you don't now, so let's stop the games, shall we?"

"You were always so rude."

"And you've always been a horrible actress." Narrowing my eyes, I stare her down. "Again, what do you want?"

"Fine." The smile drops from her face and the sourness I've been accustomed to takes its rightful place. "Did he name you his heir?"

And there it is. Just like I asked him all those months ago in a hotel lobby back in London.

Asked him if she knew. What did the mother to his non-bastard child think?

Because deep down I know she cares. Wants it for Lucas.

"Where is my brother, by the way? I would've liked to see him this trip."

"Answer the question."

"Ask your ex-husband. I owe you no explanation on my life."

"Listen, I'm doing this for your own good." Samantha sits forward then, pulling out a manila envelope from her oversized purse. With her eyes on mine, she pulls out a set of pictures and places each one face up atop the small coffee table between us. "I might not be the warmest or most caring person in the world, but I'm not the asshole you think I am. Your father is under investigation for the murder of a senator that was found dead over five years ago near the harbor. They are looking into everything he owns and are itching to pin this on him one way or another, Aurora. Don't get yourself caught up in something that will destroy you and your mother's legacy. Leave while you can and don't look back."

I don't say anything, and she walks out of the room just the same. My eyes are on the photos staring back at me of a dead body, a man in his mid-forties who looks to be entering decomposition. Then, while holding in my urge to gag, I look at the next three and they are all candid photographs of Lucas and her while out doing random things. They are being watched, and it reminds me of the messages I received.

Is this what that was about? Am I under investigation because of my familial ties?

But why mix Casper into this?

The thoughts plaguing me from all sides are making my temples throb, and I can't help but look back at my brother's face. He's just a kid—innocent and without any stress on his shoulders. It's how every kid should be at his age.

Two things become very clear to me then:

I know what my decision will be, and I can't stay here.

I SEE him before he sees me.

It also doesn't surprise me to find him here, my eyes finding his body facing my living room window as he stares out calmly, without hiding. But then again, the man's impossible to miss. Unafraid to impose his presence.

He's over six feet of solid muscle and tattoos and an aura that draws you in. A charisma that's held me captive since we met months ago.

Christ. It's been months since that night. Since I gave in, knowing the consequences. And it's that same attraction that makes me come a little closer while making little to no noise.

He's deep in thought and ignorant to my eyes. Casper Jameson stands with his back to me and wearing what looks to be a plain white shirt. It's tight to his back, every hard muscle beneath pronounced. Something that makes my mouth water and thighs clench, but I ignore it. That burn. That need.

My eyes shift to his arm and I follow the curve of a tattoo that looks new, but it's a symbol I recognize.

His newest addition is an Ouroboros and I do admire the uniqueness, the way the entire body of a large snake wraps itself around his entire arm and then disappears near the front of his hand. It's bold and done in black and white from my viewpoint, but I'm curious about the head and it's placement. I want to know how the finished interpretations looks; a snake eating its tail.

Death and rebirth in a never-ending cycle.

The early evening sunlight is diminishing as the sun sets, but for now it's hitting just right. Makes the intricate design pop against his lightly tanned skin. Skin, that shows his time out in the sun recently.

It enhances his appeal. The corded muscle rippling down his arm as he clenches both hands.

Casper takes in a deep breath while tilting his head to the side. His dirty blond hair is longer than the last time we were together, and it sweeps across his temple. He doesn't speak, waiting, but I'm in no rush.

I need my wits about me and to ask the right questions, and for it to be a successful talk, I should have a clear head. Too much has happened, and I need to process. To not demand and listen to what he has to say.

He's here for a reason, and I want to know why.

Hope that he's honest with me.

"Go ahead and yell, Gem. I deserve it." His voice is low, so low I almost miss it.

"I'm not going to scream." Leaving my carry-on by the coat closet, I turn and close my front door. Then, after a deep breath in and out, I take a few steps closer. Just a few. I stop in front of my couch while leaving him on the other side of the room with plenty of furniture between us. "To be honest, I'm so exhausted and drained that I'm not sure I'm ready to talk. Just tell me how you got in?"

"Paid a locksmith I know a hefty amount to do me a favor."

A sardonic chuckle leaves me. "At least you're honest."

Casper turns around then, his bright green eyes boring into mine. "I've never lied to you. Things have been hectic, and a promise made has interfered with my plans for us, but I am working on it, Aurora. You're always on my mind."

"I wouldn't know."

"And that's my fault. I'm so sorry, love."

Nodding, I play with the soft blanket strewn across a few decorative pillows. "What happened, Casper?"

"Can we discuss this after? I need you."

I need you.
I need you.
I need you.

Three little words, but they rub me wrong. Anger me.

"Where the hell were you when I received..." I trail off, regretting my emotional mistake. More so when his brows furrow and lips thin. When he takes a step in my direction.

"What do you mean by that, Gem? Explain." His tone is hard, and his steps are loud within the confines of my home. The shift in him is instantaneous, an angry undercurrent that sings through my every limb as I back away and begin to move toward the back of my couch. It's a barrier. A way to put distance and think clearly. "Answer me."

My eyes narrow. "Don't use that tone with me, Jameson. I don't work for you."

"No. Clearly you don't."

"What's that supposed to mean?" I hiss between clenched teeth, hands gripping the back of the sofa. "Is that some kind of a sexist joke? Like women aren't meant to lead or hang with the big boys?"

"Not at all. My mum had a better shot than my dad." And I'm so lost in my moment of indignation that I lose focus as he stops on the other side of the couch. His knee dips into the cushion, the leather groaning under his weight as he positions himself facing me and kneeling. Closer. Almost touching. "That just meant you're not afraid of me." He's quick, and before I move back, Casper's fisting my shirt in his hand and pulling me down, so our faces are but a hair's breadth away. I also don't miss the way he grits his teeth at the move.

"Are you hurt?" I ask, already lifting a trembling hand to check him. My heart can't take anything happening to him no matter how much he's pissing me off today. "And don't think about lying either."

"Clean shot through my arm. It missed the bone and no fragments were left inside."

"Am I supposed to be okay with this?"

"Not at all, but I need you to trust my word. I'm okay, sweetheart." At my *are you kidding me right now* look, he shakes his head. "I'll show you my medical report if it'll help ease your mind."

Nodding, I let out a heavy sigh. Knowing this comes with the territory. It's always a possibility. "I want a copy of it."

"Done. Now, about my earlier clarifications..."

"Yes."

"All I was stating is that people know their place when it comes to me. They're not defiant."

"Should I know mine?" I lick my bottom lip and he follows the movement, his hunger undisguised. "Should I just be a good girl and behave? Is that what you want?"

"No. Never." He leans forward, lips skimming over mine. "I like you wild and sassy and never want you to hold back." Another kiss, softly, before his teeth scrape down to my chin where he bites down. "Now, it's your turn to explain what you meant."

"You'll need to let me go so I can do that." I huff, swallowing back a moan while avoiding his intense gaze. Instead, I trail my eyes down his arm for an up-close view of the snake's head of his tattoo. It's large and encompasses his hand, wrist, and forearm—the body wrapping around his flesh and then meeting on his hand as the mouth bites down on the tail. Like the rest of the piece, the color scheme doesn't change, except for the eyes. Those hypnotizing small orbs stare back at me with the same shade of hazel as mine.

Is this saying I'm his rebirth?

"Why?" There's a minuscule tinge of amusement in his tone which indicates I didn't do as good a job hiding my natural response to his everything. To the ink on his skin that symbolizes a change in him. Possibly us. "I like you just like this."

"And I need my phone." Releasing his hold, he fixes my shirt before using his pointer finger to push me back a bit. He doesn't say anything, and I take that as my opening. My cell is inside my purse, and I walk over to the closet where I left my belongings and pull it out. Turning back to face him, I run into his chest, not having heard him move. I'm distracted. Mind overworking and exhausted. "Sorry."

Casper holds his hand out with a small smile. "Your mobile, Gem." I unlock the screen and hand it over, watching how his facial expression goes from one extreme to the next. From sexy grin to absolute fury. "You should've called me the fucking moment these came in. What were you thinking? What if something—"

"Get out."

"I'm not going anywhere."

"Yes, you are." Snatching my phone from his hand, I take the remaining steps to the door and yank it open. "Now isn't the time for a fight. I'm tired and exhausted, regretting my trip to Boston, and before either of us says something unforgivable, we should walk away."

"Aurora, we need to—"

"I'm not *asking* you, Casper. I need space…time to reevaluate a few things."

"What's that supposed to mean," he asks, tone less acerbic. Casper also doesn't back down, stepping right into my personal space, pressing his body against mine. "And I'm not angry at you. Am I disappointed you didn't come to me? Yes, but I'm more concerned by those messages than anything else."

"And you think I wasn't? I needed you."

"Then why not tell—"

"How do you communicate with someone who isn't there?" Whatever anger he holds evaporates. Metaphorically, it breaks into a thousand tiny shards at my feet. "I didn't take those texts lightly or as a joke…the people who sent them know my family and me. They seem to not want me with you."

"You know who sent them?"

I nod. "I was made aware of an investigation—"

"Into who?"

"My father."

"On what charges."

"Murder."

"I see." That's all he says, and it rubs me wrong, as if he's privy to something I'm not. It's also another reminder of how little he shares back.

"What does 'I see' mean?"

"Your father will be fine, Gem." This confirms that he knows—has known of my familial ties all along. It also shows just how thorough his investigation into me was. "Don't worry. I won't let anyone hurt you."

My smile in response is small and sad. "Can you save me from you?" *From the heartbreak you'll bring?* Casper opens his mouth to reply, but I silence him by standing on the tip of my toes and pressing my lips to his. It's soft and everything I need and hate. It's also over quickly as I pull back before he can wrap me in his arms and deepen the kiss. "I'm going to need some space."

"Gem, I—"

"Please." He doesn't like it but nods. "I'll call you when I'm ready to talk."

"I'll be in Chicago for a few days." That's all he says before proving to me once again why walking away is an impossibility. Grabbing the waistband of my yoga pants, he gives it a hard tug and I'm back in his hold—being held possessively as his mouth slants over mine. Passion ignites and burns me. His mouth devours mine in an almost brutal way and I welcome the sting, the torture as he takes and I give in, until I can't breathe. Until he takes mercy on me and pulls back. "I'll be waiting."

"I promise to call you soon."

"And I promise to always listen. I won't make this mistake twice."

I KNOW WHO she is the moment she steps a foot inside of my office at the Conte House three days later. *Christ,* there's no denying our family's genes. London Foster has my complexion, hair color, and even the slightly fuller lips that everyone this side of the family has.

And we're the last two alive to pass it on to another generation.

It's a sobering and sad fact, but I can't deny how much seeing her means to me. How much I look forward to getting to know her.

"Hi," she says, voice shy and smiling, extending a hand for me to shake while the woman with her takes a stand outside the door. From the looks of her, I think she's my cousin's security. "It's nice to finally meet you."

"Nice to meet you, too," I reply and take the offered hand, pulling her in so I can give her a hug. Furthermore, the moment we do, it brings tears to my eyes and I hear her sniffle, and instead of pulling back, we hold on tighter. Just a little longer, while a piece of my heart gets mended. "You have no idea how much it means to me that you came by today. I've been dying to meet you since Malcolm—"

"Came and spilled the beans?" London finishes for me, laughing at the truth in that. She pulls back from me but keeps my hands in hers, giving them each a squeeze. There's happiness in her face and an honest look of appreciation for this opportunity that has to mirror my own.

We are just two women who lost all we had, our mothers, and were navigating through life missing a link—a bond to the past that will help cement the future. But now we can have that. We'll have each other to keep the Conte legacy alive.

"More like he welcomed *me* to the family."

"He didn't!"

"Totally did in his own sort of gruff-ish way before leaving this office."

"Dear God." Her giggle is loud and boisterous, and she lets go of my hands to wipe at the few stray tears that have fallen. "I'm sorry." Another bubble of laugher. "He's just something else and very determined to lay the world down at my feet. I hope he didn't upset you or was rude while vetting you."

I shake my head, my own smile widening. "So, what you're saying is he's one of the good ones?"

"Absolutely…wait…is it Aurora, or can I nickname you? Because you look like a Roe-Roe to me."

"Go for it. Roe-Roe works for me, but then I get to call you Lo-Lo," I chuckle, her bubbliness reminding me so much of my mother when excited. "I was only ever called Aurora as a child when in trouble, and that was often. I'm too curious for my own good at times, or so I've been told."

"Tell me more. I want to know all about the family I never knew."

"That might take years."

"Good thing I have all the time in the world." London gets a pensive look and then walks out the door to her guard. She says something to her quietly and then comes back in after the woman gives her a nod. "Are you hungry?"

"You're kidding! That's how you two met?" I ask London after almost spitting out my Long Island; we're sitting inside of a sports bar not that far from my apartment and catching up, giving each other little tidbits of information that describe our personas. That show just how similar we are. "You were a private dancer...with a pole and everything? Not judging, by the way..." I tack on, not wanting her to get the wrong impression "...because I've been thinking about taking one of those classes as a surprise for someone."

"Malcolm was my first and last customer."

"Ever?"

"Ever." Her eyes shift around the room once and then come back to mine. I recognize the move, too. She's taking in our surroundings and making sure no one's listening or getting too close, something that the woman with her wouldn't allow anyways. That one looks like she'll snap your neck if you breathe wrong around my cousin. *I like her already.* "That man literally kicked down every door to keep me for himself. To protect me."

"And you're happy, Lo-Lo? Does he take care of you?"

"I'm his equal, Roe-Roe, and we take care of each other. He's never made me feel anything but cherished. Loved." Pausing, she lifts her pop to her lips and takes a few deep sips. "For the first time in my life, I go to bed every night knowing I'm safe. That no one can force me to do anything, and what I give him in return, willingly and because I love him with everything I am, is my heart. That's all he's ever asked for even though he's risked his life to save mine."

"Wow."

"Yes." She waves her manicured fingers in a *hurry up* motion. "Now, your turn."

"Um, what? I don't have anything like—"

"The guy you want to learn to dance for...is he your boyfriend?" she asks, smirking at me. Enjoying my impersonation of a tomato. "This has to be good if you're blushing this hard."

I shake my head, averting my eyes. "We shall put him under the *it's complicated* section for now."

"Why are you looking away?"

"No reason." Another mistake on my behalf as I look over and begin to fidget in my seat. "Quit looking at me like that. He and I are not serious." *But I want to be. Need him to want it.*

London tilts her head to the side, appraising me. "But can you see your-self with him? Like long term?"

"Yes." No doubt. No hesitation. "But who knows what the future will bring, though. Life changes in the blink of an eye and right now, whatever we are is up in the air."

It's the truth. Nothing in life is guaranteed and a relationship like ours is doomed from the very beginning. All the cards are stacked against us.

We live on separate continents.

I hate the business, and it's a huge part of who he is.

He's always disappearing without a trace for weeks as he searches for the man who pulled the trigger.

I'm afraid to fall and crash.

"Why?" She gives me an apologetic look, picking up on my change in mood. "If you don't mind me asking, of course."

"Not at all." Smiling to show her that it's really okay, I sit back and pop a fry in my mouth, chewing slowly to give me a few extra minutes to word this right and control my tells.

"You're killing me here."

"So impatient," I mock grumble, a bit chastising in genuine fun, just like my mother did to me as a kid. I have no chill. Almost zero when I'm curious about something and so far, the only person that keeps me waiting is Casper. He's become my exception to the rules on every subject it seems. "But..."

"Woman, I will throw a piece of bacon at your head."

"You wouldn't dare."

"Yes, I would." Her light blue eyes turn to slits, daring me to keep making her wait as she tears a tiny piece of bacon from her club sandwich. "Five, four, three—"

"You little shit! Okay. Okay." I'm laughing at the absurdity of this. Just how at ease I am with her and how much it's helping my self-inflicted loneliness after I sent Casper away. "I give."

"Spill."

"You and my best friend Aliana are going to get along beautifully."

"Great, and two."

"I met him in London and had a one-night stand," I spit out *a la Band-Aid* effect.

"Oh my!" She sits forward and places both elbows on the table, cradling her face and looking at me as if I'm an interesting soap opera. "Please continue."

"Dork."

"Takes one to know one, and keep going. Because he had to have left quite the impression for you to get all red and—"

"I did not."

"You did."

"Do you want the story or not?"

"Proceed."

"You're so kind." Discreetly, she flips me off and I can't help but crack up. It's insane to me how effortlessly this has all been. How fast we've clicked.

It's easy and comfortable, as if we've known each other our entire lives.

"Yup, and it was totally cliché too. Just like the movies." Closing my eyes for a minute, I'm transported back to that day. Moreover, my lips begin to paint her a picture of that night. The pub, the pulsing music blaring through its speakers, the intense green eyes watching me across the room. The connection and draw, the moment he stepped in behind me, and then the moment his lips skimmed my earlobe as he spoke against my skin.

My skin breaks out in goose bumps. My heart races.

And through it all, I get hit with a pang of longing because I'm the one stepping back.

I need to call him. I miss him.

When I'm done, I open my eyes and meet London's wide ones. She's smiling. "Not serious my ass, chick. That was hot and sexy and intense and I'm running out of words to describe a smidgen of what you just told me. Don't be blind or stubborn. Don't deny what is clear to see…that man is under your skin."

"And who's under yours, Twirl?" a male voice says from behind her, and our heads snap back simultaneously toward the intruder. When we realize just who it is, we have two very different reactions. Lo-Lo is elated, while I'm embarrassed.

How much did he hear?

"You," is her automatic response before slipping from the booth and throwing her arms around the no-nonsense CEO's neck, something that with his demeanor I'd think he'd be against, but it's the opposite. The extreme opposite.

Malcolm Asher is all smiles for his girl and doesn't give a damn who sees it. The look in his eyes is that of a man in love. The sweet kiss he gives her is drowning in adoration.

It pours from them. The love.

And seeing it with my own eyes gives me hope. Literal hope that maybe someday this can be Casper and me.

"I need to call him," I whisper to myself as the elevator door opens on my floor. It's been a long day, but amazing, and with it came enlightenment:

If we really want to, we can make this work. I had the perfect example of it in my face all evening, and everyone knows who Malcolm Asher is. What he does. What they have never been able to prove, but people talk.

And others, like my father, have done business with the man and his father before him.

"Gem," Casper says out of nowhere and I scream, a gut-curdling yell that makes him step back with both hands up. "What's wrong with you?"

"Why would...are you...you scared ten years off my life!" I'm in his face, moving in closer and fighting to ignore just how good he smells. How good he looks in a leather jacket, simple white shirt, and old jeans. My pointer finger digs into his pec as I jab him, angry that he both scared and made me wet at once. *Handsome bastard.*

"Love, I said your name three times. Is something wrong?" There's genuine concern in his tone, and my annoyance simmers into a near nothing throb. "Did you get another one of those messages?"

"No. Nothing like that."

"Then?" he asks, taking advantage of our nearness to slip an arm around my waist to pull me against his chest. And I don't fight his hold, if anything, I let him. Enjoy it. His touch.

"I met someone today that I didn't know existed."

"Met someone?"

"A cousin. I have a cousin here in Chicago and had no idea all these years."

"I'm so happy for you, Gem. Family is the most important thing in the world." Ducking his head a bit, he kisses my temple and then across to my forehead. "I like knowing you have someone to turn to here."

"Thank you." I nuzzle his chest and give him a small kiss of my own there. "Now, what are you doing here? I thought you'd wait for my call."

"Something happened—"

"You need to leave again?" Disappointment hits and he sees it. I've gone from happy to my shoulders dropping.

"They found my mum's killer in Cuba." As much as I hate it, I understand. Agree, even. Casper won't move on until he finishes what he started months ago after her death.

"Go. I'll still be here when you get back."

"You promise we can talk then? There are some things I need to explain. Plans to discuss."

"More reason for me to wait. Go," I whisper shakily, emotions rising to the surface. "Just come back to me in one piece, and no more bullet holes. If you do, I'll add the next one myself."

"Is that your way of saying you care?"

Rising up onto the tips of my toes, I peck his lips twice before speaking against them. "That's my way of saying I want to be with you."

CASPER

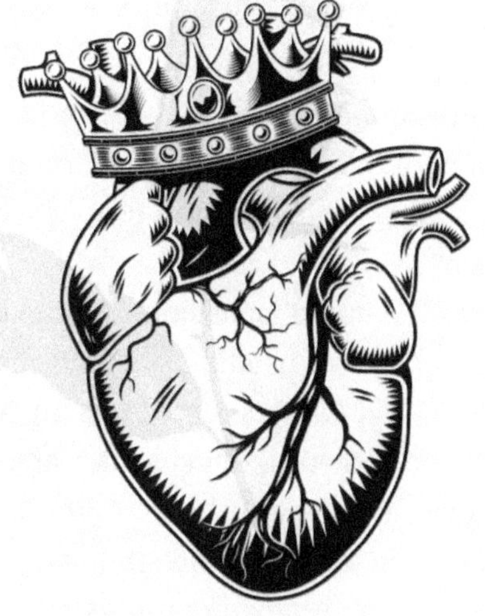

MY MOBILE RINGS atop my nightstand and I reach over, almost knocking my bottle of water to the ground before bringing the device to my face. It's a number I don't recognize but the area code is a similar one: 305, and that means Miami.

And there's only one bloody bastard that I know in the area personally.

Thiago Rivera is one of my biggest and most loyal business associates/clients. He's a man of his word and an unapologetic cunt to everyone but those closest to him, and also a damn good friend. Furthermore, in this business I only trust two men: Malcolm and him.

I pick up on the next ring. "About time you called, you arse. How's life treating you on the outside?"

"It's getting there." His voice is a bit rough, as if he's been out all night drinking, and he clears his throat. "Adjusting."

"That's good to hear. Are you free, or…?"

"Probation for two years." Through his side of the line there are some loud voices—they're yelling something in Spanish, and I sit up on the bed. I have a feeling this isn't a social call. There's too much commotion. Too much cursing.

"Everything okay, mate?"

"Is the pigeon in its cage?" he asks, and it's his way of asking if the line is safe to speak on.

"Ezra keeps it clean and maintained."

"Good." The sound of ice clinking inside of a glass follows as he moves to another room, the yelling around him ceasing as the door slams shut. "You in the States?"

"In Chicago. Why?" Without conscious thought, I grab my pajama bottoms and put them on before heading out into the main living area of my penthouse. I'm alone, but Callum isn't far with Archie. They're at the unit across from mine, more than likely sleeping after being up until three a.m. going over intel one of my men gathered on the Cancio organizations —trying to find a connection to the Savino siblings.

And we learned three very fascinating things:

That name doesn't exist in New Jersey. Not a single fucking Savino family.

Matteo wants to retire and wants his heir, *my Gem*, to take over.

I have a bullet with the name of his second-in-command on it.

He wants Aurora, and I'll have his head mounted on my wall before he lays a single finger on her. Fuck that, I'll never allow him the chance to even attempt to get close.

Dominic Bruno is a dead man walking.

"…because you're needed in Cuba tonight, my friend."

"Tonight?" I ask, walking into the other penthouse, and Callum looks up at me mid-bite. He places his bowl of cereal down—the man has an obsession with Lucky Charms—and stands, awaiting orders. "What's going on? Why is your little brother in Cuba?"

"Because Ivan has your mother's killer in a holding cell in Havana."

I miss you. ~Gem

> Wish you were here, but I understand. Do what
> you must and come back to me safe. ~Gem

HER MESSAGES COME in as I step off the small chartered aircraft we switched to after touching down in Miami the following night. It's just a little over nine in Havana when we land, and it's hot. The temperature is in the high 80s while Miami's wasn't any better. We were in the beautifully sweltering city for less than thirty minutes before leaving, and then inside of Cuban airspace a little over an hour later.

With each step down from the small plane, I feel my state of mind change. I'm wound tight and full of restless energy. Angry and needing to unleash my wrath.

To begin paying them back for what they've done.

A life for a life multiplied by my ire.

> Thank you, love, for always understanding and
> being amazing. I'll be seeing you soon. ~Casper

Then I pocket the device, putting it on silent so as to not be interrupted, at least for the next few hours as I go and make new friends.

At the end of the small private airstrip that belongs to the Riveras is an older gentleman holding a sign with my last name on it. Behind him there's a classic car, an open door, and the man I owe a very large favor to.

"It's been a very long time, Ivan," I say, extending my hand out once I reach him. "How have you been?"

"Can't complain." He smiles, and it's just like looking at a younger version of Thiago. "Happy to have him home...Mom's ecstatic and planning a wedding."

"He's getting married? But I thought—"

"Luna is giving him hell, but it'll happen." Callum stops to shake his hand and then slips inside the car, followed by Archie. Both are silent for distinct reasons. One is trying to clear his head, while the other is working with Ezra via text to wipe our information from all flight logs. As far as Interpol and the US government knows, I'm still in London. We all are.

And I want it to stay that way.

My comings and goings aren't something I want to be public knowledge or publicized anywhere. Anonymity is key in my business, and I adopted that teaching into my daily living.

The less people know, the more successful you'll be. The less you're likely to run into hypocrisy disguised as friendship.

The less bullshit tries to infiltrate your life with false pretenses.

Trust very few people and those you keep close. Because bad intentions and envy run rampant in today's society, and when the going gets tough, very few stick around.

"My money is on her drawing blood first."

"More than likely." Ivan shifts his eyes to the driver, who's already put our carry-ons into the trunk of a mint 1950s Chevy Bel Air and nods, signaling for him to get back inside and wait. "But this clusterfuck is a long time coming. He brought this mess upon himself."

"Agreed, but we both know he'll wear her scratches with a smile on his face and a drink in his hand."

Ivan throws his head back and laughs at that. "Very true."

"So, about this little visitor you have…"

He sobers at once, features turning hard. "Some motherfuckers have a big mouth and love to run it, Jameson."

"Drunk?"

"Off his ass." Stepping aside from the door, he comes and puts his hand on my shoulder, squeezing it, while his dark brown eyes meet mine. "You have our deepest condolences, Casper. What they did is unforgivable, and whatever you need to avenge her is yours."

"Thank you, my friend."

"Ready to go?"

"Please lead the way."

THEIR HOME HERE IS LARGE: a colonial monstrosity with a twenty-four-hour staff, transportation, and full-sized jail at the far end of the compound. There is one way in and one way out, with a crematory inside the same building.

No neighbors. No questions. No one knows they are here.

The government here is too cocky to realize what's happening beneath their noses. How people are slowly rising up to take back what has always been theirs. They were just too afraid to strike back without help. However, it's coming. That day that all Cubans dream of is on the horizon, with help from the Riveras and two more families silently working in the background.

They will have freedom.

We will have an open port to negotiate from.

However, this visit is for a very different purpose and as we exit the car right in front of a building's door, I walk calmly to the trunk and pop it open before their driver can assist.

I won't need much for this visit.

One gun and my two knives.

"Mate, were you able to get what I asked for?" I hear Callum ask Ivan as they come to the back as well. "How much?"

"Yes, and not a thing."

"Owe you one. Just ask." They stop beside me and Ivan pulls a package from deep inside the trunk—a box—and hands it to my cousin. I don't ask about the contents. I'm sure it'll come in handy, but for now, I take my time preparing.

My vest comes off and the all-black suspenders fall down to my thighs. Next, I remove my mobile and wallet—handing them over to Archie—and then pull out the chain inside the front pocket of my trousers. It's a special medallion my mum had blessed by the pope on a visit to England after I was born. On the round, quarter-sized piece is the symbol of Ares, the God of War: an ancient helmet from gladiator times and two swords in the form of an X behind it in white gold.

It's intricate and bold, and I very much doubt the highest-ranking member of the Catholic church noticed it when giving the blessing.

A pulsing energy fills my body and all around me the noises begin to dull. I put the piece around my neck—securing it before moving my neck from side to side. It cracks, my back loosens a bit, and I close my eyes for a minute.

That's when I hear it. This minuscule sound that I pick up while the other two continue to talk and Archie stands to the side with the two guards standing outside the door. He knows his role here—to keep watch and help them clean up after, nothing more.

This will be a family-only event.

I take a step toward the entrance and the sound becomes a tiny bit clearer. Low, but more coherent.

It's screaming. Male. Afraid.

"Ivan, I'm going to need a desk chair than can spin, please."

"I'll have someone bring one down."

"Thank you."

"Whatever you need." Ivan walks past me and his guards open the doors wide, letting us see into the long corridor up ahead. Everything is dark. In need of repairs, but then again, if you're brought to a place like this, it's for a reason. You're here to receive sentencing, not have a drink.

At the end of this hall there's a large metal door and the further inside we walk, the more his words become pronounced. Clear.

Where the fuck am I?

Let me go, cabron!

I'm going to kill you.

He's a defiant little arse, and I'm going to enjoy every minute of his end.

There is a total of twenty steps before we meet the entrance and I open the door.

At once, the scent hits my nostrils; it's putrid and stomach turning, but more than that, the scene that greets my eyes when the lights are switched on is beautiful in all its gory glory.

Mauricio is standing in the middle of the room surrounded by cells with open doors, and inside of each is an animal. Large hogs; angry and feral swine that the minute we walk in become quiet. They're deathly still and silent as we make our way toward the almost naked man with his arms bound high above his head.

Mauricio fucking Hernandez is dirty, angry, and a lot older than I thought he'd be.

"Evening," I say. His eyes snap in my direction, and he hisses as once again the brightness from the lights angled toward his face, hurt his eyes.

"Who are you?" he asks, squinting hard. "Why am I here?"

"Why is he here?" I parrot, looking back at my cousin and Ivan. "The poor man is asking why he's here? Why this is happening to him?"

"Poor lad." Callum comes to stand beside me with the package Ivan gave him in hand. "This is a horrible predicament to find yourself in."

"It is."

Ivan steps into the light, places the chair in front of Mauricio, and steps back, but not before the cocksucker gets a good look at his face.

"You," he grunts out, fighting against his bonds to reach Ivan. "You were at the bar—"

"Yes. I was." The door to this room slams shut and a lock is engaged. "And it was an interesting night, indeed. Many stories shared over a bottle of Havana Club. Do you remember that?" Ivan pulls out a remote from his pocket and hits the button at the center, dimming the lights a bit. Enough that he can now see me and pales. "Remember the story you shared of your recent time in London?"

CASPER

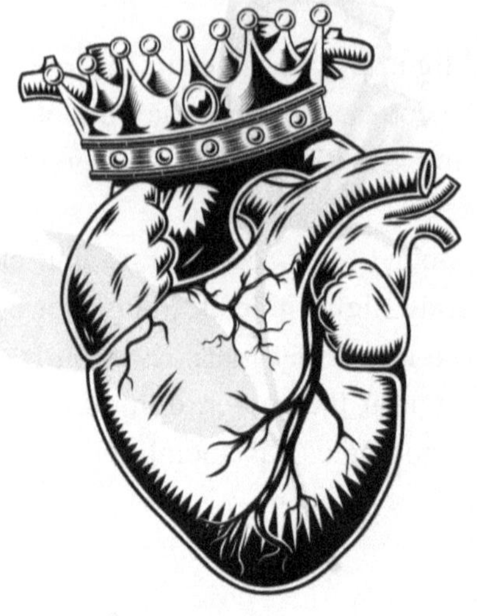

"**I** DON'T REMEMBER."

My eyes narrow, but I keep my tone of voice calm. "I'm going to give you a minute to go through your memories, Mr. Mauricio Hernandez. Use your time wisely."

"You have the wrong man," he says instead. Too quickly. Stupidly. Sweat begins to build at his temples and then the shivers begin to run down his body. With each tick of the clock, his fear is becoming all the more palpable. It's pulsing throughout the room. "I'm innocent."

"I haven't accused you of anything yet, mate." Turning my face, I look at Ivan. "Have you?"

"Not at all."

"And you?"

My cousin beside him snorts and shakes his head in the negative. "I haven't said a word."

Looking back at the guilty fuck, I shrug. "See? No accusations. However, I do believe you have a story to tell."

"I'm not him."

"Him who?"

From the corner of my eye, I see Callum and Ivan step away from us and head toward the very last cell. Once inside there's some racket, the sound of metal items being pushed around and then the wheels of a creaky old cart coming toward us. The thing is old and definitely belongs in here with the trash, but the laptop atop it is new and so is the camera hookup beside it.

It clicks then what he meant outside, and I'm glad he thought that far ahead to prepare. My father will very much appreciate it.

But first...

I take the remaining steps between us and with a quick flick of my wrist deliver the first of many cuts to come with my karambit, two identical slices behind the ankles that sever his tendons. Even if he could, the man can no longer lift his foot off the ground and walk.

"Motherfucker!" he screams out, and the agony in that high pitch does two very important things:

It makes me smile.

Makes the large hogs in the room grow loud and rowdy.

Another click of his remote and the cells close, leaving two of these beasts on the loose and roaming the room. They're running, squealing—coming closer to him but not attacking yet. They will, though. It's only a matter of time before the hunger overtakes all thinking.

An important fact about pigs; they can be cannibals. A small horde can clean a body down to the bones without any problem. For this very reason, I asked my friend to not feed his lot today after finding out that on his compound, they had livestock for different purposes.

A hungry animal is dangerous.

A hungry and agitated animal is a killer.

"I'm going to ask you one last time, Hernandez. Tell me the story you shared with my friend here? Last chance."

"He's lying!" The more he fights his bonds, the tighter they become, and I can see the tip of his fingers turning a darker purple. Take in the way the ropes are cutting deeper into the wound I created. *Ouch.* "I was just at that bar celebrating my wedding anniversary."

"Really?" Ivan looks at him from behind the laptop's screen, in his hand an HDMI cord. "Because there was no one with you but the prostitute you bought for the night. And don't worry, I left her every single cent you had in your wallet and back at the cheap hotel you were hiding in. Those two hundred thousand in cash will be used by her family and friends to survive and have a better life."

"You piece of shit...I will kill you!"

"That's a mighty big threat from an innocent man."

"Do you know who I am? I will...*fuck*!" Another cut. This time, though, to his leg, and it runs the length going from knee to upper thigh where his boxer briefs end. I went deeper this time. I made sure to take my time and enjoy the way his flesh gives way underneath my sharp blade.

The only way to describe is it is like slicing through butter, smooth and precise.

Blood rushes to the top of the wound and rolls down his leg, pooling on the floor beneath his feet. The puddle grows quickly, calling the attention of the animals. One almost gets close enough to bite, but Ivan slaps his behind hard enough that he rushes away on a squeal.

"Feel like telling me that story now? Come one, Mauricio. Let's reminisce."

"Maybe he just needs a little help getting there. Something to remember?" Callum walks over with the calmness of a saint and opens a bottle of the same rum he got piss drunk with. "Right, friend?"

"Don't. Please don't." Mauricio's head is shaking hard from side to side, his eyes on the bottle in my cousin's hand. "I'll talk."

"So you do remember?" Callum lets a small amount fall from the bottle's opening onto his leg but avoiding the cut altogether.

"Don't do this."

"Do what?" Another small stream. This time, a few drops fall into the open wound and his body bows into itself. Crying out, he blubbers something that we can't quite make out. "Repeat that?"

"I'll tell you what you want to know, just let me walk out of here alive. Promise not to kill me."

"But first, let's start with a slide show. A beautiful message from a friend?" Callum asks and I nod, loving the idea.

What do you think, Hernandez?" Ivan takes that as a cue to turn the laptop on. He does so, and then pushes the creaking cart closer until its literally touching his skin, the rust from the metal smearing across his abdomen and thighs.

And because I'm an arsehole with no remorse, I slice across his stomach—a shallow cut—from side to side right over his dirty flesh.

At his curse of pain, I smile, but I sober just as quick. He killed my mum. This bloody cunt took from me the most important woman in my life until just recently, a move she would've approved wholeheartedly if it meant her son is happy. That she would've gotten those grandkids she dreamed of and never once stopped giving me shit over.

"Where are they?" I ask Callum who looks back at the computer, pointing at the app next to the Skype button. Pressing it, I remove myself from them and let the entire album play out. I let him see just how depraved and sick I can be. I let him watch picture by picture as his good-for-nothing friend, the rubbish that got him my mother's job, is sentenced.

Felix Vega was useful until he wasn't and for his role in her death, he received a penance that no man, misogynist or not, can handle. For the couple of days that Gem made me wait for her, I tortured him. A burn at a time. A strike at a time. A loss of an appendage at a time.

Alexander is Aurora's bodyguard for a reason, and it's his brutality that has kept him under my employ. Without an ounce of concern or care, I watched the man from a comfortable seat as he cut an inch off his dick at a time. One every hour and the wanker only made it to number five before there was nothing left.

Then, he removed his balls. One at a time too.

From the very beginning to the end where Felix takes the offered gun with a shaky hand and pulls the trigger is all documented. Saved for him to enjoy, and on the second go-around, his watery eyes meet mine.

"I'm sorry," Mauricio says as I hold a hand up for Callum and point toward the laptop. He set this up so my father wouldn't miss this moment from his home in London. Everything happened too quickly for him to meet us, but this is the next best thing, and after a few clicks of the mouse, he's on the screen.

I look over and he nods in greeting but we exchange no words. None are needed at this moment.

It's a time for actions, and they speak louder than any words ever will.

Flipping my attention back to the prisoner, I raise a brow. "So, you do know who I am?"

"Yes. I studied your picture and file for two weeks before the hit took place."

"Who sent you?" He doesn't answer right away, and Callum does me the favor of pushing the bottle's opening into the wound and tipping the alcohol over. Mauricio's screams of agony rile up the hogs again; this time they begin to bang against the metal bars keeping them back, while the ones that are loose come sniffing, licking the floor, snorting, pushing forward until they are just below his bloodied feet. Just when they prepare to bite, Ivan pushes them back with a metal pole he procured while we watched the photo film. "This will only work for so long, Hernandez. Tell me their real names and not the bullshit Felix gave me."

"No one knows their real names and I didn't care enough to ask." It's an honest answer, I'll give him that, but not what I want. So to edge him along, I give him an almost identical slice across his other leg to match the first.

"Tell me what you know. All of it."

"Nico and Antonella are the children of Giada Savino. These three hate Matteo Cancio for something that happened between their father and the Boston mob boss a very long time ago. They never told me what, but from what Felix said it all started a year after Aurora, Cancio's daughter, was born."

"Matteo wasn't in charge then."

"The father. Matteo Cancio Sr. was."

"Okay." Placing my knife onto the cart, I extend a hand out to Callum for the bottle. He hands it over, and I bring it to Mauricio's lips. "Drink. It'll help."

"Just kill me."

"I will, but I need something first..."

Opening his mouth, he lets me pour a generous amount and swallows. "You want to talk about your mother?"

"She wasn't your intended target." Not a question, and he nods. "Then why shoot an innocent woman."

"They doubled the offer." He shrugs and lifts his head toward the bottle in my hand, and I pour another shot in his mouth. After swallowing, he releases a hiss as some of the spirits spilled onto his leg. "Those are a bitch...hurt like hell."

"That's the point." I hand the rum back to Callum. "Now, about the money?"

"I was supposed to receive the other half a mil next week to an account I have in Guatemala City. The national bank doesn't ask questions and after slipping the manager a couple of bucks, he speeds the process up personally."

"What day next week?"

"Wednesday."

"Thank you for your cooperation." With that, I pull out my gun and shoot him four times in the upper torso. That's the signal. The beginning of his end as Callum cuts him down, letting the almost dead weight drop to the ground without a care.

His groan is loud and pulls the attention of the two pigs on the floor. They come closer and we pull back toward the exit, and once there, Ivan presses the button on his remote that opens the cells for the other hogs to come out.

Within a minute, the screams inside the room are deafening. Would make a weaker man sick to his stomach.

Not me.

It's almost poetic, really. A disgusting cunt ending his life as nothing more than pig food.

After a minute, I step outside while the other two stay on the other side of the door talking, catching up, and I'll do that tonight, but first...

I find Archie right where we left him, standing to the left of Ivan's men and watching the door. Once I step through, he wordlessly hands me my belongings and then retakes his position. The other two give me a nod, but also remain quiet as they know to wait for all three of us to walk out before they remove what's left and dispose of all evidence.

Swiping a finger across the screen of my phone, I scroll through my contacts and find the phone number I need and type out a message.

It's time we sit down and talk ~Casper.

Within seconds there are three little dots on the screen letting me know my message was received. It starts and stops a few times, but I'm pleased with their response and agree.

Name the time and date. ~Cancio

CASPER

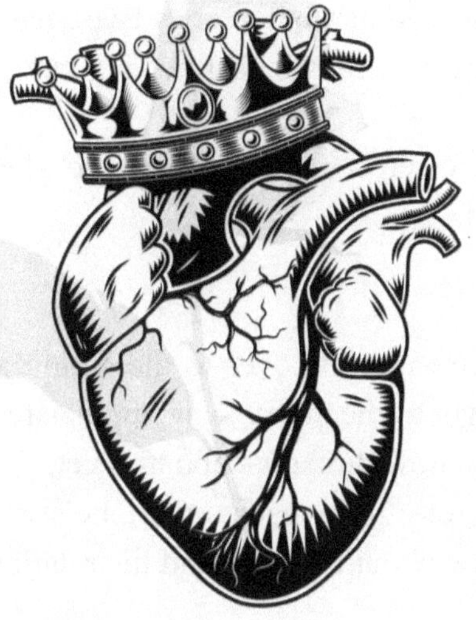

"**I**'M VERY SORRY to hear about what happened to your mother, Casper. That's unacceptable and if you need anything, let me know." Matteo extends his hand out for me to shake as we meet in the lobby of his downtown office a week after I came back from Cuba. I've spoken to his daughter three times since then, explained what happened, but I never told her I'd be coming here.

Not yet. Not until I've handled a few loose ends.

The first is making her father understand my intentions. What I think of his plans for Gem.

Hopefully, my beauty understands why I do what I do. For her. For the us we will be.

The entire top floor of this building houses Matteo's office and that of another man I'll be visiting before walking out today because I'm here for two reasons:

To lay my cards down on the table. To warn him of what's to come.

Both reasons begin and end at the exact same spot:

Don't touch what's mine.

Looking at Gem's father, I take in the similarities between him and his daughter. Like now, as I take the offered hand and give it a firm shake, his brows give a small furrow as he tries to read me. Then, there's the tightening of his jaw when I give nothing away.

Two small expressions that match ones I've seen on Gem's face whenever her piqued curiosity isn't fed. On her it's cute, on him it's amusing, but I rein it in.

"Thank you. The offer is much appreciated since we have a mutual interest to take care of."

"We do?"

"Yes."

Matteo nods and then points over to the sitting area near his floor-to-ceiling windows. "Right to the point, I can appreciate that."

He has no idea just how direct it's about to get.

We take seats across from each other; he's watching me, and I'm dissecting what I know about the man and his relationships thus far. "Who are the Savinos?"

"Savinos?" His expression is confused because that not where he thought I'd begin. If he isn't aware of my relationship with Gem, then he thinks this is about business. "I don't know anyone with that name." *My information was correct. They don't exist.*

"They seem to know you, though."

At my response, he shakes his head. "Never heard of the name. Are they from Boston?"

"From my understanding, they're from New Jersey but want a permanent seat of power here. They know you, your family, your business dealings, and want it all."

"What the fuck are you talking about? Who are these people?" His face has gone from lost to red in anger, jaw ticking. "How do you know this, and no one under my employ has—"

"I'm involved for two very specific reasons, Cancio. Both of which involve the women in my life." Sitting forward, I let my hands fall between my parted thighs. "They stole a gun shipment from me around the time you were in London a few months back."

"I had nothing to do with that."

"Something I already know, but at the time, blamed you." My phone pings with a message, and the special tone is his daughter's. For the moment I ignore it. I'll call her when I leave. "It became pretty clear soon after that you had no direct involvement and were in town for personal reasons."

"Direct involvement? I had no knowledge of anything happening."

"It involves you because of those fucking cunts. This is the second time they've tried to mix me in their mess...do their dirty work and have failed. They want you dead, want your territory, and then the male of the trio desires your daughter for himself. That last one will only happen over my dead body."

"How do you know my daughter?" As he says this, his eyes narrow. "Wait. Why are you really here? What does my Aurora have to do with this?"

"Why do you *think* I'm here?" Does he not look into her life at all? Does the bloody arsehole not care?

"Business. Maybe an expansion of operations."

"Are *you* looking to expand. Is the UK attractive to you?" I counter, instead. My expression is one of annoyance.

"Always has."

"Nice to know, but I'm not here for that...this time."

"Then why?"

"Because Aurora is mine." My tone leaves no room for argument. End of.

"Shouldn't you be asking me—"

"For shit." My voice is even, but the threat hangs in the air. I'm not a child and I ask permission from no one but Gem. Hers is the only one I need. "What happens between us is just that...between us. My relationship is with Aurora, and I will never ask nor apologize for being with her."

"And if I forbid this?" He's toying with me now—testing—and doing a shit job at it; the smile he's fighting back isn't helping his case. To him, this would play out perfectly in his desire for her to take over, and I could be the man to guide and stand with her.

Problem with this is he just doesn't realize how much of a wall I can be.

"Your approval isn't needed or wanted."

Matteo doesn't like my reply and his eyes narrow. "You have balls, Casper. This isn't England."

"I do, and I'm not afraid. Trust me when I tell you my connections run deeper than yours."

"Is that a threat?" he spits out through clenching teeth; hands are on the armrests and placed strategically to launch himself forward if need be.

"That's a fact." I shrug and then sit back to show I'm not at all intimidated. "Now, to get back on track. Nico, Antonella, and Giada Savino set things in motion to make it look like you were involved and responsible for the stolen shipment...hoping I would link you to my mum's death and retaliate. But like all rubbish, the stink comes to the top and people talk. It's how I found out about these three, the others involved, and disposed of a few."

"We're not done talking about my daughter."

"My intentions are clear, and I'm not going anywhere."

"We'll deal with that later." Matteo rubs a hand down his face, spitting out a few curses in Italian under his breath. Once he regains his composure, he looks at me again and this time all amusement is gone. The man looking at me now is the one people fear in Boston. "How do I find these assholes?"

"*We* find," I correct, and he nods, accepting my position in this. "Do those names ring a bell? Any of the three?"

"No. Not at all," he says, standing from his seat and walking over to the windows where he just looks out. He doesn't say anything. He doesn't move a muscle. Just stares until there's a knock at the door. It's timid and stops after three taps. "Come in."

The door opens and his secretary's head pops in, a woman in her early forties that looks afraid of her own shadow. "I'm so sorry for interrupting, sir. Mrs. Cancio is on line one and demands you take the call."

He doesn't turn around to address her. "No worries, Lisa. Pass her through."

"Thank you, sir."

Once the door closes, he releases a rough exhale. "Will you protect my daughter before your own life?"

"Yes."

"Will she be taken care of and respected?"

"Yes."

"Do you love her?"

"I'm not going to answer that." Matteo turns around at my reply, but before the man can utter a single syllable, I shake my head. "When I say the words, they will be to her. Not you. Not anyone. Just her."

"I can respect that."

"Good." Standing from my seat, I fix my cuff links. "Answer your call, and we'll finish this conversation at a later time. For now, you have my mobile's number and can reach me if needed. Watch your back, Matteo, and keep this information to yourself. You don't know if they have help on the inside."

"Even Dominic? I trust him and as my second—"

"Especially not him. There's something about the wanker that doesn't sit well with me, and if he ever so much as breathes wrong in her direction again, he's a dead man. A message I will be delivering personally once I leave this office."

"I can't allow that."

"Yes, you will." I crack my neck to alleviate a bit of the tension there. "For this meeting I gave you the courtesy of no guns and none of my men entered this floor. As a matter of fact, I left them downstairs waiting for me with strict instructions on how to proceed if things became *unpleasant* between us. Now, it's your turn to play nice. Where is he?"

"Just to have words."

"I'm going to kindly explain a few things."

He lets out a sigh but relents. Not that he has much of a choice. "Opposite end of the floor, only door on that wall."

"Thank you, and don't forget that your ex-wife's call is on line one."

To Dominic's shitty luck, he's not in his office when I seek him out, but I do find him a little later entering the building as I exit.

His eyes are down and oblivious to my persona as he tries to slip into my slot in the large revolving door. He's a bloody fucking idiot and it's time he learns a bit of respect.

"The fuck?" he yells the second my shoulder slams into him, sending him back onto the concrete outside the Cancio building. His phone, the one he was so lost in, goes flying toward the street and I see Callum walk toward it while a few of Cancio's guards take their positions.

No guns are drawn. Not while we're out in public like this.

Archie stands to my right with Jeffrey and a minute later Callum does as well.

I don't touch the idiot, but I do stand above him. "Get up."

There's a flash of fear in his eyes, but he hides it behind a sneer. "Touch me again, Jameson, and it'll be the last thing that you do." Those are the wrong words to tell a man like me, something he learns a second later when I place my foot on his neck. Not to choke, but to prove a point. He's still a nobody. Will never be on the same level as me. "You have five seconds to remove it and leave. Matteo will see this as an act of—"

"Matteo gave me his blessing to deliver a message personally." At this, his features harden and the hand trying to push my foot off clenches. So I do him the favor, removing it only so I can yank him up by the hand and help the tosser stand to his full height. Dominic tries to distance himself, but I don't let go, and the next time he tries to forcefully do so, I take my karambit out and flip it open while stepping into his personal space so to everyone passing by, it looks like I'm giving him a friendly hug. With my lips at his ear, I bring the blade to his neck—enjoying how hard he swallows when he feels the sharp steel—and let out a chuckle. "If you come near Aurora again, I will find out and I will kill you. Make no mistake, Dominic, she is mine and this is the only warning I will give you as the second-in-command for the Cancio family. Don't force my hand. Back down and learn your place."

Then, I step back as if nothing has happened. I even pat him on the back and wish them all a nice afternoon.

I'm done in Boston, and I have a girl to go see.

Why are you in Boston? ~Aurora

Why didn't you tell me you were back? ~Aurora

You know what, never mind. I don't like to chase people. ~Aurora

THOSE THREE MESSAGES came in two hours apart and I made the mistake of not calling her back like I promised I always would. I bodged up. Not going to deny it, but I wasn't in a good place and never want her to see me like that.

Maybe it was everything that's happened over the last few days catching up to me, or my talk with her father, or even the four pints I had with dinner, but I let myself mourn my mum. I said goodbye in my own way and privately without anyone there to witness my grief.

Her killer has paid his price for taking her life, and I said my goodbyes.

Now, though, as I dial her number forty-eight hours later and find a recording telling me that *the number you've dialed has been disconnected*, I realize my mistake. Taking the time to myself isn't the problem. Not at all. All I had to do is tell her to give me a moment and that I would get back to her.

Aurora is tired of waiting for me.

Aurora misses me.

My Gem needs me the same way I crave her constantly.

"You're in a shit mood tonight, mate. What gives?" Callum asks from beside me in a pub back in Chicago, but I pay him no mind. I'm preoccupied. Taken in by the memory of her smile when I promised outside her apartment door to always come back. I remember the sweetness of her lips as she pressed them briefly to mine and then told me to go.

That she would wait for me.

"He looks like a man who's in the doghouse." Malcolm brings the gin and tonic in front of him to his lips and takes a sip. "Want to share with the class? I'm an expert on relationships nowadays."

"Back off, Asher."

"I'm not the enemy, Casper." Malcolm regards me with a cool look, at ease. "But something is up, and it isn't business related. Fuck that—since when do you spend so much time in Chicago?"

"My apologies," I say, but I neither confirm nor deny his suspicions. "Just have a lot going on in my head."

"Want to talk about it?"

"Not really." Callum clears his throat, ready to add his two cents, but at my glare closes his mouth. I'm sure he'll bring it up again. That he'll tell me I'm being an idiot, but now isn't the right fucking time to meddle. Cousin or not, I'm not in the mood for anyone's bullshit.

"Fair enough." Malcolm then pulls out an envelope from his suit jacket and pushes it across the table. It's an invitation of some sort and I raise a brow at him. "London and I would like to invite the Jamesons to our wedding. It's taking place in a couple of months here and I'd like for you to be a part of the wedding party. It'll give you a chance to get to know London and meet her cousin Aurora. She'll be the maid of honor—"

I don't let him finish. "Count me in."

"That easy?"

"You're someone I consider family. End of." *Perfect opportunity to fix this.* "Do you know who I'll be walking down the aisle with?"

Callum coughs, and Malcolm glances back over at him with a questioning look. "You okay?"

"Yeah…" my cousin bangs a hand on his chest at bit "…beer went down the wrong pipe."

"Oi. Be careful."

"Thanks." He gives me a shitty grin. "Must be some bullshit in the air that caused it."

"You're the only tosser choking on nothing. All you, bro."

Malcolm clears his throat; the man doesn't quite know what to think. "Any request?"

"Her cousin." No hesitation from me, and if he notices, Asher doesn't call me out on it. Something I'm grateful for. "It'll give me a chance to get to know her as well." *To win her back.*

Aurora

"**T**HAT WAS A BIT extra of you, Roe-Roe."

"I agree with her, chick. A bit much," Aliana adds after London, looking at me like I'm insane for having changed my number. And maybe it is a bit much, but what's done is done and so be it. "Especially since you swear, he means nothing and isn't worth mentioning."

"She has a point." London picks up a piece of apple with Brie, pops it into her mouth, chews, and then gives me the stink eye. "Why can't you at the very least give us his name?"

We're at the house she shares with Malcolm and in the middle of some serious wedding planning. There are samples everywhere: flowers, fabric swatches, and a few place settings to choose from that the planner dropped off for us to go through. The menu is pretty much set, and I'm just adding notes for the caterer on different RSVPs with allergies while Aliana serves us drinks. Bottle number three, a light Pinot has been the group's favorite so far.

"Because it's not important."

"Says the woman still harping on it."

"That's mean, Lo-Lo."

"Calls it like I sees it." She shrugs, waving her hand in the air. "Prove me wrong. Tell us."

I shake my head. "Not happening."

"You suck." Then she's distracted by a pretty napkin and the ring that goes with it. It's in a soft champagne color with a gold trim. "I like this one. What do you think?"

"Beautiful and delicate. I'm digging it." This all feels like it's happening overnight; we met, I blinked, and they disappeared for a few days, coming back engaged. And I can't deny that a small piece of me is jealous. That I want this for myself. She's so happy, vibrating, and this newly found confidence looks good on her.

My beautiful cousin is free, and it's because those two pieces of shit are dead. *May they rot in hell where they belong.* Her past isn't pretty, but my girl has risen above the bull crap and is building a good life with Malcolm. He's good to her. Looks at her the way Casper would look at me whenever our eyes met. Like I was his everything.

Maybe I am overreacting. Maybe I should just let him explain why he went to see my father.

"You look like you want to spill," Ali whispers beside me and I jump, wanting to punch her while she refills my glass. Her giggles are not helping her one bit.

"Nope," I hiss.

"Yes," they say in unison.

"Not happening."

"Why not?" my best friend whines, and I can't stop the epic eye roll that follows. These two are relentless. "Why can't you admit you like him and tell us who he is? Do we know him?"

"Because she's being selfish." Mariah, Malcolm's cousin, walks into the Asher kitchen then with two more bottles of wine in hand and a delivery boy behind her that looks ready to pee his pants. It's priceless, what I come to expect when we convene and gossip. It's nice. Fun. We go together in a way that's seamless.

"Withholding information from friends is a punishable offense, Aurora.

I'm both hurt and disappointed," Ali says, a fake innocent expression on her face.

"Really? Who sent you a text last week that turned you tomato red?"

The other two turn their heads and narrow their eyes.

"It was a wrong number."

"Those make you blush and smile?" I question, hoping it takes the attention off me.

"Whoever it was had sent someone a dirty joke. Sue me..." Ali shrugs, trying to be nonchalant but I'm not buying it "...and I didn't know that finding something amusing was such an issue. Unlike you, I haven't been on a date in a long time. Too freaking long."

"You guys suck as friends," I say, schooling my facial features for half a second, because then like a domino effect, we all crack up. One by one laughter rings up and it's in the middle of it that someone clears their throat.

The delivery boy is still there and standing awkwardly by the counter near the fridge. "Can I leave?"

Christ. We begin all over again. I've never laughed so hard in my life.

Tears. Hiccups. The whole nine.

And right now, when I want to give in and call him—see him—it's needed. It hurts like hell, this separation, but we can't go on like this. I'm here and he's there. And while I know that it won't fix our situation, our relationship can go one of two ways at this point...

Together, or not at all. The ball is in his court, and I hope he seeks me out.

That he makes the right move.

London is the first to calm down, and her eyes gets this evil twinkle in them. "You know, Malcolm has a good friend flying in for the wedding that I could set you up with. He's handsome, in his thirties, and Asher approved."

"No."

"Why not?" This time it's Aliana.

"Prove us wrong." Mariah is looking at me with a raised brow. Knowing that if I fight it, it's because of the mystery man they're dying to know about.

I'm a cheater if I do and damned if I don't. *Fake it for now and call it off before the date.*

"Fine. I'll go on one date if he agrees." The hoots and hollers that follow make me forget we're grown women and not a bunch of prepubescent tweens at a boy band concert. "What's his name, by the way? The friend?"

"Not telling," London says with a giggle, high-fiving the other two. "It'll be a surprise."

Crap.

———

IT'S around midnight when I finally make it back home, and just like the last few days, there's a long-stemmed white rose on my door. A first, because the others have been on the windshield of my car or my office door at The Conte House.

It's taped, and with a folded note attached that I grab, opening it right there before entering my apartment.

I'M GOING TO GIVE YOU THE WORLD, AURORA.
JUST HEAR ME OUT.
LET ME IN.

The girly girl deep within makes an appearance and I squeak. Squeal. I make all kinds of embarrassing noises that I'm incredibly thankful no one sees, this display of weakness.

This little act of affection means more to me than any ostentatious gift would. It soothes me. Makes me think that maybe, just maybe, I'm wrong and he's not the jerk I've made him out to be in my head.

That maybe there's a reason for how he handled things. For why he went to see my father, a father who's gone silent since that visit. Not a single peep in days, and had it not been for Samantha letting me know to stay clear—in a text—because a mob boss from England was visiting, I wouldn't have known.

It's just too much of a coincidence, and his lack of denial is all the confirmation I need.

Or maybe I'm looking too deep into this and I just need to let it play out.

My mind likes that conclusion while my heart thunders in my chest. There's no denying that I miss Casper. That I want him here, but I'm going to need something more profound than a flower and note.

What I need is to know how he feels about me. To know that he cares.

That maybe someday soon he will love me like I already love him.

A sobering truth that sends me rushing inside and to bed. It's better to not think about things I can't fix; this is on him.

Casper needs to show me before we can move forward.

THERE'S a hard knock on my door the next morning, startling me awake. It's constant, loud, and I find myself stumbling down the hall toward the front door without a second thought.

My hope is that it's Casper, but as I look through the peephole, I realize it's a woman. She's dressed in black and looking straight ahead, letting me take in her face without her knowledge.

Light complexion, jet-black hair, and high cheek bones. Her lips are also in a bright shade of red.

I've never seen her before, and I open the door. "May I help you?"

"Aurora Conte?" she asks, and the second I nod, the woman brings her badge into view. She's BPD and at once I'm fully alert. "I'm detective Corrine Santos and I have a few questions for you. Do you have a few minutes?"

"Sure." I step to the side, giving her room to enter. "Come inside."

"Thank you." Officer Santos crosses the threshold, then waits, following me into the living room a minute after and takes a seat on the oversized chair. I take the loveseat. "I hope I'm not interrupting anything, and I appreciate you taking the time to speak with me."

"No problem." Grabbing the afghan from the back of the couch, I lay it over my lap. "I'm sorry, but why are you here again?"

"I have some questions regarding your relationship with a Matteo Cancio."

"You mean my father." My conversation with Samantha comes to the forefront of my mind. Once again, she wasn't lying.

"Yes, your father." Pulling a small recorder from her blazer, she gives me a smile. "Do I have your permission to record this conversation?"

"Yes."

"And you understand that anything you say can be used as evidence in a criminal investigation."

"Yes."

"Great. Let's begin." She crosses her legs and sits a bit forward, keeping her eyes on mine. "Once more, how do you know Matteo Cancio?"

"He's my father."

"But do you know him personally? This is a yes or no question, Miss Conte."

"He's my father."

Her eyes narrow a bit and lips thin. "What was he like as a father."

"Absent."

"And his relationship with your mother?"

"Is none of your business."

"Miss Conte, for this to work I need you to answer—"

"Why are you really here?" For a split second there's a bit of worry, a hint of fear, but she schools her expression quickly. This is all beginning to smell fishy. "What are you looking for?"

"I'm sorry..." she gives me what she thinks is a sincere smile "...but that information is pertaining to a criminal investigation and I can't divulge."

"Then I see no reason for you to be in my home, and this is where I ask you to leave."

"You need to answer my questions."

"No. I don't." At my response, she clenches the hand in her lap; her entire posture stiffens. "Leave."

"I can charge you with—"

"Nothing, Officer Santos. I have broken no laws, and at the moment, I feel as though you're harassing me. Leave my home and stay away, or I will place a formal complaint with your department regarding this visit and your treatment."

"Are you threatening me?"

"That's a promise." Standing from my chair, I calmly walk over to the front door and pull it wide open. She follows a minute later, an angry expression on her face. "Have a good day."

Officer Santos walks by me and out the door but pauses a few steps from me. She doesn't turn around. "Be very careful with the company you keep, Aurora. You're walking a fine line between loyalty and stupidity. Don't get caught on the wrong side of this war."

Aurora

I SMOOTH OUT my dress and blow out a breath.

I'm happy. I need to be happy for my cousin who's getting married in a few short hours, and although my heart hurts and I'm inexplicably jealous, I'll put on a brave face and smile for the cameras. I'll say the right things and be giddy, but I can't help but think back on what I never truly got to enjoy.

It's been months since Casper looked at me the same way, since I've seen him.

Sure, the jerk has left me roses and notes, but that's it. Nothing more. No more visits or calls letting me know he's never too far.

Why does he decide to listen to me now and give me the space I asked for?

"Roe-Roe!" London squeals as she wraps her arms around me. The hold is tight and near suffocating, but it does the job of erasing the sudden pang in my chest the thought of him brings. All the darkness is washed away by the happiness London soon-to-be Asher exudes.

"Hey there!" I am blown away by the smile on her face and I find myself matching hers. It's contagious. So honest.

"You ready to meet your date?" London asks with a waggle of her eyebrows, but then she's looking past me, and a hint of blush appears on her cheeks. My money is on Mr. Asher being close by.

I roll my eyes, suddenly regretting that I agreed to this. "Yeah. Fine. Where is he?"

"Right here," a low rumble of a voice says with that British accent that makes my knees go weak and I turn, losing the very breath in my lungs at the sight of him. In a suit. Hair perfectly styled. With that hellish five o'clock shadow that I miss between my thighs.

Christ, woman. Get a hold of yourself.

In the distance, someone calls for London and I hear her say something to me, but I can't make out the words. I'm trapped, lost in the man in front of me. In the sudden burst of desire that ignites at his mere presence. That won't let me go.

Of course Casper and Malcolm would know each other. Two peas in a criminal pod.

"What are you doing here?" I ask, my brow furrowed, inconspicuously trying to take a step back and create space between his body and mine.

He glances over toward Malcolm and London before reaching out and taking my hand. "Come," he says, pulling me away from the rest of the bridal party. Casper doesn't stop until we reach an empty corridor, away from prying eyes and ears.

Once there, I pull my arm from him and cross them over my chest. "What do you want?"

"We need to talk, Gem."

"Why now, Casper? Where have you been?"

"I've been trying to give you space," he says, and it holds a hint of bitterness. As if he hated doing so. "To not overwhelm you, but I miss you, Gem. I'm sorry if you're angry with me—"

"You know where I live."

"Yes, but I've been unable to come. I'm wrapping things up."

"Then call." It's simple. He has ways to do so.

A flash of annoyance crosses his features. "You changed your number."

"I know you could have gotten my new number if you tried."

"If you wanted me to have it, you would have contacted me."

"That didn't stop you last time."

A chuckle leaves him. "No, I suppose you're right." He steps forward then and rests his hands on my hips, fingers digging in. The fire from his touch seeps through my skin and into my muscles, and even though I shouldn't, I relax into him, my hands finding purchase against his chest.

"I was away for too long, but I swear it's for the last time."

"Months," I seethe, even as I draw closer to him. I ignore how he says it's the last time, because I don't want to believe what I know will be nothing more than another broken promise.

"Roe-Roe, where are you?" London calls out and I force myself to step away, my eyes never leaving Casper's.

We return to the group and go through the motions, my heart skipping when I wrap my arm around his and we walk down the aisle together. Each step the need for him grows. Each moment near him weakens my resolve to stay away.

To not let him in.

When the schedule for the next day is gone over and we disperse, the group all in a chatter as we depart to dinner, I fall silently behind with Casper right next to me. When they turn right, I go left, and still, he follows. And when I stop to demand he quit playing with me, Casper spins me around and I fall into his chest. A low growl rumbles beneath my hands, but I barely get a squeak out before his lips crash to mine. Hands grip, digging in, pulling me closer as he kisses deeper. Breath leaves me and I fight to control the kiss, which only makes him fight harder.

"You're mine, Gem. Will always be mine."

"YOU LOOK BEAUTIFUL, cousin. The bracelet from Grandma Isadora looks perfect," I say from behind her, watching with amusement as she adjusts the crown Malcolm demanded she wear again. He was adamant on this; no veil or anything that would cover her face because in his words: *his queen never hides*. But then again, London loves his obsession with her. How much he wants her and shows it without a single ounce of shame.

The place or time doesn't matter.

"Thank you so much for coming, and for this." Lo-Lo lifts her wrist and inspects the delicate tennis bracelet with diamonds and sapphires throughout. It's her something borrowed and blue. "Having a piece of the family to wear today means more than you'll ever know." She turns to face me then and does to me what I find myself doing all the time. It's crazy and wonderful how much we look alike. To take in the familial resemblances after spending so much time alone without knowing the other existed. "It means a lot that you could make it. That you wanted to do this."

"I'm going to flick you if you thank me again, chica. Stop it." My eyes are watery, and my bottom lip trembles a bit.

"Ass," London mutters in the same emotional tone, but before we ruin our makeup, I smack her arm.

"Dork."

"You bruise me, and you'll deal with Malcolm."

In the last few months since we connected, if she says something like this, I laugh and hit her again.

Our relationship is very sibling like.

Like what I've missed out on my whole life.

Which brings forth questions that have been plaguing me for a few days now.

How long have they known each other?

How well does London know him?

Is that why they want to hook me up with him?

"What gives? What's with the look?"

"How well do you know his groomsmen?" I ask, keeping my expression as neutral as possible.

"Which one?"

"British and a complete lying asshole." *Christ*, I suck at this. How could I just blurt that out? *Get a hold of yourself. She'll put two and two together.*

"Casper?" she asks, thrown off by my yo-yoing change in demeanor.

From almost weepy to hormonal in the blink of an eye. *I need help.* "Did he do something to you?"

"Other than exist?" And because I'm certifiable, I nod with an added huff for good measure. *Is this what an out-of-body experience feels like?* My curiosity is going to get me in trouble if I don't shut up. "We don't click."

Lies. All lies.

The way he grabbed and kissed me—full of passion and need—after the rehearsal dinner in an empty corridor re-confirmed this.

I can't escape him. I want him.

"Why? Do I need to involve—"

"No. It's me."

"Do you like—"

"I'm coming in," Malcolm calls out through the door a second before barging in, and I thank Jesus above for this interruption. The groom has the most amazing timing, and as he takes her in, I know I'm going to be asked to leave, something I'm internally doing the Nae Nae over. *Thank you and amen.* "Aurora, we need a moment before the ceremony. Please find Casper and let him know I'll be down soon."

I'm already fluffing my hair before the last word passes through his lips. "Of course. Just behave, kiddos. Leave the fun stuff for after..." I trail off, heading straight for the door because while I adore them both, I'm not trying to see what comes next.

"Oh, God!"

London moans before the door is fully closed and yup. Just say no.

NERVOUS BUTTERFLIES OVERTAKE me as I lift a hand to knock on the door of the men's dressing room. I know he's there. I can feel him near.

Sense that overwhelming electrical current that flows through my limbs each time we're near. It's palpable. Heart thumping.

My thighs clench, and I place my knuckles on the wooden door to hold myself up. I don't knock, not yet, but as if sensing me too, Casper swings the door open.

And then, I'm tumbling right into his arms. Feeling whole again.

"Get in here." His voice is gritty. Holds a tinge of near-demonic desperation that makes me whimper, and I move closer to his body. Chest to chest. His hard cock against my mound.

I can't help myself. I can't stop this.

At that moment, I thank the inventor of the high heel for making me the few inches taller I need to enjoy this. To feel him throb, pulsing against me where I'm longing to have him again.

"Please." That one word from my lips and his pupils dilate, lids becoming heavy as he sees just how much I missed him, too. How my own hunger matches his.

Then my feet are off the ground and my dress rides up, bunching around my hips as he lifts me with one arm beneath my butt. This puts him right there, my wetness to his tuxedo-covered cock, and my legs go around his waist to hold him tight.

So I can gyrate softly.

So I can quell some of this mounting heat burning me from the inside.

Casper lets out a curse and pivots us both, my back slamming against the door. "I've missed you," he whispers low, but to me, it's as if the man shouted it from the rooftops. Our faces come closer and those lips I've missed so much hover over mine. They sweep gently across once and then pull back, tempting with his denial, until I can't take it anymore and I'm the one that caves.

I submit. I can't fight this anymore.

Embedding my fingers in his hair, I yank his mouth to mine and let go. I just let go.

He has me. Always will.

Thank God this room inside the church is empty because we can't control ourselves. The bubble of lust we're trapped within squeezes tighter, so tight that as his hands wander lower, I begin to shake. As he fists the back of my lace thong and pulls, ripping the fabric in pieces, I moan. That the moment two of his fingers swipe over my wetness, I come for him.

It's automatic and wild and I can't breathe.

I can't focus on anything but his harsh breathing against my neck as I throw my head back with eyes closed. Savoring. Letting the relief wash over me while I whisper his name like a sacred mantra.

"Fuck, Gem. Give me more, baby," he rasps, nipping my collarbones while a hand takes hold of my hip, anchoring me to the wooden surface. "I want to walk down that aisle with your scent all over me. Marking me."

"Oh God." Another harsh shiver and I'm panting. I can't think as the world around us fades and the pleasure overtakes my senses. That is until he's right there.

His flesh on mine.

His cock against my entrance.

Just there. Not moving.

When he pulled himself out, I have no clue, but bless him for being coherent when I'm not. In that moment, I'm useless. His to enjoy. His to take.

And I want it that way. Crave it more than I thought could be possible.

Casper slips the head inside and it's like breathing again after being deprived of sustenance for an extended period of time. Another inch and I cry out, fingertips tugging on fistfuls of hair as my body arches, fighting his tight hold on my hips.

"Tell me you want me. That you need *me*," he demands and pulls out. My eyes narrow and my lips part, the expletives sitting on the tip of my tongue, but they die down when he pushes forward, sliding the bulbous tip through my folds and over my clit. "Say the words and I'll fuck you...break you...then when you let go, I'll put those beautiful pieces back together again."

To anyone else those words would be demanding and forceful, but the look in his eyes tells a different story. This man is barely holding on to his sanity. Showing me his weakness; my hold on him.

"From the very beginning, it's always been you. I just want you."

"Christ, I need you. We can't be apart for so long again...I don't function that way." I want to tell him that I feel the same, that I agree, but before I can, he slams in to the hilt in one smooth stroke. His hips are punishing, bouncing me on his cock at a rapid pace, and I can't do anything but hold on and let him.

My hands fall from his hair and my head bangs against the door, the sound loud. "So good. Always so good."

"Shhhh." He nips my chin and the action brings his chest against mine. This changes the angle of his thrust and I clench down hard, moaning out my approval. "Quiet, Gem. Or do you want everyone outside this room to hear how much you love my cock? How much of a filthy little girl you are." He doesn't realize how I love his dirty mouth. How wet hearing him talk makes me. "*Fuck*, baby. You like that, don't you. Like the thought of being caught."

"No," I whimper out, fighting against his hold. Wanting to move but can't.

He places his hand over my neck, gently squeezing. "Explain."

"I don't care what anyone outside this room thinks, Casper. Truly don't give a fuck." His thrusts are languid, savoring, waiting for my explanation —it's worse than when he lets go. Because right now, as he pulls all the way out and pushes in slowly, I can feel every ridge and the metal of his piercing against my walls. "You make me delirious with need. You make me wet. Your dirty words are what throw me over the edge every single time. Just you."

"You're it for me too." His hold on my neck and hip tighten, and my body responds with another rush of wetness, coating him. The groan he releases is a delicious torment before he picks up speed, angling my hips while keeping my shoulders on the door by his hold on my neck.

On the next pump of his hips, I see little white dots dance across my line of sight. He finds that spot, the one that he's claimed as his, and presses against it with each inward stroke. Hard. Precise. Each thrust holds an edge of pleasurable pain that pushes me headfirst into another orgasm.

This one is stronger than the last, and a few tears run down my cheeks. "I can't...*oh God,*" I whimper into his ear as he envelops me in his arms, pulling me against his chest as he lets go with a hissed *fuck* next to my cheek.

We don't move for a few minutes. To be honest, I don't think either of us has any strength left in our bodies, but Casper still manages to not trip and sits with me astride his lap on the leather chair across the room.

Across from a mirror. Where I can see the mess we are.

And as he releases a chuckle, it hits me all at once just what we did and where.

I'm going to hell for this.

This is so wrong.

"Quit overthinking things, Gem. Relax."

My eyes shift back to his warm green eyes and I forget my reproachful words. Instead, I go shy and feel the heat sweep across my cheeks. "Hi."

"Hello, love."

"I was sent here with a message from the groom."

"Which is?"

"He'll be back down after he sexes up my cousin." No sooner has the last word passed through my lips than the sexy Brit beneath me is laughing. Hard and long. Unrestrained. Moreover, a minute later I follow.

We are ridiculous and I love him all the more for it. I can't help myself.

Somewhere along the line without thinking, I gave him my heart and the jerk, unknowingly, won't give it back. *Now I just need to tell him this.*

It's our turn to walk down, and my hand in his trembles. The entire church is looking at us, and I can't help but fear that they know. That even after fixing what he got messy, they are judging.

Hell, I'm judging myself for just how easy I am when it comes to the man.

What is wrong with me? Why do I let him?

"Relax, Gem. I got you." His voice is soft and at once soothes my fragile nerves. He helps me breathe easier as we make it to the front where he drops me off with a kiss to the cheek that makes my face bloom.

Aliana is looking at me, but I ignore her. Instead, I focus on the maid of honor and her man walking up to the front. Mariah and Javier are adorable in that *I will cut you* kind of way. They reach the front and after Javi lets her hand go, she hugs her cousin and pulls back, wiping under her eyes.

They share a look—a silent conversation—before Mariah takes her place next to us, and then the music changes.

Every person in the church stands as London comes into view. She's beautiful. Absolutely breathtaking, and while Malcolm takes her hand in his at the end of the aisle and the priest begins his sermon, my eyes turn to Casper.

He's looking at me with a dirty little smile that makes my own lips quirk up. It's like we're having a private conversation, saying what we can't with words.

I'm sorry.

I need you.

I can't be without you.

The world around us continues, but we're lost in each other's eyes, listening as the vows are shared. The promises our loved ones make hit home for me, and as they say I do, I can't stop myself from mouthing *I love you.*

But what surprises me the most, what takes my breath away and centers me all in one breath, is his *I love you* back.

CASPER

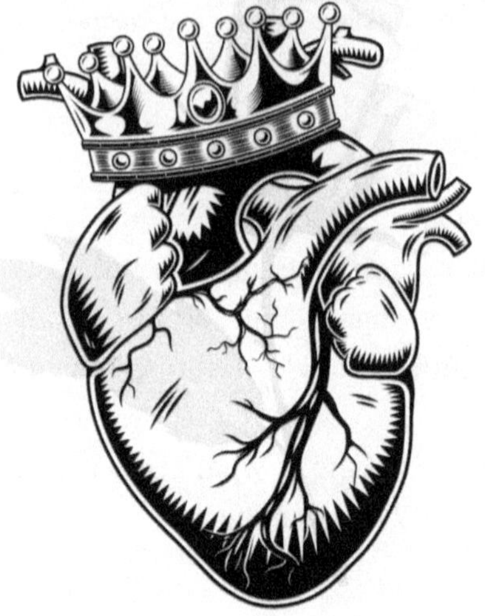

"**C**OME WITH ME,**"** I whisper into her ear, watching as the two lovebirds leave. Everyone's following them out; some wish them well while others keep to the time-honored tradition of throwing rice at the newlyweds.

We're neither of the two. Instead, we pull back and out of sight, slipping away from the group and back inside the hotel. Let them party—we have more important things to discuss.

Like the three little words we said during their wedding.

Gem places her hand in mine and gives my fingers a squeeze, not saying a word as I lead her through the open lobby where anyone could see us and right into the elevator that leads to the penthouse.

Once inside, she stands beside me and watches the numbers go up as we ascend. Little does my girl know what awaits her once inside. What I've had planned since Malcolm told me the reception would be held for the guests inside the Peninsula's largest ballroom.

They wouldn't stay to enjoy it, and as much as I care for the two, I want my girl. Alone. Unfiltered. Open to my plans.

The elevator dings, announcing our arrival, and I let her exit first, guiding her with a hand low on her back toward the room's door. This is the largest suite the hotel offers and has the most privacy. Especially for what I have planned.

I give her the keycard. "Open the door, love."

"Okay." It's shaky and low and *fuck*, she smells amazing. Like cherry blossoms and sex; a little bit of her and me combined to create the most decadent scent. The card goes in and the light blinks green, a lock is disengaged, and when I push it open for her, she gasps, seeing my surprise for her from the very entrance and leading toward the outside terrace. "Casper? What did you...how? When did you have time to do all this?"

There are rose petals along the floor, a sweet blush red that reminds me of her cheeks when I embarrass her with something inappropriate. Something that we both know she loves. Then, there's the soft glow from the lit candles placed strategically along the room to show us the way.

"I've known you were in the wedding party for a while, Gem." Giving her hand a gentle pull, I bring her to my chest. Loving how she wraps her arms around my neck loosely, because even though those sexy heels help her in the height department, she's still so much shorter than me. She always the perfect little doll to my much harsher planes. Soft to my hard. My other half. "For much longer than you think, and I began to plan that very night. I need you to know...show you...that I want this. That I want you."

"I know you do. That part was never in doubt." Her eyes are bright and her smile so fucking sweet. "I'm just selfish and want you here all the time. That's on me. I need to—"

I silence her with a kiss. Taste her the way I wanted to earlier but couldn't because of her makeup. Now, there's no photographer or people to please. No friends or interruptions and I embed my fingers in her hair, tipping her head back to my liking.

And I devour her. Kiss her with every bit of the hunger I live with day in and day out for her.

Always her. Always burning.

"I want to be with you, Aurora. Always." Turning with her lips still on mine, I guide us slowly outside, one foot at a time and between her pleas for more and my wandering hands. I touch her everywhere I can and before she reaches the open balcony doors, I lower the zipper at the back of her dress, letting the silky black fabric fall to the floor at her feet.

It pools there, and just like at the church, I place my hand beneath her arse and lift her up. One cheek in my hand, I squeeze the flesh and step over the threshold where the cool night air meets her overheated skin.

It's the perfect time of year here. Not too hot. Not too cold.

And yet, my girl shivers in my hold. Goose bumps arise on her skin and it's a motherfucking heady notion to know it's solely because of me.

"Is this going to become a regular occurrence? I can walk, you know." She's a cheeky little thing and it also earns her a quick smack to the arse, one that I soothe with the tip of my fingertips. Caressing. Massaging the sting away.

"And if it is?" With her in my hold, I take us straight toward the private jacuzzi in the far corner of the terrace and the table beside it. There, I have an assortment of fruit, cheeses, melted chocolate, and a chilled bottle of champagne, a delicious spread that I'm going to enjoy either feeding her or licking from her skin. "Do you have a problem with that?"

Placing her on her feet, I peck those bee-stung lips and then turn, picking up the bottle and pouring us each a glass. I'm also trying to calm myself, to not attack like I want to. Because dear God, this woman is a sinful delight wrapped in a pretty little bow just for me.

When did she have time to change her lingerie?

The color of her underwear—the indecent scrap of satin covering her pussy and tits—almost matches her skin tone. A light tan shade with a hint of rose. It's soft and molds over her curves, showing me every little secret she hides, like the wet spot over her mound. The proof of her desire for me.

"You like?" she asks, but I don't need to turn around to know what she's talking about.

"How did you—"

"A truth or a lie?"

"Always the truth," I grind out, bringing a hand to my cock and squeezing.

"I carried an extra set in my small clutch just in case. I knew you'd be there today and…"

Fuck, this girl. "So, you came prepared."

"Yes." Aurora's tone is a bit breathy, holds a sultry edge that brings a shiver down my spine. "And to answer your earlier question…No. No, I don't."

"Good answer." I turn then, because I just can't hold back, and groan at the sight that greets me. That barely there silk is no longer on her skin. It's on the floor, tossed without care, while the moonlight illuminates her soft skin. Aurora looks ethereal. Like a goddess.

Like my favorite kind of sin.

"You're wearing entirely too many clothes, Casper. Aren't you hot, baby?" she asks coyly, batting her lashes while twirling a long curl around her finger. The few pins that held one side back so that it all cascaded over the opposite shoulder are gone, and the loose strands now flow around her bare shoulders with the soft breeze.

"Can I have that?" Aurora asks coyly, batting her lashes.

"I'll give you anything you want." I hand over the flute, watching in silence as she brings it to her lips and takes a sip. She moans at the taste, and my cock throbs, pushing against the confines of my trousers. "I meant the words, Aurora…I do love you."

"I love you, too." She takes another sip and hands it back to me. "Hold that for me."

"Okay." And then Gem does the sexiest motherfucking thing in the world; she begins to undress me. I'd long taken off my jacket and bowtie—left them with Callum who was busy talking to Aliana downstairs—so she untucks my shirt and begins with the very last button.

One by one, and at a torturous pace. Slowly. Her nimble fingers undo each one and then push the material off my shoulders, exposing my torso to her lips. Lips that begin to kiss every inch of exposed skin.

She licks and nips. Traces the contour of my six-pack and then lower to the waist of my trousers. There, she dips her tongue beneath the edge, encountering the head of my throbbing cock.

Another lick and she hums in the back of her throat. "No underwear?"

"Don't like them." My voice is gruff, rough as I try to keep still and see where my naughty nymph is taking this. "Never have."

"Sexy." She whimpers a second before dropping to her knees. Naked, beautiful, and trusting. Nimble fingers undo the button and then lower the zipper, giving the bulbous tip another lick before pushing the material down to the floor. "Even your cock is perfect."

"The only perfection here is you, Gem. My perfection."

"I love you." Then her breath is on the head of my cock, fingers surrounding my girth in a tight grip. She pumps me once, twice, and on the third swipes her tongue over the slit at the top. "And you're delicious."

I grip her chin and force her eyes to mine. "Open, baby. Take me in your mouth."

"No." Shaking her head, she removes my fingers from her face and then comes back to my cock. Her lips are against my skin, breath kissing the tip. "I'm going to enjoy you at my pace." Gem runs her tongue over the head, swirling before going lower where she lays a tiny kiss over my piercing. "Slowly."

"Be nice, baby girl," I warn, body coiling tight as my need to take control begins to claw at me. "Just remember that I'll return the favor tenfold. I'll make you cry with desperation."

"When I'm done, do your worst," is all she says a second before taking me in her mouth, sucking me in deep and then pulling back slowly. She does this three times, hollowing her cheeks each time and then adding pressure with her tongue on the underside.

All the while her gorgeous hazel eyes are on mine, watching my reaction each time she takes me a little deeper, opens a little wider—how good she looks with her lips all shiny from my pre-come.

This woman is my demise and rebirth. My everything.

She feels so good, and yet I need more. To dominate her.

"Son of a bitch," I grunt, bringing a hand to the back of her head and pumping in and out a few times. Her fingernails are digging into my arse while a hum reverberates through my shaft. "Open wider, Gem. Let me fuck that pretty little mouth."

"*Oh God.*" It's a moan and it causes a lick of heat to rush down my spine and settle on my heavy balls. "I want to taste you."

Wrapping a fistful of hair in my hand I pull, forcing her to arch prettily for me. Her breasts are perky and nipples hard. Her inner thighs shine with her wetness.

Her lips are open and as I slide to the back of her throat, I moan. M*otherfuck.*

Warm. Wet. Fuck.

Gem whimpers around my length, the sound traveling through every nerve ending while she relaxes her throat and I slide in a little deeper. Slowly. She lets me fuck her mouth with measured strokes until her lips kiss the base and my eyes roll back.

"So close," I hiss, throwing my head back when she cups my balls. Squeezing them. "Where do you want my come, beautiful? Your tongue or tits?"

She doesn't hesitate to answer when I pull back, leaving just the tip over her lips. Lips she licks while those heavy-lidded eyes watch me. "Come in my mouth."

"Good girl. Now open wide and show me your tongue." Doing as I say, she waits with a hungry expression. Showing me that she wants this. Me.

I slide back inside and this time I'm not gentle. I use her, pumping my hips as my hand on her head pushes her forward, meeting my thrust. Her mouth is warm and her tongue eager, swirling around my length as she pulls me in deeper.

Then those lips close around my girth and her cheeks hollow.

Her teeth scrape over the piercing with the right amount of pressure to cause my eyes to roll back.

But nothing...not a motherfucking thing compares to the lust in her eyes and the word *come* slipping from her lips.

One word. Four letters.

And I give in to her command.

"Swallow," I manage to grit out, hand tightening in her hair as the first rope of come coats her tongue. The second and third do the same, but on the fourth, I pull out and dribble down her chin and onto her chest. "*Christ,* Gem. Hot little mouth."

Aurora pulls back, a sassy smile on her lips as she licks them. "Yummy."

My knees are weak and body thrumming with the aftershocks of pleasure, but I still manage to scoop her up off that floor and bring her to my chest. "You're amazing."

After what we've shared, you'd think she wouldn't get shy, but Aurora does, and her cheeks pink up. "I've been wanting to do that for some time."

"Have you, now?" I chuckle, lips at her temple. "Because I will volunteer my cock every day for the rest of my life."

"Perv."

"Absolutely." Taking us to the jacuzzi, I sit her on the edge, remove the rest of my clothes, and then get in. The water is hot, and the night air is a tiny bit cool—feels amazing—but it becomes pure perfection when I pull her to sit between my thighs. "Now, how about we talk for a bit. I have something I want to run by you."

"Good or bad news?"

"It's the best decision I've ever made."

Aurora

"YOU WOULD DO that for me?" I ask from my seat across from him in the jacuzzi a few hours later. Because a blow job led to his face between my thighs and then my body being bent over the large tub's ledge. We can't be trusted. Can't help but attack. It's the only way we can talk and be close without going at it like sex-starved animals. "Just like that? You want to step down as the head of the Jameson family, buy a house here or in Boston, and help me run my father's organization?"

"There's more to it than that, love, but in a nutshell, yeah. Pretty accurate summary."

"Why?"

"Why?" Casper smiles at me and shrugs. "Why not."

"You need to give me more than that, Jameson. Why would you do this for—"

"Because I love you. Because I want to build a life with you. Because running a criminal organization is not your dream, not where your heart lies, but it is what I know. We could do it together—grow it together—have it all, and you'd still be able to do what you love. It's a lot of work, a huge learning curve for you, and I'll help. Money isn't an issue nor is where we live. All that matters is that I come home to you and you greet me with a kiss."

"I like that," I say, but then scrunch up my nose. "I'm also scared of agreeing. He wants to hand it over in a year…I don't have a clue what I'll need to do or how I go about handing it over to you."

"I said together. We have time to figure it out."

"Thank you."

Because what he just laid out is everything I want and more than I can hope for. Especially after making up my mind regarding my father's proposal.

I'll step in with the condition he leaves Lucas alone. He's a child and I want him to enjoy that the way I never did. To just be happy and for Matteo to be there when he needs him.

To show up at baseball games and practice because from my understanding, the kid is very good.

To show up for school functions.

To show up just because he wants to see his kid and decides to kidnap him for the afternoon to go and goof off.

I want that for my brother. I honest to God do, and with Casper offering me the world at my feet, I can do this. I'll have him to lean on. To take over because that would be the best scenario for me.

"I know what I am offering, Gem. I also know that more than anything, you need me here."

"But what about your family?" I'm grasping at straws because what sounds too good to be true usually is. "Your responsibilities?" How the hell can he just pack up and go when my father married out of duty. The man always acts as if he had a gun to his head when he agreed to that sham of a marriage. "Don't they need you to—"

Casper crosses the tub, silencing me with a finger over my lips. "Breathe, sweet girl. Breathe."

"I'm fine. It's just that I don't understand how you can make a change so grand when my own father abandoned us over duty."

"That's a simple answer." He leans toward me, kneeling by my feet and with his face inches from mine. If I shift just the slightest bit forward, our lips will touch once more. "Focus, Aurora. I'll fuck you after if you behave."

My eyes narrow. "I can always head inside and take care of myself."

"But you won't. You want me to touch you...make you come." He accentuates his point while running his strong hands up my thighs, kneading the pliant flesh until he has my hips once more in his hands. Then, I'm straddling him in the water, my core over his throbbing cock.

"You're cheating." I pout.

"And I need you to pay attention to what I'm going to say." The seriousness in his tone grounds me and I stop, no more teasing or messing around. Instead, I scoot back an inch and closer to his knee, creating some distance.

"Go on."

"Thank you." Casper takes one of my hands in his and brings it to his chest, right over his heart where it pumps fast beneath my palm. "A man in love can do some crazy and stupid things. Sometimes it's a combination of both. Your father does care, Aurora, but circumstances put him in a position where he didn't have a choice. I'm telling you this because when the time comes, I need you to listen to what he has to say. Really listen and try not to judge too harshly when there was more than one player involved."

"What do you know that I don't?"

"That it's time for you two to talk without anger or guilt. For him to tell you the truth."

"You're scaring me."

"There's no need to be scared. I swear that it'll bring you peace and help you heal...and while I want to tell you, that's a conversation best had between the two of you. Trust me."

"I do." My heart knows that this man won't let me down or put me in a position to be hurt. That I *can* trust him if nothing else. "Should I just pop up for a visit or call first?"

"How about we call his secretary after we talk to someone else."

"Who?"

"It's time you meet your new family, Gem."

He had it all set up.

Sneaky, sneaky man.

After getting out of the tub, I rushed inside and straight for the shower without contemplating one very important factor...

I have no clothes here.

Nothing but the dress I wore for the wedding and that's the last thing I wanted to wear when meeting the important people in his life. Which is how he found me forty minutes later inside the bathroom near panic and trying to get ahold of Aliana to come and drop something off.

Problem is, she isn't answering her phone. Two rings and it goes straight to voicemail with that generic recording that most of the population uses for their inbox.

"Pick up, chica. For the love of all things holy...pick up," I hiss into my cell, cursing my luck for getting stuck like this without a backup. Being that the wedding was local, and I was taking an Uber home with Ali, we left our Athleta wear in the dressing room at the church. The priest's secretary told us to do as much and to just come pick it up the following day. Today. "Dammit. Where are you?"

"Everything okay?"

"Jesus!" I grab my chest, holding the towel covering me tightly. "You scared me."

"And you look like you're having a heart attack. What's going on?"

"I don't have anything to wear."

"That's all?"

"What do you mean *that's all*? I'm not meeting your family in the nude."

"Fuck and no. No one sees you but me."

"Possessive much?"

"And?" The man has no shame, even shrugs at me as if to say *so what*. "But to help you with the first part, I already had something brought up. Just come and grab it when you're ready. My cousin already called and should be here in twenty minutes or so."

"You know what? I'm not even going to question a thing." I drop my towel, turn him around, and push the man out the door. "Just lead the way and I'll get dressed."

"You're naked and that's not fair."

"Neither is my freak-out." Reaching down, I pinch his butt hard.

He yelps and swats my hand away. "That hurt."

"Don't be a baby."

"I'm going to fuck that sassiness right out—"

There's a knock at the door followed by a very loud *Oi* that blocks him from any form of retaliation. Serves him right, and I pinch him one last time after grabbing the bag on the bed and running back to the safety of the bathroom.

<hr>

WE'RE SITTING in the penthouse overlooking the Chicago skyline and silence hangs in the air. Casper just told them his plans. His desire to move to the States and help me run the soon to be renamed Cancio empire. It's the one thing I will go to war over.

What's fair is fair, and it won't just be my father anymore. It'll be a mixture of the two; the Jameson name will be just as attached and none more important than the other.

We will be one.

He didn't make some long-winded speech or gave them multiple reasons why either.

Not at all. Casper is a straight-to-the-point, take-him-or-leave-him kind of man, and I appreciate that if no one else does.

Callum is across from us, his face impassive and eyes on me. "And how do you feel about this, Miss Conte? How do you feel about my cousin coming to live in the States? Why won't *you* move to England?"

"Watch it, Callum. Don't get ballsy on me—you more than anyone should know I won't hesitate to shoot."

"Let her answer."

"She doesn't need to."

"I'm right fucking here," I hiss out, standing from my seat beside Casper and moving to the center of the room. "Callum, watch the condescending tone. All right?" Then I shift my eyes to the man I love. "Casper, I'm not a child nor do I need to be spoken for...let me say my piece."

Both men sit back and look at me while I turn my attention to Jameson Sr. He's an older version of his son with a sweet face, but I see the pain that lingers in his eyes. The sadness.

"I'm going to take this moment to extend my condolences to you, Mr. Jameson. What happened to your wife is horrible, and I'm truly sad that I will never get the chance to meet Casper's mother and tell her that I love her son." From his side of the video screen, he swallows hard and nods. The first hint of a smile appears on his lips since the video call began. "Now, as for Callum's question, which was rude by the way, my answer is simple...I cannot leave the Conte House. That place is all I have left of my own mother—her legacy—and I will continue it. As for Casper moving here? When he told me, I was shocked, happy, confused, and so on. I still don't fully understand how he could leave your family to come and help me take over the reins here, but I appreciate it more than you could ever understand. I also hope that this will be the start of a strong alliance between the two families and we can work as one to grow as an empire. Because make no mistake, I might not want to be involved in the day to day, but I will have a seat at the table. I will be made aware of important decisions and my vote will count...will be higher than anyone's outside of Casper. Is that clear enough, or do I need to say a little more?"

"No. That's enough." Callum stands from his seat and walks over to me, extending his hand. "Please accept my apologies if I offended you. I love that bloke and just want him happy."

"Accepted and forgotten."

"Well, I guess there's only one thing left to say after that." His father gives me a nod full of respect and then claps his hand once. All the men stand at that and look at me. All wearing the same shit-eating grin on their faces. "Welcome to the family, Aurora."

CASPER

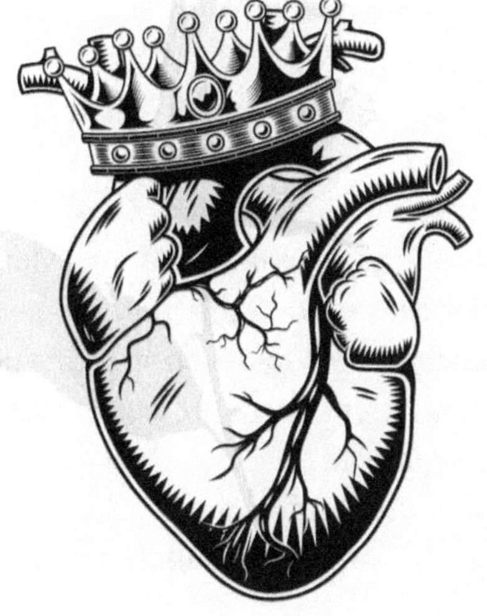

IT'S LATE IN THE evening when the arsehole leaves and I'm alone with my Gem once more. Callum has plans he's not divulging, and to be honest, I'm not worrying over it. When he's ready, he'll come find me.

Until then, I'm going to enjoy the next few days with Aurora before leaving for London. Because while Callum accepted the position to take over, I still have a few things to deal with, the main being our contracts and having a meeting with certain suppliers.

This merging of families will work for all involved and could be very profitable. Matteo has a lot of businesses, legal ones like the real estate firm where his head office is located.

The man is good with the housing market, but more importantly, moves a lot of money each month through it: bonuses, client gifts, and the cocaine he peddles through those same avenues.

I've done my research, and the arse is smart.

While he does buy, flip, and sell a lot or properties—he also has a high turn-around for failed negotiations. While to most that would be a red flag to never work with him, it's the opposite, really; those checks that go through his bank account with large sums and fall through are how he moves his product.

Those home showings are nothing more than a pickup and delivery.

And the businessman in me likes that. A lot.

Easy and once learned could be implemented across the globe through different partnerships, Miami and Vegas being the main two that come to mind outside of the Boston/London union. One is a large-quantity buyer and the other transports across state lines and into Mexico for me.

And while her father isn't retiring this very moment, it's never too soon to start putting your ducks in a row when it comes to a change in power like that. There are things Gem needs to learn. That she can only understand from a hands-on approach.

"You're thinking awfully loud in there," Aurora says, giggling as she taps the top of my head with her small fist. "Are you having second thoughts?"

"No. Not at all." Turning my head, I meet her eyes beside me on the bed. She's fresh out of the shower and as naked as I am, scent sweet and feeling like the softest silk beneath my hand. I can't stop myself from reaching out and caressing her arm and lower to her hip where her hand lies. "Just planning. Figuring out in my head how to make this merger happen quickly and without incident, because there's always some wanker that has a problem with change."

"You think we'll have some resistance?"

"Possibly, but I'll be bringing half of my men back here with me. Including the one that works for you."

Her brows do that adorable pucker in the middle that makes her look grumpy. "What are you talking about? I don't have anyone—"

"I put a bodyguard on you the very day you tried to sneak out of my house after the night we met." Gem looks at me like she's not understanding, and I lean over to kiss her cheek. "Sweetheart, just because I haven't been around doesn't mean I left you alone. You've always had someone there ready to intervene if necessary and he quite likes you, so it works out."

"He likes me. You've been watching out for me?"

I nod, happy that she's not screaming at me. "His name is Alexander, and he's the older gentleman that drove you to the hotel where you later met with your father."

"So then you know about Dominic and the weird detective who came to my—"

"I do. Does that bother you?" Turning onto my side, I bring her thigh over my hip and pull her close. Her naked flesh is against mine, though this time it's in a comforting gesture. This is something she needs to know and accept, more so as she steps into her new role. Aurora might not want to be the head of the soon-to-be-renamed Cancio family, but her role will bring just as much attention.

People who've always wondered about her affiliations with the mob will now have concrete proof and will come forward, looking for a hand-out. It might be money or a connection for something they want...but the rubbish always comes to the surface when it can bring them a gain.

"It should, but it doesn't," she says, her nails tracing the pattern of my chest tattoo. "And I was going to tell you about them. Especially Dominic's behavior. The guy is an asshole, but I'm not afraid of him. He's just another pompous jerk."

"He's a dead man walking."

"You could just fire him?"

"Or I could shoot him."

"We'll revisit him later." Her pointed look only makes my cock twitch and she notices, rolling her eyes. "What about the woman?"

"My hacker tapped into the BPD mainframe and pulled her file. She *is* a detective and has two years of experience under her belt. However, her quest for fame is your father's case."

"Samantha told me about it, but I didn't want to believe her."

"Samantha?"

"His ex-wife. She came to see me while I was in Boston." Gem is pensive and I don't interrupt her. Anything she remembers could help us get to the bottom of this bloody mess sooner. "It just doesn't make any sense to me that out of everyone, I'm the one she tries to interview. What about Samantha or Lucas? Associates and that one senile brother he has that is around from time to time?"

"Uncle? Matteo has a brother?"

"Half-brother, and the guy is weird. Has been put on a seventy-two-hour hold more than once."

"This didn't show up in the police file Ezra has been working on for days. None of those people you just named do." Tapping her thigh, I wait until she moves and I grab my phone, sending a quick email to Ezra with the new information. Something isn't right. More so when the only name that repeatedly shows up is hers.

That, and we are missing the identity of their informant. I have a feeling this is an inside job.

"WHAT DO you mean it was seized?" I hiss into the phone, pacing the length of the penthouse terrace. I'm furious. Wanting to break something, but Gem is inside sleeping, and I don't want her to worry. "When did this happen?"

"A few hours ago." Thiago's voice is gruff, thick with sleep. It's barely seven in the morning there and he's been at the Port of Miami since six thirty. "Don't worry. We got the motherfucker responsible and he's being taken to his room as we speak."

Running an agitated hand down my face, I close my eyes for a moment and think. Analyze the situation.

Transporting through state lines isn't my usual mode of delivery, unless it's a pickup from Mexico to the US and I have a courier for that, but this is different. The product is already sold, and Thiago's buyer is waiting.

This client has already paid him half of its street value and needs it for a week-long party he's throwing in the Bahamas. CEOs of Fortune 500 companies imbibe more than your average citizen and harder. They want to get high, have sex, then repeat the cycle all over again and for extended periods of time.

Hell, look at the little blue pill industry. Who buys that?

Old men with money and in copious quantities so they can fuck their newest wife like the pool boy can.

"I'll be there soon," I say after a minute, feeling her near but I don't turn around. Not until I get hold of my anger. "Please send a car to take me straight there."

"Not a problem, Jameson." The sirens of a cop car become louder on his end, and then it shuts off. "How's it looking, Officer Alejos?"

"It's hot, Thiago. You shouldn't be anywhere near here, especially if you just got out."

"And I'll stay out. Luna will kill me if I go back."

"She talking to you yet?"

"Since when have you known your niece to be anything but hardheaded." The man laughs at Thiago's statement, but quiets just as fast when his radio goes off. There are a few codes that come through, a woman letting him know there's a robbery in progress and units are needed.

"I'm out, Rivera, but I'll let you know. The initial report should be ready by tonight and it'll show what they know. You'll have the upper hand, but the window is small. Act fast." The siren blares a few seconds later and then quiets as he drives away.

"You heard him?" he asks as my girl wraps her arms around my midsection. "We need to move fast while they'll be preoccupied. Question is; how are we replacing? How long will it take?"

"Buy me a few days." My fingers entwine with hers, holding them tight against my midsection. "There's enough in Chicago thanks to a gift from Asher and it's here in a warehouse. I'll have it driven down."

"Perfect. Shoot me a message with your flight info."

"Will do." I hang up and turn around to look down at Aurora. "Did you hear?"

"I did."

"I'm sorry."

"Not your fault." Rising onto the tip of her toes, she bites my chin. "Now, let's go back inside and book your flight so I can take you back to bed before you leave. I'm thinking you owe me that wicked tongue between my thighs as an apology."

"Done," I growl, throwing her over my shoulder and heading back inside. She wants me again and I'll give her my mouth, fingers, and cock.

It's time for my breakfast.

"RISE AND SHINE, ARSEHOLE," I say, kicking the man responsible for all of this. He stirs, grunting a little as he comes to, but I don't have time for slow awareness.

My next blow comes from a closed fist straight to his jaw, causing a piece of tooth to fly out.

We're in the Rivera home in Miami. They own an entire street, no neighbors, and have a small building where they hold detainees for transport to Cuba. It's away from the main house, their adorable mum, and completely soundproof. I'm really loving the space.

It gives me ideas for my future home with Gem.

The punch to the face catches his attention and he comes to, searching for the culprit. Those muddy brown eyes land on me and widen, and as blood rushes down his lip and chin, he looks to his left and finds Thiago. "What's going on?" he asks, fear radiating from his every pore, more so when he takes in Ivan to the right and Callum behind him.

Surrounded on all sides and tied to a kitchen stool, he's bare chested and hunching over a bit, hands and feet bound by rope through the wooden legs.

If he moves wrong, he'll tip over.

If he pisses me off to quickly, I'll slit his throat.

Sitting forward in my chair, I get in his face. "How have you been, Mr. Arroyo?"

"Why am I here?" His eyes keep shifting between myself and the raging lion beside him. Thiago's looking at him through narrowed eyes and a snarling lip—it curls over his teeth at the corner while he chews on a toothpick. "Mr. Rivera, what's going on? I—"

He's cut off by another strike. This time it comes from Ivan and the four-inch blade in his hand. A quick jab and it's embedded deep into his right side, causing him to choke on a scream.

Pulling the blade out, he cleans it on the man's bare skin. "Answer Mr. Jameson when he asks you a direct question."

"Mr. J-Jameson." His voice breaks while his limbs begin to shake. *Good, he knows who I am.* "This is a mistake."

"People who usually say that without any prompting or accusations being presented are usually guilty." My eyes shift to Callum who quickly does as Ivan did, stabbing him in the back area, near the kidneys. "Now, let's try this again, shall we?"

"Yes," he cries out, body wanting to bow in on itself, but the bindings don't let him. Instead, every move he makes creates a shooting pain that races through his limbs. Causes more rivulets of red to stain the floor below.

"Good boy." And I pet his head like I do my dogs back in London. *I need to buy a house in both Chicago and Boston...bring my boys with me.* "How are you today?"

"Scared. In pain."

"Honest. I like that. Don't you, Thiago?" The man just grunts in affirmation, eyes hard on the cunt responsible. "We'll take that as a yes."

"Now, do you know why you're here?"

"No...*fuck*...okay!" Thiago chose his spot with precision, stabbing him in the thigh and with the blade inside to the handle, he twists his wrist, tearing through the muscle in the most painful way. This isn't a straight cut; it's jagged and rough. "Please, I'll tell you what you need to know."

"So speak. Tell me why you snitched to the feds, got our shipment seized, and then cost us a lot of money?" I tick each one with the tip of my karambit, slicing the very tip of my pointer as I do. "Talk."

"It was to get you out of Chicago."

"The fuck did you just say?" I'm hearing myself talk, but it sounds far away. Fury ignites within my veins, my worry for Aurora overtaking all of my senses. "You have ten bloody seconds to explain yourself."

"The Savino family paid me a lot of money to—" I don't need to hear him finish—I've already slit his throat and I'm rushing out of the room. The other three are following close behind as I leave the building with my mobile in hand.

"Call Malcolm and tell him to take her to his house." Callum moves past me, already dialing while Thiago places a hand on my shoulder to stop me. "Not now."

"What's going on? How can we help?"

"They're going after my girl, brother."

"Then we're *all* going to Chicago, Jameson. Nobody touches family."

Aurora

"S O," I SAY, drawing out the word as I stare at the rearview mirror and the man reflected there.

"So," he replies.

"Interesting to see you again."

"I saw this coming," Alexander says. He's driving me to work. It was a promise I made to Casper before he left for Miami, and the man can be very persuasive. With his mouth between my thighs, he can get me to agree to just about anything and knows it. "Besides, have you not noticed just how determined he is when wanting something?"

"Touché. But in my defense—" I'm interrupted by the ringing of my cell phone. It's a Boston area code, and I pick up. "Hello?"

"Aurora?" It's a woman, and the voice is familiar.

"Yeah. Who's this?"

"Oh! Umm, it's Lisa...your father's secretary."

"Good morning, Lisa." Alexander eyes me from the rear view, brow raised high. I put my hand over the phone's receiver. "My dad's secretary. Not sure what she wants."

He nods, and Lisa on the phone clears her throat a few times. "Miss Conte? Are you there?"

"Sorry. You caught me mid coffee order." It's the first thing that comes to mind and when Alexander snickers, I roll my eyes. "How can I help you?"

"I apologize for the interruption, but your father would like to invite you to lunch today. He's in Chicago, and wants to know if you're free from twelve to two?"

"Why is my father in Chicago?"

"There's some commercial property he's looking into buying near West Hubbard Street and would like to see you."

"Why didn't he call me himself?" Even at his most neglectful, Dad never involved his staff. This is weird. "Better yet, tell him to call me. I'll make the time if he does."

"Please don't get me in trouble." And it's the fear in her voice that makes me pause. The last thing I want to do is take my annoyance out on an innocent bystander.

"Fine. Tell him to meet me for lunch at the Mexican place. He knows which one."

Upon arrival at the Conte House, I dig into my daily tasks. Catching up on email takes up most of my morning, and shortly before noon Alexander taps on my office door, ready to take me to meet my father for lunch.

"Go get yourself some lunch," I tell Alexander, exiting the vehicle in the back parking lot area. I'm but a few feet from the door and my father should already be inside waiting. Not that Matteo bothered to call me. Lisa was the one to confirm the place and time an hour later.

"No," he says without pause.

"I'm safe with my father," I argue.

Alexander's expression is dead serious as he regards me. "No."

"Yes."

"Miss Conte, I have strict orders from Mr. Jameson to not let you out of my sight. Let's not ruin my track record here."

"You weren't there in Boston," I point out, remembering how uncomfortable Dominic made me feel. "Where were you then?"

His gaze holds a hint of something. A secret he feels ready to spill.

"The room next to yours is a storage dump-all where your father shoved whatever his ex-wife didn't take. I was in there, gun up and ready to shoot, but you handled yourself impeccably."

My eyes widen as I stare at him. "Wow." Once again, Casper amazes me. I had no idea Alexander had followed me a thousand miles to keep watch. More than that, he managed to get inside without detection in a home that should be a fortress with how serious my father takes his security. He can be a bit paranoid at times.

"He cares. Has from the very start."

My lips pull up into a smile. "I do too, you know."

"And I think you shouldn't." It comes from behind me, and before I can take in Alexander's expression, fear locks me in place. Everything happens around me in slow motion; one minute we're holding a normal conversation, and the next I'm being pushed out of the way as a gun goes off.

My head hits the hard pavement, bouncing twice, and my vision blurs a bit.

"Run!" It's my guard's voice I hear, and it snaps me out of my momentary shock. More bullets fly. Different directions. So much noise. And as I try to reach for my Glock within my purse, I'm being yanked up by the hair, forcibly shoved and made to face Alexander's kneeling form on the ground.

A strike to my cheek snaps my head to the side. A cry leaves me as pain floods in from the impact, radiating through my face.

But that pain helps me focus; it brings my attention to the woman to my right as she unloads another shot into Alexander's body.

He falls back and the gun slips from his hand.

There's no time to react, to attempt to get away—there's just a pinprick to my arm.

The last thing I remember is saying her name.

"Detective Santos?"

I DON'T KNOW where I am.

I don't know what time it is.

I can't see anything but darkness all around me.

Everything is slowly coming back into focus and my body hurts—my head feels as though it's going to explode.

Shifting to draw my hands to my temples, I realize I'm bound and the continuous movement all around me is that of a car. Or van.

I can't see, and the scratch of cloth across my skin tells me it's because of a blindfold covering my eyes. But more worrisome than anything, what has me near tears, is the hand slowly stroking my hair as if I were a pet.

An unknown caress that sends a chill down my spine while I lie as still as I can.

"I do love a woman who plays hard to get. Breaking them is much more rewarding," a male voice says and it's familiar, has a certain lilt to it that makes me cringe, and that's a huge mistake. He notices, letting out a low chuckle before there's another pinprick on my arm. "Sleep, Miss Conte. We'll be playing a special game soon enough."

"He'll find me," is all I manage to say before it all goes black.

I'M ON A BED. It's comfortable and smells clean, but definitely not one I know. That, and I'm not a fan of the harsh citrusy scent inside the room.

The more awareness looms on the edges of my subconscious, the colder I become, and the thin blanket thrown over my body doesn't help much. I don't move, though, lying completely still in order to pick up noises all around me.

It's quiet, but I don't trust it.

I don't trust anything at the moment.

It's fight or flight, and I need to keep my wits about me if I'm going to escape these lunatics. Especially the man.

There's something familiar about him, a natural disgust, that reminds me of Dominic. Even his voice held a similar tone.

"Open your eyes, Aurora." My eyes snap open and my worst nightmare is confirmed. "Hello, beautiful. Ready to get married?"

CASPER

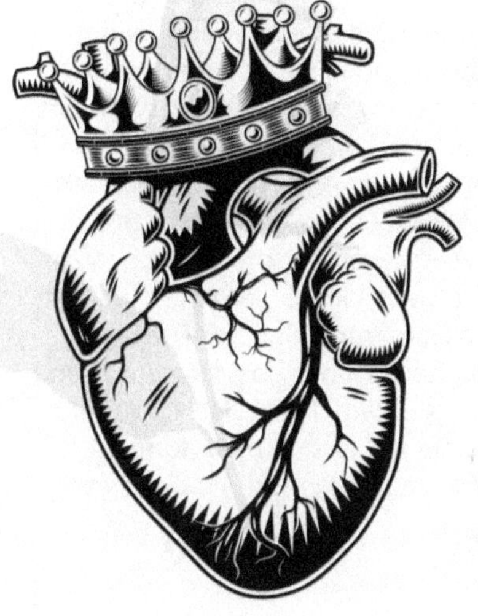

Message received at 12:00 p.m.

Mr. Jameson, I've spotted Cancio's second-in-command lurking around her apartment building. He didn't see me, but the bloke walked up and down the street twice, phone in his ear, and then left. I'm on my way to the Conte House now, and will be calling Alexander shortly. I'll await your call on how to proceed.

Message received @12:30 p.m.

Sir, I need you to call me. Aurora went to meet with her father for lunch and has gone missing. Alexander has been shot, two to the chest and one to the arm. Police are involved, happened outside a Mexican restaurant, and he's being attended at Northwestern... Casper, we don't know where Aurora is.

. . .

Message received @12:40 p.m.

Sir, it's Ezra. I was able to get through the
encryption and found some alarming facts.
Detective Santos is none other than Antonella
Savino. Her alias was given by the department
head in BPD, a family member of Matteo's
deceased mother-in-law, her last name before
marriage was Savino. Giada Savino at that. This
is larger than we suspected, more so because
she and her brother, Dominic, are the older
children of one Samantha Cancio. They were
before their marriage occurred and were raised
by a family friend—away from Matteo, Aurora,
and Lucas. Samantha is also the informant for
this case. I'll be emailing you the proof shortly.

THAT'S WHAT GREETS me as the plane touches down in Chicago. It's been five hours since the son of a bitch in Miami let me know that it was all a setup. Five hours since my world was taken from me, and I want to kill every motherfucker that so much as breathes in my direction.

No one knows where Gem is. They've disappeared.

"We'll find her, Casper." Callum squeezes my shoulder, jumping into an all-black SUV waiting for me. Jeffrey is behind the wheel and he nods in greeting, slowly pulling away from the curb as Thiago and Ivan jump into another vehicle. I don't know who the driver is, nor do I care, but my guess is my employees knew I'd want my space at the moment.

I'm not thinking rationally. The anger is consuming me.

"Head to his flat," Callum tells Jeffrey and the man nods. My place here is not that far from Aurora's, maybe a ten-minute drive at the most, and I need to head there first. "Do I bring Archie here? I'll call and have him on a plane if you think we need him."

"No. Leave him with Dad just in case." Which reminds me. "Has anyone called her father? Where the fuck is he?"

"No," Jeffrey interjects from the front. "And from my understanding, the one that called to set up the lunch meeting was the secretary. Alex was semi-conscious when I got to the restaurant, was just being put on a gurney, and he told me this. Dominic and Antonella have her."

"I want their blood on my hands," I ground out.

"Ezra's doing his thing and says he'll have something soon. He's tracking Aurora's phone signal. It's last ping was near the Missouri border."

"They're heading west." It's not a question.

"Seems so."

"Okay. Okay." I need to get home and prepare. "Get her father on the phone for me. He needs to get his arse here, and the secretary has some explaining to do."

THE SPECIAL REPORT bulletin has been running on the bottom of the television screen over and over for the past few hours. It's the same for every major news network.

And that explains where her father has been.

So far, they have no leads or motives, and his secretary is with the police. She was the last to be with him, just ten minutes prior to him leaving the building, and is being interrogated.

My money is on her being involved somehow.

I look at Callum and tilt my head in the direction of the balcony. He follows me, leaving the other two inside, passing me a cigarette before lighting his own.

"Something isn't right with that," Callum says.

"No. It isn't." Pulling the smoke into my lungs, I hold it for a few seconds and exhale. "Have you heard from Ezra? Has Samantha been found?" Because she's also gone missing, while Lucas is staying at his dad's home. The staff there is watching him—keeping him away from the news—until I know what we're facing.

Funny enough, they called me when the first report released, telling me they were under strict instructions to take direction from me—or Aurora. No questions asked. Period.

"Still gone and—" We're interrupted by the Face Time application on my mobile. I hit accept at once. "What do you have for me?"

Ezra comes onto the screen from his home office, hair a mess and bags under his eyes. "Sir, I have visual from an airport in St. Louis where Antonella caught a cheap flight out, and the destination is Vegas. The name it was booked under matches her work I.D. and Casper; she wasn't alone. Samantha, Cancio's ex-wife, boarded the same flight under the name Giada Savino."

"Both heading to Vegas?"

"Yes. It was a direct flight." There's an alert coming from his screen then, a loud blaring sound, and he looks away from me. Placing the phone down, I watch as his fingers fly over his keyboard and then a wicked grin overtakes his features. "Gotcha."

"What's going on, mate? Did you—"

Ezra cuts me off, his eyes scanning the screen in front of him. "He chartered a small aircraft in St. Louis after going their separate ways and has now been in the air for two hours. Destination is also Las Vegas."

Finally. Direction to my Gem. "You're getting a bonus for all these extra hours."

"Not needed. Just kill the bloody bastards...they deserve every last bit of karma coming their way."

THE BRIGHT LIGHTS of the Las Vegas sign welcome us six hours later. After hanging up with Ezra, we got things done quickly. A change of clothes and out the door—my only pit stop was to her flat, where I grabbed something for Gem to change into.

After the day she's had, my girl will need the comfort.

They're staying at the Venetian. Top floor. ~Ezra

The credit card on hold for the hotel is Aurora's
~Ezra

Typing out a quick "Thanks" I pocket my phone and walk out with the others. I called in a favor before boarding the plane back in Chicago to my colleague in Vegas.

Julio Villanueva is not a trafficker but a runner, and his MC is my go-between for the States and the largest Cartel south of the border. He knows people. Knows the city like the back of his hand and can get me anything I need for my buyers overseas.

Or, like now, he can find a few unmarked cars and the weapons I need.

"Good to see you, Jameson." He pulls me into a one-arm hug. "Wish it was under better circumstances."

"Me too." Walking to the trunk of the first car, I hold my hand in the air waiting for the keys—he tosses, and I catch them, popping the back using the key fob. The compartment is fully loaded. Inside, I have everything I need and a few extras: guns, bulletproof vests, magazines, cans of gasoline, and even a machete or two. "Thank you, mate. This is perfect."

"Do you know where they have her?"

"Why do people come to Vegas?" I ask instead, slamming the trunks closed. "Why is Sin City so bloody popular to tourists?"

"Gambling—"

"And bullshit wedding chapels with twenty-four-hour service." My mobile pings then with an incoming text from Gem's phone and I pull it out, opening my messages to find my suspicions confirmed.

There, with her back against a car door and with tears in her eyes, is my girl. They put a cheap veil on her and a sash that reads *Bride-to-be* over the clothes she was taken in.

But more important than that, Julio beside me cocks his gun. "I know exactly where they are. It's fifteen minutes from here and behind a dingy strip mall away from the main casino area. It's the part of Vegas most don't see. The fucker who owns it will marry her against her will. Suit up. I'll take you."

CASPER

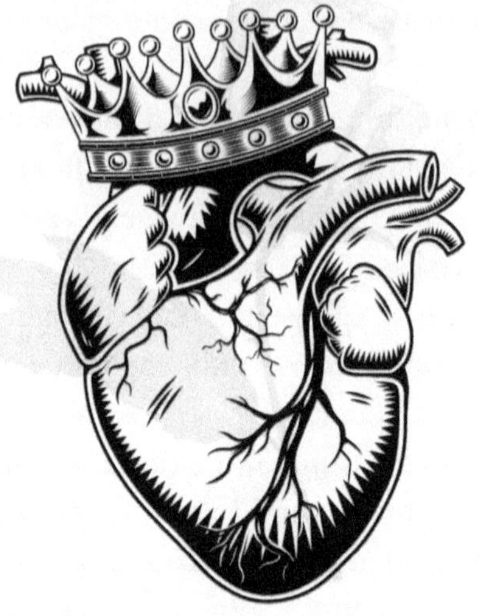

THE PLACE IS just as Julio described.

Filthy.

Bad area.

A low-level criminal's playground.

The chapel with its neon sign half working is isolated at the very end of this street and away from the normal traffic route—no walkways or performers working the passing crowds.

The place is perfect for the illicit, but today it will meet its end.

Outside the small building, we park our cars, closing in on the two already in the attached lot. There's a newer-model Mercedes and a Toyota Prius, both tags from Nevada, and Julio makes quick work of slashing the tires with the two men he brought with him.

They'll be staying outside and acting as guards because one way or another, this little family and the shop's owner won't be making it out alive.

Taking my gun from the back of my trousers, I walk up the small concrete pathway that leads toward two steps and the main entrance. The entrance is locked, and I stepped aside so Callum can shoot the lock using his silencer.

I chose not to use one. I want them to hear me.

A quick *pop pop* and he pushes the double doors open with his foot, leaving them open wide. There's no movement from inside, no running or cursing, and we walk quietly through the small lobby and right into the room where an older gentleman sits at the organ playing the traditional wedding march.

Nobody's standing, but there is a woman—familiar in her role as Aurora's stepmother—all but dragging her down the narrow aisle while a group of ten random strangers watch this all unfold.

"Don't do this, Samantha. Let me go!"

"Shut the fuck up, brat. I should've had you disposed of years ago."

No one steps in.

No one moves a muscle to help a crying woman.

And yet, when I raise my gun and shoot the officiant in the neck, all hell breaks loose.

Now, they run. Like bloody cockroaches, they try and scatter but one by one begin to fall as bullets rain down on the sick bunch. Men and women, I no longer care as I aim and shoot.

The man on the organ.

The fucker sitting near the back drinking a beer from a paper bag.

Dominic's sister who comes toward me with her own gun raised, firing off a bullet that grazes my sides as I reciprocate. "You had to make this difficult. You should've chosen me."

The difference between her and I—I didn't miss. I also don't respond to her asinine bullshit.

Antonella Savino falls to the ground with a chest wound, bleeding out fast but still trying to reach for the gun that fell from her hand a few feet away. She's determined if nothing else, dragging herself, and I follow behind her as she grunts in pain. It only takes a minute or two at best for her fingers to grip the handle, and when she does, I shoot the back of her skull, killing her instantly.

Then, there's a sound I've come to enjoy over the years. Truly savor.

A loud screech that rents the air then, an agonized yell, and I meet the eyes of someone who should've known better. Who should've protected my Gem as if she were her own.

Prim and proper looking, her face is pinched tight—pure agony in her expression—before she takes off running in a ridiculous pair of heels.

"Ivan," I yell, and he looks over. "The mom. Through the door on the left."

"Got it." Then he takes off, and as Thiago and Callum make quick work of everyone else—the entire staff on the clock included—I walk toward a scared Gem and a nearly pissing himself Dominic.

No one has touched them. They left him for me.

"Let her go."

"I'll kill her."

"No, you won't." My eyes meet Aurora's hazel ones and I smile. "Close your eyes and walk toward the sound of my voice, sweetheart." The last body falls to the ground and the men with me turn and point at him. "Trust me, baby. Nothing will happen to you."

"He's got a gun to my back," she whimpers, but I also take in how her shoulders pull back a bit. How she's fighting the natural instinct to crumble in fear.

"He'll die before a single bullet dislodges from his gun."

"I'm right here, you piece of shit."

Ignoring his idiotic cry for attention, I wink at Gem. She smiles back at me; it's a tiny one, but there, and it grows just a little bit more when a crying banshee in the form of her stepmother is dragged in a minute later.

"Nico! Baby!"

"Mom!" Dominic yells out, and it's his last mistake because he pulls the gun away from the only person keeping him alive.

The moment he does, Gem ducks and begins to crawl away as every gun goes off, emptying their rounds into his body. From the barrage he flies back against the wall, pulsating against the shattered mirror behind him.

And when the last bullet leaves my gun, hitting his mouth and ripping a part of his face wide open, his lifeless body falls to the ground riddled with holes. His blood is on the ground and splattered across the walls. His bullshit legacy, the one they were forcibly trying to create, will be nothing but a memory because in the very next moment, I have Gem back in my arms.

She's all that matters. My entire world is back where it belongs, and I never want to be apart again.

"From now on..." my lips skim down her temple and cheek "...where you go, I go, and vice versa."

"Deal." Gem pulls back and tilts her head up, locking those watery eyes with mine, and the world fades away. "I knew you were going to come for me."

"Always, Gem. I'll always be but two steps behind you." Then I'm kissing her. Completely losing myself in her taste in the middle of a corrupt wedding chapel littered with dead bodies. I ignore the hysterical step-mother and her pleas while she's being removed. I ignore someone pouring gasoline throughout the room until we need to leave.

And yet, I'll always remember the very moment I fell in love with her all over again.

Once outside, Aurora walks up to each man and gives them a hug, the last being me—she held me tighter. Longer. And when she pulls back, Gem holds out her hand for the box of matches Julio had given me when we exited the building.

"Let me do the honors," she says, and I couldn't be prouder.

In that moment, I know she'll be okay. That she'll stand beside me through anything the world sends our way.

***

WE LEAVE Vegas without looking back two days after seeing the others off. Thiago and Ivan flew back to Miami that same evening while Callum disappeared last night after dinner.

We don't know where he went or why, but the man had a look of deter-mination that rivaled mine when it comes to Gem.

On the news, the incident was reported as a gang-affiliated crime, a local dispute between the owners of the shady chapel and a meth ring that left a total of fifteen dead. The authorities are asking the community to come forward with any information that can help locate those responsible, but no one will say a word.

Not when they fear becoming the next victim on the five o'clock news.

Not when the bodies were burned to a crisp, and the medical examiner is having to pull dental records to identify each one.

"You are thinking hard again, Mr. Jameson?"

"More like missing you, Mrs. Jameson." I hum and look over, catching her wicked grin a second before she unclips her seatbelt, ignoring the sign. Then, she's up and shaking those hips, exaggerating the four steps it takes to make it across the aisle and into my lap where she burrows her face into the crook of my neck. "Are we a little needy after our nap, love?"

"Always want you close."

"I love you, Gem." Bringing her face up to mine with the tips of two fingers, I stare deeply into her hazel eyes. Let her feel the full weight of my words—almost the exact same ones— before saying I do in our private ceremony inside the Bellagio with no one but Callum in attendance.

"Gem, since the moment I saw your beautiful face across the room from me, I've been yours. Completely and irrevocably owned." Callum snickers beside us and I subtly flip him off, making Aurora giggle. *And because I'm a man with zero patience, I bend down quickly and steal a kiss. She gasps and I wink, squeezing her hands once before continuing. "You make me want to be a better version of myself each day, and I hope that over the next fifty or more years, I can make you proud to be my wife. I promise to always be faithful, honest, and more than anything else...to be your best friend and partner in crime. I love you, beautiful, and I can't wait to spend the rest of my life waking up to your smile every day that the Lord blesses me with life."*

We got married our way.

Privately, and inside the room we stayed in with an officiant that for a few extra grand made the early morning trip to see us. She wore a simple cotton dress I brought with me in a pale lavender color, and I wore a button-down and a pair of trousers, both in black. Our rings are basic and not the ones I'll have her design with me and the family jeweler, however, if I go by the smile on her face each time she sees the solid band, I'd say these aren't going anywhere.

That I'll just have to find a way to incorporate them into the new set.

"I can't wait to start this next chapter of our lives, Casper. To move on from the bad and build a new world together."

"You rocked my world in a way I wasn't prepared for, Mr. Jameson. You were determined, hardheaded..." I couldn't help but laugh at that "...and ready to bulldoze your way through all of my preconceived notions of what a man like you is and not who you are. And I couldn't love you more for that. For not giving up on me when I was lost and afraid. For not walking away when I made things tough." Aurora's voice becomes thick then, her emotions rising to the surface as I fight back my own. These words are the greatest gift she could ever have given me. "You've always had my back, let me lean on you, and now it's my turn to show you that I got you. That I'm where you can rest your head at night because I will protect you just as fiercely. I love you, Casper. Love you with every bit of my heart, and I promise to always be faithful, honest, and stand by your side through the good and bad."

And I believe her. Wholeheartedly.

Because my girl is strong. Her heart is pure.

And while the road to forgetting this entire ordeal won't be easy, she showed her determination by turning this negative into a positive. This, as crazy as it may sound, is where our life together begins.

We still have a mess to deal with back home and with her father, but we'll be okay. She'll get through the trauma, will come out stronger, and I will cheer her on every fucking step of the way because that's what love does to you. You live for your other half and become what they need at any given moment.

As long as we have each other, everything else can go and fuck itself.

EPILOGUE 1
Aurora

FOUR MONTHS LATER...

"**D**AD, THIS CAN wait. She isn't going anywhere," I say, trying to make the stubborn man back down. There's no reason, no value, in seeing Samantha at all. For me, she could rot away for the rest of her life right where she is.

A location that only Casper knows about and is keeping it that way. He's handling her. He's delivering her punishment for what he considers to be an unforgivable crime: touching me.

"No, Roe. It's time that you learned the truth on a few things. You need to hear the real story of how this mess began," he grunts from the back seat. He's still in some pain. The pothole we hit isn't helping, and yet he still wants to do this. "I need you to see...to understand why things happened as they did. To realize that I do love you and always have."

His words stop me, and I look toward the man driving us to her location. His words to me out on that private terrace slam into my consciousness and I nod.

A man in love can do some crazy and stupid things. Sometimes it's a combination of both. Your father does care, Aurora, but circumstances put him in a position where he didn't have a choice. I'm telling you this because when the time comes, I need you to listen to what he has to say. Really listen and try not to judge too harshly when there was more than one player involved.

Casper asked me all those months ago to listen. To really listen and try to understand that life isn't always a cup of sugar sprinkled with rainbows, and I get that now. After Vegas, I see the world differently.

It's one thing to know what people do and another to witness it first-hand. To be made a pawn in someone's sick game.

Turning in my seat, I look at my father in the eye. "Okay. If you need to do this, then we will go, but I need you to understand something before we enter this building...I already know you love me. You showed it by discharging yourself out of a Boston hospital against their wishes and flying to see me in Chicago three days after you woke up. You proved it when you grabbed me and hugged me tight, begging for forgiveness for a crime you didn't commit—"

"I am to blame, kid. This mess began a long time ago, and it's because of love for family that I didn't do what I should have." And that right there is his demon. The cross that he shoulders.

"Dad, I don't care—"

"We're here." Casper's voice cuts through our conversation and we both turn to look out of the car's window. The place is not what I thought it would be. Not at all, but I can see the why behind his actions.

Her home is nothing more than a private facility that takes in those that society won't. Those that, for the right price, will lock you away in a padded room with nothing but a mattress in the corner. Most people don't know that this asylum still exists; it's not open to the public, but for criminals, the rules change.

They bend and don't break.

"Nice," my father says, opening his door and stepping out without help. I glare at that, but the man waves me off and walks toward the entrance where a large man dressed in scrubs awaits.

"Name?"

"Giada Savino and the code is 1982," Casper says, stopping behind me.

He types the information into his tablet and then gives us a smile. "Thank you for your patronage, Mr. Jameson. Please enjoy your visit."

"Cheers." Then, he's guiding me forward without a word. Dad follows; he's looking around the place and chuckling to himself now and then. The place is creepy and nothing holds humor, but I can see how having a woman like *her* here is hilarious.

She went from everything to nothing in the blink of an eye.

At the end of the long hall to the right, there's an elevator and we take that to the fourth floor. The door dings, we step outside, and right across from the only way out is her room. And more than that, she's standing there looking at us through the small window.

I wave and her scowl deepens.

Casper takes a step forward, and she rushes away like the dogs of hell are after her.

He's the first to step through, and I take in the empty room with nothing but a mattress on the floor. *How the mighty have fallen.*

"Take a seat." My husband points at a small dinette set near the opposite wall that I didn't take into account, I've been too busy looking in the general direction of where she is. "That was placed here for your use only."

I take the offered seating while my father doesn't. Instead, he walks slowly over to his ex-wife and when in reach, caresses her cheek. "How are you, Samantha? How's this life treating you, princess?"

"Fuck you," she sneers and tries to slap his hand away, but that's a mistake on her part. Before she can take in her next lungful of air, my father has her throat in his hands and is squeezing, slamming her body hard against the wall behind them.

She turns red right away, her panicked eyes looking to me of all people for help.

"You do not look at her," Matteo snarls; his demeanor is one I've never seen before. Never had to experience. "How fucking dare you...after everything I gave up helping you...to save your life and that of my brother."

"Your brother?" I ask myself, not realizing I said it aloud until Dad turns his head toward me.

"I agreed to marry her because of a bounty placed on both you and your mother's head, by her father. See, being the next in line, I was promised to her without my knowledge by our fathers. They wanted to join the families —our underworld dealings with their pharmaceutical company—and take over the global pandemic that was growing at the time for opioids."

"How? But, I... what about Mom!" I'm not making any sense. This information cuts deep—is almost too much at once.

"She knew. I never hid who I was to her and after an attempt was made—"

"They tried to kill her?" I interrupt, angry at the fact that they tried.

"No." His eyes are sad. "They tried to kill you by injection at a routine doctor's appointment. I caught them, and after taking both of you home, I disposed of every employee at that office."

"Then what happened?" Because I need to know. I want to have this hole inside my chest, the one that missed her father growing up, to be sealed. My heart needs to know that he didn't abandon us. Me.

"I went back to the apartment I shared with your mother and found her bags packed. It hurt, but I understood. You were and will always be our greatest achievement, Roe, and above our love, your life came first. We spoke, planned, and made the right moves to keep you safe. If I gave in to their demands, nothing of this world would touch you."

"I'm sorry."

"Don't be. I'm not an angel and this has been my penance."

"But when you took over, why didn't you just come back? Mom would've—"

"When Lucas was born, I made a promise to God and him that I wouldn't fuck that relationship up, Aurora. I couldn't live with another child hating me."

"I don't hate you."

"Thank you." Then, he's turning to look at the woman who is close to turning blue beneath his hand. He eases up but doesn't move. "Now, for the rest of this story—"

"I have a gift," Casper speaks up from the doorway, and I never even saw him move. "This is my early birthday gift to you, Cancio. Enjoy."

No sooner has he said the words that Callum enters, all but dragging a dirty man behind him. A gasp leaves my throat because I know him. I have seen him from time to time over the years, but there's no denying the resemblance between him and my father.

"Ah, Mario." Dad looks at Casper and gives him a smile. The British bastard has officially become his favorite person. "So good to see you."

The edge in his voice causes the man to jerk back, but Callum isn't having that and shoves him forward where he lands on his knees a few feet from his brother. A move that makes whatever her real name is whimper.

Mario's head snaps up and the moment he sees her, rage builds behind his eyes. "Get your hands off her," he sneers, spittle flying from his mouth. "She's mine and you stole her from me! You took everything from me!"

"Did I?" Releasing her, he lets Samantha fall to the ground and turns toward his brother, taking the remaining steps between them. There is no remorse or pause in his actions, but Dad pulls a gun from the waistband of his pants and forces it into his mouth. "Because I didn't want to become the head of this family, but you were irresponsible and had a drug habit that would've created problems. You slept with her and got her pregnant. You refused to step forward and let them force me into that sham. You put me in the position to lose it all so your life could be spared, and yet, I did take care of *your* responsibilities and lost my world." *Is he saying that Dominic and Antonella were my cousins? That* they *had kids together?*

"But you offered me an arranged marriage to—"

"I didn't know, kid." The remorse in his expression guts me. "These two pieces-of-shit faked the children's death shortly after they turned fourteen. And I believed her. Bought the tears and screams of pain." Dad turns his eyes back to his brother. The iciness in them makes everyone in the room pause. "Your idiocy has cost me a lot over the years, but I forgave because that's what families do, but trying to overthrow me while touching the one thing I told you to never come near...you crossed the line, brother."

"Please don't. Don't take him from me, too."

"When I married you, I told you to never betray me. I took care of your kids with *him*," he sneers, "as best I could, given the situation. I maintained them while Lisa raised them. I warned you that I'd given my arm to bend once, that I signed my name on that dotted line so that both of you wouldn't be killed, to stay away from my daughter. You didn't listen, and this is your penance." Without another thought, my father pulls the trigger, ending his own brother's life.

His body falls and I'm immune to it. After what he confessed, I'm an emotional ball of a different kind. I'm angry for what they did to us—to my family—but more than that, I see a man who gave up everything to protect me. So that I could live a normal life.

That's a sacrifice most people will never have to make.

That's the most unselfish act a parent can do.

And all I can do in that moment, as his ex-wife crawls over to my uncle's dead body and Dad steps back, is rush forward and hug him tight. I understand. What he did for us... "I love you, Dad. I'm sorry it took me this long to say it back."

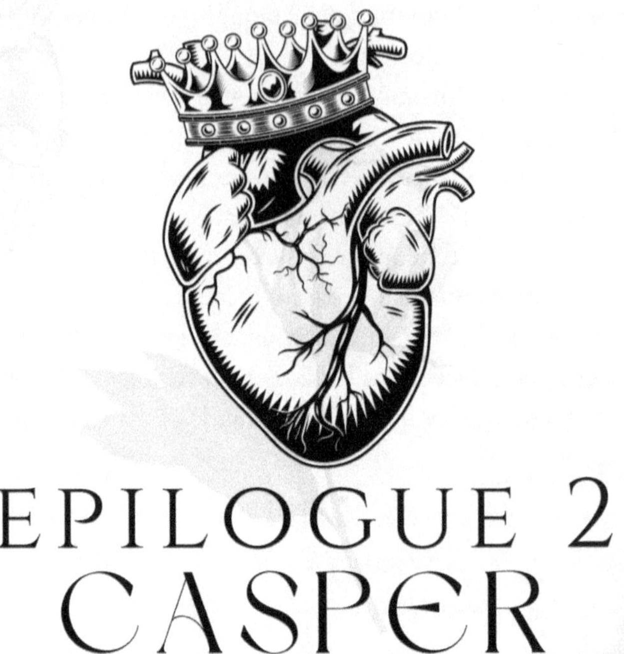

EPILOGUE 2
CASPER

FOUR YEARS LATER...

"YOU TWO WILL have issues with that one," Malcolm says from beside me. We're outside in London's childhood home barbecuing, waiting for Callum to arrive with Aliana, and for the girls to come downstairs. He's taking too long and is making the wife a wee bit antsy. Then, we have one heavily pregnant woman covering for the other who thinks she's slick and is taking multiple tests upstairs.

This family is crazy but keeps me entertained. Everyone thinks they can keep secrets, but we all know the other too well. Have too many resources at our disposal.

Aurora gave birth to our precious Penelope Bianca Jameson a little over a year ago and has already been wanting another one. She wants a huge family and I do too. With everything that happened, the heartache and obstacles, getting pregnant wasn't easy. Cost a year of tears and frustration for her, but when that little stick held those two pink lines, everything became worth it.

However, what I still don't get—what's beyond my comprehension—is how Gem thinks I wouldn't know? That I don't pay attention.

When it comes to her, I don't miss a single detail. Especially, one as blatant as chugging a gallon of water this morning without rhyme or reason.

"Why do you say that?" I ask, watching Maximus, his son, come closer to my Penelope and I smile. That little dictator-like arse is going to come in helpful when boys come knocking. Heck, he'll save me the time of shooting them myself.

Like now, Thiago's son waddles toward a sleeping Penelope in his mother's arms and Max pulls him away, all but dragging the child by the vest toward the sandbox we put up for the kids yesterday.

We're here for the next three weeks to unwind for a bit and celebrate my woman's birthday. That, and let things die down in Boston. Business is business and a dead body near the Boston harbor will bring forth questions.

Questions, that will be thrown our way because of who the bodies belonged to. Samantha and Lisa—who'd gone missing after being released from her interrogation—were both found dead and tied together last night. Both spent the last few years together inside the asylum as neighbors, like the good little cousins they were, and died by suffocation the night before being found by a worker there.

Good riddance. None of us care.

Even Matteo has moved on and likes the retired life down in Boca. He's popular among the women there and while Aurora finds that disgusting, she agrees he needs to move on.

To find someone.

"I'm going to set up a bodyguard business for Max and I'll charge you for him."

"Will he know how to use a gun?" Because Romeo has a little backbone on him already, pushing the other away so he can reclaim his spot near my little girl. *Arsehole.* "That might bring in bigger clients with heftier pockets. He'd be golden for the fathers trying to keep their hands clean."

"Maybe when he's eight." Malcolm nods; I can see the wheels already turning in his head. "London will kill me if it's before...she even made me sign an agreement on this."

"You tried teaching him?" The kid's only four and a mini replica of his father down to the attitude and brow-raising. Fuck, even the way he talks reflects the man. "That would be kind of cool."

"It is." Yeah, the lad isn't waiting, and his wife will have his head for it. "Now, back to your weirdness..."

"Speak up, arse. I don't have all day here."

"You remember my inauguration of the Hong Kong building?"

"I do. Why?"

"You said that Chicago would become your permanent home base?"

"That's because I plan to retire here...eventually." I shrug, watching the stubborn bloke trying to rouse my princess from sleep. He's playing with her toes and I want to punch the lad. "My plans have deviated a bit."

"Is this change happening any time soon?" Malcolm laughs now, but wait until London delivers his next child. A girl. "Need help?"

"When Lucas is ready, I'll be making some changes. Might settle the family here first, for a little while at least, and then move." At that, he nods in understanding. Since his mother went away and father decided to live in Florida, the kid's been with us, going to school during the day and being trained at night. Aurora was against it at first, but she sees and accepts his desire to carry on the family legacy.

And I agree. My sights are on a different city.

Much larger. Grander scale.

"Out East or West."

"East first—"

"Malcolm!" we hear the women yell and take off running.

Malcolm enters the kitchen first, coming to a stop in front of an already waiting London. "What's wrong? What happened?"

"It's time," is all she says, and he's picking her up and heading toward the front door; the man barely has enough of a conscious thought to ask that we watch Max for them. The front door slams shut after my confirmation, tires peel out, and through it all, I'm watching a smiling Gem.

"We'll be there soon, love,' I croon into her ear as I turn and place my hand on her flat stomach. "Just a few months."

"You know?"

"That's a silly question, love."

"A boy this time? To have a pair?"

"I'm happy with whatever the Lord blesses us with."

Her head turns in my direction and those hazel eyes are bright. She's smiling at me so beautifully. "I love you, Casper, and I'm so blessed to have met you."

"And I'm thankful to call you mine." Then, my mouth is on hers. Pouring every bit of the love I have for her into that kiss, because I do. I adore this woman.

She's my heart. My soulmate. The mother of my children.

And I'll never let a single day pass without her knowing this.

She'll always be my greatest treasure. My Gem.

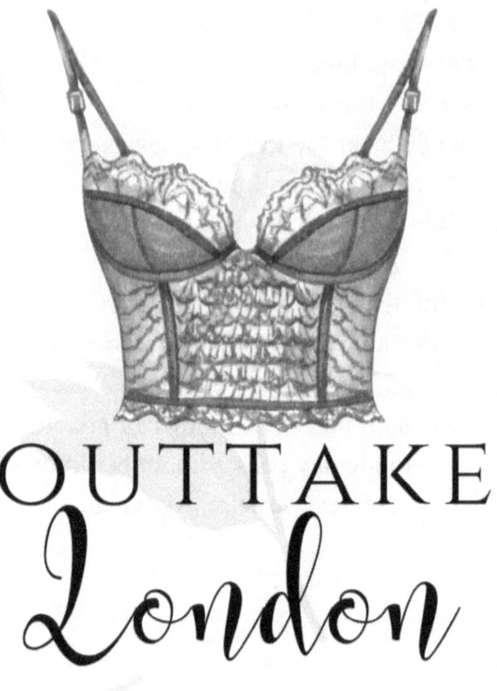

OUTTAKE
London

"**W**HAT THE FUCK?*"* everyone in the room hears Malcolm whisper-shout from his office. It's not in anger, but more of a weirded-out confusion that makes the nosy folk in this family head in his direction.

Of course, I'm the sacrificial lamb since I'm untouchable, with everyone else following close behind. Roe and Mariah are a few steps behind me, almost tiptoeing, and their men cover the rear.

Pun intended. Literally.

"Who the fuck left this in here?"

And while we're all lost, Javier is chuckling to himself. As if he knows what's happening.

"Babe? Are you okay?" I call out, announcing the brigade because the man hates people barging in. Except me. I get a total pass, and more so since he knocked me up. "What's wrong?"

However, before we can enter, the man himself appears in the doorway in all his devilish glory with a set of keys in his hand, clenching them tightly. "Is there something you'd like to explain, Twirl?"

My brows furrow, head shaking at his tone. "Not that I can think of. Why?"

"Are you missing anything? Maybe misplaced something?"

"My Chapstick, but I highly doubt you'd be upset by that." That's the only thing that comes to mind.

"I'll order five cases tonight."

I cringe. "Did I leave it on your desk?"

"No."

"Laundry?" Because that's happened a time or three, ruining a shirt or pair of pants, and all incidents damaged something of his. Not that he cared. I was more upset than he was.

"No." Malcolm shakes his head, less tense now. If I'm reading him right, he's becoming amused. "Think, baby. Are you missing *anything* personal."

"Did I leave out one of our—"

"No. Not that." This pregnancy has done a number on my memory. If it's lost in this house, ten times out of ten it's mine, but even so, I don't understand Malcolm. *What the hell did I do?*

And then the tears come.

I can't help myself.

I'm five months pregnant with the following uncontrollable symptoms: hungry, horny all day, and hormonal. I cry if the breeze is too hard while munching on my newest obsession: pickle chips.

I'm down to my last bag. Need to have more delivered.

"I'm sorry." It's a hiccup as I look up through watery eyes.

"What the hell is wrong with you," Mariah seethes at her cousin, coming to my defense, which makes me sniffle harder. "How can you pick on a pregnant woman?"

"I didn't—"

"Casper, give me your gun." That's Roe-Roe for you. After discovering her long lost love affair with the shooting range, she wants to shoot everything.

"Cool it or get the fuck out," he hisses, and another round of tears hit.

"But the barbecue!" Cause I'm also hungry.

"Oh for the love of..." my husband trails off, picking me up in his arms and walking me toward his display case inside the office. It's a creepy addition he had custom built a few months back.

The large trophy-like case takes up the entire wall to the left of the entrance and holds nothing but guns; old and new ones, some going as far back as the early 1900s which were given by a client as a gift. Then, right at the center of the case, he put his retired Desert Eagle.

The same one I used to shoot Alton.

Placing me back on my feet, Malcolm wipes the few tears that have fallen and kisses my lips. A quick yet passionate peck that makes me forget my name, and once I'm calmer, he turns me to face the glass structure. *Oh my God!*

"Hmmm," that's all I manage to get out, biting my bottom lip to fight back the laughter building. "That's..."

"So you recognize it?"

"Maybe."

"Maybe?"

"Kinda."

"Twirl?" When I don't answer, he turns me around and tips my chin up with two fingers. His lip is twitching and mine aren't any better. "How did an old and worn copy of *Emma* end up in there?"

"Are you mad? Because my answer depends on that."

"And my answer will depend on who did it."

Widening my eyes, I give him my most innocent expression. "Me?"

"Why are you framing this as a question?"

"Just in case your answer was a trick."

"Christ, baby." Then he's laughing, cracking up in a way I've never seen him do before. The serious businessman I know and love is gone, and this one is almost choking on his amusement. "London, sweetheart...you...I love you."

"I love you, too."

"And you owe me some money, Mrs. Asher." Javier says from behind me and I pout, because he was right. Malcolm isn't mad and is laughing, pulling me close to his chest and kissing my temple between chuckles.

"She owes you shit, and I should shoot you for this. This bullshit has your idiocy written all over it."

"I'm insulted." Javier's mock indignation should earn him a slap to the back of the head. He's a horrible actor.

"Try threatening him when you can breathe, babe."

Malcolm looks down at me, still wearing a grin. "Get the book out of my case, Twirl." Then, because the jerk loves to use my neediness against me, he leans down and places a kiss below my ear. "You'll pay for this tonight, baby. Over my knee and you'll count each one; ten spanks in total." I swallow hard and nod, afraid to speak. "Then, I'm going to fuck your ass slowly, agonizingly, because I want you desperate."

"Please," I whisper under my breath, hoping no one notices, but he does. His hum against my skin is the proof.

"You will beg. You will cry."

"Malcolm," I whine, at this point ready to say goodbye to everyone and take him upstairs. "Don't be mean."

"You will say my name, but more importantly...you will soak our sheets and my cock."

Okay. That's it.

"Everybody out."

"Lo-Lo, you okay?" Aurora asks, but the moment my eyes shift to hers, she gets it. I don't have to say a word because she's dragging Casper out of the room. "We'll be back in two hours. Have fun!"

God, I love her.

"I owe you double, now get lost." Javier nods, giving me a quick high-five before pulling a confused Mariah behind him. She's asking him what's going on as the door locks behind them, demanding to know why they had to leave, but I drown it all out the moment Malcolm takes ahold of my hips and grinds his hardness against my ass.

The world fades and it's just us.

"So beautifully needy." Gathering my hair, he moves it over to the opposite shoulder and nips my exposed neck, each bite a little harder than the last. "My perfect girl."

"Yes," I moan, pushing back against him. "All yours."

"To have and to hold." He walks us back to his desk, stopping once my hands find purchase on the edge.

"Always." I'm panting, skin prickling with excitement.

"In sickness and health." Strong hands wander across my chest, squeezing my tits before pinching each nipple through the thin cotton of my shirt.

"We will never part."

"Never."

"Good girl." His hands wander to the front of my maternity jeans and lowers them carefully over my belly, shimmying them down my hips and lower until they pool at the floor. I'm not wearing any underwear and he hisses out a curse in appreciation. "Now, bend over and count each one, Twirl. Let's not keep our guests waiting."

"But you...*fuck*! One!"

"I decide the when, sweet girl. Not you." His lips are at my ear, releasing a rough exhale over my skin. "This is to punish you for taking bets from an idiot." His hand comes down again, three times in rapid succession and he doesn't wait for my count. I can't. Not when he's squeezing the hot skin with one hand and rubbing my clit with the other. I'm wet and swollen and already close to the edge.

But he does that to me. Drives me insane.

Another two swats and my legs shake.

Another to the opposite cheek and my back arches.

I don't think I'll make it through the next three without coming, I'm right there and those tight circles he's rubbing over my bundle of nerves...

"Oh God!" I scream, every muscle in my body locking down as he spanks my pussy with three fingers. That's all it takes. I'm falling over the edge and crying, lost in the sensation as he gathers me in his arms and walks us around the desk to his chair.

We don't talk.

We don't move.

Malcolm lets me close my eyes and rest, giving me exactly what I've been needing for the past two hours.

An orgasm and then a nap.

And it's as I'm drifting off that I hear him, his deep baritone softly in my ear. *"I'm still taking your ass tonight."*

THIAGO
DE LEON

In Miami, I'm royalty.
The beginning and the end.
I'm the truth my queen will never escape.

Thiago Rivera De Leon doesn't believe in second chances, and I never show mercy to those stupid enough to cross me. Loyalty wins you favors but trying to overthrow the city's king will find you with one of my bullets between the eyes.

A simple promise I always keep while abiding by two rules:

I don't forgive. I don't forget.

And after spending the last five years behind bars, I'm out with two goals in mind...

Kill the bastards responsible.
Reclaim my Luna.

GLOSSARY FOR SPANISH & CUBAN SLANG:

Primo/Prima = Cousin

Viejo/Vieja = Old Man/Woman

Mierda = Shit

Bebe = Baby

Cabron = Fucker

Mamajuana =
This Comes From The Dominican Republic And Is Made By Combining
Rum, Red Wine, And Honey And Soaking The Mixture With A Special
Tree Bark & Herbs. The Color Is A Deep Red, And Some Say It Tastes
Similar To A Port.

Pincha = Work

Singao = Fucker or Asshole

Hijo de Puta = Son of a Bitch

Que Vola = What's Up

Acere or Asere = Friend

Dale = Go ahead or Give

Tio/Tia = Uncle or Aunt

Salsa Rueda or Salsa Casino =
This is a style of salsa dancing that originated in Cuba. Here, the couples form a large circle or rueda, and they execute turns, steps, and patterns in unison to the calls of the singer or leader.

THIAGO

T HE SOLE CLOCK on this floor strikes seven a.m. and my eyes snap open, neck cracking as I raise my head and wait. The shift is abrupt, harsh, and yet the rest of my over six-foot-four frame remains in place as I stare at the entrance to this cell.

A solid door made of steel with a slot at the center just big enough for my hands to slip through. It's how they move you. How they demean your manhood, exhibiting for all to see the hold they have on your freedom. How they have you by the metaphorical balls.

I'm coming for you.

It's my reprieve and penance all in one; that thought brings forth a volcanic rush of ire through my veins as a certain memory slams back to the forefront: *You broke us.*

I did this. The sole blame lands at my feet.

My hands clench and unclench, nostrils flaring. My body thrums with the violence brewing as the day before my arrest plays on a constant loop.

It's meant to torture.

Unforgiving in its detail.

It serves as a reminder of two very hard truths:

I've hurt the most important person in my life.

This is the price I've paid for being the heir to Orlando Rivera De Leon. For taking my rightful place as the head of our family.

Staring at the small metal slot on the door, I breathe in and out slowly while fighting to regain control over my impulses. I'm wound tight as the seconds count down to a day five years in the making: *my release.*

I've been a patient man.

I've been playing by a set of rules designed to make others feel falsely powerful. To feel secure. To show me their hands in a game they'll never win.

Something that ends within the next few hours as I retake my crown, because in the city of Miami...

I *am* the law.

The beginning and the end.

I. Am. King.

A second alarm blares through the dirty old speakers of this inmate housing unit, and yet, everything else remains quiet. Everyone but me, and it's as if the entire building is cowering back. Hiding.

More than that, the constant **tick tick tick** of my fingernails drumming against the heavy metal door is proof of my mood. I haven't moved from my place in front of the room's entrance in hours. I'm restless. Counting. Thinking. Angry as I taste the sweet note of freedom that cloaks my piece-of-shit cell inside this federal prison.

My home for the last five years. Where they've put me away with every intention of keeping me inside indefinitely. And yet, I couldn't give a flying fuck about the time lost because everything in my life will always start and end with *her.*

She's the one regret I have. The one I'll lay down my life to make right.

"My beautiful little Luna," I whisper, waiting for the telltale sign of movement outside these doors. I know what's coming. How this will proceed, and my lack of patience is beginning to show as the loud sound of multiple doors unlocking follows.

My muscles further coil and I close my eyes, taking in a deep breath that I let out slowly. This isn't the time to argue or break the neck of the correctional officer in charge, especially when he's under my employ. When he's kept me in the know all these years as the justice department tried and failed time and time again to keep me within these walls, by any means, and failed.

I'm a hot commodity. A known killer with mafia ties is something the United States government hates to see walk out these doors.

They've done everything in their power to pin bullshit on me. To try and take me out.

Moreover, the irony sits in doing time for a crime I didn't commit.

I'm not an innocent man. I've taken more than one life in my thirty years on this earth, but this body doesn't belong to my count. Not that it matters. What's done is done, and I made the decision to accept this as my fate.

Instead, I'm focused on the future. It's time I reclaim what's been taken from me.

"Hands behind your back and away from the door, Leon."

"Done." A lie he will never call me out on, and a few seconds later his face appears in my line of sight. He's alone. Hands shaking as he holds out a small device toward me. "Where is she?"

"At home." Officer Ortiz's voice shakes and he clears his throat.

"This is verified?"

"By your brother not ten minutes ago via her bodyguard on duty." Inmates walk past my open door and their heads are bowed, some even fidget to move faster. The officers herding the state's cheap labor department toward the early morning mass, for those that have found religion while inside their concrete cage, also look away and pretend that mine is an empty room. A cough pulls my attention back toward Ortiz. "He said to warn you. There's something going on at her job and she'll be gone all day —big meeting about a recent case—until late this evening."

I nod in understanding, but she won't be making it in today. "Turn around and stand in the doorway."

"It's a bit risk—"

"I didn't ask you for an opinion."

"I apologize, sir." Ortiz lowers his eyes immediately and follows orders, and once he's in place, I dial the ten-digit combination of numbers

I'll never forget. The series is embedded deep into my consciousness. Tattooed into my DNA.

It rings. Three in total before there's a click on the other end.

Then, there's the sound of her breathing: soft and warm from being half-asleep.

It takes her a minute or two to say anything, but when she does, I'm transported back to my youth. Back to the very first time I laid my eyes on her doe-eyed brown ones. How I stopped in my tracks.

How I knew I'd never be the same after that singular moment.

How at just one week shy of my eighteenth birthday, I knew she was special.

"Hello?" *Motherfuck.* One word from those sweet lips and I come alive in a way I haven't since my incarceration began. Every nerve ending constricts and my hand tightens around the small plastic device. It protests, but I remain in place, taking in the curiosity in her tone and then the small gasp that follows as I let out a low groan. "Thiago."

Not a question. Not a single doubt.

Luna knows me like I do her. It's always been this way for us.

A few beats of silence linger between us as I wait. Wait for the inevitable question.

"How are you calling? Why are you after—"

"Mine." It's all I say because nothing else is needed. My girl is smart.

Luna has the means to find out where I am and how I'm doing. Something that she'll deny, but we both know is the truth. Something that within the span of the last five years she's done multiple times. On a constant basis. Every four months without failure.

"Thiago, no. *No.* You don't get to—"

"My beautiful queen." My voice is rough. It holds a tinge of the demonic need that courses through my veins for her. I also don't miss the small little keening sounds that come from the back of her throat—a whimper that I'd know anywhere. It's the same one that passed through her lips when I'd part her thighs and slip inside her tight heat. The same one she'd make when I'd tell her how much my world revolves around her. "Today. Tomorrow. Always."

"Thiago, how could you let me think—"

"I'm coming for you." With that, I hang up and drop the phone to the ground, breaking it as I step on the device. Ortiz is there and his body is tense, head shifting minutely from side to side while making sure unwanted visitors to this floor don't force my hand—that I don't unleash the pure thirst for revenge that simmers beneath my skin.

Another alarm rings throughout the unit just then, this one signaling an early morning cell check before breakfast. Not uncommon. I expected this, but there's nothing that can hold me inside.

The release was processed and pushed for earlier than normal by a hefty donation from my family to the governor of Florida's reelection campaign. They need funding, and I want out of these doors before the clock strikes nine.

Because that is how the system works. I'm corrupt, but so are they. Everything done in public is nothing more than a pony show, because behind the scenes we are all dirty.

"Sir, it's time," he says low but doesn't look back.

"Handcuff me." And he does. With a trembling hand, Ortiz turns back to face me and walks over, placing the cold metal loosely around each wrist. No other words are spoken. None are needed while leading me out of the cell.

At once, the small hum of low conversations ceases to exist as we cross the threshold, and the line against the wall with inmates turns to face the chipped paint behind them. No one meets my stare. No one dares.

Instead, the corridor parts like the sea for Moses as I walk toward my freedom.

They know.

They wait.

I don't forgive. I don't forget.

The streets of Miami will run red by the time I'm through rectifying this costly deed. Those responsible will pay for every tear my Luna shed in my absence.

Luna

THE MUSIC INSIDE the Leon home is loud tonight and so are all the grinding bodies—unfamiliar faces—dancing and drinking in the downstairs area of the house. These strangers are celebrating, imbibing, and they all give me a glassy stare as I make my way through the crowd.

No one stops me or makes small talk, but I can't help but feel as though they're following my every move as I reach the first-floor landing. It's empty, something I am grateful for, but where are the people that live here?

Where's Maritza or Ivan? Thiago?

Something is going on that I'm not privy to.

Something that isn't the norm for me. For us.

It's the opposite.

I'm family. Have been one of them since day one.

And more importantly, it'll be official next year when we say *I do*.

Then why has he been avoiding me for weeks? I shake that thought out of my head and focus on what I do know. What I've seen with my two eyes.

Thiago hasn't proposed yet, but the ring is inside his sock drawer.

He hasn't gotten down on one knee, but he's never shied away from telling me that I'll always be his. His beauty. His queen.

That I'd become the mother to his five children one day, and we'd raise them together. Never apart.

Because I don't care that he's been crowned the head of Miami's largest mob family. That he's killed for profit and does things that are both illegal and immoral. No one is a saint, and anyone who claims to be lives inside of a glass house.

My own family has more than one skeleton in its closet.

My uncle Edgar, Natasha's father, might work for Miami PD now, but everyone in our family knows that in the Dominican Republic he had certain business practices that were lucrative yet dirty. Extortion being one he favored in his youth, forcing Mom and Pop bodegas to pay a monthly stipend in order to avoid violent encounters with him and those under his employ. They paid him to be left alone.

He was never arrested or convicted in D.R. *but* it doesn't negate his past.

Then you have his brother. My father. He takes bribes from both criminals and those with money needing favors from the city council. Lobbying is real, and it doesn't occur just in our nation's capital. Local government facilitates ordinances and bends the law for those who fund their reelection campaigns.

No one's a saint, and that's a truth I accepted a long time ago.

We all have secrets. A dark side.

Accepting his was never my problem—I embrace *him* as he is, as long as he comes home to me every night. As long as he doesn't let the family business keep him away from the one we'll create some day.

That's what I hold on to when my own home life is in shambles.

My mother hates my father.

My father is unfaithful and proud.

And yet, even as misery drowns them, they stay. They tolerate and pretend because it's convenient for their lifestyle. He has the perfect doting wife for public functions, and she gets to spend his money while pretending to be happy.

I don't want that. Never have.

Material items mean crap when you're unhappy. Alone.

I want more for myself than to conform to an idea that some antiquated bastard created. Something that I share with the man I love beyond all comprehension. We want a happy life, not something fake or superficial.

"Thiago, stop!" I hear a woman giggle as I reach the second floor of their home, and I pause. In that singular moment—that laughter and *whom* it belongs to stops me cold. My prior thoughts of beautiful days filled with love and memories shrink to the point that my body coils into itself.

A sinking feeling hits my chest and I shake my head.

He wouldn't.

He couldn't.

"Don't overreact, Luna." There has to be an explanation as to why he's with her—someone I despise and who constantly tries to infiltrate our inner circle—of all people in his room. A room that, from where I stand, has a closed door.

"Quit it!"

"Behave, little girl." Thiago and his *guest* say in unison and time ceases to exist; I close my eyes for a brief second. The world disappears. All I hear is that annoying laughter, and I move on autopilot.

I blink and I'm at his door.

I inhale and push it open.

I gasp and the ground beneath my feet feels unstable.

The sight that greets me shatters my heart into a billion and one minuscule pieces. But more than anything, his unapologetic face will forever haunt me.

Those hazel eyes I love watch me standing in the doorway while his arms hold Amberlyn tight, an intimate embrace, with no remorse or care as they lie in his childhood bed. Thiago doesn't let her go. Instead, he pulls her in closer to his naked torso and kisses the crown of her head like he's done with me so many times in the past.

Her head is hidden inside the crook of his neck, but those fire-engine locks and the cheap tattoo of a dragon on her shoulder blade that she got done her senior year of high school are visible. Then there's that ever-present giggle. Obnoxious and loud as if she's being tickled, but the cause isn't his fingers digging into her sides.

No. It's the effect of whispered words that I can't make out.

There isn't an *I can explain,* or *It isn't what you think.*

He doesn't care.

My bottom lip begins to tremble, and a lump lodges itself in my throat. It hurts. Everything in that moment hurts as I watch the man I thought I'd spend the rest of my life with lying in bed with another woman.

Tears gather at the corner of my eyes, but I don't let them fall. I won't give him this too.

No. I've given enough.

I won't stay or accept this. I won't become my mother.

"You broke us." Are my parting words before I rush down the stairs and out the front door without looking back. She can have him.

I'm done.

THIAGO

"**G**OOD TO SEE you on this side, brother," Ivan says, pulling me in for a hug the moment I'm within reach. It's the first one in five years and I squeeze him just as tight, holding on for a few seconds before pulling back to take him in.

He looks the same, yet older. More mature than the last time we were face to face.

At twenty-six, Ivan looks like a younger version of me: same height, slightly smaller build, and with the kind of tan that comes from spending continuous hours under the sun. In my family, though, that golden tone comes naturally.

It's in our Cuban blood. The Caribbean in us.

"It's good to see you, too."

"Even if I'm not as pretty as Luna?"

"I'm going to ignore that and thank you for the clothes instead." I was arrested while drunk at my parents' home a few hours after Luna ran out with tears in her eyes—taken from my childhood room in nothing but a pair of black boxer briefs and socks because I was in no shape to drive to my penthouse. Those assholes didn't give me a chance to so much as put a shirt on, and my release would've been in that piece-of-shit orange jump-suit if it were up to the state.

The grey sweatpants and white shirt that Ivan brought, as plain as they are, feel like heaven after so long.

"No worries. Besides, la vieja would have a heart attack if you showed up in whatever hand-me-down crap they gave you." His hazel eyes, a shade or two darker than mine, look toward the back end of the SUV he's driving, and I take account of two other vehicles. They're similar to his and have two men sitting inside of each awaiting orders.

"Speaking of the women in my life...how are they?" I ask as both cars flash their lights in greeting. "Is Luna still home? Is Mom using this as an excuse to throw a party?"

"First..." he holds a finger up "...would it matter if she wasn't?"

"No." Nodding at the cars, I turn my head toward Ivan again. There's no doubt he's talking about my beauty. "I'd find her anywhere."

Ivan smirks, amusement covering his expression. "Nat left about an hour ago, and she looked pissed."

"She'll get her moment." They're upset, and while I understand, moves had to be made to protect those I love. My beauty knows the truth. More-over, even if it was after and it hurt her, that choice served its purpose. *I'm going to make it up to you, baby. I swear it.* "And Mom? Has anyone reeled her in?"

"That would be a negative. She's Hispanic, bro. There is no reeling her in."

"How many times has she called you in the last hour?"

"At the very least fifteen times."

"Just fifteen?" I chuckle, knowing just how extra the woman could be. "That's nothing when it comes to her."

His phone rings then and Ivan snorts. "Make it sixteen."

"Still a small number." Shaking my head, I focus on his phone and how much they've changed since my arrest. The cheap prepaids I've been using are nothing like the Apple device in his hand. "Did you bring my cell?"

"I did." He pulls open the passenger side door, and sitting atop the seat is a wrapped box with a large bow in all white. I don't have to ask to know that this was Mom's idea, but I shake my head nonetheless. "We should go. The meat has been marinating for two years now."

"That is quite a while." I take him in once again. He's the nicer one of the two, and while the thirst for blood runs in our family, *his* is just a bit tamer than mine. However, that shitty grin and the nervous tick that makes him crack his knuckles, which he's unconsciously done twice now, are still there. I haven't seen him or the family in a while, per my orders, but I've missed them all.

"Too long since you've played," he says low, eyes on something behind me. Following his line of sight, I find a small audience where there shouldn't be one near the rear entrance of the building. "Let's get out of here. It's not—"

I shake my head and he closes his mouth.

I choose to stare at the cameras instead and he steps aside, taking his rightful place behind me and to the right. It's a statement of unity and rebirth with my release.

I'm still sitting at the head of this table.

The De Leons aren't hiding. We don't bow.

Head on and held high, and because I'm an asshole, I wave. Cocky and with a smirk, I give each camera attention while the hijo de puta at the center of this impromptu news conference glares at me.

Openly. Full of hate.

While the man sputters and gestures wildly with his hand, I hold myself back from snapping his neck like a twig. The reporter closest to him notices the mayor's actions and elbows his cameraman to get the shot. They do, and it takes everything in me not to laugh or shoot him where he stands.

Ivan's car has more than one gun, and I've already seen mine close to my gift.

Ulysses Senot is a close friend of Luna's father, holds office in Miami, and is someone I plan to visit soon. To have a one-on-one. Like men. Him, and that pussy son of his that they tried to set up my beauty with.

Because that's his horse in the race. He'll do favors for his friend as long as my Luna's hand in marriage is on the table. The two old men want to unite the families, and that will never happen. Not in this life or any that follow.

Soon. Holding my palm out, I shift my eyes toward my brother and raise a brow. "Keys."

"In the ignition."

"Get in." He does so without any more prompting, and I follow suit, slamming the door closed before giving a final look at the group watching.

"Do you know where we're going?"

Turning the fob, I close my eyes for a second and bask in the silence that follows his question. Just a miniscule moment where I thank God for Luna and my freedom—this will be my lone instance of empathy and compassion.

I have a job to do and emotions have no place in my decisions, and while family is family, what led to my incarceration was an inside job. A setup. The attempt was made to end the life of Orlando and Maritza Rivera De Leon, and when that didn't go as planned, I was framed with the death of another man. The hired hitman. A man whose body was found inside my penthouse hung and missing limbs on a night where I'd been elsewhere.

Neither were my doing.

Moreover, whoever is responsible—family or friend—will face the consequences.

My wrath will bathe the earth in their blood.

Opening my eyes, I stare ahead and into my freedom. "I'm in the mood to look at ships."

THE PORT of Miami hasn't changed much since the last time I was here. It's still hot under the mid-morning sun and full of employees covering every single square inch.

They all have a job to do and are paid by either the US Customs administration or independent contractors to do a certain task. They are here to unload, load, and stop people like me from slipping illegal substances in through them and onto the city's streets.

They hope to make a difference. To clean up our country.

Yet, if you pass over a stack of bills to the right employee, all others fall into line.

Now, you become who makes the rules.

Now, they turn a blind eye when your container arrives or when certain meetings need to take place aboard a private ship a few miles offshore that is owned by a diplomat from Panama, a friend of mine that I've personally done favors for—taking the life of the man stalking his daughter and being the provider for his drug of choice.

Cocaine: that lovely white powder that so many covet and pay ridiculous amounts of money to get their hands on.

He owes me, and my collection comes with immunity from searches by US officials while aboard this ship that secretly belongs to me. His name is attached only for legal purposes because the two countries have an agreement, a lobbying interest, and his property is not to be touched while inside the United States.

Money is a dangerous commodity that everyone wants. They crave it. Want the power that comes attached to the said price tag.

A price tag that helps one nation with its debt and the other with exporting goods.

One gives an unwavering alliance, while the other secretly conducts moves to monopolize a market in their backyard. And while this is going on, I use the discretion to my advantage.

Something that at the moment is very useful with the eyes of the city on my back after my release. You can't get inside the port of Miami without searches, identification, and stating your reason for business here. Failure of any of those three, and you will be removed.

No excuse. Unless...you are a De Leon.

Moreover, *if* I conduct business while on international waters, I can't be convicted.

These workers know who I am.

They know why I am here.

And the moment I drive onto the large concrete floor of this port, all work stops and people begin to scatter. Even those that work for our government step back and look the other way as I exit the vehicle and five doors slam closed behind me.

It's almost comical, really. Local authorities—those self-righteous and low on the totem pole—hate me. Yet, you ask the governor of Florida and higher, and I'm just a businessman.

Everything depends on who you have in your pocket. Who owes you. Who you help fund to keep in power.

It's one of the many reasons that Luna's father hates me. I'll never fund the waste of sperm.

Not after he broke her heart by cheating on her mother. Not after the time he tried to smack her during an argument, and I broke his hand before he could ever lay a single finger on her skin.

My men surround me as I walk across, taking my time until we reach the stairs that lead to a lower deck that not many have access to. Taking the few steps down, we reach one of my favorite toys: a boat.

One of the many that I own, but this particular one I've never seen.

I'd left Ivan in charge of buying this powerboat and also with naming her. Little Moon has been sitting here looking pretty, and I let out a whistle of appreciation when I fully take her in.

All black and shiny, she's beautiful and sleek. Meant for racing or fast rides across open water. Perfect for what I need. For transporting myself along with two of my men across open waters where those wishing to put me back behind bars have no jurisdiction.

Climbing aboard, I turn and point at the two men standing to the right of Ivan to follow me. They do, and so does my brother, while the others stay behind to remove the cars and store them nearby for when we return.

"She's beautiful," I tell Ivan while the engine comes to life, purring beneath my feet and into the ocean below as I pull out of the dock. The salty breeze feels good on my face as does the rush of adrenaline that follows when I punch the accelerator and let this boat do what it's meant to. Fast and smooth, we glide over the water, barely touching the surface as we make our way to the ambassador's ship. "Good choice."

"It's my gift to you," Ivan says, the roar of the engine and the sound of crashing waves as we slice through the ocean, forcing him to yell from his seat beside me. "The least I could do." There's a tinge of regret in his tone, and while I know the *why*, I ignore it for now. We'll talk, but this isn't the right time.

There are twelve nautical miles between me and international water, and while those around me hang on to the interior handles or their seats, I relax my stance and let my mind focus on one thing and one thing alone: vengeance.

There's a shift in me the closer we get. A change in energy that brings forth a near demonic rush of rage to my veins. I throb where I stand. I feel the world begin to slow and my breathing with it.

This meeting is a long time coming, and I am due payment.

Ismael Navarro did something he shouldn't, especially since he knows me—my family—and yet he decided to play God for a few extra zeros in his bank account. That betrayal will never be forgiven. More so after I took him under my protection when he was still in high school and his family died in a car accident.

Ismael lived with us. Ate with us. He called my mother *Mima* yet pulled a gun on her from a moving motorcycle the day after her birthday two years ago. His second offense, and for that one, I could no longer wait for retribution.

Unforgivable; the little bitch created his own death certificate that day and the only thing keeping him alive since then is my missing signature.

He's been stewing in his own filth for two years now awaiting trial.

Once near the large vessel, I pull in beside a platform near the back that has one of my men near the controls of a hydraulic lift. I hold a hand up and the movable flat section that resembles a stage begins to descend, slowly, and when it's just within reach to walk across, I hand over the controls to a man who's worked for my family since before I was born.

Miguel is old school, someone I trust, and loyal. He's also who taught me how to drive a boat, and as I move from behind the wheel, he takes over. "Have fun, sir," he calls out as I step onto the steel surface, stopping at the center while the others stand behind me.

It's secure and sturdy and I give the signal to ascend. The rise is slow, but the higher we go, the more I give in to the needs I've kept under lock and key for the last five years.

This is a piece of me. This is who I am.

It's who I'll always be, and as I reach the top, I welcome my demon back.

A killer. Someone without remorse for what must be done.

The somewhat large platform is open and my men, those who stay on this ship for extended periods of time between Miami and pickup locations throughout Latin America, greet me with respect as we board the ship. Heads are bowed and they chant my name lowly as I pass, but I pay no mind for the time being.

Instead, I walk toward the center of the ship and down a long set of stairs that lead to an open ring. Here, I lose the all-white T-shirt and toss it somewhere behind me. I flex my arms and shake out my limbs to expel some of the adrenaline flowing through my system.

This is my playground. My place to let go, and as I step foot into the octagon-shaped area and close my eyes, a feeling of home overtakes my senses and the noise dulls. Here, my other instincts come alive:

I hear the low whimper from nearby.

I breathe in the stench of blood, urine, and chlorine.

I feel the shift in the air as a body is thrown at my feet.

The body tries to crawl away, but my men surround us. The person begs out a broken *please* and a sardonic laugh rumbles through my chest a moment before I settle my eyes on his pathetic form.

Broken. Bleeding. A shell of the man that I grew up with.

"Ismael fucking Navarro." At the sound of his name, another pitiful noise escapes the back of his throat and scared brown eyes look up at me. They're bloodshot and the one on the right has a deep gash over the brow. It looks disgusting: infected and dirty. "How have you been?"

"Thiago, I didn't—"

"Silence."

"Please, I...*fuck*!" he screams out as my foot comes down on a bruised ankle. It snaps—the bone giving way under the force of a single blow—and he learns to listen. Those cracked lips snap closed, and he cries in silence. *Good boy.*

"You messed up, Ismael. There's no coming back from this." I walk around him, taking inventory of the weight loss, the rough scars down his bony back, and the singular open puncture wound on his side. "What you did..."

"It was a mistake. I would've never gone through with it, Thiago." His tears, the way his bottom lip trembles, fail to move me. If anything, it renews my anger. His audacity to ask for any clemency from me burns through my patience like acid on flesh. It bubbles, unleashing its toxicity, and I react. "I swear. Y-you gotta believe me."

"Do I?" Grabbing a fistful of his hair, I yank him up to his knees and bring my face closer to his. Nose to nose. "Give me a reason. Just one."

"I'll tell you who put the hit out. Tell you where he lives."

THIAGO

IKE DEAD WEIGHT, I let his body fall back to the ground. The thud and the following whimpers of pain he releases are loud inside the hollow space. "Speak."

"Please. No more."

"Speak," I repeat, moving in closer to his head while Ivan steps to where his broken ankle limply lays. It's rapidly swelling, the previously healed cuts reopening and staining the already filthy floor red. "You have sixty seconds to say your piece."

The men surrounding us create a barrier. They are quiet but slowly begin to stomp a single foot against the floor. It reverberates throughout the room. It drowns out Ismael's pain.

"Will I walk out of here alive?" I tilt my head at his question, eyes narrowing at a man that I once considered family. He had access to the most important people in my life because of me. Because I saw potential in a kid that needed direction.

"No." No point in lying or giving him false hope.

"Can you make it quick?" A harsh shiver racks his body and his teeth clatter; his lips look to be turning a little blue, too. "Just end it."

"That depends on you." With the toe of my sneaker, I open his mouth and push down on his bottom jaw. Stretch it to the point that the very corner of his mouth tears, becoming red. His life's essence doesn't streak as the cut's isn't big enough, but it has to sting. Feel uncomfortable. "Tell me what I want to know."

He tries to talk around the leather of my Nikes, but instead gags, coughing up what looks to be a large amount of bile and more blood.

A lot of it.

From where I stand above him, I can see he's malnourished. In pain. Spiritless.

And yet it's not enough. Nothing short of his last breath, and that of those involved, will ever be.

I remove my foot, seeing what's in Ivan's hand from the corner of my eye. "You have two choices: merciful or vengeful. Up to you." As the last word slips past my lips, Ivan brings the sledgehammer down on his knee. It's on the opposite leg from the one I broke, but his screams of pain are just as loud.

"FUCK!" Ismael bellows, body writhing, and that brings with it more pain. The change in position forces the shattered pieces of bone to rub and cut flesh, to ruin tendons and ligaments he'll never have use for again.

Kneeling near his head, I block his view while holding one arm back. "Next blow will be to your skull." On my next inhale, I feel the cold against my skin from my weapon of choice and it warms my limbs.

There's nothing like the heavy weight of this metal in my hand as my fingers slip through each hole with ease. The fit is snug and I make a tight fist, savoring this extension of who I am once again. *It's been too long.*

The asshole swallows, grimacing as he fights another bout of gags. "I'll tell you everything."

"Your time is almost up." I bring the custom, solid gold brass knuckles into his line of sight, turning my hand slightly so the lighting in the room glints off each curve. These were a gift from my queen: a solid gold pair of brass knuckles in the shape of a crown with my name in Old English scripture at the center. They're sharp and heavy, and I've broken more than one skull with them. "Five, four, three…two—"

"Alfredo Gaytan." *Is a dead son of a bitch.*

I know the name. Know exactly who he is. But more importantly, I know who he works for.

Gaytan is under the employ of the Senot family—to be more precise, he's the head of Ulysses' wife's security. A man she's been fucking for years without her husband's knowledge because he's too far up the ass of his good friend, Antonio Alejos.

My queen's father.

"Say that again." My voice is gruff, lip curling up at the corner into a snarl. "Say that name again."

"It was Alfredo Gaytan. He hired me to kill the hired hitman and deposit his body in your apartment, and since I've crashed there in the past, no one questioned my coming and going."

"Why kill him? Why not try again?"

"They were losing time." Ismael tries to shrug, but grimaces instead. "He failed to take out his mark, but if they could lock you away, not all was lost." The trembling in his body increases, his entire frame going into shock, but I'm not done yet and signal one of the men near a large industrial hose to bring the extension to me.

"Open it," is all I say once it's in my hands, and within a few short seconds the rumbling of water shooting through a pipe at high speed infiltrates the room. This isn't your average variety garden equipment. No, this is high-pressured and cold—a direct hit hurts like a bitch, and is perfect for rinsing off an enemy's blood from my floor.

The first stream catches the shaking man off guard and he screams, agony riddling the high-in-pitch sound as it reverberates in the once-again quiet room. The jet is heavy and direct; it further opens the wound at his side, splitting the already sensitive skin wide open.

He bleeds onto my floor. He screams my name in a last-ditch plea. "Thiago, por favor. No mas."

I nod and the water is turned off.

I step over his body and his eyes widen.

I fist his hair, yanking him into a half-sitting position, and he closes his eyes.

"Look at me, Ismael." Bloodshot brown eyes shoot open, meeting my hazel ones, and in them I see a mixture of fear and resignation. Understanding and acceptance. "Did you show my mother mercy when you emptied your magazine into her armored vehicle? Did you come to me—show gratitude and loyalty—when Gaytan offered you the job and money?" His mouth opens, his reply sitting on his tongue, but it's not something I need or want. I have the file. I know every detail of the events that lead to the attempt on myself and my family. "The answer is no, old friend. You saw dollar signs and didn't give a single fuck about the people who took you in."

"I'm sorry." It's a broken whisper, a sob catching in his throat.

"No more than I am." With that, I lean over and kiss his forehead before forcing his head back in an uncomfortable-to-swallow position. His jaw and neck are exposed; the last bit of fight left in Ismael comes rushing through as he weakly attempts to fight my hold. Nails dig into my skin, but don't break the surface. Thrashing commences but dies down when my hold is unrelenting. "I'll see you in hell one day."

I bring my brass-knuckled fist down against the lower half of his face, effectively breaking his jaw. There's a crunch from breaking bone, fragments of teeth falling to the ground, and then blood.

Bright and almost glowing, it flows from his now-useless mouth. His screams become muffled because:

He can't fully open his mouth. He can't move it. He can't swallow.

And then I do it again. And again. Each strike consistent in intensity, I don't stop, nor do I wipe away the splatters of red that now paint my skin. Ismael is almost limp in my hold, and yet, his body weight isn't a hindrance for my grip. My fist comes forward again, this time on his cheek and the skin breaks wide open, exposing another piece of broken bone.

Moreover, as his head snaps back and movements still—as his breathing slows—I toss him at Ivan's feet.

I've done my damage. He will die.

Not as fast as a bullet or a knife wound, but the man is slowly choking.

"Do you have anything to add?" I ask my brother, giving him the opportunity for a final act of retribution.

"No, sir." That *sir* serves a purpose as well. It's him officially welcoming me back—not that it's necessary, but more of a show of respect. This motherfucker is someone I trust with my life, and while behind bars, he was my eyes and ears. Following my orders from within, working day in and day out to both keep the family safe and the business running. Because of my father and Ivan, we still hold Miami's drug scene in an iron grip. "But a beer would be nice."

A gurgling noise from below makes me smile. "First round on me after…"

"You go see your girl."

"Pretty much." His phone chimes then and he digs into his back pocket, pulling it out and swiping a finger across the screen. Ivan laughs and shakes his head, tossing me the phone so I can see for myself what has him so amused.

There, in a series of texts from our vieja, is a veiled threat and it's hilarious.

> Tell that boy of mine to make it right and kiss her culo if he has to. No excuse. Tomorrow we party and Luna better be with him. ~Mami

> You show him this, Ivan. ~Mami

> Did you do it? Tell me. Is he still handsome? ~Mami

Christ. I'm cracking up before finishing that last one. It's so like her.

Forceful yet loving. A don't-mess-with-me-or-mine attitude that I learned from her.

My father might've been the leader of the De Leon cartel, feared by many, but my mother was worse. She could forgive any indiscretion except the touching of her family. Blood is sacred.

Mami, I'm here and I'll see you tomorrow. Love
you, but I make no promises on Luna. She's
stubborn. ~Thiago (your favorite)

The body on the floor groans, and I shift my eyes to him. He's bleeding and fighting to swallow. The floor beneath his head has a puddle of red saliva.

Another ping comes through, pulling my attention away.

Mi hijo! I love you so much. Can't wait to hug
you. ~Mami

Me too. ~Thiago

Okay. Go…but drag her back home if you have
to. *kisses* ~Mami

That, I can do. See you all tomorrow. ~Thiago

Tossing the phone back to my little brother, I call forth a younger man I've never seen before. At no older than twenty, he stands to the side with a tray which holds a bottle of water and a towel. "Thank you…" I say and wait for his name.

"I'm Junior, sir. Miguel's son."

"How long have you been with us, kid?" I knew of his father having a son but was under the impression he lived with his mother in California and was a lot younger.

"Two years, sir." Junior swallows nervously, eyeing the splattering of blood on my hands and chest. "The day I turned eighteen, I left my mom's house and came to live with him. I couldn't deal with her addiction problems anymore."

"Understandable." Taking the bottle, I twist off the cap and pour more than half its contents onto the folded cotton on his tray. "And do you like working for us?"

"Yes, sir."

"Did you learn anything today?"

"I did, sir." While I clean my hands with the towel, I raise a brow and wait for him to elaborate. He's smart and catches on quickly, squaring his shoulders while his eyes focus on the man beneath us. "You don't betray the hand that feeds. You don't go against family. You don't sell yourself for a quick buck, especially when it *will* cost you your life."

"You're going to make your father very proud, kid."

"Thank you—"

"More than one person wants her, Thiago." This comes in the form of a murmur from the floor below—broken and so low that I almost don't make out the words, but I do. It's a warning. The last words before the light leaves his eyes and a vacant look takes over. There's no more breath. No more movement. At 10:08 on the Tuesday morning of my release, Ismael took his last breath, and I feel nothing.

No pity for the twenty-five-year-old.

No moment of reflection.

No forgiveness.

Moreover, while those around me begin to dispose and clean up, I focus on the last words of a dying man that confirm what I already know. There's more than one player in this game, and the prizes differ. However, the one unifying factor is my queen, and it hurts to accept that someone within my own familial tree did this. That they covet what is mine, but they do, and I'll uncover their tracks if it's the last thing I do on this earth.

No one will ever take me away from her again.

Not even God himself, if it came down to it.

Luna

"**I**'M COMING FOR YOU."

Those words run through my mind on a constant loop. Four simple words that once put together in the minuscule span of a few minutes have flipped my world on its axis. I'm left standing, unable to move, lost within my head, but the somewhat closed wounds of a few years ago reopen and it knocks the very breath from my lungs.

It shows me how, after all this time, what he did—his lack of faith in us — still hurts.

Moreover, these tumultuous emotions always lead me back to him. Thiago Rivera De Leon.

My soul's other half. My lion.

A man whom I've loved since our adolescence, and I've never learned how to stop doing so. He's my truth that will never change, and a response that I can't duplicate with anyone else. Even at our worst moments, I've always been his.

Something I know deep in my soul will always be a fact even if a part of me hates him just as much. No man measures up, and the very thought of trying to move on has been unacceptable. My own body rebels against me and cries out for his warmth, those strong hands that knew how to touch me, how to drive me crazy with just the faintest hint of a caress.

How to bring me to the highest peak of pleasure with filthy words and a telling grunt that would build in his chest and rumble past parted lips when he found his own release.

Then, after leaving me a boneless mess on his sheets, Thiago would wrap his arms around me—pulling me in close and tipping my face up to his. His eyes would hold warmth and love. His lips would kiss mine with a softness that always made my chest ache.

Because for all the ways he could be an asshole to the outside world, with me he's always been a giant teddy bear. My everything.

Which brings me to the following truths. Two things that I can't deny and are just as hard to swallow.

I miss him.

I'm not ready for him.

My hand vibrates then and I look down, taking in the phone and flashing lights of the screen. I know the name, know that I need to pick up, but can't seem to hit the answer button.

I'm here, but not.

My entire being is assaulted from all angles with flashes of memories; a movie reel that starts at the very beginning and highlights our best moments. It's fast and hard to keep up, but I do and a small sob catches in my throat as I follow his transformation from handsome teenager to a devastating god of a man.

But then that same movie reel of wonderful images reaches its end and a single tear rolls down my cheek. I'm living it all over again. That day. The very moment he broke my heart.

I see it.

Take in every last detail as if I were inside his bedroom and not my living room.

However, the difference between *then* and *now* is the truth. He betrayed me in a way that I don't know if I'll ever forgive.

Thiago didn't trust me. He chose to lie instead of letting me stand by his side as the queen he always claimed me to be. *He* forgot every promise ever made and chose to steal my choice in the matter.

He didn't cheat. I know that.

I knew it deep within my soul after I cooled off, but by then it was too late. Thiago made me believe so by playing on my deepest fears; that I wasn't enough. That the cursed circle made by my parents would follow me like a crucifix into every relationship.

It hurt. Cut deep.

It took Amberlyn and Ivan months to make me realize that I'm not *them*. It took her opening up, and my noticing that the brother she was in love with is Ivan, to let her in.

Thiago broke us to protect me, and it seems I'll get the explanation I deserve today.

Bang.

Bang.

Bang.

The sudden loud noise within the space causes me to jump and I drop my cell, taking with it the half-empty coffee cup on the table as my hands flail in an attempt to catch the device. I fail, and once more curse the man I love for the mess on my hands. Piping hot liquid spreads quickly in an uneven shape on the soft carpet beneath my high-heeled feet. It's bathed my phone and ruined the leg of my high-waisted white dress pants.

"Dammit!" I hiss as the heat seeps through, burning my skin, and I pull the fabric away as best I can. They're ruined. There's no way to salvage this large of a stain, and I kick off my shoes to begin disrobing when there's another series of hard knocks.

"Lulu, open up!" Nat yells through the door, her voice full of concern. "Are you..." I rush across the room and yank it open before she finishes "...*fuck*."

"Yup."

"Thiago's already out?" Amberlyn asks, peeking in from behind her, worry written across Nat's soft features. "Did any of them contact you?"

"What're you guys doing here?" I ask them, then pause. My brows furrow in confusion. "How do you know?"

"First, good morning-ish." Natasha ticks off with her fingers. "It's already almost ten, and Thompson sent me to check on you." She's dressed for the office; her signature black trousers and blazer look on point. So is Amberlyn. She doesn't work with us in the forensics department but at a bail bonds office nearby.

"Almost ten?" *How long have I been stuck inside my own head?* "What the—"

"And second? Everyone's talking about it. Have you not seen the news this morning?" When I shake my head, Nat huffs, fully walking into the room and straight for the remote on the coffee table. Amberlyn follows her, my mess plain to see, but neither mentions my more-than-likely ruined phone or the spilled disaster, which I'm grateful for. Instead, they focus on the TV screen after Nat turns it on, flipping the channel until we reach the largest Spanish-speaking network and I see his picture. It's one I know very well as it came from my camera and I own the only other copy.

Back in the days when owning a photography studio was my dream. When it was my passion and not just my opening to keep track of Thiago. I became a crime scene photographer to get those charges dropped because while I'm angry at him, the evidence taken from his penthouse wasn't conclusive.

Someone wanted him gone.

"Wasn't that at Maritza's fiftieth?" Amberlyn asks then and I nod, once again living through a memory.

"Mijo, don't be so difficult," his mother whines while I use the power of my pout to persuade him. "Just one. It won't kill you and Ivan already took his."

"Ivan's an ass kisser, Vieja. We both know this."

Her eyes, an almost identical shade of golden honey, narrow. "So are you when you want something from my Luna."

His stare shifts to me and I fidget, the telltale blush sweeping across my skin. There's hunger in those beautiful orbs, but just as powerful is his love for me. It's there. Wide open and never hidden. "I'll never deny kissing her as—"

"So," I interrupt, mock glaring at him because the man has no shame, and this is his mom. Though, by the low giggle she emits, I'll say she's amused by us. "A picture? Just one?"

"This will cost you." Thiago bites down on his bottom lip, eyes roaming my smaller frame. His heated gaze lingers at the strap of my expensive camera that falls over the swell of my breast. "Are you willing to pay?"

"Name your price," I say, but my tone comes out a bit breathy and not one bit the unaffected woman I am trying to portray.

Something he notices, and his smirk deepens. "You know what I want."

"To give me grandchildren?" Maritza interjects, and I am so thankful for that. Because I know what the jerk wants.

His price is my ass; literally.

"Among other things." Thiago raises a brow at me. A challenge. The man knows I'll never deny him anything. "It's a simple yes or no, baby girl."

"Are you serious right now?" I laugh, but it's a nervous one. Embarrassed. Wanting to both strangle and kiss that stupid grin off his face.

"Yes." No hesitation.

"Thiago!" I throw a hand up in exasperation. "That's cheating and you—"

"Nothing's fair in love and war, Luna. Remember that."

When all was said and done, Maritza got her picture of him dressed in the standard Cuban Guayabera with a Corona in his hand, the waves behind him crashing upon the shore. Handsome and a bit arrogant, he smirked at me while a continuous blush bloomed across my cheeks as I fought my need to taste his lips.

Or bite him until the jerk bled a tiny bit.

But then again, Thiago enjoys putting me on the spot. He enjoyed my tendencies to be a little violent—to leave the perfect indentation of my teeth all over his upper body when angry or aroused.

Christ, I need help.

"What are you going to do, Luna?" Nat bumps her shoulder with mine, bringing me back to the present.

"This is my favorite picture of him, you know."

"I do. The fact you still keep it on your nightstand is proof of that."

"Guilty." My eyes shift to my cousin and I give her a sad smile. "When developing the film, I made a copy. The original is his mother's, my gift to her."

"That still doesn't answer my question, Lulu. Help me help you."

"Back then we had it all. We were inseparable." However, a few months after his mother's birthday it all came crashing down at my feet. Natasha opens her mouth then, and I can literally see the questions in her worried gaze, but I shake my head. "Nothing's changed. I expect he'll swing by at one point today."

Because I'm not an idiot; he's kept tabs on me through his younger brother, Ivan. Through guards. Through my uncle. *He just never bothered to call me.*

Crossing her arms over her chest, she puffs out her cheeks. "You're not going into work, are you?"

"No."

"How long?"

"A few days. Tell them I have food poisoning."

"Are you sure? Want me to stay?" Nat moves to stand in front of me, effectively blocking my view of the TV, and places a hand on each shoulder, giving them a squeeze. "Thiago has a date with my foot up his butt. Let me have my moment."

Shaking my head, I let out a chuckle. "Another time."

"One punch and I leave?" I get her need—her anger at someone she once considered a brother. Natasha has seen me at my best and worst, stood by my side when my mother made snide comments and my father shouted his disdain. She's my person through thick and thin. "Pretty please?"

"The first blow is mine."

"Rock, paper, scissors?"

"Mine, babes. You can have a go after...I promise."

"Fine, but I'll be holding you to this."

"You have my word..." looking behind her, I notice how late it already is "...you guys should go. Let's not make it any worse. Thompson's already going to be pissed with my not coming in and..." I turn my head toward a quiet Amberlyn "...how are you here without issue?"

"Day off." That's all she says, but I have a feeling it's more than that. While she isn't the most vocal person when it comes to feelings, actions prove her loyalty. It's written on her face. In the way her brows pinch and lips thin into a line. "Just thought I'd hang out with you...you know? Girls' day."

"Thank you, but I'll take a raincheck."

"Are you sure?" Her eyes plead with me to accept, but this situation is best faced alone. Just me and him. "I know how to hide a body, get us bailed out, and then not get caught while skipping it."

At that, I laugh deeply, loudly, bending over and placing my hands on my knees. This day just keeps getting more ridiculous by the second. "I love you guys so hard."

"I'm serious!"

"I know," I manage through my laughter; it takes me a minute or two, but I manage to get myself upright and wipe my damp eyes. They're both looking at me like I'm crazy, and maybe I am, but I see the amusement in the twitch of their lips. "God, I needed that."

"Glad we could amuse you." Nat gives me a final puppy-dog look, her last-ditch effort at convincing me to let them stay, but I shake my head no. Her shoulders slump and lips purse. "You suck, and fine. I'll cover whatever comes up."

"Thanks, prima. I'll owe you." Pulling her in for a quick hug, I then turn to Amberlyn and give her one as well. "Both of you mean so much to me. Love you." With that, I rush them out the door before they can pitch another attempt, promising to call them later. Much later. Maybe *after a warm bath and a few shots of rum* later.

Agreeing with myself that it's the best strategy I can come up with on short notice, I undo the button on my pants and shimmy out of the ruined garment. Leaving them where they land, I make my way toward my room at the back of my apartment and straight for my shower.

The coffee is still sticky on my skin and I could use a long soak beneath the hot waterfall showerhead. Which is what I do. Taking my time, I strip the remaining garments and fully step inside.

I let the near-boiling water hit my golden skin, relaxing the muscles of my back the longer I stand there. I let the sweet scent of coconut and lime calm my racing heart and then take with it my worries as I rinse off. Time ceases to exist, and I forget the world for that period of time. Twenty minutes or an hour, I have no clue how much time has passed as I close my eyes and breathe in deep through my nose.

Then out through my mouth.

Slowly. Without rush. For that small reprieve, I stop wondering about *him* until there's a sudden knock on the door. The person on the other end is impatient and I turn the water off, grabbing my towel from the rod. I wrap it around myself and step fully onto the mat but have to pause.

Reality is a fickle bitch, and she smacks me with the full force of a freight train and I begin to shake.

Another knock and I walk out of the room on unstable legs.

Three quick raps and I almost stumble, catching myself on a small accent table in the hall.

"Luna, are you in there, sweetie? I have something for you." My neighbor Cicely, an old and cranky lady that's taken a liking to me for some reason, calls through the door, and the sudden bout of nerves evaporates. Just disappears.

"Sweet baby Jesus," I breathe out low, softly banging my forehead against the wall. "I'll be right there!"

"No need to rush." *Then why the hard banging on my door?* "I'll leave the zucchini bread here...drop by later if you get a chance. My Netflix logged off again."

"Give me thirty!"

"No rush but before five, please." With that, she walks away and I turn back to my bedroom on steadier legs. It's the second largest room in the apartment and comes with a balcony attached that wraps around the side of the building, connecting with the living room. Open space and soft colors; it's all pink and white with a touch of gold—a large four-poster bed and armoire.

A small sitting area within and deep walk-in closet. Large windows that overlook Brickell Ave. near downtown Miami.

It's my sanctuary, and as I open the top drawer of my dresser to get a clean pair of panties, I change my mind. A nap sounds like heaven right now, and with Cicely not being in a rush, I slip on the pair of hipsters and walk back to bed.

The moment I crawl under the sheets, the pure exhaustion brought on by his release has me drifting into the state of sleep called limbo. I'm not fully under or awake. I'm not analyzing my life or playing out reunion-like scenarios.

For the moment, I'm just being. And when my stomach rumbles some-time later, I ignore that too for another few minutes until there's a sudden knock at the door.

"I thought she said no rush?" Throwing my legs over the edge, I stand and grab the silk robe laying at the edge of the bed, wrapping it around myself. The belt is barely secured—not even a full bow in place—when I rush out and down the hall, pulling the door open before she begins another series of knocks.

However, in my stupidity, I'm half-naked and regretting it immediately.

Because the person on the other side is not my neighbor or Natasha or Amberlyn. No. This person causes my entire world to stop. Everything around me disappears and my chest grows tight because there, in all his handsome glory, is the man I've vowed to forget and failed.

The man I don't want to love but do.

"I've missed you, baby girl," Thiago says, his voice deeper, richer than I remember, and a shiver runs through me. He's bigger too. All muscles and tattoos and a sinful smirk that causes a rush of wetness to seep through the lace of my panties and coat my inner thighs.

He doesn't say anything, but the way his nostrils flare and hands clench at his sides give away his intentions. *I'm in trouble.*

Damn him for being just as delicious as always.

And God help me too, because while my body cries out for his touch, while my heart nearly beats out of my chest, another emotion pushes all the others back.

I'm angry. Full of ire with my next intake of breath and I can't stop myself. Won't.

I smack him.

THIAGO

I'VE BEEN FOLLOWING her all day. Since the very moment she walked through the large double doors of this pretentious high school where I am a king. Almost worshipped out of a raw fear that comes from knowing who my family is.

What we're capable of. We don't hide it.

We are criminal. Miami royalty.

In a city like this one, nothing stays hidden and I learned from an early age to be proud of each life I've taken. At almost eighteen, I'm far deadlier than my old man, and those around me know this. Fear my temper.

It's why so many try befriending me; they believe doing so will give them a free pass. It's also why the basic females at this private school nearly stampede over each other to be seen with me. For a chance to be with me.

Have I fucked a few? Yes, but they meant nothing.

Not one has stood out among the sea of nobodies like *her*.

No one has ever stopped me in my tracks with just one look.

Like now. The beauty turns her head back in my direction and her brown doe eyes meet mine, causing the world around me to stop. All noise ceases. It's just us inside of this hallway while my heart, that cold bastard, almost beats out of my chest. While my palms sweat and mouth goes dry as I take her in once again.

She's short but curvy, beautiful in a way that's near angelic while the glint in her eyes threatens mischief. She looks soft and her skin holds this golden touch that creates a hunger—the need to taste the exposed skin of her neck where the uniform shirt is unbuttoned is near maddening.

I want her.

I'm also fucked.

I know this, so when she turns back to face the door just a few steps away from her, I pull out my phone and type out a quick message to my father.

> Viejo, I need info on a new student. Everything.
> Her name is Luna Alejos. ~Thiago

His response is quick and just what I expect.

> Important? ~Dad

> Yes. ~Thiago

Because this is. My gut tells me it's unbelievably so.

> Done. It'll be delivered within the hour. ~Dad

Pocketing my cell, I do what I've done all day and follow her into class. The seat behind her in biology is empty and I slip into it, leaning forward so I can take a lungful of the sweet scent of coconuts. Her long black hair is down with loose ringlets bouncing gently while she shifts, fighting the more-than-likely urge to tell me to fuck off.

She doesn't, though.

Instead, she emits a low huff and faces forward. Ignoring me. Making this so much sweeter without trying.

I will make this beauty mine.

PRESENT...

THE FEEL of her palm connecting with my cheek brings me back to the present and creates two instant problems:

I'm hard.

I'm amused.

She hasn't changed, and her proclivity for just the right amount of violence forces me to react. To take a step forward and then another, giving my beauty no other choice but to retreat into the apartment, and giving me the perfect opening to follow.

She's trying to evade what's already set in stone. Us. This. The uncontrollable hunger—the almost crippling need we have for each other.

I am hers and she is mine.

Always will be.

"Stop right there, Thiago," she says, expression hard and lips in a thin line. It's cute. Adorable how she follows the demand by holding a delicate hand up between us as the front door closes behind me. *Nothing could stop me from coming for you, beautiful.* "I didn't invite you in, and this..." she points at herself, then me "...isn't happening."

"I've missed you." It comes out gruff, full of every bit of the hunger I've kept buried deep—a need so palpable that she shivers, and her expression softens. Because no matter how angry she is, and justifiably so, she needs this too. Me. Us.

"Liar." The tinge of venom in her tone causes my chest to ache, but I don't outwardly show the effect. "All these years and not so much as a damn phone call, Thiago? Not a letter or note or smoke signal. Nothing."

"I saved those to give you in person." Taking another step into her home, I take off the collared pullover I'm wearing and toss it somewhere behind me. Her eyes wander my chest and lower, cataloging the newest additions to my artwork, something she's trying to avoid but can't control.

It doesn't take long for her to find the feminine crown over my left pec and her name above the five points in her penmanship, a little favor that Ivan managed to pull off when he helped her find the apartment she lives in.

This building is mine and was purchased when her intent to move out of her parents' home became known two months after my sentencing. Plans that she confided to Amberlyn after a big fight with her parents, who continued to celebrate my demise. Little did she know that her new best friend, after I sent her to expose the truth, let it slip to Ivan by mistake.

He likes Amberlyn even if he hasn't admitted it to himself, while she's been in love with him since high school. A fact that's beneficial to me, and I'm not the least bit ashamed of playing dirty when it comes to my queen.

The contract she signed was nothing more than a bullshit pretense necessary at the time, and each month when she pays rent, it goes into a savings account with only her name on it.

However, I think she knew. It's the reason she went along with everything and never put up a fight.

"I don't want them." *Liar.*

This pull between us is palpable. Growing. Fucking torture as I try not to lose the last shred of control I have when it comes to her.

Luna's always been my kryptonite.

We're a lost cause. An unavoidable explosion.

A game we both know will end up one way; with her bent over or riding my cock.

Either way, I'll have her.

"That's a nasty habit you've picked up in my absence."

"Amuse me." Hackles raised, she places a hand on her hip and the robe shifts, giving me a peek at her upper thigh. "What *nasty habit*?"

"Becoming a fraud."

"What did you just say?" There's that fire again. That spark that always made my cock throb, swell to the point of pain. "I'll need a repeat."

I hurt for her. Can feel each bead of pre-come as it rolls down the head and then length, disappearing into the fabric of my boxer briefs.

Luna licks her lips, and I follow the movement with unrestrained hunger. "You'll never be over me, baby girl." This leaves me on a groan, a sound that causes her breath to hitch. "Quit lying to yourself."

It also serves to prove how affected Luna is by my mere presence, and when the two little tight nips appear through the thin material of her robe, I take in the rest of her.

Fuck. Just fuck.

Because the good Lord doesn't have mercy on me, and words will never suffice to describe the perfection before me.

Sinful and every bit of the temptress she is, my beauty stands in the middle of her living room in nothing but a satin robe and a pair of hipsters the color of lust. Red. Thin. Lace. Almost see-through, she's all curves and tan skin on display. All warmth and that ever-present scent of coconut swirling around her.

She's toner than I remember, too, but still thick where I love. Where I love to grab onto as I maneuver her hips over mine.

Slow to the point of madness.

Fast to the point of delirium.

Her belt slowly starts to come undone, the soft fabric parting and exposing her midsection. However, my eyes settle on her right hip bone and the small tattoo visible just over the waistband of her panties. It's my initial, in my penmanship, with the intricate and bold face of a lion beside it.

Leon is the Spanish translation for lion, and Luna always said my last name couldn't fit me any better. That I remind her of a vicious predator, and I take that as a compliment. As a challenge.

I remember the day she got it, too. It was her eighteenth birthday and against her parents' wishes. They wanted more for her than me, the son of a mob boss and next in line to take over the family's dealings.

Hypocrisy at its finest since her dad is a chauvinistic and corrupt member of the city council. Then you have her mother, Yvette; religious and stuck somewhere between duty to her beliefs and hating the male species.

Both stuck in a loveless marriage where appearances are all that matter.

My eyes travel lower, just a tiny bit, and stop at the juncture of her thighs. Christ. From where I stand, I see the wetness coating her upper thighs and can just make out the pink flesh through the soft lace.

My mouth waters. My muscles coil to the point of pain and I tremble as a deep rumble vibrates through my chest. This moment is five years in the making.

Days and nights of denying myself her taste to protect my family. To keep Ivan out of jail.

She's my reward.

My treasure.

Mine.

"Leave," she says, breathing a bit choppy.

"I can't do that." My own chest expands, hands clenching and unclenching at my sides—fingernails digging into my palms. "I'm not leaving you again. Never. Fucking. Again."

"Please." She's trembling, goose bumps breaking out across her skin. For as much as she's angry, she's missed me too. Needs me. "We'll talk later. After I—"

Whatever bullshit excuse my beauty tries to use dies when my eyes snap to hers. "No."

"Thiago, please..." she swallows hard, squeezing her thighs "...this isn't the right time. Be reasonable."

"I love you." Those three words are my truth and her breaking point.

"No. No!" Luna's head shakes from side to side, the flip in her mood instant. This is the effect of a yo-yoing rollercoaster of emotions, and I see her intent before she reacts. With her next intake of breath, she reaches over and grabs a heavy glass vase, hurling it at my head. "You don't get to do this after what you did. What you tried to make me believe."

It misses the mark as I duck, and it smashes into the wall behind me. "I had no choice."

"There's always a choice!"

"And I took the one that mattered. I pushed you away to motherfucking save you."

"So you keep saying!" This time it's a picture that barely misses me. "From who?" She's exasperated, and in her annoyance makes another mistake. Her movement, that explosive rage rushing through her Latina blood, exposes her left breast, and I lick my lips. Mouthwatering is the best way to describe her.

She's always been perky: a heavy handful with the most tantalizing shade of dusky pink nipples. They're perfect, a bit fuller than the last time I had the privilege of licking—biting—each tight little tip.

I swallow hard, eyes closing for a second. Needing the moment. "I'll tell you everything, but not now."

"Yes, now. You owe me—"

Holding a hand up, I cut her off. Then, desperate hazel meets sacred brown and I hold her stare. I let her see me. Open myself up to the only woman I will ever call mine.

"I owe you more than I will ever be able to repay in fifty lifetimes, Luna." The anger she tries desperately to hold on to begins to melt; it's still there and fighting to resurface, but her own feelings for me won't let them. "I love you and always will, baby girl, and that won't change. Not today or tomorrow."

"Don't do this to me."

"I'm never leaving you again."

"I deserve more than that, Thiago. Need more than words after—"

"And you'll get it all. My life if you so much as ask, but right now..." I trail off. The sight of her soft skin on display, the way her chest rises with every sharp intake of breath, is killing me. Destroying my very will. She's claiming me—tattooing herself into my very DNA without a single touch.

"What?" Without conscious thought, Luna raises a hand out toward me. It hangs in the air between us, her beautiful eyes on my face. "What about right now?"

"Right now..." I lick my lips, almost tasting her in the air around me. Luna's sweet and perfect and the hint of coconut lingering around me is driving me insane, especially when I know that she's decadent everywhere. "I'm going to start by righting the five years' worth of orgasms I owe you."

Her lips part but no words come out. She's stunned into silence, eyes wide, and the small object in her hand—another projectile—slips from her tiny fingers.

The muted thud is loud inside the room.
So is her whimper as I close the distance.
There's no running or escaping. No more denying.
We need this.
We'll talk later. Much later.

THIAGO

A SINGLE TOUCH.

That's all it takes.

The world dissolves into a low hum the second my fingers wrap around the back of her neck, gripping her just the way she likes: hard. Because for as much as I love her violent tendencies—that passion that only I can bring forth—Luna loves my domination over her much smaller frame.

The way I can bend her to my will.

Maneuver her like my precious little dirty rag doll.

"So beautiful," I croon low, welcoming the electric current that bounces between us; this warmth travels throughout my limbs and then settles on the tip of my engorged cock as I yank her against my hard body.

Chest to chest. Breathing in her every exhale.

Savoring each shiver.

Loving the gasp and then whimper she fights to hold back.

"It's been too long since I've had you like this, beauty."

"Thiago." It's sweet and full of fear; she doesn't want to give in but can't fight the yearning. She doesn't want to need me but can't deny her hunger. "This...*oh God!*"

"I love you." My lips skim from her temple to cheek, pausing at the corner of her mouth. There, I breathe in her intoxicating scent. Coconuts and lime. My demise. "I missed you."

"We shouldn't." It has no conviction behind it. Luna isn't pushing me away but gripping the waistband of my pants. She isn't yelling but giving in. She isn't fighting my hold but inching her way closer.

Each inhale is a silent *more*.

Each exhale is a needy *plea*.

"Look at me." At my command, her head shifts slightly and those sweet lips hover over mine. Right there. I can feel the warmth of her breath on my face, the memory of her naturally sweet mouth causing the last cord of sanity to snap.

I force her back, not stopping until her body meets the wall, pinning her in place with my own hips while my lips descend on hers. My eyes close of their own accord, groaning as her decadent taste brings me back to a different point in time. Back to the first time I kissed her.

The effect is the same after all these years. I become manic. Desperate. Insatiable.

I massage her tongue with my own, reacquainting myself with an addiction that I've been deprived of. Feening for five motherfucking years.

They stole that from me. Us.

Lord, forgive me now because I won't ask for repentance later.

"Please, Thiago. We—"

"Need this." I finish for her because it's the truth. Our love is a gift and a burden. Our weakness and anchor. "Are you going to continue denying it?"

Her response comes in the form of a harsh bite to my bottom lip. It stings, and the lick that follows only makes me harder. Thicker inside my jeans.

My fingers dig into her neck, limiting her eager mouth from moving over mine. "Answer me, Luna. Say it."

"No."

"Is that so?" My eyes leave hers and traverse lower as I take a step back. She's tiny. Small compared to my over six-foot-four frame, and as those beautiful brown eyes darken to almost black, I release my hold on her neck. For now. Only so I can skim a single finger down to her right shoulder and then the left, savoring the way her delicate skin breaks out in goose bumps.

Pushing the soft material off and down her arms, I wait for a protest that never comes. There isn't a single sound of complaint, and I let the material catch at her elbows before undoing the belt at her waist that is holding on by an almost nonexistent bow.

It loosens and I watch as her arms shake before they fall, giving the garment the give it needs to fall at her feet. It pools there, and then she's naked except for the small scrap of indecency she calls underwear.

Her legs squeeze together.

Her abdomen clenches.

I haven't touched her yet.

But then I do.

With the very tip of two fingers, I slowly make my way down the center of her chest while ignoring the two tight tips begging for attention. I'm not ignorant to the way they throb for my touch, but I have a point to prove and don't pause until I reach the edge of her panties. Right at the waistband where I slip those same two fingers beneath the elastic with my eyes on hers.

Watching her. Daring her to deny me.

Instead, Luna parts her legs in offering and moans deep in the back of her throat when I cup her wet cunt. She's soft and swollen and ready for me. She's arching into my touch while her hips gyrate, and I'm a weak man for her.

Another swivel of her hips and I fall to my knees, yanking that offending piece of lace with me. It tears, the sound loud inside the quiet room until...

"Jesus, Thiago...*fuck*!" It's her first scream for me after so long. Nirvana.

I bury my face between her legs. No waiting. No teasing. Fuck, no. I'm a man possessed with years' worth of hunger to make up for.

"My queen," I hiss against her tender flesh, licking a path from her entrance to clit and back again while I undo the button of my jeans. My cock is hard and throbbing, pulsing, and while I enjoy her sweetness, I lower the zipper and pull my length out, fisting it tightly. For every swipe of my tongue, it's a stroke. For every moan, it's a swipe across the swollen-to-the-point-of-pain head with my thumb, spreading the beads of pre-come down my shaft before pumping again.

I fuck her with my tongue slowly. Maddeningly. Punishing us both.

"Please."

Her hips buck and I turn my face, biting the inside of her left thigh. "Patience, baby girl. I'm in no rush."

A hiss escapes the back of her throat then, her fingers fisting my hair and tugging on the dark ends. "Can't wait. I need—"

"Me," I snarl, lip curling over my teeth, and I refocus my attention on what's mine. What she gave me and I'll be the last to ever taste. To fuck. To love. "You need me, and I need you. No one else, Luna. We begin and end with each other."

"You left me," she hisses, pulling my face closer by the hold on my hair. It stings, her fingernails scratching my scalp, but I could give two royal fucks if she makes me bleed. I love her like this: wanton and desperate. Riding my tongue as I slip the tip inside her tiny hole. "How could you do that to me?"

"I'll make it up to you."

"How?" Luna's close, the way her breath catches and thighs tighten around my head tell me as much. "How do you make us right?"

"Like this." I sit back just as the first rush of wetness coats my tongue. The first few drops slide down my chin, and before my girl can protest, I release my cock and smack her clit with the same fingers that just a second ago were jerking my dick.

Her reaction is instant. She comes hard; head thrown back and eyes closed—with those lips I adore open in a silent scream.

"Beautiful," I croon, standing to my full height. My pants fall, pooling at my feet as I take her in—drink in the pure look of rapture on her exotic features. "But now it's my turn, Luna." With one of my hands, I pin both of hers before she can react. As she shivers, I press my hard body against hers. As another moan meets my ears, a shuddering breath leaves my chest. "Does that turn you on, baby girl? How much I want you?"

I'm on fire. Hurting. Unable to comprehend anything past the burning in my veins and the pulsing of my cock.

Her face turns, lips once again hovering, but I don't kiss them. Instead, I rock my hips, pushing my cock deeper into her stomach, leaving a trail of my essence over her skin.

"Thiago." My name tumbles from her lips like a mantra. A sacred prayer.

"Answer me, Miss Alejos. Admit that you'll always be my dirty little whore."

"Yes." But it's too low and I need more. Her admission needs to be loud enough that every neighbor on this floor can hear. Fuck that. Let the world know.

She's mine.

"Not enough."

Those brown orbs snap open and meet mine; in them, I see my future. Our life together. "I hate that I love you."

My lips crash to hers, and I release her hands so I can cradle the back of her neck, positioning her to my liking. We're passion and fire. We're licking and biting and drowning in everything that we've missed.

But then the other hand explores, caressing the tender skin of her breast before pinching a nipple. Her tiny gasp into my mouth is delicious, and I need more of that sound. How she whines after for more of my touch. Always so greedy.

On her next intake of air, I hoist her up and wrap those thighs around my waist. She's hot and right there, but I refocus on her breast, licking a path down her chin and neck, nipping my way down to her cleavage.

Her back arches in an offering and I accept, taking a tip between my teeth while twisting the other between two fingers. Wetness coats the trail leading to my cock, and I bite down hard. Her hips undulate, and I flick my tongue against the pebbled flesh.

"Just fuck me, Thiago. I need it." *Motherfucking finally.*

Her admission makes me feel one hundred feet tall.

"I've always loved that mouth of yours," I say against her supple flesh, giving the pebbled tip a final nip before releasing both. She trembles. Watches me. And I love it, that near crazed look in her eyes as I sweep the expanse of her midsection, fingers spread wide over each rib and lower. I'm reacquainting myself with her curves, paying homage to a body I've missed every night. Because since the age of eighteen, she slept in my bed up until a week before my arrest. When shit went down, I removed her from my life. Made sure that she couldn't be implicated or attached to me.

"I'm not going to beg."

"Just tell me what you need." I hold her above me, tip at her opening. "Say it again."

Luna is a siren, a beautiful demon sent to destroy me, and when she cups my jaw forcibly, the words *fuck me* slipping past her lips...

In one deep stroke, I bury myself to the hilt, ripping a scream full of pleasurable pain from her. *Christ,* she feels amazing. More than. This is my home and heart and everything good in my life. She's perfection. My queen.

The picture on the wall near her head falls and the glass shatters, a piece or two slicing my shin, but I don't stop. Instead, I pull out and drive back in with the same angry intensity. There's the sound of her wetness each time I enter; the slickness runs down my shaft and balls, soaking us both. There's the way her fingernails dig into my shoulder blades, breaking the skin as she holds on to me while I snap my hips into hers.

I can feel the few beads of blood as they roll down my skin.

I love how she tightens, swiveling to meet each of my punishing thrusts.

But more than anything, I love how she brings her mouth to my chin and bites down.

It's what I've been missing all these years. The feel of her slick cunt bouncing on my dick while her mouth is on my skin.

In and out, I ride her without mercy, getting lost in her body. Positioning my hips in a rough rhythm that causes her eyes to roll back and walls to tighten around my dick. And while I fuck her, I don't stop looking at her.

Memorizing every feature. Counting the small smattering of freckles over the bridge of her nose that she hates and I find adorable.

I've missed you. "Open your eyes, Luna."

She does as I ask, her chocolate orbs heavy-lidded. "I'm so close, baby."

That word. The term of endearment. Four letters.

It shatters and puts me back together again.

Releasing her hip, I bring a hand to cup the back of her neck. "I love you, Luna." Her walls squeeze me at that, tightening to almost the point of pain while I peck those kiss-swollen lips. Once, twice, I sweep across them —back and forth before nipping the top one. "I'll be yours in this life and every reincarnation that follows."

Lips parting, I see the unspoken reply. Her desire to say the words back, but the sweetness of her breath grazes my mouth and I tighten my hold, angling her to my liking. Her own tongue peaks out, swiping her bottom lip and the very edge of mine.

"Kiss me." It leaves her on a throaty moan, and I give in without a second thought because I know my girl. Know that Luna's fighting a war within herself—heart over mind—on how to accept my presence back into her life, and this is her giving an inch. It's her olive branch, and I take it. I'll give her the world if she so much as asks, and on her next intake of breath, my mouth slants over hers while my hips pick up the pace. While our tongues battle for domination, I bring my hand on her hip between us and circle her clit. *"Please."*

"That's it, baby girl. Fuck, you feel so good." Tight little circles, three of them, and her walls tighten. They pulse—massaging my cock while my eyes roll back. Luna's milking me, placing me a hair's breadth from the edge, and then she tips me over with a tiny little mewl. It's her tell. My favorite sound in the world. "Son of a bitch," I hiss out from between clenching teeth, slamming in a final time to the hilt as I spill inside of her.

"I can feel you, Thiago. *Oh, God.*"

Rope after rope fills her pussy and I press my palm down against her clit, rubbing her in time with every pulse of my release. "Come for me, Luna. Give me what's mine." Slick with her juices and my come, I pull out just enough that I can bring two fingers down on her clit and tap the sensitive bundle of nerves. Her thighs around my waist tremble, and I do it again. Harder. Enough that the stings cause her mouth to slacken and a soundless scream to escape as her release coats my cock.

We're a mess and panting and I bury my face in the crook of her neck, scraping my teeth over her collarbone as the pulsing—tightening around my length—pulls forth another violent wave of pleasure from me. My fingers hold her hips in place, riding out the second wave in agonizingly slow strokes while her moans turn to whimpers.

It takes a few minutes for her breathing and mine to slow, for the shudders to cease and the deep-seated euphoric feeling of exhaustion to take hold, but when it does, I'm also reminded of another part of us that I've been without for too long:

The after.

That time between coming down from the natural high and the nap she always takes after. And when her body slumps in my hold, I know exactly where I'm heading next.

Luna's room is at the very end of the hall. Even from my jail cell, I took care of what's mine, and her apartment is the best.

Largest bathroom.

Largest bedroom.

The latter is where I'm heading, and it's the right choice because a second or two later there's a low snore from her. It's tiny and cute and it fills my chest with another emotion altogether.

I'm finally home.

Luna

I'M ROUSED FROM sleep by kisses on my shoulder and the warmth of a hard body behind me. I'm disoriented and stay still; I have no clue what time it is, and it's something that, along with the soreness between my thighs, scares me. Freaks me out.

But then I hear him.

That low, raspy voice that brings back the memories.

It brings back his near desperate touch after so long. His reverence the second our eyes met.

And now, there's the way he curses me in English and then prays to me in Spanish.

I'm his *weakness* and *Tesoro*.

"You're my motherfucking world, beauty." There's so much emotion in those words, and tears spring to my eyes. More so when Thiago's lips kiss an addition to my tattoo collection that he hasn't seen. Or at least, I don't think he's paid attention to.

It's another mark that represents him. It exposes my weakness.

A pair of MMA gloves like the ones he uses in fights; the difference is the heart at the center where the real pair has his name.

Christ, I want to contradict him. Deny and rage and let go of five years' worth of loneliness, but I don't. I can't.

Not when his arm around my waist tightens and I'm once again drowning in us. In memories that are both painful and a blessing. Not when that same mouth sweeps across my shoulder blade while whispering my name like a blessed mantra.

Thiago's words become a faint whisper then and I can't make out what he's saying, and stupidly, my heart tells me to revel in the moment and forget what brought us here.

And more importantly, I listen.

Against better judgment, I melt into the broad chest pressed against my back and let nostalgia kidnap my senses.

This has always been my favorite place to be and Thiago knows this. It's been our ritual after an encounter like the one we had a while ago. Because after sex, after claiming my body as his, the ruthless killer likes to cuddle. He loves my body against him, fingertips caressing my skin while whispering filthy nothings in my ear.

It's a weakness and need, and I've yearned for another moment like this one. It's why I stay quiet. Why I swallow back my emotions while closing my eyes.

I'm not ready to hash it out.

I'm not ready to send him away.

So, I let his warmth and masculine scent take me under. Let his touch relax me while I pretend it's another place and time. When we were happier. Heading toward a long and happy future together.

I've missed you so much.

It doesn't take long for his rhythmic caresses to become faint—soft. They lull me into a state of complete relaxation, and just before sleep takes me under, I hear his low chuckle. "I've missed you too, beauty. Stubbornness and all."

THE NEXT TIME I open my eyes the room is dark and the bed's empty.

My sheets are cold and the apartment quiet.

And yet, the scent of his cologne embraces every square inch inside the room.

I feel him and don't; it's a limbo I recognize. One that stole months of my life after his arrest and then sentencing. Those days blended into each other, where nothing made sense and I couldn't process my new life.

A *me* without him.

"Damn you, Thiago," I hiss under my breath, ignoring the discomfort and my nakedness while scrambling into a sitting position. My mounting ire doesn't care if I should be reaching for the Tylenol bottle instead of a robe; all I know is that he isn't here.

That he left me again without explanation.

Throwing my legs over the edge of the bed, I stand without looking at the clock or grabbing my phone. Instead, I put on a silk wrap and rush out of the room like a demon out of hell and straight into almost complete darkness. The only source of light is coming from the moonlit sky through the sliding glass door.

An open sliding glass door.

The further I walk, a soothing, salty breeze follows, sweeping through the living room. I follow its path, one foot in front of the other until I'm standing in a doorway with a vast view of the open water off Brickell.

It's beautiful but missing someone, and once again a pang of loneliness hits me in the chest. My balcony is empty, crushing my hope, and I step out onto the veranda while staring ahead.

Is that all he came for?

Is that all I've become?

I'm trying to put my emotions into perspective. I'm trying to understand why I let this happen.

Insecurity is a heinous bitch and I hate her with the passion of a million keyboard warriors.

"I'm an idiot." Leaning with my elbows on the railing, I breathe in and out slowly. Once, twice...six times, I don't stop until the lump in my throat recedes, and mentally repeating *this is not my fault* helps.

"I'm here."

"Fuck!" I yelp, clutching my chest as I whirl around to find him in the doorway, a bottle of beer in his hand. At once, the reproach on my tongue dies and I'm swept away by his handsome features. Even fully dressed, the man is dangerous for me.

Thiago Rivera De Leon is tall, dark, and wickedly handsome. He's all muscles and tattoos. He's the promise of nirvana and heartbreak all rolled into one.

The best of everything. What you shouldn't want but can't walk away from.

His face is partially hidden by the shadows of the night, while his jaw and lips curl up at the corner into a sinful smirk. His eyes have this glowing effect in the moonlight, and they shine with mirth and appreciation.

They roam my body from head to toe, the near-nakedness that is silhouetted by the same moon his focal point. He sees me. The want is in his stare.

And if I don't stop this—us—I'll find myself on my knees worshipping at his throne.

"Stay." It leaves me in a shaky voice.

"Why?" Thiago takes a single step forward and once again, I'm a tumultuous rainbow of emotions—wants and needs and truths that make me weak and at the same time stronger because he's here.

I can stand without him, I've proven as much, but just having him close brings forth a part of me I'd shut down years ago.

"Because you owe me this."

All amusement falls from his face and those hazel eyes pierce mine. "There's so much I need to make amends for."

"Then you can start by giving me a minute while waiting in the living room."

"Is that what you need?"

"It's part of what I deserve."

"Okay, beautiful. No argument from me, but..." he trails off and my lips part, the *but what* sitting on the tip of my tongue as he bends at the waist to place his bottle down on the floor. Then, I blink, and he's sauntering across the space dividing us. His swagger is sexy, and so is the way he doesn't ask for permission when stealing a kiss. One second I'm cursing his handsome face, and the next I'm melting into him as his warm lips meet mine and a hand cups the back of my neck.

It's soft and sweet and torture all at once. It's small nibbles and a caressing tongue against my own. The cold beer only enhances his natural decadence—a unique taste that I've missed.

Dreamed of.

Passion ignites in my veins and I tremble, hands fisting his shirt while he holds me just as tight. Chest to chest. His breathing and mine in sync.

"Thiago," I say. It's breathless and I can't take back the neediness that seeps through each letter. Loving—belonging to this beautiful sinner will only continue destroying me, and it's inevitable.

"*Fuck*, baby girl." It rumbles through his chest; the vibration causes my thighs to press together. He notices this and slows the kiss against my protest, nibbling on my bottom lip while his hand—the one on my neck— keeps me in place. I'm being denied and the pout that follows is almost embarrassing. "If we don't stop, Luna, I'm going to strip you. I'm going to put you on your knees, and I'll let this pouty *mouth...*" he accentuates the word with a swipe of his tongue across the abused flesh "... kiss my cock before I slip inside and let you reacquaint yourself with my weight on your tongue." A shiver rushes through me, and my nipples, the stiff little satin- covered peaks, rub against his chest. "I'm seconds away from mounting you, my queen. From fucking you on all fours with the night's sky and the open water as our backdrop. Is that what you really want?"

"You know what my answer would be."

"Just a second ago you were telling me to give you a minute."

"You knew what kissing me would do."

Thiago nods and the hand on my neck skims from cheek to jaw, his thumb rubbing across my mouth. "But how angry would you be afterward if I didn't step away now?"

"Very."

"That's why that kiss was just to tide us over." His smile is sad but understanding. He's giving me what I need even if my body rebels against the very notion. "I'll be inside waiting. Take your time."

"Okay." That's all I can say, and with one last look, he leaves me to my thoughts. Thoughts that are chaotic and ever changing. One second I'm that girl—the one head over heels in love, but then just as fast I'm angry and bitter. Two sides of a coin with no place to land because either way it falls will hurt. "I need to be honest with him," I mutter low, rubbing my cheek where his hand had been. "It's all I can be."

A moment, a deep breath in, and I turn to face that open glass door. Standing there, I square my shoulders and fight back my desires to forgive and forget. To start over without any more delays.

My heart wants him, but my mind can't stop torturing me with a singular word: distrust.

Thiago's distrust didn't allow me to stand by his side during a challenging time.

Thiago's distrust didn't allow us to face this bump in the road together.

He didn't trust *me* enough to stay.

Luna

A TRUTH I can't ignore, and it hurts.

Internally, I crumble where I stand, but on the outside my posture stiffens. In the blink of an eye I go from aroused to exhausted. From happy to near angry tears.

My chest expands and the scent of him surrounds me—even the small breeze coming off the water can't dilute its effect, something that further incenses me.

In the time that he went inside and I turned around, I've become a lit fuse and I stomp inside, hellbent on getting answers. "Why?"

"Take a seat, Luna."

"Don't tell me what to do, Leon."

"Been a while since you've called me by my last name. I've missed it." Alluding to my use of Leon when angry doesn't help his case. Neither does his small smirk.

I watch him through narrowed eyes. "Why?"

"Sit." Thiago isn't moved by my annoyance and pats the cushion of the chair across from his, right beside a table where an ice-cold Corona waits. "Take a sip, breathe, and I'll truthfully answer anything you want."

"I'm not playing—"

"I know. Just humor me, bebe."

With a huff, I walk over, sit, and then cross my legs. I make sure the material of my robe exposes my upper thighs and covers where his eyes wander to continuously. "Talk."

He licks his lips. "Where do you want me to start?"

Pausing with the bottle at my lips, I raise a brow. "At the beginning."

"That night?"

"Make me understand, Thiago," I say after swallowing, my tone a bit biting. "Why would you try to make me believe you cheated?"

"It started three weeks before the night you walked in on me with Amberlyn." I give him a blank stare. There's no reaction from me; I already know that nothing happened. "Do you remember the commotion downstairs and my having to leave?"

I'm nodding before he finishes. It was an ordinary Saturday evening and we were getting ready to go to our favorite club for a night out when screams rent the air. His mother was angry, crying, and Thiago left without so much as an explanation. No one talked about or explained what was happening; his parting words were spoken through gritted teeth and over his shoulder. *Don't leave the premises, Luna. Code Black.*

That meant a loved one was hurt. It meant total lockdown.

Thiago was going to take over soon, but his father still held the position as head. And as such, Ivan and Orlando were on their way home from a fishing trip with an associate. There was a car accident and a few injuries, but things changed after that night. He changed.

The next day, I went home to my parents' house with an empty promise to talk later. That "later" turned into three days without a word, a few excuses over being busy, and then total silence.

"I do."

"And you remember how Dad stepped down right after."

"Yes. The exchange of power happened within seventy-two hours."

Thiago rubs a hand down his face, the muscles in his forearm taut with tension. "There was never a car accident, Luna. He was shot." A gasp escapes me, but he stops me from asking questions with a shake of his head. "There was a hit carried out. They tried to kill him and failed."

"Who would do that?"

"I'm working my way through the list as we speak."

"I need more than that, dammit. Who?"

"You do, but I'm asking for time."

"Give me a good reason as to why I should do give you anything."

"Because there was another attempt made while I was in jail and this one was—"

"Maritza." He gives me a quizzical look, but I take a moment to gather my thoughts. Beer in hand, I take a deep pull while wishing it was something stronger, something to numb me before the pain of what lies ahead hits me in the chest. Those few seconds also help me piece together what I've always found odd. "Your mom called me two years ago and told me to be careful, that she had this bad feeling nagging at her right before her birthday. And you know how she is?"

"I do."

"Once something is off, it's time to be on alert. The woman is rarely wrong, and I listened." Closing my eyes for a second, I take in a deep breath and let it out slowly. "We talked every day, you know. We even met up for lunch on her birthday, but the next thing I know, Ivan's calling to inform me she fell and couldn't see me. We never made plans after that, and this explains so much."

"I told her to stay away."

"Why would you do that?" That stings—cuts deep, and I press my free hand down over my chest. "Do you know how much I've missed her? Needed her when—"

"Keeping you out of the picture wasn't easy, baby girl. Not on them. Not on me. Not on you…" Leaning toward me, Thiago takes the bottle from me, places it on the table, and then takes my hands in each of his. I don't fight him. I don't so much as move while he gives each a squeeze because I'm almost afraid that if I pull away, he'll stop talking and I need the truth more than my own dignity. "I know this is hard, but I had no other choice. Not when I wasn't here to protect you, and keeping you safe is all that's ever mattered to me. Not when it was one of mine, someone I considered family, that pulled the trigger on Mom."

That confession stuns me. Takes away every single recrimination and leaves me shaken. My mind is racing and my heart aches.

"Who?" is all I manage through the sudden lump in my throat. *Who stole you from me?*

"Ismael *was* the sicario."

"Ismael?" I ask, and I also don't miss the emphasis on the word was. Past tense. Not that he deserves anything less after the Leon family took him in. After Thiago treated him like another little brother. "Why the hell would he do that? Who would dare—"

"Money." There's a slight tick of his jaw and I still in my seat, waiting for the next invisible blow. "They dangled a diamond-studded carrot and he bit. It was one of Senot's men that made the call on both accounts."

"Senot? You…that…Thiago, he's my dad's best friend!"

"Does the name Alfredo Gaytan ring any bells, Luna?" he spits out, dropping my hands and rising to his full height. It's intimidating, but I don't shrink back. And if there's one thing I still trust about the man, it's that he would never lay a hand on me. So I watch him, never taking my eyes off him as he walks away and over to the open glass door, his hands clenching at his sides. "Does it?"

"Yes." Because it does. I've seen the man a few times here and there over the years, especially when Jasmine Senot is present at functions. He's her guard, a job that never made much sense to me when no one really cares about the mayor's wife. They dislike him at times, but she's left alone to be clueless and pretentious. "How is he involved? He's Jasmine's shadow."

"He hired both men."

"Both men?" Christ, nothing makes sense. How much has been kept from me?

"The night Dad was shot and we covered with a car crash, the hitman failed because Ivan reacted at the right moment. He pushed the old man down, covered him the best he could, and then unloaded a magazine in the direction the asshole was shooting from." There's a tinge of shame and anger in his tone. His posture is tense, muscles bulging underneath the fabric of his shirt. Even the tattoo sleeve seems to portray his ire; all black with soft shadowing to contrast the features of this ominous painting representing death. "This happened after the fishing trip, late at night as they were leaving Versailles. Video of the parking lot shows them parting ways with our visitors, walking toward their car after theirs exited the lot, and then three gunshots. The first two missed and the last shattered Dad's knee."

"Christ," I breathe out, feeling more than a little overwhelmed. My mind is going in so many directions that I just don't know what to think. "Why would Gaytan do that? Do you think it's a setup?"

He senses my distress and looks over, the shadow on his face making his eyes almost seem glowing in the moonlight. "Not at first. Unfortunately, and I know you don't want to accept this, but I wouldn't make an accusation like that without solid proof."

"At first?"

"When the guy failed to execute Dad, he was disposed of by Ismael and the body placed inside my home. He was dismembered, with bullet holes that came from Ivan's gun—recovered at the scene—but pinned on me. That's why I served time. Not for any of the shit I've done, but because someone wanted me out of the picture."

"Who?"

"The list is long, but Senot is at the top."

"I'm not saying he wouldn't, but—"

"Luna..." The way he says my name, the sadness in his voice, makes my heart clench. "Baby girl, I've had the video of this transaction taking place outside of The Acere Bar, *my* fucking bar on 36th street, for years. Since the night before Ivan picked up the traitor and took him offshore on holiday. They, Gaytan and Ismael, were caught discussing payment and their target: my mother. Their faces are clear to see, and ironically enough, all of this on the side of the building where everyone believes there are no cameras."

"I'm sorry, Thiago. So sorry this is where we stand."

He turns to fully face me. "It's not your fault."

"No. It's not." Standing from my seat, I slowly make my way across the room to him. Because while I am still mad at the way he pushed me aside—made me doubt us—what's been done is more than a disrespect. It's personal. I can see it in his eyes how Ismael's betrayal cut deep, and while the world might not see his heart, it's always been open to me. Reaching him, I wrap my arms around his midsection and bury my face in his chest. "You have every right to feel as you do and handle their punishment as you see fit, Thiago. I'll never begrudge you that."

"But can you—"

"I wasn't done." Inhaling deep, I take his masculine scent deep into my lungs and tears spring to my eyes when I feel his lips at the crown of my head, he too breathing me in. It's sad and telling. Right now there's too much for me to process, and forgiveness isn't something I can promise. *I need time.* "I'll give you that things were hectic. That you were busy keeping everyone safe, but that still doesn't explain—why shut me out? Why abandon me?"

Two fingers appear in my line of sight a second before he's tipping my face up to his. He doesn't kiss me, but for a moment just stares. Eyes locked and my heart racing, I gift myself the luxury of getting lost in his hazel orbs. The world around us moves, time continues to tick, but when we are like this, nothing registers.

"...kill you."

"What?" I missed everything he said except for those two words and I step back, disentangling myself from his arms. "Repeat that?"

"You were the original second hit." That realization is my breaking point. My body begins to shake, and my knees feel weak. "I broke us to protect you."

"Leave."

"Bebe, we should—"

"No, Thiago. I need you to leave." Turning from him, I walk toward the front door and open it, holding on to the knob to avoid grabbing him. He's behind me; the sound of his heavy footsteps and dominating presence gives me goose bumps.

His hand grips my forearm, but he doesn't turn me around. Just holds on. "Luna."

Just my name. A raspy reverence.

"Time," I say, voice low yet firm. There's no anger, but more of an overwhelming need to breathe without his presence choking me. Distracting me. "Give me time to think and make sense of everything on my own, because right now I'm lost. In less than twenty-four hours you've come back and brought with you a truth I've both longed for and at the same time, feared. Please, just leave and wait for me to be ready."

"Okay." Then his body is right behind mine; heat sears my near-naked form as his broad chest presses into my back, his lips skimming my temple. "I'll leave, but this isn't the end, nor will it be for long. I love you, Luna. Please remember that if nothing else."

A kiss to my cheek.

Another whisper of my name.

And then he's gone, leaving me an overwhelmed ball of emotions that leads me on shaky legs to my kitchen. There's only one thing I need and without pause, I open my fridge and pull out the bottle of Mamajuana I keep inside. The Brugal rum and spice mixture has to help—make me forget for a little while the chaotic mess my life is.

Twisting the top off, I bring the bottle to my lips and take a large sip. It doesn't do more than burn a tiny bit going down, and before the mellow warmth can spread, I take three more pulls the size of a shot to speed the process along.

The alcohol rushes through me and on an empty stomach, the effects start after another minute. Once the buzz kicks in, I walk back to the living room and while taking a smaller sip, I park my butt on an oversized chair and make a silent toast.

For the Leons.

For my broken heart.

For my own list.

Because Thiago is right about one thing; revenge will be sweet.

THIAGO

IT'S BITTERSWEET PULLING into the driveway of my childhood home thirty minutes later. I've missed the place and the people inside, but my mind is elsewhere. With her.

Always Luna.

Anger and hurt are a deadly combination, and my queen is drowning in both. They're feelings I expect, know she'll hide behind until ready, but I won't let her wallow in.

Hate me now, but our love will never die.

When I left, the betrayal—the fear I played upon that day more than five years ago—had reopened like a wound, and she's dealing with the aftermath. Confronting what she's buried deep inside all these years while accepting the reality she was ignorant to.

Her words cut, but I'll proudly wear the scars. It's a necessary evil in order to heal and let go of the past. She'll have her moment, a chance to clear her head, but then I'm coming back.

Turning off the ignition, I undo my seatbelt and open the door, placing a single foot on the pavers below when the front door is thrown open. At the entrance is a short Latina in her early fifties with a megawatt grin on her face. Her chin quivers, and she rushes down the three steps, almost tripping in her haste.

"Mi hijo!" she yells out, tears running down her cheeks. Her light hazel eyes with a touch of green in them are taking me in—from head to toe—and cataloging the subtle differences. I was never a small guy, my stature and love for mixed martial arts kept me in shape, but with not a lot to do in jail I picked up another hobby. Lifting weights kept me focused. Kept me from snapping the neck of every cocky cop who quickly learned to lower their heads and keep walking. "Orlando, hurry up. My baby is here."

Those words have barely left her lips when she crashes into me. Her arms go around my midsection and a sob shakes her much smaller frame.

I hug her back just as tight. "Mom, I'm okay. I'm here."

She slaps my arm and then goes back to hugging me. "Let me have my moment."

A chuckle escapes. "Please, take your time."

"Always my smart ass child," my vieja says, and I can hear the pain in her voice. Feel the tears soak my shirt. "But these five years were hard, Thiago. What those assholes did—"

"No more of that tonight." At my interruption, she looks up with a raised brow. Because no matter how old you are or how feared you are, Cuban mothers demand respect. However, when you're her oldest and favorite, you get away with certain things. No flip flops will be thrown at my head nor will a flying hand go to the back of my head. Instead, there's the tremble at the corner of her lips and then the full-on smile when I kiss her forehead. "I love you, Mom. Missed you and your cooking."

"Oh my God! I'm sorry, kid." And just like that she's flustered and moving back, heading back inside while my father stands at the top of the landing with a smile. Maritza De Leon is on a mission now and doesn't stop until she reaches the door; there, she turns to look back from over her shoulder. "Your favorite on the menu; white rice with black beans, picadillo, and sweet plantains. I'll be in the kitchen getting you a plate…give me ten."

"Sounds perfect." Not that she heard me. The flash that nearly tackled me is gone and the door slamming behind her is all the proof I have that she was ever here.

"That woman is something else." The admiration in my father's tone makes me look over and I catch the smirk on his face. Orlando De Leon has always been larger than life in my eyes. A man of his word and loyal to those he loves. A man that will end a life without a second thought and then go home and kiss his wife goodnight.

I lean back against the side of the car. "Quit being a creeper, Viejo."

"Kid, it was cute when you were younger, but quit calling us old." The hold he has on his cane is firm and there is very little hobble in his step. He begins to walk toward me, and I don't argue. He's a proud man, and this is his way of showing me he's okay. "Because this old bastard can still kick your ass."

Smirking, I raise a brow. "I'd like to see you try."

"Punk."

"So testy."

"Come here, asshole." Dad stops in front of me, pulling me into a bone-crushing hug. "Good to have you home, son. We've missed you."

"Miss you, too. All of you." My arms wrap around him and hold him just as tight for a minute before stepping back. "How has she really been? Anything I should know about?"

"Your mother is a warrior, Thiago. A rock." He looks behind him toward the house and smiles. "She's angry because of what's been done and expects answers soon. This is your warning. The questions will come."

"I know." As soon as the last word leaves my mouth, both demeanors change. His and mine. The seriousness of the situation and what's to come isn't a game. Someone tried to hurt us—kill and dismantle us—and it's not something I will ever let go of. "Ismael is dead."

"We kept him alive for you. Trust me, I'll share the video with you at another time of his stay with us." In his brown eyes there is no warmth; the instincts of a killer are very much present. "That hijo de puta fucked with the wrong man's wife. He was lucky I left him for you—my wrath would've dismembered him an inch of flesh at a time while feeding the bite-sized pieces to the local predators."

"Have Georgie and Kline gotten bigger?" Those two gators behind the house do come in handy from time to time. "When I left, they were about five feet give or take."

"About eight now."

"Good." Rubbing my chin, I consider my options when it comes to the next name on my list. His connection to a certain family. His loyalty to the whore he fucks behind her husband's back. "Stop feeding them for a few days."

"Yes, sir." There's a bit of a chuckle in his tone, but I can also see the pride on his face. And while they kept a firm hold in my absence—Ivan and Dad—I'm now here to right this wrong. To send a message to anyone opposing our control over the city of Miami. "Anything else for your first night back? Which we didn't expect you for, by the way. We thought you and Luna would—"

"She needs time, Viejo." Throwing an arm over his shoulder, I turn us toward the stairs and begin to ascend. "A lot was hidden and now thrown at her. Luna just needs to cope and wrap her head around the truth."

"You make sure Luna's here on Saturday?"

"I'm picking her up before five."

"Good." he says, voice firm. "She belongs here with us. She's one of us."

I rub my other hand over my chest, where her name is etched into my skin. "Something else I'll be making official soon enough."

Mom appears at the doorway and waves us on before the man can comment. "Food's getting cold. Hurry and wash up."

"You heard your wife. Move it or I'll carry you."

"Try it and I'll shoot you." Raising his cane, he tries to hit me with the solid teak end, but I duck out of the way. "Now go and eat. We can continue our talk after dinner. There's something I want to show you."

"Should I be concerned?"

"It's about your cousin Jadiel and his sister's boyfriend."

"Talk business later and let's get him fed, Orlando. That mierda he's been forced to eat the last few years is unacceptable." At Mom's reproach, I give the old man a nod to let him know I heard and agree. We'll talk. I'll assess.

And God help that singao and whatever crap he's caught up in now.

"THAT WAS AMAZING, VIEJA. THANK YOU," I say, sitting back and patting my stomach after my second plate of home cooking. It's one of my favorite meals and a hot seller in two of our restaurants. "That hit the spot, and it'll probably put me to sleep in a little bit."

My phone atop the table vibrates then and I pick it up, the name Malcolm Asher flashing across the screen. It's his second call in the span of thirty minutes and I pick up while holding a finger up to my mother. Her nose and mouth scrunch up and her chin juts out in the *who is it* expression. I mouth *Malcolm* and she goes back to the counter near the stove where a large flan sits and coffee is percolating.

"News travels fast, Asher?" I say in greeting before taking a sip of my drink and placing it back atop the table.

"When dangerous men are released? Faster than you think." He chuckles, what sounds like a chainsaw in the background. There are birds in the distance; it doesn't sound one bit like he's in the city. "I'll be heading your way tomorrow. Are you available?"

I scratch my jaw, contemplating my plans. "After midday and not for long."

"I won't hold you up, then, but we do need to talk." There's something in his tone, an almost urgent quality—as if he needs to do this but rather be elsewhere—that catches my attention.

"Then I'll see you tomorrow."

"Thank you."

The tone of the call isn't a social one and I hang up, placing the device on the table before looking toward my father who's standing at the fridge, beer in hand. "Asher will be here tomorrow."

"For the reunion?" he asks, taking a sip. "Didn't your mother tell you it's been pushed back to Saturday?"

Before he's done, I'm shaking my head. "Business, and I have a feeling this has everything to do with the Fosters."

"Why don't you invite him to stay a few days." This time it's Mom who speaks. "You know I'd love to have everyone over." There are a few associates that I welcome into our homes, those that have been in business with us for years, and Malcolm is one of those. A crazy fucker, but honest and dependable.

"I'll extend the request."

"It's been so long since I've seen him and Mariah. Since you've been able to relax, Thiago…have a drink and a decent meal with the family. The bullshit they put you through and…" Mom trails off as her bottom lip trembles, a small sob causing her body to shake, and at once, I stand from my chair. The legs of the chair scrape against the travertine tiles before tipping over in my haste to reach her. She's across the large kitchen and standing by the sink, gripping the dishrag tightly in one fist as she stares at me. "Everything was a mess and I worried—prayed every single night that Papa Dios would keep you safe."

"He did. I'm home, and everything will be okay."

"Ivan hasn't stopped beating himself up over everything and I couldn't help him. Or you." Dad tries to grab her before I do, but the shake of my head stops him. He slips out of the room after giving me a pointed look, but I ignore him and focus on Mom. Those watery hazel eyes and the sadness in them cement my resolve to bury every motherfucker involved with my incarceration. "I'm sorry."

Two words. Two simple motherfucking words, and they are the wrong ones.

They stop me in my tracks just a few steps from her. Close enough that I grab the rag in her hand and toss it before taking both her hands in mine and closing my eyes. Then, I breathe in and out.

I keep in mind where I am and why.

God, not today.

I'm not asking for patience nor understanding. I'm not asking for anything but the will to calm myself while I reign in my sudden bout of ire. Because I'll be damned if this woman ever apologizes to me without just cause, especially for shit she has nothing to do with.

A couple of seconds and my eyes snap open, nostrils flaring as I say the next words slowly. As calmly as I can muster. "I never want to hear you say that again, Maritza De Leon." What I just did is a cardinal sin for Hispanics everywhere. We don't use our parents' Christian names. Never.

They are Mom and Dad until *they* die and even then, there is no pass go and collect fifty. "Understood."

However, her reaction is worthy of whatever reproach I receive next, especially as her shoulders square and chin tips up. "I'm going to pretend I didn't hear that."

"And I'm going to pretend you forgot who you are."

"I know damn well who I am, Thiago." Her hands slip from mine and she reaches up to cup my chin. "Don't confuse my tears for anything other than anger for my family."

"Good." I kiss her forehead and then pull away, standing to my full height. Her eyes narrow for a second as I watch, impatience starting to color her features. "Because I need you strong for what's to come."

"This family stands behind you."

"I know."

"Are you prepared to make those decisions when the time comes? No matter who it is?" She's alluding to the Senots and maybe even Luna's family, but my suspicions run deeper. Much deeper, and maybe even closer than they think.

"I am."

Her head tilts to the side, studying me. "Something else is on your mind, Thiago." Not a question, but more of a perception.

"There is, but I need you calm and collected first."

Without a word, she walks over to the sink and opens the faucet, letting a bit of water pool in her palms before bringing both wet hands to her face. She does this a few times while I watch, and the old man sneaks a look in the room while her back is turned.

He mouths the words *dead motherfuckers* as I wave him off with two fingers. She's his wife, and I get his need to step in, but I have the perfect way of distracting her.

"Whatever you need, I can handle."

"Luna."

From the corner of my eye I see my father throw his hands up as if saying *hallelujah* while she begins to smile. A devious one at that. "Whatever it is, consider it done."

"Good, because that's one woman we can't show any signs of weakness to." At that, Mom throws her head back and laughs. Her entire body shakes and when she looks at me again, her red-rimmed eyes shine with amusement now. "She's as stubborn as you are and is angry. I get that. I accept my part in the mess I didn't originally create but made worse by pushing her away instead of explaining. However, and this is where I need you; there are things that you can explain woman to woman that will come off as condescending from me. She doesn't need for me to explain her role or the difficulty of war, but you can listen and give her guidance as someone who knows this life."

"Her forgiveness won't come easily."

"I know, and that's another battle I'm prepared to bleed for."

THIAGO

I
T'S A LITTLE after ten a.m. and I'm standing outside her door, breakfast in hand. I know what she likes, what she'll need, and can motherfucking guarantee that her hangover will thank me for the gesture. Because I know my queen, and the Mamajuana she likes to keep in her fridge was pulled out last night. Just like I know she drank more than she first intended.

Her drink of choice, Brugal, is a traitorous bastard. The Dominican rum on its own is strong, but when steeped with this special blend of spices, it can knock you on your ass. There's no longer a harsh burn or taste and there in itself lies the problem; you don't feel it until it's too late.

"Rise and shine, baby girl," I say while making my presence known; three quick raps against the door and I hear movement from the inside. Nothing loud, but more like a distant grumbling, and I smile. Another hard knock and the word *motherfucker* follows shortly after.

"I'm coming!" Luna calls out, then there's a crash and the sound of glass meeting the floor seconds before the door is thrown wide open. My queen stands there with her eyes closed and a hand rubbing her right temple, face a little wet from washing. She's wearing an oversized shirt —*my* shirt from my time on our high school baseball team—and a grumpy expression.

No makeup and hair a mess, Luna is a vision and my cock swells, pressing against the inseam of my dark grey slacks since I'm not wearing any underwear. *Motherfuck* is right, and my need for another taste almost drops me to my knees.

So close to what's mine.

So close to my version of heaven.

It's also the second time she opens the door without looking, and her gun is nowhere in sight.

"Nat, I told you to please back—"

"Open your eyes, beautiful."

"Lord," she says while tipping her face up, "this is not the time for jokes."

"Never thought that a personal delivery of pastries from Vicky Bakery and a Starbucks coffee would be considered anything other than glorious. From what I remember—"

Luna holds her hand out, looking at me through narrowed slits. "Gimme and go."

"I want a kiss for my troubles."

"Thiago, I swear to God now isn't the time to mess with me." That small hand smacks my chest, and my cock gives another harsh jerk. I can feel the bead of pre-come at the very tip and bite back a groan when it rolls down the underside. "Hand them over."

"Which ones?" Lifting them out of her reach, I take a step forward. "Guava and cream cheese or just the quesito? Maybe you're in the mood for something a little more indulgent?"

Luna doesn't back away and that sweet, sleep-rumbled scent of her skin assaults my senses. "I'm not a toy, and you need to learn some patience."

"Love you too."

"I forgot how much of a morning person you are. *Stubborn too.*" The last part is mumbled under her breath, but I heard her loud and clear. Her sass is adorable. "Thank you for breakfast…yada yada…goodbye."

"I would believe the put-off act if there wasn't a smile curling at the edge of your lips."

There's a sound that leaves the back of her throat, this wild mixture of a scream and curse word, before she stomps back inside. I'm watching her sweet ass—following the naturally exaggerated sway of her hips—when she steps right over the small broken glass figurine that somehow managed to break a few steps from the doorway.

"Shit!" She hops on one foot, bringing her injured one up. Blood is already seeping from the cut, and before she can fully assess the damage, I'm dropping her breakfast on the accent table near us and then picking her up in two strides.

At first, she tries to fight my hold, but one kiss to her bare shoulder where my shirt has slipped off and a low *shhh* has her settling down.

Her kitchen isn't far from where we are and I walk over, placing her atop the cold granite counter. Luna sucks in a breath at the contact, but I don't acknowledge the sexy sound. Instead, I take her foot in my hand and place a kiss over the large hibiscus flower tattoo at the top. It's bright and large and holds a special meaning for the two of us.

In the large garden at the back of her parents' house a week after I met her, surrounded by this very flower, I stole my first taste of her lips. While Luna's father was at work and mother out shopping, I kissed her for almost an hour, hand on her perky tit, until we were both out of breath and smiling.

"Perv."

"For you, without an ounce of shame." The cut looks to be a little deep, but nothing that will require stitches. "Hold on and don't complain."

"What are you going to do?"

"Take care of my girl." Picking her up, I bring us to her large farmhouse sink and place her sideways atop the countertop with her foot inside the basin. She hisses when I turn the water on right over the cut, but it's a necessary evil in order to make sure there isn't any fragment of glass left inside. With the very tip of my pointer finger, I feel over the cut while washing away the small rivulets falling down her heel. "No glass inside and it isn't deep, baby girl, but you will need a Band-Aid."

"Thank you." Her voice is small and holds a tinge of fear, and I know it has everything to do with her lack of clothes and my proximity. She's not ready, and that's okay. I'm here to make my presence known and show that I'm not going anywhere. "My first-aid kit is in—"

"Drawer on the left side of the fridge." At my response, she gives me a quizzical expression. "You've always put one in that drawer, Luna."

"That's not true."

"Bebe…" I raise a brow and begin to tick off each place by wiggling one of her cute toes "…at my old penthouse, my parents' house, and yours. If you opened that drawer in particular after you've been around, there's a good chance you've moved it there or brought one with you."

"I—"

"Quit arguing and be a good patient." Turning the water off, I lean over and place a chaste kiss at the corner of her lips. "Stay put."

A nod is her response, but she doesn't question me when I walk out of the kitchen and toward the front door. There, I grab her breakfast, make sure the door is locked, and go straight for the magic drawer. Her eyes are on me the entire time, or more specifically, the bag in my hand, but I'm already grabbing the kit and turning back to her.

Then, there's a bit of trepidation as I place all of the items down beside her. "I should probably do this myself."

The "myself" has more to do with her dislike of pain and the one time I disinfected a cut by pouring alcohol straight into an open wound.

"Relax, Luna. This won't hurt."

"That's what you said last time when—" I silence her with a quick, harsh kiss as my mouth slants over hers, swallowing the gasp that escapes. This isn't slow or sweet; it's a claiming of those petal-soft lips, and a deep rumble builds in my chest when a soft mewl escapes from the back of her throat.

She gives in to my possessive need. To how my fingers wrap around the long strands of her hair, tipping her head back to my liking. The angle puts her at my mercy with her pretty little throat exposed, an expanse of skin that calls to me and I run my teeth down her chin and over the base.

"Fuck, Luna. Just fuck," I groan, licking her fragrant neck where her mouthwatering scent is the strongest. It's her and coconuts and this faint hint of lime that makes me throb against her cabinets. "You'll always be my biggest weakness and treasure. I love you more than my own life."

"This isn't taking care of my foot," she moans, the fingers of her left hand gripping my long-sleeved shirt right above where it's rolled at the elbow. It's pulling me closer. Holding me against her. "Maybe you should stop."

"I will." My teeth scrape across her collarbones. "I am."

"Please do."

"As you wish." Yet I don't move. Not yet. Instead, my hand caresses her leg from shin to thigh, gripping the firm flesh just shy of painful. "Right now."

Another nip and she lets out a sigh.

Another inch higher and the heat from her pussy sears me.

Another needy sound and I pull back, removing her grip on my shirt before grabbing the first-aid kit and opening it. Inside she has the basics and an addition that makes me chuckle.

"Not that funny, jerk." There's no real annoyance in her tone, though. The mirth is there and so is the bit of sparkle in her brown eyes that are looking at me with warmth. "You know I hate the alcohol wipes. They sting."

"So you decided to trade it for the smallest bottle of hydrogen peroxide I've ever seen?"

"Yes. No shame either." Luna's perfectly sculpted right brow rises; the look she's giving me would make a weaker man step back or fumble. Me, I like the challenge. The daring attitude. "It's painless and bubbles up to let me know I won't lose a limb. Win-win if you ask me."

Unscrewing the top of the bottle, I hold it over her injured foot before she can pull away. "I didn't, but I'll take your word for it."

"Jerk."

"More like Dr. Leon." Then I pour. She flinches a tiny bit and I raise my own brow, silently calling her out on the bullshit she spewed earlier. "Thought it didn't hurt?"

"Not as much," she spits through clenched teeth. "This time it did, though."

"Of course. It's a one-time thing." A little more of the hydrogen goes on the faintly bleeding wound. "Now, sit still and let me finish."

"Finish what?"

I don't answer her. Instead, I grab one of the cotton rounds inside of a small Ziplock bag and wipe the bit of blood still flowing. It's not a huge amount and the cut is as clean as can be. No glass or dirt and after drying it off, I open her antibiotic ointment, smearing a bit across the gash. It seals and no more drops of blood flow, letting me place a Band-Aid on.

The ones she has are...*entertaining*, to say the least.

SpongeBob. A lot of them. An obscene amount, and I grab one with the yellow sponge giving a cheesy grin to the wearer.

"There. All better." Lifting her foot out of the large farmhouse sink, I kiss the small bandaged cut before turning her to face me. Her legs go over the edge of the counter and I step between them. Then, we're face to face and I place a chaste peck to her lips. "How're you feeling, beautiful?"

"The truth?"

"Always."

"At peace for the first time in years."

Placing my forehead against hers, I close my eyes. "I've missed you too."

"Thiago, I'm not ready—"

"I know." Sliding my fingers from her calves to thighs, I grab one in each hand and easily lift her up. She wraps them around my waist, legs crossed at the ankles while I grab her breakfast with the hand not supporting her weight.

Her face burrows into my neck as I walk us out and I don't miss the tiny kiss she gives my neck. Pleasure rocks me at the simple gesture and my cock flexes against her heat, but neither of us comments on it.

We just enjoy the moment and then I hold her for a minute or two longer once I'm at the foot of her bed. Just standing with her in my arms is enough to get me by for the few days I'll be away.

Forty-fucking-eight hours of agonizing hell.

Bending at the waist, I place her on the mattress with the bag beside us. Once she's on, I point to the headboard. "Get situated while I take things out for you."

"I can do..." Luna trails off at the look I give her. Turning onto her hands and knees, the vixen crawls across the bed and it takes every bit of the near nonexistent strength I possess to keep me from following.

I grit my teeth.

I press down hard on my throbbing length to alleviate the pain.

Nothing works, and by the look on her face, the little brat knows exactly what she's doing to me.

"Shut it."

"I wasn't going to say anything."

"You just did."

"Can you feed me now?"

"One day soon you'll pay for that, beauty." Walking around the bed, I take my time and I also don't hide just how hard for her I am. Her eyes immediately drop and then widen before her small pink tongue makes an appearance. Right to left, my queen licks her bottom lip before taking the lush flesh between her teeth. "Eyes up here."

"Not apologizing." A hint of pink sweeps across her cheeks.

"Didn't ask you to." Opening the large plastic bag, I pull out a drink tray and the small box with her pastries. There are even a few toasted pieces of Cuban bread with butter and a pinch of salt still slightly warm inside of their aluminum foil wrapping. Everything is sealed and while the piping hot coffee kept every-thing warm, it's cooled enough to be drinkable. "Want me to grab you a plate?"

"Gimme."

"You'll get crumbs—"

"Clean later, eat now." As she says this, I pass over her salted caramel mocha latte. Her small hands wrap around the cup while I pull the comforter over her exposed legs. For my safety—sanity—not hers. "How is this the perfect temp?"

"Bought it hotter than hades so it'd be kid's temp by the time I got here. I remember your tricks."

She takes a sip, a small smile on her lips. "Good, because I really needed this."

"Glad I could offer you some comfort after a night of drinking."

"It was needed."

"That bad?"

"Memories, videotapes, and a visit from an ex will do that to a woman."

"I'm your always, not an ex." My phone vibrates inside my pocket and I pull it out, giving it a quick glance.

> Sir, just a reminder that Mr. Asher's plane is due to land soon. ~Miguel

"Everything okay?"

At her question, I pocket the device and nod. "Just have a meeting to attend." *Or several.*

"So soon?'

"Malcolm is flying in," I say, opening the box of pastries and placing them beside her on the bed. Her TV remote is also on the bed, but not within reach and I rectify that. "He needs to talk and said it was urgent."

"Be careful."

"Is that concern I detect in your tone?"

"Get out."

"You're adorable." Bending over, I tip her face up to mine with a finger and kiss her lips. A soft peck, and then I pull back. "Eat, relax, and then catch a nap. Be lazy, and I'll have dinner delivered tonight."

"That's not necessary—"

"I take care of mine. End of."

"But I'm…" she trails off, and we both know it's because she can't say the words.

"Not going to deny me." I can see the urge to do just that, to lie to me, but my queen remains silent instead. *Good girl.* "By the way, beautiful, Mom's expecting you this weekend. It's my welcome home and she wants the entire family there."

A flash of hurt crosses her features; I know being kept away hurt them both, but we need to start mending fences. She loves my mother and my mother adores her.

"I'm not sure that's a good idea. Not yet."

It's hard, but I hold back my amusement. I knew she'd say that. "She also sent a warning attached to that invite, babe, and if you're not ready by five on Saturday, she'll come pick you up herself."

Luna huffs, but there's no real anger there. "Maritza is more stubborn than you are."

"She is." Not going to refute that.

"What if you tell her I have plans with my parents?" At my incredulous look, her shoulders slump. "Never mind. That's a shit excuse and she'll never buy it."

"Exactly." It's hard, but I hold back a smirk. "I'll be here at four-thirty. Be ready."

"I'll drive myself and Natasha will be coming with me."

"I'll pick you up and Natasha can drive herself."

"Be reasonable!"

"Be happy that I'm not kidnapping you now and dragging you everywhere with me. I'm more than impatient to have you back where you belong. With me. With our family." Another kiss, I steal a quesito pastry, and then I'm walking out of the room. Her offended yell follows me out of her sanctuary and then apartment door. My beauty is still as stingy with her sweets now as I remembered, and I adore her all the more for it.

My Luna is hurt, but there. She's still the same girl I fell in love with.

THIAGO

"**H**E'LL BE LANDING soon, sir," Miguel says as I slip into the all-black SUV waiting for me outside of Luna's building. Leaving her again this soon isn't something I want, but I understand her need for space. To wrap her head around the truth, and while the choices I made cut deep, I always knew that I'd be back for her.

Nothing could keep me from taking care of her, and now that I'm free, I'll make her my wife.

"How soon?"

"ETA is thirty."

"Then I want to be walking inside in fifteen." Looking outside my window, I take in the blue waters glistening between two buildings as he pulls away from the curb. How the waves crash upon the rock formation that serves as a wall, leaving behind a fine sea mist in the area that infiltrates the senses and gives you a sense of calm that's fraudulent. The ocean isn't to be trusted.

It's volatile and unpredictable and a silent killer.

Moreover, it reminds me of the beautiful woman I left stewing in her emotions; peaceful yet dangerous. Luna is my perfect storm.

Her soft face this morning after a drunken trip down memory lane made me remember nights out partying in the past.

The warm smile she naturally gifted me as I cleaned the small cut made my heart thump.

The way she burrowed her face into my neck, admitting in her own way that she missed me—made my cock throb.

"And will we be entering from the back entrance or...?" His question pulls me from my thoughts, and I meet his eyes in the rearview mirror. He knows where my mind is. He knows *her*.

I smirk, brow raised. "The front. I'm not hiding."

"I'll make the necessary arrangements." We're at a red light near the entrance to I-95 and he pulls out his phone, sending out a quick message before placing the device inside the vehicle's cup holder. A ping comes through a second later and he spares the screen no more than a glance before nodding. "No traffic and an announcement has been made. Just walk through."

"Thank you, old man." A car pulls up alongside us and the driver's completely unaware of my being. Maybe it's idiocy. Carelessness. Or maybe it's the conversation he's having with a woman, Mrs. Senot herself, and it seems heated. His hand slams down on the steering wheel while she frowns, eyes flicking around to make sure no one's taken notice of Antonio's hostile, emotional state.

However, my father-in-law is unmistakable in his pompous suit, now waving a hand in the air as the light turns green and Miguel places his foot on the accelerator. And that's when his face turns, and he notices my driver. He knows Miguel and at once turns a bit further in his driver side seat to look into the back windows that will never show my identity. The tints won't allow it, and even though I'm tempted to lower my window and extend a greeting, I just watch his minor freak-out. *Guilty is a very ugly color, old man.*

"My pleasure, kid." At Miguel's response, I turn my attention back to him. He's the only one outside of my parents that can call me that, and it's because I see him as family. Not that he would in front of anyone; he lives by a code of respect. The man's worked for us long enough and has been more than loyal; I owe him. It's because of him that my mother is alive and without a single scratch. Miguel maneuvered them away, broke through an abandoned building with the front of her armored vehicle before taking a swift right that knocked Ismael off his bike while knocking him unconscious. "It's good to have you home. We've all missed you and Luna."

"Miguel, what you've done for—"

"I'd die for the Leons." I give him a nod because words aren't needed. I know where he stands. I trust him. Miguel focuses on the drive while I dissect the reason for the visitor touching down in my city within the half hour.

The world and its inhabitants revolve around one sole purpose: making money. It's the reason why people get out of bed, go to work, kill a few people, and then lay their heads down at night with a few extra zeros in their accounts. It's why men like me exist.

Illegal business practices aren't abnormal. They are the *norm* so many fail to see.

Greed.

Sex.

Drugs.

They go hand in hand and play inside the most out-in-the-open playgrounds. Criminals don't hide. Not anymore.

Instead, we move in social circles where excess is common and discretion is key. We own legitimate ventures and filter our *dirty* funds through them. It's a simple concept, one that my visitor is all too familiar with.

Malcolm Asher takes, launders, and repeats without failure to produce perfectly accounted-for wealth. Through a few well-played moves, he turned our side ventures into multiple avenues to clean our illegal gains. Any business qualifies as long as you move cash, high quantities, and through a few family-style Cuban restaurants, three bars, real-estate in lower income areas, and a laundromat; we have more than enough.

He's a friend, dangerous, and someone I treat like family.

Someone who watches my interest with a certain piece-of-shit asshole that tried to steal from me while I was in jail—that I plan to dispose of after I deal with more immediate issues.

I think he's planning on doing that himself, and I wouldn't complain if the price is right.

"Thiago, we're here."

"I'm going in alone." Inside the gift box Ivan had for me were extra magazines for my Ruger SR9, my new iPhone, and a pack of gum. I appreciated all three, and before opening the door, I tuck my gun into the waistband of my pants and pocket an extra clip. "Stay close. I'll call."

"Of course." The SUV pulls away a few seconds after I exit, blending in with the light-for-a-weekday traffic.

Then, I walk through the main doors without pause.

No one stops me or asks questions, but they all look. Those who live here know me, fear my last name, and they should. So when they move to step out of my way, I smirk. When they rush to tell tourists to move, I give a nod.

Respect is something earned, and I appreciate those with enough common sense to not piss off a killer.

"Welcome back, Mr. De Leon." Ninette says as I approach the TSA checkpoint. She's a friend of my mother's, and one hard-ass old lady. They went to school together in Cuba, and both families fled with the Mariel. "We missed you."

I'm smiling at her, and once close, I give her a hug. The woman is like my aunt and I've missed her too. "You okay? Treatment going as planned?"

"Not leaving this earth yet, Thiago." She pulls back and cups my chin, her eyes watery. "The devil isn't ready for me yet. Thinks I'm too mouthy."

At her response, a chuckle escapes. "Is that why Miguel hasn't put a ring on it? You whine too much?"

She smacks my arm. "Brat."

"And yet you still love me?"

All amusement drops from her face then, and before I can ask what's wrong, she's hugging me again. Tightly. Ninette burrows her face into my chest, but I can still make out her muffled words loud and clear. "Those responsible don't deserve to live, Thiago."

Giving her a final squeeze, I put my mouth close to her temple. "They'll get no mercy from me."

"Good." Righting herself, she discreetly wipes her cheeks before signaling for me to pass. "Go through. There's a table waiting for you at The Clover.

Bending a bit, I kiss her forehead and walk through the TSA employees only entrance. Those in line murmur and other agents look at me, but I make it to an empty monorail cart without further delay.

Malcolm hasn't landed but will do so shortly, and a few minutes after I reach the terminal bar, I spot him. He's not alone, but Carmelo and two others stay a few steps behind, the former carrying something in his hand.

His eyes meet mine and he enters the establishment, bypassing the hostess who's all too eager to assist.

"I'm not surprised by your call," I say with a smirk, amused by the look of disappointment on the girl's face. That, and I have an inkling as to why the sudden visit, because men in our position are only motivated by two very powerful reasons:

Money.

A woman.

Not that I call him out on this. Instead, I raise a brow and wait.

"Good. Then you know why I'm here." Malcolm extends a hand, and when I grab it, he pulls me out of my chair and into a man hug. "Happy to see you out, Rivera. That was a shit case and setup."

"I know." Nodding, I give him a tight squeeze and let go, taking my seat once again. There's no point in correcting my full last name: my father is De Leon, I'm Rivera, and Ivan is Junior to them. "It's cost me something far more valuable than time."

A waiter stops by then with two pints of stout and menus, but I wave him off. I won't be here for long. He bumps into Carmelo as he scurries off, and I'm not surprised by Malcolm's man slipping him a few bills to stay away.

"Then I won't take any more of it." Malcolm holds a hand up and Carmelo gives him a folder. It's a quick transaction, and then he's gone. Back to his post as security with the other two who stayed outside.

"I want to liquidate their debt. The Fosters will owe me." His tone is one of finality, and I'm half tempted to knock him down a peg. The only thing that stops me is our friendship.

I've known him for years, and he's not a man to react without reason. Whatever this is about has to be important.

"Why?"

At my question, he slides the folder over. "Open it."

And I do, ire overtaking my senses. My eyes harden. "That poor girl is innocent," I hiss out. "She's nothing like them."

"She's mine." At his words, my eyes snap to his and I see so much of myself in him at that moment. Malcolm might be older, but that's the reaction of a man protecting what's his. "Their lives will end by my hands. Agree or don't, Thiago, it makes no difference. This is a courtesy visit because of our friendship, but my compliance with our agreement died the very minute they touched her."

I'd kill anyone that touched my Luna. And it's that thought that keeps me from having a reaction of my own. This isn't Chicago where he is feared. Malcolm is in my playground, but the motives behind the words are the bruises on London's face in these photos.

I accept that without a single hesitation.

I understand him because if it were me, I'd have killed them already and just delivered the heads.

"Fuck the money." I sit back, my large frame causing the back of the chair to protest. My hands are clenching and jaw ticking. "Keep it, burn it...donate it for all I care."

"Then what do you want in exchange?" he asks, mimicking my position. For a moment I watch him. Unwavering. Calculating. "If not money...?"

"I'll be there to witness." Not up for negotiation.

"Done."

"Good." I stand then and Malcolm follows, walking out after tossing a few more bills to cover the untouched drinks and their discretion. "Are you heading back home or staying in Miami for a few days?"

"My flight leaves in half an hour."

"Mom will be sad she missed you." I chuckle, scratching my jaw. "She's on party-planning crazy mode."

"Wish I could, but London needs me." He does look a bit contrite; the man loves my mom's pernil and congri with yuca. She makes the dishes for him every visit without fail.

"Say no more. Next time." I give him a slap on the back, but my eyes narrow on the next breath. London doesn't need more bullshit thrown at her. "Be good to her, Asher. Or I'll shoot you myself."

He pulls back, matching my smirk. "Are you going after Luna?"

"I am." *I already have.* My phone beeps then and I pull it out, reading a text from Ivan.

> Senot Junior just arrived at Luna's with flowers.
> Red roses at that. ~Little Bro

A dark cloud overtakes my senses and the plastic in my hand groans under the pressure of my hold. "Call me when you're ready to proceed." It's a barely contained snarl, tinged with the storm brewing within.

Malcolm's smile drops, concern overtaking his features. "You okay?"

"Just have a girl to reclaim and a motherfucker to kill."

Luna

AND THEN HE'S gone again, leaving me a confused, hungover ball of a mess.

When I opened the door earlier, I thought it was Nat or my mother, both of which pestered me all day yesterday for similar reasons. One, demanding to know how our tumultuous reunion went—to know if I cursed him out or kicked him in the balls—while the other all but warned me to not see him again.

Little do they know I did neither.

I gave in to Thiago's touch like a whore who hasn't seen a man in a decade. Like an addict feigning for his next hit.

Hungry.

Desperate.

Almost begging.

It's why I've avoided them. It's also why I mistook Thiago for them.

I'm still struggling with the reality that he's back.

The front door slams shut behind him and I close my eyes, taking in the emotions that having him close again evokes. There's love and butterflies and worst of all…fear.

Not of him per se, but the hurt being an *us* could bring.

I hate him for putting me in this position to begin with, because had he spoken to me—explained the situation—we wouldn't be caught up in this mess. Waiting for him would've never been an issue; my trust in him before that day had been unbreakable.

Now, though, I'm not sure how to feel.

Why was it so easy for me to believe the worst? Why did I fall for that bull crap so easily?

"This is such a mess," I whisper to the empty room and do something that's both equally stupid and heartwarming. Grabbing the remote from beside me, I press the play button like I did last night and scoot down a bit to get comfortable.

A few seconds later the TV flickers and we appear on the screen. We're younger, a year or two at the most after meeting, and laughing at something Natasha is saying on the other side of the camera. His arm is thrown over my shoulder while holding me close; he's chuckling into the side of my head after one of his baseball games.

One where the winning home run was his.

Where the city's dark prince dedicated the moment to his beauty.

On the screen I'm wearing one of his shirts while he looks handsome in the team uniform; the name De Leon and the number twenty-four on both our torsos in a large and bold font. Moreover, it's the sight of us happy and carefree that pushed me toward drink number six or ten late last night.

I lost track after a while.

Going through family videos and watching us grow up together—cheer for the other during important milestones—hit me hard in the chest. I ached. I cried. I cursed.

More so when we were so close to having it all before it was snatched away.

The phone beside me vibrates and I look over, grimacing when my father's name flashes across the screen. He wants the same as my mother, more so, and I have no desire to speak with either of them and fight. It's just not worth it.

Answer your phone, Luna. ~Dad

Quit avoiding me. I will show up at your
apartment. ~Dad

My reply is quick and the same one I've given every time he tries to communicate. He's not the same man that raised me, his position here in Miami has gone to his head, and I'm only his daughter when he wants something.

Can't. I'm washing my hair. ~Luna

Call me back, child. We need to talk. ~Dad

Sure... ~Luna

Maybe next year? Instead, I exit that video and go back to the file with the name Mrs. De Leon on it. There, I click on the last video which was from our trip to the Dominican Republic five months before his initial arrest. It starts before takeoff, just the two of us, and he's getting situated in his seat while I'm smiling into my new video camera, the one he'd given me the night before for my birthday.

People continue to pass by us in our first-class seats. Some look, but most avoid eye contact while the twenty-five-year-old heir of the De Leon dynasty looks at me with equal parts hunger and adoration. With his unfiltered love, my heart pitter patters now like it did then, and more so when he turns my face to meet his lips.

Bringing a hand to my mouth, I touch the same abused flesh that still tingles from his earlier kisses. His taste lingers. His masculine scent surrounds me.

"How do I let him go?" The answer to that is that I don't think I ever can.

A deep and tired sigh escapes me at that large tidbit of truth, and I fast forward the movie. Now, we're at the hotel that same evening, walking down the privately owned beach belonging to the resort so I can catch the moonlit sky and the waves crashing upon the shore.

That trip had been my heaven, a much-needed recharge after an exhausting semester of college, and immediately I'm transported back to that night.

My excited ramblings make him laugh as we make our way to the shore. There's minimal lighting, the moon and stars guiding us down the private path, and only once we cross onto the sand do I stop. Miles of gorgeous beach stretch out on either side of us while I take it all in: the salty breeze, the soothing sound of waves crashing, and the warmth of the muscled body that steps behind me, his mouth at my ear.

A shiver rushes down my spine and a small gasp leaves my throat; I almost drop my camera.

Thiago's quick hand snatches it mid-air while chuckling. We're not in the shot, and I'm not going to stop it from recording the conversation. "Careful, baby girl." He hands it back, bringing it over my right eye. "I want to explore the functions later tonight and can't do that if it's full of sand."

"What do you have in mind?" My hands shake from his proximity as I take the small device, the picture on the screen jerky and out of focus. There's the water and dark endless sky, but you can't quite make out the details, and yet at that moment, I'm standing there with him and nothing else matters.

The palpable need is burning bright, our love stronger than ever.

"I want you to ride my cock out on the balcony with the tropical view as a backdrop." It leaves him on a groan, a rough exhale against my neck. He nips at the skin there between words, licking the tender flesh afterward. "I want to capture you falling helplessly—see my little cock slut give in to my demands and then cry out with a need so desperate to come that you give in to the delirium. Crazy beautiful and accepting of every touch and kiss, I want to record your fall as I pull each orgasm from your body."

"Thiago," I whimper, the camera shaking from the trembling in my body. "Can we go back now?"

A deep laugh rumbles through his chest. "Patience, beautiful. Let's get your footage first."

"You always put me first." My voice is low, and I'm nearly languid in his hold. How he does this to me I'll never understand. One minute I'm

desperate to feel him between my thighs, taking me, and the next I'm a lovesick, swooning mess. He's my devil. My weakness. The best thing that's ever happened to me. "Thank you so much for bringing me here."

"I'd do anything to see a smile grace your lips, my queen. Anything to make you happy." His lips skim down my temple and toward my cheek, and when he pauses to breathe me in, goose bumps rise. I feel his grin against my skin. "Besides, I have a payment plan already set up for you. I even have the perfect outfit for you to wear while servicing my needs."

"Jerk!" I'm not mad, and he knows it. There's no hiding my own smile as I smack his arm.

"Your jerk."

"And that's all I'll ever need." It's breathy and a bit whiny as he lavishes my throat with open-mouthed kisses. "Just you."

"Keep talking like that and we'll get married before leaving the island." The seriousness in his tone causes my head to tilt in order to give him better access and a rush of wetness to ruin my panties. "The part of your family I like is already here, bebe, and we can turn the reunion into a wedding without much difficulty."

"Don't tempt me."

"I'm not waiting forever to make it official." More kisses before he runs the tip of his tongue back to my ear and exhales. It's a rough one. One that tells me he's already planning. In his head, our nuptials are a done deal.

Turning in his arms, I stand on the tips of my toes so I can reach his lips. A mouth that's smirking down at me while those hazel eyes, the brightest shade of honey, show his true emotions.

He's happy. In love. Hungry for me.

"I love you, Thiago."

"You mean everything to me, Luna."

"And someday soon, I'll wear a pretty white dress and walk down the aisle toward you. I want to be tied to you, Mr. De Leon, in every way humanly possible. To be your wife."

"I approve of this plan. You have until the end of the year to be my wife." His mouth lowers to mine under the Dominican sky before I can give him a smart-ass retort about putting a ring on it.

Then everything changed. Drastically. Without warning.

One minute we were the perfect couple, and then…*nothing.*

But as I watch this video—take in every single second and revisit with my love—one of the many holes left behind by his absence begins to heal. The pain is less. The hollowness doesn't feel as suffocating.

There's no rush or worry as we embrace, we're taking our time and while all you see on the large screen is the sand or the occasional tan flesh of his arms and our feet, the love between us is palpable. We're not in most of the shots, and it's so out of focus most people would say it's crap, but to me it's a prized possession.

Knock. Knock. Knock.

The sudden banging on my door pulls me from my thoughts and I pause the video. The person at the door is a bit impatient and I look over at the clock on my nightstand, which reads a little past noon.

I'm not expecting anyone at the moment and once again leave the sanctity of my bed, stumbling over a small gift that I know for a fact wasn't there before.

"He's killing me," I mutter under my breath, annoyed and excited all in the same breath. Fingering the small bow around the palm-sized box, I pull on one end when there's another set of hard knocks. "The hell?"

Determined to not make the same mistake again, I hobble over to my armoire, careful not to reopen my cut, and open the third drawer where I keep my workout clothes. At the very top sits a pair of purple yoga pants and a black tank top with a built-in-bra that I recently purchased, and I whip off *his* old shirt before shimmying into my clothes and making sure everything is in its rightful place.

I'm not wearing underwear, and whoever is on the other side of my door impatiently knocking doesn't need a show.

"I'm coming," I yell out, and the insistent thumping stops. "At least they have common sense." Rolling my eyes, I stand against the solid wooden door and look through the peephole. There's a shadow there, definitely male by the size of its silhouette, but I can't make out just who it is. I also know it's not Thiago since our agreement stood for this Saturday.

An entrance table near me has a small drawer that's just the right size to conceal my Glock, and I step over to it slowly without making much noise.

Slowly, I pull it open and take out my piece, check the safety, and then do what most women wouldn't do in my position.

On the count of ten, I unlock my door and then step back, pointing my firearm straight at the entrance. "Come in."

Within the span of four heartbeats, the knob begins to turn and the door is pushed open, revealing a very confused man holding a large bouquet of red roses. "Luna, what the?"

"Claudio, what are you doing here?" I lower my gun and without taking my eyes off his, put the safety back in place. I'm not putting it away —showing—anyone where I hide my weapons—but I do take precautions, especially when I see how nervous it makes him.

I'm not a fan of the man, but I hold no ill will toward him as of yet. He's just creepy. An ass kisser. Someone that, unfortunately, I've had to be courteous to over the years when at a family function and his family is present. Or while attending some bull-crap reception for the city as a favor to my father when we're on speaking terms.

His brown eyes watch my hand where the Glock is firmly in my grip. "I just thought you'd need some cheering up with *you know who's* recent release."

"That's very thoughtful of you, but I'm more than okay."

For the first time since opening the door to a weapon being aimed at him, his eyes snap to mine. "Are you sure? My father and yours said that—"

"Our fathers needs to learn how to mind his business." *And watch his back, because if I find out he's behind Thiago's arrest, I'll kill him myself. Him, and anyone else involved.* There's a tick of his jaw at my words; he doesn't like my unapologetic response, and I shrug. "Are those for me?"

"Yes." Another tick as he hands them over, his fingers lingering a bit longer than necessary against the one not holding my gun. "Can I come in?"

"Sure." My smile is politely forced, and had he not been a man so full of himself, Claudio would see this. But then again, what can you expect from an over-privileged kid whose father's political career has given him a veil to hide behind, and that alone makes his common South Florida good looks unattractive. "Please take a seat while I put these in water."

"Thank you. Some coffee would be nice as well."

The urge to roll my eyes is strong, but I keep a game face like a true champ. "Sorry. I'm all out." I even add an apologetic shrug. "Need to go grocery shopping. My maid refuses to do so for me."

"Good help is hard to find," he says, his expression one of complete understanding, and I bristle internally. My sarcasm has gone completely over his head, and that response is generic at best. It's what people who undervalue their employees or the working force of the country like to say in order to disguise their greed and asshole mentality. "I have a girl that could probably help you once a week if you're interested. She picks up my laundry, groceries, and details my car."

Silently, I ask the Lord to give me strength. I'm tired, moody, and Thiago leaving me a bit horny doesn't help. Because while I might not like my papi at the moment, whoever set him up has to pay, and I will gladly help us get the retribution we deserve.

Moreover, my first opportunity to do so is now. Claudio likes to talk an awful lot and could share something useful. Something to help put the timeline or direction of these puzzle pieces in order.

If they're involved, he's too cocky not to gloat if I goad him just right. I've avoided all talk of Thiago for years, and today that ends. I'm not wasting any more time, especially since it's his mother's guard who ordered the hit.

Why, and under whose direction?

"Give me a moment," I say instead while holding out the flowers. "Let me fix this."

"A glass of water is fine, too."

"Sure. Coming right up." Turning toward the kitchen, I head for the sink and place my gun atop the counter. There, I make a show of opening the faucet and letting the water run to just the right temperature while thinking of ways to bring up the topic of my ex without being too obvious. That, and come up with a list of viable reasons as to why he needs to go immediately after.

So far, I have a stomach virus or contagious rash of some kind at the top of my list.

The latter of the two will need some name made up for it, but it shouldn't be too hard. I'm more than positive that keeping up with medical terms for diagnosis isn't something he does.

"Where to put these?" I remember there's a small vase inside the cabinet below and to the left of me, and I bend to grab it while muttering a low curse under my breath. This visit could've happened at any other time and I would've been appreciative. Prepared. Entertaining anyone is the last thing I want to do, especially when I think about the video on pause inside my room.

Thiago did make good on his promise on the beach that night. He made me cry out in a prayer to his name over and over again. *Get it together, woman. Now is not the time.*

"Easier said than done." Opening the wrappings, I find some old leaves, dying stems, and a few rubber bands holding the bouquet together. I'm wondering where he bought these. They don't seem all that fresh, and I'll have to cut a good chunk off the bottom to keep up the pretenses before putting them in water. *So much work for something that'll just go in the garbage once he leaves.* Turning to grab my garbage bin from under the opposite counter, I'm stopped in my tracks when I find Claudio at the entrance watching me. "Is there something you need?"

He shakes his head, smirking at me. "Just enjoying the view."

Standing back up, I narrow my eyes. "Don't start."

For years my father has tried to push me toward him, talking him up at every opportunity and as a dig at the De Leons. Not that it ever fazed Thiago. He knows where I've always stood—that I don't find this man-child the least bit attractive—and following my father's wishes to gain approval isn't something I care for.

Claudio's mouth goes from lazy smirk to a thin line. Exasperation marring his features. "When are you going to give me a chance, Luna? I've been patient and—"

"I wouldn't finish that if I were you."

"Why not? We could be so good together."

"Leave."

Men suffer from one particular issue that becomes a downfall in most cases. Their egos are fragile. Unable to handle rejection without spewing vitriol back to appease their own wounds. This will be one of those cases.

I can see it.

The change in his demeanor. The harsh breathing and hateful retort brewing.

"Stop being stubborn and proud for one second. Thiago isn't coming back for you." The way he spits out his name, the venom coating each letter, makes me angry—furious that the idiot considers himself above him, but I merely raise a brow. This is what I'll need; a careless moment from him. "What you had is done and soon enough, he'll find himself a new plaything. That's what all men like him do. They use and then discard."

"Is that so?" My tone is mocking as I drop the bouquet, not caring where it falls, my arms crossing over my chest. "Do fill me in on how men like him work. This is riveting stuff."

"He'll do it again." It's a barely contained snarl, lips curling over his teeth. "You should be thanking his enemies for their prayers."

"Prayers? What prayers?" *Keep talking, idiot. Confirm what Thiago said.* "What does that even mean?"

"It means God listened, and those with the means to do so helped expedite that excrement of a family's downfall."

"Get out," I hiss out through clenched teeth, my fury rising to the surface in a volcanic rush, and I take the few steps between us to jam my finger in his chest. He staggers a bit, his face contorting, but the pain registers on my next intake of breath and I'm the one jumping back. *"Fuck."*

It's a mistake. Because in my tumultuous ire, I didn't pay attention to the small box there.

Another box with a bow. Another box with a bow and sharp corners that has dug itself into my cut and at once, it reopens. Blood rushes to the surface, saturating the bandages Thiago put in place for me, dripping onto the floor below. I'm now hobbling, with my foot raised high as I curse my luck and watch the jerk before me grin.

Not a normal smile. This one is creepy, and I move back when his hand reaches out for me. "Let me help you with that."

"No."

"Luna, you need—"

"I'll give you exactly thirty seconds to walk out this door before I shoot."

OUR EYES SNAP toward the magnificent force standing a few feet from Claudio's back. His Ruger's raised and pointing straight at the now paling man, cocked and ready to shoot without a single shred of remorse in his eyes. "Ten, eleven…fourteen."

"Luna, are you just going to let him—"

"Seventeen, eighteen," I count for Thiago and Claudio's eyes narrow, the hate in them clear as day to see. "Go, and don't come back. Spare yourself the embarrassment."

"This isn't over," he spits out and turns, running into a hard wall the size of a man who is breathing harshly and glaring. "Excuse me."

"Of course." Claudio fixes his tie and then makes to walk around a motionless Thiago. He makes it a step past, just a single one, when Leon speaks again, causing Claudio to look back. "But before you go, I have a message for your father."

"My father doesn't have time for…fuck!" Without warning, Thiago brings the butt of the gun across Claudio's face, breaking his nose and more than likely his cheekbone. A deep gash opens across his face and he screams, a pitiful sound that hurts my ears. His skin becomes saturated by the crimson gushing from the cut; his clothes are also ruined. Not that it deters the mob boss. Instead, he gets close to the whimpering fool and whispers a parting threat that sends a chill through my bones. "This is just a hello from me, Jr. Just a friendly reminder to stay in your lane and keep those putrid eyes off what's mine. Do that, and you'll avoid a lengthier conversation. Understood?"

"Yes." It's low and meek.

"Now, as for your father…" Thiago lifts his gun once more, this time placing the barrel right under his chin while turning them sideways. So I can see. So that a large open wall is their background, and I cock my head to the side. *What is he doing?* He pulls the trigger, and nothing comes out. Does it again, and I think Claudio is close to pissing himself.

"Leon, let him go. Please don't—" The heated stare he sends me shuts me up. It's not anger in his eyes, but more of an animalistic hunger that almost pulls a low moan from me.

There's a smirk on his lips when he turns to look at the man he's holding. He's aware of how much of a turn-on seeing his devilish side is, and even after all these years, it still has the same effect. My skin erupts in goose bumps and my thighs clench—heart races. "Let him know I'll be dropping by his office this upcoming week and will come bearing gifts. The largest one in particular will leave him speechless."

Claudio hasn't realized that Thiago moved the gun just enough out of the way, that when he pulls the trigger, the bullet lodges itself into a wall instead of his head. Nothing registers, and the look of pure terror on his face will forever be etched into my mind. Eyes wide and with a scream caught in his throat, I don't think he's breathing, and it isn't until Thiago taps his chin with the hot metal that he reacts.

Without looking my way, he rushes out the door without closing it.

Something that Thiago remedies quickly after. I count to ten, and the entrance slams shut and the lock is engaged.

Another few seconds pass, and he's back inside the room. It's just the two of us.

The tension is palpable. Our hunger near demonic.

I breathe in and it's his scent that surrounds me once again. That unique scent of man and woods with just the right hint of citrus that makes me react. On my next inhale, my body moves without permission and I launch myself into his arms.

I kiss him.

There's no pause or remembering what brought us here or even asking every single *why* question that floats through my mind. Instead, I give in to my needs without a single care as to the repercussions.

He catches me easily, devouring my mouth as I give in to my need. Forget the bloody cut on my foot or the reason why I shouldn't—right now none of that matters.

Not a damn thing.

All I can focus on is his taste and the feel of him pressing against me. How he came into my home like an angry beast and showed Claudio out.

How he told him that no matter what…

I. Am. His.

And I'm almost ashamed to admit how much that affected me. I needed to hear that even if I'm not ready to get back to the us we once were.

"Motherfuck, beauty," he growls, hands splayed across each asscheek and squeezing when I nibble on his bottom lip. "I need you. Let me feel you."

He's hard against me. Throbbing.

And I gyrate, giving myself a taste of what I can't deny wanting.

My eyes roll back, that small thrust of my hips adding pressure against my clit, and a rush of wetness soaks my yoga pants, the thin material doing a poor job of separating us.

I feel him. His thickness. His heat.

It helps to remind me of something I've missed all these years and my mouth waters.

Thiago is delicious from head to toe and the silkiness of his cock on my tongue is orgasmic in itself.

He grunts as I run myself over his cloth-covered length, fingertips digging into my skin. "Behave. I'm trying to give you the time you asked for."

"I'm going to need you to break that promise..." my mouth trails open-mouthed kisses across his chin and then lower over to his Adam's apple

"...just for a little while. Just a quick. Hard. Ride." I punctuate each word with a flick of my tongue over his skin, a reminder of what I've done to his swollen, reddish-purple head before taking him down my throat.

No gag reflexes. Something we discovered the first time I gave him a blow job.

"*Fuck*, you're dangerous." Not a complaint, and a second or two later we're moving toward my living room where he lowers me to the ground. He takes a step back. Just one, and I hate it. "Are you sure, Luna? I'm going to need you to say you want this."

I don't answer. Instead, I give him my back and find the large sectional a few feet from me, the armrest being what's closest. His heated stare follows me as I walk to it and pause. The heat of his hunger licks at my flesh.

My skin prickles with excitement. My heart flutters with emotions I'm not ready to visit.

So I give in to my need without pause or thought.

Bending at the waist, I bite my lip to hold back a grin when he groans. My hips shimmy and I dip a finger beneath the waistline of my pants, lowering them slowly, revealing the curves he's worshipped since we were teens.

His low *son of a bitch* sends a thrill of excitement through my small frame and goose bumps rise. A shiver rocks me, his name tumbles past my lips, and then his hands find their home as he grips my hips.

His hold is strong. Fingers digging in to the point of pain, and I welcome the sting because it proves he's really here. With me.

"Finish lowering them, beauty. All the way to your ankles." One hand releases its hold, while the other bends me forward. All the way until my cheek rests against the leather and my pants fall to the floor.

Without panties, I'm easy access. Open for him.

Lifting my face a bit, I look back and take in his reaction. Take in the way his eyes roam down my body and he licks his lips.

"Like what you see?"

"You've always been my definition of perfection." His other hand is behind me, palming a cheek before coming down on a single hard smack. It stings, but I welcome the bite. Welcome the heat that follows and the wetness that pools at my entrance as he undoes his belt and lets it fall to the floor.

That clang makes me bite my lip, eyes on his. I follow his every movement, count the seconds that it takes for Thiago to pop the button of his slacks and then lower his zipper.

He's taking his time. Savoring my need.

And I'm soaked for him.

I'm desperate to feel him inside.

My eyes close as I shake. I'm trying to calm down—to breathe through this manic yearning burning my veins.

Another smack. Then another.

"Please," I whimper, eyes snapping open.

"Keep them on me, bebe." He alternates between the two cheeks and then skims his finger lower where he encounters my wetness. His hum of approval makes me clench. The lone finger he dips inside makes me moan.

But nothing excites me more than the feel of his blunt head parting my folds, spreading my wetness, before snapping his hips forward. One swift thrust and he's buried to the hilt, my walls gripping him tight.

"Can't go slow, Luna. Forgive me."

"Thiago, I want...*fuck*!" It's a scream as pleasure and pain crash into each other, leaving me gasping for breath. I feel every ridge of his cock—every throb as he pulls out and slams back in without pause. His rhythm is near punishing, fast and hard and *oh so good* that my toes curl.

Long fingers grip around my dark hair, wrapping the strands around his fist. One harsh tug and my back arches, head tipping back to an almost uncomfortable angle.

"Thank you." I know why he says that. I can feel it in his touch. The reverent way his lips press against the tattoo in his honor at the back of my neck. Up until now he hasn't seen it, but now it's staring at him in the face.

Thiago doesn't pause his strokes—the fast pace in which he rides me—while mouthing the words *I love you* against my skin. Each syllable, his tight hold, marking me as his.

Those deep strokes cement my truth; I'm his girl, his future, and his willing whore.

My lips part but no sounds come out as he bends his knee a bit, changing the angle. He's right there, pressing against the one spot that causes my eyes to roll back and hips to buck in desperation. I'm tightening around him. I can feel my walls try and to pull him in deeper.

"You feel so good, mami. So tight and wet...like heaven." The hand at my hip slips between my body and the couch, his fingers rubbing tight circles where I'm most sensitive. Two more strokes and I'm standing at that precipice, teetering on an orgasm so strong my eyes tear up.

"Please." It leaves me on a shaky whimper, my hips pushing back against his. The *slap slap slap* of our skin is loud, and beads of sweat roll down my back. "Need more."

"Give it to me. Let me feel...*fuck*, yes...again." His hips push harder, pistoning at a pace that leaves me on the tip of my toes and fingers digging into the armrest. "Come on my cock, Luna. Mark me."

That's it.

Two words and I'm thrown over the edge. My moans are loud and yet, even at my highest peak, I hear his accompanying grunt a few seconds later. The sounds of his pleasure break me all over again, and I clench around him as another wave of bliss rocks through me.

I'm left gasping and sweaty and completely sated. I'm left accepting that no matter where life leads us, I'll always end up right here. Beneath him. Reveling in his touch.

It takes a while for my heart to stop racing and for the shaking of my limbs to cease, but when they do, reality sets in and I can't stop the words from escaping. "How do I forget, Thiago. How do I let the anger go?"

He doesn't answer right away. Instead he pulls up his pants, leaving them open at the waist and then pulls me to stand with my back against his chest. His warmth seeps into my skin, and it's a balm to my soul. His lips press against his tattoo on my neck and I sigh.

"I know this isn't easy, Luna." Thiago's voice is softer now than I've ever heard it. It's a mixture of apologetic and full of regret while keeping that raspy quality I find sexy. "I'm not expecting you to forgive me or let this go overnight, but I will tell you that I'm not willing to back down or let us end. We will never have an expiration date nor go our separate ways, beautiful. Not now. Not ever."

"So then you are *expecting* me to just forgive and forget," I accuse, turning in his arms and jamming my finger into his chest. "Be honest. Admit it."

There's a tsk that comes from the back of his throat and my eyes meet his. "Nothing in life is easy, and what's worth fighting for is always hard." Strong hands cup my face, and Thiago's thumbs caresses my cheeks. His face is so close, and yet, he doesn't move to kiss me. I'm both thankful and full of denial that it's exactly what I need. "All I need from you is to believe that I'll fight for you. For us."

"I know you will." My indignation evaporates at those words and I melt into his touch. "You're more stubborn than I am."

A ghost of a smile crosses his features before they harden once more. Not in anger, but in determination. "If you asked me to, Luna, I'd burn the world to ashes if it meant I have your heart again." My eyes close at the heaviness—truth—in his words. They fill my heart with joy and on the same breath, I hate that we're here to begin with. That life threw us into this messed-up loop. "I'm sorry I hurt you. Sorrier than you'll ever begin to comprehend, but I'll make this up to you. As God is my witness, I will earn your forgiveness through actions, and in the meantime, I'll just have to wait for you to catch up."

THIAGO

T HE SOUND OF voices rumbling meets my ears as I come to a stop a few feet from a large room on the top floor of our transport vessel. We're off the coast of Miami, back out on international water, and the people on the other side of this metal door are awaiting my entrance.

They're loud, some throwing out a curse or two in Spanish while they argue over the Caribbean Series that Cuba lost back in February to Panama. Ironic since this large ship belongs to a diplomat from there. At least, that's what the United States government chooses to believe.

From beside me, I catch Ivan shake his head at the ridiculousness and I roll my eyes in silent response before pocketing my phone after texting Luna. I haven't seen my queen in two days, forty-eight hours where I've given her a break from my presence without being too far away.

I'm in the flowers that arrive each morning along with breakfast, and then at night, on the note scribbled over her favorite wine's label. Just a simple *I Love You, Beauty* that I know she enjoys. Her response every time a delivery shows up gives that much away.

The text messages with emojis.

The one picture of her in my shirt while sipping from a glass.

The smile in her voice during our five-minute conversations whenever I get a chance, is proof that I'm wearing her down.

"Cabron, you still owe me money from the series before that. Get out of here with that mierda," comes from inside the room, and I know the voice. I almost laugh because my father takes this too seriously as do most in Latin American countries.

These are grown men, some even family—the kind of assholes that will take a life if necessary without blinking twice, but when it comes to base-ball, they lose composure faster than a bullet dislodges from my gun.

"Go ahead and give me two," I say to my brother and Miguel, who follow my instructions without a backward glance. The large metal doors open, and the room grows quiet; they know I'm here—what I expect—and my men don't disappoint.

My father was the same in his time as king of the 305.

Respect. Silence. Loyalty.

No excuse. Either you are with the De Leons or you're viewed as an enemy.

As they slip inside and the doors close, no one asks where I am. Instead, the constant thud of fists meeting solid wood reverberates throughout the floor and I smile.

It's their greeting. A welcoming.

It's one I embrace as I pull open the doors, walking inside and straight for the head of a large, teak table that's currently full. Men gather all around it, standing while those fists never stop pounding. They're smiling as I take my seat: a large chair that resembles a throne in all black that's carved out of imported ebony wood.

And it's only once I've taken my place that the noise stops, and my men sit.

"Gentlemen," I say, looking each one in the eye. The men here are a group I trust. That I've personally vetted with Ivan's help. "Before we begin, I want to thank both my brother and father for stepping in when I couldn't personally attend. For following my instructions and keeping this family strong, proud, and feared."

"Leon Pride," they chant in unison.

"Over the last five years, I've set in motion a change to our structure that will take effect immediately. If you aren't within these walls, sitting inside this room, then you're not one of us." Grabbing my glass with four fingers' worth of rum inside, I lift, and the others follow. "It's time to grow, and so will the profits. It's time to burn our names into the history books as the largest cartel operating within the US."

"Leon Pride."

"There will be changes," I say, meeting my father's eyes. He nods at me, raising his glass a little bit higher. Total trust in his eyes. "Blood will be shed. There will be motherfucking anarchy in this city by the time I remove all the filth, and then, it'll be our family that cleans up the mess. To the victors of war go the spoils, and ours will be cleaning out every dirty city official's office."

"Leon Pride."

"Leon Pride." With a smirk on my face, I bring the glass to my lips and take a sip before holding a hand up. It's a signal for Miguel, who leaves the room and comes right back with the help of his son, dragging with him the kind of scum we will begin disposing of.

He's my gift to the group. Where this mess began.

The man kicking and screaming—the one being pushed toward me— works as an office assistant for the judge that convicted me, a man with ideas of grandeur and rising to a higher rank by winning favors not by merit. He falls to his knees at my feet, scrambling to move back, but Miguel's presence keeps him right where he is, crying and praying to a man that will not show mercy.

He's also the one who recommended his deceased cousin to Senot as a hitman, and in return, he'd get a job with him as the Director of Public Affairs. A job that's way above his skill set and knowledge, and while I'll never knock someone's hustle, he stepped outside his lane and bit off more than he could ever hope to chew.

His cousin was the same man found dead inside my penthouse.

He's the man that will die tonight.

"Where did you find him?" Dad asks, his hand at his waist where he pulls out a 9mm and points it at Roger's head. "This son of a bitch owes me one."

"Where do all little boys go when they're scared?" Pushing my chair back, I turn enough so that I'm facing the whimpering bitch.

"His mother's house in—"

"Texas," I finish for my viejo, taking another sip from my glass before cutting my eyes to the guilty guest at my feet. "Isn't that right, Roger?"

"Please don't hurt me." Without prompting, he's crawling toward me and once at my Ferragamo loafers, he kisses each one. "I made a mistake… I'll work it off. I'll do anything you want me to."

"Is that right?"

"Yes. Anything." I'll give the asshole a few points for being smart enough to not look me in the eye.

"Tell me who approached you."

"W-what do you mean? I-I—"

"Someone told you to entice Ulysses because we both know you aren't smart enough to concoct this yourself." If he's offended by my slight, Roger hides it well behind a quivering lip and the snot rolling over it. *Disgusting.* His mouth opens to reply, but before he does I hold a finger up, silencing him. "The truth, Mr. Charles. Just confirm what I know, and we can all move forward with our day."

"It was Jasmine Senot." The information given to me in jail regarding his involvement was missing one tiny detail that I now see plain as day. His motives are obvious. Simple. Somehow, he fell for her, too, and this was the idiot's way to win some brownie points. It's written all over his face— this hurts him to give her up. "She wants her husband dead and used his dislike of you in her favor."

Infatuation is a dangerous thing and often overlooked as nothing more than a crush or basic attraction. To me, though, it goes deeper. Much deeper. A person believing themselves in love will do just about anything for the object of their desires:

Lie.

Cheat.

Steal.

Kill.

All apply and none are off-limits.

"I appreciate the honesty, Roger. So much so that here's what I'll do for you."

"Thank you. I'm so sorry and I'll—"

"Close your eyes when speaking to me." He does as I ask, and ten seconds later, I give the nod of approval.

Roger Charles doesn't see the first bullet coming nor the next. They hit him so fast as every gun inside the room empties a magazine, producing life-ending holes throughout his tall and lanky frame; by the fourth gunshot, and with eyes wide open, he's dead.

Blood stains the floor, rivulets that wet the soles of my dress shoes, and as the last shot rings out, I take a final sip of my drink.

Let them come for us now; I'm prepared and will kill anyone who stands in my way.

Even if that means I put a bullet between my father-in-law's eyes. Because that motherfucker isn't innocent in all this, and when the time comes for retribution, they'll all fall.

My Luna will know how dirty his, Ulysses, and Jasmine's hands are compared to mine.

"DID you make it to the safe house okay?" I ask Ivan, placing my cell with the secured line between my right shoulder and ear. It's a little past eleven a.m. the next morning, and I'm overlooking a medium-sized shipment of illegal firearms being brought aboard by a group of Dominicans via a yacht. This delivery is a gift for a favor. For the protection of an underground manufacturer's family from the Philippines that uses the D.R. as a hub —his wife and young daughter—while they were on vacation in Miami three months ago. I gave the okay from my cell, and this is his token of appreciation. "Were they right?"

"Yeah, that son of a bitch is here. Mauricio Hernandez was drunk off his ass and partying it up near the Malecon when I arrived." He's in Cuba now, having left immediately after the execution of Roger. It's how we planned it after word came in yesterday morning from my men on the island of what this piece of shit had done. What he proudly told anyone who would listen.

Casper Jameson is a good man. An asshole. The British motherfucker is part of my family, honest, and someone I do business with on a regular basis.

What's been taken from him isn't something that any of us in this unified circle can ignore, nor will we want to. You don't harm the women in this lifestyle. They are respected, if nothing else.

Mother or wife; they are never to be touched.

What Mauricio has done deserves nothing short of a painful death, and that's something he knows.

It's why he's hiding from the Jamesons. Why he's living his life up zero to a hundred without pause because you can only go undetected for so long.

His biggest mistake was going to Cuba.

He signed his death certificate the very moment he stepped foot onto its soil.

"You grabbed him?" I say before clearing my throat and taking a sip from the ice-cold glass of water I'm nursing. It's one of Luna's rules: a night out drinking equals two bottles of water and ibuprofen before bed.

"Within the hour." There's the sound of someone yelling in the background, a male voice on the verge of panic and a thump on metal shortly after. "I'm delivering him to the compound now and then awaiting Casper's arrival...." there's a pause on his end and then the firing of a gun "...*not so mouthy now, asshole?*"

"Difficult guest?"

"The crying is getting on my last nerve. I would've shot him by now, but Casper deserves that honor."

"Agreed."

"Can you text me his ETA once you get it, bro?" he asks before saying something to our personal driver over there.

"Done." The last of the crates is brought below and the large metal ramp used just above sea level is closed. "Expect my call within the next half an hour."

"Thanks. See you tomorrow."

"Cuidate."

"Always." The line goes dead then and I turn, leaning back against the railing. The waves below are a bit choppy, slightly rocking us, and I crack my neck. It's been a long night and I haven't slept as of yet, celebrating with those following me into this next stage of our growth. We toasted to our future. We disposed of a body.

I set my plan into motion.

Pressing the number eight on my screen, I wait for the phone to ring. It does so three times before there's a click on the line.

"About time you called, you arse. How's life treating you on the outside?"

The smile in his tone, even as he mourns his mother, makes me chuckle. "It's getting there. I'm adjusting."

"That's good to hear. Are you free, or...?" In other words, can you work or are you playing the role of a good boy?

"Probation for two years." The few men cleaning the other side of this top floor don't see me and their discussion on some unimportant bullshit becomes loud. As the volume rises, there are a few curse words thrown about—a threat or two—and I leave my place by the railing. All it takes for them to become silent is a mere five steps: the sight of my hulking frame makes them mute.

"Everything okay, mate?" he asks, more than likely having heard the small commotion.

"Is the pigeon in its cage?" I say instead, glaring at the young bunch. They're new, that much is obvious. They're nothing more than hired help to do the grunt work.

They need better training. A hands-on approach.

"Ezra keeps it clean and maintained." His tone isn't as jovial anymore. He's all business now.

"Good." The sound of my ice clinking inside of the glass becomes loud as I move this conversation inside. Opening the door, I give the soldiers a final glare and let the door slam shut behind me. I'll deal with them later. "You in the States?"

"In Chicago. Why?" Casper sounds as if he's moving around a room, almost agitated, and I wonder what has him in this state. He doesn't know that my brother flew out once we got word of the unwanted visitor on the island and the crimes he's committed.

"Pack a bag and head to the airport because you're needed in Cuba tonight, my friend. Ivan will be there to pick you up."

"Tonight?" There is the opening and closing of a few doors and then what sounds like his cousin talking. "What's going on? Why is your little brother in Cuba?"

"Because Ivan has your mother's killer in a holding cell in Havana."

Luna

CHRIST. IT'S AS if nothing's changed.

As if the years haven't passed us by.

As if Thiago didn't leave for five years and this is just another weekend.

The long entrance winds as we drive toward the De Leon house Saturday mid-afternoon: an ostentatious home sitting at the center of a seven-acre lot with nothing surrounding it.

No neighbors close enough to hear or see.

No trespassing by those wanting to make friends with the notorious family.

The car stops and the man beside me squeezes one of my hands—the same one he's held on to since we left my apartment—and then turns off the ignition. He's watching me. Looking for any sign of distress.

There isn't any. Not a single twitch.

To be honest, this reminds me of every other dinner I've attended since meeting Thiago. The same expensive cars fill the roundabout driveway.

The same crazy bunch of characters milling about on the front wrap-around porch with his parental figures at the center. Always at the center.

Orlando and Maritza look the same, just a smidge older. Same smiles. Same soft eyes. Same welcoming expression.

They're watching us inside of a vehicle I didn't know Thiago still owned. From my understanding, after Ivan let it slip in conversation, his brother sold everything he owned before his sentencing. His penthouse, multiple large SUVs, and a boat named My Beauty.

All gone. All our memories forgotten.

A small pang hits me at the center of my chest, that sadness that I can't escape, but I push it back. Instead, I focus on what still remains. What I'm sitting inside of.

This car is special; a fully loaded all-white Audi that was given to him as a gift his senior year of high school. This car was witness to many kisses, his expert hands fondling out front of my parents' house. Our school. All over the city of Miami.

It's where I gave him my first blow job overlooking a high-end restaurant on Collins Ave.

"And you say I'm the perv?"

"This is new," I say instead, fighting to control the soft heat sweeping my cheeks. "Did you have it tricked out à la *Pimp My Ride*?"

It's been kept pristine in his absence. Customized with everything the latest model has.

I should know, I own one.

"Quit stalling." His tone is playful, and so is the smirk on his lips. He's so handsome.

My attraction to him is just as strong. It makes me weak. But I don't show this and instead roll my eyes. "I'm not."

"Then what are you doing?" Lifting our joined hands, he turns our wrists and lays a kiss to my knuckles. "Because it looks like you're avoiding."

"Feeling lucky, Thiago?"

That makes him pause and his right brow lifts. "What do you have in mind?"

"Five hundred dollars says your Mom rushes over within the next sixty seconds."

"I'll take that bet, but I don't want your money."

"What do you want, then?" I ask with more excitement than I should show. My curiosity is piqued and thighs clench at the heated look that follows. Thiago's eyes sweep from the very top of my head to my exposed legs in the small sundress I'm wearing. Nothing fancy; a soft cotton coral number that drapes over my curves in a flattering way. With a sweetheart neckline, a tight bodice, and flowing skirt, it's comfortable while still being sexy. It's accompanied by tan wedge sandals, a pair of hoop earrings, my signature winged liner and lip gloss combo, and the man is struggling to keep his eyes off.

The desired effect I am after.

He licks his bottom lip, head tilted to the side as he lingers at my knees. "A date."

"A what?" Because I need to hear that again. Just to make sure. I'm also ignoring the small thrill of excitement that flows through me at that. "We're playing for money, not—"

"A date, Luna. I want to take you out on a date." The last word hasn't fully passed through his kissable lips when my door is wrenched open and I'm being pulled from the car by a walking floral scent that I'm familiar with.

Maritza doesn't say anything once our eyes meet, but her smile matches the one breaking free across my face. It's sweet and warm and everything I've been missing for the past few years. A maternal love that you can't duplicate or falsify.

Hazel eyes that look so much like her son's become watery and her bottom lip trembles. "Mi Niña." *Her girl.*

That's all she says. Two words.

In an instant everything rushes to the forefront.

The feeling of abandonment.

The resentment at his idiotic betrayal.

The love that will always be there for his family.

Tears fall from my eyes without permission; I feel vulnerable. My emotions are running rampant—fluctuating between hurt and love. Between pulling her in for a hug and running away.

Not that it matters as a second later Maritza takes the decision from me, wrapping her small arms tightly around me as a small sob escapes.

"None of that, beautiful. We don't deserve them." At her response I open my eyes, not realizing that I'd closed them. There's no one. Not even Thiago. From one end to the other, I look for his family members but come up empty. "Thiago signaled for them to scram. His pissed-off face actually sent them running. It was hilarious to see."

Pulling back, I settle my stare on her as my lips twitch. I'm sure I look a mess, crazy with tear tracks, blotchy skin, and smile. "Why?"

"Why do you think," she counters, her perfectly sculpted brow raised. *She's where he gets it from.*

"Mari, at the moment, I have no idea what to think or which way is up. Struggling is more like it. Confused definitely. But understanding him? Yeah, that's something I lost five years ago."

"Is it something you want to reconnect with?"

"I still love him, but—"

"Then follow me. It's time you hear something."

"Where are we...*okay*." She takes my hand in hers and all but drags me behind her, around the side of the first floor and to a door not many have access to. If your name isn't Maritza or Orlando, you don't dare enter. This is their office, and like all the main rooms, it has a door to be used in case of an emergency.

Without pause, she keys in the code and walks in after a series of beeps. Once inside, she signals for me to take a seat. "A drink?"

"Rum, please."

"Brugal or Havana?"

"Hostess choice." Maritza nods and brings out a special edition Havana Club they keep for important occasions. The Maximo Extra version is worth a few grand and this household from what I remember always keeps a minimum of three bottles at all times.

Pouring three fingers' worth into a set of snifters, she closes the bottle and walks back over, taking a seat on the large couch. The room is on the larger side for an office with a full sitting area in front of the large windows and a fireplace that's nothing more than a decorative piece.

I take the offered drink. "Salud."

"Salud."

That first sip goes down smooth. The sweet notes of fruits and vanilla are pleasant and mixed with the smokiness of the old wooden barrels it's produced in, becoming a soothing mixture. Not a single flavor overpowers the other and I hum, taking a second and third taste before placing the glass atop the coffee table.

Mari does the same, her body turning to face mine. "I know it's hard, mi Lunita."

"More than hard. I feel lost."

"But this doesn't have to be the end." There's something in her tone that causes me to tilt my head to the side, and I'm left trying to decipher what she means. Because she's talking as if—what it seems like is—she's been in my position. *That can't be right. Orlando adores her.* "All couples go through rough patches, sweetheart, and trust me when I say I've wanted to kill my husband a time or two in the last thirty years. He's messed up. I've messed up. It's life…our life," she says, taking my hands in hers and giving them both a squeeze. "Not a damn thing has been easy for any of us, and if Thiago is guilty of one thing, it's being too overprotective when it comes to you."

"He didn't even give me the chance to choose him." My voice betrays me, and she hears my pain; understands the betrayal.

"And that's what hurts the most, isn't it? You feel as though he didn't trust you to stay." She hits the nail on the proverbial head and tears fill my eyes once again, my chin trembling. The look she gives me is soft and full of understanding. "Let it out, Luna. It's okay to be mad. It's okay to feel how you do, and anyone saying otherwise deserves to be shot."

A small giggle escapes, but just as soon that amusement dies. This rollercoaster is taking its toll on me. Within the span of a few days my world—the normal I fought so hard to build for myself—has shattered into a million and one pieces.

"Why?" At my question Maritza nods, understanding me without further explanation.

"My son is the best person to explain this."

"He claims he didn't have a choice."

"That's not what I meant." A final squeeze and Maritza releases my hand, shifting forward so she can reach a small remote atop the coffee table in front of us. She presses a few buttons, sits back, and I'm met with a voice I know. A younger version of the one that showed up at my door less than a week ago.

One I both love and hate. That I can't live without.

I love him now just as much as I did years ago.

"Mom, this isn't easy for me. Hurting Luna wasn't..." Thiago trails, his voice a bit slurred. There's a tinge of pain and self-recrimination in his tone, and the faint sound of ice clinking inside of a glass fills the silence. *"Everything is fucked up. A complete and utter mess."*

"You could go see her," his mother says on the recording, a bit of a scold there. *"Explain."*

"And say what?" It's a tortured yell and I feel the weight of emotions crushing my chest. It's palpable and haunting and my heart breaks for him. For us. *"Am I supposed to tell her that some asshole put a hit out on her? Admit that I failed to protect my family...that I can't find the son of a bitch who shot Dad?"*

"Son, this isn't your fault."

He scoffs. *"Right now we have no idea what tomorrow will bring, Vieja. I'm being investigated, Dad is injured, and Ivan blames himself for leaving behind evidence at the scene that brought the MDP to my door. I'm the suspect of a crime I didn't commit but the Major has a hard-on for."* The ice clinks again and then he sighs. *"Pushing her away, no matter how much it hurts, is all I have left. I'm not doing it for shits and giggles or because I'm an untrusting asshole. It's the complete opposite, Mom. With her out of the picture, they'll turn the focus back on us. They'll come for me and not her. She'll be safe and that's all that matters."*

"But you're not giving her a choice."

"That's where you're wrong."

"Son, I don't understand. Help me out—"

"A long time ago, I explained to her that at times things are not what they seem. That I'll need her to trust me blindly." Something rustles and

the recording goes quiet for a minute or two. Utter silence that takes me back to that conversation. To my agreement and then his promise. *"My heart is hers to keep safe,"* he says so low, but I hear. I feel the depth of those words now as much as I did when we were kids. *"I trust her to remember that. To know that I'll always come back. That what I've done is to keep her safe."*

"Speaking of...?" His mom's voice wavers with emotion on the recording, and I look over to see the same tears in her eyes as I have in mine. *"Security? Are you leaving her unprotected?"*

"Never." I can almost see his handsome face send her a glare. *"She'll have someone around at all times. Not disclosing who, but Ivan has instructions and he'll explain things eventually. For now, everyone needs to fall the fuck back and not make it any worse."*

"Why are you making it sound as if you're going away? Like you won't be able to fix this in a few weeks?"

"Because I've made sure the target is on my back now."

Maritza hits a button and the recording stops. Her eyes are on me. Waiting for my reaction.

The truth is that right now I'm caught between love and loss. Between confusion and running out of this room in search of Thiago so I can kiss him stupid.

I feel like a jerk.

I feel too much at once.

"Did that help at all?" she asks after a bit, her phone in her hand as she types something out. "Are you ready to see him? Because I can only keep him at bay for so long."

Turning the screen in my direction, she lets me see his texts.

> What's taking so long? ~Thiago

> Is she okay? ~Thiago

> What did you do? ~Thiago

"When did those come in? I didn't hear your phone."

She shrugs, smiling. "A few minutes after you went mute."

I'm embarrassed and nod. "How long was that?"

"Say ten minutes, give or take."

Not horrible. "Tell him to cool it. I'll see him in a bit."

"Okay." And she does just that, hitting send and then tossing the device on the oversized chair across from us. "So, what now? Do you think you'll get past this?"

"Maybe."

"*Maybe* you will after making the man work for it?"

Twisting in my seat, I give her my undivided attention, hands crossed over my chest. "Keep going, Mari. You seem to have a plan."

"Lunita, I want you to forgive my son and move on more than anything, but…" she leans over, in her eyes I see that devilish glint her boys are known for "…he has some atoning to do. You both do." After hearing his confession and recalling our conversation years ago, I should've demanded the truth and not swallow his idiotic mistake. "He let you down and you forgot that as his queen, you come before everyone… including myself. Two wrongs don't make a right, but that doesn't mean that he should get off completely easy. Make him work for it. Chase you."

"You mean make up for the five years of radio silence." That devious side, that coquettish part of every woman's personality steps to the forefront and my shoulders square. My chin juts forward. One of my fears in seeing Maritza today; the defending her son without considering my feelings.

That his side is all that matters.

And I was wrong. Completely.

"Exactly." Standing up, she holds a hand out, pulling me up when I take it. "The women in this family are fierce, strong, and don't take bull from anyone. Especially their men. We are fifty-fifty partners and it's time you show him as much."

"Making him suffer a bit would make me feel better." *I'll make up for my mistake later. Much later and with my mouth.*

"Good. Because I want grandkids and soon, Luna."

THIAGO

"**W**ELL, THAT DIDN'T take long at all, primo."

I turn my head slightly, acknowledging the intruder while keeping my focus on the door to my parents' office where I know Luna is. It's the best place for their conversation. For her to calm down without everyone being in her face.

Maybe I should check on them?

"Something on your mind, Jadiel?" My cousin is not alone, and the man beside him takes a step back at my brusque tone. "Speak."

"Just wanted to say hello, boss." The amusement in his voice grates on my nerves. But then again, I've never liked him either. Tolerated is a better descriptor of our relationship. "That, and introduce you to my future brother-in-law. He works for me."

I don't miss the false bravado. I see his cocky expression.

Jadiel Gomez is the spitting image of his father with illusions of grandeur that don't belong to either of them. He's the son of my father's sister and a man who considers himself more than what he will ever be.

It's one of the reasons that neither was present for the meeting held a few days ago.

My aunt, God rest her soul, was a beautiful human being who married Andres out of love while he saw an opportunity. They are her heirs. They are nothing but trouble.

And I have my eyes set on both while they covet my position. Believe that it belongs to them since he is older by three years. A belief that makes no sense as his mother was never interested or in line to take over. That place belonged to Orlando as the oldest and now me as his son.

Ignoring the idiot, I turn my attention to the man standing slightly behind him. "Name."

"Sergio, Mr. De Leon. I'm Celeste's fiancé." Celeste, Jadiel's sister, is nothing like them. She's a sweet girl with the disposition of her mother and terrible taste in men. Men like this asshole who thinks he's special. Someone who will try and manipulate her with the help of the other men in her life.

If I angle my gun just right, I could kill them with one bullet.

"Is that so?"

"Yes." So enthusiastic. A pathetic puppy.

I take two things away from his sorry introduction; he doesn't belong, and my cousin is pulling the strings. Sergio doesn't step forward to extend a hand nor does he look at me in the eye. Instead, he flicks his eyes toward Jadiel for approval.

My cousin gives a minute nod, and he speaks.

My cousin coughs, and he focuses on the wall behind me.

"And you work for Jadiel?"

"I—"

"Before you answer, you do understand I'm his boss? That my word is law?"

"I'm—"

"Cousin, don't be—" they begin in unison, but I hold a hand up, effectively silencing them.

"Teach your pet some respect, cousin." Finally, there's a reaction from Sergio and his hands tighten into fists. His lips thin, and mine stretch into a smirk. "Your job is a simple one and doesn't require a personal staff. You manage transport. Nothing more."

"Thiago, I do a lot more than schedule deliveries," he sneers, stupidly taking a step forward. Close enough, but I want to see how far he'd like to take this.

"You're a glorified errand boy. You do what I say."

Another two steps, his hands clenching. "Fuck—"

He doesn't get to finish his sentence as my hand shoots out, grabbing his neck and squeezing. My hold is tight, his face turning red. "What were you saying? I can't hear you?" I lift him off the floor, his feet dangling a foot or two off the ground. "Fuck me? Was that it?"

"Let him go," Sergio says, and it's the wrong move. Rule number one in this life: pay attention to your surroundings. Ivan cocks his gun right before pressing it to his neck, digging the barrel in deep.

"Kneel at his feet."

"Ivan, we—"

"You have ten seconds before I pull the trigger." My brother removes the gun but keeps it aimed for his head. "Get on your knees."

Sergio does so, his face ashen. His body also begins to shake. "Don't shoot me. Please."

Fucking pussy.

"Shut the fuck up and speak when spoken to," Ivan hisses out, finger twitching on the trigger.

In my hold, Jadiel becomes a bit limp and I let him drop. His head hits the expensive flooring and the sound of the crash is loud, but with the office being soundproofed, they won't hear a thing. No one to protect him. No one to feel bad for him since my aunt is dead and his father is an alcoholic asshole.

Crouching down, I watch him splutter with a hand on his throat as he fights to get enough air into his abused lungs. There's a bluish tint to his lips, his body writhing, and I feel no remorse.

He is my blood, but there is no love in me for the egotistical bitch.

Running the family is his ultimate hard-on, and our business interests don't align. The De Leons move drugs, weapons, and control the port by force and fear. Racketeering. That's how we hold this city hostage. Why everyone bows down.

Without our approval, getting a product in is difficult and bringing it down through the state's interstate leads to other complications. Being caught is one of them.

So they pay. A lot.

We don't traffic in humans. We don't kidnap pretty girls to sell them overseas.

I'll kill him first.

"Let's try this again, shall we?" His answer comes in the shape of a groan, and I take it under consideration. "What is your role in the De Leon Dynasty? Title and explanation."

"Lieutenant in charge of logistics."

"What else?" Pulling my phone out of my pocket, I wave him on before sending a text to Mom. "Give me the specifics."

"I make the schedules, coordinate the movement of merchandise, and send out soldiers to collect payments."

"What else?"

"That is it." Voice low. Meek.

"And who do you work for?"

"You."

"You're a member of this familia, Jadiel, but that doesn't give you leniency or protection against discipline." Condescendingly, I smack his cheek a few times, the force behind the hit just shy of painful. "Blatant disrespect won't be tolerated. Not by you, your father, or the gopher marrying your sister. A sister that wouldn't appreciate this sort of behavior."

"Apologize, asshole." My eyes shift toward Ivan and I stifle a chuckle. The man is near pissing himself. "This is our boss, and you'll lick his boots if asked."

"I'm sorry."

Pathetic at best, and I shake my head at him. "You don't seem to under-stand the severity of this infraction. Take him out back. We'll discuss his role with Celeste before I head out tonight."

"Understood." Ivan looks down at Sergio, his expression one of disgust. "Get up."

"Please, it's a misunderstanding."

"I said get the fuck up."

"What's going on here?" a voice says and my brother looks toward the opposite entrance where the foyer is. I don't waste my time. I don't owe him an explanation.

"Mind your business, uncle. This doesn't concern you."

"This is my son and—"

"Unless you want to end up on your bad knees, turn around and walk away," I say, standing to my full height and placing my shoe on his son's chest. Jadiel groans, his much lankier frame protesting. That's another difference between us; he's an office guy, while I like to dirty my hands. "You're only making it worse."

"Today is about celebrating, Thiago. No need for violence." His hands are up, eyes on Jadiel. They share a look; a warning from one man to the other. "Apologize to him. Now."

"I'm sorry, boss. I was just trying to be funny and it got out of hand."

I remove my shoe and step back, extending a hand. My cousin takes it and I yank him up with one harsh pull, bringing him close in what looks to be a man-hug, mouth near his ear. "I'm going to pretend this didn't happen, but you ever step out of line again, and you'll be joining me out at sea for a hosted event. Understood?" Even if he tries to hide it, I still feel the shiver that runs down his spine. He's afraid of me. Not even close to being able to handle being inside an octagon with me. "Cousin or not, I will kill you, your father, and the sack of mierda looking to marry Celeste. Watch yourself and don't ever let this happen again."

When I let him go, his father is there but Sergio and Ivan are nowhere to be seen.

"Can we be dismissed, sobrino? I'd like to discuss my son's behavior with him."

"You do that." Walking over to Andres, I kiss his cheek. "Because my patience can only run for so long."

They walk out and I stand my ground. Watching the door. Thinking.

Puzzle pieces start making sense, and that's when the danger begins.

They have no idea of the target on their backs.

"Run, motherfuckers," I say, and there's a click of a lock disengaging not far from me. The door to my mother's office opens and she comes out, smiling at me in a way that says *you're in so much trouble* and then continues on her way toward the back. No words. Nothing.

Not that it matters, because I'm already looking at the doorway awaiting her appearance. And when she does, all smiles and that sassy, defiant look in her eyes, I'm done for.

Luna arches a brow and I bite my lip.

She walks past me, and I'm following close behind.

There's somewhere I should be, but I don't give three flying fucks, and just before exiting through the kitchen and out onto the terrace, I stop to grab us two ice-cold beers. This takes a total of sixty seconds, that's it, and when I step out and people begin to clap—whistling obnoxiously loud—I smile.

Not because of the welcome back.

Not because of the people here.

I'm smiling at the sight of my father embracing his daughter after so long and the warm way her eyes meet mine. They're happy and bright, and I'm to going destroy the lives of so many to keep that lightness there.

Some of those assholes are here. Watching. Muttering under their breaths.

But all in due time.

Ivan now stands near the back and to the right with a woman beside him that I recognize from the file upstairs. He tilts his head in the direction of the far end of the lot where we keep a special housing unit that resembles an old-school jail. Dirty, rank, and with special inhabitants that feast on anything within reach.

He mouths the words, *Miguel* and *Sergio* while holding up two fingers. Cell two and Miguel is handling him.

I'm in no rush. The asshole can wait.

Scratching my chin, I look at the faces of each and every one in attendance. Friends, associates, foot soldiers, and family. All smiling. All waiting on some big speech.

"I want to thank you all for attending the celebration of my release from the state hotel." Silence meets my ears. Not so much as a bird chirp.

"My stay was fun. Enlightening. But most of all, it gave me time to think. To prepare." Raising my bottle, I settle my eyes on Luna while those around us mimic my action with their own drinks. "To the future." This time I receive a unanimous chant while she gives me a nod. "To a new era of violence in Miami." A yell in support while her eyes show understanding. She knows I'll never hurt an innocent, but may God have mercy on those responsible because I never will. "To the death of our enemies, because this is my public declaration of war to those that have done us wrong."

I don't miss how two figures shrink back and subtly walk away from the group celebrating. I don't miss Celeste's strange reaction or how she looks for Sergio through the throngs of people. Over a hundred in attendance, and three are missing. Three that are connected. Three with my eyes now on their every move.

For today, I'll play along, but come light tomorrow I'm going on a hunt and the woman standing beside Ivan with a scared expression on her face is the key to my success.

THIAGO

PEOPLE BEGIN TO disperse when I make my way across the terrace to Luna. She's all I have eyes for at the moment, the only person that deserves a detailed explanation, but it'll have to wait. At least until my personal guest leaves.

"That was some speech, *boss*," she croons, hand on her hip, accentuating her curves. My parents move away, entertaining a few associates and their wives while I ignore the world around us for just a few more seconds. "Invigorating."

"You know, you're the only person in this world whose sarcasm I find amusing. Cute, even."

"That's because I'm adorable in every single way." The way she bites her bottom lip makes me want to fuck that pretty little mouth. Watch her lips stretch around my girth and choke as I hit the back of her throat.

"Is that so."

"It is."

"You are very dangerous, beauty." I move closer, crowding her space.

Her heat sears me as I press against her, chest to chest. Lips hovering. "And I love the way you bite."

She places a hand on my chest, right over my beating heart. "This conversation feels very familiar to me. A repeat of every family function right before you say the words..."

"I have a meeting to attend." There's no anger or reproach, but I do see the burning curiosity. "And while this time is no different, I want you to accompany me. It might help keep the person calm."

"Are you serious?"

"I am." I've made mistakes, plenty of them, but knowing that she doubted my commitment to her is the one I regret the most. Before, I kept her from the darker side of the business. Kept her in the know without any gritty details, but that ends now. "Come on. Let's go talk to her."

"Okay. Sure, let me..." Luna trails off, her face scrunching up in confusion. There aren't many women in this industry, and the few we are aware of don't make moves outside of the West Coast. "Her?"

"Gaytan's wife is here."

"Carlotta is here?" I'm not the least bit surprised by her question, or more importantly, that she knows the woman's name. My girl is smart, cunning, and has access in different forms to the MPD database. "Why?"

I don't answer her, but I do extend a hand and wait. This is my asking her to trust me and follow my lead. To stand by my side.

A deep exhale follows, but my girl slips her hand into mine and lets me lead her away. We pass nosy guests, those who want to talk business or kiss ass, as we head toward the back building. The closer we get, the more guards stand at the post.

There are five of them up the cobbled path leading to the door and two more blocking the entrance. They all move aside as we walk straight through and up a small stairway off to the left that leads to a conference room.

It's not fancy or meant to entertain important acquaintances; it's an interrogation room before the horrors below swallow you whole. This is where my family gives you a chance to stop being a singao and take responsibility for your actions.

This is our confessional. Your last rights.

Upon entry, we find her and Ivan sitting at the far end of the long table, one on each side. They're not talking, but he was kind enough to find her a bottle of water and a few napkins to dab her red-rimmed eyes.

"Evening, Mrs. Gaytan." At the sound of my voice she startles, almost knocking the bottle over. "I apologize now for the less-than-stellar accommodations for this impromptu meeting."

"No apologies necessary, Mr. De Leon. I'm used to living in a less-than-safe neighborhood with my two children." Tears well up in her eyes and spill, but Carlotta is quick to dab her eyes. "My husband is never around. Never calls. He abandoned us."

"Have you taken him to court?" Luna asks and Carlotta gasps, noticing her presence. She recognizes Luna. Not that it deters my queen. No, she just walks toward where Ivan sits and takes a chair beside his. His eyes meet mine, but I shake my head. The reason that Luna is here will be more than self-explanatory in a few minutes. Once seated, she meets Gaytan's wife's stare head-on. "Because I can assure you, he makes very good money being the personal guard to Mayor Senot's wife."

"The courts stand with those who work for the city. Technically, he protects an official and as such, they seem to have immunity when it comes to child support cases or divorce."

"You've tried to divorce him?" Luna pushes the box of Kleenex closer to her.

"Twice now, and it was thrown out of court because the man refuses to sign. He actually had the audacity to tell the judge he was trying to win me and the children back." The venom in her tone doesn't surprise me. That piece of shit deserves every bit of my wrath coming his way. He's going to burn alive for his sins.

"How can I help you? Maybe I can talk to someone down at the precinct—my uncle is MDP and can help get the case given to another judge." My queen is beautiful in her anger for this woman, in the way she's helped calm down a fragile victim who up until now had no one in her corner. No one believed her.

But unfortunately, wishful thinking isn't how the world works.

People in power don't help or care unless it has some kind of personal gain attached.

"Where do you live, Mrs.—?" I begin, but the shake of her head cuts me off.

"Please don't attach me to that man's name or crimes. I have babies to take care of and feed."

"Of course..." I offer her a reassuring smile instead of a correction; she's dealt with enough. "But I do need you to answer the question, Ms. Suarez. Where do you live?"

"A low-income housing project at the center of the city." Her answer is succinct and doesn't give away her location. Nor does she ask how I know her maiden name. She's trying to protect her kids in case something goes wrong, and I don't press because after today, it won't matter.

"Okay." Pulling the chair out, I take a seat and lean back, scratching my jaw. "Are your kids somewhere safe for the next few hours?" Luna gives me a strange look at that, almost pleading with me not to scare her.

"Yes, sir." Carlotta isn't, though. If anything, she sits straighter in her seat. Brave woman. "I've done as you asked me to. I dropped them off before coming here."

"Good." Opening the laptop in front of me, I press my thumb to the scanner for access and pull up a tracking app. "When did you last see him? Do you know where your husband is today?"

"I do. It's a workday and *she* loves meeting up with friends for dinner," Carlotta spits out before taking a sip from her water bottle. I'm sure this is all weighing heavily on her head; the first time you help end a life is never easy. However, her husband's betrayal is burning her from within, and it's the dominating emotion she's focusing on. The years of hurt and neglect are cutting deep. "Ivan gave me the small tracker yesterday. I knew he'd show up if I mentioned going to social media to blast him via our text exchange, especially since our oldest has a vitamin deficiency and asthma. Within half an hour he was pounding on my door, smashing my phone and laptop and then pushing me around. My neighbor, a small-time dealer at that, stepped in and threw him out on his ass. While they fought, I slipped the small device onto the Mercedes symbol of his car."

There on the screen of my computer is a bright green light alerting me to his location. It's moving, traveling through Bal Harbour as we speak.

"I'm going to be very blunt with you, Ms. Suarez." She nods and sits back, her expression showing a hint of fear. "Your husband won't make it past the next seventy-two hours. He's done things that are unforgivable; hiring a hitman to kill my father and mother is one of them." Her bottom lip trembles but she keeps her tears at bay. Accepts this with as much grace as she has left. "He will pay with his life and you will disappear. Leave Florida. Start over wherever you want with the two million I've deposited into your account. There's nothing left for you here in Miami."

"Can I bring my mother? She's old and—"

"Yes."

"Thank you."

My eyes shift to Ivan's and I make a circular motion with my hand. "Get her to safety and ready your most trusted. Pick him up, no witnesses, and drop him off at the old stadium."

"I'll message you when I have him, brother." As he stands, Carlotta does the same, but pauses just before reaching for her purse. Her focus is on Luna. Just her.

"I'm sorry, Ms. Alejos. I'm so sorry that your world has been flipped multiple times because of the pure selfishness of others." Carlotta takes a deep breath and lets it out slowly while trying to find the right words to express herself. "I know it's going to hurt, but open your eyes, *please*, because those that hide behind the veil of righteousness are the vilest." Opening her large handbag, she pulls out a slim plastic case and walks over to me, pushing it into my hand. "My plan was to give this to you and ask that you share it with her. There are things on this recording that you both need to see. To hear."

I grip the case, eyes on hers. "Thank you."

"What's been done isn't right, Mr. De Leon. The people they've hurt...it needs to end." Carlotta's voice is just above a whisper toward the end, her eyes growing misty. "You know, when I married Alfredo, I was completely head over heels in love with him." The ghost of a smile appears for mere seconds. It's gone just as fast. "Blind and giving and forgiving, but the version of the man who said, 'I do' and the one on this recording— cheating and snorting coke—are two very different people. Money changes people, and it's made him unrecognizable to us."

"I'll make it look like a car accident. Your children will never know the truth."

"Thank you." Her eyes close then and the tears fall. Her body shakes, the sob escaping, and it's my queen that comes around the table to provide comfort.

Her arms encircle the crying woman and hold her tight, whispering something too low to make out. And that's more than fine with me; her compassion and beautiful heart is one of the things I love most about her. Carlotta pulls back slightly after a few minutes, nodding to Luna. "It'll be okay. I'm going to be okay."

"Yes, you are. Never forget that."

Mrs. Suarez's eyes flick to mine, a clear mixture of gratitude and sadness in the chocolate orbs. "She's a keeper. Don't ever let her go." Without another word, she turns and walks out to meet Ivan on the landing.

My beauty is silent, contemplative, as I take the few remaining steps between us and wrap my arm around her shoulders. "Are you okay?" I ask, laying a kiss to the side of her head. "Need anything?"

"A full hug and a beer would be nice." She shrugs, looking up at me from beneath long lashes. "These last few days have been something else."

Wrapping my arms around her, I tuck her under my chin, lips against her hair. "Not all bad, though? Right?"

"Nightmarish is more like it." My eyes narrow, but she doesn't see this. Instead, she's burrowing deeper and giggling to herself. However, that amusement dies just as fast and she pulls back enough to look me in the eye. "Why do I feel like this is just the tip of the iceberg? Like what's coming might break me?"

"I'll always hold you together, beauty." I lower my head to hers and peck those sweet lips once. Just a quick press. "Even the crazy pieces."

"You jerk!" she spits out, smacking me in the chest. Her mind moves from plaguing thoughts to abusing me, and I'll gladly take that heavy load and make it mine. I never want to see that sad and worried look on her face. "The only insane individual here is you."

"Is that so?"

"Yes, it is."

"Run."

"What?" she half laughs, half splutters.

"Run, little Luna."

"Do you think you'll catch me if I do?" She's already moving toward the exit, a small step at a time.

"Always." As I say this, her hand reaches back for the door. The doorknob twists but I see no rush in her. Instead, I feel like she's tempting. Wanting me to grab her. "You have five seconds."

"I only need two," she yells and then she's gone, rushing down the steps while I wait another beat and follow. Luna is halfway down when I step over the threshold and see her looking back at me with mirth in her eyes.

Wrong move. She stumbles, but rights herself and I find that as my opening. Grabbing onto the metal railing, I go down a few steps and then jump over, landing on the floor below. I hear her gasp without looking up, but I do catch her arm as she tries to zoom past me.

One gentle tug and I have her in my embrace again, looking down at her. "Gotcha."

"That was cheating," she gripes, trying to pinch me. Violent little thing.

"Nothing's fair in love and war." I know I've said those same words to her in the past, and I meant them then as much as I do now. I'll do whatever it takes to keep her. To always call her mine. "Now, let's go. We've been gone long enough."

With my hand on the small of her back, I guide us outside of the building where the faint pulsing beat of salsa hits us. It's slow at first: a bob of my head and the swing of her hips. Next, we hear the laughter coming from the guests back at the main house and the clapping of hands.

She looks up at me.

It's a silent request. A plea to drop everything for a while and enjoy ourselves.

And I do, pursing my lips and then bumping her shoulder with mine. "Five hundred bucks says my father is going to start a rueda before I can take you out myself."

"I'm not taking that bet."

"Why not?" I'm grabbing Luna's hand, twirling her around as we make it to the edge of the now-lit yard. There are twinkling lights all around us and a few couples showing off their dance moves as we reenter. Everyone notices us, they're smiling, all except my old man who looks ready to pull his favorite daughter away from me and out onto the dance floor.

"Because he'll do just that and then I'm—"

"Bebe, the only man you'll be dancing with right now is me," I croon and then turn her again, pulling her against my chest. "Are you ready to show these people how it's done?"

"Do you even remember how?"

"Wrong words." Before she can reply, I'm tipping her back low. Low enough that her hair skims the ground before I bring her back up, body pressed tightly against my own as our feet move.

It's synchronized perfection.

A sensual cadence burns from the inside as I follow her, moving to the island beat while people gather around. Their clapping matches our moves, the noises becoming one as she turns, her back to my front.

Those hips gyrate and her hands are in mine as she drops low and then rises, pushing her ass against my hard-as-steel cock. It's sexy. Mother-fucking beautiful.

And more so when she turns a second later with fire in her eyes, teeth embedded in her bottom lip.

It's a look I've seen before a hundred times.

It's want. Hunger. *Trouble.*

"Come a little closer, Thiago." Luna crooks a finger. "I don't bite."

Grabbing her other hand, I turn her once, twice—five times in fast succession. Her giggles ring out, her eyes bright each time she catches sight of my shitty grin. And when she wobbles a bit from the speed in which I turn her, I bring her back to my chest with my lips at her ear. "I proudly wear your marks. Do your worst."

Luna's lips part, her sweet breath fanning across my mouth, but before she can reply…

"May I cut in?" My father stands to the side of us with a proud grin on his face. He's oblivious to our exchange and I just barely hold back my smirk. "I need my dance partner, son. To show these people how it's done."

It's comical how her lips snap shut and eyes widen. I can almost imagine the inappropriateness of whatever retort she has on the tip of her sweet tongue.

"If the lady wants?" At my response, her eyes narrow and she subtly brings her high-wedged foot down over mine. It doesn't hurt like she thinks, but instead sends my receptors into overdrive. Pleasurable pain traverses through my over six-foot frame and settles on the tip of my engorged cock, causing it to give a harsh jerk behind the metal of my zipper. "Well, Luna? Do you?"

"Orlando," her voice is soft, the perfect innocent vixen, "can you have them play *Llororas*?"

Dad's eyes flick to mine and you can see the mirth in them. Asshole. "Of course, mi niña." He extends his hand out and she places hers in his, but then pauses and turns back to face me. Rising on the tip of her toes, she presses her lips to my chin. Just leaves them there, her flesh on mine and my nostrils flare, her scent pulsing through my veins.

"Luna." There's warning in my tone, but she doesn't adhere to it. Instead, she nips the skin there and pulls back enough to once again meet my heated stare.

"Enjoy the show."

THIAGO

MY EYES FOLLOW her every move across the decent-sized dance area my parents set out for the gathering. It's made from some kind of wood flooring, interconnecting pieces, and designed by a family friend that's an architect in South Florida when he remodeled the home a few years back for my mother's fiftieth.

Hendrix Parker is also the man responsible for designing my new home.

A body sidles next to me and I cock my head to the side. I've been expecting her. "Let me have it, Nat."

"I'm still mad, asshole." Natasha pinches my side and I laugh, swatting her hand away. "You hurt us all by doing that crap and then leaving. She was a wreck, Leon."

"I know." I can feel her eyes on the side of my face, how she's fighting to keep her voice down. Not that I care either way. She's Luna's cousin and I care about her like I do my own family, but right now, what she has to say doesn't matter a single lick to me. My eyes are on my girl. On how she throws her head back and laughs at something my viejo says.

How her hips sway perfectly in time with each beat as the singer declares that the girl who's done him wrong will cry. Suffer like he did.

It's a jab at me.

Her way of flicking me metaphorically off while saying *eat your heart out*.

What she fails to understand is that I would rather eat her instead. Lick. Bite. Devour.

"Are you even listening to me?"

"Not really." Not going to lie to her.

There's a huff and then another pinch. "Can you look at me, dammit?"

"Taking my eyes off Luna is nearly impossible after so long, Nat. Sorry." My beauty accepts the hand of another dancer, my godfather this time, and is turned three quick times before following his quick footwork. They push back and come forth on the count of three, turning to the right as the circle around them does the same. Six couples on the floor and all moving in one unified choreograph.

A quick hand movement—extending her away from her dance partner—and she's back with my dad now.

"Looking at her like that isn't helping me stay mad," Natasha deadpans after a lengthy sigh. "I know you love her, Thiago, but—"

"No buts." For a brief moment, I look over while ignoring someone's high-pitched whistle. Sounds like it came from my mother, and her loud *dale* a few seconds later confirms it. "I've loved—love her now as much as I did when we met in high school. That will never change, Nat." Her eyes soften and the harsh line her lips were set in quirks up just the tiniest bit at the corner. "And I'd also like to think you know me enough to know that I couldn't give a flying, bloody fuck about who doesn't agree with our relationship. I fucked up, I let her down in one aspect, but she also forgot to trust me. Forgot every single thing I've told her over the years."

"Wait, I think your mis—"

"Am I?" I narrow my eyes. "Isn't this where you tell me to leave her alone?"

"Not at all, jerk." Natasha's eyes grow misty, her expression sad as she punches the same side she's pinched twice. Violent family.

"Hands to yourself, Alejos. I take the abuse from her and no one else."

"Shut up. You owed me that last one."

"Keep it up and I'll tell your father who crashed his '69 Stingray your senior year."

"You wouldn't."

"Try me."

"Fine." She even makes an exaggerated show of putting her hands behind her back. "Better?"

"Much." At her dramatic action, a chuckle escapes me, causing her to giggle. It's stupid and makes no sense why I find it so amusing, but I do. It reminds me of all the idiotic conversations I've had with her over the years. How close our little group has always been. She's been like a little sister to me and always in our corner; someone I trust. My laughter ceases and I clear my throat. "I'm sorry, Nat. Hurting either of you wasn't my plan, but at the time I had no choice but to make things appear a certain way. With everything going on, and the MDPs detectives sniffing around, I needed her away from this. From me. Should I have come to her, yes, but at the same time, we both know she would've fought me tooth and nail to help. I was working on borrowed time and leaving her alone…caught in the middle, was unacceptable to me."

She nods, her body language a bit less stiff. "What about having men put on her for protection? To keep her safe while you were—"

"Who says I didn't?"

"Then why?" she asks, and Natasha doesn't need to elaborate for me to understand.

"Because I needed the hit placed on her head back on me. It's all I had at the moment, Nat, and in order to keep her safe, I made it seem as if she was nothing to me when in fact, she's my world."

"But why go the cheating route?"

"Because it works. Plain and simple." It sucks, but it's the truth. No sugarcoating. "The same night Luna found me with Amberlyn, the hit shifted back to my family. We knew that would happen and took the necessary precautions, like armoring the vehicles."

"Like Maritza's."

"Exactly."

In a move I'm not expecting, Nat hugs me tight once before stepping back and as she does, I catch Luna's eyes. Her smile is bright and cheeks flushed. She's also holding a thumb up at me which makes me roll my eyes.

"Go to her."

"What?" Luna crooks a finger behind my father's back and mouths the words *come get me*.

"…all I want is for you guys to be happy." I catch the end of Natasha's words and pull my eyes away from the woman I love beyond all comprehension. "I also want my cousin to smile every single day like she's been doing since news of your release broke out. And while I might still be a smidge mad at you, Leon…" she holds up two fingers to show just how tiny her anger is "…I'll never stand in the way of her happiness."

"Thank you, Nat."

"Just never break her heart again."

"Never again will we ever be apart," is all I say before making my way toward the coquettish woman daring me to steal her away. And I do just that. Without giving the old man a chance to refuse or block my attempt, I have her in my arms and holding her close as a bachata begins to play. Her body and mine are one as we move. Her mouth, those berry-colored lips parting as I grip her hip and anchor her to me. "You're mine now."

"I've always been yours."

"Wake up, asshole," I sneer early the next day while grabbing a bucket full of dirty mop water and throwing the contents at his head. The wetness spreads all around Sergio, one rivulet coming to a stop just in front of my all-white Pumas.

At once, Sergio sputters as a few drops of water rolling down his face slip between parted lips. His face scrunches up before his taste buds fully decipher the nasty taste; it's the same water used to clean the mess my large hogs leave behind on the premises.

"What the fuck?"

I toss him an old rag. "Sit up and clean your face."

Sergio glares at me, not fully taking me in as I stand in the doorway to one of our detainment cells. The bright Florida sun is harsh on the eyes and he begins to squint soon after. "Who the fuck is there? I demand to be—" His words die as I take two steps forward, my hard stare meeting his now scared one.

"Good. You're learning some manners." The table is an old, scratched up wooden piece of shit in a hideous pine color and the dirty water from the bucket pools at the center. The walls are an off-white that now seems yellow in the daylight, and the only thing dry is a chair against the wall and I grab it, flipping it around so I can sit backwards. "Full name?"

"Where am I, Thiago? Where's Jadiel?" His eyes shift around nervously, taking in his surroundings. "What day is it?"

Miguel, who stands behind him, reaches out and grabs a fistful of his black hair and yanks back on his ponytail, causing Sergio's neck to extend into an uncomfortable position. He stares at my guard, mouth agape, throat bobbing harshly as Miguel's hand comes down across his cheek. "Only answer what is asked. Nothing else."

"Okay." That earns him another strike. Sergio's face is now red, and the fingerprints left behind are becoming more pronounced.

"That's enough." At my mock admonishment, my guard lets him go, pushing him forward and toward the Ruger now atop the table. "Let's give the man a chance to answer." Scared eyes meet mine. He's sweating. "What. Is. Your. Full. Name?"

He swallows hard. "Sergio Martinez."

"And your age?"

"Twenty-nine."

"Where were you born?"

"New Jersey."

"Where in Jersey?" I ask, even though I already know the answer. I also know that's not the last name on his birth certificate. Martinez is his deceased grandmother's maiden name.

Why's he choosing to lie? Don't know, but it won't remain a mystery for long. Today is his only warning because Sergio Martin, not Martinez, is from the same city as my Luna.

He hung out at the same places. He was friends with her male older cousin from her mother's side who passed away from a car crash the night of his twenty-second birthday.

They weren't close—he barely knew my queen—but I do remember her sad eyes when they found out. I remember Yvette dragging her and Natasha back to Westfield for a weekend of mass, a vigil, and then burial.

"Westfield, New Jersey," Sergio coughs a bit, his mouth still tasting like shit from the filthy water. "May I have a drink, please?"

"Only because you said *please* so nicely." I tap the back of the chair and stand, heading toward the far end where I keep a small refrigerator. It isn't plugged in, but there are two water bottles inside that are just a bit over hot. "I apologize for the lack of provisions. This is all I have."

Sergio grimaces when his fingers wrap around the water bottle. "No worries. I understand, sir."

My eyes shift to Miguel, who's holding back a laugh, then back to him. "Go ahead and drink up, Sergio. We need to wrap up this little chat."

I'll give him points for keeping the disgust out of his expression while taking a large gulp of the old water. I have no idea how long that's been there nor do I care; it serves a purpose.

"Now, are we done?"

He drains the entire bottle. *Guess hot beats dirty.* "Yes."

"Good." I don't retake my seat, choosing instead to walk around to him. The closer I get, the more he shrinks back and when I stop just within reach, Sergio almost falls over.

And in that moment of fear.

That singular second of realization...

I strike.

Grabbing his wrist, I slam it against the wooden table with one hand and take my Ruger with the other. The barrel against his skin gets his attention. "Don't fucking move." He doesn't listen and I lift the gun, bringing it down with force against his knuckles. Once. Twice. A total of five times, breaking the bones there.

His scream rents the air. His sob follows. *Pussy.*

"Fuck. Please...*please* stop," he cries out, fighting to pull his hand from my grip. If anything, he further injures himself. Dislocated his wrist. "We're family!"

That one pisses me off and the next strike is to his mouth and then neck, causing him to choke. To shut the fuck up and lose a tooth in the process. There's spluttering and gasping and even blood dribbling from the split lip, but I'm not done.

Before his next intake of breath, I'm jamming my Ruger just under his chin. "We're not family, *Martinez*. Dating my cousin doesn't make you one of us. That shit is earned." My finger twitches on the trigger while his body shakes, the pain radiating from his expression. "Now, answer my next question."

"Anything. I don't want problems."

It's meek and I crack a smile. "Why did you move here?"

"For school, and then I liked—"

"The truth, Sergio," I cut him off. "Don't let me be the reason my cousin doesn't finish planning this wedding."

"I moved here to follow a dream."

"So you're a chaser now?" My phone vibrates inside my pocket and I let him go, taking a few steps back. I pull it out and read the message.

> Pick up is done. Dropping off the sack of potatoes now. ~Little Bro

I type my reply just as fast.

> Thank you. See you soon. ~Thiago

"Yes."

"Okay," I say and let him go, stepping back to accept the small towel my guard has for me. My hands have a little blood on them and so do my new sneakers. *Fucking asshole.* "Let's get him cleaned up and back home within the next twenty-four hours. If anyone asks, he was busy doing a little favor for me and fell on the job. Understood?"

"Of course, boss. We all know the man can be clumsy."

"I didn't hear your response, Sergio. Understood?"

"Yes, I'm clumsy and fell."

I walk out without another word and find one of the two watchmen standing at the ready. He doesn't ask questions, but once I move past him, goes inside to help Miguel.

There are far more important things to focus on today than Sergio, even though my eye is on him. He's full of shit, and his secret isn't as hidden as he thinks.

He's useful at the moment, I'll give him that.

Easy to break.

However, Jadiel is what keeps him alive, but once I discover how deep his betrayal runs, I'll break both their necks personally.

THIAGO

IT'S THREE O'CLOCK by the time I arrive at an abandoned stadium near Jackson Memorial Hospital on Monday. It's old, unsafe, and dirty. It's full of rats and used needles—random articles of clothing thrown about different areas of the premises.

Sad. This place wasn't always like this.

In its heyday, the stadium was used for spring training by some of the largest baseball associations nationwide; it's also where the home team began as a minor league club.

Now, though, it's a condemned site and only a few brave crackheads come inside to use or fuck. Then there's me and my family. When we occupy, the surrounding population scatters and hides—they pretend the giant eyesore doesn't exist.

I like it that way.

It's why I haven't torn it down.

As of 2001, while being nothing more than a kid, I'm the owner. A gift from my father when the city wanted to blow it up, taking with it memories of Miami's baseball dreams.

Before our team became a major league threat.

Before we won championships.

I'm a baseball fan and the city cashed in on the much-needed relief from the self-made debt that the then mayor at the time was responsible for. The transaction was all in cash. No traces, which served him just fine as he escaped a lengthy prison sentence due to the miraculous funds he "proved" to just be misplaced by the last auditors.

Stepping through the hole in the shitty fencing, I make my way in through the main doors. They're busted, rusted, and useless, but I don't keep the place for its beautiful facade.

This is an untouched territory in the heart of Miami, and right at the center of what used to be the luxurious lobby is an almost naked Gaytan. He's tied up, hands above his head on a large truss that's seen better days.

There's a *drip drip drip* above him. Most of the ceiling is gone and what's left doesn't protect him from nature. That, and somewhere above is a leaking pipe that's unleashing its torment, one drop at a time.

Right over the same spot now for three days.

All day.

Every few seconds.

Softening the skin at the crown of his head.

His eyes widen when he fully takes me in. Recognition takes over; he sees his death in my eyes. "Evening, Alfredo," I say, stopping just a few feet from his filth. There's no one else here besides me. It's unnecessary when the people in Allapattah and surrounding areas mostly work for you in one capacity or another. "How's your day going? Are you hungry or thirsty?"

"Let me go." His fight or flight has kicked in and he struggles against his bonds.

"Why would I do that?"

"This is a mistake. You're making a terrible mistake!" There's fear in his eyes and his body gives a slight shake when I pull a few things out of my pocket: phone, money clip, and my brass knuckles. "The Senots won't take—"

"Quiet." His lips snap shut, eyes shifting away from my glare. "Not another word unless I ask a direct question. Understood?" Gaytan is smart enough to nod his head, the action causing his face to contort in pain; there's a large bruise on his neck. "Good boy."

He doesn't like being addressed like a dog, and I could give two flying fucks.

Giving him my back, I turn and grab a small wooden stool Ivan left for me. I drag it slowly toward him, pushing aside whatever garbage is in my path—the noise loud inside the large, open, and mostly dilapidated structure.

Then I place it a few steps from him. If he'd been loose, it'd be within reach.

Close but not.

A taunt.

One that I bolster by placing my items atop it before adding my loaded gun to that same pile.

No safety. A quick pull of the trigger and one of us would be dead.

"You never answered my questions, by the way," I say and get no reply. "How are you? Hungry?"

"Are you offering me a last meal?" Alfredo's reply—the sarcasm—grates on my nerves, and before his next intake of breath, I backhand him across the mouth, fully aware that my gold rings will knock out a tooth or two. The two at the front bear the brunt of the force, the metal breaking them in half.

Leaning forward, I smirk. "Want it to be?"

"Fuck you!" It leaves him on a bloody lisp, his lips split where the broken teeth embedded. I don't reply, but I do grab my gun, pointing it straight at his head with a brow arched. "Please don't."

"What happened to *fuck me*?" A pull of the trigger and a bullet dislodges; it barely misses his arm. Just barely.

"Are you insane!" Arching, he fights to pull away—stresses his shoulder and pops the one on the left without me placing a single finger on him. "Son of a bitch." It's a hiss, teeth clenching tight as his position only adds stress to the dislocated area. "You're going back to jail where you belong. Mr. Senot can—"

"Suck my dick." The next bullet exits the chamber and lodges into his thigh, the same side as his dislocated shoulder. His scream of pain is loud, but I'm not moved at all. Instead, I give him a bored look. Dramatics bore me. "Are you done?"

No answer. Not any that I can decipher as he writhes, blood flowing from the wound, complaining in gibberish that only he can understand. Sure, there's a *fuck* here or there thrown about, but the rest is a bunch of nonsensical groans that add up to shit.

So, I fire again.

The third bullet grazes his side over the bluish marks on his right ribs. There's a bit of red that rushes to the surface, the heated burn of the bullet leaving its marks, but no deep cut or puncture. It's a flesh wound, but if you go by his pathetic wails, you'd think I cut off a limb with a rusty saw.

Pussy. Tilting my head, I lower my Ruger to the area just below his belt and wait.

"Please don't." Sweat forms at his brow and upper chest now, the hairs at the latter matting against his tan skin. "Not there."

I almost chuckle. Almost. He acts as if he'll have the chance to use it again.

"Then don't test my patience again." At my words, he nods and I lower my weapon. It takes its place once again on the stool as I remove my shirt, the white Ralph Lauren polo going with the rest of my belongings. "Now, are we ready to play twenty questions? Will you behave?"

"Yes." A low whisper, his body shaking as reality sets in.

"Okay." Walking closer, I take inspection of the damage already inflicted and roll my eyes at my brother's handiwork. There's a ring all the men in my family wear, a thick gold band with our last name branded over the top with a yellow topaz on the left of the large "D" for my mother's birth month. It's gaudy, very Cuban, and mine is retrofitted to carry Luna's stone on the right.

Ivan's, though, is a bit more eccentric.

A bit more brutal.

His letters are in 3D and pointy; they embed the letters onto the skin if he throws a punch and it lands at just the right angle, a perfected bitch-slap that marks Gaytan right over the back of his shaved head.

"First question." There are bruises across his back large enough to come from a shoe sole and the cut over his left eyebrow that's swollen, but his eye is fine. "Why are you here?"

"I don't know." The first sign of a liar is the inability to look you in the eye. His shitty eyes look past my shoulder and focus on the entrance.

"Final warning." My tone is icy, dripping with the ire I have the power to unleash at any moment. "Answer the fucking question."

"I'm telling you the...*Jesus*," he cries out, body fighting to pull away from the hand I've placed over his injured shoulder, digging my fingertips in to the point his body shakes from the pain. His teeth grit together so hard he cuts his own tongue. Tears well up in his eyes as I watch him, and just when his lips part to speak again, I kick his legs further apart so his weight drops, forcing his bonds to stretch the muscle. "It wasn't me."

"What wasn't you? Be specific, Alfredo." The rope cuts into his wrist and he winces when I finger the bound flesh. "What is it that you didn't do?"

"I-I didn't..." Alfredo pauses, swallowing hard. His mouth is bloody; rivulets stain the beard at his chin and then neck. "I didn't hire Ismael."

"Hmm." That's all I say. I'm not here to comfort him.

"It's the truth."

"Are you sure about that? Last chance."

"Yes. It was..." He mumbles the name I need. It's low, almost too low for me to hear, but I do as if Alfredo shouted it.

"Louder." Just because I can. Because we both know there's no feasible way that it'll stay hidden for long.

That *she'll* stay hidden

"I'll pay with my life to save—"

"Your bitch the heartache? A death sentence?" My glower alone forces him to arch away, adding more pressure to the joints of his arms. "Because we both know Jasmine doesn't give a fuck about either of you."

"She loves ME!" Gaytan suddenly yells out, his own anger bursting forth. The idiot still doesn't see how he's been played in all of this. "She approached me before Ulysses asked me to do so—to fucking end your piece-of-shit family—but when I said no, he promised me something I couldn't deny. We were banking on you discovering his plan and ending him. That you would set *us* free."

"And yet here you are, just like Roger." With a quickness Gaytan doesn't expect, I pull out a small knife from my front pocket and flick the blade open. I'm quick with it, my arm slicing through the air and across the ropes tethering him to the truss. A single slice cuts through the rope just below his right wrist, while the second motion breaks what's left around the wooden beam. He falls, his bruised and bloody body meeting the dirty concrete floor below. "But then again, she probably made him feel important. Blew him while professing some poetic shit that made his simpleton mind bow at her feet."

Gaytan's eyes are closed now, his body trembling. "Roger?"

"Was fucking her too," I answer, breaking the last of his spirit. "He thought himself in love until the very end, but then self-preservation kicked in and…"

"He gave us away." So much sadness in his tone. Heartbreak.

"He gave *her* away." Because Alfredo needs to understand that he's of no importance. To me. To her. To Roger. To his kids that'll grow up in a safe and healthy environment after his death. "You're nothing but an over-rated gopher who drank the Kool-Aid and bought the bullshit attached. You were a pity fuck. A necessity in order to achieve compliance from a man not worth pig shit."

"Roger was my friend." Tears drop from his eyes, his face contorted in anguish. In mourning, and I smile. I find his emotional pain amusing.

"Is that betrayal I detect in your voice?" With a smirk on my face, I place a foot atop his torso and press down right over the flesh wound. It bleeds, opening just a little bit deeper. "Do you need a hug or pat on the back? Do you need me to supply the fake condolences?"

"I cared about him."

"Roger is dead and on his way to being shark chum off the coast of the Bahamas."

"Just end me." It's a whimper, pathetic and unmoving.

"With pleasure…" he nods, closing his eyes in wait "…but not yet."

Gaytan frowns. "Why are you prolonging—"

"Because I can. Because the family you abandoned also deserves some retribution." Brown orbs snap open and meet my amused ones. His shock is evident. He didn't think me to be so thorough. "Those kids will never know how much of a scum you were. They'll grow up happy, healthy, and Carlotta will find a man worthy of her. She'll never depend on a man again. She'll never put up with scraps in order to maintain those kids. They'll move on while you rot. They'll truly live while you become nothing but an unpleasant memory not to be revisited."

"How much do you know?"

And there's the fifty million dollar question.

How much? How little? Why am I fucking with him?

"You're alive just to confirm what I already know." Bringing the hand with the knife in my grip up, I turn the blade, letting the sunlight filtering through a hole in the roof glint off the metal. "Nothing more."

Gaytan coughs then, his abdomen constricting, and he grimaces. Tries to fold into himself.

He's in pain without reprieve.

He's facing his reality without an ounce of hope.

It takes him a moment to compose himself, to stop squirming beneath my foot on his torso. "Jasmine never hid her lovers, you know. I accepted them."

"Why?"

"Because she promised me that I'd always be her number one."

"And Ulysses? Does he know?"

"He does." A cough escapes again, a bit of blood in the spittle. "He's not man enough to satisfy her and at the same time likes to watch. Ulysses enjoys being her bitch. Her cuckold husband."

"But if you're an employee and not her bull, who is?"

Say it. Say his name.

"Antonio Alejos." He's grown a bit pallid and sweat forms at his brow.

"Thank you, Mr. Gaytan." I remove my shoe, take a step back, and raise my knife by the very tip of the blade. "Your death is only the beginning."

"Wait!" he yells out suddenly, more panicked than he's been thus far. Maybe it's the delirium from blood loss. Maybe he's afraid to die. "Let me just say goodbye—"

A quick flick of the wrist and I embed the blade three inches deep into the center of his neck, cutting off his nonsense. Alfredo's reaction is automatic, to grip the base, but before he can pull it out, I have my hand on my gun and I'm firing round after round.

I don't stop until his body lies motionless and he's looking back at me with horror in his expression. He's bathing the ground with his life's essence. Paying for his crimes against my family, but I wasn't kidding when I said this is just the beginning.

I'm going for the head of Medusa.

I'm going to break her and then watch the rats try and scatter.

Luna

I HAVEN'T SEEN Thiago for more than a few minutes here or there since Saturday night.

Since he dropped me off at home a week ago with a toe-curling kiss that weakened my knees and left me a panting mess when he left. He didn't try to have his way with me. Nor did he come inside my home.

Instead, against my closed door his hips pinned mine while his mouth reaffirmed what I already know is my truth...

I'm his and he is mine.

I am totally failing at this making him chase me thing. I need to be stronger.

"Feeling better, Alejos?" my boss asks, bringing me back to the present and I look up, catching his stern expression. Today, though, behind the serious look, there's a touch of amusement. It looks weird because I don't think I've ever seen my boss so much as smile. "That must've been some virus you caught. Used up all your vacation time this year."

We both know it's a lie. I'm sure the opinions running rampant in this precinct alone placed doubts on my sudden bout of "sickness" as well as reputation. While most officers here treat me with respect—they know who my father and uncle are—I'm still looked at differently. Judged as the ex-girlfriend of a notorious mafia boss and not trusted.

I'm sure that my absence was spoken about, but I just don't care. This isn't my career path for life, just until I find what I came looking for.

"I'm better, sir. Just a small twinge of queasiness left behind."

"You want to be benched today?" he asks, taking a sip from the most hideous mug I've ever seen. It's a toilet. Literally. His daughter gave it to him as a gag gift two years ago on his birthday, and the crotchety old man loves it. Drinks his coffee from it every day.

"Not at all." Sitting back, I keep my expression cool while avoiding the piece of ceramic I wish to smash with a hammer. It's gross. Looks gross. However, I do see the folder in his other hand, the label in the color red that is his way of coding priority levels. Depending on the scene, if first responders tampered with the evidence, and lastly, if we're looking at a case with a fatality. "Whatcha got for me?"

The color he's holding is for fatality.

"Are you sure?" Thompson has never, not even when I came in with a broken index and middle finger from a fall, asked me this. *What's his deal?* "You could help the crew in the back with the physical cataloging of—"

"I'm sure. Not a doubt."

"Fine." The man mumbles the word *stubborn* under his breath. It's low, but I catch it and decide not to question him. "We got a Jane Doe out in Sweetwater. Call came in about fifteen minutes ago." He's watching curiously while extending the file out toward me. As he does this, I catch for the first time since taking this job the sight of a set of numbers tattooed on the inside of his wrist.

I've seen that before. On multiple people. On *his* people.

The hell?

"Sir, what's that on—"

"Are you taking this case, or do I send Walker instead?" My eyes snap back to him and he shakes his head. He's telling me to drop it for now, and I do. *For now* being the operative words.

Someone has some explaining to do.

Someone has been keeping tabs on me.

Someone never stopped taking care of me.

It shouldn't warm my heart, but it does, because it's just another sign that Thiago didn't just leave. That he thought ahead. That he had more faith in me than I had in him.

I never thought twice when the sudden position as a forensic investigator became available for me. When my uncle pretty much walked me inside after graduating and gave me the paperwork to sign, without so much as an interview. At the time, I took it as he spoke highly of me and cleared the pathway I needed without my asking.

He and Natasha are the only two people that knew of my plans. Who knew that I wanted to clear his name and then shoot him myself for the stupidity he pulled.

Because even angry at him—hurting—I needed to help him in any way I could.

There's a lightness in my heart right before it clenches with the disappointment that follows.

I didn't trust him, and yet, my papi knew I'd do this. That I would take the challenge on.

And I've risen to the challenge. Two of the detectives working his case have been fired for tampering. The judge who sentenced him was caught with two prostitutes out on Biscayne Blvd in a seedy motel, pants around his ankles and with his hands dipping into the cookie jar—two street workers whose cases had been dismissed inside his courtroom.

Those pictures hit circulation quickly. Every single local news station played that story at the beginning of each broadcast for weeks and put a giant question mark on all his previous convictions.

And yet, it's still not enough. I'm after the head of this snake, and up until yesterday, I'd been looking in the wrong direction. At the wrong people.

"I'll take it."

"Good. Good." The tension in his shoulders drops a bit. "Officer Alejos will be escorting you, and Natasha is on her way now to handle the written documentation of the scene. It's a gruesome one, and this needs to be handled quickly as it's near an elementary school."

"When do we leave?"

"Now, kid. Let's head out," Uncle Edgar says from behind me and I turn my head, taking in his expression. He looks so much like my father, but that's where the similarities die. He's happy and down to earth, and the only thing he's ever cared about is my and his daughter's well-being. "You ready?"

"Yeah. I'm ready." My equipment is the first thing I prepare after clocking in, and my bag is ready to go. Pushing my chair back, I stand and grab it from the corner of the small desk I use here. We don't talk as we head outside of the building; there's so much to say, but with ears around, it's best to keep our lips shut.

However, that changes once inside his unmarked car. Because while it still belongs to the city and it's loaded with cameras and audio, talking in code is something my family has perfected over the years. He's a cop with a shady past, my father is a city council member with enough sins to ruin his hope of a future governor position, and then, you have me.

The once-almost wife to Thiago De Leon. A known criminal. A known killer.

We're dysfunctional as fuck.

"Missed you at the family dinner on Saturday, Tio." My first words are generic, to be interpreted as an Alejos get together. "Hot date kept you away? Who's the new flavor?"

"Was busy. I *am* seeing someone, but it's a short-term thing." He shrugs, reversing the car and then shifting into drive. The exit is on the other end of the lot, and as he passes a group of rookies standing beside a square car, they all pause to look. At me, not him. "Blind dates usually don't go past that."

In other words he was working, but for Thiago, and blind date means delivery of goods.

"Oh, I know. Your daughter has tried a few times to get me to fall down that rabbit hole and I refuse."

"Has she, now?" He grumbles something under his breath. "Need me to tell her to back off?"

"Not really."

"Are you sure?" His eyes shift over briefly before facing forward, turning right and merging with traffic heading toward the expressway. "I know firsthand how Natasha can be at times."

"After Saturday, Nat got the message loud and clear." My uncle nods, seemingly at ease now, but I'm not done. "Your presence was missed, though. I would've loved to see you there…to hang out like we used to."

Before everything went down, we were all so close. Him, Natasha, and me.

He's who I trusted and came to when my parents were unbearable. When they put down my relationship with someone they see as unworthy. Uncle Edgar has always been in my corner and I took it a bit for granted, gave him crap for picking a side that wasn't mine, when it's the farthest thing from the truth.

And I'll admit that it's my anger that got in the way.

"Hazard of the job, Lunita. You miss important occasions."

"You sounded like your brother just then," I say, trying to crack a joke, but at once I see that it falls flat. His hands tighten around the steering wheel and nostrils flare; the look he gives me alone is one I've never been on the receiving end of.

Before addressing me, I watch discreetly how he elbows the door, giving it one solid thump with his elbow. To the naked eye, it seems that he did it by mistake, but then another sound fills the air—a low buzz, and then as if an old VHS tape slid into a VCR player.

"Look straight ahead and not a word. Understood?"

"Yes."

"Good." A second thump a second or two later, and the whizzing sound picks up in speed. My eyes shift to the passenger side window then, taking in the scenery that in Miami means nothing more than a few thousand vehicles on the road with angry drivers inside. People here drive with a purpose, and mostly a *get out of my way* mentality that very few can handle.

We're special like that. I wouldn't change my home for the world.

And it's also where I truly believe that the expression "road rage" was invented.

It takes about a minute for the whizzing sound to stop and for him to look my way. I can feel his stare and turn to catch his glare.

"What was that?"

"Never compare me to that *asshole,* sobrina," he grits out instead, choking back a curse word or two. "Your father is a self-absorbed cabron that doesn't deserve you as his daughter."

"Tio, I never meant it—" I'm interrupted by the sound of his radio crackling and the operator shooting off a few codes along with the location of a robbery in progress. It's near the Bayside Marketplace and all available units are being called in. At once, three other squad cars respond, confirming their location and in route process toward the clothing store.

For a few beats after we stay quiet, listening to the communication between officers and dispatch. His expression says it all, though. There's guilt there and something else that I can't quite identify.

"I'm sorry."

"I'm sorry," we say in unison, and I chuckle. The amusement dies down quickly, though. "I really am, you know. Sorry, that is."

"You did nothing wrong, Luna. Nothing."

"Not for the bad joke, Tio, because that's all it was, but for the last few years. If I ever hurt you or was a jerk, I apologize."

"Not needed, but accepted since I never gave you the chance to pull away."

"You are stubborn."

"Ditto." Edgar chuckles, but that turns into a heavy sigh near the end. "I shouldn't have given you the attitude, Luna. My anger toward my brother shouldn't fall on you." He reaches his right hand out and gives my arm a squeeze. "Mine and Antonio's relationship isn't in a good place at the moment. Let's leave it at that for now."

"Will you two ever be okay?" He shakes his head in the negative at my question and I nod. "Can't say I'm surprised. He's become someone I no longer recognize."

Edgar looks like he wants to add something to that, but a rough exhale escapes instead. "To answer your earlier question; Thiago had this car, and a few others on the force, retrofitted with special blocking devices. Once that goes on, it records the driver for sixty seconds and reports the playback to the department. It'll play in real time and on a constant loop."

"When the hell did he do that?" I play along, dropping a subject I can see plain as day he doesn't want to visit. "The guy has been out for a little over a week."

"This was seven days after his sentencing."

"That makes no sense."

"Doesn't need to." At my incredulous look, he rolls his eyes and waves one hand in the air. "Francisco, the mechanic at the precinct, is on the Leons payroll. You've been around them longer and can fill in the rest better than I can."

"Christ." My emotions are spinning between heartache, confusion, amusement, and lastly…I'm in awe of him. It's getting harder and harder to not let my love for the man dominate me blindly, and while a part of me longs to let go and do just that, his mother's advice still rings true in my ear: he needs to see me as his equal, too.

They've been a constant companion as of late, those words, especially after listening to the recording of him before jail. It's made me think. Made me accept that I too, am to blame. And while I don't agree with his lying, with letting me think the worst of him, I forgot my own promise to him.

To trust him. To know that I am his one and only.

"He's always one step ahead, Luna. Always."

"Funny you say that…" I trail off, turning my attention back to the main road. It's busy and full of loud music—life going on as if nothing's changed—while I'm battling this yo-yoing effect. Inner demons that whisper words of fear, revenge, and love.

"Why is that?"

"Because the more I sit down and think, the more obvious things become, and I feel like an idiot. So many changes, and I never once questioned what was happening around me because truly, it was convenient."

"Sometimes our minds protect us that way."

"Or maybe it was too painful to accept that the man I love more than life itself was close but on the same breath, unreachable." And that sums up my emotions to a T. I'm not an idiot, and yet, I chose to follow blindly without questioning a single move when I damn well could have. To Ivan. To Maritza. To my uncle. To Thiago himself, but I zipped my lips and just kept walking to the tune of someone else's song because I didn't want the truth to hurt worse.

It angers me.

It disappoints me.

It's shifted my outlook a bit from Thiago and more toward myself.

I didn't fight for us; to let me stay by his side. I accepted the apartment without asking about the owner—why do I have the largest one or the entire floor to myself? Why does the unit across from me remain empty after all these years? Why have I seen two men following me at all times when out and not once confronted them because of the tattoo on the inside of one man's wrist? *One just like my uncle. My boss. Like the ones soldiers working for the Leon family all receive when accepted.* Why I am still his emergency contact after all these years according to the police database that I borrowed the login for?

Why?

Why?

Why?

So many questions that I've left as is, and for what? I'm not this woman. I'm not afraid.

"We're here, kid," my uncle says, and I'm pulled back to the present. "You ready?

My head shifts toward him, meeting his eyes from the corner of mine. "I'm sorry, what?"

"We're here."

Luna

THE SECOND MY feet meet the asphalt, I'm stopped in my tracks by an uncomfortable feeling. Thoughts of my personal life vanish as a shiver rushes down my spine and the soft, downy hair on my arms stands on end.

There's an eeriness to this crime scene. Ominous. Bone chilling. It grips me—this invisible, crushing weight on my chest that makes me pause with my hand on the door's frame. I've seen things over the years. Know what the depraved side of humanity is capable of.

These are memories that I'll never forget, and yet, this one already feels different.

Haunting.

Darker.

"You okay?" my uncle asks again, from beside me now, and his voice is full of concern. "You're a little pale."

"I'm fine. Just got a weird feeling." I'm looking out toward a small, empty field at the far end of the large parking lot. My unease is coming from that direction, an empty area that's been taped off as a second evidence site. "Ignore me."

"Weird feelings are nothing more than warning signs."

"It'll be okay." Even as I say this, I can't shake the sense of foreboding.

"And I'll be keeping an eye on you. First sign of distress and I'll pull you out."

"Deal." I won't argue his call. He's not being difficult, I know this; it's protocol to pull any department employee—officer or otherwise—if under sudden distress as this can prohibit them from completing their tasks. Some of which could literally mean life or death.

We're inside of one of South Florida's largest outlet malls and behind a popular retail clothing store near the building's center. The entire place opens within a few hours, and yet, I'm concerned about two things: the elementary school nearby, and the morbid onlookers that will try and catch a glimpse of the crime scene.

Because humanity cannot help itself when it comes to death. They all want to see it—experience it—without being the party impacted by the catastrophe. Sadly, curiosity can make an asshole out of the nicest people, and with the rise of social media, people fancy themselves reporters.

As long as they get thousands of likes, they don't care about safety, empathy, or impacting my lighting if the camera picks up a millisecond of flash from their phones.

With the location being a high trafficked one, it's going to be a tight deadline to catalogue, collect, and move the deceased before any interruption can delay everything.

My eyes shift from the back lot to the large white sheets blocking what I can assume is the victim—like a canopy with a makeshift wall—and then the back door of the store. Already we have three employees congregated there, cigarettes in hand as they point and talk. Speculate. Form a twisted version of this poor person's demise.

I need them gone.

"Remove them from the premises. The dumping of ashes could contaminate the scene. It's windy, and I need to secure the integrity of each item before the others collect."

"Go ahead and set up. I'll take care of that." He turns to walk away, but then pauses a mere three steps from me and looks back from over his shoulder. "Something about this call has felt off since it came in. It's why I drove you here. It's what my *boss* asked me to do, and above the badge, I'll protect my family, Luna. If at any moment I say *out*—"

"We out."

"Good." Within a few steps, he's over to the other officers and pointing toward the group of onlookers—yelling something that makes those trying to record run back inside. No one says anything to him, and the louder he becomes, the more proactive the men in blue become.

"Bet you twenty the younger one pees his pants a little?" Natasha says from beside me suddenly and I jump, almost dropping my bag. It droops a bit in my hold, but I reaffirm my grip before glaring at her. "Someone's off her game."

"Should I put a bell on you?"

"Not my fault you're distracted."

"*Not my fault you're distracted,*" I parrot back while she rolls her eyes. "You just have a bad habit."

"Of walking and talking?"

"Shut it." I leave her standing by her father's unmarked vehicle and step under the yellow tape that marks the perimeter containing the body. There's blood all around the victim, a line of red that makes me think she was dragged here. Nat follows me over, in her hand a few items from her own kit. "Young, or?"

"Mid-twenties according to the first responders team, but I've been waiting for you to mark this area. The other site, at the back end, is done and ready for film."

"Anything in particular we need to focus on?"

"My first analysis is inconclusive. I'm needing a second opinion on whether that's the murder scene."

"All right." This is something we've done plenty of times before; it's why we work closely together and often. Natasha has an impeccable eye for evidence. Spots traits others miss, and while I fell into this out of a need to clear Thiago's name, I took to the training Thompson gave me himself rather quickly.

Another thing I haven't questioned until now. And those numbers on his wrist—

"You okay, prima?" The concern in her tone pulls back to the present. "Something up?"

"Just contemplating my approach." I say instead, refocusing myself. This is neither the time nor place. "What's back there?"

Whatever she sees in my expression makes her back down. Nat grimaces and I still myself for her answer. "Her organs."

"*Christ.*"

"Among other things." Nat moves past me and at the end where a small puddle of red sits, she places a plastic marker on the ground with the number thirty-six on it. The numbers prior must be out in the other field. "It's not pretty, Lulu, and watch your step. The small area is contained, but messy. This sick fucker has anger issues that are more than prevalent in his tactic."

"Crime of passion?"

"I'm leaning more toward hate."

"Got it." I don't know which one is worse: passion or hate? They're both extremely powerful emotions that can catapult even the nicest of people to commit horrendous acts of violence. "I'll be back in a bit."

"Take one of my extra-large rulers." She stands then, walking over to a small table set up beside the makeshift structure protecting the corpse. Taking her gloves off, she tosses them inside of a bin for disposing hazardous material and cleans her hands. "With the brightness out..." my cousin calls over her shoulder, "...you might get a clearer reading on camera with it."

"I have two with me, but another never hurts."

"I'll probably toss this one after this scene."

"That bad?"

Walking back after zipping her bag, she holds it out for me. "One of the worst I've ever worked."

"Good morning to us," is all I say and take it, turning around with my own equipment in tow toward the lot with overgrowth. I leave her to it. To set up my shots and get this done as quickly as possible without being neglectful to the most minute detail. It's her strength, while mine has always been capturing what's in front of me through a lens.

From where I am, I can just make out a section that's cleared out except for a lone tree at the center, as if it were placed there for shade when the surroundings are nothing but sandy dirt. The police-standard yellow tape greets me at the edge and as I step under it, the wind carries a wave of putrid—decomposing stench that is unique to flesh, or in this case organs, rotting under the sun for a while.

I don't even need to look at the evidence to know that this isn't a fresh kill.

This poor woman has been deceased for more than twenty-four hours. If not longer.

"Miss Luna Alejos," my name is called from the left and I turn my head toward the voice, ignoring the area where the smell is coming from. It's better this way. I'm disconnected. The voice, though, does have my attention since it's male and unfamiliar. "We're ready for you. Do you need any assistance?"

The badge on his shirt reads "Young" and I quickly run through everyone I've worked with in the past. He isn't one of them. The way he shifts from side to side, right hand shaking, isn't boding well for him, either. Puts me on alert.

How does he know me?

"No." Letting go of my rolling bag's handle, I take out my cell and press the number four. "Who are you?"

"I'm sorry. Maybe I should've introduced myself." Young comes forward with the intention to shake my hand, but I hold up my palm. He's smart enough and stops. "Is something wrong?"

"A few things." No sooner has the last word passed my lips than Edgar rushes over. Ignoring Young for a second, I look over at my uncle before either man speaks. "You know him?"

"He's a transfer from North Carolina. First week on the beat..." Edgar pauses, looking over at him "...and not quite used to how we run things."

"Okay. Fair enough." The others, a few officers that know me, chuckle under their breaths. One glare from me and they turn away quickly. It's one of the few things I took from the De Leons over the years; how effective a single look could be. How it cuts through people's defenses and exposes their weaknesses, because most people don't like confrontation. Those who constantly bark have no bite. "Officer Young, while I appreciate the offer, I'm going to have to decline. As I work to capture this scene, please keep yourself and others at bay. No one other than myself or a forensics specialist is allowed past those lines until we are done. Understood?"

"Of course, Miss Alejos."

"Then do so." I'm being a bitch, I know, but something about him isn't sitting well with me. And as he goes, a forced smile on his face, I hold up a finger toward my uncle. "Check him out," I say, voice very low. "He knew my name without an introduction and my name tag is inside my shirt."

"The others with him know you very well."

"And yet, they don't fidget around me. Avoid? Yes. But their hands don't shake, nor do they shift their weight from foot to foot."

"Say no more. I'll take care of it."

"You calling *him*?"

"Yes."

"Good. I'll start here while you do that." He turns from me then, maybe takes two steps, and then stops. In his hand he has paper, pulled from his pocket and folded in half; I move closer to reach for it. My fingertips grip the single sheet, head down as if looking at it, but I know he wants to say something. "What?"

"You're more like him than you want to admit." Then he's gone, leaving me with that thought and paper in hand. The note is written in Thiago's handwriting and I find myself reading each line over and over again.

A GIFT FOR MY QUEEN.

OPEN THE LEFT SIDE POCKET WHERE YOU USUALLY KEEP A SET OF
BRUSHES
TO CLEAN YOUR LENSES AND YOU'LL FIND A SURPRISE.

LOVE,
YOUR KING

"What did you do?" I say under my breath, turning back to my forgotten bag. It's where I left it, and right in the line of sight of the few officers standing guard on the other side of the caution tape.

They're watching me and I don't go for the pocket with the gift—instead, I take out my camera and attach the lens I'll use—a normal with a micro attachment to capture the smaller details.

Camera in hand, I test the shot. My first two are of the view from where I stand toward the mall parking lot where Nat is. The brightness of the morning sun demands that I adjust, and with a small turn of the dial it shifts into complete focus. Clear.

The next one is of Officer Young who looks uncomfortable under the scrutiny of my lens. He should be.

And it's only once I'm done with my test run that I allow myself to look toward the markings on the ground. *Jesus Christ.*

There are no words.

Nothing can describe the image laid out before me.

The blood is the first thing I take in. The amount; dry or coagulated and with flies flying around it. Then, there's the pattern:

Everything that should've been inside the body is in a consciously formed circle. Her organs, now dirty and decomposing, have manually been moved and placed—almost as if it were an artistic expression—and on the direct opposite side of her intestines are two markers.

Two shoe prints.

Two very distinctive shoe prints in varied sizes.

I focus on those first, snapping pictures at different angles before placing my large-numbered ruler beside them. I'm right about them, about the discrepancies, and jot down a quick note to confirm with Nat.

The organs are next and the splatter all around them confirm my suspicion about the body being moved. It also makes me look up where I notice a thick branch—the support used, and a bit of rope looped around it.

"Motherfucker," I whisper, angling my camera up to take in the full scene. This is where this Jane Doe lost her life, only to be dragged across a large parking lot to be left as a display. Looking back over to the men waiting for me to finish, I meet the eyes of the newbie on the force. "Officer Young."

"Yes?" he calls back, not coming across the tape but stepping close enough to clearly hear me.

"We'll be listing this as place of death."

"Are you sure?"

"Yes."

It's sickening.

Sad.

And as I finish, collect my items, and head across the lot back to Natasha, that sense of foreboding grows tenfold. More so when I catch her and Edgar's expressions as I approach.

The woman on the ground is uncovered and staring at the sky without eyes. Just empty sockets and her mouth parted in what I can only imagine is a silent, horror-filled scream.

However, that's not what shakes me to the core.

It's her resemblance to me.

A Latina at no more than five-foot-two with dark hair; she had my complexion and build. A beauty mark over her upper lip on the right side that I do as well. Our tattoos were different but placed similarly.

This Jane Doe graced me with a glimpse of what my own corpse would look like someday.

THIAGO

THE BUZZ OF the tattoo machine always seems to lull me into a state of relaxation. It's one I don't indulge in often but I trust him, and after visiting Malcolm in Chicago to drop off my wedding gift personally—a quick trip in which he had his own token of appreciation for me in the shape of Foster's head—I'm back home and find myself needing my friend's assistance.

I've known him for years, and even while locked up, he's the one I had brought into the prison via backdoor entryways to work on the symbol of Luna on my chest.

Talan Cox has done every single piece, the largest being the back one we're finishing today. It's taken two months to complete, hours upon hours of taking a needle to my skin in a very old-fashioned ritual like the warriors of the past would do to get my homage to justice done right.

The large scale sits above the head of its two owners: the devil and his angel. They're both holding the large staff that extends high and distributes the weight evenly. It symbolizes a partnership. How in my world Luna is the good side of me. The one that balances me out and who rules beside me.

The needle digs a little deeper on the curve of my spine and I grit my teeth a bit; it's not that it hurts, but that the area is sensitive and feels as if the flesh is burned. "How's it looking, bro?" I ask Ivan who is also in the room, standing on the opposite side of Talan. He too wants to book in a date after this, has something in mind that when he showed me, I approved of completely. "Think Luna will flip her shit?"

"Most definitely and in a good way."

"She forgave you already?" Talan asks, wiping my back. The paper towel is a little rough on my skin, but at the moment, silk would feel like that. The shading is always worse than the line work. "Cause when I finished the gloves on her neck, my girl was here, and she wasn't cheery at all when it came to you, Leon."

"I'm working on it."

"He's begging her," Ivan and I say in unison, which prompts me to flip him off.

"Can you hurry up," he says, chuckling a bit. I've known the man for years, hung out together as teens, and I've never seen him this far gone for anyone. You can see it on his face just how in love the asshole is. "Maya and I have a bet going and the stakes are high, my friend."

"How high?" Sitting up, I turn toward him with my brow raised. The stretching after being on the table face down for the last two hours without moving is a bit bothersome, but I ignore it. "What will you win?"

"Complete servitude for a month." *This sly motherfucker.* A laugh comes from the reception area just then, very girly and loud. "And that will be her. Guess she's out early."

"Where does she work?"

"School, and working on her Masters," he corrects, smile wide and proud. "Future Mrs. Cox will be a marine biologist."

"How the hell did she end up with a bum like you, Talan?" I ask, fucking with him, but instead, the man just shakes his head and then pounds his chest once.

"Not a fucking clue, but I'll never let my Bitty go."

"Then you'll understand the lengths that we go through to keep them safe and ours."

At my words, he tilts his head to the side, appraising me. "Ask and it's done."

"I'm going to request your presence at my home tomorrow around three in the afternoon. It'll be for an overnight stay."

"With Maya." Not a question, and I nod. Talan and I have a few more things in common than just our appreciation for tattoos. We have a similar build, skin tone, and hair color. With the right clothes and a hat, he could pass as my double for the night. "We'll be there."

***

"Hands up where I can see them and don't move."

"What the?" Luna shrieks, dropping her handbag and keys. Her head snaps to the left, brown eyes meeting mine from over her shoulder. She goes from worry to pissed within seconds—whirling around to greet my smirk with a scowl. "I should smack you for that."

"Please do." I take a step closer and then another, pushing her back against her driver's side door. "Slap. Bite. Scratch. Anything and everything, my beauty."

"Don't start. Not today."

"So I heard." The smile slips from my face and I focus on why I'm here. "You okay?"

"Not really." Her response is so honest. Her need for my comfort is humbling. But more than anything, the exhaustion she exudes is palpable, and I don't wait another second to do what I came here for.

Before she can protest, I pick her up and turn around. She's in my arms, not the least bit protesting my kidnapping as I walk us away from her building. Instead, she's burrowing against my chest with her nose in the crook of my neck.

Every little puff of breath escaping her feels like a heated caress—reminds me of those gasping breaths between curses for more. Of me. Of the pleasure only I can give.

It's hard to do, especially when her finger plays with the short hairs at the back of my head, but I ignore it. Ignore the throb of my cock and how good she feels—even the scent of whatever chemicals she uses at work couldn't dull her natural sweetness. It makes my mouth water, but what Luna needs right now is love and support, not my cock.

I push my hunger back, lips at her temple while placing a soft kiss or two. "I got you, bebe."

"Thank you." Her voice is low. Barely a whisper.

"Even when you don't see me, I'm there. Please believe that." My car isn't too far from hers and unlocked, making it easy to open the door of the SUV and place her on the passenger's seat. "You're not alone."

Luna gives me a nod and lets me buckle her in, more compliant than I've ever seen her. It worries me. What she saw today will leave a haunting expression that will never be erased.

I saw her pictures; Thompson sent a copy of the file over right after Luna left. And while I hate that she's witnessed humanity at its vilest, I'll never stop her from doing what she feels she needs to.

Because this is her way of doing for me what I do for her: protect.

Before closing the door, I peck her lips once. Just a tiny kiss that pulls a sweet sigh from her lips, and then I get inside myself, pulling out of the parking lot faster than I should and taking the turn down the street that will lead me toward the expressway.

It's a bit busy for the time of day, with the rush-hour traffic at its peak, but I manage to get us back to my home in the La Gorce Island private community within half an hour. She's been quiet beside me as I drive, not caring how close I come to clipping a car or three as I weave in and out of the busy road, but the second I come to a stop at the gated entrance, she looks over.

I've been watching her. Taking in every single breath and the rise of her chest with it. The way her lips, succulent and sweet, thin out as she thinks —contemplates what she saw today. However, what I see now is curiosity in her expression, and I'll take that any day over the sadness. Over her worry or fear.

The motherfucker that did that—stole that young woman's life and scarred my queen—is a dead man. He shouldn't fear the police; I'm his biggest threat. Enemy. My men are looking, and Satan himself will welcome his soul by the time I'm personally through with him.

"Ummm, Thiago?"

"Yes." Lowering my window, I flash a security card in front of the reader. The gates open, but I don't press on the accelerator. I wait for her question with my eyes on her curious face.

"Where are we exactly?"

"Patience." With a grin on my face, I drive through and toward the very opposite end of this island near Miami Beach and park in front of my surprise. It's located near all major points in Miami and with something that is rare to find: a large lot, sitting at over two acres of land and five hundred feet of water-frontage with connections to the ocean and intercoastal waterways. It's private with no neighbors on either side as I bought them out, and the homes will remain as guest houses for family, associates, and friends when needed.

The home itself was large, but outdated, and was taken care of by Hendrix Parker of H.P. Builders. Gutted until the only thing left was the foundation, he brought to life a contemporary-style home with protection being the main focus but without losing its modern appeal my girl loves.

Floor-to-ceiling windows, clean lines, ample natural lighting throughout; the open spaces merge into a large communal space that is perfect for entertaining, while the upstairs is reserved for us.

This home also comes with two hidden rooms that no one will have knowledge of outside of Luna and me.

"Welcome home, baby."

"W-what? I don't...*huh*?"

A chuckle escapes at her adorableness and I turn in my seat, cupping her cheek with my palm. "This is where I plan to grow old with you. Where we'll have babies and become strict parents."

"So cocky." A tinge of pink warms her cheeks and her eyes brighten. For the moment, the sadness is gone and my sassy queen takes her place. "I feel bad for your future daughters."

"*Our* daughters won't be allowed to date until they're at the very least forty."

"What makes you think I'll still be around past—"

"Luna, where you go, I go, and vice versa. This is it for us." A small smile tugs at her lips, and no matter how hard she tries to fight it, it grows until it matches my own. "I'm never leaving you again."

And just like that, the warmth is gone. "You said that once before."

"I did, but back then certain things were out of my control."

"And now they aren't? You have the bull by the balls?" she asks, a weird mixture of incredulousness and worry in her tone. Because even when trying hard to hide them, her emotions have always been easy for me to read. I know her. Her tells. Like now, the way she bites the inside of her cheek when trying to control her facial features.

"More than." I caress her cheek with my thumb. "When I'm done, we'll own the world."

My plans reach far outside of Miami, the state of Florida, or even the United States. What I'm after is a global dominion. To build a worldwide empire.

Imperium.

"What does that even mean, Thiago? What are you up to?"

"All I need from you is to trust me. To know that I'll always come back."

"Like a roach? Those fuckers are persistent." The slick insult is meant to throw me off, but I roll my eyes at the lame attempt. However, I won't call her out on it either. Not today, when I know it's been a rough one.

"I forgot how much of a brat you could be at times." Turning the ignition off, I exit my car and make my way around to her side. My intent is to be a gentleman and open her door, sweep her off her feet, and maybe kiss her breathless at the threshold of our new home, but that doesn't happen. I'm met by the sight of her foot on the pavers and a smirk on her face. "No patience either," I tsk, rolling my eyes.

"But you love me this way."

She takes the hand I extend, letting me pull her out and close the door. One tug and her chest is against mine, my lips hovering over hers. "I adore every single inch of you."

"That's always the right answer."

"It's the truth."

Her bravado slips for the briefest of seconds, and I see the girl in her eyes from five years ago make a small appearance. "I've missed you so much, papi. More than you could ever begin to comprehend."

My arms encircle her small frame and lift her off the ground, feet dangling. "And I love you more than anything in this world. I'd give my life for you without hesitation." She nods, her eyes growing a bit misty, and I carry her up the small set of stairs that lead to the entryway. The house is unlocked and the food I left cooking on low should be ready to eat by now, but I don't pause to check.

Tonight is about pampering her a bit. Taking care of her needs, and I plan to spoil the fuck out of her.

Our bedroom is up the grand staircase past the foyer and I take them two at a time, not pausing to show her a single room out of the eight or the pictures on the walls. They can wait. Maybe even later tonight if she's feeling better.

The lights come on as I enter our grand master. Her head shifts on my shoulder, just a tiny bit, and I know she's taking the space in—the soothing colors that I chose with her in mind, a stark contrast to the furniture in a dark mahogany. It's white and a shade of grey that I know she likes because of its subtle hint of purple.

There are pillows everywhere, too.

Just how she likes it.

Her kiss on my cheek makes me smile. "You like it?"

"It's beautiful."

"It's ours." Placing her down on the extra-large bed, I take a step back and just take her in. Take in the way she looks there. How right this is. "I'm going to need your nosy butt to stay right where you are for the next few minutes. Can you do that for me?"

"Maybe."

"Get up and I tickle you."

"That's not nice."

"When have I ever played nice?" I ask, a slick smirk on my lips.

Luna licks her own, eyes on my mouth. "With me or the general public?"

"I won't dignify that with an answer, bebe." And just because I'm an asshole without an ounce of shame when it comes to her, I pull my shirt off and toss the thin cotton at her head. "Now, are you ready to get wet for me?" It hits her on the forehead, and still her eyes wander, from my mouth and lower to my chest where her tattoo is. Luna's teeth embed in her lip. "Sweetheart." I get nothing. Not even a *huh*. "Yo, shorty?"

That does it. Her eyes snap to mine and her face pulls into a disgusted expression. "Don't do that. Just no."

"Then stop objectifying me."

"Are you...? Did you just...?"

"Yes. I did." Taking the few steps between us, I crawl over her body, effectively pinning her down. Her chest rises with each harsh breath, lightly pressing over my bare one. The blouse she has on doesn't do much to stop the heat coming off her skin from burning mine. "*Fuck*, I want you. Need you, beautiful."

"Then take me."

"I want to." Lowering my face to hers, I nip her bottom lip and then lick the abused flesh. "God knows I do."

"But?" She drags the word out, a bit breathy at the end. Her sweet breath is a temptation. "Because I feel as though you're about to drop one."

"Maybe..."

"Thiago, I swear—" I silence her with a quick yet harsh kiss. It's lips and teeth with a hint of that desperation that seems to never ebb. She moans into my mouth and my hips buck, spreading her thighs wider apart as I settle between them, her hot core to my throbbing cock. Her little needy noises vibrate against my chest. Slipping a hand beneath her head, I tilt her head back while fisting the long locks—dominate the kiss and steal the very breath from her lungs as our tongues intertwine.

My other hand wanders lower and to the button of her black trousers, popping it open. My hand slips beneath the waistband when a loud buzz comes through the intercom, stopping me in my tracks. It's the alarm I set for the food. *Son of a fucking bitch.*

It hurts to do so, but I move back. "Stay, and don't move."

The way she brings a hand to her lips almost breaks me. "Where are you going? Why are you going?"

"To get your bath ready and then check on dinner."

"You cooked?" It's been a long time since I've done so. It's one of the things I've always enjoyed doing. "I did. Your favorite, too."

"Then go. I'm starving." With her knees, she pushes herself higher on the bed using my midsection for leverage. Luna doesn't stop her seductive wiggle until she's at the headboard and looking back at me still kneeling on the bed. "What are you waiting for?"

"You will drive me insane one day."

"Good. Because I'm already there."

Luna

I'M IN HEAVEN.

In complete and utter bliss as I lay inside the large, freestanding clawfoot tub in the middle of his bathroom. My body has lost the rigidness I've been carrying since working the crime scene a few hours ago when I closed my eyes and let him disrobe me. Since my mother sent me a message to call her or else, right before Thiago picked me up. My troubles stayed at the door as soon as I walked inside—vanishing as my body succumbed to the warm, and sudsy water.

Now, my attention is solely occupied by him.

His presence. What he calls our home. All the troubles he's gone through to make me feel special with something as simple as drawing me a bath after a hard day.

A bathroom that's filled with the soft scent of lavender and honey invading every square inch—every available surface overflowing with flowers and candles. It's sweet and relaxing and decadent; I never want to leave, and more so when the man I love walks back into the room a second later while holding two champagne flutes and a box containing chocolate-dipped strawberries.

He's still bare-chested and I watch with hunger as the ripped muscles of his upper body contract with every single movement. How they flex and show off what years of bulking up behind prison bars can do for a body.

My Thiago has never been skinny or considered small, but this is more. His strength and size are overwhelming me in a way that my breathing becomes a bit labored, chest rising out of the water's edge faster as I wander lower. Down his chest, my tattoo, and then the eight-pack of his stomach. His abdomen tightens under my gaze and one of my hands slips beneath the water.

"Don't." It's a hiss. A warning.

"Don't what, Leon?" My words are a bit breathy. A low whine behind them. "Be more specific."

"If you touch that sweet little cunt, I will spank you." There's no hiding the shiver that rushes through me at his gruff words or the way my skin breaks out in goose bumps. "Now, be a good girl, and hands above the water at all times. I'll take care of you, beauty."

"How do you plan to do that?" A few stray hairs fall from the messy bun my hair is in. Hazel eyes follow each one as they caress my shoulder; he licks his lips. "No answer? Can't?"

No answer to my taunt. Nothing. Instead, the handsome devil doesn't answer.

He takes the remaining steps between us, extending one of the glasses to me once reaching the stone tub. I've never seen one as big as this and so sleek in its design.

His fingers skim mine in an innocent way, and yet, as he hands over the crisp champagne, I feel as though he's touched me everywhere. It heats me from within. It makes me feel delicate and small and fucking protected by his domineering presence.

Setting his own glass and snack down on the low wooden stool beside the tub, he undoes his belt and then drops the leather accessory beside the sparkling wine.

His pants stay on, just become undone at the waist, and his shoes have long been removed. Barefoot and with his chest expanding, he motions for me to scooch up a bit and then slips in behind me. The water rises and overflows, and yet his hands grip my hips roughly and position me over his pant-covered legs, making a larger mess.

Our breathing matches. Our movements are almost desperate as I spread my legs for him, begging silently that he touch me.

"Fuck, Luna. What you do to me, bebe." His hips buck beneath me and I feel him. *Oh God*, I feel him. "You're a temptation I could never deny. A need I could never satiate."

"Please," I whimper, arching my back while sitting upright so I can rub myself over his length. The glass in my hand tips over a bit, the cool drops rolling down the center of my chest as he throbs beneath me, pulsing with the same want I have. For a release. For the connection. "Touch me."

"I've always loved you like this." Strong, calloused hands leave my hips and skim down to the middle of my thighs where he squeezes. His touch borders on painful, but I welcome the sting and the small marks that are sure to be left behind. "Love all the little noises you make."

"Thiago, I—"

He quiets me with a quick nip to my shoulder and then the slow lick that ends at the nape of my neck. "Drink."

"I need to...*fuck*," leaves me on a breathless moan, his teeth digging deeper just below the tattoo there. "Papi, please."

"Drink." One of the hands on my thighs grabs the glass and brings it up to my lips, holding it against my mouth. "A little sip just for me."

I'm powerless and do as he says, taking the cool refreshment as his other hand cups my core beneath the water. He holds me in his palm, adding pressure over my clit as my body reacts, gyrating against his hand. I swallow, and he parts my slit with a finger before tapping the sensitive bundle twice. Then again. For each sip I take, he rewards me with added pressure—with tight little circles that within seconds have me close. My body contracts in his hold and I move my hips—rub his thick cock with my cheeks as I search for the release I crave.

"How?" That's all I can manage through gasping breaths and the electricity that thrums through my veins. And all because of him. Because of his skin on mine. His touch that with each passing second that ticks on the clock becomes rougher. More. Everything.

"Because I own you." Thiago slips a finger inside of me and pumps a few times. Slowly, almost leisurely, before adding a second. Then third. My body leans back against him, head tipping back when he holds them there and kisses my cheek tenderly. "Because no one in this world will ever be able to satisfy you like I can."

I can't help but close my eyes at his words, and it's when I do that, he tosses the glass onto the floor. It crashes, shards skidding across the floor, but that's not what my attention focuses on.

No. I'm caught by the act of his now empty hand covers the expanse of my neck and tightening its hold. How his chest rumbles behind my back with a loud growl that shakes me to the core.

Thiago has me at his mercy and he knows this. Enjoys it.

"Say it, Luna."

"So close."

He pulls his fingers out and I want to cry. "Say it." Soaking wet fingers land on my clit with force and I shake, walls tightening in search of those delicious digits that now evade my entrance. "Give me what I want." Two passes over the length of my pussy, from clit to just over my other hole and a small tremor rocks me. "Admit who you belong to."

"Y*ou*!" It's a sob of defeat that he rewards by slamming those long fingers in. All it takes is four quick pumps and I fall as another wave of pleasure crashes—makes me lax in his hold. I can't stop the words that tumble past my lips nor the way I reach back, squeezing him through the wet pants that hide nothing from me. "I'll always belong to you."

"Son of a bitch," he hisses, pulsing in my hand the very second after that bit of truth slips past my lips. Thiago comes inside his pants as I ride out every last drop of the relief he pulls from my body, not giving me a second of reprieve as he continues to work me with slower strokes. And as I succumb to my exhaustion of the day, to his power over me, I close my eyes. Time stills as I do, and the noise level around me—his breathing and the open hot water tap—become muffled and low. The last thing I hear makes me smile. It gives me just what I needed to let go entirely. "One day soon, I'll be standing at the end of a long aisle waiting for you. You'll wear white, and I'll put on one of those tuxes I hate but makes you happy. You'll call me handsome, and I won't be able to form words because your beauty always brings me to my knees, but that day, on that blessed day, I'm going to be the happiest son of a bitch as I make you my wife."

I AWAKE to the sound of a stomach rumbling; it's getting louder, and it takes me an extra second or two to realize the sound is coming from me. I haven't eaten since he fed me a few of the chocolate-dipped strawberries before tucking me in hours... *Crap, what time is it?*

There are a few seconds between my eyes adjusting to the darkness and my noticing that Thiago isn't in the room. The sheets are cold beside me and I frown. This is the second time he's done this to me since his release.

"Where are you, jerk?"

"Right here."

I give a small jump at the sound of his voice, eyes snapping toward the direction of the doorway. He's standing there in nothing but low-hung pajamas pants and a smirk. "Quit sneaking up on me!"

"Only when you stop being adorable."

My eyes narrow. "You're up to something. Spill it."

Because I know him. Know his tells.

And right now he's exhibiting the signs of a sexy man with a secret. The seductive grin, the cocky posture, and then there's the heated look he's giving me.

How he takes in my naked form, a bedsheet all that stands between my skin and his sight. Not that the Egyptian cotton does much to hide me.

He too sees me. Sees the way my nipples tighten; the stiff peaks throb for a single lick from his mouth, to feel his lips wrap around the nubs and his tongue to soothe the sting of his bite.

He's my weakness. I'm powerless here.

"What makes you think that I'm up to something?"

"I can always go home."

"Or you can come downstairs with me for a quick bite and then—"

"You did mention something about my favorite meal."

"Your favorite?" He shrugs. "Maybe."

"Did you or did you not make arroz imperial?" Climbing off the bed, I slowly make my way toward him, swinging my hips in an exaggerated manner. "Don't mess with me, Thiago. I'm starving and your mom's recipe is the bomb."

"Follow me and find out for yourself."

"And clothes?"

"Completely unnecessary."

"I don't think so, perv." Turning toward a tall armoire, I open the third drawer from the top and pull out a plain black T-shirt. It's where he's always kept them. The order is always underwear, socks, and then under shirts—every drawer is always the same no matter the piece of furniture. Slipping it over my head, I undo my loose hair bun and fluff the ends a bit. "Now we can go."

"Or maybe we should stay." He pushes off the door's molding and saunters toward me, stopping only when his arms reach me and fingertips grip my hips. They dig in, his touch just shy of painful, and I shiver. Shake in his arms. "What do you say, beautiful? You can crawl back up that bed, lay flat, and spread those thighs so I can eat you instead?"

"What about me?" I bite my bottom lip. "I'm starving."

"I have something to fill that pouty mouth. To stretch..." dipping his head, he kisses me sweetly—teasing the sensitive flesh "...those pretty lips with."

"It's been a while since I've had a taste."

"Too long since I've felt you choke." Thiago turns us slightly, walking us backwards and after a few steps, the back of my legs bump the bed. "What do you say, Luna? Want to play?"

"I do, but—"

"But?" His right brow arches and grip eases. That's how I find my opening, and in a move he doesn't predict, I turn and crawl over the mattress. And maybe it's the sight of my naked cheeks on display as the shirt rides up or the way my hips swing that delays his reaction, but I'm on the other side before he comes to. "The fuck?"

"Maybe later? Feed me first."

"Luna—"

"Thiago..."

"I'm going to enjoy leaving a red handprint across each ass cheek."

"You'd have to catch me first." I take a step toward the door and then another, pausing when I reach the end of the bed. We're an even distance, his longer legs giving him an advantage. "Think you can?"

"Always." He's eyeing me. Letting me advance another two steps without so much as a muscle twitch. "And to prove my point...*run*. Run, bebe." Mouth twitching, he rubs a few fingers over his lips. "A thirty-second head start is the most I can do."

"What will that prove? I don't know my way around—"

"You won't make it to the stairs before my mouth kisses your pussy."

Luna

"YOU LOOK BEAUTIFUL," Thiago says from the bottom of the stairs as I descend a few hours later. I've been holed up inside what he loves to call our bedroom and getting ready after a delicious lunch made by his hands. I was fed the rice dish by his fork, drank sparkling water from his cup, and was then surprised with a large box and a note that demanded I kill him without mercy. Moreover, the way he's staring at me now with those hooded eyes and the kind of smirk that destroys my self-control proves I've done just that. "Simply stunning."

"Thank you." My response is a bit breathy. A bit exposing as I take him in, my own desires plain to see. He's in a three-piece navy suit with a crisp white shirt and a burgundy polka dot tie; the miniature circles are the same shade of blue as his clothes. In the small pocket next to his left lapel, he's tucked in a neatly folded handkerchief and I smile at the old-school touch. Classically handsome from head to toe, Thiago looks like a delicious sin, and the way his eyes roam over me warn of his true intentions. "And you look very handsome, Leon."

He's the predator, and I am his willing meal.

And the way I watch him admits my own defeat.

"Come." He extends a hand out to me, beckoning me closer. And I do; I take the remaining steps slowly, making sure to add a little extra sway to my hips, an exaggerated movement that he follows with undisguised hunger.

The second I reach him, Thiago takes my fingers in his and turns me. He admires every angle of my body, of my exposed skin and the curves hidden beneath a thin layer of fabric. Beautiful and shiny sequins shimmer in the light and highlight the almost indecent cut of this garment.

I don't know where we are going, but I'm succeeding in my quest to drive him past the point of gentle and into the realm of animalistic yearning in an ombre minidress. It's in a golden berry combination with a pair of strappy sandals in the same shade as the bottom half of the skirt, while my makeup is simple: a smoky shadow, winged liner, and nude lips.

I'm not wearing any jewelry except for the thin gold chain with a vintage key pendant that he gave me on our one-year anniversary. His eyes linger on the piece, too, and I see the approval in his expression.

The heat of his stare licks at my exposed skin.

It causes my thighs to clench, and the low groan that follows weakens my knees.

A second turn and then I'm face to face with him, breathing in his masculine scent. "Hi."

"My queen." His lips hover over mine, just a hair's breadth away so as to not ruin matte lipstick, and I wish more than anything that he would do just that. Wreck my makeup. Mark me. "You are a true test to my self-control."

"Ditto." And because I can, I kiss him. Leaning forward just a smidge, I touch my lips to his and hold them there. Just feel him. I enjoy the way he trembles and both hands land on my hips, his hold strong, and my need grows to almost painful as an animalistic growl builds in his chest. It vibrates against my closed mouth.

"We should go. We're going to be late."

"Lead the way."

"Of course."

"Then step back."

"*Fuck.*" One of his hands leaves my hips and grasps the back of my neck, tilting my head to the side. Anchors me to him. "Dangerous fucking creature."

"I—"

"Let's go." A harsh step back and Thiago turns, my hand in his as he walks us out the front door. There's a Rolls-Royce Cullinan in white waiting out at the curb with Miguel standing beside an open door. This is all very formal, nothing I haven't been treated to in the past, but I'm on alert within seconds because he's not alone.

Something's up, and I'm confused by the other occupants in the driveway. *Talan and Maya?*

"What's going on, Thiago?" I ask before they reach us. "Are they coming with us?"

"No." That's all he says because a second later he's shaking hands with our tattoo artist and meeting his girl. "Thank you both for the help tonight. I appreciate it."

"All good." Maya giggles, her mischievous eyes on me. As if she knows something I don't. Since getting the gloves done on my neck, I've been to Cox tattoos a few times with Nat and Amberlyn and even had lunch with Maya twice. She's sweet, studious, and has the kind of attitude that keeps Talan on his toes. I like her, genuinely do, and we're going to have a conversation when I get back as to why she didn't warn a girl on this man's plans. "I'm going to make use of your private stretch of the marina and get some homework done. Do you guys get dolphins out this way? Do they get close to the dock?"

"We haven't lived here long, but they might," Thiago says, his thumb rubbing over my knuckles in a soothing gesture. "It's not something that uncommon."

"Your nerdiness is adorable, but they need to leave." Talan puts his arm around Maya, tucking her against his side, his tone both proud and amused. "Say goodbye and go explore the water, Bitty."

"Bye, guys." Maya elbows Talan's side and steps forward, giving a smiling Thiago a handshake before turning slightly and wrapping her arms around me. Her hug lingers for a moment as she sways me in that way that all women do when excited. "Have fun, girl. The man's gone all out from what I hear," she whispers the latter and then steps back, trying to take a backpack from Talan who grumbles *it's too heavy for you* and hitches it back up his shoulder.

Her eye roll reminds me so much of the ones I've given Thiago in the past, and I laugh. "Men."

"Amen."

"And on that note, we are out. I'll be in contact, Cox." Thiago's large, warm hand settles on the small of my back as he ushers me forward. "The yacht out back is yours for the night."

Talan nods, moving himself and Maya to the side. "Thank you. You two have fun."

A final quick wave is all I have time to do as a second later, I'm inside the car and heading down the long driveway. No one speaks as Miguel drives, nor as he merges onto the expressway and follows the signs that lead us to Kendall. The closer to our destination we get, the more my curiosity is piqued, and when I turn to ask Thiago where we are going, I find myself with some kind of fabric placed over my eyes.

"A surprise?"

"A surprise." He replies before tapping my lips once with his finger, silently telling me to not ask any more questions. And behind the veil of total darkness, I indulge him and sit, waiting as the car speeds up, slows down, turns a few times, and then stops altogether. The drive feels long but at the same time short, and I start to believe we're heading toward Collins Ave. for dinner when two doors open and I feel a soft breeze sweep across my legs.

Then I wait. And wait.

I'm becoming a frustrated ball of energy when once more a door opens, and this time it's on my side. "I've got you, beautiful. Trust me." His scent invades my senses and I can't stop my hum of approval. Neither can I hold back the small squeal that escapes as his arms wrap around my shoulders and thighs right before I'm picked up and carried bridal style toward our next destination. I count the steps. I try to listen for something familiar and I get nothing.

Not a clue.

No music. No people. Nothing...until I feel us ascending a set of stairs and I'm met with the pleasant scent of vanilla right before we're sitting with my body astride his lap.

"Thiago, where are we?"

"Just a little longer. Please."

"You are going to owe me for...what the hell!" I whisper yell as I feel the sudden vibration of a plane's engine. It's not harsh or loud, but the constant thrum causes me to pull the dark sash away from my eyes and meet his before tossing the fabric somewhere across from us. His hands tighten around my midsection, anchoring me to him, and I while I try to find the right words to say without the added curse word thrown in, we begin to taxi down the runway. *I'm going to kill him.*

"Can it be after we get back from a quick trip to New York?"

"What are you...why are we going to New York?" I turn the question around because that I know of, I have nothing there that merits this trip. "Explain."

"You said you wanted to kill me..." his kisses my cheek "...and this is a date."

"A date? In New York?" Christ, everything is happening so fast, but things are slowly beginning to make sense. The phone call from my boss giving me a few days off because of my reaction to the scene, according to my uncle's report. Talan and Maya showing up out of nowhere and the small resemblances between us. We share similar heights and builds; Maya's hair is even dark like mine.

If anyone is checking his house, they'll see a couple at home and think nothing of it.

Girl, pay attention. Your kidnapper is talking.

"I'm sorry, what? Repeat that, Thiago?'

"I said..." his smile widens "...a date and show on Broadway."

"Are you taking me to? Every show is sold out!" I can't hide the excitement in my tone or the smile that breaks free.

"It's a possibility."

"Tell me."

"This is too fun to stop now." Thiago licks his bottom lip and then bites on the plump flesh. "Maybe if you beg prettily."

"Thiago, don't play with my emotions," I hiss out in mock outrage, jabbing a manicured nail into his side and causing the large man to squirm back, a chuckle escaping. "Are you taking me to see Hamilton yes or no?"

"And if I am?" The more he moves while trying to evade my poking, the more my ass wiggles over his quickly hardening cock. I'm not in the least bit of a hurry to move from my place and enjoy watching as the amusement dies and his lust takes over, his always palpable need that feeds into my own. "Do I get a reward?"

We can go from laughing to loving in the blink of an eye.

We can forget the world and its troubles by just locking eyes.

Utterly consumed and powerless to stop it.

"You can have anything you please if the answer is *yes.*" I'm taunting him. Pulling the lion's tail while giving in to my own wants. Because it's more than the gesture—the whisking me away for an out-of-state trip with the destination being something I've wanted to do for a few years now. It's because once again, he's showing me that while away, incarcerated and paying for a crime he didn't commit, Thiago was watching. Always paying attention to my wants and needs. "Now will you tell me? Pretty please and with a cherry on top?"

"Be careful, Luna," Thiago grunts, voice husky and dangerous. "That's a very dangerous offer to make a man like me." He punctuates his warning with a thrust of his hips, large hands pinning me in place. I can feel the flexing. How he throbs. "Take it back."

"I have no regrets or concerns on the matter." Goose bumps break out across my skin as I watch his beautiful hazel orbs become hooded. The tick of his jaw as I gyrate—push him just a little bit more. "None whatsoever."

"Welcome, Mr. and Mrs. De Leon. I'm Silvia and I'll be your in-flight server today," a woman suddenly interrupts and we both turn our heads, pausing the conversation. She's older, maybe in her early forties and wearing a very large smile. It's the kind that all people in the service industry—those with years of experience under their belts—perfect over time. "Can I get either of you anything to drink? An aperitif?"

I'm confused by this and it shows on my face. "Aren't you supposed to wait until after takeoff?" Beneath me, Thiago shakes with silent laughter and I poke him once again, digging my fingernails deeper. "Are we not taking off for a while?"

Silvia's smile is indulgent and just shy of amused. "We've been in the air now for fifteen minutes and have reached cruising altitude, Mrs. De Leon."

"What?" I glance toward the window and sure enough, the evening sky is starting to fade as it merges with the endless darkness of a late summer night. *How can I get so lost in him?*

Lord help me. Help us. "This is your fault, Thiago. All on you."

"What is?"

"Distracting me." I'm trying to stand and take the seat beside his, but the man's hold won't allow it. "Once again taking over my world."

"And I'll take full responsibility for that." Tucking me against his chest, Thiago kisses my temple. "I've had a bottle brought on board for this flight. Please serve us each a glass and prepare a charcuterie plate to accompany."

"Of course, sir. I'll be right back with both."

Once she's out of earshot, I tip my face up to him. "You know, this isn't fair to me. What if I get used to you being here, always with me, and then you leave..."

"We don't get much of a choice in this matter."

"How so?" My defenses are low, and I'm fully emerged in the moment. Overwhelmed. Lost. Letting go. And while my mind still tells me in the background to be cautious and not forget so easily, my heart is louder. Reminding me all we were and could be. Of why life is short and could drastically change in the blink of an eye. "How do we not control our present and future?"

Silvia returns then, his requested items on a silver tray. "We're due to land in Teterboro Airport on schedule by seven p.m. where a car will await you on the private landing strip and it will take you onto your next destination." With utmost care, she places the drinks and plate down before pressing a button—a hidden panel within the wall of the jet—and the table begins to shift closer. It's motorized, and when within reach, she lets go and takes a step back. "If you need anything for the remainder of your flight, please press the call button as I will give you both the privacy requested."

"Thank you." Thiago takes a wine glass and hands it to me before grabbing his own. "We appreciate it and will call if need be."

"My pleasure."

The door to the pilot's small cockpit closes and his head turns toward me, lips close. "There's never been a choice because I was made to worship you. There's never been a choice because your heart will always recognize mine." Bringing his glass to my lips, he offers me a sip and I mimic, holding the rim of mine against his mouth. "There's never been a choice because we fight, rise above, and more than anything we love each other through everything. Life will never be perfect, Luna. I'll fuck up and so will you, but it won't diminish how deeply connected we will always be."

"Salud."

"I love you, bebe." Gently, Thiago tips his glass and I do the same. We share the white wine and I'm the one to steal kisses between sips, but more importantly, this feels right. Like this is where I'm supposed to be. Like I've just recovered the part of my heart that died five years ago. "And to answer your earlier question…"

"Quit toying with me," I mock whine. Not that it matters at this point; we could turn around now and go home and it'd still be our best date to date. The thought behind this counts more than the actual trip. He has no idea how much I'm team Thiago already. *That I've always been.*

THIAGO

WITH MY HAND on the small of her back, I walk us through a private entrance of the Richard Rodgers Theatre in Manhattan. I've purchased every box on either side of us and asked for specific refreshments to be made available on demand. I want her to enjoy the show and not worry about getting up at intermission or be recognized by a nosy theatergoer.

It's something she doesn't fully comprehend yet, but she will. My return and reconnection with her will not go unnoticed by her peers, job, and family. Antonio himself will have a coronary when I make my presence known both publicly and in private.

I want the media to speculate, follow, and confirm.

I want him to choke on his fury when he realizes that I've never truly left her side.

There's a low thrum throughout the building, people finding their seats and excitedly watching the stage. They talk but keep it low so as to not disturb, while a few others look toward the top box where the light of the entrance hall now shines through. They can't see us, as I purchased every other private balcony on this side and across the theater, but I'm scanning the crowd nonetheless and looking for anyone that I might know in attendance.

People fill every area and my eyes settle on another man with his wife taking a seat almost directly below us. He can't see me, not with the darkness of my box, but still looks around as if he feels my eyes on him. Ulysses and Jasmine Senot are in attendance and she looks every bit the whore she is, while he, *he* seems worried. Fidgety. Afraid. Those beady eyes shift around the room while Jasmine is unaffected by her missing bodyguard/lover and the distress clearly visible on her husband's face.

This is something I didn't expect; I thought we'd bump into some kind of reporter or a business associate passing through the city, but never *him*. It comes in handy, though. I'll kill two birds with one stone.

Woo Luna.

Deliver a personal message to the Senot patriarch.

"This place is packed," Luna says while taking her seat, in her hands one of those old-school-looking glasses that I had my cousin Celeste find in a vintage store. It's solid gold and a bit heavy, but my queen got a kick out of the pair. "How long before the show starts?"

Turning my face, I give her my full attention. "Ten minutes or so. Why?"

She smiles. "Because I'm excited and extremely impatient."

"Are you sure you don't need anything, bebe?" We haven't had a heavy meal since this afternoon and the charcuterie plate on the plane was just to tide us over. "Hungry or thirsty? The show starts in a few minutes, and I'll have something sent up if you wish."

"Is that even allowed?" At the look I give her, she rolls her eyes. "Never mind, and the answer is no. We can grab something after."

"We have a reservation at The View for ten tonight."

"Isn't that the place with the revolving view? That makes a full 360-degree turn every hour?"

"It is."

"Very nice, Leon."

I can't help myself and lean over, kissing her lips, nipping her bottom lip once. "And don't worry about being late if you wish to meet anyone from the cast after; they'll hold since it's a private rental."

"Tell me you didn't rent out..." And I lose her. Just like that.

The curtain rises and the first actor steps on the stage; I'm a forgotten thought as she visits another place in time. While she sings along to every song. It's nerdy and cute and I want to bite her, but an hour in and when I am close to taking possession of her mouth, someone else decides to remind me they are here.

From the corner of my eye I catch Ulysses standing and sliding past those in the row with him. He's interrupting, phone in hand, and heading toward the upper exit.

"I'll be right back, Luna."

"Everything all right?" she asks, but her eyes remain on the stage. Riveted. Adorable.

"It's perfect." Standing, I bend and kiss the top of her head before exiting. I follow the corridor that leads here but turn toward the theater's lobby instead of the private entrance. He's just a few steps ahead when I spot him, on his phone and not paying the least bit of attention.

"What do you mean his wife and kids are missing?" he snaps at the person on the other end, gripping the cell phone tight. "Someone has to know. Alfredo wouldn't just leave like this."

Ulysses continues walking right out the front doors and I follow him all the way to the stage door on the left side of the massive building. This is where people gather when waiting for the actors to sign playbills, and other than those specific moments, it's a desolate area. Out of the way and private.

"Claudio, I will not..." my hand shoots out and grips the back of his neck, slamming him face first into the concrete "...the fuck!"

"Long time no see, Senot."

"T-Thiago," he stutters, fear in his tone as the phone slips from his fingers. In the distance, I hear his son asking what's going on and yelling out *Dad* but it just adds to the moment. Let him hear; this will just reaffirm my warning when I caught him in Luna's house demanding something that'll never be his. "What are you doing here? How did you get out of Miami?"

Pulling his face back a bit, I reacquaint him with the wall a second time before turning the piece of shit to face me. His eyes are wide and sweat forms on his brow. "I flew."

"You are breaking the law and I can have you arrested for this." The threat doesn't do what he hopes; I'm not afraid. Unmoved. Smirking as I pull out my Ruger and push it into the dear mayor's neck. "*Please*."

"Weren't you threatening me a minute ago?"

"Thiago, let's talk. It doesn't have to end like this."

"End?" I take a step back, removing my gun and then tapping his forehead with the barrel. "This is just the beginning."

Limbs shaking and swallowing hard, Ulysses keeps his eyes on mine. "Aren't you going to kill me?"

"No."

"Then..."

"I'm just here to set a date and time for a meeting at your office." The next strike is hard enough to break skin, and blood spills from the wound. "Nothing more."

"Please stop."

"Date and time, Senot."

"A month from now, I have an opening," he says, looking past me and I follow his line of sight. There's a small group standing at the edge of the alley: two men and two women. They're talking. Laughing. Doing everything but paying attention to the assault being committed. Ulysses sees this as an opening and opens his mouth to yell, but I backhand him hard enough to cause his head to snap back. For his teeth to bite down on his tongue hard enough to cut.

"I'm starting to lose my patience." Stepping back, I pull the handkerchief from my breast pocket and wipe my hands. "Date and time."

"I'm going to be out on vacation for two weeks starting Monday." Asshole sounds as if he had a lisp, and I bite back a chuckle. "I won't be back for two weeks, De Leon. Will that work?"

"Perfect." Condescendingly, I pat his cheek and he flinches, almost swaying on his feet when I bend at the waist and pick up his phone, placing it back in his shaking hand. "See you then, and enjoy your holiday."

Then I head back inside just as I exited, making it to my seat as the show comes to an intermission. Luna eyes me with suspicion, more so when a few minutes later we hear the high-pitched voice of the mayor's wife demanding to know where her husband was. Why he looks like—in her words—shit.

It's an unmistakable accent the one Miamian's have. It's Spanglish with a hint of southern and valley girl combined that makes the women of South Florida very unique. Easy to pick out of a crowd.

Luna spots her and doesn't voice her questions aloud but chooses instead to give me a look.

Not a warning, but more of a *you will explain,* and I nod. I'm not hiding anything. This was just a coincidence that I took advantage of.

"Are you enjoying yourself, beauty?"

"Very much so." There's mischief in her eyes as they meet mine. No reproach. "And I have a feeling dinner conversation will be very enlightening?"

"I'd like to think of it as informative."

"Then by all means, Thiago. Blow my mind."

THERE'S a warehouse I own in the city of Hialeah. It's right below the bridge that turns 103rd in the N.W. area into 49th street and is a highly trafficked area with people from both cities rushing back and forth to fulfill different needs: food, shopping, and work. However, more than anything, that stretch right after you cross the bridge is a small industrial area where a lot of textile and automotive shops are located.

There are a lot of abandoned buildings from where businesses have gone belly up or have transferred out of the country. There are junk yards, rental equipment warehouses, and the mom-and-pop shops that service those nearby with everything from dive bars to illegal gambling.

From second-hand items to guns, the latter being my reason for being here.

In the center of this cluster of warehouses is a street desolated and owned by one family: mine. We operate a scrap metal recycling shop that both moves my money and gives customers access to my ghost guns. Here, a client can come and inspect merchandise, buy and load up, then drive off the lot as if they've traded their catalytic converters or clean copper for cash.

This is also where my gift from the gun manufacturer has been for weeks and I'm personally meeting a new potential buyer—an aficionado of artillery who runs a militia in a South American jungle fighting social injustices.

Whatever his reasons are, he comes bearing cash and that's all that matters in my world.

"Thiago, I have what you asked for." Ivan holds a folder out to me a week after my trip to New York, and I lower the Mac-10, placing it back in its individual case. The supplier is very meticulous, clean, and cares about the quality of his product. I appreciate that. *And to think a few weeks back they were nothing but scrap metal in this very yard.* "You were right."

"Together or separate?" Taking the folder, I open to the front page and skim down the report, taking in the transcript of the most recent conversation with Jadiel. My free hand tightens into a fist and my veins throb with the ire coursing through them. With the audacity of these three and their aspirations. Two horses in the race and each vies for my queen's hand in marriage, something her father is all too willing to help them obtain for a price, my head being the ultimate goal. "Is this everything from their talk?"

"Separate, and we have audio from both locations. Same day, but four hours apart."

"Eyes on them at all times. I'll listen to this later."

Ivan scratches his jaw. "Each of them has a tail."

"Good." Closing the file, I place it down a second before the large metal doors open and in steps Alejandro Lucas, a decorated military man in his native country of Colombia who now runs an independent military larger than all his neighboring countries combined. His presence is meant to be imposing and the others in the room immediately go on high alert.

A shake of my head holds them back, but I can see the glint of each weapon.

Know their positions and capabilities.

They relax when they see I'm not intimidated in the least.

Alejandro's not alone. Walking just behind him is a group of men wearing camouflage and high-round artillery. Their expressions are emotionless. Their body language is almost robotic.

The perfect killer has both of these attributes.

He stops two steps from me and extends his hand. "Nice to finally meet you, Thiago. I appreciate you meeting me personally and on such short notice."

Taking his hand, I tighten my hold against his firm grip. "I make it a habit to meet all potential buyers."

"That is a smart thing to do. A lot of criminals out there." As he says this, all of his men raise their weapons and point them at me. I don't flinch, but I do release a chuckle. "Something funny, De Leon?"

"Extremely." Because this won't be the first or last time any man stepping through my doors to buy this kind of merchandise attempts to rob me. In this life it's killed or be killed. Take what you want and walk over the corpse of any man standing in your way. But just like him, I come prepared, and my bite is worse than his bark. A quick glance at Ivan and he gives the signal, forty of my own soldiers showing themselves—they're scattered throughout the room and holding the kinds of weapons that he's here to buy. Anything and everything; M1911, M-10, AR-15, Uzi, and the last and most amazing is the military-grade tanker with a functioning missile ready to fire if need be.

Would we all die? Yes.

Would I back down? No.

Instead, I call his bluff and raise a brow. Wait. Watch.

Alejandro's smile grows as the seconds tick by until the asshole is laughing, full on and deep as he releases my hand. "You are one crazy son of a bitch!"

I shrug. "So I've been told."

"It's a quality I admire in those I do business with." His militant employees lower their guns and stand in place, posture rigid and body alert. Alejandro then gestures to the case still open with the Mac-10 inside, silently asking if he may take a closer look and I nod. "As you can imagine, a man in my position needs to surround himself with people unafraid to make difficult decisions."

"Understandable." I take a step back and my men part, lining up in a row on either side of us. "Now, shoot it."

"Do you have somewhere in mind?" His dark eyes, an almost black shade, meet mine as he tests the weight of the piece in his hand. "Is there a range on the premises?"

"Depends on you, Alejandro." He's perplexed by this, and I give Ivan the second signal. There's a door on the far back wall and from that entrance a man is dragged inside beside a movable target that they put in place rather quickly. The paper we give him has ducks on it. It's one Luna would pick whenever we'd go out to a range in the past. "Human or—"

"Let me go!" The man struggles, and my client's face is one of incredulity. This asshole is his right-hand man and the father of his sister's unborn child. He's also a married man, and not to the bright-eyed-eighteen-year-old he seduced with the lies of getting a divorce. He's also someone with a heavy hand who hurts those defenseless against him, and when the wife and his sister confronted him, Chiquito hurt them both.

Separately and in locked rooms, for over twenty-four hours he physically assaulted them, and this is retribution. I will never condone raising a hand to a woman, and when the day comes that I deal with Jasmine Senot, it will be my mother or Luna who decides her fate.

Alejandro doesn't think twice. Face hard and the devil in his expression, he whistles loudly. The sound reverberates throughout the large building and his old friend snaps his head up, giving him the perfect opening. My detainee opens his mouth and mouths *Alejandro* as my client's finger twitches.

One bullet. One intake of breath.

Chiquito Salazar slumps over still in my men's hold, head blown back and brain matter scattered behind them.

"I'll take them all." Alejandro turns to look at me, a smile of satisfaction on his face. "Everything you have."

"You know the price." At this, a lankier man from his entourage comes forward, two briefcases in his hand. He places them atop one of the cargo boxes and flips them open. "There's two million dollars there and eight more if we can triple this order within the month. There's a radical movement growing, and I sit at the helm of this war. My men will need the best to fight."

"Done."

He extends a hand out once more and I shake it, but then he pulls me into a man hug. "I don't know how you knew about him or why he was here, but that son of a bitch has been avoiding my wrath for the last two months. Thank you for this kind gesture. I appreciate this, and you've won my loyalty."

"You're very welcome." Taking a step back, I look him in the eye. "Ivan, have everything loaded and the body of Salazar also on his truck."

"Of course, brother."

"How did you know?" he asks, curiosity getting the best of him.

"I make it my business to know who I am making transactions with, Mr. Lucas. What he did was sick and unacceptable—could not go unpunished—and when I put my men on a search mission, he evaded us too, until appearing at a hotel on South Beach that's owned by my family."

"Hijo de puta," he spits out, accent thick, and I nod. The man was scum. "If you ever need my help, Thiago, it's yours. I mean that."

"And I hope I never have to take you up on that offer." Not because I don't appreciate the offer, but because that means shit's gone south and out of my hands. "Will you be staying in town or leaving immediately?"

There's a look that crosses his face. It softens for a fraction of a second, and I recognize it. "There's someone I need to see first. I may be here for a day or two depending on the outcome."

"Then I say good luck, and enjoy some good food while you're at it. The Cuban Lion on Collins Ave. will hold a table for you for the next few days."

"I might just check them out."

"Tell the chef to make you my favorite." I pat his shoulder twice and then walk out of the building and toward the office I keep on site. Listening to those recordings are my top priority, and I watch Ivan grab them and head this way after giving out orders.

Antonio Alejos is now dead man walking.

Luna

I look at the text and my brows scrunch up in confusion. I don't know the number and I'm almost positive that this isn't for me, but then a second message comes through answering my unasked question.

But then again, how would I know after communication between us ceased. After Maritza, she shortly followed, and I left it alone. No fight. No questioning. Nada.

Three small dots appear at the bottom of the screen as I'm saving her info into my contacts. They come and go a few times before the reply follows through.

> Yes, silly. Last year at some point. LOL ~Celeste

> Are you hungry? Working? Want to meet up?
> ~Celeste

Do I? Maybe. At the very least to ask her why she ghosted me too.

And besides, technically I am off, having been at the site of an abandoned car that caught fire. Not a huge crime scene as the main item burned to a crisp, but the surroundings held a few interesting facts: footprints, a small water bottle which reeked of fuel, and a bandana with the could-be assailant's bodily fluid. As if he blew his nose and then didn't think that the piece of cloth would survive the fire, so they tossed it carelessly.

Items like that don't magically appear at crimes the likes of arson, and most importantly, not together. That car fire wasn't a coincidence when all three pieces of evidence are found atop a small concrete block to the right of the Honda Accord.

It's also another crime scene where Thiago has somehow managed to sneak a little gift into my equipment bag. Four gifts now that appear out of thin air: an intricate vintage key, a new bracelet, and charms—a baseball, a camera, my age when we met, my age now—a pair of Hermes sunglasses and today…Chapstick and gum.

"He's keeping me on my toes," I mutter low before reading the newest text.

> Are you even off work? ~Celeste

> Early morning call means I get off soon. Does
> one work? ~Luna

> Can we make it a girls' lunch? ~Luna

I'm already walking outside the building and almost jogging toward my car, intent on cutting off Natasha who left a few minutes prior. The parking garage isn't far, but it's large, and I cut between two rows before spotting her and Claudio, who's a little closer than I'm comfortable with. While she's walking toward her car, he comes toward me, and I notice then he's not alone.

This puts me on edge. I've known the woman for years, but she's never sought me out or really talked to me. She was always around my father. Talking to him. Laughing at something he said.

Jasmine Senot is looking at me with an annoyed expression. Like I'm beneath her.

Her mere presence puts me on edge, and when her son tries to grab my arm and halt my steps, I hold a hand up. "The answer is no and don't you dare touch me. I have nothing to say to either of you."

"Watch your tone, Luna. Your father wouldn't approve of this."

"I didn't ask, nor do I care."

"Luna, please—" Claudio tries to grab me again, but stops mid-sentence, looking past me and shrinking back. His mother does the same. Then another step; their faces a bit ashen and whoever has spooked them deserves a cookie from me. However, I'm not concerned with them either way. My target is in a hurry and walking way faster than normal.

"Don't come near me again. Next time, I *will* shoot you and claim self-defense."

"This isn't over," Jasmine sneers, pulling her son back another pace. "You will see me again soon enough."

"No. I won't. Back off." I don't stay and chat, hurrying after my cousin.

Natasha's almost at her BMW parked three down from mine, and I place two fingers inside my mouth—the loud whistle rents the air, making her and two other people pause and look back.

"Lunch?" I call out, catching up. "Just got an invite from Celeste."

"Thiago's cousin?"

"Yes."

"Have fun."

"*We* will."

> Sounds perfect. I have some exciting news to share. ~Celeste

Turning the screen toward her, I show my stubborn cousin her reply. "See…she has some exciting news!"

"Lulu, I have plans and—"

"With whom?"

"Noneyabusiness." Nat looks away for a second, a small hint of a blush on her cheeks.

"Who?"

"I'm out."

"No, you're not." Looping my arm through hers, I turn us both and all but pull her to my passenger-side door. "Spill."

"Why should—"

My facial expression stops her idiotic reply in its tracks. It's a combination glare/annoyance. "This coming from the woman who blew up my phone the day of Thiago's release, day after, two days after that, and let's not forget the party at his parents' home."

"Which you still haven't given me all the details about." Nat stops and turns to face me, pulling her arm from mine so she can place it on her hip. "Amberlyn and I have been more than patient."

"And last week after our date," I continue as if she hasn't said anything. She's made a fine point, but that doesn't mean I have to acknowledge it.

"Which all I got was…" she holds up a finger to tick items off with "…handsome papi, suit, Hamilton, and hottest kidnapping ever."

"And you want more?"

"Yes." No shame in her *nosy* game.

"What are you offering up in exchange?" At my question, she narrows her eyes. "Come to lunch and I'm willing to share almost all the details. We'll play twenty-nosy-questions after."

"But Ignacio—" She slaps a hand over her mouth and my smile grows. Nat is screwed and knows it.

There are only a handful of Ignacios that we both know and only one is under the age of forty. Moreover, his father and my uncle don't get along for a reason none of us are aware of.

"Ignacio Perez, Natasha? Really?"

"Not now."

"Oh my God! It is!"

"Quit it." She smacks my arm hard. "You know how hard this shit is better than anyone."

Nat's right and I nod, my expression contrite. "Sorry. I'm being a jerk, aren't I?"

"Kind of."

"Forgive me?" I give her my best puppy-dog eyes. "Pretty please, and I'll buy the booze for tonight's sleepover."

"What sleepover? We're not ten anymore."

"The one we are going to have because it seems we're keeping secrets and that's not our thing."

Nat grimaces and nods. "Will it be copious amounts?"

"Do you know any other way?" I ask, giving her the *really* look.

"Then you got yourself a deal."

"...AND then he said I had the prettiest eyes he's ever seen!" Celeste giggles and we all laugh with her. Not in the way she thinks, as if we find everything she's saying is *the cutest anecdote ever* but more of a *what the fuck is going on here* way?

As a matter of fact, I think everyone inside of the busy sushi bar in Coral Gables feels that way. People are whispering, turning to look and slyly pointing while Thiago's cousin is oblivious to it all. And that is the only part of her that hasn't changed; her personality is still the same—sweet and happy—while her outward appearance gives off a different impression.

Celeste has always been beautiful. In all the years I've been with Thiago, she was never one to boast or show off—use her name to her advantage. However, the woman sitting in front of me gives the appearance of something she is not.

Her lips are over plumped, and she's had some unneeded work done.

Her shirt is nearly see-through, and her skirt is too short.

Her laugh is borderline obnoxious with that look-at-me quality that annoys.

What happened to her?

Amberlyn is to the right of me and pinches my arm. "Is she on something?" she whispers this behind her glass of water, keeping up the pretenses by taking a few sips. Because she too had taken Natasha's stance, and the only family member she's kept a relationship with over the years is Ivan. *He's* someone she could never stay away from without a catastrophic reason. "She wasn't like this."

"I wouldn't know." I've finished my tuna roll and I push my plate away, focusing on my iced tea instead. Prior to her text, the only other time I've seen her was at the De Leons house for Thiago's welcome home party, and Celeste avoided me then. One second she was outside, and the next, gone like her father and brother—something that in our teenage years wouldn't have happen.

"That's very sweet, Celeste." Nat does me the favor of engaging her because I'm thrown off by what I'm seeing. "And where did you guys meet?"

"Oh! That's the cutest part!" She waves at someone past us, overeager and smiling from ear to ear. "We met during a family trip to New Jersey."

What the hell were they doing in Jersey?

"And it was love at first sight," a male voice says from beside me, but I don't look back. My eyes are on my cousin's expression and the shock in them. "One minute I was helping one of our servers with a large party, and the next, I was overtaken by her beauty."

"Sergio," Natasha says, dropping her chopsticks. Her eyes flick to mine briefly. "It's been a long time."

"Very." His presence looms behind me for a fraction of a second longer than I am comfortable. Just a minute and internally I'm cringing, letting out a rough exhale when he comes around and stops at Celeste's chair, bending at the waist to kiss her forehead. This is a boy I remember all too well—pushy and obnoxious and conceited—who professed his love to me before my family moved. "Since Luna's freshmen year of high school."

"You mean *our* freshmen year?" I interject, and his eyes settle on me, his look intense. "Last time I saw you was at my cousin's birthday party out on the shore. About two weeks before we moved."

"Sounds about right." Sergio's jaw ticks, and Amberlyn pinches me again. She's picked up on his slight agitation. "Good times."

Bullshit. It wasn't a good time, and I broke his nose with a straight jab to his face when he tried to force a kiss from me. When he threw me back against a wall and tried to pin me with his weight, I was lucky that Natasha walked in at that very moment and shoved him off, adding a second kick to his groin after my own.

"Well, this is pretty cool. You all know each other," Celeste says, her face pinched tight while rubbing her fingers with an ostentatious ring over his casted hand. "What a small world."

"Is this your fiancé?" Both their eyes settle on me, but it's hers that I focus on. I see something in her I've never noticed before: jealousy mixed with fear and worry all in one. *I need to speak with Thiago about this.* Something just isn't right. How she's moving closer, almost at the edge of her seat and falling in order to cling to his limp arm, throws off warning signals. "Was this your big surprise?"

"Yes." There's a hint of defensiveness in her tone, an almost silent accusation that I don't understand. "Sergio Martinez is my soon-to-be husband and I wanted you to meet under less stressful circumstances. You know how the family is. How your boyfriend can be."

Martinez? Why would he lie about his last name?

"When did you—"

"So, I fell head over heels in love with Celeste and after a week of being unable to be apart, I sold the family business and moved here. I haven't looked back since."

"Wow," I mutter under my breath, but Celeste caught the movement of my lips and I stand, coming around to her enthusiastically before she can question me. "Wow, guys! Congratulations!" Pulling her away from his side, I maneuver us a few steps back and hug her. "I'm so happy for you."

After the female squeal/excitement dance, which I fake to death, Celeste pulls back to look at me. "Do you mean it?" I'm caught off guard by her question. She doesn't know my history with him, and while just being near him gives me the creeps, for all I know he does love her. He's changed. It's plausible even if I doubt it. "Are you happy for me?"

"Of course I am." Behind her Natasha and Amberlyn move toward us, each coming to stand on either side of us. "True love is a beautiful thing."

"It really is, Celeste." Amberlyn kisses her cheek. "We're all so happy for you."

"Thank God." Her reactions don't make a lick of sense, and Celeste continues with her explanation before we can ask. "If you're on my team, maybe you can help me with Thiago? He's not a fan of Sergio...I mean, look at his hand. It's broken, and it's my cousin's fault. *He* sent him out to do grunt work and my hubby got injured."

"Celeste, that's not up to me. You know how the hierarchy works better than I do."

"I know that." Celeste turns her head, looking back at Sergio who's watching us. Something passes between them, and she nods her head minutely before turning back to me. It was a quick shift of her head that the others didn't see, but I do. "I'm not asking for preferential treatment, Luna. Not at all. Just his safety at all times."

The words, *then don't work with the family* sit on the tip of my tongue. I'm so close to calling her out when my phone pings. It's the work ringtone, and Nat follows me as hers does the same.

One unopened message from: Thompson Work

> Mandatory meeting tomorrow. Be here @9 a.m.
> Confirm you received this. ~Thompson Work

"Shit. We need to go, Luna."

"I just saw," I say, following my cousin's lead. "Guess it's going to be a long day."

"Don't tell me you're leaving. I thought you were out for the day." At my raised brow, he tries to backpedal. "At least that's what my baby girl said—I was hoping for a longer reunion."

"My apologies, but unfortunately, work calls." Sliding my cell into my back pocket, I grab my wristlet and walk over to Celeste. "We'll talk more soon, okay? I promise."

She lets out a sigh but offers me a smile. "Maybe dinner later in the week?"

"It's a date, sweetie." From where I am, I look at Sergio and wave. "Nice seeing you again."

It's a lie. Completely and Utterly.

"Likewise, Luna."

The other two say their goodbye and we walk out, not looking back, but I can feel the stares. It makes me as uncomfortable now as it did back then.

"What a creeper," Amberlyn hisses, opening the door so we can walk through. "That guy isn't right. The bad vibes he gives off..."

"He's always been that way." Turning right at the short entrance walkway, we head toward the parking lot. We're almost there, just a few steps from my car which is in the first spot and first row, when I spot someone I'd know anywhere. I stop us, holding out a hand to each and *shhh* them.

Nat's looking at me. "What is it, prima?"

"It's Dad, and he's not alone." Before the last word, Amberlyn whispers *shit* and Nat finds them.

"What the hell is he doing with—"

"I don't know, but I'm sure Thiago doesn't either. Jadiel has no business meeting him." It leaves me on a hiss, and I don't think twice when instead of getting into my car, I cross the street. I'm a few steps behind them, so close to the Mediterranean restaurant, when a black SUV blocks my path. "Watch it, ass...Leon?"

He's driving, smirk on his lips. "Get in, beauty."

"But...my dad...what are you—"

"Trust me to have a handle on everything." His hazel eyes are so beautiful, literally pulling me toward him as if hypnotized. "Get in."

I'm already moving toward him, one hand on the handle, but I pause right before pulling it open. "But my car?"

Thiago looks past me, and Nat takes my keys from my other hand. "Drop the car off later tonight. I'm sure you both have plenty to talk about." My cousin says something that resembles an agreement to my ears, and he laughs, a deep chuckle before locking sights on me again. "Get in."

"But—"

"Get. In." There's heat in his tone. A want that licks at my skin and makes shiver.

And I do just that without another complaint. I'm in his car and buckling in as the girls say goodbye, giggling as they walk away. I'm watching him drive and the world disappears—my mind and body giving in to my desires, but right as we stop at the next red light, I snap back into focus.

"Thiago, my dad was with Jadiel and—"

"I know." He's not upset. Angry.

"You do?"

"Bebe, I think it's time you listen to the recording Carlotta gave us."

THIAGO

"ARE YOU SURE you want to hear the rest," I ask, seeing the distress on her face. The hurt. "We can stop here, and I'll take care of everything."

"Let it play." Luna's voice is strong, and to anyone that doesn't know her, uncaring. But she can't lie to me. Hide from me. "Please, Thiago. I need to hear it all for myself and not get the abbreviated version from a worried boyfriend."

"I'm more than that and you know it." Pressing the play button, I sit back and pull her into my side. I'm here to comfort her. Be everything she needs.

"Those dumbasses have no idea what's coming their way," her father says. You can hear others laughing in the background and water splashing. The music is loud, and very faintly you can hear the moan of a woman. *"Even Luna needs to learn her place, and that's to spread her legs and be bred by who I choose as her owner. Her husband will be beneficial to my campaign, an asset in business, and not that piece-of-shit thug she thinks will be her husband. I'll kill him myself first."*

"I thought that's what Jadiel or that other idiot was for? To kill them all." Senot's wife's voice is now unmistakable. She sounds high. Almost maniacal with a hint of jealousy. *"God knows my son would gladly do it for the little tramp."*

"Watch your mouth, sweetheart. Never speak ill of my daughter." There's a whimper of pain from her and a jumbled *I'm sorry* that sounds as if he's gripping her face—cheeks hard. *"Your son doesn't measure up. Like father, like son. Both are too pussy to take ownership of the women they love."*

"Fuck, papi. Mas duro." This time the moan is loud as she asks for it harder. *"Hearing you speak like this is such a turn-on. I need you."*

"Such a cock-hungry whore." The sound of a strike follows, and her squeals quickly turn into cries. Once. Twice. Eighteen times until Jasmine Senot is a blubbering mess and begging for him to fuck her, but all Antonio does is laugh. Taunt. *"You're not worthy of my dick today, Jasmine. At best, I'll let Gaytan fuck you and leave you wanting. Isn't that right, Alfredo? Tell her you'll never be enough, and I'll let you come inside her used cunt."*

"I'm not enough."

"Again. Louder."

"I'm not enough."

"Good boy."

Her father's laugh makes her shudder in disgust and my girl holds a hand up. "No more. Please…no more."

"I'm sorry, love." Pressing my lips to her temple, I lay a tiny kiss there. And then another. I litter a line from her forehead to cheek with small signs of affection. "I'm so sorry you had to hear that."

"How can he…why?" That's the million-dollar question and I have my theories, but I don't think she wants to hear them. At least, not today. Tomorrow when she's had time to process, I'll tell her exactly what I think. Tonight, though, she needs to mourn a relationship that she still wants— wishes were different. "And my mom? *Jesus Christ*, does she know?"

When I first met Luna, her father was her hero. He was someone she looked up to, that she wanted approval from in every facet of her life. I changed that dynamic. I took away the hooks he's cemented deep with years of bullshit teaching that did nothing but break her mental state and left a young girl behind that needed permission for everything.

To talk on the phone.

Whom she could become friends with.

If she could step a single foot outside her home.

His hold was like a noose, and when I came into the picture, I broke those bonds. Because to men like him, children aren't anything more than pawns to be moved in whatever direction best suits his needs. Antonio Alejos lives in a world where the parent is always right, and his word is the only one that matters.

He doesn't care if she's happy, loved, and cherished—his political career is what matters. The connections to the rich and powerful—the pathway to D.C. he will never have. A motherfucking idiot, because I could've helped him in so many ways.

"I think she knows, Luna, but is in no position to protest. She's made her bed and lies in it because it affords her the life she wants." Her eyes close and she nods, tears escaping. Each one breaks my heart. Makes me want to go out and beat the fuck out of them both for hurting my girl. "There is nothing you can do to change them, bebe. I'm sorry."

"I know." Her sigh is heavy, and she leans further into me. "Are you going to kill them?"

"I can only promise to speak with you before my decision is made."

"That's more than I can hope for after what I just heard. What he's done to—" The words die then as sobs take over. Luna's entire body shakes, the enormity of the situation hitting her hard, and I pick her up. Flipping her to face me, I turn her so she straddles my lap and pull her chest to mine. Her breathing is choppy and face splotchy—tears soaking my shirt—and yet she's the most beautiful thing in my world. Seeing her this distressed doesn't help her father's case.

Instead, it further burns my blood, but I bite back the emotion. This isn't her fault, and the added pressure of my decision will only hurt her. Because his death certificate sits at my desk awaiting my signature.

For her, though, I'll postpone the inevitable. Not forever, but long enough for her to cope.

"It's okay, baby girl. All will be fine...I promise."

"It won't be, Thiago. We both know that." She looks up at me, her eyes so sad. Full of hurt. "This can't end well."

"What would make this easier for you? What can I do to ease your mind?"

"Don't kill him. Anything but that."

"Luna, I can't make a—"

"Just promise me…" she takes in a shuddering breath "…that if it can be avoided and it's not in self-defense, you'll bury him in court or expose him. Let death be the last option on your list."

"I will try." It's the best I can do, and she knows this. Luna nods then and leans forward, placing her lips on mine briefly before burying her face in my neck—letting go of the pain and embarrassment this has brought her. And all I can do is hold her. Let her know that I'm here for and will support her in whatever she needs.

"Thank you." That's the last thing my beauty says, because a few minutes later she's asleep. Standing with her in my arms, I walk us to our bedroom and gently lay her down before slipping in behind her, her back to my chest and head nestled beneath my chin.

Her rhythmic breathing lulls me into a semi-calm state, but one thought continues to roam in my head. It worries me that she isn't addressing what Antonio said about her on that tape. How he intends to sell her to the most useful bidder.

Something that will never happen, but has to sting, nonetheless.

***

THE PHONE RINGS atop the bedside table pulling me from a semi-deep sleep, and I look over at my alarm clock. It reads a little after five in the morning and at once, I'm up and careful not to wake Luna up. Not after our discussion yesterday and having to cancel on Natasha, who seemed more concerned than upset when I gave her a very abbreviated version.

That's Luna's story to tell, and I respect that. She'll share when ready.

Before it rings for a fourth time, I'm pressing the green button and throwing my legs over the edge of the mattress. "Speak."

"S-sir, we have an issue." It's Miguel's son and he sounds scared, his breathing harsh. "They've taken it all."

"Slow down, kid. Who's taken what?"

"The feds. They're all over the port."

"When?" Anger ignites in my veins, my entire being vibrating with ire. "How long ago? Why are you even off the ship?"

He's set to stay aboard for another week before taking some time off to go see his mother in California, something I know Miguel isn't too happy with.

"The guys on the ship sent me out for a food run, and I was on my way back from picking up the order when I almost ran into the commotion. Feds are everywhere, and I was lucky enough to be confused with a delivery boy." There's some kind of commotion around him, but the voice of a man comes through loud and clear: *Get a count and load up this haul. We did good today, boys.* "That's the man in charge, but he's following the lead of another man." He's whispering now, his voice almost shaky. "I'm hiding behind a container from China just to the left of them. I'll send you the picture now."

"Do that and don't get caught. I'm on my way, kid."

"Thank you, sir."

"You did good." I hang up, then and press the number two on my speed dial. It takes three rings, but Ivan answers groggily.

"You okay?"

"Heat at the port." I've already grabbed a pair of sweatpants and t-shirt, slipping them on and then grabbing my Pumas. I'm in a hurry and rush downstairs, slipping them on at the bottom of the stairs. "Meet me in thirty."

My phone vibrates with an incoming text and I pull it away from my ear, looking down at the screen. It's the photo that Junior promised me, and the hijo de puta on the screen isn't a stranger. I've used him in the past to run deliveries for me.

Joel Arroyo is a dead man.

"Motherfucking cocksuckers."

"Something like that." I left my SUV sloppily parked after coming home with Luna and with the key fob inside the cup holder. It's a keypad entry; my pin is the day we met. "Bring a few with you."

"Got it. See you in a bit." He hangs up as I turn the car on, but before I pull out, I send my sleeping girl a text.

> Trouble with a delivery at the restaurant. Be home soon. Love you. ~Thiago

Tossing my phone aside, I peel out of my roundabout driveway. At the end of the long entrance stand four men and I roll my window down, pointing at two. "Get in." They do as I say without a word, getting into the back while the other two straighten their postures. "If anyone shows up, you call me. No one is allowed on the property without my or the wife's approval. Understood?"

"Yes, sir."

"Good." I'm a good twenty minutes from the port and as I get out of the community, I make the turn toward I-95 West then South, hitting speeds of over a hundred miles per hour. The motherfucker responsible will not make it off the port. "Guns ready and be stealthy. We're here to pick up and not be seen."

"Yes, sir." These two are a bit new to the family, only a year in, but came with high recommendations from the Perez family. Another prominent family, from the same province in Cuba as my family, and who've made a name for themselves through somewhat legal ventures.

They deal in fraudulent activity: insurance, credit, and hacking. Their son Ignacio is a good guy and does jobs for the family from time to time.

He's in charge of all surveillance equipment at my house. He's also had his eye on Natasha for quite some time.

Biscayne Blvd. is completely empty at this time of the morning and as I pass in front of the Freedom Tower, I make the sign of the cross. I'm proud of my heritage and I know the sacrifices my family made for freedom.

The light turns red up ahead and I slow down, coming to a complete stop as two MDP SUVs blow by the intersection, their lights off and heading toward the American Airlines Arena where they make a sharp turn left.

They're heading for the port. I'd bet money on it.

I also know that taking my car too far inside is a mistake, and after turning on Port Blvd., I park at the farthest lot out and beside a waiting Ivan. Everyone exits the car slowly, careful not to make too much noise, and we take a private side entrance onto the main hub.

There's so much commotion past the door we're standing at; I can just make out the orders being shouted—*check that container* and *tear every last bit apart*—but that's not what stops me. No. Not at all.

What stops me in my tracks is the two men blocking that entrance. One unconscious, while the other has a gun raised and pointing toward that same door which separates us from the feds.

Junior looks scared, near pissing himself, but holding it down for me. For our family. And while right now isn't the time to ask him the "how," I'm sure it's a very interesting story.

His relief at my presence is palpable; a single snap of my fingers and my men begin to drag the unconscious asshole out. At the same time Ivan is there to help Junior out, the adrenaline of the moment wears out quicker than it arrives, and I take his gun as his arm goes limp.

He's done his father very proud and has earned himself a token of appreciation.

THIAGO

"WHAT DO YOU mean it was seized?" Casper hisses into the phone, and I can hear the wind rushing past him as if he's pacing. His tone holds anger, but it's not directed at me. I feel him, though. My own need to break something is near overwhelming. Could land me back in jail if I'm not careful. "When did this happen?"

"A few hours ago." My voice sounds gruff to my own ears, thick with sleep as I overlook the main hub and the dying activity. They've done their damage. Took my shipment, and yet they'll never be able to pin it to me. The manifesto is made out to a phantom company. Nonexistent. Fake office. Fake Florida license. A figment of the imagination.

"*Fucking shit*." It's grumbled under his breath, and I'm not all that sure he meant to say it aloud.

Seagulls fly overhead, and I squint my eyes. It's barely seven in the morning here and I've been at the Port of Miami since a little before six. "Don't worry. We got the motherfucker responsible, and he's being taken to his room as we speak." I rub my jaw, scratching the stubble there. I'm thinking. Contemplating my options since the merchandise taken had already been sold and my buyer is waiting.

My favorite CEO of a Fortune 500 company has already paid me half of its street value and is expecting delivery to a hidden property he owns in the Bahamas, his yearly orgy with his newest wife and friends.

"I'll be there soon," he says after a minute, his tone more controlled now. I don't think he's alone. Might even be that woman—Mrs. Asher's cousin—that I saw him with at the hotel Malcolm held his reception dinner. I saw them on my way out, but they didn't see me, and it was amusing to watch the self-assured British asshole chasing her around. And had the place not been watched, I would've stayed long enough to give him shit for it.

"Please send a car to take me straight there."

"Not a problem, Jameson." I'm about to say something else, but an unmarked cop car interrupts. It shuts off and the door opens; one of my favorite people steps out. "How's it looking, Officer Alejos?"

"It's hot, Thiago. You shouldn't be anywhere near here, especially if you just got out." He means: *my niece would be so pissed at you.*

"And I'll stay out. Luna will kill me if I go back."

"She talking to you yet?" I almost laugh at his poor acting. He's one of the few that knows the truth; my baby girl loves me. Is back where she belongs.

"Since when have you known your niece to be anything but hardhead-ed." *She would also knee me if she heard that.*

Edgar laughs at my bullshit, but quiets just as fast when his radio goes off. A woman shoots out a few codes, a robbery in progress and back up is needed. "I'm out, Rivera, but I'll let you know. The initial report should be ready by tonight and it'll show what they know. You'll have the upper hand, but the window is small. Act fast."

Then he's gone and I run a hand down my face. "You heard him? We need to move fast while they'll be preoccupied." Ivan points toward a now sleeping Junior inside my car, silently asking if we wake him up, but I shake my head in the negative. He more than proved himself tonight and deserves the small break. "Question is; how are we replacing? How long will it take?"

"Buy me a few days." A woman's voice comes through Casper's end of the line, soft and low. I can't make out what she says, but his grunt—how he says her name in response—confirms my suspicion. "There's enough in Chicago thanks to a gift from Asher, and it's here in a warehouse. I'll have it driven down."

"Perfect. Shoot me a message with your flight info."

"Will do."

THE INSIDE of this building reeks of rotting flesh, urine, and the pathetic tears of my enemies. And yet, it's so close to the main house where my mother's in the kitchen cooking a large meal for Casper and his entourage.

She's planning to spoil them before they leave and any other day, I'd find it funny. But not today. No, at the moment I'm sitting inside of a building staring at a man whose blood will stain the blade of my knife. *His life for the money lost.*

It's dark and dirty where we keep detainees; here they confess and receive sentencing. They beg and cry and make promises they can't keep before transport to Cuba or the morgue. You either work off your debt or die, but then again, that all depends on the infraction.

On how much you tried to take from me.

If the people of this upscale community knew what happens here, they'd vacate the city. As is, they mostly keep away, and those that lurk close enough eventually scurry off soon enough.

Because fight or flight always kicks in.

"Rise and shine, arsehole," Casper says, kicking the rat on the side of his leg. The bitch stirs, complaining a bit as he comes to, but my British friend has as much patience as I do. The next blow comes from a punch, closed fist, to his jaw. His head snaps back and a tooth falls.

Joel comes to, startled—eyes shifting nervously around the room. Those brown eyes land on Casper first, widening while his mouth drops open. The split on his lip tears a bit more and blood dribbles down his lip and chin.

"What's going on?" Then, that fearful stare lands on me. His body shakes. His sweating becomes profuse—his fingers and legs twitch as if his intent is to flee, but in reality, he can't. Ivan is to the right of him and Callum directly behind; each one is staring at him with the same anger I'm battling with—with the ire rattling the cages of our individual demons. He's surrounded on all sides and tied to a kitchen stool; it's dawning on him just how fucked he is.

"How have you been, Mr. Arroyo?"

"Why am I here?" Bare chested, we have him bound in a way that has him hunching over a bit, hands and feet secured by rope through the wooden legs. Casper sits forward, his face now right in his, however, his eyes keep shifting toward me. My eyes are narrowed and lip curling up at the corner in disgust. Anger. My family has done a favor or two for this piece of shit. When his mother got evicted because of a small kitchen fire in her efficiency and no nursing home would take her in, my mother helped find her a place, threatened the owner into taking her in for free. "What's going on? I—"

He's cut off by Ivan's four-inch blade. A quick flex of his arm and it's embedded deep, the pussy choking on a scream. "Answer Mr. Jameson when he asks you a direct question." My brother pulls the blade out, glaring at Arroyo while cleaning it on the man's bare skin. "Understood?"

"Mr. J-Jameson." The way his voice breaks grates on my nerves. How his limbs begin to shake makes me want to break each one so the nervous twitching stops. "This is a mistake."

"People who usually say that without any prompting or accusations being presented are more than likely guilty." Casper looks toward his cousin, Callum, who does as Ivan did. His puncture is in his back and lower, near the kidneys "Now, let's try this again, shall we?"

"Yes," Arroyo cries out, body fighting to bow into itself but can't. His bindings won't let him. Instead, the jerky movement causes more blood to drip and stain my floor. *Not enough.*

"Good boy." Casper pats his head as one would do a pet, and I hold back a chuckle. "How are you today?"

"Scared. In pain."

"Honest. I like that. Don't you, Thiago?" At his question I grunt in affirmation; I'm not in the mood to talk to the imbecile. "We'll take that as a yes. Now, do you know why you're here?"

"No... *fuck*!" I can't control my reaction to his bullshit any longer and stab him in the thigh, twisting the blade so it tears through the muscle in a very painful way. The cut is jagged and rough. "Okay! Please, I'll tell you what you need to know."

"So speak. Tell me why you snitched to the feds, got our shipment seized, and then cost us a lot of money?" Casper asks, ticking each item off his fingers with the tip of his karambit. "Talk."

"It was to get you out of Chicago." Arroyo's voice is low, almost too low to hear, but we all do, and crystal clear.

"The fuck did you just say?" The concern in Jameson's tone catches me off guard. *The fuck is going on?* "You have ten bloody seconds to explain yourself."

"The Savino family paid me a lot of money to—" He doesn't finish. Casper slits his throat and the next second is rushing out of the room. I catch him just outside the doors to the building, barking orders into the phone, and place my hand on his shoulder. "Not now."

"What's going on?" I ask when he looks back at me, his eyes tormented. "How can we help?"

"They're going after my girl, brother."

"Then we're all going to Chicago, Jameson. Nobody touches family."

WE'RE at a private airstrip in Kendall an hour later, waiting for our jet to be ready when my phone pings. It's been doing this off and on for the last thirty minutes, all incoming messages from Luna who I told in a rushed conversation that I'd be back as soon as I could.

> What's going on? ~My Beauty

> Are you okay? ~My Beauty

> Why are you leaving? ~My Beauty

Looking down at the screen in my hand, I swipe my finger across it and read her latest text.

> Meet me outside by the left side of the building in five. ~My Beauty

What is she doing here?

> Bebe, things are hot right now. Please pull back. ~Thiago

> No. You need to listen to what I have to say. ~My Beauty

"Everything okay, bro?" Ivan asks, stepping in beside me while Casper paces and Callum barks orders into his cell phone. "If something came up and you need to stay, I'll--"

"Luna is here."

"Oh. Ummm." He doesn't know what to say; her stubbornness in that she's determined to come with me is unbreakable. It's why I lied. I know her and had no choice. "Where?"

"Outside. Says she wants to talk." Casper looks over at me but I shake my head. He nods and continues to walk the length of the room from one end to the other. "I'm going to need a few minutes, and while I'm outside, call Miguel and put everyone on red alert until we come back. Dad will step in. He has his orders, and Miguel needs to oversee that security is on heightened alert at all times."

"And Luna?"

"Two men on her at all times. No one comes within five feet without my knowing."

"Even her own family." Ivan is asking about her parents, not Edgar or Natasha.

"Especially them."

"All right. I'm on it." He pats my shoulders once, already pulling out his phone as he walks away.

Casper looks my way once more and I point to the outside, silently telling him I need a breather. The beginning of a smirk appears at the corner of his lips, but it dies down immediately, and he looks away. It's almost as if he knows, but can't allow himself to feel happy for me when his girl is missing.

She was taken from outside a public parking lot behind a popular Mexican restaurant and in broad daylight.

Casper doesn't want to hear comforting words, and I understand that. In his position, I would've shot anybody that so much as said hello.

Exiting through the automatic doors, I turn left where the sidewalk begins and find Luna already there. She's standing in front of the building as opposed to the side and extending one of her dainty hands out to me. I reach her in a few strides, taking her hand in mine, and it's she who pulls me toward our meeting spot.

We don't talk. No pleasantries exchanged.

Nothing until we turn the corner and then I find myself pressed against the concrete wall, her mouth on mine and legs around my waist. My reaction is instant and full of hunger; the swipe of her tongue across my lips almost blinds me as the ever-present need—that palpable force that thrums when we are close—rages into a near-blinding inferno. But then again, it's always been this way. Our love is both brutal and worshipping. Both giving and selfish.

Before Luna can protest, I flip our positions, forcing her back against the wall. There's a small whimper that escapes her hungry mouth, the sound settling on the tip of my engorged cock that flexes against her core.

I can feel her heat through her short cutoffs she's wearing, and I grind my hips harder. Rub her pretty little pussy and swallow her moans of pleasure. "Luna, love...*motherfuck*, I can't think straight when I have you like this." Another swivel and she throws her head back, lips parting as she takes in a ragged breath. "When you come looking for me, nothing else matters. All I see, hear, and feel is you. Nothing fucking else.

"I'm so weak when it comes to you, Thiago."

"I feel the same. Always have."

"I know." Luna opens her eyes and meets mine. There's something in them, though. A softness I haven't seen in a very long time and my heart thumps harshly inside my chest. "You've always been mine, Thiago."

"I am."

"And I love that." At her words, my hands go from frantic to gentle. From demanding, to rubbing soothing circles against her hips bones with one hand while the other cradles the back of her neck. "I need you to know this, Thiago. I need you to understand that while I'm not happy with how things were handled, *by the two of us*, I've never stopped loving you. It's impossible for me to do so."

"Beauty, what's going on? You know I'll be back, right?" Because I need her to know that I will be back. For her. For us. That my plans far outreach where we are, and I want the dreams of the past to become our future.

Marriage. Kids. Ruling by my side.

"You're your mother's son and that woman is stubborn, papi. There's no doubt in my mind that you'll be back." Bringing her lips to mine, she kisses me again but this time it's softer, slower as she caresses her tongue with mine--tastes me and hums in satisfaction when I bite her bottom lip. "But that's not why I'm here."

"No?"

"No."

My thumb rubs the area where my tattoo is at her nape. "Talk to me, Luna. What's up?"

Her eyes become shiny and her bottom lip trembles. "I love you, Thiago."

"*Christ.*" Her words. They shake me to the core and my hands tighten their grip, the need to keep her where she is overwhelming. "Bebe, I love you more than anything in this world. Would do anything for you."

"We have so much to talk about, Leon. To make up for, but before you go, I needed you to hear those words. To know that I'll be waiting for you to come back so we can begin the next stage of our lives."

My grin is cocky as I nod. "Is this your way of asking me on a date?"

"No."

"Again with the *no,* beautiful."

"That's because I'm not asking, Thiago. I'm telling you." Before stepping back, the brat nips my bottom lip hard. "I'm also quitting my job, too. Just thought you'd like to know."

THIAGO

WE GO FROM Miami to Chicago to Las Vegas within the span of six hours. Casper's man has located his girl and the shit-for-brains family who's taken her, while we're following a friend and local runner with strong connections to a large Cartel south of the border. Julio Villanueva knows people. He knows this city. And more importantly at the moment, his MC is supplying us with a few unmarked cars and the weapons we need.

"Good to see you, Jameson," he says, pulling Casper into a one-armed hug before holding a fist out for me to bump. We've been around each other more than a few times before my incarceration—he's someone I'll call if there's a product I need and fast—and I'm thankful he's picked up on my need for silence. My boy's girl was taken and I'm here to do what-ever he needs me to, not chit chat. "Wish it was under better circumstances."

"Me too."

Ignoring the rest of their conversation, I grab a vest and two Glocks the moment the car's trunk opens. The compartment is loaded almost to the brim with everything from different sized guns, bulletproof vests, a machete or two, and to the right side, two ten-gallon cans of gasoline.

Ivan follows suit and so does Callum, each taking the piece they want with extra clips and protection. The few men with Julio also suit up and then everyone steps back to give Casper some space, not out of fear, but because we understand.

He's the last to reach for anything, and as he grips his weapon of choice, his phone pings. Dropping the 9mm, he pulls out his phone in haste and we all watch as he reads the message. Casper's expression goes from hopeful to full of ire within the span of a second, his hand tightening around the plastic as he takes in whatever is on the screen.

"Casper?" I ask, worried now that we're too late, but then he flips the screen around. *Sick motherfuckers.* Aurora's inside of a car with tear tracks— her fear—clear as day on her face, but that's not what makes me pause, my own anger growing. What these assholes have done goes past horrifying; they've put a cheap veil on her head and a sash that reads *Bride-to-be* over her shirt.

"I know exactly where they are." Julio's standing beside me now, looking at the picture. "It's fifteen minutes from here and behind a dingy strip mall away from the main casino area. It's the part of Vegas most don't see, and the fucker who owns it will marry her against her will. Suit up. I'll take you."

THE PLACE IS DIRTY: a seedy little strip mall in an area not heavily populated by those traveling to sin city. Exiting the car, I take in the surroundings—the local watchers and the users all trying to act as if they're not watching this unfold. Trying to pretend that we don't see them.

Fucking idiots. No matter who they work for, no one inside that building outside of Aurora will make it out alive. No one.

The chapel at the very end of the street where we park is small, and the neon sign above it barely works. There's also a newer-model Mercedes Benz parked out front with a Prius right beside it that Julio and his men make quick work of. Every tire is slashed, and the gas tank punctured below; the accelerant quickly spreads as it drips, and the broken asphalt absorbs it.

As we leave them to guard the front parking lot, we walk over to the door and listen for noises coming from the inside. There's music playing, a low rendition of the wedding march, and Casper steps aside so Callum can use his silencer to get us in.

We have the upper hand here; they have no idea just how close they are to their deaths, and people react violently when cornered. The last thing we want is Aurora injured.

Two quick shots and Callum pushes the double doors open with his foot, leaving them wide open for everyone to pass. No one's heard us as of yet. There's no screaming or trying to get away, but knowing how fast that can change, Ivan repositions himself with me to take out the runners quickly.

We walk through the small lobby and right into the salon where an old dipshit is playing the organ. He's not good, and the seediness continues as the grimy room and its "witnesses" become my focal point. Casper will get his girl, but the rest of these rats will become nothing more than a game between brothers. Nobody's noticed us as of yet, but that ends rather quickly when an older woman walks in all but dragging Aurora down the aisle.

"Don't do this, Samantha. Let me go!"

"Shut the fuck up, brat. I should've had you disposed of years ago," the dead-woman-walking spits out, her hand raised high as if to strike her, when Casper raises his gun. One bullet and the officiant is dead; a bullet hole to the neck is our signal for the fun to begin.

Now, they all run. Try to scatter, but I unload the first magazine into the upper bodies of three males who almost made it to the door. Their bodies fall and a woman a few steps back screams, the obnoxious sound muted by Ivan's gun.

It's not something we normally do, but when a family member is hurt, normal procedures change.

I'm grateful when the organ player's head slams into the old instrument, his head half missing from the high-caliber round that ended his life.

Another woman rushes past me and I don't blink, shooting her quickly in the back and then stepping over her as she bleeds out.

The officiant we thought to be dead shifts on the floor, coughing up blood, and I catch his movement a second before a younger woman, the other Savino sibling, rushes Casper.

She's yelling obscenities. She's crying that he should've picked her, but my friend doesn't spare her a second glance as they exchange bullets. He doesn't miss and she falls to the floor, trying to crawl toward safety, but Casper ends her hopes quickly. A second bullet to the back of the head, and she's dead.

A loud screech rents the air then, and before I end it myself, some idiot rushes me. For a second, I slip, almost falling to the floor, but I manage to flip our positions and land atop of some young thug spitting curses at me.

"You killed my best bitch, asshole."

"It doesn't matter when you won't be alive much longer." Reaffirming my grip on the gun's handle, I bring it down on his head. Once. Twice. Ten times until the bone of his temple cracks and his eyes bulge out of their sockets. And because I'm a nice motherfucker, I stand up and end him before he can take a final breath on his own.

My hands are bloody when I stand and Casper yells out, "Ivan...the mom. Through the door on the left."

"Got it." Ivan takes off and Callum and I focus on ending the last few stragglers wounded and hiding. The entire staff and those sitting down on the shitty pews are dead, and only then do we join Casper, who's staring down Dominic.

Aurora is being held by him, fear in her eyes.

"Let her go."

"I'll kill her," the near pissing man says, his voice shaking.

"No, you won't." Casper focuses on his girl and smiles at her. "Close your eyes and walk toward the sound of my voice, sweetheart." The last word hasn't fully passed my British friend's lips when I change my clip and join Callum in pointing our guns at Dominic. "Trust me, baby. Nothing will happen to you."

"He's got a gun to my back."

"He'll die before a single bullet dislodges from his gun."

"I'm right here, you piece of shit."

I almost laugh when Casper chooses to wink at Aurora instead of acknowledging him. And she smiles back, more so when her stepmother is dragged back inside by my little brother.

"Nico! Baby!"

"Mom!" Dominic yells out, letting Aurora go, who scrambles away as fast as she can. Smartly, she ducks and begins to crawl away—once she's out of the danger zone, we unload every single bullet left in our guns into the man's body. His lifeless body smashes into a mirror behind him a second before Casper has Aurora back in his arms.

The moment is sweet. As sweet as they sometimes come in our world, and I know it's time for me to leave when they begin whispering their promises to one another. I don't regret helping my friend—would do it again in a heartbeat—but I miss my own and after what she said before I left, it's time we lay the cards down on the table.

I want my ring on her finger.

I want her out of her apartment and moved into our home.

I want her by my side always.

Luna

"WHERE HAVE YOU been, Luna?" This comes from behind me, my key not fully inside the lock after driving back from the airstrip. It was a necessary trip. An exhausting trip for me. Not because I finally allowed myself to say the words back, but because I had to let him go after just getting him back.

Right now, my heart and mind are in sync, and neither comprehends his having to leave and the possible danger he's putting himself in. Do I understand his need to help Casper? Yes, I do, but that doesn't mean that I don't worry. Because the Lord knows that I care.

Always have and always will.

"Are you even listening to me? I've been calling you for days."

Then, there's the picture I took from the still unsolved case. Jane Doe was found organ-less inside the parking lot of the Sweetwater mall, and I see myself in those vacant eyes. In her hair color, stature, and slim build. There's something about that case that I can't forget and has been nagging at me.

The crime scene was careless and the killer almost taunting the police with his cocky display. How they still haven't identified her after so many days. There's been no missing person's report that fits her characteristics nor loved ones asking about her.

Nada. Not a peep for a Latina whose life was taken much too soon and now sits inside of the morgue awaiting her fate. Either she's claimed within the time limit, or cremated by the state. It's sad, and even in death, her rights have been taken away.

This world is cruel and unforgiving.

"Luna, you have thirty seconds to answer me. Where have you been?" I still don't answer her, something my mother hates, and the accompanied huffs confirm she isn't alone. But then again, this doesn't surprise me. *He* uses her for these types of visits, the unpleasant kind. Dad will rile her up so she'll start running her mouth—nitpicking my life apart—and then come in to mediate the situation as if we are children.

It's manipulation at its finest. A sick game.

And it takes everything inside of me to not open my door, find my gun, and shoot him where he stands. What I heard on that tape is something I've been pushing back—avoiding until I'm ready to face the reality that my father is a vile human being. That he's not the man who took me to the beach on the weekends and came home every night with a treat from my favorite bakery in Jersey.

He's changed, and that hurts. That my mother is a possible accomplice also cuts deep. However, what bothers me isn't the fact that he's a dirty politician or cheating his way to the top; I'd be hypocritical if I did. No. What hurts is his wanting to use me as a pimp would. That I'm his ticket to finding an idiot to do his bidding, and he could care less about my happiness.

Antonio will try to kill me or Thiago to get his way, and deep down I know that when the time comes, I'll have to accept the outcome. I'll back the De Leons because my father brought this upon himself.

Pushing the door wide open, I step inside and pause right at the entrance to face them. "How can I help you, Mother? And by the way, you've sent me one text. *One.*"

"Niña, don't get smart. Answer me...where have you been?"

"At my *pincha.*"

"That's not our vocabulary," my father spits out like I knew he would, once again showing his disdain for Thiago. This time in his culture. But then again, Antonio Alejos hates anything that isn't prim and proper—fake. I could use the Dominican, Cuban, or Chinese slang word for work, and he'd still have an issue. "You're a college graduate. Act like one."

"I'm tired and don't have time for your rudeness. Mind *your* manners or I'll close the door." My father moves his foot a bit, a minute shift, but I catch it. "I wouldn't do that if I were you, councilman. Unless invited, you will not enter my home."

"Are you kidding me, Luna? I am your father and you will respect—"

"Nothing." Squaring my shoulders, I let my handbag drop to the floor. I'm facing them head on, looking into their eyes so lifeless that it hurts. "I will do nothing."

"Luna, you're out of line. Your father and I—"

"Have no place in my life. Not after our last conversation."

"This again," she hisses, exasperation coloring her features. "He's a criminal! There is no future for you with him that doesn't consist of pain, cheating scandals, and low self-esteem."

"Those are three things that I don't suffer from, Mom."

"You will."

"Do *you*?" I snap, tired of the never-ending go around with them. "Are you projecting on me once again? It was your M.O. when I was a kid—"

"Enough." My father's voice thunders, eyes narrowing on me. "I'm sick and tired of this attitude and the complete disrespect that the De Leon family has instilled in you. I am your father, Luna. Remember that, and life will go much easier for you. Not all men put up with a mouthy woman, and your future husband will knock some sense into you if need be."

"Leave, and don't come back."

"You will regret this, child. Choose your side wisely before it's too late."

"I chose a long time ago, Antonio." My mother gasps at my use of his first name, her eyes showing a hint of fear, but I don't linger on her as my father shoots out his palm toward my face. His intent was to slap me, but I duck back and with my hold on the door firm, look him in the eyes. "Do that again and it'll be my bullet that ends you. Watch yourself."

"Your insolence will cost you highly." His hand grips my mother by her elbow, his fingers digging in to the point that she winces. For the first time, her usual stoic personality is showing emotion. She's scared. "How much do you love him?" my father asks, pulling my attention back to him, a sneer on his face. "Want to keep him safe?"

"Careful, Daddy. Your arrogance might just be your end."

"Luna, please. Stop this." Mom's pleading, trembling. "Family sticks together. We—"

"The next time you want to see me, Mom, come alone."

"Lunita, please stop this. Let's all just—"

"Your mother does as I say." I ignore his idiocy. If my father worries about anything, it's public appearance and she's always been the perfect public wife. He won't give that up, but it doesn't mean that I wouldn't want her to leave him, and I'll find a way to talk to her without him there. Today isn't that day, though. "Something you need to learn and accept. You will do as I say."

"No, I don't. Goodbye." Taking a step back, I slam the door in their faces and bend to grab my phone that's fallen out of my purse. Thiago's busy and I won't bother him, but that doesn't mean I won't let him know what's going on.

> Parents showed up. We fought. Call me when you can, papi. Love you. ~My Beauty

I grab my purse and walk inside the large apartment that feels empty. It feels off. Someone is missing—our home is what I want—and before I chicken out, I pull up his contact info. Thiago gave me his number, asked that I use it for whatever I may need, and my heart stops racing the moment I hit send.

> Miguel, can you please come and take me home? ~Luna

LIPS SKIMMING down the center of my back rouse me from sleep. They feel amazing, loving, and I find myself snuggling closer to the body. I know it's Thiago without looking at him.

I know his touch. His scent. His dominating presence that both overwhelms and brings me peace.

"Either you're home early, or I overslept?" My voice is heavy with sleep, yet I've never been more awake. Aware. "Everything okay? Did Casper—"

"Shhhh…later. I'll explain later." The blanket is pulled off me and his warm, just-out-of-the-shower body covers mine. From head to toe, we are one and I part my legs beneath him, spread them as wide as he allows, and lift my ass in offering. "Tell me again. Say the words."

"I love you."

"*Christ*, I'll never tire of hearing you say that." His thick cock flexes, slipping between my slick folds and then pauses at my entrance. Thiago holds himself there while draping himself over me; his lips are at my ear. "I'm nothing without you, Luna. I live for you."

"Papi, I…*oh God*," It's a helpless whimper as he buries himself to the hilt in one smooth thrust. Every single muscle in my body clenches—the pleasurable sting of stretching around his girth feels like heaven. It pulls from me a rush of wetness that soak his cock and my inner thighs.

Thiago doesn't pause or let me adjust. Instead, he pumps his hips without mercy, and I can only fist the sheets below. I'm holding on, trying to meet his thrusts, but can't when he flattens me to the mattress.

This is a claiming. A stamp of ownership.

"*Fuck* you feel good, beautiful. That's it…squeeze me just like that." His thrusts are purposeful—hard—while his hands leave behind an imprint on my flesh that I never want erased. Fingertips dig into my hips, his hold almost painful—it teeters between pleasure and pain and I moan for him. "Show me how much you want this. Who owns that sweet little pussy."

"You. All I want is you." He rewards my needy mewl by moving me up the mattress—my face almost hitting the headboard—with a slam of his hips. My thighs shake and eyes close; I'm already so close. It's building and making it hard to breathe, and I never want him to stop.

Using one hand for leverage, I swivel my hips. And I do it again when he groans above me, when his hand comes between us and he stops, placing his thumb on my clit while smacking my ass cheek with the other.

"Ride my cock." There's a bit of a challenge in his tone, and I look back at him from over my shoulder. Brow raised and smirk on his lips, he rubs my clit in tiny circles and waits. Leaves me on that proverbial edge. "Make yourself come, Luna. I want to feel your pussy flutter around my dick and squeeze me to almost the point of pain."

"No."

"No?" he hisses, and that earns me another smack to the opposite cheek.

"No, papi," I mewl, a needy sound that he enjoys, and use it to my advantage. "I want you to take me. Own me. Make me come so hard that I forget...*yes*."

"Then I apologize ahead of time." Thiago hooks my arms by the elbows with his and pulls me up, forcing my back to arch and bottom to stick out. I'm almost in a sitting position, his lips at my cheek and our breathing ragged. "I love you, Luna."

Then he fucks me. There's no other way to explain the way he takes me.

Every pump of his hips is brutal, a never-ending pleasurable punishment that slams into me with the force of a freight train. His hips slam into me...the *slap slap slap* of skin on skin is the only sound heard inside our room because I can't form a single sound.

My mouth is open, but words don't come out as I'm holding on by a very thin thread.

I can't stop it. Don't want to.

"I will always own you." It's almost an angry snarl as he lets go of one arm and slaps three fingers over my clit. My eyes squeeze shut, and my chest seizes, everything around me disappears as I come for him.

It feels never ending and I know someone is crying out, but I can't stand upright any longer and fall to the mattress. There's a *shhh* sound coming from above me and sweet words that prolong my pleasure as muffled curses follow.

I feel warm and tired and satiated.

I feel sleepy and give in to the feeling.

The last thing I consciously remember hearing is *I was never going to let you go.*

———

THERE'S something glinting in my face and it's annoying the crap out of me. I move my head, not ready to get up, but it's there and unescapable. Lazily, I swat at it with one hand and I'm met with a chuckle.

"Thiago, stop. I'm tired."

"You said that thirty minutes ago." He sounds amused and the light refocuses right over my right eyelid. *Jerk.* "Time to get up, bebe."

"How about forty more minutes."

"You said *that* over an hour ago." Now I have his mouth on my shoulder, working its way lower and taking the comforter with it. "There's something we need to discuss."

"It can wait," I whine, trying to wiggle away from him. It sucks because my side of the bed is warm and I'm now wiggling toward cold sheets. "Maybe after breakfast."

"How about now?" he says, following me across the bed. This mattress is larger than your standard king, and we both like to sleep on the right side. All night, we were one cocooned mass of limbs and covers with the occasional petting.

"No."

"No? Are we starting the day off like this?"

"Yes."

"Now you want to *yes* me."

"It's too early for you to—" I'm interrupted by the sound of an alarm. It's loud and at once, Thiago's up, slipping into a pair of sweatpants and grabbing his gun from the nightstand. He doesn't so much as look at me, but I do catch the way he points toward the table and I see the second Ruger there. "What's going on?"

"Get dressed." Then he's out of the room and I jump into action, following his orders. There's a pair of yoga pants and a tank top with a built-in bra that I left out for an early morning run. Putting them on, I forgo the shoes and follow the sound of noises downstairs.

No shots have been fired, but at the bottom of the stairs the sight that greets me is my Thiago with a crying man on his knees. The anger on one man's face and the fear in the other. All the guns drawn, including my own, ready to end a life.

And when they notice me, I can't help the shock on my face for two distinct reasons:

There's a large diamond ring on my finger, and it's weight finally registers.

The intruder is someone I recently met and had a bad feeling about.

What the hell? "Officer Young?"

THIAGO

"Name?"

"This is all a mistake. Please—" He's cut off by the sharpness of my brass knuckles across his cheek. There's a gash that forms right over the bone, the fourth now on his face. He's bloody. Swollen. A literal mess as we've been at this for an hour now. "No more."

Luna's with me, standing just to the right of us while I interrogate the bastard cocky enough to try and break into my home. She's not speaking, hasn't said a word after identifying him as someone working for the MDP.

"Name?"

"We can cut a deal. I'll—" Another strike, this one to the side of his neck, and he stiffens. The officer chokes from the shock of pain, and then his eyes roll back. The blow was hard enough to hit the Vagus nerve where, I knew it would cause a blackout.

"How long will he be under?" Luna says then and I look over, catching the small smile curling at her lips. She's fingering the ring on her left hand, turning the symbol of my love from side to side. "Because you owe me an explanation."

"Do I?"

"Yes, you do."

"I believe it's self-explanatory." One of the guys who captured him steps forward, offering me a wet hand towel to clean my hands, but I shake my head. Not yet. Not until I end this. "Is Ivan on his way?"

"Should be here within the next fifteen minutes," the guard answers, retaking his place against the wall of my guest house turned temporary jail.

I would've loved a custom-built basement, but it's not feasible on this property. So instead, I had my developer convert this originally four-bedroom guest house into a large open space with two jail-grade cells. There is drainage on the floors, an indoor irrigation system on the roof and walls, and complete soundproofing. No one can hear you from the outside. Not a single peep will pass through.

"Thiago."

"Yes, love?"

"Why is there an engagement ring on my finger?"

While the man in my chair fails to regain consciousness, I take the remaining steps between my girl and me. My hands are filthy and I'm sweaty, but I still lower my face to hers and take her lips in a sweet, soft kiss. Just a few pecks. A little something to hold me over until later, when I make love to my future bride.

Her small hands reach out for me—she tries to pull me in closer, but I shake my head. "Not while I'm like this."

"But...ouch!" Beautiful brown eyes narrow at the harsh nip to her lips. "That was mean."

"That ring is on your finger because it belongs there. Because I plan to make you my wife very soon."

"Would've been nice to have you ask..." she trails off, a slick little grin that matches my cocky one on her plump lips. This crazy, gorgeous, and perfect girl isn't worried about what I'm doing—my breakdown of the intruder—but is focused on her engagement ring.

But then again, she's never judged me.

"I did ask."

"When?"

"At your college graduation a few years back." And I did. Right there in the open field and on one knee after everything was done and the place was empty. At least at the time, we thought it was. In our minds, we were the only two, but two women decided to stay behind and be nosy. I never told anyone, but they smelled blood and captured the private moment. Luna doesn't know this, but I have the pictures inside our office to prove it. "Or did you forget?"

"I remember every single moment of that night." She's looking at me, hands absentmindedly caressing my chest. "You were so handsome in that dark suit and crisp white shirt sans tie."

"Do you remember your answer?"

"I told you then that I'd marry you today, tomorrow, and always." Luna is nodding at me, smiling so big that one would think we were on a romantic getaway and not dealing with a home breach. "Guess this means we're getting married soon?"

"Very soon."

"How much time?"

"Three months to the date and not a second more."

"Okay." Standing on the tips of her toes, she kisses me again. This time with more passion. With a promise of something delicious later. "It's a date."

"Something you two want to share?" Ivan says from the entrance and we look over, my eyes going straight to a box in his hand.

"What's in the box?" Gone is the playfulness and my queen takes note, quickly stepping back and retaking her prior position. Ivan smiles at her and walks over, giving her a quick kiss on the cheek. "Something that will explain who the hell this dumb fuck is, and why the Texas native is roaming the streets of Miami posing as an officer of the law."

"Show me."

The guards in the room spring into action immediately and without my saying, pull over a small table I asked to be put against the wall. Once in place, they step back and Ivan places the items face down atop the wooden surface.

His eyes shift to mine. "Can you promise to keep your cool?" he says this lowly so no one else hears. The question catches me off guard and I tilt my head, appraising him with a cool expression. "Thiago, what's in here is both useful and would piss any real man off. Don't scare her."

"You have my word."

One by one he flips the items collected over: pictures, videotapes, files with notes and information on the mayor, my father-in-law, Luna, and my family. He's been following them, while my family's information comes from articles: national headlines, local newspapers, and a printout from Wikipedia. Everything is detailed, cataloged by date and holds some very damaging information on the families of some highly regarded city officials and their corruption.

Everything I could ever want and more, but more importantly, his information on Luna is limited and all comes from her job with the forensic department:

Date of birth.

Listed home address, which was still listed as her parents home.

Height.

Weight.

Then, there's a couple of pictures of her doing everyday things. The most recent is of her casual lunch with my cousin and her piece of shit fiancé.

"He gave me bad vibes that day out on the field," Luna says, coming to a stop beside me. Her hand is on my back—scent calming me—as the urge to wake him up and show him what pain really feels like rises to the surface. I've been patient thus far, more level-headed than normal when it comes to her, but only because Ivan is right. She knows me as her man and not the demon my enemies meet. "Even newbies know not to interfere or ask to help the forensic team. We know how to photograph the scene and have very specific ways on how to catalog, then file the evidence. He was too overeager. Seemed almost desperate to help."

"That's because he's not a cop," another male voice interjects, and I find Edgar at the door. Her uncle is furious. Near shaking with rage. "I did some digging of my own after Ivan called me and came across his rap sheet when running a facial scan. Scott 'Young' Rogers is from Houston, and on the run for a litany of crimes. He's wanted for everything from a carjacking, to the homicide of a woman whose crime scene looks very similar to what we found with our Jane Doe."

"Jesus," Luna gasps, hand clutching her chest. "This guy is completely sick in the head."

"Wake him up."

"Yes, sir," both guards answer in unison. The younger of the two drags Young's chair away and toward the farthest corner where a high-pressure spigot sits above his head, while the other man opens the drain and sets the water temperature to ice-cold. There's something about water that always gets the point across in one way or another; be it cold and hard or a tumultuous wave. It makes you calm, but that's the danger within it lurking. Water drowns. A single continuous drop on the same section of flesh can puncture a hole through you.

A single large wave can decimate an entire village and every being in its path.

As my men do this, Ivan grabs everything and puts it away and out the door, only coming back after my evidence is secure.

Then, we all stand across from him, just a few feet apart, and watch as the first jet hits him in the face. Scott sputters, coming to fast and fighting not to drown as the heavy flow soaks him from head to toe. The pressure from the water further opens his gashes, especially the one on his temple and cheek.

"What's going on...*fucking* stop! Help!"

"Why would I do that?" Scott stiffens. You can see the exact moment he remembers just where he is. What he did. He searches for me, following the sound of my voice, but can't keep his eyes open past the water. It's a strong jet the size of my wrist and very cold.

"I'll tell you anything you need to know."

"Will you, now?"

"Yes."

"Okay." Holding a finger up is my signal and the water shuts off. "Now, tell me why you're here, Mr. Rogers. Enlighten me with a story." Coughing, he chokes out a reply I can't quite make out. "Again, louder this time."

"Antonio Alejos hired me to kill you and then deliver his daughter to a property he owns in Tampa."

"That son of a bitch!" Edgar bellows, rushing toward Scott and knocking the tied man to the floor. I don't stop him. No. I feel his anger, his total disgust.

After he's laid a couple of good punches in, I look at Ivan and tilt my head for him to get him off. He resists at first, getting to land an elbow across the bridge of Scott's nose, but stands up after my brother whispers something to him.

Edgar's eyes go to his niece, who is now shaking in my arms. *Take her*, I mouth, and he comes over, pulling her from me—at first, she fights it, but goes after I kiss her temple and rub my thumb over her finger.

"I'll be up in a minute. Go with him."

"Will you be okay?"

"Always, beautiful. I got you."

"Okay." And it's only after they walk out that I crack my neck and let go. With a quickness that Scott doesn't expect, I flip open a blade I've had in my back pocket and stab him right between the legs. His mouth drops open, the silent scream caught in his throat, but he can't hold it back any longer when I twist the knife.

Then, his scream rents the air. Loud and full of pain and still not enough, so I pull it out and repeat the process five times. Blood soaks his pants and drips onto the already light pink water below.

"How did you get the job?"

"No more. Just no more."

"How did you get the motherfucking job, asshole? Don't make me ask again."

Scott's bottom lip trembles, limbs shaking from the shock trying to set in. "Alejos paid the chief of police to get me in under the pretense that I was a family friend just transferred. It was a favor-for-favor scenario."

"What did the chief receive?"

"A no-holds-barred night with Senot's wife."

Those sick fucks. "Is there proof of this?"

"There's a video at my apartment in Midtown."

"Already have it," Ivan says from behind me. "Everything useful is already in our possession."

"Thank you, brother." Taking the knife out, I bring it to his neck and press it against his Adam's apple. "Why did you collect all that information, Rogers? What was *your* plan in all this?"

"At first, it was money." His crying, the blubbering is getting on my nerves, but I grit my teeth and ignore. His time is almost up. "Alejos offered me a mil and then a way out of the country. But then…"

"Then what? You decided to extort him for more?"

"I decided to kill him and keep his daughter for myself."

Bending a bit, I get right in his face. I let him see the devil that resides within me. "You will never taste her sweetness." The knife goes in with just a small amount of strength from me, slicing right through his neck and causing him to choke. No air. No way of talking. Nothing.

Scott "Young" Rogers will die being the miserable cunt he is. Alone. Without mercy.

He can go ahead and make space for Antonio, because he will be following him shortly.

THIAGO

SUNDAY'S LUNCH AT my parents home a couple days later is a loud, boisterous affair. People are sitting around a large grouping of tables lined up in a row and talking amongst themselves. I'm at the head with my queen to my right and my parents to the left.

Then there's Ivan, Natasha, Amberlyn, and anyone else we could fit between myself and Jadiel and company, something that I think they're picking up on.

There's fidgeting.

A constant refill of their drink.

Excessive trips to the bathroom.

Even Celeste, who's unaware and blinded by her love for Sergio, looks uncomfortable. But that's on her. I'm a strong believer in self-awareness and being independent, two traits she's missing. The older she gets, the more she's becoming her mother.

It saddens me but doesn't have any weight on my decision. One that's made, and I have the backing of those who matter.

"Who's ready for dessert? I made a huge flan this morning?" Every hand but mine raises, and as they all focus on my mom taking inventory of how many servings she needs, I press play on my phone.

There's a crackling coming from the speakers and the sound of barstools scraping against tile follows—those at this table go quiet.

"Fucking asshole thinks he can treat me like shit," Celeste gasps, listening to her brother spew his true feelings on this recording. Her reaction is to be expected, and I do feel bad for her in this instance, more so as every head turns in his direction. He's pale as a ghost, stiff in his seat. *"I'm going to enjoy putting a bullet in his head, then one in Ivan and tio Orlando. Every fucking male with the last name De Leon needs to die within the next two weeks."*

Jadiel won't meet my eyes.

He's sweating, hands shaking as he grabs his beer.

"Calm down, Ivancito. You'll get your chance to do just that...Alejos paid us a great deal to end his daughter's suffering." They snort a second before a male waiter introduces himself at a sports bar on Biscayne Blvd. It's a place I am familiar with. Know the owner. *"Two Heinekens and a sampler for now. Nachos too."* That comes from my uncle, who thanks the man and then coughs. It's a distinct one. Like someone who's smoked three packs a day for thirty years. *"What's the next step, though? I haven't spoken to Antonio in weeks. Have you?"*

On the tape someone sucks their teeth, a trait my cousin has. Whenever annoyed, he falls back to this habit.

"Yeah, and he's on my ass about this. Something about time running out and pitching his campaign soon; he wants her married and compliant by then." Their drinks are served, and the waiter tells them the food will be right out. *"Something I agree with. The little bitch has been taunting me for years and I plan to make her pay. Make her my personal fuck doll."*

Beside me Luna grabs her can of Coke, gripping it so hard that it over-spills, soaking the white linen cloth. I place my hand atop the table, palm up. An invitation she accepts a few seconds later, intertwining our fingers.

"The broken ones are always fun."

"After Thiago's death, she'll be an easy target."

I press the stop button and bring my beauty's hand to my lips, kissing her soft skin. No one makes a sound, but I do see their intent loud and clear. Some are ready to jump up and grab them, while the two in question are dealing with their fight or flight response.

To run.

To lie.

To kill me for exposing them.

Winking at Luna, I stand and place a hand on my Viejo's shoulder, giving it a squeeze as I make my way around the table. No hurry. No outward display of anger.

I take my time in making my way around the table to Jadiel, reaching him just as he tries to stand. With a hard shove, I sit him back down. "Sit, primo."

"Thiago, that was just me talking shit. I didn't—"

"Silence." My voice thunders, causing him to make a whimpering sound. He's afraid, and the man should be. "I'm only going to make the following offer once, so accept and pray to God that he helps you." Those around the table in the know stand, pushing back their chairs and moving four paces back. "You will be ready at five this upcoming Friday and not ask questions. You will board my cargo ship, get ready in a private room, and meet me in the ring. Two five-minute rounds will decide your fate and mine, Jadiel. Beat me, and the position as head is yours. Nod if you understand." He does, practically squirming in his seat to get away. "Good boy."

And then I leave him there, ignoring his father and sister and the dumbass who I'm coming for next. Everyone standing follows me inside and the sliding glass door closes.

Our position has been made. My offer is valid.

Casualties in this instance can't be avoided, but his sister is the only person I'll welcome back into the family after the chains holding her down are broken.

ULYSSES SENOT's office is closed that Thursday, but we both know that's a lie. The sign is there to deter visitors, me to be precise, but I knew the very moment he stepped foot inside of his floor in the Government Building which holds his office.

Today is the second time he showed up for work since we bumped into each other in New York.

He's been hiding by taking an extended vacation and then faking a bout of sickness upon his return. He's been staying inside and avoiding all types of outdoor activities that require an appearance by the quote-on-quote *good guy*.

What he fails to understand is that while being patient, I've done my homework. That I have eyes everywhere. That I've studied every bit of evidence I'll use to bring them all down, one by one.

Tapes upon tapes of people plotting my family's demise. Our deaths.

Pictures upon pictures of these upstanding citizens doing lines of coke and fucking—sharing what shouldn't be shared and treating this pathetic excuse of a man like a personal punching bag.

And no, this isn't a kink or a mutual agreement between consenting adults. Antonio and Jasmine treat him like shit, beat him, and then laugh at the bruises while he's forced to watch them together.

The only person that still cares for him is his son, and when things come to light, he'll be sitting in a jail cell and serving time for years to come. He'll never see the light of day again—Claudio will carry the burden for his father, I'll make sure of that.

They judge me, but two of those involved who are still alive want to run a sex trafficking ring in the 305 and hide it behind their political personas or affiliations. They have enough pull, know enough corrupt city employees to make that happen. A favor for a favor, and those sick fucks will get away with it because Senot is afraid to say no.

In all of this, Ulysses is the lesser of the scum. An easy target.

But more importantly, my name will be cleared by the end of the day.

I bypass security—a woman whose husband works for me at the port— walking right through the lobby downstairs and right onto the elevators. His office is on the top floor and no one dares to stop me or Ivan, not even the secretary that at the sight of me looks away and pretends we aren't here. This visit is a long time coming, and I warned him years ago to expect me to pass him the bill for my county stay.

"What the—?"

"Hello, Mr. Senot. Might I have a minute or two of your time?"

"Thiago, what are you doing here?" He reaches for the panic button to the right of his leg, but in his nervous haste spills coffee all over himself. "Shit!" His hands grab a wad of Kleenex beside a cup full of pens, dabbing at his desk and the sheet of paper he was reading. "How did you get by security?"

"Just walked right on by." There are two chairs opposite his desk and we take one each. My brother also places our gift atop the table. It's a small box, nondescript and wrapped in black paper.

He eyes the box, his hand trembling as he grabs more tissue and dries the no-longer-there puddle. "How can I help you, Mr. De Leon? I'm a very busy man and—"

"My family would like to extend our deepest condolences on the loss of your long-time employee and wife's fuck toy."

"Thank you. We don't know what...did you just say fuck toy?" Face red and eyes wide, he stares at me with the same horrified expression Gaytan wore right before I ended his life. "What are you talking about? My wife—"

"Is a narcissistic bitch that humiliates you by sleeping around with any willing dick," I finish for him. Beside me Ivan snickers, but rights himself quickly when I look his way from the corner of my eye. What they've done to him is messed up. He is the epitome of an abused husband, but that doesn't negate the fact that he could've said no to attempting to kill someone I love and sending me to jail. That falls on him. "Now, with that being said, I'm here to offer you a one-time-only deal, Senot. Are you listening?"

"I don't make deals with criminals." His self-righteous attitude, that chip on the shoulder that all politicians carry, rises to the surface. He looks downright offended by my words. "We're done. Go."

"Within the next sixty minutes my Luna is delivering two special packages to both the District Attorney's office and the largest media outlet in South Florida. Those two gifts contain pictures of threesomes, foursomes, and your humiliation at Antonio Alejos' hands. Then, there's the audio of backdoor deals being made with my cousin Jadiel—who I've kept out of this to deal with him personally—including my incarceration and the hitman hired to kill my father. I have confession tapes from those parties, given to a now deceased Gaytan as he ordered the hit on your behalf."

"No. NO!"

"Yes." Ivan pushes the box in his direction. "You are implicated in multiple counts of perjury, fraud, illicit activity, and consuming of illegal substances. The same ones you took an oath to combat when you took office. Then, there's the sex ring you're helping to both build and hide for your wife and best friend."

"Thiago, this...how did...don't do this."

"It's already done."

"We can work something—"

"No. We can't." Crossing my leg at the knee, I scratch my jaw. "There is nothing you could do for me that will stop this from happening. And while I may be a criminal, I would never hurt an innocent."

"This is all a misunderstanding. I would've never gone through with it."

"Liars never enter Heaven's gate," Ivan deadpans; it's an old saying my mother would regularly use to try and get us to confess as kids. To scare us into admitting whatever prank or mischief we were up to. Leaning forward, he opens the box and begins to lay out every single item within. The more Ulysses sees, the more he begins to sweat. The more he pulls at the collar of his ugly pinstriped shirt that's seen better days. "Deny it now?"

"I-I—"

"Can't," I end the statement for him. "But here is what you *can* do, Senot."

"Anything."

"Leave."

"What?" he sputters. "What do you mean, leave?"

"I mean grab whatever shit you can fit inside of a duffle bag and get out of Miami." We stand then, and I lean over his desk, placing a single finger atop the picture of Gaytan after his execution. A silent warning and admission from me. "Don't let them drag you down further."

Just as I turn to head to the door, my phone beeps with an incoming text.

> Done. It'll begin playing shortly on media outlets. Once one station grabs a story, they all jump on it. ~My Beauty

> An arrest warrant is the next step from the DA. Should be ready within the next 24 hrs. ~My Beauty

I flip my phone around so that Ulysses can read it. His expression says it all: he's scared.

> Thank you, love. ~Thiago

It's not easy on her. I know this.

Her tears on my shoulder two nights ago as she went through each item Ivan collected broke my heart. Loving someone is hard, and more so when they're hurting because you feel their pain—want to take it away and make them smile. You want nothing more than to erase the disappointment and loss.

And while I begged her to let me handle things, Luna once again showed me just how much of my equal she is. Chin jutted out and hand on her hip, I was told she needed to do this. That it's her duty as his daughter to put a stop to his disgusting plans, especially the ones that include her.

"Within the next twenty-four hours your world will implode, Senot. Heed my warning now and disappear because no one outside of your son will miss you."

We leave, and shortly after midday the breaking news headlines begin to appear with the politician scandal. Every news station is reporting. Every name involved is shared. Their long list of charges and the DA's involvement follows—the news of arrest warrants possibly being granted later this afternoon by a judge in the county—are the cherry on my cake.

However, there's a twist in this story come the ten o'clock hour. A breaking news alert that doesn't surprise me as the reporter on the screen begins to deliver the accounts of what's occurred.

Miami Mayor Ulysses Senot is dead after a confrontation in his home tonight. The politician, who's at the center of a huge criminal investigation as of a few hours ago, was shot and killed by his wife, who later turned the gun on herself. At this time the details of this gruesome ending are vague, and we will continue to report on this story as more details emerge.

THIAGO

IT'S LOUD INSIDE of the cargo ship the following night as people find their seats. Some are drinking. Some are gambling. Some look like they're ready to piss their pants.

The latter being Jadiel who has tried to have my mother intercede twice. She didn't, hanging up the phone and refusing to allow him or his father on her property.

Claudio who tried to run away after the news broke out of Senot's death and then the active warrant for both Antonio and the surviving Senot.

My eyes scan the crowd from my seat on the right side of the ring. In the past, when I've fought, it was for fun—sold-out underground fights whose chump change I'd donate to a charity of my choice.

Tonight, though, there's no fanfare. No bright lights or someone announcing each fighter. No trash talking, gloves, or the illusion of protective gear and a clean fight.

I want his blood on my hands.

I want to feel the very moment death takes him when I snap his neck.

No mercy tonight.

"Will you be okay when all is said and done?" Luna's soft voice pulls me away from the sight of my uncle trying to pep talk his son.

"Yes."

"Okay." Her lips skim my forehead and down to my ear where she pauses, her small exhale is sexy. "Come back to me unscathed and you'll get a reward. Something we both need."

"For me to bend you over and—" She covers my mouth with her dainty hand, my ring on her finger cool against my lips.

"I was thinking more of a honeymoon."

"That's still a little under three months away, bebe." Too long when I'm ready to give her my name now. When I want to start trying for a baby. "We might need to discuss that after. That date is too far off."

Instead of an admonishment not to rush our special day, my girl just giggles. "Finish the fight, Leon. Make it quick and trust me when I say it's in your interest to do so." A bell sounds over the loudspeakers then and she steps back so I can stand, giving me a sweet smile when I look over.

"I love you."

"I love you, too."

This ring has no bars, cage, or ropes; a small barrier no higher than someone's waist is what separates us from the crowd, and I lift Luna over it so she can take her seat behind me. My mother and father are there beside her, and so are those closest to me and mine. Like Ninette and Miguel who sit with Junior; the kid has grown so much since my release and is no longer on the boat. He will begin working with me in two weeks as a personal driver, while studying finance at night at a university nearby.

Ivan appears next to me, a bottle of water in hand. He's laughing at something and when I raise a brow, he shrugs. "I have ten grand on this not going past the minute mark."

"Really? You see him making it that far?"

"I'm hoping for something interesting here." He's lucky he's my brother or I'd toss him off the ship. "Besides, I'm going against Amberlyn, and knowing her, she won't let go of that money easily. I already have a counter offer she can't—"

I shake my head. "Out of the ring and shut it."

"Just help a guy out."

"I'll see what I can do." The second bell sounds and all noises cease. The lights dim all around us and the center stage ones shine brighter. It's just the two of us, looking at the other and focusing on the other's moves.

He's anticipating me to rush him, but I won't. Instead, I begin to stalk forward, my footwork lazy because he is no threat, and I stop two steps from him.

"Hit me."

"Thiago, enough. Let's talk about this."

"Hit me. You get one free shot." Closing my eyes, I relax my stance and lower my guard. "Make it count, Jadiel...it'll be your only opportunity."

"This is a trick." Losing your sight helps you focus on your other senses, and when he moves the waistband of his pants, the material makes a crinkling sound. *Fucking moron.*

His fist connects with the side of my head, the metal barely making contact and he has no weight behind the blow. It's a soft touch with the weapon and I almost feel bad for him.

So much so that I crack my neck and stiffen my jaw. "Again."

I take two more before my eyes snap open and make connection with his. He has a pair of brass knuckles on, a cheap version of mine, and on backwards. The thick metal that should go above each knuckle is inside his palm.

"Even when given a chance, you fuck it up." My hand snaps forward before he can duck, and I grip the base of his neck—squeezing until breathing becomes difficult and his hands begin to claw at my arm.

Sadly, that might be the most damage he causes.

"Okay," he sputters, face turning red. "I've learned my lesson and you've had your fun. I know my place."

It comes out as a bunch of broken garbles with a squeak, but I understand, going as far as to nod and then toss him aside. "Get up."

"Are we good now?" Jadiel is rubbing his neck. "I promise it won't happen again."

"Get up."

"Not until you...fuck!" A single kick hits his midsection and he's crying, curling into himself right before I land another, this one to his head.

I stand back. "Get up and fight or I'll slit your throat right now." His father in the background tries to rush me, but two guards grab him, bringing him to his knees. "Or better yet, I can make you watch as I blow your father's head clean off."

That gets to him. You can see the anger simmering; it overtakes his *pussy-like* qualities and Jadiel stands on wobbly legs, his hands up as if preparing to throw a punch. "Touch him and I'll kill you."

One of the guards strikes my uncle, breaking his nose.

"You were saying?"

"You're a dead man," he screams, rushing forward and connecting with my body. I stumble back a bit but catch my footing and turn us. His body hits the padding below hard and a grunt leaves him, but for once in his miserable life, he doesn't give up.

Jadiel throws an elbow up that connects with my mouth, splitting my bottom lip. I taste the blood and smile, letting him do it again before I fully mount him.

My right leg pins both of his, making it hard for him to move as I take the dominant position. He has no way of defending himself other than those bony elbows, while I position myself to pound his face in.

The first direct hit stuns him. The second makes him cry out.

I use my full force behind each strike, taking pleasure in the way his face begins to swell and break, his blood staining my hands and chest. My elbow comes down on his right eye and I feel the moment the orbital bone breaks. There's a give in the firmness of the bone, the eye moving loosely right before it bulges out.

Jadiel can't focus. He's squinting and fighting to protect his face, but I'm not done and land a second elbow just below the opposite eye. The swelling comes on quickly. His vision looks to be a bit dizzy, and I move into the side guard position. This gives me the space needed to hook his arm, bring my leg over his head, and turn my body.

At once his scream rents the air, the pressure I'm adding creating stress in three places: the elbow and shoulder joint plus the upper arm bone. He's tapping. Begging beneath me. I pull back harder and all three pop; the bone being the last as it breaks in two.

The crowd, who had been quiet until now, begin to stomp the floor, a low chant of *end him* filling the room. It grows louder with each second. The women are louder than the men—they're pissed for more than his betrayal. They're mad because of his plans to hurt my queen, someone everyone in this room loves and respects.

Releasing him, I stand and then fist his hair in my hands, dragging him along behind me toward the center of the ring. People stand. They wait. And when my father calmly walks over and shoots Jadiel's father in the head, he gets a standing ovation.

One down, a few more to go.

My cousin can't quite make out what's happened over the swelling, but I'm kind enough to bend a bit and relay the scene. "My deepest condolences, primo. Your father is dead." His body shakes, his chest caving as a sob bursts forth. I'm not moved, nor do I care. "You rose against me, Jadiel, that was your first mistake. The second was selling the logistics of my shipments to the feds, helping Arroyo fuck me over. Your cockiness has been your downfall. Believing me stupid enough to not check the video feeds make you an amateur. See you in hell."

Standing to my full height, I tower over him and snap his neck. He's gone in the blink of an eye and falls to the floor, eyes wide open as a group of employees from this cargo ship come into the ring to take the body out. These are the same men that a few weeks ago were goofing around while others were busy loading my gifted guns aboard.

"Let this be a lesson," I say, my voice loud enough to carry over the room. "Betray me and death will be your end. Fail at the job I've entrusted you with and this is your fate. Anything less than respect and loyalty is a direct disrespect to our name and oath."

Luna

FORTY-EIGHT HOURS have come and gone since the Senot homicide/suicide. The city is buzzing. It's all anyone can talk about, more so after Claudio's arrest at the airport. He tried and failed to pull a runner after being tied to a third of the crimes committed by our families. And while I am glad that justice is being served, that Thiago's case is being reviewed so those charges are expunged, I'm more concerned at the moment with my mother.

She's not answering her phone which is unusual for her. That damn device is her saving grace and Pinterest is her home. The woman has more boards than anyone I know and hasn't updated a single one since before things went boom.

Mom shares them on her private Facebook and IG almost daily, showing off her ideas for decorating next season. For the changes to her hair she's considering or the DIY bullshit she'll never attempt because it's cute to say you're handy but not so much to actually get dirty.

Her words, not mine.

"Anything yet?" Thiago asks, coming to lie down beside me on the couch. I'm completely moved in now and hanging out atop a monstrosity he had to have for our media room. I won't deny it's plush and comfortable and I sink in like no one's business, but at the moment, I feel off.

Restless.

Worried.

Wondering where the hell my father is hiding and worse, did he do something to my mother. Because bad parent or not, I do love the woman and wouldn't want her harmed. To me she's just as guilty in the sense that she kept her mouth closed and went along with what he said for appearance's sake—accepting the lies and affair with Jasmine Senot—but all physical evidence tied to the crimes shows her noninvolvement.

My phone rings again, and I sigh. It's a local number, the same one trying to get a hold of the daughter of the ex-commissioner since the story broke out.

"Nada." I toss the device aside and turn onto my back, looking up at the ceiling. "It rings three times and sends me to her full voicemail."

"My men are looking for them," he says, voice low while draping an arm over my waist. It's a bit heavy with his muscles, but I don't complain and let him pull me in closer. Breathe me in. "I'll turn this city inside out to find her for you."

"I know you will. I'm probably worried for nothing."

"Intuition is a nagging little voice that makes us rationalize the situation without second guessing or rational explanation. We just know." Turning my face toward his with the tip of a finger, he stares into my eyes. The hazel orbs are full of so much compassion and empathy. "Tell me, bebe. What does yours say?"

"That they're home."

"You think so?"

"Everything in me believes it and I can't explain the why. It's a gut feeling that I can't shake, Leon—"

"Get up and get dressed. We leave in twenty."

"What do you mean? Where are we going?"

"Right where you know we should be."

"But?"

"I'll have Ivan and Edgar meet us there. Let's go."

"Thank you," I whisper, my emotions rising to the surface. He's not making me feel like an idiot or telling me to wait or saying it'll be okay, and he'll take care of it. My papi is validating me with something that most would laugh at and tell me to trust his men, or the police. Our story hasn't been easy, at times painful, but at this very moment I fall in love with him all over again. "I love you, Thiago. Always and forever."

"Always and forever, beautiful." He grabs my hand and leads me up the stairs to our room. There are still a few boxes with my things that need to be put away and my clothes from the night before strewn about, but I've never felt more at home than I do with him. And before I let go of his hand to get dressed, I turn in his arms and rise onto the very tips of my toes so I can reach his lips.

"I want to get married in our backyard thirty days from now."

"My queen deserves—"

"This is just your formal invitation, Mr. De Leon. I've already taken care of everything."

"Have you, now?"

"Yes, now let's go find my mom. I'd really like her to be present at my wedding even if it's bitching the entire way."

THE HOUSE IS EERILY quiet when we arrive around five that evening. There are no cruisers watching the residence or nosy neighbors outside like I expected.

To be honest, I've never seen this street so desolate—empty. *Where is everyone?*

Thiago parks his car behind my mother's silver BMW, leaving the engine running just in case. All the window drapery is open, parted so you can see inside, and I take in the lack of lighting or movement.

I'm the first one out of the car and up to the front—three car doors open and close—their footsteps loud up the paver-lined driveway.

They stand behind me, their support giving me the strength to open the door using a key code combination.

"I think he's here too," Edgar says, and I grip his hand. This is his brother. Flesh and blood. No matter what they've done, how shitty my father is, it still hurts. "I'm thinking—"

"The cottage at the back of the property."

"What cottage?" Ivan asks, walking past me with his weapon drawn. He's followed by my uncle, and Thiago takes the back. I'm surrounded by them as we enter, and the stench inside makes me gag. It's the foul smell of spoiled food, something left out for days, and I follow the smell to the kitchen. The culprit is atop the stove; a large batch of some kind of soup that's turned sour in this heat.

"Christ, that's foul." Thiago's nose scrunches up, and he draws his own weapon, looking at me, so I take mine out as well. He always makes sure I carry, that I'm protected. "Stay vigilant. Safety off."

No A/C has made the house stale too. No electricity running throughout the house means no cameras are running. It's a good thing past this horrible smell; we'll have the element of surprise if they're on the premises.

Nodding, I look back at his brother. "My father built a man cave out back, past this home's property line and in the middle of the undeveloped land behind this lot. It's completely decked out; all utilities working, full living room and bedroom with a functioning bathroom."

"And no one knows about that place?" My brother-in-law's incredulous look would be funny any other day. Not today, and I shrug.

"Those that do are either dead, in this room, or freaking out they don't get involved. As of this morning, two other names have been added to the investigation: the police chief and the judge that sentenced Thiago."

His eyes narrow and he shakes his head. "And we're the fucked-up ones?"

"Hypocrisy is usually wielded by those afraid to look in the mirror. It's easier to cast stones than to accept responsibility."

"Very true, my queen." My fiancé passes me, intertwining our empty hands as he goes. We leave the kitchen and check the den, the family room, and find no sign of life outside of the empty bar. Every liquor bottle is missing. "That's not normal."

"No."

"Should we still check upstairs?" I look at Thiago and shake my head. It's useless and a waste of time. They're not here. "Okay." Looking at

Edgar and Ivan, he motions for them to head out back and we follow. No one talks. We just walk as quietly as possibly, not wanting to alert them to our presence.

The lawn is overgrown, and the pool is green—the algae reproduction consuming every inch. Even my mother's hibiscus plants that she loves so much are now dead.

"What the fuck happened back here?" Edgar stops just at the tree line, taking in the density. That, and a small trip wire that glints with the sun's position in the sky. "It's not high. Step over it."

We follow him over and search the ground nearby for more. There isn't any, but we're careful nonetheless as we walk through and find the cottage, a little one-bedroom unit that I hear music coming from and detect the scent of food being cooked.

"You were right, Luna." Thiago lifts his gun, aiming it for the door, and the other two follow him. I stay back. Not because I'm afraid, but because they're more equipped to handle this type of situation than I am.

I'm not looking to let my emotions cause someone harm.

My fiancé raps the ground three times, and on the last, kicks the door in. Three screams follow: two male, and one female. The place is dingy when we rush in, garbage and empty liquor bottles littering the floor, and the people inside reek.

How long have they been back here? This is more than a few days-worth of filth.

I'm taking it all in. Everything. From my father's hate filled eyes as he sits on a tufted blue chair that's seen better days—to Sergio on an ottoman with a crying Celeste holding two plates filled to the brim with hot food.

Her hands shake, spilling what looks to be a pasta dish on Sergio, and his automatic reaction is to lift his hand, swinging it back as if to hit her. Wrong move. Sooner than I can blink, the angry brothers beside me shoot him. They both empty an entire magazine, littering his body with holes from his head to midsection.

It's all happening so fast; one minute he's sitting, and the next slouched on the ground at an odd angle while my father has his hands up and is glaring at his brother.

"You'll pay for this, Edgar. You, and my traitor daughter." There's so much venom in each word. His desire to reach for the shotgun to his left against the wall is plain as day to see. He'd kill us if he could. "Mark my words, you'll both regret the day you chose *them* over your own blood."

"Funny, brother. Because it's hard to draw revenge from six feet below."

"Fuck you," my father hisses out, making a move to stand, and a shot is fired. Just one, and he cries out. It's then that I look over, meeting his eyes the same shade of brown as my own. They're lifeless, empty, as blood stains his dirty shirt at the left sleeve and shoulder. "I'm going to—"

I tune him out for my own sanity. He's not going anywhere, my uncle will make sure of that, and I look over at a furious Thiago. He's keeping it together for me. He's not personally ending my father's life because of the promise he made me. And while the man deserves whatever life throws his way, if it came down to it, I'd rather it's Edgar or myself that pulls the trigger. Something, that I know my papi will understand.

"Check the room down that small hall. My mom..." I trail off as my voice cracks and he walks over, placing a kiss on my forehead.

"Help Celeste, and I'll check the back with Ivan. We'll circle the outside too if we find nothing."

"Thank you." As they head toward the back, I turn my focus to Celeste who hasn't moved an inch. "I'm sorry, sweetie. I got you."

She's a bundle of nerves, the eruption almost violent as shock settles quicker than I can react, and she sways. The plates slip from her fingertips, crashing to the ground and dirtying both our legs. A few shards cut her while my sweatpants have stains, but I jump in without a second thought. Right before she crashes to the ground, I grab her, pulling her into me and away from the bloody scene and food.

There's a small patch of clean flooring to the right and when I can't hold us up any longer, her weight in this state too much, I lower us. "It's going to be okay." I'm rocking us from side to side after placing my gun on the ground, not wanting to freak her out further. "You're safe."

"Am I really?" Her voice is small. Shaky. Timid.

"Yes, we'll take care of you. Help you." Her arm shifts a bit and I ignore the stretch, thinking nothing of it, when time stands still for a second time and my gun is pressed below my chin. My eyes close and I fight the urge to look into her eyes. "Why?"

"Because everything that's gone wrong in my life starts and ends with you." Celeste's hand is shaking. You can tell she's never really held a gun before, much less shot one and I'm not surprised. Not with a sexist father and brother. "All the men in my life have fallen for you, and I've taken the brunt of their frustrations."

"Bebe, she's here!" Thiago calls out, but I don't move or answer. "Did you hear me? She's—"

All eyes are on us now. They see the gun.

My father laughs and then he doesn't. A body crashes to the ground and feet come closer. Multiple bodies surround us, and guns are cocked.

"Celeste, please think this through. This isn't you."

"Prima, don't force my hand."

She ignores Thiago's warning, her tears falling on my shirt. "Because of my brother's obsession with you, Thiago killed him. My father too. I've lost it all, Luna. Every-fucking-body that I loved."

"Drop the gun and step back."

"That's not true. We're all here for you," Leon and I say in unison; I'm calm while I have no doubt in my mind he'll pull the trigger. Something that will break his heart because he does care for her. We all do.

"Dale, Celeste. Stop this...no more blood needs to be shed." Ivan tries to step closer, but I feel her finger shift around the trigger, and I hold a hand up. He stops but doesn't move back.

"I knew about Sergio's obsession with you a week after we met, you know. It's why I told him to change his last name." She pushes the barrel just a little bit deeper, and it's uncomfortable to swallow. "Your father sent him pictures of you from family affairs, graduation...vacations. He fed my love's obsession in hopes that he'd kill Thiago and bring you back under his thumb. You were to be his plaything, and yet, I was still going to marry him because that's what love is. You accept the other half of your soul with all their baggage and fuckups."

"That's not love, sweetie. You deserve more."

"Shut up!" Her scream at my ear hurts, and I move back, grimacing—a natural reaction—and it sends my head back and chest away from hers. That slim opening is all Thiago needs, and two shots end her life.

I don't want to see and close my eyes. Her blood is literally on my hands and shirt. So when two masculine hands grab me and pull me off the floor, I fight back.

At that moment my mind goes blank and the world dissolves into loud noises and panic. I can't get air into my lungs.

"Breathe, Luna. Fucking breathe!" The sound of a door opening and closing follows, and then birds in the distance. My feet don't meet the ground, but it's his muscular scent that grounds me. It's what I focus on as his hands grip me tight—encircle me in his hold.

Every breath slowly becomes easier.

Every word he says becomes clearer.

"Breathe, baby. Just like that." Another soothing caress up and down my back, figure eights that begin to relax me. "That's it. Come back to me, love."

"I'm here," I say and it's low, but by his reaction you'd think I would've yelled it.

"Thank God." His lips meet mine. The kiss is sweet—electric, and my shaky hands come up gripping the back of his neck. Behind us, feet approach the cottage at a rapid pace; they pass by and head inside while we stay in this moment.

The kiss calms me. Gives me what I need to lose the tight noose that was slowly choking me.

"Put him in the back of my car. I'm taking him in myself." My uncle's voice registers sharply, though, and I pull back just in time to see Antonio Alejos: unconscious, in handcuffs, and over some man's shoulder. "Ivan, please get Yvette to the main house. She needs medical care and an ambulance will be here in a couple of minutes!"

"What's wrong, Luna?"

"Shit." I'm pushing against him, wiggling in his hold as I fight to get down. "My mom! What's wrong with my mom?"

"Broken leg and a concussion from the looks of it, but—"

"But what?"

"Bebe, Yvette's been doped up pretty hard." At that I gasp, my chest burning from the previous panic. "We found her with a needle in her arm and slumped over. Ivan will ride with her."

"Let me go. I need to—"

"Stop."

"But she needs—"

"Her daughter to not pass out and to meet her in the hospital later. To breathe. To be there for her. To help her in the next stage of her life because everything she's always known is gone." My body becomes languid with his explanation because he's right. Things won't be easy for her, and mending our relationship won't happen overnight...

So much has been said. Done.

"Thank you." And I mean it. Because this man has always been my rock. He looks out for me, loves me, and accepts me as I am. He gives me the world and asks for nothing but my heart in return. And while our love story had a sad intermission, the act that followed has been worth it all. "I love you, Thiago."

He lays his forehead against mine; and his gorgeous hazel eyes have gone soft. "Forever and always."

And while around us chaos ensues, bodies are removed, and the building and everything inside is set on fire, I close my eyes and let him carry me away.

He is mine and I am his.

That's all that matters.

It's how it was always meant to be.

EPILOGUE 1
THIAGO

"**I** CAN'T BELIEVE you're making me late to my own wedding, papi. Seriously, we need to be...oh *God*!" One stroke and I'm deep inside her tight little pussy, the bottom of her dress being held in one hand while I grip her hip with the other. She's tight and wet and has been begging me to take her like this since late last night.

It's all in the way she moves.

A simple bend at the waist while I'm watching TV, small indecent boy shorts riding up and exposing the new tattoo at her hip. My initials. In my writing. And more provocative is the way she got them.

Sneaky and serving me a dose of my own medicine, Luna asked me to sign a few documents atop her desk because she'd forgotten to send them herself. They were for her new gallery downtown. The contracts for my contractor to start the build for a very detailed and specific darkroom she wanted in the back of the space.

So, I did what all good hubbys do and I signed/initialed whatever she needed me to.

Three days later, this was my surprise.

I also spanked her until the sweet little globes became hot to touch and then fucked her like the bad girl she is. Luna drenched my sheets. Clawed at my back. Met me thrust for thrust while begging in that pretty voice of hers for *more*. Always more.

"Thiago," she mewls, clenching around my girth when I bend my knees a bit, changing the angle. My thrusts are deeper like this. Hitting that tiny spot inside that makes her...*Christ*, Luna flutters all around me and I close my eyes. "Harder...just a little bit *more*."

"So greedy, baby girl." Her exposed back is a temptation I can only withstand for so long, and I bite her. Little nips all over the expanse—wherever I can reach. "But remember that you made me do this. You're the reason we'll be late to our wedding today...all those guests downstairs waiting out on the lawn while the sun begins to set." Each word is followed by a punishing thrust. She clenches, thighs trembling, but I don't slow down. It's the opposite. "They're mingling while I fuck you. They're speculating about our delay while I imbibe of my gift a little early."

The last few weeks have been hard for her. Exhausting, but she took charge like the queen she is and took care of her mother while planning this wedding. I stepped in where I could, when the withdrawals kicked in and Yvette lashed out at her and the hospital staff, but Luna never took it personally. Her empathy knows no bounds and she proved that while making sure her addict mother—a habit forced by her husband, and at time chosen by herself to numb the pain—got the help she needs.

Moreover, while their relationship might never mend—Yvette chose to stay at the treatment center and not celebrate with us today—I know it brings Luna peace of mind to be there just in case. The same cannot be said for Antonio, though. No. Never him.

Edgar has personally seen to the destruction of every asset the man ever had. Their sibling rivalry surpasses what most experience, and we've come to learn that it's because he loved Yvette first. Antonio stole her from Edgar, and when they got married, he made his brother promise to always take care of his family first. His failure to do just that is what finally broke the camel's back.

Antonio Alejos will rot away in his cell before taking a trip to the morgue where they'll cremate, and then bury him in a plot for those who have no family to claim them.

"Please," her hungry little whine makes me tremble, my fingers at her hip digging in to the point she'll have marks on her skin. Always my mark. My love. Me.

"Take it." Another nip, this time to the center of her spine. "You knew exactly what you were doing when you designed this gown."

Her dress is simple in its elegance and fitting of her curves. A long white silk slip gown with minimal beading at her chest and a long train that begins in a ruching detail at her tailbone. The bodice is tight, sexy, while loosening at her hips to give a slight mermaid feel. At the least, that's how she explained it to me the day she gave me the concept. Designers from all over the country were tripping over themselves to design it, but Luna went with a local seamstress and her own original.

One fitting and she knew it was the one. I agree. It's her. It's beautiful.

But more importantly, I'm going to enjoy tearing it from her body tonight.

The six-inch heels on her dainty feet add the perfect height, and I bend over her just a little bit more. Our bathroom, her makeup vanity has the perfect chair for this. A plush mini replica of my throne-like chair on the cargo ship, and it cushions her while I fist the long, curled locks. I pull her head back, arching her against me and kiss her neck. Our eyes meet and in them, I see the same emotions reflected back at me.

Love. Loyalty. A never-satiated hunger.

"I can feel you're close, bebe." I breathe her in, that ever-present scent of lime and coconuts making me throb. Beads of sweat form at my brow and one drop falls to her neck; I follow its descent down her chest, disappearing into the soft fabric of her dress. "Come for me. Mark your husband."

Luna's mouth opens in a silent scream. Not a sound comes out as her entire body goes rigid. She's not breathing, clenching so hard around my cock—a nearly choking grip—and it's exquisite. Almost painful in its beauty, and on the next flutter of her walls, I feel the warmth of her juices doing exactly what I asked her to.

"Son of a bitch," I hiss out through clenched teeth, fighting to keep my eyes on her through the mirror as she milks me. She pulls the come from my heavy balls; it's a perfect mess. I stay buried deep until the very last drop of my release fills her body.

Our breathing is hard. Her hair is a tousled perfection. There's also someone calling our names from the bottom of the stairs because they're not allowed on this floor, and I feel like the luckiest son of a bitch alive.

"Can I marry you now?" Luna giggles from below me, her eyes sparkling in the mirror. "Or do you need a minute to recover." My response comes in the form of a glare and a single swat to her ass cheek before I pull out, tuck myself in, and lower her dress. She can't wear panties with it, and I rather like the idea of her walking toward me with my release coating her thighs. "That stung."

"Then don't be a brat." Turning her around to face me, I pull her into my embrace. Hug her tight to my chest and bend my head to reach her ruby red lips. "I love you, Luna. More than my own life. More than any man has ever loved a woman."

Instantly, she melts against me. Her sassy smirk turns into a soft smile. "Forever and ever and ever?"

"Past this life and the next." Then I kiss her inside of our room, slow and sweet and with more passion that I ever thought possible. "Now, are you ready to sign your life away to the devil himself? To spend two weeks with me on a private beach in Cuba?"

"Would you let me go if I said no?"

"Never."

"And that's why I will. Because even when I'm lost, you stick by me and fight for us."

And that's exactly what she did.

At forty minutes later on the dot, Luna became my wife. My partner in crime. My right hand and the rightful queen of the De Leon Dynasty.

EPILOGUE 2
THIAGO

THE IMPERIUM...

THIS DAY HAS been a long time coming. Every man within this room rules his domain with an iron fist and loyalty to those they care about. We all bring something different to the table—money, weapons, and the most profitable of all: drugs. An obscene quantity of drugs, that when our resources are pooled together, would overtake every other syndicate fighting for the scraps we leave untouched.

Ninety percent of all production and distribution would go through us. The De Leons have channels in Cuba and Panama, while the Jameson brothers have Boston Harbor and the U.K. Then you have Malcolm, a cold and calculating man with an empire far reaching what the United States can control.

And yet, he wants more. To control worldwide monetary needs.

All profits would be equally shared.

One family.

One kingdom.

One power.

"Who's in favor of this merger between families?" Malcolm asks, hand held high with a glass of Gin in a toasting manner. We're inside my cargo ship in open water with more men surrounding this vessel than the national guard patrolling nearby knows what to do with. Then again, they wouldn't harass the newest mayor of Miami.

The 305 made a deal with this devil when the residents chose me to clean up their streets. To bring in more jobs and money. And I've done that in my own way. Bringing in businesses funded by myself under fake LLCs that pay its employees well to, not knowingly, launder my money.

A win *win* if you ask me.

"Aye." I don't think about it twice, raising my own. These are men I know and trust—family—and this merger will be beneficial to me and mine. My legacy was cemented a very long time ago, on the day I was born and laid out by my father, but this is different. My two year old son has been born into an opportunity not one criminal organization has yet to accomplish. They've tried—more times than I can count on one hand—and eventually failed because of greed.

Because the need to overthrow your neighbor always comes forth.

Kings cannot rule within the same city or state. Each one of us has an established family and territory with room to grow. Respect is key. Respect is what keeps us in business.

We each understand what it takes on our own, but together we cannot be stopped.

"Aye," Casper and Callum follow in unison, their pints almost gone, but the gesture is there nonetheless. I know Casper's long-term plans, and this fits his need for growth. Lucas will take over Boston eventually and then he has a bigger city in mind. Brighter lights and loud crowds make for a solid investment.

"Aye." The last and to my right is Ivan. He's ready. Has been for over a year since settling on the island. We have plans, and he has a political aspiration to run for president in Cuba. Out with the old and in with freedom, prosperity, and the largest transport channel to the states our U.S. government has ever seen.

"Then it's settled." Malcolm smirks, throwing back what's in his glass. "To the Imperium, gentlemen."

"The Imperium." we chant.

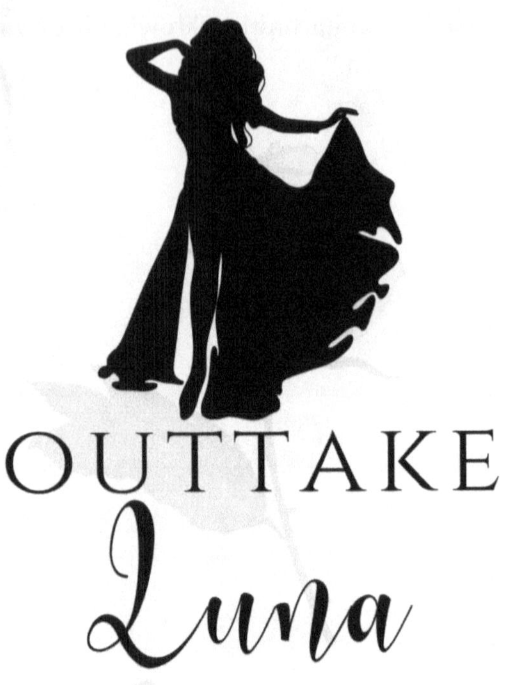

OUTTAKE
Luna

HOW THEY MET...

"WHY WON'T HE stop looking at me?" I whisper to my cousin Natasha, giving her the universal sign for *look but don't look* while passing in front of said boy's desk before exiting the classroom. The same *guy* that hasn't made a single attempt to hide his staring—an annoying habit that's had me on edge since walking into my first class.

It's been like this all day.

Every class inside of this private school. Every single time I look back...

He's there. Watching me.

An expression on his handsome face that I can't quite decipher.

Because there's no denying that he's cute. That I felt my cheeks heat up the second our eyes connected; dark brown on a hazel so vibrant I've never seen before. But more than that, they remind me of a lion's eyes.

The large dominant feline male that you see at the zoo or on a Nat Geo documentary.

For someone my age, there's this hint of something dark behind his stare. Something accentuated by the way people have been flocking to him all day.

I know this because I've been secretly watching too.

Have seen the way the other girls look at him.

How the boys try to constantly engage him in conversation.

He's popular. Respected. A hunter.

But why am I letting him get to me?

"At least he's hot, Lulu." She shrugs, fixing the strap of the oversized book bag over her right shoulder. "Remember Sergio from down the block?"

At that, another face comes to mind and I pause at an area between the hall of classrooms and the girl's bathroom; the hallways are near empty as most students have taken off for the cafeteria. "Please don't remind me." A shudder of disgust runs through me at the mere thought of that jerk. "It's the only silver lining to our move from Jersey to Miami: no more creepy kid following me around like a lost puppy."

From the moment puberty hit, I became his target. Two years older than me and pushy, he's not my type at all with a pimply face, shorter-than-me stature, and a pompous attitude that screams of entitlement. And all that arrogance just because his parents own a local pizza place/arcade that's popular where we lived.

Sergio Martin constantly asked me out on a date that'd never happen, tried to steal a kiss or two and failed—left notes inside my locker declaring a love I wouldn't return. He was a problem I didn't want or need, and it's made moving so far away from my friends a good thing.

It's the only reason I've kept my displeasure to a minimum, well that, and my uncle allowing Natasha to come live with us instead of staying with our grandmother while he handles a business problem in the Dominican Republic.

But now with—

"See, prima. That's called a silver lining."

Rolling my eyes, I slap her arm. "I'm not the only one that had an admirer."

"Mine wasn't so bad." She shrugs, rubbing the spot I just hit. "Kind of sweet actually."

"You say that now!" I whisper yell, taking two steps back while she tries to jam a finger in my stomach. "Quit it."

"Make me."

"I'm ticklish and hate it."

Natasha takes one step forward of her own. "I know."

"Keep at it and I'll trip you."

There's a gleam in her eyes when she comes at me again and I turn, looking over my shoulder to flip her off as I duck out of the way. "You suck—" And that's as far as I get, because while trying to avoid her, I run straight into a hard body.

A body whose scent smacks me in the face and my head becomes light. That causes my knees to weaken, something I always thought to be made up by the Spanish soaps my mother watches.

The reaction's automatic and scary, and I don't understand it. Neither do I hide the small gasp that escapes my throat when I meet a pair of amused hazel ones that have been following me all day.

"Hello, little queen?"

"Little queen?" I squeak, enjoying the way his warm arm feels as he wraps one around my lower back and pulls me in closer. Liking how good I fit against his side—taking in the moment—when I should be pushing him away.

Demanding he let go.

That he leaves me be.

But I don't. Can't. Instead, I once again inhale his masculine scent while biting my bottom lip. I refuse to let out another sound. To show how much he's getting to me.

"Yes, little queen."

"Is that supposed to mean something?"

"One day it will."

"I need more than that." It comes out breathy, and he gives me this tiny little smirk that makes the butterflies in my stomach take off. *I'm in trouble.* "Thiago...that's your name, right?"

"Yes."

"You need to explain—"

This handsome jerk that I don't know, that's been watching me all day, leans in and lets out a low hum of approval while placing a kiss on the shell of my ear. A move that brings a hot flash of want through me. It catches me off guard and I almost miss his whispered words, but when they sink in, my world changes.

"It means one day you'll sit by my side as Mrs. De Leon."

ABOUT THE AUTHOR

Elena M. Reyes is the epitome of a Floridian and if she could live in her beloved flip-flops, she would.

As a small child, she was always intrigued by all forms of art: whether it was dancing to island rhythms, or painting with any medium she could get her hands on. Her passion for reading over the years has amassed her with hours of pleasure, but it wasn't until she stumbled upon fanfiction that her thirst to write overtook her world.

She's a short and sassy Latina with an adorable pup, a kiddo that keeps her on her toes, and a husband who claims she'll cause him to go bald prematurely. Lol

Email: Reyes139ff@gmail.com

FATE'S BITE SERIES

LITTLE LIES
LITTLE MATE
HALF TRUTHS DUET
HALF TRUTHS: THEN
HALF TRUTHS: NOW
OMISSION:
PART 1
PART 2
COME TO ME (2026)
THE HUNT (2025)
TERO (TBD)

<u>BEAUTIFUL SINNER SERIES</u>
<u>Each book is a standalone.</u>
<u>Now Live!</u>

<u>SIN (#1)</u>
COVET (#2)
<u>MINE (#3)</u>
YOURS (#4)
RISQUE #5
OWN #6
Beautiful Sinner Spin-Off
CORRUPT
MY SINFUL VALENTINE
SAVAGE KISS

ONE RULE

MAKE YOU MINE

(Marked Series)